PATRICK LAPLANTE

PANDORA
UNCHAINED

aethonbooks.com

Aethon Books
www.aethonbooks.com

Print and eBook design and formatting by Josh Hayes.

Published by Aethon Books LLC.

ALSO IN SERIES

Pandora Unchained

Pandora Unchained 2

Check out the entire series here! (Tap or scan)

THE EVIL CALLED HOPE

"The basis of cultivation is that human potential is unlimited. By unlocking that potential at the various cultivation stages, we inferior humans can bridge a portion of the gap separating us from the unreachable gods.
I have dedicated my long career to advancing human cultivation, but my efforts have been hampered by the accidental discovery of locks inhibiting human growth. The deities of Pandora have forbidden further research on the topic, so I can only pursue the answers in secret."

– Sirius Abberjay Kepler, Pandora Medical Research Institute, 42 years before the Cataclysmic Emergence.

Frozen grass and iced-over puddles crackled under Sorin's feet as he made his way down a winding clay road on the outskirts of the Blood-wood Outpost. It was late autumn, so the weather was finally turning. The Evil called Disease was at its peak during the hateful transition between summer and winter.

Despite being located outside the outpost walls, the Temple of Hope was as lively as ever. There was no shortage of the terminally ill, the disabled, or people who were just down on their luck. Sorin took note of the ill and listed off their symptoms in his head out of habit.

The wasting, final stages, thought Sorin as he picked out a gaunt face amongst the beggars and petitioners. *It is slightly contagious, but the patient is still sane and maintaining self-isolation.*

Not far away were a man with an amputated leg, a woman with a half-burnt face, and a man crumpled over in pain from a crush injury he'd suffered three months prior. Sorin was familiar with that case because he'd been the one to treat him in the clinic.

Unfortunately, much like in the other cases, there was nothing to be done for such an injury. The man would need to suffer unbearable pain for the rest of his life, however long that was.

"Physician Sorin?" called out a sickly woman holding a bundle in her arms. "Physician Sorin, is that you?"

"You have the wrong person," said Sorin in a rough voice. He pulled his hood down to obscure his handsome, albeit pale face, and hardened his heart to the pleading of the common people. Here, in the Temple of Hope, he was just like them: a gambler who'd come to put all his chips on the table for one final bet.

Past the beggars at the entrance were the people with wishes to make. Most were farmers whose crops had been devoured by lesser demons, plagues, and corruption, but there were guardsmen, youths with entirely too much money, and adults looking to gamble away their savings for a small chance at a big win.

Whether they were wishing for good business opportunities or begging for heavy snowfall or rain, each of them knew that their chances were slim; the temple granted wishes according to luck and fate and never in the way one expected.

"Next!" called a young priest. His eyes were bright and filled with prospects. But Sorin knew that this spark would soon fade. He would become like the rest of the temple's cynical priests, a shepherd who led sheep along a misty cliff to the market, knowing that only a few would ever make it.

A supplicant arrived at one of the two minor altars. He was a baker who owned a shop not far from Sorin's clinic. Times were hard, so people had been cutting back, even on necessities. Even a fat and successful baker now had trouble making ends meet and could only burn joss sticks to a tricky fox in the hopes that good fortune would carry him through the winter.

"Next!" called a priest at another secondary altar. This one smiled sadistically as a young man set fire to his life savings and muttered a prayer for three minutes straight. In the end, he was just like the baker. The altar remained unmoved. His prayers had gone unanswered.

Sorin's destination was the main altar of the temple. According to his late grandfather, the chances of having one's wish granted were much higher there than anywhere else. But the minimum offering was higher as well. Sorin had squirreled away money for three whole years to be able to afford it.

"Next!" called the seniormost priest presiding over the main altar. He was an older man with a gentle and kindly demeanor. A teary-eyed woman pushed past the priest and ran out of the temple, and the look he gave her was nothing if not sympathetic. "The next supplicant can come forward to make an offering. Remember: The Temple of Hope makes no promises or guarantees. Everything will be done according to the will of the Eighth Evil."

Sorin's heart clenched as he realized that *he* was the next supplicant. Moreover, he had come to offer everything he had. If this offering failed, his short lifespan would run out before he had enough money for another gamble.

The Bloodwood Outpost's Temple of Hope was smaller than the ones found in proper cities. But just like the larger temples, it was built of sturdy stone and only minimally adorned. The temple had no need for wooden pews like those found in the old world's cathedrals or for sculptures depicting the triumph of the gods. The gods were long dead, and only the Eight Evils remained.

Said Evils were carved upon the walls of the long corridor leading to the main altar. Jealousy and Hatred incited war, while Strife, Violence, and Madness dispensed it. Death and Disease followed closely on their heels, while the greatest Evil, Hope, fought against all seven of them.

"Present your offering on the altar and state your name and your wish before lighting up the kindling," instructed the kindly priest. "All wishes made at the main altar are private, so I will remain outside the room. I will open the door in exactly five minutes, regardless of your success or failure. I wish you luck in your endeavors." The priest hesitated before offering one final piece of advice. "Your cultivation might be crippled, Physician Kepler, but your profession is honorable. I don't normally discourage people from making a wish, but in your case, it might be best to count your blessings."

"Many thanks, Priest Harold," said Sorin. "But every person has their struggles, and all humans are equally entitled to seek Hope."

"My apologies for forgetting my station," said Priest Harold. "I will do penance for three days and three nights as an apology." He walked out the door, and a loud click indicated that the door was locked and that Sorin was free to make his offering.

Kindling had already been piled up on the altar by the temple's staff. Included in the offering were carvings of the seven lesser evils, along with a small kindling platform on which the offerings would be made.

Sorin directly upended a pouch containing dozens of one-star demon cores and a single two-star demon core. He'd been purchasing them since his arrival at Fort Bloodwood using what money his parents had left him and hadn't been taken by his greedy relatives and what little he'd earned for working for three years as a physician in the outpost.

"Sorin Abberjay Kepler offers sincere greetings to the guardian god of humanity," said Sorin, grabbing one of the twelve wish-fire torches on the altar. "My wish is simple: I want to know how my parents died. I want to know if any foul play was involved in their deaths. And if so, I want to know who killed them."

The hot white wish-fire spread from the torch to the altar as soon as these words were spoken. It snaked up the kindling and onto the demon cores, releasing powerful mana fluctuations and acrid smoke that assaulted Sorin's damaged lungs.

The man felt a stab of pain in his chest as unhealed wounds ripped open. Yet he did not dare look away from the carvings of the seven evils as they burnt away into nothingness. Minutes passed as the fire slowed, and only small bits of wood remained. Before long, only a few embers remained, and these two went out one after another until only darkness and smoke remained.

It looks like it wasn't meant to be, thought Sorin with a sigh. *But Grandfather warned me: The fox is fickle and will seldom answer even the simplest requests.*

Five minutes hadn't yet passed, but with the wood all burnt out, there was nothing left for Sorin to do. He turned towards the door and was about to knock on its smooth, bloodwood surface when suddenly, his hand passed *through* the door as though it were air.

A black mist billowed across his feet, sucking in whatever light had managed to creep its way through the cracks beneath the doorway. A deep darkness invaded the room, and a chilling cold gripped Sorin by the feet and worked its way up his broken body, lingering briefly on a half-healed scar on his solar plexus where his mana sea had once been.

"Sorin Abberjay Kepler," hissed a voice from the darkness. "Son of Lorent Abberjay Kepler and Maria Doyen Kepler. Descendent of Sirius Abberjay Kepler, heretic of the church and visionary of humanity. Cultivation: Crippled. Organs are highly damaged. Life expectancy: 3–4 months. Once evaluated as a genius physician. Born under the constellation of the Black Star and blessed with a second-stage soul at birth. Potential at birth: Unlimited. Current potential: Uncertain."

The darkness gathered above the main altar. Two bright red eyes lit up the altar and the chamber walls with an eerie light, revealing nine chain-like tails that reached out endlessly. It was thanks to these chains tying down the fate of Pandora that humanity had survived, or so the legends said.

Sorin's bladder almost gave out, but thanks to his strong soul, he was able to compose himself quickly. He felt the urge to prostrate himself but managed to find his dignity before his knees hit the floor. "Sorin

Abberjay Kepler greets the Greatest of the Evils and offers his profuse thanks for the kindness of granting his wish."

"Kindness?" spat the fox, revealing a mouthful of razor-sharp teeth. "You expect kindness from the trickster fox? The swindler? The manipulator of fate? Kindness is not my business, Sorin Abberjay Kepler. You knew it walking into this room, and now, speaking to my likeness, you have forgotten the warnings of your ancestors."

Sorin cursed inwardly at his misfortune but noted that the fox *had* appeared. That could only be a good thing. Hope hadn't outright refused his offerings, which meant that there was room for negotiation. "If my offering displeases you, Lord Hope, I can secure additional demon cores."

The fox snorted. "I have no use for such petty things. Moreover, you're a broken wretch who has a half foot in the grave."

"Then I—" started Sorin.

"No. Do not try bargaining," the fox said, cutting him off. "Do not try haggling. I know you inside and out, Sorin Abberjay Kepler. I know your past, your present, and the few pathetic futures you would try to influence.

A black mist billowed out from beneath the fox and tightened around Sorin. It didn't probe him like the cold mist from before but was actively squeezing the life out of him. "I did not appear because of your offering, mortal. I appeared because your request *insulted* me. What do you take me for—a shady backstreet information dealer? A broker of secrets? And even if I were one of these lowlifes, aren't your offerings too pitiful?"

Sorin was very close to blacking out, but he resolved to hold on till the last second. Spots began appearing in his eyes when the black mist hand suddenly threw him across the room and onto the temple's plain stone floor.

Sorin nearly fainted from the impact. *No fractures, but possible hairline cracks on my ribcage,* he instinctually assessed. *Stitch*ed wounds have ripped open and will require re-suturing. *Internal bleeding will need to be assessed and remedied to prevent excessive blood loss.*

His entire body was afire with intense pain, but Sorin mustered his remaining willpower to pick himself up and stare up at the monster hovering above the altar. He remembered his grandfather's words about the fox, the many wishes family members had made, and the kinds of requests the tricky fox liked most.

"My payment is lacking, and I have nothing to my name," Sorin admitted. "My parents are dead, and my inheritance was taken away. My cultivation is crippled, and I can't even control my hands properly.

"I am desperate, Lord Hope. You are the only chance I have. Is it arrogant for me to make a request? Perhaps. But you're all I can rely on. You're all the hope I have."

His words seemed to pique the fox's interest. "It *is* the desperate I serve," confirmed the apparition. "And the lost and the vengeful and the broken. So tell me, Sorin Abberjay Kepler: What is your *real* wish? What do you request of your Lord and Savior, the Greatest of the Eight Evils?"

"I want a chance to start over," said Sorin without hesitation. "I want a sliver of a chance at life. I want a tenth of that chance to discover what happened to my parents, and if there was any foul play involved, a tenth of that chance to avenge them."

As these words left his mouth, the black mists in the temple billowed. Sorin could swear he heard a scream as the nine-tailed fox pulled with his chain-like tails. "Quiet, wretched world," spoke the fox. "If there's something I want, you're not qualified to prevent me from taking it." He then shoved a claw into a slit in the fabric of reality and pulled out a sickly green orb. It was the size of Sorin's fist, barely a marble compared to the fox's immense stature. Golden runes floated inside it.

"Your request has been heard and accepted," said the fox. "By my authority as the Eighth Evil, I grant thee *hope*." A stream of information surged into Sorin's mind, severely taxing his powerful soul. The knowledge threatened to slip through his fingers, but Sorin held on to every last bit of it and forcefully incorporated it into his spiritual sea.

"Divine Cultivation Art: The Ten Thousand Poison Canon?"

muttered Sorin as he picked himself off the ground. His body shivered as he growled at the Eighth Evil, who was currently grinning ear to ear. "I asked you for hope, not mockery. You dare give me, a cripple, a suicidal cultivation technique?" He'd just briefly looked over it and could immediately tell that cultivating it was the same as seeking one chance at life amongst nine chances at death.

His rage was so great that, for a moment, Sorin forgot himself. A vicious backlash from the fox deity struck him and thoroughly ripped open the wounds on his torso. He fell to his side in agony and barely managed to catch his breath as the fox leaned over the altar and growled at him.

"I am the Evil called Hope," said the fox imperiously. "I am the greatest deity of this world and will not tolerate your petty mortal complaints. You asked me for hope, and hope I have given you. Whether or not you can grasp it, it is of little consequence. You can roll over into a ditch and die for all I care."

Then, as though it had all been a dream, the darkness lifted. Sorin found himself kneeling before the altar in a puddle of his own blood. The door to the chamber creaked open, revealing the old priest. "Physician Sorin?" said the shocked priest as he hurried inside. "Are you all right? Do you require treatment?"

"I'm fine," said Sorin, picking himself up. "These are just flesh wounds. I'll recover in no time."

He then pushed his way past the priest and made his way down the mural-covered hallway. Upon seeing his bloodied appearance, expectant looks changed to gazes filled with pity.

But Sorin was used to such looks. He ignored these people and made his way back into the outpost. It was morning, and these small wounds were far from enough to keep him from opening the clinic.

2

THE CRIPPLED PHYSICIAN

A physician's ability could be summarized using three measures: the process in which they diagnosed their patients, the speed and accuracy with which they wielded their scalpel during surgery, and their skill at applying medicines and acupuncture needles to treat their patients.

Sorin had once been praised to the high heavens for his dexterous use of the scalpel, which was why it was so painful that, according to his current skill at wielding one, he would only be considered a middling physician.

Always make the shallowest incision, Sorin remembered from his father's lectures as he ran his knife over taut and bulged skin. *Doubly so when removing tumors and corruption. To rupture a mass is to spread it. To spread a mass is to doom the patient.*

A red line appeared on the skin, then two more. Sorin used forceps to pull back the skin and pin it, revealing a black, demonic abscess the size of a chicken's egg that was on the verge of bursting.

Sorin gently prodded at the mass with the side of an acupuncture needle, revealing the acupoint the mass had chosen to inhabit. If left untreated, the mass would use this point to constantly accumulate mana and demonic corruption until it eventually metastasized, provoking organ failure on a massive scale and killing the patient within hours, if not minutes.

"This is a lot less painful than I expected," confessed the adventurer, whose name Sorin had already forgotten. "I was told it would feel like a stab wound and take me a week to recover."

"Your case isn't bad, so it's less painful and will require only three days of light recovery," answered Sorin, as he wielded his scalpel to cut away at the mass's minor attachments, leaving only the 'corruption point' the mass had used to start growing in the first place.

"Physician Sorin is just being modest." It was Gabriella, Sorin's apprentice, who spoke these words. In truth, she would never have been his apprentice in a proper city, as they were roughly the same age, but she was talented, so he'd made an exception. "You'll find it difficult to find anyone more skilled in removing corruption in the surrounding outposts and cities."

"Nonsense," muttered Sorin as he continued his work. The attachment was tricky, and Gabriella's words had distracted him—another reason why she should never have been his apprentice. Gabriella was a blessing to the clinic and a light in Sorin's dark days. She had fiery hair that reached halfway down her shoulders and pale skin that should not have been possible outside a major city. She was also the gentlest and most kindly person Sorin had ever met.

"Really?" said the adventurer. "But I heard he was a—" Her words cut off before she said something insensitive.

"It's fine," said Sorin, who had long since grown used to his condition. "My cultivation was crippled; you heard it correctly. But you should also know that this means I used to be a cultivator, which means my hands will be steadier and my spiritual strength much vaster than any Blood-Thickening cultivator in this outpost.

"Still, I need to apologize," said the adventurer. "Mentioning such a thing is in poor taste."

"Silverspire Grass extract," said Sorin, holding out his hand to Gabriella. She handed over a vial, and Sorin twisted the top before taking out three drops with a needle and placing it directly on the exposed connection point.

"Ouch, that *smarts*," said the adventurer, flinching from the pain. But a second later, the mass fell off, and her eyes widened in disbelief. "How? It was latched on so tight I thought it would pull my entire skeleton out."

"Silverspire Grass has mild antidemonic properties," explained Sorin, removing the pins in her skin and stitching the wound closed. "The recommended practice is to directly cut at the connection point to stop the corruption in its tracks. But in mild cases, it's more efficient to frighten off the accumulation of demonic energy. In this way, one avoids damaging the patient's acupoints and meridians." His words sounded like they were from a textbook because they *were*. He'd practically memorized his entire medical reference library.

Sorin's practiced hands took no time at all to stitch up the incision. "Gabriella, if you would?" The apprentice physician placed a pale hand just beside the cut and began guiding life mana to where the skin had been peeled away. "Don't fully heal the wound. Only go to 80 percent. Otherwise, the wound will scar and make moving it difficult. It's far better to let the wound heal naturally while the patient exercises."

The adventurer winced as she flexed her hand and rotated her wrist. Scabs had already formed on the incision and wouldn't hinder her as long as she stayed away from adventuring for the next three days or so. But Sorin didn't say so because adventurers rarely ever heeded that advice. "Try to take it easy for the next few days," he said instead.

"How much do I owe you?" asked the adventurer.

"Ten silver," replied Sorin.

The adventurer frowned. "So little?"

"I charge an appropriate amount for services rendered," replied Sorin. "To do otherwise would go against a physician's ethics."

The adventurer shook her head and took out the ten silver pieces. "You're undercharging, Physician Sorin, just like they said you would."

Sorin shook his head. "I'm just charging what I should. The clinic is doing well, and I see no need to increase our fees anytime soon."

"Even so," the adventurer said, removing two bottles from her pack, "I was told you were stubborn, but I was also told you were in need of some Mugwort extract. I had a friend bring me their stock before coming."

Sorin hesitated but accepted the bottles. "I have some clients in need that will be very thankful for your thoughtful donation." He might not accept additional fees, but some medicines were in short supply at the outpost. They were the kind that were difficult to gather and were useful in treating non-cultivators.

"You have a heart of gold," said the adventurer. "I'll make sure to tell others to come here instead of the other clinic."

"Physician Lim is a fine practitioner," Sorin lied. "There's no need to do such a meaningless thing." At the very least, Physician Lim was a *passably competent* practitioner. But he wasn't too greedy and did treat those who were lacking coin.

Sorin cleaned the treatment area as the adventurer left. He took his time before moving on to his next patient, a familiar face in this clinic. "Lawrence, what have I told you about peeping and the inevitable consequences of such activities?"

"That it would imbalance my yin and yang and lead to reproductive issues?" said Lawrence, looking cheerful despite the boils covering his face. "It was just a small peep. Definitely not deserving of whatever she did to me."

"She obviously sprinkled powdered Crimson Rash Flower onto her fence and her windowsills," said Sorin. "And somehow, you practically smashed your face all over those two things. Gabriella!"

"No, don't call *her*," said Lawrence. Unfortunately, Sorin's tolerance for Lawrence's antics had hit rock bottom. He wouldn't refuse him treatment, but he would make the procedure as painful as possible.

"It's you," said Gabriella coolly as she entered the room. "Who was the poor victim this time? And how painful should I make it?"

"Go for maximal punishment," instructed Sorin. "This is a good opportunity to get to know the human nervous system and explore the pain tolerance of a patient. Zero anesthetic is required, but you can experiment on the effectiveness of different doses." He then looked to the nervous rogue. "Well? You never answered her question."

"This…"

"Gabriella, would you be so kind as to get the torch and the lancing kit?" said Sorin. "It'll leave dreadful scars on the poor man's face, but alas, we have so little information to go on."

"It was Margorie!" Lawrence confessed before Gabriella could leave. "And I wasn't exactly *peeping*. She had clothes on! She was just folding laundry in her backyard! Is that really a crime punishable by poisoning?"

"Even doctors use poison on occasion," said Sorin, though he paused and frowned as the words poured out of his mouth. The Ten Thousand Poison Canon had been weighing on him these past few days. In fact, he hadn't slept much since then, because the canon wasn't nearly as crazy as he'd made it out to be.

"Lawrence, you're *sixteen*," said Gabriella, taking out a set of silver needles from her belt pouch. "Grow up already, will you?" She leaned over to treat the boils, and Lawrence leaned in to take a peek. But Sorin was prepared and stuck a needle in Lawrence's neck, paralyzing him temporarily.

He watched on approvingly as Gabriella pierced the individual pustules and used her precious life mana to heal his flesh. Redness remained, but the poison and pus were both removed. There would, unfortunately, be no scarring after her expert treatment.

Knowing the treatment was as good as done, Sorin's mind reflexively began to calculate. *Iron-Melt Poison and Flesh-Melt Poison are indeed incompatible, but could I use another mediating poison to balance out their effects? And is it possible to use such poisons to clear out damaged flesh and cells?*

"Physician Sorin?" The man blinked and looked into Gabriella's too-blue eyes.

"Yes, Gabriella?"

"The treatment is finished. Could you look over the result?"

It only took a quick scan to confirm that she'd done the best job possible. "Passable work," said Sorin. "But you might want to work on the depth of your lancing." As much as he liked Gabriella, he was a perfectionist. And physicians needed to constantly criticize themselves to prevent complacency.

"Noted," said Gabriella. "Next time you do something like this, Lawrence, I'm going to go out of my way to cause you pain."

"Thank you so much for the rescue doctors," said Lawrence, hopping off the treatment bed. "No need to see me out. And please don't mention this to anyone. Patient confidentiality and everything, you know?"

"I'm a bit worried about him," said Gabriella once Lawrence had left the clinic.

"So am I," said Sorin with a shrug. "But it's better that he learns a lesson now than when he goes out adventuring."

"Will he really?" asked Gabriella.

"There's not much else to do in the Bloodwood Outpost," said Sorin. "His father was an adventurer, and so was his father's father. And from what I can tell, he's got the talent, if not the brains, to do well at it."

The clinic was empty, so Sorin moved to grab a broom, only for Gabriella to yank it away and give him a *look.* "You know you're not supposed to be doing unnecessary manual labor," she said, glancing at his chest. "Your wounds—they've reopened again, haven't they?"

"They're fine," said Sorin. He made to take the broom back but winced as pain radiated down his pectorals.

"*Men,*" said Gabriella. She stomped over to the door and flipped the sign. She then lowered the curtains and pulled Sorin to a bed. "Sit down," she commanded, and Sorin could only resign himself to his fate. He unbuttoned his shirt, revealing a mass of scars. Three bright red wounds had never fully healed. He had used stitches and a cheap healing ointment to keep it sanitary and prevent infection.

Gabriella traced his wounds with concern. "The surface should heal up within the week, but there's not much my life mana can do for the deeper cuts."

"Spare your mana," said Sorin, pushing her away.

But Gabriella stubbornly pushed back. "We don't have any patients now, so I have mana to spare." She began pouring said mana into the deepest wounds that had reopened, then proceeded towards the shallower rips—these were much easier to treat—continuing outward.

She continued in this way for a full half-hour until, finally, Sorin was forced to stop her. "You've used up 95 percent of your mana," said Sorin. "If you use up more, you'll overtax yourself and affect your cultivation."

"But I can't cultivate *all* night," said Gabriella. She'd reached the sixth stage of the Blood-Thickening Realm and was finally starting to see diminishing returns in her cultivation.

"Becoming a physician also needs careful study and memorization," said Sorin. "Have you finished the reading I assigned?"

"*Yes*, I finished studying up on meridian theory, including the twelve primary meridians and four extraordinary meridians," said Gabriella. Sorin knew there were actually *eight* extraordinary meridians, but he did not correct her on the matter. The top cultivation families carefully hoarded such knowledge. At her level, she was better off not knowing.

"Then today, you'll read up on Remus's theory of poison application," said Sorin. "What? Do you think you won't learn anything?"

"It's not that," said Gabriella with a grimace.

"Then what is it?" asked Sorin.

"Well… poisons are things that assassins use," said Gabriella.

"Margorie used poison against Lawrence," Sorin pointed out.

"That's *different*," said Gabriella.

"I don't see how," said Sorin.

"Anyway, poisons are what demons use against humans," Gabriella continued. "And they're also what some particularly hateful humans use against other humans."

"Poisons are a key part of your studies," said Sorin. "You must recognize them to be able to treat them, and you'll also need to be able to use poisons to fight off various afflictions." Seeing that she was still unconvinced, he sighed. "You're a bright girl, Gabriella, and I'm happy you chose to study medicine. Instructing you these past three years has been a blessing I never expected. But there's something you need to realize: You're also a kind girl. *Too* kind."

"Is there such a thing as being too kind?" Gabriella pouted.

"There is," said Sorin. "As physicians, we amputate limbs to save lives. We cause pain to heal wounds. And sometimes, we cause irreversible injuries to our patients. We need to hurt people to be kind to them at times. With your current state of mind, you're completely incapable of making such decisions."

He then walked up to the clinic's bookshelf. "So... Remus's theory on poison and application, and Warren and Rice's debate on the ethics of poison and their use in the medical profession."

"But that paper is considered trash," said Gabriella.

"It's only trash if you treat it like trash," said Sorin. "There's something to be learned wherever you look." He sighed as he felt his wounds and assessed his condition. His hands were trembling, so he couldn't hold a scalpel. His mind was also tired and preoccupied with the 'gift' Hope had given him a few days prior.

The Ten Thousand Poison Canon is insane, no matter how I look at it, thought Sorin as he reviewed the medical theories he'd learned. *To balance poisons is one thing, but to use one's blood to replace one's mana sea? Madness.*

Yet his subconscious mind was slowly warming to the idea. Just because he'd never heard about such a thing, it didn't mean it wouldn't work. And as long as the poisons were balanced, there should be no threat to his life.

"Sorin?" asked Gabriella, snapping him out of his reverie.

"Sorry, I got distracted again," said Sorin. "And I'm clearly in no state to practice. I'm going to go home and rest."

"That would be for the best," said Gabriella. "Do you want me to walk you back?"

"I'll be fine," said Sorin. He walked over to the door and put on a thin coat. The nights were getting chilly, and his health was not what it used to be. "You can send for me if there's an emergency you can't handle, but I anticipate you'll be fine." Gabriella was a smart girl and would be able to handle most patients that bothered coming to this rundown clinic.

3

SEEKING LIFE THROUGH DEATH

The Kepler Manor was located on the outer rim of the Bloodwood Outpost, not far from the towering wall built entirely of demonic wood obtained from Bloodwood Forest. It was much larger than the lower-quality dwellings in its surroundings and had at one point been the Governor's Manor.

Thanks to huge investments from the guilds and corporations ten years back, the outpost had undergone a complete makeover. The Governor's Manor had changed locations, but the Kepler Clan had bought the old manor at a bargain.

Only three people lived in the Kepler Manor: Sorin Kepler, the master of the house; his butler, Percival; and his maid, Clarice. It was a small house, given the status of Sorin's family, but much larger than most in the outpost.

In Sorin's opinion, it was a complete waste to live in said house. He didn't *need* such a huge house for the three of them and would have been much more comfortable in smaller accommodations. But his family's obsession over face and reputation trumped his own desires for modest, so here he was, in a house he couldn't afford with a staff whose wages he couldn't afford to pay, working for a clinic that barely made ends meet.

"Young master, you've returned," greeted Percival as Sorin walked in. He was a forty-year-old man with black hair tied back in a simple ponytail. His clothes were old but well-maintained. He wore tailored black pants with a matching vest and a white shirt with lace on the neck. "My apologies, but we hadn't expected you so early. I can prepare you a spot of tea and some light snacks if you'd like."

"That's fine, Percival," said Sorin. "Be at ease. I just had some thoughts that I wanted to confirm in my study."

"I'll have the tea and snacks ready shortly," said Percival, ignoring Sorin's refusal.

The house was huge and had a total of twenty rooms, all lit by expensive mana lamps that delivered a yellow light that was easy on the eyes. The study was located between Sorin's room and the library, which contained hundreds of medical reference books and assorted research notes.

He walked behind his desk—an expensive thing made of sable oak, a rare spirit wood that kept the mind fresh and focused. He pulled a book on the reference shelf containing a small selection of reference books. A hidden compartment opened, revealing a safe that could only be unlocked via bloodline authentication.

It accepted a drop of his blood before popping open, revealing a precious golden tome. The book was called the Divine Medical Codex, and only high-ranked members of the Kepler Clan were allowed to read it.

Sorin opened the cover to the first page, which contained a note and introduction by his family's founder, Sirius Abberjay Kepler. He was not the only author of the book but a major contributor.

Thanks to his ancestor's teachings and successful policies enacted by his many descendants, the Kepler Clan now held enormous influence in the medical community. Even politicians and major organizations would need to consider their opinions when deciding policies.

The Divine Medical Codex was a complete work that included a section on the human body, a section on cultivation, a section on ailments, and a section on treatment methods and medications. Sorin turned to a page illustrating the human body's meridian network. The twelve main meridians and eight extraordinary meridians were high-lighted and described, along with 361 acupoints that were used both in medicine and cultivation.

Each cultivator was born with naturally open meridians. The more naturally open meridians one possessed, the greater the cultivator's talent. Sorin himself had been born with all twelve primary meridians naturally open. With the help of his father, he'd managed to open four of the eight extraordinary meridians, establishing an unshakable foundation for his future advancement.

Unfortunately, Sorin had yet to advance to the Bone-Forging Realm when he received news of his parents' deaths. A few days later, he suffered an unfortunate "accident" that destroyed his mana sea and delivered a fatal blow to his internal organs.

Since he belonged to a family of physicians, he was able to escape with his life, but his cultivation remained crippled, and his life expectancy was greatly diminished.

He was no fool. He knew the branch families were behind the inci-dent. He was also certain that the Council of Elders knew as well. Alas, his parents were dead, and he was now useless. The elders had unani-mously decided that his uncle, Reeves Mockingjay Kepler, would be the next head of the family.

But Sorin no longer cared about such things. It was all in the past. His life was ruined, and he accepted that. What he did *not* accept was that he was fated to die a useless wretch. He was determined to discover what had happened to his parents. If they were also the victims of his uncle's machinations, he would surely avenge them.

Balancing poisons is no longer an issue, thought Sorin as he reflected on the Ten Thousand Poison Canon. *I've gone through the calculations several times, and the Divine Medical Codex agrees. The main problem with cultivating the Ten Thousand Poison Canon lies in acquiring so many unique poisons. Stronger poisons are required for each cultivation realm, and these things aren't easily acquired even by master alchemists and physicians.*

The second problem laid in the approach to cultivation. To Sorin's knowledge, cultivation was done from the inside out. A cultivator circulated mana through their naturally opened meridians to move ambient mana into their mana sea. By increasing the density of their mana, they were able to thicken their blood, thereby passively strengthening their organs, their flesh, and their bones in preparation for the next cultivation realm.

Each cultivation realm had ten cultivation stages. The first cultivation realm was Blood-Thickening, followed by Bone-Forging and Flesh-Sanctification.

Blood-Thickening was the first step. By reaching the first stage of Blood-Thickening, one would officially be considered a cultivator. It should be noted that only one in ten people could cultivate, and among these people, most only had one or two meridian channels open.

Where the Ten Thousand Poison Canon confused Sorin was that it didn't mention how to circulate mana through one's meridians, nor did it mention the all-important mana sea. Instead of storing mana in one location, as every single other cultivation method Sorin had ever heard of did, the Ten Thousand Poison Canon relied on the physical body to store mana-infused poisons. This would directly thicken the blood, thereby granting the cultivator a large mana pool with the innate poison characteristic.

Most cultivation methods required a compatible set of unblocked meridians. The Ten Thousand Poison Canon was the exception to the rule. Did meridians not matter, or did it simply assume fully unlocked main meridians? Cultivating, according to the canon, might be suicidal for Sorin, given the state of his collapsed mana sea and his stagnated and damaged meridians.

There were also Sorin's physical problems to worry about. His internal organs were on the verge of failure and might not be able to tolerate even a perfectly balanced cocktail of poisons. His life expectancy of 3–4 months could easily turn into 3–4 hours. Cultivating the Ten Thousand Poison Canon might be the last thing he did.

It was well into the evening when Sorin heard a knock on the door.

He put down his pen as Percival entered and brought in a plate of cold dinner. "My apologies for bringing it up so late, Mr. Kepler," said Percival. "I assumed you were fully conscious when you said you'd be right down for dinner. It's been a while since you were so immersed in a puzzle that you didn't pay attention to your surroundings."

"It's a puzzle, all right," said Sorin, accepting the plate of food. He shoveled root vegetables and garden greens into his mouth without tasting them, then pushed away the perfectly cooked pork chop because cutting it up was far too troublesome.

"Allow me, Mr. Kepler," said Percival, taking up the knife and fork and cutting the pork chop into small pieces.

"Please stop calling me Mr. Kepler, Percival," said Sorin. "Mr. Kepler is what you called my father. I might be sixteen, technically a man, but I'm not even half the man my father was at that age."

"Alas, decorum ties my hands, Mr. Kepler," said Percival, pushing over the plate. Sorin had no choice but to shovel down the pork under the butler's watchful eye. "Besides, I think you're devaluing yourself. Even with your *condition*, few one-star physicians possess even half your skill."

"I'm just a ticking time bomb," said Sorin. "A cripple on the last of his days. It won't be long now before I leave this world. Ten years later, I doubt there'll be anyone who remembers me." He closed his eyes and sank deep in thought. That was another thing to consider—his condition. Since he didn't have a lot of time remaining, why *shouldn't* he take a gamble?

"Percival?" said Sorin, opening his eyes.

"Yes, Mr. Kepler?" replied Percival, who'd yet to leave the room.

"Could you fetch me a few books from the library?" asked Sorin. "I'm looking for *An Analysis of Fort Bloodwood's Flora and Fauna and their Demonic Mutations* and *An Adventurer's Guide to Poisonous Herbs and Creatures*."

Percival raised an eyebrow. "I take it you've run into a unique medical case, Mr. Kepler?"

"Something like that," muttered Sorin. "The local beauties have started using poisons to deter perverts and peeping toms. They have no idea what they're doing, so I'd like to prepare for the worst."

"I have to ask—why bother?" said Percival. "Lawrence's antics are well-known throughout the outpost."

"Because a doctor should have a caring and open heart," said Sorin.

"Your father would spank you for saying such a drivel," said Percival.

"Fine," said Sorin. "It's a puzzle. I'm interested."

"A much more reasonable answer," said Percival. "I'll be back in a jiffy."

Percival returned a short while later with the requested books and retired for the evening. As for Sorin, he stayed up late into the night. Calculating. Thinking.

I'm dead either way, aren't I? thought Sorin as he measured his options. *I've only got a few months left to live. What can I even do with that?*

Since he was at the end of his rope, he might as well gamble. And if his gamble paid off, those three to four months might become thirty to forty years. He would also obtain the power he needed to get the answers he craved.

Having made up his mind, Sorin made his way down to the basement of the manor, where the laboratory was located. What he was attempting was very dangerous, and any external attempts at saving him would greatly reduce his chances of success. He locked the door and then immediately got to work.

"Seven-Star Lung Corroding Lily... Four-Leaf Blood Purging Clover..." muttered Sorin as he looked through the glass jars and vials above his workbench. There were dozens of poisons in the manor's medical stores, but unfortunately, only two poisons—Seven-Star Lung Corroding Lily extract and Three-Flame Ginseng powder—could be balanced between his yin and yang organs.

The Seven-Star Lung Corroding Lily extract was useful in dissolving lung mucus that would otherwise prevent patients from breathing. As for the Three-Flame Ginseng powder, it had various applications but was predominantly used to purge out harmful bacteria and demonic qi invasion in the large intestine.

Both poisons were not potent enough to enact the changes required by the Ten Thousand Poison Canon, but the text described a way around this. Sorin carefully measured portions of each poison and stirred them into liquified mana extract, a violet-blue liquid that could assimilate with virtually any material.

He waited as the beakers hissed and bubbled. The blue-violet liquids slowly changed color until each one was a different shade of sickly green and a fifth of its original volume. He then loaded thirty-one syringes made from mana-infused glass and one-star grade mana-tempered mithril. The seven-star poison required eleven injection points along the lung meridian leading down the arms, while the three-flame poison required twenty injection points that also ran along the arms, albeit through a different path.

With preparations complete, Sorin used liquified mana extract to trace a pattern over his body using a needle. Some spots were difficult to reach, but Sorin had dexterous hands; thanks to two opposing mirrors, he was able to complete the mysterious pattern illustrated in the Ten Thousand Poison Canon.

This is it, thought Sorin as he disinfected his acupoints. *The point of no return.* Whether he lived or died was up to fate. Regardless of success or failure, there would be no going back to his profession. There would also be severe political ramifications.

Sorin gritted his teeth as he injected poison into his left side using his right hand. He did the same to his right side with his left, making sure to balance the poisons properly.

His hands shook, but he forced them to remain steady. His body became a battlefield between hot and cold, yin and yang. His blood, which had lain dormant for the past three years, began to seethe with excitement.

The pain was excruciating, but Sorin was used to pain. He bit down on a leather belt and used his spiritual strength to maintain consciousness. His body twitched, and the two poisons invaded his body, compromising major organs and destroying significant portions of his flesh.

Little by little, he saw his odds of success grow slimmer as his body became a cesspool of fatal toxins. His heartbeat slowed, and he lost all feeling in his limbs. He felt cold. So cold, despite the ingredients burning his innards.

It was in this moment, when his life hung on by a thread, that he realized how foolish he'd been. How could he, a cripple, possibly change his fate? A part of him wanted to give up, but fortunately, a much more stubborn part hung on for dear life. It was that same part that had pulled him through when his cultivation was destroyed, and his lifespan severely injured.

It was during that moment that the destruction came to an end, and the poison finally fused with his blood. His mana changed, and the combination of blood and mana surged through his body, nourishing his flesh.

Dead nerves regained their function, and muscles regained their strength. They greedily drank in the poisonous mana and incorporated it into his starving cells.

Mana continued to build up within his body until suddenly, a few blockages that had existed for the past three years collapsed. Mana surged through two of his dormant meridians. The two meridians in question were Sorin's lung and large intestine meridians. Mana flowed through these two organs and breathed life into their dead flesh.

With this sudden reversal, Sorin felt his body's condition improve for the first time in years. He recovered a portion of his lost strength and no longer felt the fatigue weighing down on him like a suffocating blanket.

For the first time in three years, Sorin breathed in a proper breath of fresh air. All felt right in the world for approximately ten seconds, at which point his vision blacked out from overexertion. Sorin's exhausted body collapsed onto the cold stone floor of the laboratory as it continued strengthening itself and transforming.

4

THE ADVENTURERS GUILD

Sorin woke to a gentle knock on the laboratory door. "Mr. Kepler?" came Percival's worried voice. "Mr. Kepler, are you all right?"

"I'm fine," rasped Sorin as he picked himself up off the basement's stone floor. He'd been so tired that he'd passed out.

On instinct, Sorin assessed his body's situation. His neck was sore from having slept in a slightly off position, but he was otherwise fine. In fact, he was better than fine, he realized as he scanned himself from head to toe. Mana was now circulating in his body through his lung and large intestine meridians, filling his arms with a familiar strength.

"Are you sure?" came Percival's voice. "Breakfast is ready if you care to have some."

"I said I'm *fine*," repeated Sorin. Percival was a wonderful person, but he was also extremely perceptive. Moreover, his work wasn't limited to being his butler and guardian; he was also spying on him on behalf of the Kepler Clan.

The two unlocked meridians were the least of the chances in Sorin's body. Most important was his thickened blood, which had jumped up two stages thanks to the infusion of poison and his cultivation prior to being crippled.

In fact, his blood contained much more mana than when he'd first started cultivating. This was all thanks to the Ten Thousand Poison Canon. His blood had changed on a fundamental level and now incorporated the essence of the two poisons he'd assimilated.

Sorin's cultivation experiences relied on having a mana sea, but to his relief, controlling the mana in his blood came naturally. A sickly green gas surged out of his hands and formed two orbs. He accustomed himself to the feel of the poisonous mana by twirling the orbs around his fingers, then tossing them up and down before pulling them back into his body.

Having confirmed that his body was functioning better than ever, Sorin walked over to a corner of the room to a humanoid mannequin. He summoned poison into his right hand and struck the mannequin with a poison-infused palm. The palm print he left on the mannequin hissed and sizzled. Moreover, the artificial 'veins' on the mannequin turned black as the poisonous mana infiltrated its system.

Sorin took notes as the poison worked its magic on the mannequin. The mannequin was a magic treasure that was more valuable than anything in the manor, save perhaps the Divine Medical Codex. *I wonder how long I'll get to keep it,* thought Sorin. He'd long since memorized the codex, but it was the principle of the thing.

Earning back his physician qualifications was now all but impossible. Physicians required life mana, and few exceptions were ever made. But he still had all his knowledge and training and was able to quantify and analyze the mannequin's symptoms.

"Symptoms are not limited to the lung and large intestine meridian contact points," he muttered out of habit as he took notes. "A poison mutation has likely occurred, creating a compound poison that is stronger than the two originals."

The next test he performed was on a series of test papers that could be used to identify poisons and diseases. He soaked the papers in various test solutions and then flicked a drop of poisonous mana on each of them. Intricate lines appeared on the papers as the poison either consumed the test medium or ran its course.

The results surprised Sorin. Somehow, the poison was much stronger than he'd expected. *The sum of both poisons can't possibly be this powerful,* he thought as he analyzed the test results. *This can only mean one thing: The Ten Thousand Poison Canon not only assimilates and combines poisons, but it also concentrates and amplifies them to scale with my cultivation.* He was only a second-stage Blood-Thickening cultivator. The difference between a second-stage Blood-Thickening cultivator and a tenth-stage Blood-Thickening cultivator was like night and day.

The poisons had definitely merged, but this begged the question: could they be split up again? Sorin urged out another globe of poisonous mana. Then, using his powerful spiritual strength, he split it apart into two separate green globs, one pale and one dark. He performed the same tests as before and discovered that, while they were the same poisons as he'd originally mixed, they were much more potent. Moreover, their quantity was seemingly endless. His body wasn't just amplifying these poisons but also producing poisonous mana on a massive scale.

This both gratified and worried Sorin. Poisons were dangerous and had to be carefully controlled. Using poisons was one thing, but accidentally poisoning innocent people was the gravest of taboos that could result in a cultivator being crippled or killed to set an example.

Sorin practiced for several hours before he was satisfied with his new abilities. Not only could he manipulate the poison mana like life mana, but he could also pull it back into his body and relieve poisonous symptoms.

In fact, his abilities weren't just limited to his personal poisons. He tested out a theory with several other poisons and discovered that it was possible to absorb poisons into his own body. The downside was that his poison-resistant body would have to suffer some of the effects of the poisons as he assimilated them.

Like life mana, it was also possible to project a small amount of mana on physical objects. With his strength, a small dagger was the limit. Fortunately, he'd been trained to use daggers for self-defense ever since he was little. He was also experienced enough with needles to throw them at targets at very short range.

Yet all this was theoretical. In the end, Sorin had been trained and had practiced as a physician. Physicians preserved lives for a living. And now, thanks to the Ten Thousand Poison Canon, he would be taking them instead.

The Adventurers Guild was the busiest location in the Bloodwood Outpost. Adventurers were essential in clearing out the demons of Bloodwood Forest. Only then could loggers peacefully cut down trees and prepare the land for purification.

Unlike the Temple of Hope located on the outskirts of the outpost, the Adventurers Guild was located at the heart of the bustling town, just opposite the Governor's Manor. It was constructed from the demonic bloodwood obtained in Bloodwood Forest and positively reeked of blood and iron.

A steady stream of adventurers poured into and out of the complex, turning in beast cores and beast parts for their corresponding rewards. There were also people turning in herbs or simply providing proof to obtain bounties. All sorts of missions were issued in the Adventurers Guild, some on behalf of the government but others on behalf of organizations or individuals.

The Adventurers Guild was dirty, busy, and chaotic. *Not enough soap. And definitely not enough protocols surrounding demonic contamination,* thought Sorin as he pushed his way through a mass of adventurers reviewing jobs posted near the entrance.

He felt several pairs of curious eyes settle on him as he lined up at the reception. Sorin wasn't exactly an unknown figure in the outpost; many adventurers here had either suffered grievous wounds or absorbed too much demonic energy. Adventuring was a dangerous profession that could render a person broke if they made the slightest mistake. It was these kinds of people who usually turned up at Sorin's clinic, desperate and unable to pay for treatment.

"Physician Sorin? Is that you?" asked the receptionist when he arrived. She was a dark-haired girl with shoulder-length hair whom he often saw frequenting the bakery a block away from his clinic.

"I'm sorry, it's been a while since we last saw each other," said Sorin. Also, he was terrible with names and didn't bother being coy about it.

"I'm Grettel," said the receptionist. "And I must say that I'm quite surprised to see you here. It's typically your nurses or Gabriella who come here to post requests. Are you in need of some medicinal ingredients or demon parts? Or perhaps you're here to advertise your services?"

Sorin cleared his throat. "Actually, I've come to apply to join the Adventurers Guild." The room quieted the moment he said these words, and Sorin suddenly wished that he'd come at a less busy time. "Perhaps I should stop by in the afternoon?" he said to Grettel.

"Unfortunately, it's always this busy," said Grettel apologetically. "And I'm sorry to say that I can't make exceptions, even for a wonderful physician like yourself. Licensed adventurers *must* be cultivators. For safety reasons. I'm sure you…" Her voice trailed off as Sorin summoned an orb of sickly green mana.

"I've run into a small bit of fortune and recovered a portion of my cultivation," Sorin said to Grettel. "Could I trouble you to sign me up for the next evaluation?"

"I… Of course," said Grettel, picking up a stack of papers on her desk and passing it to him. "Actually, it's just an hour from the next assessment. You'll be the sixth person in this assessment group, although you *might* want to wait till tomorrow." She gave him a meaningful look.

Sorin's eye twitched. As much as he'd love to accept her advice, he'd already attracted too many eyes. It wouldn't be long before others knew Sorin had regained his cultivation—more than enough time for Percival to find out and prevent him from taking the examination.

"The next assessment is fine," said Sorin.

"Then please fill out your information as best you can," said Grettel. "We understand that some of these answers might be difficult to answer; the assessor will fill out the blanks during the assessment process."

Sorin took the stack of paper and moved over to a table to fill it out. Most of the people in the common room were eyeing him strangely and joking about the idea of a *physician* going adventuring.

They probably can't tell the difference between life mana and poison mana, thought Sorin. Both were green in color, and both were exceedingly rare.

That being said, he *did* notice a few fearful adventurers glancing his way. They were some of the more experienced adventurers, the kind that made a habit of *not* running their mouths off about everything.

Name and cultivation stage are all straightforward, but this? thought Sorin. *What does any of this other stuff even mean?* His education as a physician was beyond excellent, but his knowledge of adventuring was lacking.

Class, skills, spells, and abilities. These things confused him. From what he knew, adventurers were formal in how they classified cultivators, but Sorin had never paid attention to his tutors, and they had never pressed the matter.

Sorin only had the most basic idea of classes, and he had no idea what his class might be. He wasn't a mage or assassin like most poison-wielding adventurers were, nor could he be classified as a rogue, an archer, or a warrior. If anything, he was a cross between a rogue and a poison mage who could dabble as a field medic.

Unsure of how to proceed, he left this section blank. And when it came to skills and abilities, he just wrote down poison, medical knowledge, and basic martial arts. There was a section for detailed descriptions, but he ignored them. The assessor could worry about that.

The last document to be filled out was a contract. Specifically, it was an indemnity contract stating that neither Sorin nor his relatives could hold the Adventurers Guild responsible for his death or any injuries he might suffer. There were also clauses on privacy, but as far as he was concerned, there was no protecting information once it was written on paper.

"Here you are," Sorin said, handing back the papers to Grettel.

"This…" Grettel said, grimacing as she looked at the class and skills section. "You *might* want to wait until tomorrow. The instructor this time is extremely picky."

"Who's picky?" a sharp voice snapped from behind her. Grettel jumped as the speaker snuck behind with a shadow-related movement technique and grabbed the registration folio and Sorin's information file.

"Look at what we have here," said the speaker with a grin. "Someone who has *no* idea what they're doing. I think this assessment is going to be a lot of fun. Don't you?"

"Please be kind, Assessor Haley," winced Grettel. "He's a nice boy, and everyone at the guild would be happy to see him come back in one piece."

"I'll see what I can do, but I make no promises," said Assessor Haley. "Now, what are you all waiting for? If you're not lined up in the next ten seconds, you *fail*!"

5

FIRST COMBAT

A light blue mana shield rippled as their group of seven left the protection of the outpost and entered demonic territory. A wild and chaotic mana replaced the gentle and calm mana characteristic of human-inhabited territories.

Cultivation and energy recovery grew several times more difficult, and their emotions, already in high gear due to the impending exam, suddenly grew unstable. "We'll stop here to regulate our emotions," said Assessor Haley. "Remember that this is fall, which is very different from either summer or winter." Summer was the domain of Violence, while Winter, the deadliest of the seasons, fell under the influence of Madness.

It took a few minutes for their makeshift team to grow used to the pressure. Sorin was not an adventurer, but his late father had taken him out into the wilderness on several occasions. He was, therefore, the second to rehabilitate himself after Lawrence, an unexpected acquaintance for this trial. It was clear that Lawrence had also been trained by his father in preparation for his adventuring debut.

"Communication with the outpost will become difficult going forward," explained Haley. "Only precious consumable treasures can be used to communicate, and even I only carry three on my person. It is, therefore, important to remember that anything that happens in the wilderness is likely to stay in the wilderness.

Haley led the way, and the rest of their group, still struggling with the emotional impact of the demonic forest, followed. They were mostly silent and kept to themselves, though Lawrence approached Sorin and gave him a thumbs-up.

"Physician Kepler," said Lawrence. "Out of all the people I know, you're the one I least expected to see here. Have they started bringing physicians along to look after the wounded?"

"I'm not a physician anymore, so please call me Sorin. Besides, we're the same age. Addressing each other with titles is just uncomfortable."

"But Sorin just sounds *wrong*," said Lawrence. "It's hard to face a person who's seen your privates and busted your boils a half dozen times without a certain degree of separation."

"Deal with it. If we're adventuring together, it's very likely that at least half of these people will see you naked by day's end."

"True," said Lawrence. "Though my father always said that half of being a rogue lay in not getting hit."

"And what about the other half?" asked Sorin.

"That... well... it involves seeing *other* people naked while also maintaining a pure and unsoiled body," said Lawrence. "Eeek!" He suddenly froze as a sharp projectile flashed by his ear and drew a stream of blood. "Assessor Haley, how could you!"

"If you keep spewing nonsense during this assessment, I won't hesitate to fail you, even if it *is* the tenth time you've taken this assessment," said Haley, not even deigning to look back.

"She's a vicious assessor," whispered Lawrence. "Which is why my dad said I couldn't take the test from anyone but her. He also said that in all these years, he's the only one to have seen her—"

"Lawrence!" snapped Haley. The rogue wisely shut his trap and fell in line.

"Now that we're a fair distance away from the outpost shield, let's get down to the meat and bones of this assessment," said Assessor

Haley. "You're all here to take the Adventurers Guild examination, and as far as I'm concerned, it started the moment we set foot outside the Adventurers Guild. And Daphne?"

"Yes?" said the mage in their group, blinking.

"Are you daydreaming on me?" asked Haley. "Because in my eyes, that's already a failing grade. You've got a lot of negative marks to make up for."

Surprisingly, the mage took it in stride. "All right. I'll do my best." Her eyes glazed over as her mind drifted once again.

Haley put her hand to her forehead. "Fine. If you die, my conscience is clear. Vetner?"

"Yes, Assessor Haley?" said a nervous-looking warrior. He wore chain mail and wielded a sword and shield.

"As the only person who seems to be able to take hits on this team, it falls to you to be the tank of the party," said Haley. "Daphne, hold your spells and only use them if you have to. Lawrence, keep an eye out for sneaky demons and potential ambushes."

"Yes, ma'am!" said Lawrence. He was amazingly quick and blurred off into the distance. It was only thanks to his strong spiritual perception that Sorin could make out his shadow flitting from tree to tree.

"Janice, you're a healer, so you won't be expected to defeat any monsters individually," continued Haley. "Just focus on providing support and use your mana sparingly. You'll fight in a group with Vetner when the time comes. Gareth?"

"Yes, Assessor Haley?" said a sharp-eyed youth. He was a dark-haired boy with golden eyes that never seemed to stop moving.

"I see that you've already taken stock of our surroundings," said Haley. "Keep at it and grow into your role as we move."

"Yes, Assessor Haley," replied Gareth. He began paying more attention to their backs and sides, leaving the front for Lawrence, and probed in detail.

"That just leaves Sorin," said Haley. "Sorin Kepler. Any relation to the Kepler Clan in the capital?"

"Regretfully," said Sorin.

"Then, given your origins, I'm sorry to say that I've never seen a sadder application," said Haley. "No experience? No training? Did you think that since the classes at the Adventurers Guild were free, they weren't worth taking? I'd at least expect you to pass your family's screening. Don't you know that can cause huge issues for us?"

"That... my situation is a little unusual," said Sorin, but Haley cut him off before he could explain.

"Save it," said Haley. "You're from a big family. You feel stifled. I get it. But that also means the bar is much higher for passing than it would normally be. You'd better be damned impressive, or you can forget about getting a passing mark. Is that understood?"

"Yes, Assessor Haley," said Sorin.

They were less than twenty minutes into the forest before Lawrence came rushing back, and Gareth, the group's archer, called them to a stop. "Our flanks are clear. Lawrence—what did you find?"

"Three minor demons, horned rabbits," reported Lawrence. "Shouldn't be too difficult to take care of them alone, but I figured it was your call."

Gareth looked to Haley, who nodded to him. "Vetner, take point. I'll cover you with arrow fire. Serious wounds are unlikely, but Janice, please keep an eye on him. Lawrence? Approach from the right and take out one of them. I want to familiarize myself with your movements and attack speed. And Daphne? Hold your fire. Daphne?"

The mage blinked and looked at Gareth. "Yes?"

"No spells, please," said Gareth.

"Okay!" said Daphne, giving him a thumbs-up.

"That just leaves Sorin," said Gareth. "I have no idea where to fit you, so act how you please and don't get in the way."

"Understood," said Sorin. He would take the chance to try out his abilities against living targets if he could. Demons had different physiologies than humans, and mana interacted with them very differently.

Lawrence led them into a clearing. Upon seeing the three-horned rabbits, Gareth called a stop and signaled for Vetner to initiate.

The warrior began to glow with a soft blue light as he activated a combat skill. Sorin thought it was overkill against minor demons, but he took out his dagger and needles and prepared to fight if required.

Demons had keen instincts and immediately reacted to Vetner's charge. The three-foot-long creatures channeled demonic energy into their horns and aimed their attacks at Vetner's torso.

"Shield Extension!" shouted Vetner, pouring mana into his arms and through the shield on his left arm. A mana projection twice as large as the shield appeared to block two of the rabbits. As for the third, Vetner swung his sword down and took a chunk out of its cheek.

The two rabbits Vetner had blocked bounced back quickly. One of them tumbled into a tree and used it as a springboard to attack the unprotected Daphne.

An arrow came flying out of Gareth's bow and struck the horned rabbit in the neck. It tried to get up, but Sorin flicked a crystal needle imbued with poison into its neck, extinguishing the last spark of life in its corrupted flesh.

The rabbit Vetner had chosen to fight was putting up a fierce struggle, so he had no time to block the remaining rabbit. Fortunately, Lawrence had recovered from the loss of his initial target; he appeared behind the stray rabbit and struck it cleanly between the shoulder blades.

This only left Vetner's rabbit. They stood back as Vetner finished it off. He took a blow to the shoulder in the process, but fortunately, his chainmail absorbed most of the blow.

"Clear up the battlefield and inspect all wounds," ordered Gareth. "Sorin, I hear you're good at surgical work. Get their cores and their horns, will you?"

Sorin shrugged and did as he was told. The anatomy of a horned rabbit wasn't complicated, and he quickly located the small demonic crystals in their skulls. Their horns were thick but hollow, so he had no problem using a scalpel to retrieve them.

It was only when he'd finished his retrieval work that he paid attention to Vetner. The warrior had gotten supremely unlucky in his exchange, as his shield extension had failed just as the horned rabbit was making a dying lunge. His chainmail was currently stripped back, and Janice, the healer of their party, was pouring ridiculous amounts of mana into the shallow wound.

"That wound doesn't need that much healing," Sorin interrupted her. "You'd be better off preserving your mana for something else."

Janice frowned as he approached. "He's clearly bleeding quite a bit. Blood loss can become a real issue if not taken care of promptly."

"It won't be an issue," said Sorin. He unsheathed his dagger and cut away Vetner's shirt around the wound, revealing a small hole where the horned rabbit had stabbed him. Sorin then poured a disinfectant solution over the wound and then did the same to his knife and left hand. Then, to Vetner's horror, Sorin reached into the wound with his fingers.

"Are you insane?" shouted Janice. She tried to pull him away, but fortunately, Lawrence was around and stopped her.

"Just let the doctor do his thing," said Lawrence. "He knows what he's doing."

"Horned rabbit horns appear to be solid, but they're actually hollow on the inside," said Sorin as he rummaged under the man's flesh. Vetner gritted his teeth, but the pain wasn't so serious since Sorin had stealthily rubbed a powerful anesthetic on his fingers. "The horns easily splinter when piercing into flesh, aggravating the otherwise shallow wounds that they cause."

His fingers finally found what they were looking for—a chunk of bone lodged into muscle. He yanked it out and placed a finger over the wound and the man's three torn veins. "Treatment is simple," continued Sorin. "Extract the bone fragments. Stitch the veins. Apply healing potions as required or apply a healing salve or small amounts of life mana to staunch bleeding. Stitch and heal over torn muscles. A healing salve will be sufficient for superficial wounds. Janice?"

"Y-Yes?" stammered Janice.

"I already finished stitching up most of this," said Sorin, tugging on a needle and thread and snipping through it with a pair of surgical scissors. "Three units of life mana should do the trick." *Two if she was half-competent,* thought Sorin but decided to keep that part to himself.

Thirty seconds later, Janice was done healing most of the damage. Vetner winced as he rolled his shoulder but grinned. "Nice! It's good as new!" he said.

"Warriors typically regenerate quickly, so you should be right as rain within the hour," said Sorin. "Apologies, Janice, for usurping your role. I'm just quite fearful about what other threats we might face and thought it best to preserve your life mana."

"Is everyone done?" asked Haley once Vetner put his chainmail back on.

"Yes," replied Gareth. "We've recovered and are ready to move out."

"Not so fast," said Haley. "This was your first fight coming out here, so it doesn't count towards your actual assessment. But I must say—this was one of the most disgraceful fights I've ever laid eyes on." She *glared* at Vetner. "Your shield skill is unpolished. When did you learn it? Three days ago?"

"Four," admitted Vetner.

"Rookie mistakes like that will get your friends killed," scolded Haley. "Use only skills you've practiced. If it's a minor encounter, let others know that you're practicing something new so they can back you up." She looked at Lawrence next. "Lawrence. Not bad this time around."

"Thank you, Assessor Haley," said Lawrence.

"Gareth," said Haley. "Keep this up, and you'll fail."

"Yes, ma'am," said Gareth, accepting her criticism.

"Do you know what you did wrong?" asked Haley.

"I didn't fully familiarize myself with the team and inquire as to their specific abilities," said Gareth. "I assumed they would fall into specific roles, but I should have verified before the first combat."

"At least you have the self-awareness to admit it," said Haley. "Normally, it's either a warrior or an archer that leads the team. Archers are typically most observant, so they'll call shots mid-battle." Her eyes roamed to Daphne, who was yawning, then Janice, who averted her eyes. Then they fell on Sorin, who was still figuring out how he fit in the group. "Sorin?"

"Yes, Assessor Haley?" replied Sorin.

"Good work on the stray bunny," said Haley. "It was the only thing you did right in the entire fight. Daphne's so oblivious the half-dead bunny would have probably gored her. I'm a *little* surprised at your lack of reaction to killing a demon. Did your parents send you to the arenas for training in the big city?" Sorin confirmed this. "Gareth?"

"Yes, Haley?" said Gareth.

"Sorin is a close-quarters poison user," said Haley. "Short-ranged or point-blank support as required. Situational medic. Squishy but very strong against tougher demons. Work him into the team."

"Yes, ma'am!" said Gareth. He then called the team together and began running them through a series of questions. Thirty minutes later, they ran into their second minor encounter.

6

FAILURE?

Over the next half-day, the team practiced their battle formations and respective abilities. Much of their nervousness faded as the examination turned from a life-and-death struggle into a casual walk through the bloodwood.

But only some of their battles were easy to win. A fight with six red-eyed saber wolves proved more challenging than those before.

"Vetner, what are you doing wasting your time with those small fries?" shouted Gareth. "Tie up the alpha now, or we're done for!"

"Fine!" shouted Vetner. He used his shield to bat away a lesser wolf and broke through the remainder of the pack to arrive at a wolf that was a full head taller than the others.

"Don't forget to taunt!" shouted Gareth. Fortunately, Vetner was already ahead of him. Blue mana coiled around his body and the opposing wolf's, preventing it from focusing on anyone else.

As the alpha swiped at Vetner with its mighty paws, the others were able to relax somewhat. Lawrence took the opportunity to appear behind a wolf sneaking up on Daphne and stuck a dagger in its spine, killing it instantly.

"Sorin!" shouted Gareth.

"On it," said Sorin. He was less useful against weaker opponents, but against stronger demons, he was quite effective. Lawrence's attack happened to open a gap in the encirclement, which Sorin used to approach the alpha wolf.

Three poison needles shot out from his sleeve. Two of them rattled off the silver wolf's tough fur, but the last one lodged itself into its front shoulder muscle, throwing off its balance. Vetner used the opportunity to land a vicious cut on the wolf, pulling back its attention. Sorin used the opportunity to cut a deep gash in its side with a poisoned dagger.

Black lines of corruption spread out from the wound on the alpha's side. Its movements became sluggish, and Vetner's job became a little easier. But landing that hit had provoked the rest of the pack—the smaller wolves focused on Sorin, forcing him into a passive position.

There were four wolves left, not counting the alpha, and they forced Sorin back towards his much larger opponent. The alpha swiped at him, but Sorin rolled beneath its legs and slashed once more at its torso, doubling up the dose of poison that slowly leeched away at its life force.

"Awooo!" The alpha, finally realizing how dire the situation was, let out a howl. Demonic energy erupted from its four companion wolves, allowing them to dodge Gareth's arrows and break past Vetner's attempt to block them.

They were fast—too fast to dodge. Sorin knew that even at his peak, he wouldn't be able to block them. And that was when alarm bells went off in his head, and he rolled away just in time for a large Fireball to light up three wolves, blasting them backward. They yelped as their fur melted and their flesh burned to a crisp. Daphne's sudden spell had completely neutralized them.

"Duck!" Daphne called out, three seconds too late.

"Warn me next time!" shouted Sorin, raising his dagger to defend against the fourth wolf. It fell to the ground, dead, thanks to Gareth's triple shot to the back of its neck.

Seeing its entire pack fall at once, the alpha was enraged. Demonic energy spread out from its forehead, covering its body in corrupted runes. "It's going berserk!" called out Gareth. "Defensive measures!"

They fell behind Vetner, leaving the empowered alpha no choice but to attack the armored man. Its empowered claws smacked away the shield, and its teeth sank into Vetner's chainmail.

Fortunately, Janice had been waiting for just this moment. She cast a minor regeneration spell on Vetner as Lawrence pulled him back. Gareth took advantage of the opening to let loose three more arrows into its open mouth.

The alpha recoiled, and Sorin saw an opportunity and launched himself forward. He channeled a full quarter of his poison mana into his palm and slammed it into its side.

Black lines spread out from the point of origin and combined with the original poison that had been slowly sapping away at the alpha's head. It staggered, and three seconds later, it collapsed, coughing up black blood.

Everyone's mana was limited, and Sorin's was no exception. Fortunately, his experiences as a doctor gave him a way to recover some of his expenditures. He placed a hand on the dead alpha's corpse and summoned his poison out of the wolf's body. In this way, he was able to recover a quarter of the mana he'd expended.

"Sorin, he's bleeding pretty badly," Janice called out. "I think you should take a look at him."

"Sure thing," said Sorin. Their team was now used to peeling away Vetner's chainmail, so it was off in seconds. Blood was oozing out of the wound in spurts, despite Janice's best efforts.

Sorin frowned. "The wound is *very* deep. Stand by because I'll need your help." Demonic corruption had begun setting in, so he used his poison qi to eat it away, then used a disinfectant solution to protect the wound from further infiltration.

The teeth sank into his main arteries, thought Sorin as he made some hasty stitches. "Does anyone have a healing potion?" he asked the party.

"I have one, but keep in mind that they're expensive," said Gareth, tossing him a bottle.

"Vetner will owe you then," said Sorin, catching the bottle. He unstoppered the cork with his mouth and carefully dripped half its contents into the worst wounds. They began healing over, but that alone wouldn't be enough.

Sorin made some quick sutures to assist the healing, then used his spiritual strength to find five tiny spots hiding deep inside the wound. He used a scalpel to cut away the corrupted flesh, then dabbed a bit more potion into the deep wound, finally stanching the bleeding.

"He'll need your heavy attention," Sorin said to Janice. "I don't think he'll be able to fight for the next week, at least."

"Are you guys done fumbling about?" asked Haley, appearing beside them. She was covered in sweat, and it was clear that she'd been chasing off other demons to allow them to complete their assessment in peace.

"Apologies, Assessor Haley," said Gareth. "The alpha's strength was a greater threat than we expected. Vetner is out for the remainder of the assessment."

"Don't lie to me," snapped Haley. "I hate it when people lie."

"This…"

"If you don't want to trash-talk your teammates, I'll do it," said Haley. "Vetner?"

"Yes, Assessor Haley?" said Vetner, picking himself up. His arm was no longer usable and had been safely tucked away in a sling.

"You're out," said Haley. "Not just from combat duty, but from this assessment."

Unsurprisingly, Vetner accepted the assessment without a complaint. "Yes, Assessor Haley. I'll polish up my skills for a month before trying again."

"Make it two," said Haley. "And remember, just because you're a tank, it doesn't mean you need to take damage. Blocking, dodging, and even parrying are much-preferred alternatives. Next up is Janice. Is there anything you'd like to say?"

Janice looked down. "I'll go find some better spells and make myself more useful."

"Spells are one thing," said Haley. "Common sense is another. It wouldn't be a bad idea for you to spend some time at Physician Lim's clinic or at the Adventurers Guild to treat emergencies. Contrary to what some might think, you're not just a life mana battery. You need to know what you can heal and what you can't. If a mortal doctor and a healing potion are better at your job than you are, what's the point of even having you on the team?"

Her eyes then fell on the last three in their team. "Daphne."

"Yes?" said Daphne.

"By all rights, I should fail you," said Haley. "But I respect someone who can blow up three one-star demons with a single spell like you did. It's not something just any fire mage can do. Your aim isn't bad, but try to give some warning. If Sorin hadn't dodged, he would have been burned to a crisp. Bare pass."

"As for Gareth, your team coordination and support are top-notch. You had a rough beginning, but you really stepped up. It's not your fault that Vetner got hurt over and over again but his own. You did the best you could with what you were given."

"Thank you, Assessor Haley," said Gareth.

"Oh, um, yes! Thank you!" said Daphne, then returned to muttering to herself about stupid party members getting in the way of her burning down the world.

"That only leaves Sorin," said Haley. "Overall, not bad. You're a better medic than the team's healer."

"Thank you, Assessor Haley," said Sorin.

"But you're still lacking when it comes to your main role, which is dealing damage," said Haley. "Your footwork is garbage for closing distance, and you avoid fighting way too much. You hit that wolf about three times, but really, you could have struck him with that palm at the beginning and saved Vetner some trouble."

"That... with all due respect, Assessor Haley, the alpha, was still not completely tied down by Vetner," said Sorin. "I wasn't confident in being able to dodge any counterattacks."

"Excuses," said Haley. "It's something you could have easily done with more training. So, as it stands, you fail."

Sorin gritted his teeth but could only accept her harsh judgment.

"That being said, you're not half bad. Earlier, while you were fighting, I happened to run into an interesting demon. Follow me, everyone."

She led them five miles away to an open meadow. In the middle of the clearing, they saw a tuft of seemingly harmless grass. But around said grass, there wasn't anything growing. The grass was poisonous and had killed all other plants within 150 feet of it.

"Iron-Melt Cloud Grass," muttered Sorin.

"That's right," said Haley. "It's a poisonous herb that is beneficial to certain demons. She threw a dagger out towards a patch of grass, causing it to collapse into a pit. A spider demon with a glossy black exoskeleton jumped out, its dozens of eyes watching them warily.

"So, my question is this, Sorin: How badly do you want to be an adventurer?" said Haley. "Are you willing to risk your life for it? That spider is a one-star demon called a Flesh-Melting Demon Spider. It will likely be resistant to your attacks. Its poison is quite potent, so if you get hit more than once or twice, there's no way I'll be able to save you.

"Are you willing to fight it? If so, step on up. If you win, I'll not only give you a pass but also the poisonous herb it's guarding. You've got ten seconds to decide. Nine. Eight. Seven..."

It was a frightening opponent for Sorin. As Haley said, the spider would likely be resistant to his poisons. Taking it down might take several minutes. He would have to dodge the spider's tricky attacks as he waited for his poisons to take effect.

The smart thing to do would be to retreat and polish up his skills. He could then take the assessment again and become an official adventurer. The problem was that his family would surely intervene; they had already done so much to cripple his cultivation and make him lose his position as family head and wouldn't want him rising up again.

Even the mighty Adventurers Guild wasn't immune to corruption, but it was very protective of its members. The reason he'd been so keen on taking the first assessment was because there was a big difference between barring someone from a big family from taking an assessment and stripping a member of his designation.

Then there was Haley and her seemingly one-sided treatment of

Sorin. This was especially the case when contrasting with Daphne, whose only skill was mindlessly—albeit very proficiently—setting things on fire. Haley was from the York Clan, a large and prosperous clan that would undoubtedly know about his difficulties. Moreover, the York Clan didn't have strong diplomatic ties with the Kepler Clan, which made manipulation unlikely.

Sorin had no idea what Haley's angle was, but there was nothing he could do about it. The choice to accept a more difficult assessment was his to make. "Fine," said Sorin. "I'll do it." Cultivating the Ten Thousand Poison Canon had been a calculated risk, and so was this.

"Are you sure?" asked Haley. "It's no shame in retreating from a stronger enemy. Your life is precious, after all."

"But not more precious than my freedom," said Sorin, taking out his dagger and a handful of needles. "May I begin, Assessor Haley?"

Haley smiled lightly. "Don't think I'm being hard on you for no reason. You're a member of the Kepler Clan, after all. And like all major clans, they like to meddle in the affairs of their members." Her words further reaffirmed to Sorin that she wasn't meddling out of spite. There were details here that he wasn't privy to; the advanced assessment would be difficult, but passing it might bring him unexpected benefits.

"Sorin, I highly recommend that you don't fight that spider," said Gareth before he could step up. "It's a one-star demon because it's immature, but it will eventually grow into a two-star demon. In terms of threat, it would be better for our entire undamaged team to fight it. Even then, we would probably avoid it because its poison is difficult to treat."

Sorin shook his head. "I've made my decision, Gareth. I risked my life to regain my cultivation, and I won't let anyone, or any*thing,* stop me from moving forward again."

7

FIGHTING POISON WITH POISON

The Flesh-Melting Demon Spider crouched as Sorin approached. Venomous secretions oozed out of its fangs and coated the dozen or so spikes on each of its eight legs. Approaching the spider and applying the first batch of poison would be tricky, no matter which attack angle he chose.

He advanced until the hairs on the back of his neck stood on end. Any further, and the spider would attack him without mercy. In that moment between life and death, Sorin wondered whose poison was stronger, his or the spider's? A brief consultation with the Ten Thousand Poison Canon quickly answered his question: it was spider's without a doubt.

Mana-infused blood pumped through Sorin's body, delivering energy to his legs and uncoiling them like a spring. He approached the Flesh-Melting Demon Spider from the side and swung out with his dagger.

The spider was agile, and it was far easier to rotate on an axis with eight legs than to take the long way around with two. Its mouth opened and shot a web out at Sorin, missing his torso by a bare millimeter. Then it blinked just in time to deflect three poison needles Sorin had stealthily sent its way.

Sorin hadn't expected his trick to work, so he moved onto plan B.

The spider's blink meant temporary blindness, and he used the opportunity to cut at the creature's foreleg with his poisoned knife. The knife cut a shallow gouge in its joint between two thick layers of chitin. But unlike the demonic wolves, the spider was unaffected by the poison.

There were two possibilities: one was that the spider was completely immune to his poison, and the other was that the spider's anatomy made it difficult to spot whether or not the poison was working. If it was the former, Sorin was dead, so he assumed it was the latter and continued fighting with everything he had.

He jumped back as the spider's leg swept forward, but was unable to avoid getting nicked by the barbs on the spider's leg. A shallow gash appeared on his forearm, and the spider's black poison attempted to melt its flesh, succeeding for about half a second before Sorin's own poisons moved to negate it.

I can't be cowardly, thought Sorin as he sliced at the retreating leg, leaving another small nick on the spider's flesh. *I need to take every advantage I can get to win this.* If he played things safe, he would die. The only chance he had was to take some risks.

The spider dove in to bite him with its two venom-laced fangs, but Sorin avoided them by rolling beneath the spider's belly. *Eat poison!* he thought as he slammed up with a poisonous palm. The spider shrieked as his palm hit and jumped up from the ground.

Sorin dodged as best he could but was unable to avoid getting nicked by the barbs on the spider's legs as it jumped up. The spider moved in to bite him when it landed, but he slashed upwards with his dagger and cut off the tip of its mandible. The spider shrieked and retreated momentarily to reevaluate him.

The fight with the spider made Sorin appreciate how valuable the Ten Thousand Poison Canon really was. The canon's strength didn't lay in its ability to control poisons but rather in its ability to assimilate other poisons. He wasn't *immune to* poisons, as they would still affect him, but their effects would gradually decrease as his body got used to them and finally began to secrete them.

Sorin's dagger moved ceaselessly. It was one weapon against two or three potential legs at a single time. That wasn't even mentioning the creature's deadly mandibles, which, wounded as they were, still reeked of deadly poison.

I can't... let myself... get... It was only when his surroundings began to spin that he realized that the spider's poison had unknowingly begun to affect him. The dizzy spell threw off his reflexes, rendering him unable to avoid two more shallow cuts.

Too slow, thought Sorin, backing up. He tumbled to the ground but managed to avoid the spider's descending leg just in time. *At this rate, it'll corner me and land a bite. Then I'll be as good as dead.*

The main issue, Sorin immediately identified, was the difference in their cultivation and the sheer quantity of mana the spider had to draw on. The herbs in his pack and the healing ointments he'd brought were useless. In fact, it was questionable whether Haley could even save him.

The only way I can win is to take a risk, thought Sorin. *My mana isn't assimilating the poison quickly enough, so I need to speed things up.* The spider moved in to bite him once again, but this time, Sorin didn't roll beneath it but stepped back. At the same time, he crouched and picked up the sharp, venomous mandible tip he'd cut off earlier and threatened the spider with it.

As predicted, the spider feared its own poison and gave Sorin a wide berth. Sorin forced himself to ignore the melting flesh on his hand, gritted his teeth, and then... stabbed himself! He roughly jabbed 14 different positions that mostly conformed to a series of acupoints.

Flesh melted where he'd stabbed himself, leaving large skin-less welts that were expanding rapidly. Red veins spread out from these initial points as his blood carried the poison to the rest of his body.

"Are you insane?" shouted Haley from afar. "This fight is over. Try not to die before I extract you."

"I'll be fine!" Sorin shouted back to Haley. He focused on circulating his mana and used his spiritual strength to urge the poisoned mana into his clogged-up liver meridian in an attempt to unseal it.

Fortunately, the spider was confused by Sorin's actions. It was likely the first time it had ever seen its prey intentionally poison itself, and it wanted to see where this was going. Its cautious nature was what gave Sorin the opportunity to not only fully clear a meridian channel leading down to his legs but also further fuse his combined poisons.

This… is a lot harder than I thought it would be, thought Sorin as he painfully guided the poison. Stabbing himself so roughly with a fang wasn't very precise, and, as such, he had damaged his meridians and his flesh. The poison wasn't just seeping into his mana and his blood but into his muscles and skin as well.

Sorin teetered on the brink of unconsciousness, doing his best to guide the venom along its way. Then, when darkness began creeping into his vision, he suddenly felt something shatter. The clog in his meridian opened up like a dam.

The spider, noticing that something was amiss, moved in for the kill. Yet before it could reach him, Sorin burst forward with a speed that was 20 percent faster than he'd shown previously. His movements became more elusive, and he was now able to turn much more rapidly.

At this rate, I won't be able to outlast it, thought Sorin, avoiding its attack. *I've taken a fatal dose of its poison. That means there's only one way for me to get out of this alive.*

He strengthened his resolve and charged at the spider with the fang tip. To everyone's horror, Sorin stabbed it just beneath the spider's jaw, suffering deep gashes on his arms as the spider bit down on him.

His skin began to melt away, exposing muscles, nerves, and bones. Sorin's poisons were doing the best they could to counteract the sudden infusion of flesh-Melting poison, but there was only so much they could do against such a terrifying opponent.

"Sorin, you idiot!" shouted Haley. She appeared beside Sorin and took out an anti-venom potion. She tried to shove it in his mouth, but Sorin slapped the vial away and ran towards the stalk of Iron-Melt Cloud Grass. The situation was risky, but with risks lay opportunities.

Iron-Melt Cloud Grass was extremely effective against any gear made of metal; the moment he entered its range, the buckles and buttons on his pack and clothes melted. Even his dagger began to erode from the fierce, poisonous mana the herb gave off.

But it won't melt flesh, thought Sorin as he grabbed the herb with his bare hands. *And it won't melt stone or crystal.* He took out a mortar and pestle and quickly made a paste using a small amount of water. He then shoved a handful of crystal needles into the paste and slowly inserted nineteen of them into his arms.

His poisonous mana cycled through his three open meridians and forced their way toward a fourth obstructed meridian. Doing so melted a great deal of dead flesh, thereby neutralizing a portion of the spider's venom.

The two poisons also happened to neutralize each other. Sorin knew this because he'd looked it up in the Ten Thousand Poison Canon. The spider had clearly wanted the herb because it could use it to temper its venom and nourish itself to the two-star state.

Sorin's body shook as both poisons, initially resistant to assimilation, became docile lambs. They fused with his mana, then his blood, then his flesh. His dormant blood awakened from the tempering of the two poisons, thickening it by not one but two stages at once. In an instant, he reached the fourth stage of Blood-Thickening.

His body transformed. His muscles regained a portion of their lost life. The two meridians he'd cleared were the spleen meridian (a yin meridian) and the small intestine meridian (a yang meridian).

But Sorin didn't stop there. There was still an excess of external poison in his body that needed to be consumed. He took a handful of needles and ran them along his arm to coat them in his own poisoned blood, then proceeded to pierce twenty-seven points on his kidney meridian and forty-four points on his gallbladder meridian over the next few minutes, fully cognizant that every second he wasted would bring him dangerously close to passing out.

The process was slow and painful, made much more so by his delirious state. His hands shook with every needle, but he persisted in using them to guide the poison in his system toward obstructions in his body.

The direct infusion of poison shook up the debris that had accumulated in his once completely open main meridian channels. By using a sudden surge of mana from every cell in his body, he was able to force open a tiny channel and clear away obstructions in two additional meridians. The channels widened as he circulated his mana, slowly but surely neutralizing the aggressive poisons in his blood.

Minutes later, he'd fully neutralized the poisons. What remained nourished his blood and his starved body. His damaged muscles and nerves began to repair themselves at a steady rate, and his internal poisons, now the product of four poisons, slowly replenished themselves.

It was several hours later when Sorin opened his eyes. His clothes had rotted away, as had his pack and his dagger. The others were sitting by a fire just at the outskirts of the clearing, a fair distance from what was left of the Iron-Melt Cloud Grass. A small pack had been placed not far from his location.

Sorin grabbed the pack and donned a fresh set of clothes, courtesy of Lawrence, who was of a similar build. He then grabbed what remained of the cloud grass and sucked up its poison, then did the same to the demon spider before cutting out the one-star demon core on its head.

Only then did he move towards the campfire, where his companions were roasting what seemed to be demonic wolf meat over an open flame.

"Stop right there," said Haley as he reached the outskirts of the camp. Sorin swung his dagger out by instinct, shattering an item midflight. To his surprise, a cleansing cloud erupted around him and melted away the blood and grime from his skin. "If you're going to continue being that disgusting in the future, you should probably carry some clearmist vials on you. Otherwise, there won't be any teammates willing to take you on."

"You mean…" Sorin started.

"You obviously passed," said Haley. "You did something incredibly

stupid and risky, but you didn't put anyone in danger. And most importantly, you won.

"Sometimes, adventuring is about making the right gambles at the
right time. You sought an opportunity to break through in battle and then
used the fact that you were lethally poisoned to absorb a *second* poison
and make yourself stronger. Who can fault you for that?"

Sorin relaxed when he heard her words. "And here I thought you
were going to punish me for slapping the antidote away."

"Oh, I'm still going to punish you for that," said Haley. "You like
messy and dirty things? How fortunate. The guild's outhouses happen to
need a heavy cleaning. Unless you're not up for the challenge?"

Sorin shuddered but resigned himself to his fate. "I'll accept the
punishment."

"Smart man," said Haley. "Now come on over and eat up. We
collected those wolf corpses and roasted one of them while you were
cultivating. You ever had a roast wolf before, rich boy?"

Sorin wanted to say he wasn't rich, but he was so hungry that he
directly dove into the food. The rest of the group began to pester him
with questions about the fight. That included Vetner and Janice, who'd
failed the examination. It was during this conversation that he learned
that his once blue eyes had turned bright green.

It was evening when they finally returned to the Adventurers Guild.
The streets were dim, and an eerie silence clung to the city like a wet
blanket. A few of the city guards patrolled the streets, but they were just
a formality; the outpost was practically lawless at night.

The door to the guild opened as they arrived. "G-Guild Master?!"
Haley exclaimed as a large man with a stern gaze and a chiseled jaw
walked out. "I thought you were on vacation this week."

"I was," said the guild master. "But unfortunately, one of your
charges has given us a great deal of trouble." He pointed to the five
other examinees aside from Sorin. "You five, please come back
tomorrow to collect your scores and your badges, assuming you've
earned them. As for you, Sorin Kepler, someone from your family

decided to pay us a visit. I'd very much appreciate it if you tagged along and cooperated with the guild on this matter."

"Relax," whispered Haley into Sorin's ear as she pushed him forward. "The guild might have political ties with all the big clans but have no doubts: we protect our own."

Sorin steadied his breathing and calmed his mind. "Of course, Guild Master. Please lead the way, and I'll do my best to clear up any misunderstandings."

8

FAMILY INTERVENTION

The guild master led Sorin to a small waiting room before bringing Assessor Haley into his office. There were two people already in the waiting room: Sorin's butler, Percival, and a man who wore physician robes embroidered with the Kepler Clan crest.

Percival looked extremely guilty about the entire affair, but Sorin understood. His family provided funds and a butler not to "maintain the family image" as they'd claimed but to keep a close eye on him. The only reason they hadn't had him killed was likely because it would upset some of the old timers in the family.

Regardless of what happened to Sorin's parents, it remained that his uncle was now the head of the family, and his son was next in line for the position. But Sorin's claim was substantial, as he could trace a direct line of descent from his ancestor, Sirius Abberjay Kepler. His uncle— once removed—had quite a strong claim and, more importantly, the power to back it up.

It was very likely that they'd mobilized someone from the family the instant they'd heard he could cultivate again. There was a big difference between a crippled potential inheritor and one that was able to cultivate.

Ten minutes trickled by at a glacial pace. The man in physician's robes continuously probed him with his spiritual senses—a very rude practice by anyone's standards—and repeatedly failed to thwart Sorin's spiritual senses. As for Percival, he wisely kept his lips tight and made no attempts to communicate with Sorin.

"You can all come in," the Guild Master finally called out from his office. Haley opened the door for them and motioned for them to take a seat. The guild master was seated closest to the door, in the host's seat, while the representative of the Kepler Clan took the opposite seat.

"Please sit," Haley said to Sorin. "And you too," she said to Percival, gesturing to a seat closer to the Kepler Clan representative. "We don't have much classist nonsense around here, and I get twitchy fingers whenever someone gets forced to stand around and wait."

Percival looked to the physician in askance. It was only when the man gestured for him to sit down that he did so.

Sorin sat at the middle of the table but edged slightly towards the guild master and Haley. He was sure that, given their positions, his gesture would not go unnoticed.

"As you might all know, I am Guild Master Roy," said the guild master. "This is Haley York, a two-star assessor at this branch guild, and she has appraised me of the situation out in the field. Now, forgive me for my rudeness, but I have no idea who you are. All I've been told is that you're from the Kepler Clan. Would you care to introduce yourself, Mr. Kepler, as well as your employee?"

"Please call me Physician Marcus," said the man. "And this is an employee of the family, Percival Dunstring. I am a two-star physician from the nearby city of Dustone. I came to this outpost today because I received troubling news: a lost sheep in the family decided to challenge the Adventurers Guild assessment without his family's permission."

"I'm not a minor," interjected Sorin. "I turned sixteen just this year, and I am legally allowed to make my own decisions."

"But as you might know, the great families have agreements with the guilds and associations to prevent their members from tarnishing their reputations," said Marcus. "Our family requires that anyone who wishes to become an adventurer first be vetted by the family."

Guild Master Roy cleared his throat loudly. "I think we've started this meeting off on the wrong foot, Physician Marcus. My intention was for us all to make introductions, not for you to take the floor in my own office."

"Apologies, Guild Master," said Physician Marcus. "I'm sure you can understand that we take such cases very seriously."

"That I do understand," said Guild Master Roy. "But before we proceed any further, I'd like to pass something on to my little friend Sorin. Ms. York?"

Haley grunted and tossed a bag over to Sorin. A certificate of assessment, an identity badge, and five gold coins lay inside.

"What's this?" asked Sorin, gesturing to the coins.

"Your partial bounty for the Flesh-Melting Demon Spider," Haley explained. "Strictly speaking, the assessment was not to include more than one bounty-level target. It was my prerogative as an instructor to increase the difficulty of your test and verify your aptitude. But since you killed it, the bounty is yours.

"As for the core, you can do whatever you want with it. Spend it, use it for potions, or gamble it at the Temple of Hope for all I care. Normally, you'd need to get it verified and stamped as proof that you killed it, but since I was there as an eyewitness, that won't be necessary."

This time, it was Marcus who cleared his throat. "I'm sorry, but I seem to be misunderstanding something. It sounds to me like you're all going against our family's right to vet potential trial-takers."

"Yes, that *does* sound like a misunderstanding, doesn't it, Physician Marcus?" said Guild Master Roy. "I would fully understand your position if Sorin embarrassed you. In that case, we'd strike the trial off the records and require proof that he's passed your internal audit before he takes the trial again.

"But in this case, he didn't just pass the trial—he distinguished himself before his peers. This fact was witnessed by our most excellent assessor in the entire branch. Moreover, she is from the York Clan and is, therefore, quite familiar with the requirements of a great family. And unlike the Kepler Clan, the York Clan specializes in adventuring."

Everything now made sense. It was as he suspected: Haley had made his assessment more difficult for a reason. It was unlikely for him to defeat the creature, but by at least exchanging a few blows with it or surviving for some time, he would have been able to show off both his bravery for having attempted the feat and his wisdom for having backed off. Either way, she would have been able to use the fight to showcase his ability and justify his acceptance into the guild.

"As Guild Master Roy explained, I'm fully aware of a large family's requirements for associations and guilds," said Haley. "His assessment was documented in detail. Here is the assessment grid that I completed, along with a complete report of the trials he faced."

Marcus glared at her but accepted the folio. He frowned as he looked through it, and his frown deepened the more he looked.

For a while, no one spoke. They gave Marcus ample time to use the communication device he'd brought with him to exchange messages with the family leadership. Finally, after a good ten minutes of back and forth, he nodded. "Very well. It was our mistake," said Marcus. "Everything with the assessment seems to be in order. Would you mind giving me a copy of the assessment?"

"We have a copy," said Haley. "You can keep the original."

"Then I believe congratulations are in order, Sorin Kepler," said Marcus with a smile. "I wish you good luck in your bright new adventuring career. A poison user, are you? You realize the ramifications of cultivating such a path, don't you? Both within the family and within the Medical Association?"

"I do," answered Sorin. He'd known it before he even began cultivating the Ten Thousand Poison Canon, and he had no regrets despite knowing the challenges he would face.

This time, it was Guild Master Roy who frowned. "That's it? Nothing more? No outrage and no political ramifications?"

"It's just as you said," said Marcus. "This was all a misunderstanding. We of the Kepler Clan were only concerned about our family's image. As you well know, Sorin's cultivation received a huge setback, and we were afraid that we might be biting off more than he could chew.

But if Miss York's report is accurate, and I trust that it is, then it seems we have nothing to worry about."

Guild Master Roy let out a sigh of relief. "If that's all, then I guess it's settled. I take it you'll be going back to Dustone soon?"

"I'll actually be sticking around for a while," said Marcus. "The family has been thinking about expanding the clinic in this area. The increase in demonic activity of late has the family worried, and as you both know, the outposts always receive the brunt of it."

"Our guild would most certainly be grateful for such a thing," said Guild Master Roy. "Will that be all then, Physician Marcus?"

"It will," said Marcus.

"Then Sorin, you are excused," said Guild Master Roy. "Haley, stay behind."

The meeting ended on a much lighter note than Sorin had expected. Of course, he wasn't so naïve as to think everything was over.

Marcus waited until they were out of the office before greeting Sorin with a smile. "I'm afraid we never had the pleasure of meeting," said Marcus, holding out his hand. "I'm Marcus, from the Sovinger branch."

"Sorin," said Sorin, accepting the handshake. "Abberjay branch." A stream of life mana and spiritual sense drilled into his body from Marcus's, and Sorin, not wanting to be impolite, mobilized his own mana and strong spiritual sense to push back.

"I realize your station in the family exceeds mine, but I don't think you quite realize how problematic it might be for you to cultivate poison," said Marcus. "In fact, only death mana would be a greater affront to the family."

"And how brave of you, touching a poison cultivator directly," said Sorin. He chuckled when Marcus jerked back his hand. "Relax. My mana control is exceptional. I *was* trained by the best, which is far more than you can say."

"How funny," replied Marcus. "It's been a while since a Blood-Thickening junior bared his fangs at me."

"In the Kepler Clan, it's actually you who's the junior," Sorin countered. "As you already admitted."

"But in the cultivation world and all the associations, it's the other way around," said Marcus. "Please excuse me; someone's trying to contact me." He retrieved a jade slip from his belt, and his smile deepened when he saw the contents. "Apologies, I only received the briefest of orders during our meeting. There are further developments, it seems. You can expect something in writing sometime tomorrow."

"There's no need to beat around the bush, Marcus," said Sorin. "I'm aware of how the family works."

"Then I won't keep you in suspense," said Marcus. "Henceforth, you are forbidden from practicing as a physician. The Medical Association has officially stripped you of your honorary designation, which had been tenuous ever since the loss of your cultivation."

"Justification?" asked Sorin.

"Incompatible mana," said Marcus. "Poison mana is only moderately useful in treating wounds and deadly if misused. As you surely know, the Medical Association issued a blanket ban on physicians with poison, death, and dark-type mana around a hundred years ago. A written exemption is required to do otherwise. Feel free to apply for such a thing if you think you have the clout to pull it off."

Sorin nodded, as he'd already expected this assessment. "Anything else?"

"You are also forbidden from instructing students in medicine," continued Marcus. "Gabriella Michka will be reassigned to a more competent instructor."

"As long as she is agreeable to the matter, I have no objections," said Sorin. "She is a talented future physician, as your assessment will likely indicate."

"I'm sure," said Marcus. "Now, it probably doesn't come as a surprise that the clinic will need new management. That duty, it seems, will fall to me. Further, several family assets will be confiscated. Your Divine Medical Codex is the primary item, but all controlled medicinal ingredients, all magic treasures related to the practice of medicine, and all tomes related to the practice of medicine will also be taken."

"I wouldn't expect anything less," said Sorin. These things had been given to him by his family in the first place, so it only made sense for them to take them back.

"That is all," said Marcus. "And I must say, you're taking things a lot better than I expected."

"That's because everything that's happening now is within the realm of reasonable expectation," said Sorin. "Also, I believe the perspective of someone who's already lost everything is quite different from that of someone who's never encountered any setbacks."

"Well, I'm personally glad you're taking things so well," said Marcus. "The family cares deeply about its image, so you will be allowed to keep the manor assigned to you and will continue to receive a stipend for its operation. Percival and Clarice will also remain behind to take care of you. Their salaries will continue to be paid by the Kepler Clan."

"Sounds about right," said Sorin. "Anything else?"

Marcus's eye twitched. "Is that *really* all you have to say? You finally screwed up and had everything you had left taken away from you, and you're not even losing your temper?"

Sorin smiled lightly when he saw Marcus's reaction. "To someone like you, who struggles day and night to climb up the family tree, it might seem like a big deal. But to me? I stopped caring about all this nonsense three years ago."

"But you were a cripple then," Marcus pointed out.

"Yes. I was," said Sorin. "I lost my parents. I lost everything. I saw people I called friends turn their backs on me and people I called family kick me when I was down.

"I've long since accepted my fate, Marcus. It's my uncle who controls the Kepler Clan, and it's his son who'll be taking over after him. These facts can't be changed. Not by me. Not by anyone else."

"It's good that you know this," said Marcus.

"To be clear," continued Sorin. "I know you'll be staying here to keep an eye on me. I know that Percival is going to keep reporting on my activities. I know that everywhere I go, there will be eyes on me, reporting my every move to the Kepler Clan.

"So please include in your report that I'm fine with that. I've given up. If the Council wants, it can even excommunicate me from the family. I won't even fight it."

Having said his piece, Sorin left the Adventurers Guild. It was raining outside, and the cobblestone streets were slick with mud that had yet to wash out into the cracks. An umbrella popped open above his head, shielding him from the elements.

"I don't blame you, Percival," said Sorin to his butler as they walked. "I don't blame anyone. It's like I said to Marcus: I've been hurting for so long that I don't feel anything anymore."

"But you love the clinic," said Percival.

"Losing the clinic hurts," Sorin admitted. "But it's nothing compared to being crippled, losing your parents, and learning that everyone you ever cared about didn't care back. Don't worry. I'll be fine. More than fine. I finally have my life back, along with a little bit more freedom than I had initially."

"You know they'll never let you get too strong," said Percival.

"Then let's see exactly how they keep me in check," said Sorin. "I finally earned my freedom after three long years of suffering. If they want to take it back, they'll have to kill me first."

9

MITHRIL STRING

The next day, Sorin returned to the Adventurers Guild to meet with Lawrence and the others, as well as to run a few errands. Most of his equipment had been destroyed, and Lawrence had ideas on where to replace them.

He was about to leave when suddenly Percival arrived and whisked Sorin away. Sorin sighed as he returned to the Kepler Manor at the butler's urging.

What Sorin saw was within expectations. It was as though a storm had rampaged through the manor's spacious halls, ripping up walls and peeling up carpets.

"The first thing they took was your books," explained Percival. "They couldn't retrieve the Divine Medical Codex from the safe, so they ripped the entire thing out of your office."

"They didn't even spare the young master's desk," said Clarice, who was currently sweeping up rubble into a pile so it wouldn't get in everyone's way. "Also, please avoid the basement for now. It's full of broken glassware contaminated with chemicals. Fortunately, I stopped them from ruining your bedding while they upturned your room, looking for anything you might have squirreled away."

"Mr. Kepler..." said Percival from behind Sorin. "You don't need to bother yourself with all this. Clarice and I will pick it all up. I just thought I'd let you know so you didn't walk into a nasty surprise upon your return."

"I just wonder… why bother?" said Sorin, shaking his head. "This place has always been a prison. It's only now that it looks the part."

After witnessing the aftermath of his family's raid, Sorin was in no mood to shop for replacement equipment. He retired to his bedroom and pulled out bandages and a weak healing ointment, then began to gingerly pull away bloody bandages from his arms.

Deep, stitched-up wounds were still oozing small amounts of blood and puss. It was only thanks to Sorin's innate poison secretions that the wound left behind by the Flesh-Melting Demon Spider wasn't infected.

Having reached the fourth stage of Blood-Thickening and having unblocked six primary meridians, Sorin's self-recovery abilities were over ten times faster than those of a mortal. Even deep wounds like these would eventually regenerate.

Even so, he carefully cleaned up his wounds with water and applied ointment to the raw flesh that was in the process of regrowing. You could never be too careful because you never knew what new ailments Disease might come up with.

Once his bandages were changed, Sorin inspected the rest of his body. His mana was finally flowing semi-smoothly thanks to his opened-up meridians. There were only six main meridians left to open, but these would require a more concentrated form of mana and some medical assistance to force them open. He would attempt to do so once his cultivation increased by another grade or two.

As for his extraordinary meridians, those were more complicated. For one, they could only be opened once the original twelve main meridians were fully opened, with exceptions being made for those opened congenitally. For another, each person had a limit to the number of extraordinary meridians they could naturally open. For Sorin, this was four.

Opening additional extraordinary meridians would require alchemical pills, medical intervention, and, most importantly, luck. Unfortunately, Sorin was sorely lacking in all three departments.

One pleasant upside of his increased cultivation was his much-improved organ function. The Flesh-Melt and Iron-Melt Poisons in his blood had fused to form something extremely corrosive, and his body had naturally made use of it to clean up his system.

Not only was his general health improving, but his other meridians were also on the verge of clearing up. *Maybe I should be selective with my poisons in the future.*

Time waited for no one, and repetition was the mother of learning. He performed a series of mana manipulation drills, first generating small balls of mana that he rolled across his finger, then generating a needle of mana that he tossed up and down like a toothpick.

My poisonous blade, poisonous palm, and poisonous needles are only the most basic applications of mana. Since I don't have any skills for my poison mana, I can only rely on these basic forms for now. But lacking ranged attacks wouldn't do. He needed to think of a solution.

The range limit of his poison needles was roughly ten feet, barely better than attacking with his dagger. During his examination, Sorin had noticed that opportunities often presented themselves within thirty feet. *Some rogues use darts and crossbows as weapons. Either one would work for my purposes. But high-quality and fast-loading cross-bows are too expensive. Darts might be the more affordable alternative.*

Sorin spent the next three days training and stabilizing his cultivation. Since he was basically re-training and reinvigorating his blood, consolidating his cultivation took little time. But suddenly increasing one's cultivation, like he was doing, was risky. Slowly imbibing poisons over time might be a better alternative.

"Mr. Kepler," greeted Percival as Sorin came down from his room on the morning of the fourth day. "Breakfast is ready, and you can begin at your convenience."

Breakfast wasn't something Sorin typically ate, but seeing the spread of food on the table, his stomach growled, leaving him no choice but to sit down and eat up the entire thing.

"Perhaps you would like some fruit or some tea to finish things off?" asked Percival.

"I'm fine," said Sorin. "I'll be taking off to do some shopping soon. Feel free to relax while I'm gone." It was a clear dismissal, but Percival blocked Sorin's way out. "What is it now?" asked Sorin.

"It occurs to me that I've yet to thank Mr. Kepler for the ordeal three days ago," said Percival.

"Thank me?" said Sorin, surprised. "For what?"

"Well, it isn't unusual for masters to discipline their servants when they have wronged them," said Percival. "I fully expected some sort of reprisal but have received none whatsoever."

"That's because none of this is your fault, Percival," said Sorin. "You were just listening to orders from above."

"Even so, Clarice and I are thankful, so we went through the trouble of putting together a package for you. A small gift to express our gratitude. We would be ever so grateful if you accepted it."

Percival handed Sorin a worn leather pack. It was a large adventurer's pack, complete with a bedroll and a small tent. It wasn't magical, but the materials were well-made, albeit worn like the pack.

"You shouldn't have," said Sorin, his heartwarming for what seemed like the first time in three years.

"You should open the pack and go through its contents before leaving," said Percival.

Sorin took the pack to the table and began taking out items one after another. Inside was a mana-lighter, much more reliable than flint and steel, roughly ten days of dried rations, and a slightly magical water purifier. There was also a medical kit of acceptable quality.

But what caught Sorin's attention weren't these things but a dagger and a long piece of string. "Both are made from corrosion-resistant mithril," Percival explained. "As you might know, mithril is an excellent metal for accepting mana. Back in my adventuring days, I made use of metal-aligned mana to amplify their power."

"You were an adventurer?" asked Sorin, surprised.

"Clarice and I both were," said Percival. "Did you ever wonder how she can clean so quickly? It's all thanks to her magic spells. She used to be a mage—not a great mage, mind you, but an acceptable one given her one-star ranking."

"How about you?" asked Sorin. "I've never been able to tell your cultivation."

"I was almost a two-star adventurer once upon a time," said Percival. "But I got injured one too many times and had to liquidate most of my possessions to pay my hospital bills. It's actually how I ended up in the Kepler Clan's employment."

He ran his finger along the dagger, then picked up the mithril string. A weak current of mana poured out into the string, causing it to whip about in a seemingly chaotic manner. "Metal infusion allows a string to cut through flesh and bone. As for poison infusion... I frankly have no idea. You'll have to experiment.

"But before you experiment, I first advise you to master these basic movements. Wrapping." The silver string reached around a chair leg and made twenty turns around it before Percival yanked the table into the air, flipped it over three hundred and sixty degrees, and adjusted its position ever so slightly so that it landed in the same spot it had been in originally.

"Lashing," Percival continued. The string uncoiled from the leg and drew back like a whip. It struck the table clean in the center, leaving a deep gouge that looked intentional on its polished wood surface.

"Trapping." The string suddenly shot to a side of the room before cutting a sharp angle and crossing it along a different path. It did so two dozen times before the entire length of string was used up.

The sweaty butler, clearly exhausted from manipulating the string, tossed an apple at one of the strings. The apple was cleanly cut in two, and these halves proceeded to strike other strings in succession. In the end, there were a total of twelve apple pieces lying neatly on the floor. Percival picked one up and ate it before retrieving the mithril string and handing it over to Sorin.

"I'll practice using it every day," Sorin promised solemnly.

"I do not doubt that you will," said Percival. "Adventuring is a hard life, but it can be oh-so rewarding. One last thing. Take this." He tossed a pouch at Sorin, who caught it. Within it lay ten gold coins. There were a hundred silver coins to a gold coin, so this was twice as much money as Sorin had to his name.

"I can't accept this," Sorin said, pushing the pouch to Percival.

"I'm afraid you must," said Percival, pushing the pouch back. "You see, Clarice and I have been skimming off the top this past year without you noticing. Given recent events, we felt bad about it and decided to return the funds to their rightful owner."

Sorin shook his head. "It's the Kepler Clan that pays for the manor."

"But as far as we're concerned, the Kepler Clan should have belonged to you," said Percival. "So anything we can obtain for you from the Kepler Clan can be argued to be legitimately yours. Please don't argue with me on this matter."

Sorin wanted to push the pouch back but ultimately chose to keep it. By banning him from practicing medicine, Marcus had cut off his meager source of income. He would need to go adventuring and risk his life to secure the funds he needed to increase his cultivation.

"Thank you," Sorin finally said.

"Thank *you*," replied Percival. "Will you be coming back for dinner tonight?"

"I'm afraid I promised Lawrence I'd see him at the Adventurers Guild later. Something about a lucrative mission."

"Then promise me to prioritize your safety. Get yourself some light armor if you can. Adventuring is a brutal profession, and the slightest slip-up can cost you your life."

"Don't worry, I'm very hardy," said Sorin. "If someone tries to take this life of mine, they'll be in for a rude awakening."

"I'm sure they will be," said Percival. "But your life is precious, and Clarice and I would very much like it if you kept it."

"I'll keep that in mind." He finished re-filling the pack and slung it over his shoulder before walking out the door.

His destination: the Alchemists Guild.

THE ALCHEMISTS GUILD

A strong medicinal scent assaulted Sorin the moment he walked through the bloodwood doors leading into the Alchemists Guild. It was a large guild, given the size of the outpost, but still much smaller than you'd find in a proper city.

The building was made of stone and had far too many chimneys. It was split into two parts: the storefront in the front and the workshops in the back and upper floors.

"Welcome to the Alchemists Guild," greeted the shopkeeper standing guard over shelves of prepared medicines and exotic medicinal ingredients on display. "Whatever you're looking for, I'm sure we'll be able to find what you—*Physician Sorin*, what can I do for you today?"

"I'm not a physician anymore, Henry," said Sorin, walking up to the counter. "Given your connections, I'm sure you've heard why that happened and how."

Henry laughed uncomfortably as he scratched the back of his head. He was around thirty years old and had a cultivation stalled at the peak of Blood-Thickening. "I heard there was a commotion at the Adventurers Guild last night. Something about the Kepler Clan. But I didn't connect the dots until this morning, when a red-eyed Gabriella came to fetch some potions and pills."

Sorin frowned. "She's doing courier duty? Doesn't one of the nurses usually do that?"

Henry shrugged. "I have no idea what's going on, but she didn't look too pleased about it."

Sorin made a note to visit Gabriella in the future after things calmed down. Visiting now would only further incriminate her in Marcus's eyes. "Let's not talk about such things for now. I'm here for business."

"Tch. You act indifferent, but I know you care," said Henry. "You should talk to her, Sorin. Let her know your difficulties. Let her know you're there for her."

"The day I start taking love advice from you is the day the Seven Evils awaken," said Sorin wryly. Henry had a reputation for failed relationships. "Besides, nothing is going on between us. And I'd like to keep it that way—for her own sake."

"Fine. *Fine,*" said Henry, holding up his hands. "I won't get involved in your mess. Hope only knows how many hearts I've led astray. So, business it is. You've regained your cultivation, and I've heard that you're now a poisoner. Quite a big change in profession, I'd say."

Sorin shrugged. "We do what we need to survive, Henry. My path as a physician was obliterated long ago. Fortunately, those skills are still useful in my current profession. Tell me—do you still carry Fossilized Cockatrice Grass?"

"Fossilized Cockatrice Grass," said Henry, tapping his fingers on the store's wooden desk. "I think I recall seeing something like that in the back. Not many people look for it—it's only useful in the most extreme cases for a doctor, and only a few two-star alchemical recipes require it. So, the ingredient is rare, and the price won't be cheap."

"Then I'll trouble you to bring me ten stalks," said Sorin, who'd long since grown used to the man's rambling.

"Ten stalks? I don't think we have that much. But let me check," said Henry.

"Then bring out the weight difference in Breathstop Mint," said Sorin. "On second thought, make it a half-and-half mixture." He probably couldn't afford to use only Cockatrice Grass. The Ten Thousand

Poison Canon was extremely useful in this regard. It not only described poisons in vivid detail, but it also described their sub-types and compatibility.

Henry returned five minutes later, holding five thin boxes and one larger box. He popped open one of the smaller boxes and allowed Sorin to inspect its contents.

"How old *are* these exactly?" said Sorin, gingerly poking a piece of grass with a crystal needle. A piece cracked off and crumbled into dust that settled onto the bottom of the case.

"These were obviously the freshest goods, obtained only a few weeks ago." Henry lied as easily as he breathed.

"Oh?" said Sorin, poking the grass again. It broke in half. "If that were the case, this stalk would be no more than three months old. How curious that its medicinal properties have degraded so much that a small needle prod can break it." He then opened the next five boxes and grunted as he inspected them. They weren't much better off. He then opened the box of Breathstop Mint and snorted when he saw the contents. He might barely have enough active ingredients for his purposes.

"Throw in a half liter of liquified mana extract, and I'll give you thirty gold," said Sorin.

"Thirty gold?" replied Henry. "Why don't you just rob me?"

"You and I both know this is expired inventory," said Sorin. "By all rights, you should be throwing it away."

"Tch." Henry shook his head and picked up the six cases. "Fifty gold, or I'm putting them back."

"Thirty-five," countered Sorin.

"Forty, and I won't go any lower."

Grimacing, Sorin took out a one-star demon core. "Would you take a one-star Flesh-Melting Demon Spider core?"

"What did you say?" said Henry, grabbing the core with a gloved hand. Exactly how he'd put on the glove so fast or how he'd fetched the magnifying glass from the back counter, Sorin had no idea. "Hm. A juvenile."

"Otherwise, it would have been a two-star core," said Sorin. "I might be new to adventuring, but I'm not an idiot." He'd done some reading up on the creatures native to Bloodwood Forest before heading out.

"I can reluctantly accept this as payment."

"The going rate for a core like that is seventy gold."

"Then you can try selling it through your storefront," said Henry with a grin. "Oh, wait. You don't *have* a storefront."

"Throw in twenty more gold as change."

"No."

"Ten more, then."

"N. O. No."

"Cheap bastard," muttered Sorin. "Fine. You win. But I need glassware that can handle these poisons, the liquified mana extract I asked for, and a workstation for the next six hours. That's my bottom line."

Henry hesitated but reluctantly agreed. After all, this deal wouldn't really cost him anything extra. "Fine. Someone with your background surely knows how to use glassware, and we happen to have a workshop available. Just don't kill anyone. Or hurt anyone. And if you break the glassware, you're paying for it."

He first had Sorin sign a contract before leading him to the back of the guild to what looked like the smallest, dirtiest laboratory Sorin had ever seen. The glassware had yet to be cleaned since the last usage, so he would need to spend an hour cleaning things up. But beggars couldn't be choosers, so he swallowed his complaints and took over the workspace.

An hour later, everything was in order. Mixing medicine was complicated, and for someone like Sorin, who didn't control the wood, fire, or water elements, properly cleaned and functional equipment was paramount.

The first thing he did was heat a beaker of liquified mana extract. Mana extract was strange in that it didn't have to be one state or another at a given temperature. Once it was liquified, it would stay in that state regardless of how much you heated it. And in a gaseous state, it wouldn't condense no matter how much you cooled it.

Sorin adjusted the flame and heated it to maintain a temperature of 235 degrees. He then walked over to a fume hood, removed the Fossilized Cockatrice Grass stalks from their cases, and crushed them using a jade mortar and pestle. He ground them to a fine powder, then meticulously cleaned off the mortar and pestle before moving on to the Breathstop Mint.

The two powders easily dissolved when added to separate beakers of liquified mana extract. Sorin simmered them for three hours before filtering out the solids and tossing them into the disposal chimney. He was left with a glowing beaker of thick white liquid and a minty-fresh beaker of Breathstop Mint. Breathing in fumes from either liquid would stop his breathing for several seconds, so he made sure to use a fume hood as he dripped the Breathstop Mint extract into the white liquid.

Poisons, alchemical ingredients, and medicine reacted differently than normal chemical reagents. With chemicals, you only need to worry about various reactions like acid-base reactions, polymerization, substitutions, and so on.

But when mana got involved, you needed to know the specifics of what you were dealing with. These two poisons, for example, were in a compatible category and capable of devouring each other. Sorin planned to use the Breathstop Mint extract to revitalize the expired Cockatrice Grass extract.

Sorin fed the white liquid until it suddenly let off a soft green glow. *Looks like I calculated it correctly,* thought Sorin. *The ingredients in the Breathstop Mint are exactly what the Cockatrice Grass needed to revitalize itself.* It was only thanks to the Ten Thousand Poison Canon that he knew about the predatory nature of these respective poisons. The stronger poison on the food chain would devour the weaker one.

In the end, he was left with a hundred milliliters of opaque green liquid. The reagents had absorbed the rest to revitalize themselves.

Sorin waited a half-hour before the liquid was fully cooled. He stoppered the contents in ten vials, then dropped the remaining few drops onto his skin. His flesh solidified for a few seconds before the poisons native to his body rushed in to devour the intruding poison and carry it off for assimilation.

Even with the Ten Thousand Poison Canon, it took time to assimilate poisons. Sorin carefully observed his body and took notes as the small amount of Cockatrice Grass extract was 'digested.' *It'll take an hour to assimilate a milliliter in the beginning, but as I get used to it, my rate of assimilation should increase.* Moreover, doing so in this way would give him time to get used to mana as it changed and solidify his cultivation as he progressed.

Satisfied with the result of his trip to the Alchemists Guild, Sorin packed up the ten vials into his pack using a sturdy case and tidied up one final time before heading out.

11

DIFFERENCE IN REALMS

The Adventurers Guild was quiet when Sorin arrived shortly after dinner time. The day was over, and most of the adventurers had either gone home or retired to an inn or pub.

"Over here!" Lawrence called out as Sorin walked in. The young man was holding up a pint of ale from the Adventurer's Pub, which opened up after the guild closed down, or whenever the owner felt like opening it.

"Should you really be drinking, given the antics you usually get up to?" asked Sorin, taking a seat. "And don't know you the Adventurer's Pub charges double for beer compared to the other taverns?"

"You don't come here because it's cheap; you come here for the atmosphere!" said Lawrence, taking a deep drink from his mug. "Ah! The others are here too." He waved at the two new arrivals: Gareth, the archer from their assessment, and an oblivious-looking Daphne, also from their assessment, who'd just been distracted by the custom lighting the Adventurers Guild used when their pub opened.

Gareth pulled the dazzled Daphne over and had her take a seat. "Just the four of us then?" said Gareth to Lawrence. "Sorin," he said with a nod. "It's been a while."

Lawrence took another swig of his mug before answering. "Another!" he called out. A waitress in full adventurer's garb came over with a foamy mug.

"How about you three?" asked the waitress. "Surely you won't let your friend drink alone?"

"I'll take a whisky," said Gareth.

"I'll take hot water with ginger and honey," said Sorin, too broke to order alcohol. In fact, he hadn't even gotten dinner and would only be eating once he returned to the Kepler Clan after their meeting.

"And you?" the waitress asked Daphne.

"I… um… I'll have whatever," said Daphne, her eyes glazing over in their usual fashion. "Fire," she muttered. "Yes, maybe if I add some conflagration runes, I could…" The rest was lost to them as her words devolved into incomprehensible mumbling.

"Sure," said the waitress, giving her a strange look. "I'll be right back with a whisky, a hot water with ginger and honey, and a… *whatever.*"

"Is that actually a drink?" Sorin asked Lawrence when she left.

"I think Daphne's in for a big surprise," said Lawrence. "Should we warn her?"

"No," said Gareth. "It'll teach her to pay more attention to her surroundings."

The waitress came by a few minutes later with their drinks. Gareth waited until they each had a drink before continuing. "So. Lawrence. You said there was a bit of special work coming up that you wanted to collaborate on."

"That's right," said Lawrence. "It's my dad that landed this gig for us. He's an old buddy of the guild master and has a lot of pull with the mission desk."

"What kind of mission are we talking about?" asked Sorin. He had his preference for missions, as he could double dip by gathering poisons out in the wilderness.

"I honestly have no idea," said Lawrence. "I was just told to come wait here around this time."

Gareth raised an eyebrow. "Are you saying you invited us for a mission, and you don't even know what it is?"

"It's not a mission, per se, but an *opportunity*," corrected Lawrence. "An opportunity for many missions." He cut off as a sudden crash hushed all conversation in the Adventurer's Pub. Three seconds of silence later, another crash sounded, this one much closer.

"That sounds a lot like fighting," said Gareth. His hand wandered over to his bow, which he'd placed just by his seat."

"Seems like my old man wasn't mistaken," chuckled Lawrence. "Looks like we're in for a good show." A third crash sounded in the room, this time accompanied by the breaking of a wall. A man in half-plate tumbled into the guild lobby but instantly picked himself up.

"You're being unreasonable, Sister!" shouted the man. His hair was mixed black and blond, and he was completely covered in wood chips. A large dent could be seen on his chest armor. Surprisingly, he wore no weapons, yet Sorin could feel a strange yet powerful aura oozing from him.

"You're the one who's being unreasonable, Stephan," came a familiar voice. Assessor Haley stepped out of the hole in the wall, rubbing her fist. "The clan told you that I would be managing your train-ing, and you accepted. Whatever I say goes, and if you disagree, I'll just beat you more. Understood?"

"I refuse to be bullied like this," said Stephan. "Eat a Lunisolar Paw!!" Mana poured into the man's right hand, and to Sorin's surprise, fur and claws grew out of it.

"A beastshift warrior," muttered Gareth. "Rare in these parts. Rare overall. But can he really fight a two-star adventurer?"

"We'll see soon enough," said Sorin. "Daphne? Daphne, do you even have any idea what's going on?" The mage was currently muttering to herself, and a matrix of magical runes had appeared before her. Sorin shook his head and continued watching the show.

The man called Stephan accumulated power for three full seconds before stepping forward. The ground creaked under his weight, and mana crackled around him as his movements accelerated. "Lunisolar Paw!" the man shouted as he attacked a bemused Assessor Haley.

"Childish," said Haley, stepping towards him. She didn't even pull a weapon and instead caught the paw with her bare hand. The collision caused a current of air and mana to sweep through the room, knocking a few mugs off a waiter's tray. "You're just a Blood-Thickening cultivator, Stephan. You might be more talented than me, but an entire realm separates us. I don't even specialize in brute force, but I can *still* overpower you."

"Tch." The man called Stephan turned around and walked away. To others, he seemed fine, but Sorin's keen eyes could see that the hand he'd used to strike her was trembling. "Fine. The strong get to set the rules, so I'll listen. For now. I'll take a team out for a few exercises and show you I'm a big boy."

"Excellent," said Haley. "They're waiting for you at that table over there. Enjoy." She walked back through the hole in the wall, then used strings of mana to pull a large chunk of the wall back into place.

Having been berated and scolded in public, Stephan's pride was brought down a notch. He was, therefore, much humbler when he approached Sorin's table. "Stephan York," he said, introducing himself. "It seems we're going to be companions in the future, if you'll have me."

"What did I tell you guys?" said Lawrence. "An opportunity! Stephan here is a genius from the York Clan, and he's been sent out to this outpost for some training."

"A genius is stretching it a bit," said Stephan. "I can't even compare to the true geniuses from other families. Just think of me as a fairly strong one-star adventurer."

"I'm not against teaming up," said Gareth, draining his whisky. "A bear-type beastshift warrior perfectly makes up for our lack of tank and power. We might not have a healer, but beastshift warriors regenerate quickly. And with Sorin on our team and a few potions, we should be able to get by."

"No healer?" said Stephan, pulling up a chair between Gareth and

Daphne. "Is there a shortage here or something? No matter. It's doable with the right team. Oh, thank you!" He accepted a cup that Daphne pushed over with a finger. "I'm afraid I'm at a disadvantage. You know my name and my class, but I know nothing about you all."

"I'm Lawrence. A rogue. Scouting with an assassination specialty."

"Gareth." He raised his hand for another whisky. "Archer. No specialization. As for the lady who's not paying attention to our conversation, she's Daphne. I *think* she specializes in fire. Anyway, she's strong for a mage. Just needs a little guidance, that's all."

Then came Sorin's turn. "I'm Sorin. Poison user. I'm also somewhat skilled at emergency medical care, though I lack the mana to play the role of a life mage."

"Interesting," said Stephan. "Well, I look forward to working with you all then. We can set off in the morning once we're all rested."

"Sounds good," said Lawrence, raising his mug. "Since we've agreed, I think this calls for a toast. To a wonderful working relationship and lots of fun and adventures together."

"To fun and adventures!" shouted Stephan, pounding the mug back.

Sorin and the others exchanged a strange look but repeated the toast and took a drink from their cups. On the other hand, Daphne took something out of her robes: a piece of toast. She took a bite from it before placing it back.

"Whoa!" said Stephan, putting down his mug. "That... what *was* that?" His face began to turn red-hot, and smoke began pouring out of his mouth. "H-Hot! Water!" A waitress appeared beside him and handed him a pail of water, which he dunked his head into and began drinking like a madman.

"Let that be a warning to you all," said the waitress to them. "*Whatever* is not a drink. Leave it up to me to pour a drink for you, and I'll give you a nice surprise. By the way, that drink will be three gold pieces." To their surprise, a delicate hand shot up towards the waitress and presented exactly three gold coins. The hand was Daphne's. "Looks like someone knew what she was doing," said the waitress with a chuckle.

Stephan finally pulled his face out of the bucket. There were blisters on his lips, but nothing lethal to a cultivator. "I see how it's going to be. Very well. If it's a war you want, it's a war you'll have."

Lawrence burst out laughing. "You've gotta have fun while you can, don't you think? It's all blood and gore out there, so we might as well cut loose while we're still in town."

"Indeed," said Stephan, calling the same waitress over. "Do you know how to mix a gold shliter around here?"

"A gold shliter?" said the waitress with a raised eyebrow. "You sure?"

"For that man over there," he said, pointing to Lawrence.

"All right." A smile tugged at the waitress's lips. "One gold shliter coming up."

The drink was exceedingly tame despite the price and completely defused the situation. They continued for a few more rounds till it was time to call it quits. It was only when they were settling the tab that Lawrence stumbled out of the bathroom, looking extremely peeved.

"How was it?" asked Stephan with a grin. "It's not as nice on the way out as it is on the way in, is it?"

"You know this means war," Lawrence said to Stephan.

"I never back away from a challenge," replied the man. "I might come from the big city, but that just means I know all sorts of big city tricks."

"Before we forget," Gareth cut in. "We should set a start time. How does an hour after dawn sound? Here at the guild, same table?"

"It'll probably just be an extermination mission," said Stephan. "So let's just meet at the northern gate to save time. Haley will pick whatever mission she thinks we can handle. You should all be familiar with her temperament by now. She's insane, but she won't make us do anything impossible."

Speak for yourself, thought Sorin. His arms still itched where the flesh-Melting spider's fangs had bitten him not long prior.

12

BONECRUSH DEMON PYTHON

It was halfway to noon when Sorin and company crossed the mana shield into Bloodwood Forest. Having learned from their previous experience, the entire group steeled their minds and awaited the onslaught of Violence.

Stephan was the first to regain his senses, while Lawrence was the last of their group to stabilize. "What a pitiful entrance," said Stephan, looking around. "There's no graded acclimatization zone? No guards posted to eradicate demons that draw too near?"

"Did you really think a small outpost would be the same as a dungeon?" It was surprisingly Daphne who spoke up.

"Of course not," said Stephan, a little embarrassed by his snobby comment. "Perhaps this is why my family sent me out here in the first place."

"What's a dungeon?" asked Sorin, rubbing his head. Violence was something he struggled against given his abrupt change in occupation.

"Is he serious?" asked Stephan.

"He's serious," said Gareth. "Until less than a week ago, he was just a crippled physician. He's completely new to the world of adventuring."

"A physician who uses poison," muttered Stephan. "*Right.* You're the one from the Kepler Clan that caused this guild branch a lot of trouble a few days ago."

"I wouldn't say it was *me* who caused trouble," Sorin corrected. "But my family, very much so."

Stephan seemed to sympathize with this explanation. "The great families of Olympia are all rather unreasonable in that way. If not for the guilds watching out for others, they'd long since have controlled this entire continent. Even so, their influence, including my York Clan's influence, is quite substantial.

"To answer your question, dungeons are located on demonic sources. The Seven Evils are too powerful for mere humans to defeat, and even the seeds of evil they sow can only be sealed away and their demonic energy harvested periodically. Dungeons were created as an outlet for these evil seeds by Hope himself. We adventurers are responsible for constantly cutting down the demons that spew forth, and we are rewarded with demon cores, which we can submit to the Temple of Hope for rewards."

"Are there any dungeons near here?" asked Sorin, intrigued by the concept.

"No," said Stephan, shaking his head. "And there probably never will be. Seeds of Evil are rare, and no new ones have been discovered in over a century. Now, let's stop here and take a break. There's something I need to do."

Stephan undid his pack and pulled out a small pouch. He sprinkled the pouch around their group before replacing it in his bag. "Demon repellant," he explained. "So we don't have to fight troublesome lesser demons. It's only useful against demons below a one-star rating that don't produce demon cores."

"I'll lead the way!" said Lawrence, zooming ahead.

"I'll keep an eye out on our surroundings," said Gareth, falling into his usual role. He didn't seem to mind being demoted from party leader to party scout.

"That just leaves Sorin and Daphne," said Stephan. "Sorin, I don't suppose you have special scouting skills?"

"None," Sorin answered honestly.

"Then your role will be to guard Daphne if something pops up, unless Gareth or I say otherwise," said Stephan. "As for Daphne…" His eye twitched as he noticed she wasn't paying attention. "Daphne?"

"Hm… yes?" replied the girl, not even looking up at him.

"Daphne? Are you seriously reading a book?" asked Stephan.

"It won't be a problem." She pointed her finger at a tree and shot out a Fire Bolt. It burned a hole all the way through the tree. "See? Spell. Very useful in combat."

Stephan shut his eyes. "If you were seriously studying, I might allow it, but this?" He yanked the book out of Daphne's hands and revealed it to the rest of the group. "The outside cover is that of a spellbook, but this is clearly a trashy romance novel."

Daphne fumed. "I'm studying human physiology. There's nothing wrong with studying!"

"Well, I'll be confiscating this book on human physiology, as well as any others that you take out," said Stephan. "Unless you have a problem with that?"

Daphne glared at him. "Fine. Keep the book. I'll be expecting it back later." She let out a loud *humph* and followed Gareth, who'd wisely chosen to distance himself from the situation.

Stephan was quite pleased with how the interaction turned out, but his smug smile soon faded. "That's…" The moment she was out of earshot, Daphne summoned what looked to be a cubic puzzle made of magic runes.

Sorin shook his head. "There's no helping it," said Sorin. "She did the same thing during our assessment, and Assessor York passed her despite the bad habit." Seeing Stephan's disappointment, he added an extra detail. "She blew up three one-star demons with a single spell."

"I suppose that counts for something," Stephan grumbled. "Oh well. I have to play with the cards I'm dealt."

Having used the demon repellant, they encountered only a few lesser demons, and those they did fled the moment they realized they were outmatched.

But their trip could have been more peaceful. Stephan was having an increasingly difficult time, courtesy of Lawrence. "That's it!" yelled Stephan as he crawled out of a pit. "You do this one more time, and I'm cutting you out of the team, Lawrence!"

"I didn't do anything," said Lawrence, popping out from behind a tree. "Honest! Gareth, you tell him!" Gareth looked away and pretended he hadn't heard him.

"Listen, Lawrence," said Stephan. "In town, I'm game. In the outskirts, I'm also game." He yanked off a beetle that had bitten into his arm. "But this deep in the woods, it comes to a stop. One small prank could kill off the entire team."

"Fine, *fine*," said Lawrence. "I guess we're sort of even for the gold shliter incident now?"

"If you think we're even, you're dreaming," snapped Stephan. "But alas, vengeance will have to wait until we get back. Understood?"

"Fine," said Lawrence.

"Great. Now look over there," said Stephan, pointing to a tree that had appeared around three-hundred feet away. Thick mana surrounded the emerald-leafed tree, and not a blade of grass grew within a three hundred feet of it. Plump red fruit hung from its branches, and some had even condensed violet runes, indicating that they were ripe for picking.

"Manasurge Persimmons," said Sorin. "I see at least thirty ripe ones. If I recall correctly, those sell for about ten gold apiece."

"Twelve if you have the right connections," corrected Stephan. "Conveniently, this tree should have guardians. We're in need of a good opponent right now to test out our group's cohesion before completing an actual mission together. Gareth?"

Gareth's eyes turned azure from the mana he was channeling through them. "I see it. A single one-star demon, sleeping on a branch not far up."

"Monkey or snake type?" asked Stephan.

"Snake type," said Gareth. "Has plates all over its body. It's roughly twenty feet long and about a foot thick. Should we come up with a game plan before engaging?"

Stephan shook his head. "No need. It's probably just a Bonecrush Demon Python. It's a higher-tier one-star demon. But with me around, it can only dream about hurting anyone. Let's see how everybody does in this encounter. Daphne? Put away that damned puzzle!"

"*Fine,*" said Daphne, putting away the cube and lazily taking out a wand.

"Gareth? On my mark," said Stephan. "One. Two. Three!"

Gareth pulled an arrow back and poured azure mana into his arrow. The arrow let loose at several times its original speed, courtesy of his skill, Quick Shot. Blood splashed onto the ground, and moments later, an enraged thirty-foot demonic snake descended from the tree and headed straight for them.

"I'll hold it back," Stephan said to them. "As for the rest of you, go wild." He pulled his hands back and roared as fur covered his entire body. He grew two feet taller in less than a second, and his arms, chest, and legs were all at least 50 percent bigger.

The python was quick, and Stephan had just finished his transformation by the time it arrived. It bit at Stephan with venomous fangs, but Stephan ignored it and grabbed onto its neck. The python reflexively bit into Stephan's collarbone, further trapping itself in place.

"What are you all waiting for?" Stephan called out. "Kill it!"

Lawrence appeared behind the snake less than a second later. He stabbed into it and retreated as the snake's tail violently whipped about. An arrow struck the snake's long body just as Sorin moved in and slapped a poisonous palm onto the snake's skin, injecting it with a strong dose of his poison.

Unfortunately, Sorin wasn't as agile as Lawrence. The python whipped its tail at him, and seeing that he couldn't dodge, Sorin gripped his poisoned dagger and prepared to trade blows.

"Idiot!" yelled Stephan, pulling at the snake. Sorin slashed at it with a poison-filled dagger before rolling away.

Two more arrows zipped past Sorin as he retreated, and Lawrence appeared once again to land a critical hit on the snake. It was now writhing in pain but could do nothing to free itself.

Having nowhere to run, the snake suddenly erupted with great power. "What are you all waiting for?" yelled Stephan. "It's trying to crush me using its berserk state!"

As predicted, the snake used its explosive increase in strength to wrap around Stephan's enlarged body and squeeze tightly. It had abandoned defense in favor of perishing with its opponent. Madness burned brightly in its demonic eyes.

Unfortunately, being coiled up so tight meant that Gareth no longer dared fire arrows at it. Daphne was likewise hesitating to cast spells at the target.

Sorin could only grit his teeth and jump in. He slashed multiple times at the snake's skin, and seeing that this wasn't quick enough, he grabbed onto the skin and poured his poisonous mana directly into the snake.

The sudden influx of mana caused the python to panic. It tightened its grip on Stephan and exerted all its strength to crush every bone in his body. "Damn it! Lawrence! Sorin! Anyone!"

Stephan was turning purple from the python's crushing pressure, and his bones were starting to crack. Fortunately, it was then that two Fire Bolts struck the serpent straight in the eyes, destroying its brain in the process. The snake fell limp onto the ground, and so did Stephan.

"What the hell was that?" said Stephan, glaring at all of them.

"In our defense, you're the one who said we didn't need a plan," Gareth pointed out.

"I was trying to conserve my mana," said Daphne. "But I got him in the end, didn't I?"

Stephan raised his arm but let it fall. "Fine. The fault is mine. But seriously, you guys can't even handle a single snake when I've got it tied down?" He felt at his collarbone. Black veins were spreading from the two bloody points where the python had bitten him. He pulled out an antidote and was just about to apply it when Sorin caught his arm.

"No need to waste a powerful antidote," said Sorin. "Or a healing potion, for that matter." He touched his arm to the two puncture wounds and sent a surge of poisonous mana into Stephan's body before pulling it out along with a glob of venom. "Unfortunately, it's a pretty weak venom. Not even worth drinking." But money was money, and Sorin dripped the snake's venom into a vial, then tossed that vial to Lawrence. Do you mind milking that thing?"

"I'm not milking snake fangs," said Lawrence. "Do it yourself." He hummed to himself and went to carve out the creature's core. "Too bad the leather's ruined. Maybe we can get enough out of it for a few pairs of boots?"

"It's not worth the trouble," said Stephan. Once again, he reached for a potion, but Sorin pushed him down.

"Money is money, and we're not all rich like you," said Sorin. "What did that demon repellant pouch cost? Five whole gold pieces? And that healing potion looks strong. Probably a hundred gold. Now, hold still while I stitch you up." A needle and thread appeared in his hands. He stitched up Stephan's nicked artery in a matter of seconds. As for the rest, he didn't bother since the beastshift warrior's skin was already healing over.

Fifteen minutes later, the battlefield was all cleaned up. The snake had its venom taken, its core extracted, and half its skin removed. As for its flesh, they chose to leave it behind. While demons could be eaten, carrying around their meat could easily draw predatory demons in on their party.

"There are thirty-five ripe fruits in total," said Gareth, hopping down from the tree with a bag full of them. Should we mark it?"

"It's already been marked," said Stephan, shaking his head. "I have a few more locations marked on here that we can check out. Maybe we'll find something good there, assuming other adventurers haven't done so already."

Sorin and the rest of the team were quite open to the suggestion. With the exception of Stephan and Daphne, none of them had any magic items. Adventuring was very expensive, and any gold they gained could be used to increase their strength.

"Then, since everything's taken care of here, let's take a short break," said Stephan. "If we're going to work as a team, we need to fix our bad habits.

"Let's break everything down and see what we can improve upon."

13

A CULTIVATOR'S DISPOSITION

"Each of us can be classified according to our base classes," said Stephan, taking a seat beside them as they rested. "You, Gareth, are an archer. Lawrence is a rogue, Daphne is a mage, Sorin is a variant, and I am a warrior. Regardless of the specifics, each of us needs to fulfill our respective roles; otherwise, the team will collapse. At least one of us will die, and we'll be forced to either retire or find another team."

"I'm a variant?" asked Sorin. "What does that mean?"

"He means that you don't quite fit into a category," said Gareth. "Some rogues, assassins, or archers will specialize in poison like you do, but they usually do it to enhance their roles."

"That's correct," said Stephan. "You fight like a rogue, but you can't dodge or hide like one. You can infect enemies with poison that causes damage over time, but your attacks aren't as lethal as plague mages are. You're mixing it all up, and to be honest, it's messing up the team's dynamics. Anyway, let's keep the most complex case for later. Gareth, what are your thoughts on fighting the python?

"My thoughts?" said Gareth with a frown. "I felt stifled, to be honest. You grabbed onto that snake. I couldn't take a shot."

"Couldn't or wouldn't?" asked Stephan. "Please. It's an important distinction."

"Wouldn't," admitted Gareth. "To be honest, hitting a moving snake isn't hard for me. I wasn't worried about hitting you—you were standing still. I was more worried about hitting either Sorin or Lawrence."

"That's fair," said Stephan. "And I'm relieved that you can shoot so accurately at near point-blank range. Many archers can't." He then turned to Lawrence. "Lawrence, if he fired his bow at you, could you dodge it?"

"Me?" said Lawrence. "*Maybe*. I mean, I've got a few skills I can rely on. Assuming he's shooting right at me."

"And if he isn't?" pressed Stephan.

"If he isn't, it won't be a problem," said Lawrence. "Worst case, I'll just pull back from whatever attack I'm in the middle of pulling off and try again later."

Stephan nodded. "Sorin, what about you?"

"I can't," said Sorin, shaking his head. "My spiritual senses are strong enough to know he's going to shoot, but my reflexes can't keep up."

"So what you're saying is that you wouldn't be able to react once he shot?" asked Stephan. "Then you wouldn't change your behavior at all?"

"I suppose I wouldn't, now that you mention it," said Sorin. "Why react if you can't do it on time?"

"There," Stephan said to Gareth. "So out of the two you're worried about, the one that can actually react to your shot can dodge if he has to, while the other one is too slow to react," said Stephan. "As for me, I'm *definitely* too slow. Also, I'm durable, so you don't have to worry too much about accidents. Go ahead and shoot me."

"I see what you're saying," said Gareth. "I'll take more shots in the future. I think it'll also get easier the more I get used to everyone's movements."

"Good," said Stephan. "We'll move on to Daphne. Daphne?"

"Yes?" said Daphne, looking up from her puzzle.

"Do you have anything to say for yourself?" asked Stephan.

"Nope," said Daphne. "I did nothing wrong."

"How so?" asked Stephan.

"Because if it were up to me, I would have killed it before it even bit you," replied Daphne, putting away her puzzle. "Your intentions were clearly to test our skills and teamwork, which I allowed. Had I acted earlier, the battle would have had no suspense."

"Well analyzed," said Stephan. "Then let's talk about you, Lawrence. What is your favorite thing to do in battle, and why is it running away and hiding?"

"I'm good at running," said Lawrence. "I have a lot of experience with it. And I'm great at hiding, don't you think?"

"But do you really need to use a cloaking skill and retreat so far away from a tied-down python?" said Stephan. "Couldn't you just cut it a few more times instead?"

"It's the principle of it," said Lawrence. "My father always said that a good rogue never shows himself before he strikes."

"Which is great in theory," said Stephan. "If you were an actual assassin and killed your enemies in one massive burst of mana, that would be a wonderful way to operate. But you're *not* an assassin. You don't have the skill set. You're a typical rogue that hides and lands sneak attacks on an opponent's weak points. Don't think I didn't see how you targeted those spots between the snake's vertebrae."

"Fine," said Lawrence, rolling his eyes. "I'll work on it."

"Excellent," said Stephan.

"Pardon, but I think much of this battle was your fault as well," said Sorin. He didn't like Stephan's one-sided approach.

Surprisingly, Stephan didn't argue with him. "You're right. I intentionally fought badly to give you guys all a chance. If I had used my full strength, I would have torn apart that snake with my bare hands."

"Fine," said Sorin grumpily. "What about me?"

"You…" Stephan winced. "Have you ever learned any spells?"

"I've dabbled," said Sorin. "Mostly healing spells." Seeing Stephan's disbelieving expression, he explained. "I used to cultivate life mana. Not anymore, so the runes, seals, and mana patterns are completely off. I have fundamentals but no way to apply them."

"And skills…"

"Broke," replied Sorin. "I can only play it by ear."

"And that dagger technique…"

"Improvised from basic mana manipulation on a scalpel," said Sorin. "I can do the same with needles and throw them. As for the palm strike, it's also just dumping mana into someone else's body, much like I would with life mana."

Stephan put his hand to his brow and massaged it lightly. "Well. That explains it all. Your battle sense is completely off because you were a physician, and your techniques aren't up to par because you're just learning your abilities. You reached the fourth stage of Blood-Thickening very quickly because you're just recultivating—and trust me, that's not completely uncommon in big cities. As for your techniques themselves, they're the techniques of a physician. That includes your footwork, which is clearly geared towards self-defense."

He looked to Daphne. "I don't imagine you have any poison spells in that spell book of yours? Acid Orb? Acid Dart? Poison Spray?"

"Nope," said Daphne. "I just learned Magic Missile because sometimes fire doesn't work too well. Aside from that, I'm pretty much all fire-based."

"That was just wishful thinking on my part," said Stephan. "Sorin, I can't help you with dagger arts, and Lawrence can't help you either because he cultivates the shadow element. That's not a very good parallel to poison. So it falls to *me* to give you some pointers, strange as that might seem."

"You?" said Sorin. "You're going to teach me to fight like a beast-shift warrior?"

"Not at all," said Stephan. "But it occurs to me that you've probably never seen a proper application of a palm strike. I happen to excel at swatting things with my paws. Like bears do. Observe."

Sorin squinted as mana appeared on Stephan's hand, and it grew hair and claws. "What exactly do you expect me to…" His voice trailed off as he saw that additional mana patterns that shouldn't be there had appeared on Stephan's palm. Stephan winked at him, then turned to a tree.

"Healers need to be gentle," Stephan continued. "Warriors, not so much. Watch." Mana activated in his body, working through his legs and his other meridians. Once again, barely perceptible patterns appeared on his body to illustrate the movement of mana in his body. They were so faint that Sorin realized perhaps only he and his powerful spiritual perception could make them out.

Stephan charged up power for an exaggerated amount of time before swinging forward with his paw and striking at the tree he'd chosen. His paw smashed right through the tree, breaking it in half. Splinters of wood rained down from the sky.

"Now, I'm not completely sure how someone like you would do it, and I can't teach you my family's techniques," said Stephan with a toothy grin. "But if you were to happen to watch me fight and gain some inspiration, who would be able to say anything?"

Sorin's eyes widened. *No wonder those faint patterns appeared. He's teaching me while maintaining plausible deniability. He's not showing me his skill manual, but he might as well be!*

"Many thanks," said Sorin to Stephan. "I'll learn what I can."

"Not at all," said Stephan. "There's no helping it since we're in the middle of Bloodwood Forest. See what else you can find to imitate. Also…"

"Yes?" said Sorin.

"I hate to say it, but as a physician, you surely have a good knowledge of anatomy," said Stephan. "I'm sure that even extends to demon anatomy as well. Healing is one of your strengths, but we're adventurers."

Sorin winced. Stephan had struck the nail right on the head. He was, in fact, purposefully avoiding his medical arts. Physicians weren't supposed to harm anyone, demons included. Using what he'd learned in this fashion went against most of what he'd been taught—though he had a feeling his father would have approved of Stephan's statement.

"I'll take your words under advisement," Sorin said to Stephan.

"Good," said Stephan. "Then I'll finish off with one final bit of advice, something your family might not have had time to teach you."

"I'm all ears," said Sorin.

"Cultivation is a choice," said Stephan. "A choice to bravely move forward. Cultivators risk their lives with every step they take. They stake everything on their future improvement."

"Adventuring is also a choice. We go out, and we fight demons. We fight demons for money. We fight demons for glory. We fight demons for justice and all sorts of other reasons. Every time we go out, we're facing possible death. That includes our deaths and the deaths of our comrades as well. So it's very important to maintain the right mindset: the mindset of a cultivator."

"The mindset of a cultivator?" joked Lawrence. "What kind of metaphysical bull crap is that?"

"Quiet when the adults are speaking," said Stephan. "The mindset of a cultivator is just like I described. Risking one's life to advance. Putting all one's chips on the table. Knowing that one day, you can be doing quite well, but the next day, you can lose everything because of a simple mistake."

It finally dawned on Sorin that perhaps he'd been a bit too naïve. By adventuring, he wasn't just risking his own life but also the lives of those around him. "That reminds me of something my father used to say," said Sorin softly. "In all aspects of life, one must adopt the mindset of a physician. A single mistake can cost a patient's leg. A single mistaken acupoint can ruin a career. A single second's delay can kill a patient."

Stephan nodded. "It sounds like you know exactly what I'm talking about then. Adventuring is not so different from doctoring, it seems. In both professions, you need to use all the tricks you have in every fight. Otherwise, someone will end up dying."

14

STEELFEATHER SPARROW

A screech pierced the cold morning air, rousing Sorin from his slumber. He reached beneath his pillow, grabbed his mithril dagger, and crawled to the side of his tent to peek through its worn canvas walls.

The campfire was on its last embers, and the sun was starting to rise above the forest canopy. A sickly haze of demonic mana clung around their campsite, threatening to engulf them if the morning came late.

Sorin looked from tent to tent and saw that Stephan and Lawrence were already awake and battle-ready. Daphne and Gareth were keeping third watch; one had his bow in hand and an arrow nocked, while the other had the tired eyes of a person who'd been secretly napping, as well as a ball of fire in hand, ready to chuck.

A second screech sounded, and this time, it was followed by a gust of wind. A large avian demon dove toward their camp, wings spread, and razor-sharp claws extended. Gareth loosed an arrow at its soft underbelly, only to see it bounce off without accomplishing anything.

"I can't do anything," Gareth called out to Stephan as he walked out of his tent.

"That's only natural," said Stephan. "A two-star demon's defenses are difficult to pierce."

"Watch while I turn that two-star chicken into a roast chicken," said Daphne, pulling back her hand.

"Hold!" commanded Stephan. "Fire can work, but it'll be impossible to hit it unless it's mid-dive.

"Wait, are you saying we're going to fight this thing?" asked Sorin. "That's a two-star demon!"

"I don't think we have a choice in the matter," said Stephan. "Unless you know of a cave nearby where we can hide? Lawrence, this should be a Steelfeather Sparrow. Tell me its weak points."

"Like you said, fire should do the trick," said Lawrence. "It's also much weaker on the ground than in the air, assuming we can keep it tied up. Its weak points are its wing joins and the area just between its legs. The eyes, of course. Vertebrae, assuming you can pierce its steel feathers. Arrows will be useless unless you can hit its eyes. Sorry, Gareth."

"That's life," said Gareth.

"Wait a minute," said Sorin. "Why don't we try something the next time it comes down? You said it's a Steelfeather Sparrow? How literal is that name?"

"Fairly literal," said Stephan. "The wings are made of metal. Not steel, as the name might imply, but pretty close."

"That sounds perfect," said Sorin. "Gareth? Ready an arrow. Try to hit its wing. Everyone else, get ready to duck." The steel feather sparrow circled above them and let out a screech as it prepared to dive a third time. Sorin grabbed a knife and cut his hand, then smeared it on Gareth's arrowhead. The metal smoldered under the effect of his poison.

The sparrow was over ten feet wide and far too powerful for any of them to take head-on. It was, therefore, taken completely by surprise when Gareth stood in its path and let loose an arrow at its right wing.

The archer rolled out of the way of its talons, and the bird, not to be deterred, made a wide circle before coming back. It had just begun its descent when suddenly, it faltered mid-air. "Nice!" said Lawrence. "Poison blood for the win!"

"Daphne!" shouted Stephan.

"Fireball!" intoned Daphne, launching her most potent spell. The bird, clearly worried about the dissolving feathers on its wing, didn't notice the spell in time to dodge it and was knocked out of the sky.

"Let's catch it on its way down!" shouted Stephan. "Lawrence, keep it busy! Gareth, get more of Sorin's blood!"

"Way ahead of you," Sorin said to Gareth, tossing him a vial. He'd already finished bandaging up his palm.

Gareth let loose three arrows this time, and the sparrow, enraged by its ruined wing and its half-Melted feathers, barely noticed when the arrow struck into the featherless spots on its body.

Lawrence followed up a half-second after Gareth's attack, but when he attempted to stab into its back, it spread its wings out by instinct and smacked Lawrence aside. But that was when a second Fireball struck it, melting another portion of its feathers together and completely grounding it.

The Steelfeather Sparrow let out an angry screech and zeroed in on Daphne. Yet before it could attack her, it found itself under siege by 400 pounds of armored bear.

"Lunisolar Paw!" roared Stephan. The attack smashed the sparrow into the ground, damaging its beak. It cut at Stephan with its sharp claws as it rose from its prone position and cut a deep gouge into his bear leg before smacking him aside with a wing.

"Careful!" shouted Stephan. Daphne's eyes widened as the wounded bird picked itself up off the ground and flapped its wings to close the gap. It reached out with its steel-like claws to crush the life out of her.

Fortunately, Gareth had already expected this. He shot out an arrow from behind Daphne and knocked the sparrow back with a gust of wind. Sorin took advantage of the opening Gareth had bought him and circulated mana according to the method he'd observed from Stephan's technique. "Poison Palm!" he shouted as he slammed his hand into the creature's chest right where its lungs should be.

A white poison rushed into its body and infiltrated its internal organs. The bird twitched and shivered, then staggered as its body stiffened.

"It's paralyzed! Attack while you can!" shouted Sorin. He shot out a thread and used his mana to tie several loops around the creature's body. Poison poured from Sorin into the bird through his connection to the mithril string and reinforced the paralysis.

Several more arrows landed with a thunk, missing Sorin by a few scant inches. Gareth had improved his shooting skills significantly over the past few days.

Spleen. Heart clavicle. Gizzard. Sorin's dagger pierced out with deadly precision along the vital spots he'd identified with his initial palm strike. Identifying a patient's physiological structure and internal condition with a single touch was a core skill for physicians, and now he was using these precious healing skills to kill.

Yet Sorin had miscalculated the toughness of a two-star demon. Though his poisons infiltrated its internal organs, they weren't nearly as effective against it as they would be against a lesser demon. Even the paralytic Sorin had applied was wearing off despite the mithril string. A sharp claw came tearing towards Sorin, and it was only thanks to Lawrence quickly pulling him back at the last minute that he was able to escape.

"Keep at it," called out Stephan. "It's in no shape to fly, and we can kite as need be." He launched himself at the bird and began mauling it with his paws. He suffered several deep gashes to his shoulder and even suffered heavy damage to his chest armor in the process, but in exchange, he bought time for Sorin and Lawrence to land their attacks.

Heart paralysis, thought Sorin as he stabbed its dagger straight through two of the bird's ribs and injected another dose of opaque white paralytic poison. The sparrow twitched as it lost control over its body, and its heart contracted abnormally. *Temporary petrification is technically more accurate, but the effect is pretty much the same.*

In its incapacitated state, the bird was ripe for Lawrence to wail on. He stabbed the creature multiple times in the back of the neck, where a few feathers were missing. A two-star demon's vitality was impressive, and the bird still wasn't about to give up. Yet two Magic Missiles in the eye didn't leave it much choice in the matter.

Blinded, crippled, and mostly featherless, the sparrow thrashed about until it expended the last of its energy. "Don't touch it yet," said Sorin, stopping Lawrence just short of the bird's reach. "It's faking death." They waited two full minutes until, finally, the bird shivered one last time and slumped to the ground, dead. "You can go ahead now."

"We're rich!" shouted Lawrence, rubbing his hands gleefully. "Rich!"

"It's just a two-star demon bounty," muttered Stephan. Yet even he looked quite pleased by the result. "Adventurers at our level rarely run into two-star demons so easy to handle." Then he sighed. "The meat is ruined, and most of the feathers are gone. And my armor..." The shoulder of his half-plate was a mangled mess, and he had been forced to peel it off. Sorin shuddered to think of how much the damage would cost to repair. "The only thing of value is the two-star demon core and the bounty. Both are worth somewhere between 500 and 1,000 gold apiece."

"Hey, let's not forget the feathers," said Lawrence. "Those are perfectly good materials for smithing, even when melted."

"But they're very troublesome to remove," said Stephan.

"We'll take what we can, but we need to leave soon," said Gareth, looking around worriedly. "Ten minutes tops."

"Good point," said Stephan. "Other two-star creatures might come sniffing about." He grabbed his bloodied shoulder and winced. "As much as I'd like to patch up my wounds, let's get out of here first. And Lawrence, what in Hope's name are you doing?"

"I'm a bird!" said Lawrence, flapping about his arms with a handful of undamaged steel feathers. "Look at me, I'm a bird!" Even Sorin had to admit that the childish act was getting annoying.

Sorin made quick work of his tent and packed up his belongings. The others weren't finished, so he walked up to the bird's corpse and began cutting it apart. *The paralytic poison wasn't as effective as I thought it would be. Is it a mana issue or an application issue?* The tissue was too badly damaged to answer the question, but he made a few careful inquisitions to confirm its inner structure before putting away his knife.

"You know, you don't have to kill it a second time," said Lawrence as he removed feathers from the beast. "As much as I hate it, I wouldn't stab its corpse. It's insulting."

"It's called dissection," said Sorin. "Your attacks are very dependent on striking critical areas, and the texts in the guild are far from accurate. Shouldn't you be joining me instead of criticizing me?"

"I don't think I have the stomach for it," said Lawrence. "You let me know what you find out, though. I'll wholeheartedly accept your recommendations."

Sorin shrugged. "Suit yourself." He continued cutting up the demon's corpse until the rest of them were gathered.

"Everyone ready?" said Stephan as the rest of their party trickled in. "Gareth, any luck?"

"Empty nest," said Gareth, shaking his head.

"Too bad," said Stephan. "Demon eggs are worth a fortune even in big cities."

"So where to next, boss?" asked Lawrence. "I thought you said we were going to go do an actual mission."

"That's the plan," said Stephan. "There's an extermination request for a nest not far away. But I'm wounded, and Daphne's out of mana."

"What's the target?" asked Gareth.

"Rats," said Stephan.

"Rats?" said Lawrence. "Gross."

"Seconded!" said Daphne in a rare show of opinion.

"Well, too bad," said Stephan. "Rats are a big problem every demon tide. Whenever a nest gets found, it needs to be exterminated."

"Because of Disease?" asked Sorin.

"Because of Disease," confirmed Stephan. "Rats are weak, but a common tactic in a demon tide is to throw rats at a city and let plague break out. Disease fans the flames and makes the plagues much more virulent.

"Sometimes, the residents manage to survive the demons but lose half their population. Besides—weren't you all telling me how money is money? Well, one-star rats are five gold apiece, and their cores are worth about the same. Not bad, given that there'll probably be well over a hundred of them."

Everyone grew solemn when they heard the number. "A hundred rats? Isn't fighting that many insane?" said Lawrence.

"Not all at once, obviously," said Stephan. "But I digress. We should find a place to rest before making our way over. If we try storming the nest now, we'll only be feeding them our corpses."

15

VISION OF FIVE POISONS

Their group found a small cave to rest in before making their way to the rat cave. Stephan's wounds were worse than initially expected due to an infusion of high-grade corrupted mana.

"We should rest at least a day before proceeding," said Sorin, using a combination of poisons, herbs, and acupuncture to chase out the corruption before cutting away at the last of the corrupted flesh. "Otherwise, the purity of your mana will be affected." Mana corruption was taboo for cultivators since it would prevent them from advancing between cultivation stages. Many geniuses had fallen from grace because of it, and their talents were doomed never to recover.

As was his practice every time he rested, Sorin absorbed more of the Cockatrice Grass extract to strengthen his poison and evaluated his combat tactics. *My footwork is still sloppy because of my clogged meridians. But that can't be helped. I'll still need two more days to finish absorbing the Cockatrice Grass extract. Only then will my mana be strong enough to purge additional meridian channels.*

Speaking of Cockatrice Grass extract, he was quite pleased by the performance of the paralysis poison he'd used on the Steelfeather Sparrow. While it had taken an injection of poison directly into the lungs and heart, the paralysis effect had lasted just long enough for their team to finish off the demon.

But Sorin naturally knew that this wouldn't work on other two-star demons. He'd only succeeded because the sparrow was injured and on the ground. Many different factors contributed to their victory over the creature.

Two more things needed to be addressed. First, the crystal needles. They were growing increasingly ineffective as they fought stronger monsters. He needed to find an alternative and fast. Second, he'd been neglecting the mithril string Percival had given him and needed to continue practicing.

"Is that a mithril string?" said Stephan, walking up to Sorin as he practiced lashing rocks.

"It is," said Sorin. "A friend of the family gave it to me. He said it might be useful if I learned to control it."

"I'm sure they meant well, but I'm of the opinion that you're using that string entirely wrong," said Stephan. "Mind if I see it?"

"Suit yourself," said Sorin, passing him the string.

The string began to shiver violently the moment it entered Stephan's hands. It coiled several times around his unwounded hand and coiled into a long bundle.

Stephan swung the bundle at a rock, and the rock crumbled from the impact. "In my hands, the string isn't that useful either. I might as well be wielding a club. All I can give it is weight, which isn't compatible with its flexible nature."

He coiled the string up into a ball and tossed it back to Sorin. "Let me be straight with you, Sorin," said Stephan. "I like you. You're an unpretentious physician who does good work, no matter what your family says or what your qualifications are. You're hard-working. You practice when others rest. You're also talented—you managed to imitate that paw strike after a single day."

"But?" asked Sorin.

"But you're going to have to change in some way," said Stephan. "That thing with the arrows and your blood was quick thinking, but it's not enough. In the future, Gareth could buy poison for his arrows, and that would make you redundant."

"Got it," said Sorin. "I'll think of something."

"I hope you do," said Stephan. "Because after this mission, we'll be going back. If you haven't found your direction by the time we're out of these woods, I'm going to have to replace you with someone else. For everyone's sake."

Sorin nodded. "I know what I need to do."

Stephan nodded and returned to the back of the cave to continue his recovery.

Danger was the best way to unearth one's potential and stabilize one's mana. It was apparently also great for Sorin's poison uptake rate. What had been a milliliter an hour, ten times a day, suddenly grew to ten milliliters in a single hour. His body also showed no signs of rejecting the poison, so he drank it voraciously.

Three hours passed by in this fashion until Sorin finally felt an uncontrollable thirst. Only two vials remained by then, and like a parched desert traveler who hadn't drunk anything in days, he hastily broke off their tops and downed their contents.

The poison burned as it traveled down Sorin's throat, leaching into his blood through his esophagus. For a few seconds, he couldn't breathe. He couldn't speak. His blood bubbled as the fifth poison fully merged with the others, and his cultivation broke through to the fifth stage of Blood-Thickening.

This time, he didn't even have to direct his mana. It automatically revolved through his six open meridians and began aggressively attacking the unopened ones. He had already opened the large intestine, lung, small intestine, spleen, kidney, and gallbladder meridians.

Now, his liver, bladder, stomach, and heart meridians all shook and burst open like dams. His newly invigorated mana flowed through his five yin and five yang organs, removing any unnecessary tissues and regenerating their missing chunks.

The commotion didn't stop there. With Sorin's organs now healthy and balanced, his mana flow was strengthened even further. Pressure built up in his body, and his mana attacked the last two remaining primary meridians: the pericardium and triple burner meridians.

Sorin coughed up a mouthful of black blood from the impact. These were impurities that were forced out of his body. This mana impacted the two meridians three more times. On the fourth impact, all blockages were resolved. His body finally felt like a complete whole.

Yet Sorin quickly realized that the poisons in his body weren't done quite yet. They began to accumulate where his mana sea used to be, forming an image that shifted constantly between five forms.

A stream of information poured into his mind as the Ten Thousand Poison Canon, which had always been more of a reference book inside his head than anything else, suddenly unlocked.

There were five yin organs and five yang organs. There were five fingers on each hand. There were five mortal cultivation stages and five stages in the realm beyond.

Time was measured in five twelve-year cycles, and the Five Elements were the root of all creation. Seeking life through death was the way of the Five Poisons, and that was the root of the Ten Thousand Poison Canon.

Countless thoughts ran through Sorin's head, clearing up much of his accumulated confusion. The Ten Thousand Poison Canon suddenly didn't seem so revolting anymore. Snake, scorpion, centipede, toad, and spider. These were the five poisons in classical medicine. Sorin would need to choose one aspect before progressing in the cultivation technique.

He immediately chose the snake. The snake had a special place in Sorin's heart; the coiled snake was the symbol of the Kepler Clan and was also the symbol of the Medical Association.

The moment he made this choice, the image in his mana sea solidified and took the form of a viper. It wasn't aggressive like he'd initially imagined, but peaceful and kind. It hunted rodents but wouldn't do anything to humans unless provoked.

Moreover, there was something strange about this image—something that touched on the divine. Whether it was the golden pattern on its leathery skin or the wise and knowledgeable look in its eyes, it appeared like something untouched by corruption. Something that had come before the Evils had taken over Pandora.

The appearance of the viper had a cascade effect. Sorin felt his muscles grow stronger and more flexible, and his blood became more rigorous. The mana flow inside his body twisted and diverted to adopt a new pattern more suited to his chosen aspect.

The flow of poisonous mana in his hands also changed. Poison now accumulated in his hands instead of spreading out evenly throughout his body. Instead of pouring a slow and steady trickle of poison into his targets, he would be able to unleash a large dose in an extremely short amount of time.

"What in the name of Hope is going on?" came a voice, interrupting Sorin's trance. The physician's eyes shot open, and they spotted Lawrence not far away. It was a night out, and Sorin had drawn his dagger. "At least warn someone before a breakthrough, will you? Sorin? Sorin?!" Lawrence appeared in front of Sorin and waved his hand in front of his face. He moved to flick Sorin's nose, and Sorin's hand shot up to intercept him.

"Sorry about that," said Sorin, releasing Lawrence's hand.

"I never knew you had such a strong grip," Lawrence complained as he rubbed his wrist.

"Neither did I," said Sorin. "I just broke through, so I still don't know my strength."

Sorin could feel his four limbs bubbling over with energy. He felt like a coiled spring that could strike at any moment. And to his surprise, his mana was acting in much the same way. Unbeknownst to him, a potent amount of poison had already accumulated on the dagger he'd somehow drawn. His mithril string was coiled around his left wrist and looked like a snake, erect and ready to strike.

Yet before he could apply said energy, Sorin realized that he'd somehow exhausted all his mana stores. The mithril string went limp, and the poisoned dagger in his hand went dull.

"You all right, Sorin?" asked Lawrence as Sorin fell to the floor. "Need some water or something? A potion, maybe?"

"I'll be fine," said Sorin. "My mana reserves are just depleted."

"Well, you'd better recover quick," said Lawrence. "Dawn is coming pretty fast, and Stephan said he wanted to start up bright and early." Sorin looked back to see three sleeping figures. Stephan was snoring loudly, and Daphne, who *should* have been on watch with Lawrence, was muttering something about burning an entire filthy rat nest to the ground under her breath.

"It shouldn't take too long," said Sorin. "Sorry, I skipped watch."

Lawrence shrugged. "It happens. When someone's in a meditative state, you've got to roll with it. Waking them up is usually a bad idea."

"I'll recover for an hour and keep watch with you once I'm done," said Sorin.

"Is an hour going to be enough?" asked Lawrence skeptically.

"It will be," confirmed Sorin.

Sorin sat down and entered a meditative state once again. Thanks to his fully unblocked primary meridians, mana flowed freely into his system and his blood, reinvigorating it.

Originally, he'd thought the Ten Thousand Poison Canon was some archaic cultivation manual from ancient times. It was only now that Sorin understood that Hope's 'gift' was not as simple as it appeared.

16

ENTERING THE NEST

The entrance of the rat nest was situated at the base of a rocky cliff. A small cluster of bloodwood trees with rough bark and thick, red sap provided convenient visual cover for the man-sized hole that served as an entrance. At the same time, the bloody smell secreted by the trees masked the pervasive smell of rat droppings coming from the cave. It took them six hours to find the place, despite having a map showing them where to look.

"The landmarks all match what's on the map," said Gareth, looking up and down from a sheet of beast hide. "I also sense no other threats in the vicinity. What are your thoughts, team leader?"

"This is the place," confirmed Stephan. "Our mission is simple: to exterminate every last rat in this hole and collect their cores as evidence. Yes, Daphne?"

"I don't blame you if you don't want to answer this, but... is there a chance that your sister might want you killed?" asked Daphne. Then, looking around at everyone else's shocked faces, she shrugged. "What? It's a legitimate question. This kind of thing happens all the time in... historical records. Yes, that's what we'll call them."

Sorin had been the target of such an operation, so he could see the rationale behind it. Fortunately, Stephan wasn't at all concerned about such a thing. "My York Clan does things a little differently from the other clans," said Stephan. "We decide succession based on strength and potential. I'm currently fifth in line for the position of clan leader, so I'm very unlikely to be chosen for the position. As for my sister, she ranks twentieth. Her cultivation is high, but her talent is lacking. Does that answer your question, Daphne?"

"Almost," said Daphne. "Now, what about inter-branch strife and the like? What's that like in your clan?" She took out a notepad and pen. "I'm asking for science, of course. Not for story ideas."

"I think we might be getting a little off track," said Sorin. "Also, I think Lawrence is back."

"Really, Sorin?" said Lawrence, appearing out of the shadows next to the cave. "Did you really have to ruin my entrance like that?"

"It's for your own good," said Sorin. "Stephan's clearly getting sick of your antics, and there was a risk of Daphne blowing you up, thinking you were a rat." He nodded towards Daphne, who'd actually summoned a ball of fire and was halfway through throwing it. "See? I'm helping!"

"Just give us the rundown, Lawrence," said Stephan, massaging the space between his brows. "And try to be professional for once? This *is* an actual mission, and I'll have to report everything as it happens."

"Fine then," said grumbled Lawrence. "I'd be more than happy to explain, but I think visuals will help us greatly." He snatched Daphne's notepad and began drawing with confident strokes. They waited five whole minutes for Lawrence to hand the pen back and show off his masterpiece."

"That's the ugliest map I've ever seen," said Sorin.

"Not for me," said Gareth. "But it ranks in the top five."

"This is a perfectly legitimate map!" said Lawrence.

"I think he tried to draw a fork in the road," said Gareth, grabbing the paper. "Three-pronged? No, wait, is that a *face*?"

"You're all insufferable," said Lawrence, grabbing the notepad back and then tossing it to Daphne. "The place is basically just tunnels crisscrossing through the rock. The rats are confirmed to be Rockgnaw Rats, with teeth as big as Stephan's abnormally large hands. The smallest come up to my knees, but the biggest come up to my waist."

"Thank you, Lawrence," said Stephan. "Did you locate any smaller nests? Are there any rat variants to take note of? Traps?"

"They're *rats*," Lawrence said flatly. "The dumb, garden variety kind, in case that wasn't clear."

"Then we'll have everyone take one of these," said Stephan, tossing out a bottle to each of them. "We have three pills each, one per day. If we can't finish by then, we pull out, and the mission will be reported as a failure. Sorin, any thoughts?"

"None," said Sorin. "Are these Plagueward Pills, by the way? Mid-grade?"

"Yes," said Stephan. "I'm surprised you recognize them."

"I'm surprised too," said Sorin. "We typically don't see anything this expensive out here."

Stephan coughed lightly. "They're a necessity on a mission like this. Aren't they?"

Lawrence patted Stephan on the arm. "I'm pretty sure you're getting preferential treatment, Stephan."

"Anyway, the mission is pretty straightforward," said Stephan. "The key to completing it will be to advance slowly and methodically to make sure we take out all of them. There's a reward for every head. Also, creatures like this tend to pick their nests for a reason. There's a good chance we'll find something good in there. Gareth?"

"I think I'm out of my element here," said Gareth, shaking his head. "You call the shots, and I'll only speak out if I see something."

"Sounds good," said Stephan. "The plan will be a simple one: I'm bait, and you guys kill things as they come. Lawrence will scout ahead, and if he finds big groups, it'll be up to Daphne to initiate. Sounds good? Yes, Daphne?"

"Permission to scorch freely, sir?" asked Daphne.

"Permission denied," said Stephan. "We're going to be in tight quarters, so we'll want some advance warning before you light anything up.

Anything else?" This time, it was Sorin who raised his hand. "Yes, Sorin?"

"As everyone likely knows, I just broke through in my cultivation technique last night," said Sorin. "I just wanted everyone to know that it was a drastic change. You should all be on the lookout for different attack patterns than last time."

"If you say so," said Stephan, looking unconvinced. "Either way, I'll take the front. Gareth, you take the back, and see if you can find opportunities. Sorin, act as you see fit. Now, if that's everything, let's go collect ourselves some rat cores.

The cave was dark, damp, and very unlike the magical caves in Sorin's imagination. The mana-infused crystals he'd dreamed of were non-existent, and the only way for their team to fumble forward was with the help of two light sources: a reusable light stick belonging to Stephan and a small light cantrip powered by Daphne's mana.

Speaking of Daphne, she had undergone a transformation over the past few days. Her obliviousness was selective, it seemed, and the mention of rats had roused her fighting spirit. She was completely focused now that they were in a dangerous situation.

"How does Lawrence even manage to see without a light stick?" Sorin grumbled as they walked. Spiritual senses were fine when it came to spiritual entities, but in the darkness? They were practically useless.

"He obviously has some kind of dark vision skill," said Gareth. "Not uncommon for shadow cultivators. But quite expensive since the demand is so high for it."

"How expensive are we talking?" asked Sorin.

"I'm not exactly sure," replied Gareth. "But it's at least 1,500 gold. Maybe as much as 2,500 gold."

Sorin whistled. "Looks like his old man broke the bank for him."

"That he did," said Stephan from the front. "His movement skill is also top-notch for the Blood-Thickening Realm. His attack skill, on the other hand, is a total mismatch. His father must have prioritized his survival and cheaped out on the rest. Probably to stop quick success from getting to his head."

"What about your techniques?" asked Daphne. "Aside from shifting, I haven't seen you use anything but that Lunisolar Paw."

Stephan's eye twitched. "I was only given Lunisolar Paw and this armor. And until I pay off the loan, I'm not allowed to get anything else."

"Fascinating," said Daphne. "I didn't know the big families could be so stingy."

"They're usually not," said Stephan wryly. "But my mother is a strict woman, and my father won't dare go against her."

Seems to run in the family, thought Sorin, remembering the 'kind treatment' Stephan had received from Haley. It was a large contrast to the Kepler Clan, which gave away everything their children needed to learn their craft. But if their children failed performance assessments, they would find themselves cut off from *any* funding. The Kepler Clan didn't foster failures.

"There's about a dozen rats up ahead," said Lawrence, suddenly appearing out of the tunnel before them. He shrank back as Daphne aimed a burning finger at him. "Don't *do* that!"

"You're the one that's sneaking around!" she accused.

"That's literally my job!" said Lawrence in exasperation. "I can't kill them stealthily like I did the ones at the entrance, so I'll need to hide until Stephan engages them."

"Should we just have Daphne torch them directly?" suggested Gareth.

"No," said Stephan. "This is just the warmup round, and there's no telling when we'll run into a large crowd. Daphne, please try to limit yourself to simple, non-consuming attacks with your wand. Well-aimed Magic Missiles or Fire Bolts should be enough to take them out. Gareth, nock an arrow and see if you can hit anything in this lighting. Sorin, since we're short on melee fighters, you'll need to guard these two from the back."

"Got it," said Sorin. He tightened his right hand around his mithril dagger and felt at the string coiled in his left hand.

"Then let's kill ourselves some rats," said Stephan. Hair grew out of his body, and claws grew out of his hands as he assumed a half-bear form and charged ahead.

A symphony of squeaks sounded out as Stephan made contact. He directly swatted a Rockgnaw Rat into the cave wall and moved to swat another.

Two rats attacked Stephan's legs, but their teeth only found metal. The remaining rats, seeing that their opponent was too tough for them to chew on, charged towards the back, where Gareth, Daphne, and Sorin were located.

Daphne launched three consecutive Fire Bolts out of her wand. But her aim was dreadful, and out of three shots, only one hit a rat; another hit the cave ceiling; and the third actually hit Stephan.

Two rats were down, and two rats were tied down. A third rat died as Lawrence appeared behind the rear-most rat and dispatched it with a dagger to the back.

Gareth took down a fourth rat with an arrow but was unable to pull back in time to avoid the rat behind it as it threw itself at him. It was at this time that Sorin surprised everyone present, including himself.

Viper strike! His body, arms, and legs darted forward with speed that eclipsed even Lawrence's top speed. He was a coiled, viper striking out at his prey. His dagger pierced the large rat's neck, injecting a large dose of poison and pulling back just as quickly.

Another rat was closing in on Daphne, and the pyromaniac, committed to keeping her spells for a much larger crowd, was doing her best to keep it at bay. *Python Coil!* thought Sorin as he poured mana into the mithril string in his left hand, granting it a snakelike appearance as it shot out and wrapped around the rat, completely tying up its movements.

Adder Rush! Sorin crouched down and moved through the tight tunnel like a snake. He appeared beside Lawrence, who'd just stabbed a rat, and struck out like lightning once again. A rat fell from his knife as he pulled it back and assessed the situation.

Seeing that everything was under control, Sorin pulled the rat he'd tied up with mithril string towards him with unusual strength and slammed a dagger into its skull. A one-star demon core popped onto the floor, and the rat itself fell to the ground, limp and lifeless.

ENCOUNTERING A RAT LORD

"I *hate, hate, hate* rats!" Daphne said through gritted teeth as she gingerly cut out a core from a rat she'd burnt down. The core was low-quality, cracked, and barely recognizable. They'd be lucky if the mission officer accepted it.

"Good work, everyone," said Stephan. "Your aim... well, let's work on that when we get back."

"I was scared," said Daphne. "They're filthy rats!"

"Then why did Gareth not miss?" asked Stephan. "He clearly hates rats just as much as you do." He then turned to Sorin. "You, sir, are just full of surprises. What happened just now?"

Sorin shrugged. "I figured out a way to make the best of my abilities." The truth was, he was also frightened. They'd just entered combat when three techniques suddenly popped into his mind.

"Well, whatever you did, keep doing it," said Stephan. "Swift and decisive strikes and entanglement are all legitimately useful skills. That movement skill you were showing off wasn't half bad either."

"Thanks," said Sorin. "Need stitches?"

"No," said Stephan. "These wounds will heal up in no time at all. He'd suffered a bite through a gap in his half-plate, which didn't fully cover his body in his half-shifted state. "Lawrence?"

"Just came back," said Lawrence, popping out of the tunnel. "A group of eight coming up, but the fighting space is smaller. You might have to handle them all by yourself if you want to conserve Daphne's mana."

"Fine," said Stephan. "Then let's speed things up. Sorin, guard my back. Daphne, if you throw as much as a single Fire Bolt, I'm breaking your wand." There was a scorch mark on his shoulder where her stray spell had gotten him.

They advanced at a much quicker pace than before. Now that Sorin could effortlessly dispatch smaller numbers of rats, they made quick work of the group without suffering any injuries. They only stopped for a few minutes to collect rat cores before pressing forward.

It wasn't long before the number of rats they killed was well over a hundred. "This is a way bigger job than you said in the beginning," said Lawrence. "I'm not sure if you're aware, but there's a *big* difference between a nest of a hundred rats and a nest of five hundred."

"Don't I know it," muttered Stephan. "Isn't there a saying, Gareth?"

"A hundred rats to a lord," said Gareth. "A thousand rats to a king."

"How likely exactly is there to be a Rat King?" asked Sorin.

It was Daphne who answered the question. "Not so likely. Look here." She passed a book over to Sorin. To his surprise, it was a portable demon reference book.

"Rat Kings can control anywhere between 500 and 10,000 rats," read Sorin. "Controlling hordes over 10,000 requires a Rat Emperor. Characteristics of a Rat King are: Firstly, high coordination between members; secondly, nest-wide special abilities; thirdly, increased body size; fourthly, possible increase in intelligence. Rats under the influence of a fully grown Rat King will be 50 percent larger than normal." Then Sorin frowned. "These Rockgnaw Rats are around two feet tall, but some of the bigger ones are almost three feet tall."

"Now you see why Lawrence is worried," said Stephan. "While I'm confident that there isn't a fully grown Rat King here, evidence points towards a juvenile Rat King."

Sorin passed the book back to Daphne and fell back into formation.

There was a group of six rats ahead, and this time, the cave was much larger. The rats weren't foolish—they bypassed the sturdy member of the team by running along the walls and trying to take down Gareth and Daphne.

Yet, as soon as they jumped into the air, an arrow and a Fire Bolt took down two of them. Sorin struck two with his dagger before they even hit the ground and lashed the fifth with his mithril string, pulling it back before it could bite Daphne.

As for the sixth, Gareth avoided it. Lawrence appeared beside it and struck it in the neck. They spent two minutes gathering cores before setting off once again.

Lawrence stopped them again fifteen minutes later. "Big group up ahead," he said. "Thirty in total."

"Thirty in a single group?" said Stephan, frowning. "Is there a lord with them or a juvenile Rat King, at least?"

"There's one that's about twice as big as the normal rats," said Lawrence. "So maybe?"

"What are your thoughts?" Stephan asked Gareth.

"My thoughts are that I'll finally get to shoot something," said Gareth. "In fact, it'll be difficult to miss. That includes Daphne, of course. This is why she's here, after all."

"The only problem is holding them back," said Stephan. "Lawrence, you said they were all in a cave. How wide?"

"About three bears wide, give or take," said Lawrence.

"Hm…" Stephan scratched his chin. "Then Sorin and I should hold the pass.

"Me?" said a startled Sorin. "I'm not exactly good at taking hits."

"But you're stronger than you look," said Stephan. "I'm not sure if it's the cultivation technique you practice, but haven't you noticed that you're much stronger than Lawrence is?"

"Twice as strong?" said Sorin, frowning. "Hasn't Lawrence reached the seventh stage of Blood-Thickening?"

"That has nothing to do with cultivation stage," said Stephan. "Well, it kind of does. But Daphne and Gareth are much weaker physically than Lawrence is, and they're around the same cultivation-wise."

Sorin had a late start, so out of everyone in the group, his cultivation at the fifth stage of Blood-Thickening was the weakest. Fortunately, there wasn't a huge difference between the cultivation stages within a realm. One's mana density and their corresponding abilities increased roughly 10 percent with each stage.

"I'm not convinced," said Sorin.

"Fine," said Stephan. "Lawrence, pin him."

"Awesome!" said Lawrence. "And it's even an official order!" He blended into the shadows and tackled him from the side a half second later.

Sorin acted without thinking. The moment Lawrence grabbed him, he reached out and *twisted* his body like no human should have been able to. He then pushed Lawrence's arm behind his back at an angle and pinned him to the ground. "This proves nothing," said Sorin. "It was all technique."

"Nice wrestling technique for a physician," said Stephan. He lowered into a crouch and ran towards Sorin. He did so too quickly for Sorin to evade. Sorin could only bring him his hands and grab Stephan's to push him back.

For a moment, they were deadlocked. But before long, Stephan began pushing him back steadily. Yet it wasn't as one-sided as Sorin had expected. When Stephan let go, he nodded at Sorin. "Not bad. If you're up for it, you can defend the pass with me. I'll block a larger area, and your mission will be simple: kill anything that gets near us while the others blast them from behind. Lawrence will be our last line of defense. Anything that gets past you, he'll kill."

With so much evidence staring him in the face, Sorin could only agree to Stephan's proposal. They approached the cavern as closely as they could without attracting attention, then stopped for Lawrence to place caltrops.

Once the man was done, Sorin sent out his mithril string and charged it with white mana. This was concentrated paralytic poison, which he'd separated from his combined poison. Anyone or any demon who touched the thread would find the limb that touched it stiffening for several seconds.

The string was about thirty feet long, so Sorin stretched it across three-quarters of the opening before doubling back. If the rats somehow avoided the caltrops, they'd be very likely to trip on one of the wires, thereby slowing down the entire group.

"Are we ready?" asked Stephan. "Daphne, are you done over-charging your spell?"

"Almost," said Daphne through gritted teeth. "Believe it or not, this is a lot harder than it looks. She wasn't just holding a Fireball in her hands like she normally did but she was currently building a spell array to support and launch it. "Ten more seconds. Nine."

"Gareth, nock your arrows and get ready to fire as quickly as you can," commanded Stephan. "Four. Three. Two. One!"

"Fireball!" shouted Daphne. The flaming projectile shot towards a cluster of eight rats and blasted them to oblivion. The cavern shook, and a stalactite fell onto another group of three unfortunate rats. The others quickly awakened and, upon noticing their group at the entrance, charged at them with blind rage.

Gareth loosed three arrows shortly after Daphne launched her Fireball. He felled two rats and wounded a third. He then pulled back for another shot, but it was then that the first of the rats reached the trip wire.

"Kill anything that moves," said Stephan, growing claws and swatting a rat as it leaped for his neck.

Sorin's instincts took over once again; he stepped forward and stabbed with his dagger, catching a rat in the neck. He then did the same to a second rat that tripped over the cockatrice poison wire.

Another Fireball launched out from behind them, and so did three more arrows. Seven more rats fell under the combined attack. Only a large rat survived the explosion. It was a head taller than Sorin and stood on two legs.

"You take care of the rest of them," said Stephan, charging out at the

Rat Lord. This time, he fully adopted his bear form and pulled the rat into a tight bear hug.

Blood spurted onto the ground as the rat's sharp teeth sheared through Stephan's half plate and bit into his neck. A thunk sounded as an arrow struck the rat's thick hide. It barely drew blood before falling to the ground, useless.

Sorin wanted to charge out but knew that if he did, the others would be attacked by the remaining rats. So he stood his ground and cut down whatever rats came his way.

This freed up Daphne to tackle the Rat Lord with Stephan. Fireballs were not effective against such an opponent, so she began throwing Magic Missiles at its exposed back, drawing tiny rivulets of blood wherever she struck.

As for Gareth, he also changed his approach. He no longer nocked three arrows at a time and accumulated mana for three whole seconds before letting loose with a Power Shot. The wind howled as the arrow stabbed into the Rat Lord's side.

The rat growled in annoyance and tried to free itself from Stephan's grasp. Yet, as soon as it managed to extricate itself, a Lunisolar Paw came down on it, slamming it to the ground.

"Lawrence, block those rats coming in," said Sorin. "We need to kill this thing quick." It was no longer thirty rats they were fighting but the entire horde that was pouring in. Thanks to the panicked screeching of their leader, rats were arriving through several entrances and charging towards their group.

Lawrence and Daphne were forced to focus their attention on the incoming rats. Smaller Fireballs blasted four at a time, and Daphne, now running low on mana, was forced to take a sip from a mana potion.

When Sorin arrived at the Rat Lord, it had already picked itself up. His mithril string struck out like a viper, but it was unable to pierce the Rat Lord's leathery hide. He, therefore, tucked away the mithril string and committed all his attention to his dagger. He lunged at the rat and stabbed into one of its open wounds.

The rat squealed as Sorin injected a heavy dose of poison between its rib bones, then retreated before the rat could bite him. Unfortunately, he was unable to avoid a claw to the chest. His leather armor was split open, and blood splashed onto the cavern's stone floor.

"I'm fine," said Sorin when Stephan pulled back to defend him. "Hold him in place so I can land a few more hits.

Viper Strike was taxing. Against smaller rats, Sorin only used a smaller dose of poison, if any at all, but against a Rat Lord, he didn't dare hold back.

Now! thought Sorin. The rat dodged Stephan's Lunisolar Paw and darted toward Sorin's original position. But Sorin had already stepped forward with Adder Rush; he struck the rat straight in the neck when it overextended itself.

The mithril dagger struck bone and injected paralytic into the wound. The rat staggered, and Sorin used the opportunity to send out the mithril string to tangle up the rat's front paws, then *pulled* as the rat tried to free himself, barely keeping it in place as a Lunisolar Paw came crashing down on its skull.

Once. Twice. Thrice. It was a tough rat that refused to give in. Yet its bones could only take Stephan's heavy blows for so long before it collapsed into a bloody heap.

The remaining rats in the cave, having seen their leader perish, fled back into the tunnels. "Don't chase," said Stephan. "Let's regroup and take care of our wounds." He abandoned his bear transformation and splashed half a healing potion on his bloodied neck, then tossed the remaining half to Sorin.

18

COORDINATED HORDE

With the Rat Lord dead and the lesser Rockgnaw Rats gone, Sorin was finally able to take stock of his injuries. *Heavy damage to the pectoral muscles,* he thought as he looked over his wounds. *Potential nerve damage to the right arm. Chipped bones on the upper ribs. Estimated recovery time without healing potion: three weeks plus rehabilitation.* He took the healing potion Stephan had tossed him and carefully applied it to his open wounds. He then stitched them up with a needle and thread to ensure they were healing properly before examining the rest of his body.

Healing is going much faster than expected. Is it a side effect of the Ten Thousand Poison Canon? Increases in strength in speed have also been observed. Further analysis is required. A full adventurer's assessment is recommended.

"Thanks," Sorin said to Stephan when he opened his eyes. The healing potion had all been used up.

"Don't mention it," said Stephan. "It's coming out of the group pot. A potion like that is worth about 100 gold.

Despite the expense, there was no denying that defeating the group of rats had been well worth it. There was a five-gold bounty on each rat, and their demon cores, weak as they were, were still worth about five gold apiece. The entire group, excluding the Rat Lord, had been worth about 400 gold.

"This Rat Lord is an upper-level one-star threat," said Stephan, "We'll get a 100-gold bounty for it at least, though the core will probably only be 50 gold."

"Why the disparity?" asked Sorin.

It was Lawrence who answered him. "Bounties are awarded according to threat level, both present and future. But cores are only worth as much as the demonic energy inside them. Have you never gone to offer cores at a temple?"

"Once," said Sorin. "For a wish. But never like adventurers do." It was a well-known fact that the greatest customers of the Temple of Hope weren't the poor and the unlucky but adventurers, especially after a big haul.

"We'll go there as a group after everything is said and done," said Stephan. "But for now, it's best to figure out how we're going to tackle the rest of this nest."

"We should scout ahead and see if any tunnels become dead ends," advised Gareth. "Make a proper map of the place like the one I've been keeping. Once we clear off the side branches, we'll make our way to the bigger clusters. Given that we just ran into a Rat Lord, there's a hundred percent certainty of us finding at least a juvenile Rat King."

Their team spent the next hour salvaging the battlefield and three hours recovering their energy. Fighting in evil-occupied territory meant exposure to corruption, and it was necessary to expel this corruption to maintain the purity of their mana. But when Sorin sat down to expel his own corruption, he discovered something shocking.

There's... none? Sorin realized. He scanned his entire body to make sure. Typically, corruption started in the mana and then worked its way into a cultivator's blood before infiltrating their meridians, bones, organs, and acupoints. Yet, try as he might, he found not a trace of corruption in any of these, which is amazing even by the standards of a city-dwelling cultivator with a top-tier cultivation method.

It's not just my mana and flesh that are absent of corruption. Even my clogged-up extraordinary meridians are loosening up. My blood and mana are eating away at the corruption.

This was both a wonderful thing and a worrying thing. Wonderful because it meant that Sorin's cultivation method and the mana it granted him were truly overbearing, but worrying because of the greed someone might feel if they ever discovered this.

Sorin decided that this matter was best kept secret. If anything, he needed to find an opportunity to cleanse impure in public and show off the amazing skills of the Kepler Clan in clearing out corruption. This was the Kepler Clan's signature skill, and his family wouldn't be able to openly criticize him for doing so, at least in theory.

After the three hours were up, their group continued the extermination. Gareth and Lawrence identified branch paths from the main cavern that they carefully explored and purged out before proceeding down the main tunnel.

The walls were made of stone, not earth. Rockgnaw Rats had hard teeth that could eat away even volcanic rock. Their digestive systems secreted mana-rich acids that could melt most of it away. And what they couldn't digest was excreted into rat 'piles' that were kept in separate caves within the complex.

"I'm surprised at the level of intelligence they're showing," said Sorin to Stephan as they finished clearing out one such cave. "To keep one's waste separate from one's living space isn't something rats typically do."

"Now that you mention it, that *is* rather odd," said Stephan. "Gareth, any insights?"

"Doesn't it all come down to having a king again?" said Gareth. "A Rat Lord would make them stronger, but only a king would make these rats more intelligent. Also, it seems like Lawrence is rushing back. I wonder if he tripped a trap or something?"

"We hit the motherload!" exclaimed Lawrence as he arrived before their group. He was out of breath and hadn't even bothered hiding his presence. "There's a large mana crystal on the ground. A huge one. Biggest I've ever seen."

"Calm down," said Stephan. "You said you saw a mana crystal on the ground."

"Yes," said Lawrence.

"Crawling with rats, I presume?" continued Stephan.

"No!" whispered Lawrence excitedly. "It's like they don't even know it exists!"

Sorin frowned. "That doesn't sound very smart at all."

"They're rats!" said Lawrence.

"Sorin's got a point," said Gareth. "And them ignoring a giant mana crystal would also run counter to the observations we've been making so far. Plus, congregating near mana crystals is basic demon instinct."

"I scouted out all the caves leading into and out of the room, and there was not a rat in sight," reassured Lawrence. "Maybe they hate mana crystals! Maybe it scares them. Either way, we can jump in and excavate the mana crystal, then retreat. We'll come back later to clear out the rats."

"But then we'd have failed our mission," said Stephan.

"Not to mention, this whole thing smells like a huge trap," said Gareth. "Daphne, back me up."

"What?" said Daphne, who was currently making marks on the wall with a dagger. "Oh yes. Huge trap. Typical adventuring storyline." Then she paused. "How big of a mana crystal did you say it was?"

"Barely portable," said Lawrence. "Just standing there in the room. I think it's connected to the ground, but mithril knives and a bit of elbow grease should pull it out."

"Be specific, Lawrence," said Stephan.

"Oh. The size of two human heads," said Lawrence.

Stephan hissed. "That's got to be worth about five thousand gold pieces. What do you think, Gareth? Is it worth the risk?"

Gareth hesitated. "We could look, but I still smell a trap. We should be ready to bolt at a moment's notice."

"I'll lead the way!" said Lawrence excitedly.

They soon arrived at a large cavern measuring 300 feet across with a stalactite-covered ceiling thirty feet above their heads. The bottom of the stalactites was conspicuously chewed away. It was clear that the Rock-gnaw Rats often frequented this space.

As for the mana crystal, it was in the center of the room, as Lawrence had said. Moreover, his scouting of the tunnels a second time indicated there were no rats over 300 feet in every direction.

"All right," said Stephan, shaking his head. "Let's do it."

"You sure?" asked Gareth.

"They're *rats*," said Stephan. "How dangerous could their trap really be? Moreover, they need time to pull it off. But looking at that crystal, I can probably yank it out of the ground with my bare claws."

"Fine," said Gareth. "I'm in. Any objections?" Sorin and Daphne exchanged a look but did not dissent. That chunk of mana crystal was worth 1000 gold each, after all, and Sorin was in no position to refuse extra wealth. "We'll aim to go in and out in two minutes tops. Move!"

Their group sprinted into the room and arrived at the mana crystal. Stephan assumed his bear form and hugged the crystal while Lawrence pulled out a dagger and began cutting away at the stone, trapping it. As for Daphne, Sorin, and Gareth, they looked around the room with furrowed brows.

"Something feels off," said Sorin.

"The rat smell in this room is too strong," agreed Daphne, wrinkling her nose.

"My instincts are telling me we're surrounded," said Gareth. "But I have no idea *how* we're surrounded."

As soon as the words left his mouth, the walls trembled. The rocks on one wall burst open, revealing a group of twenty rats that came pouring into the room. "It *was* a trap!" swore Gareth. "Weapons out, everyone! We're cutting a path out of this mess!"

Stephan had already dropped the mana crystal, and Lawrence, vexed that his plan had been ruined, stopped chipping away at the rock. "How was I supposed to know they were hiding in the walls?" complained Lawrence. "That's not typical rat behavior."

Another rumble sounded as several dozen more walls crumbled. Rats came pouring into the room, cutting off their retreat and completely encircling them. "There's hundreds of them," said Stephan gravely. "A completely unmanageable number."

"I can kill us all and take them out with us," suggested Daphne. "If that's something everyone would like to consider," she added, noting their shock.

"How about we try to get out of here alive if we can?" suggested Sorin. This was his first real adventure. His life was finally turning around, and he wasn't going to give up on it now.

"Hold formation," said Stephan as Gareth pulled his bow back. "They're not attacking on sight, and I'd like to avoid forcing the point."

It was only when the last of the rats poured out and quieted down that they heard scurrying on the far end of the tunnel. A small group of rats poured out, complete with three huge rats that were clearly Rat Lords and a much *smaller* rat, barely the size of a fist.

The rats parted respectfully for this group. The three large rats and the smaller rats trotted up to the mana crystal, and the smaller rat hopped *onto* the mana crystal and used it as a podium. It began squeaking imperiously at Sorin's group.

"Does… Does anyone here speak rat?" asked Lawrence uncertainly.

"Stephan must," said Gareth.

"I'm a beastshift warrior, not a druid," snapped Stephan. "What about you, Daphne? Don't you have a spell or something?"

"Translation is a Tier 2 spell," said Daphne, shaking her head. "I'm smart. *Very* smart. But the only Tier 2 spell I've managed to learn is the authentic version of Fireball. And unlike the knockoff I use, it takes my entire mana stock to pull off."

Seemingly enraged at their lack of comprehension, the rat 'king' squeaked and pointed to a group of rats. The rats kowtowed to their leader in a seeming demonstration.

"I think it wants us to pledge allegiance," said Sorin. "What a strange fellow."

That wasn't the only thing Sorin felt. Looking at the creature, he didn't feel awe or respect. Instead, he looked down on the creature. That mouse was *prey*, so it should behave like prey.

"Well, we can't pledge loyalty to rats," said Lawrence.

"And why not?" asked Gareth. "I like my life, thank you very much."

"It's the logistics of it," said Lawrence. "Would we ever get any real food? Would we ever get enough sunlight?"

"Would we remain disease free?" Sorin chimed in. "Sorry, I thought that was the most salient point. I'm personally not for pledging loyalty if we can help it. Assuming it's a group decision."

By now, the Rat King was infuriated. It was shouting at the Rat Lords in his escort and pointing at them. Surprisingly, the Rat Lords were completely subservient to the tiny creature they could gobble up in a single bite.

That being said, the Rat King was currently the only thing stopping the horde of rats from eating them alive. Since that was the case, it was clear that the Rat King was their ticket out of there.

"I have a plan," said Sorin. "And it's a risky plan."

"That's more than what anyone else has," said Stephan. "Speak away."

"I also have a plan," said Daphne, raising a finger. "Like I said, I can kill us all along with these rats."

"Well, I have a workable plan," said Sorin. "One that involves us staying *alive*. But to pull it off, we'll need to capture the king."

19

CHAOTIC BATTLE

"You want to take a hostage?" whispered Lawrence. "Wait, that's a good idea. Why didn't I think of that? How about I do it?"

"You're making a kidnapping sound like a heroic deed," Sorin told him. "But no. It's best if I do it. For some reason, I have a feeling that this rat is nothing but prey to me. If I capture it, it'll be very obedient."

"Hm…" Stephan looked between Sorin and Lawrence. The latter was objectively the best option since he could use his movement skills to evade capture while he went for the tiny rat. "We only get one chance at this, Sorin. How confident are you?"

"Seventy percent? Sorry, this is all instinctual."

Surprisingly, Stephan accepted this explanation. "So we'll get you to do it. Lawrence, cover him. As for Daphne… this idea of yours: it involves the mana crystal, doesn't it?"

"It does," confirmed Daphne.

"How far away exactly should we be if we want to survive this plan of yours?" asked Stephan.

"According to my *very* accurate calculations… *not in this room* should be far enough away," answered Daphne.

"All right," said Stephan. "Then be careful when you—Sorin?" But Sorin had already bolted, and so had Lawrence. The two figures closed the gap between them and the three Rat Lords. Lawrence snuck past the Rat Lords but dodged when a claw came at him from behind. Another claw nearly caught him but found only a shadow.

Sorin was the slower of the two of them. He struck a Rat Lord in the neck with a Viper Strike, then used Adder Rush to dodge its counterattack and the other Rat Lord. Yet, despite his best efforts, he couldn't approach the tiny mouse. It mockingly squeaked at him as he was forced to retreat.

Yet its mockery turned to horror as a mithril string tightened around it. Sorin yanked the Rat King out from between its guards and pulled it into his left hand. "Everyone stop or your king gets it!" shouted Sorin. "Tell them, or I'll break your neck!" The snake in his body let off an intimidating pressure that horrified the tiny Rat King. It hurriedly let out some squeaks that brought everything to a halt.

Sorin retreated to his group, who'd been seconds away from waging an all-out war against the rat horde. "I know you can understand me," he said to the rat. "So you're going to translate everything I say, word for word. Got it?" The rat shivered and refused to answer. Sorin tightened his grip, and the rat squeaked out what appeared to be an affirmative.

"We mean you all no harm," said Sorin. He waited a moment for the Rat King to translate his message before continuing. "We did not understand that this wasn't a small rat infestation but rather a glorious rat kingdom. We cannot, in good conscience, continue fighting against such a wondrous kingdom and wish to leave in peace."

One of the Rat Lords squeaked back aggressively, and Sorin, having no idea what he said, turned to the others. "Who knows," said Stephan. "Just tell them you can't understand. By the way, good improvisation." He gave Sorin a thumbs-up.

"I can't understand anything you are saying," Sorin continued. "Communication is impossible. So this is how things are going to go. We shall be taking the Rat King with us." The entire horde squeaked aggressively once the Rat King translated. "But *only* until the entrance of your nest. Once we get to the cliff face entrance, we will release him. Then we will retreat from your territory and never come back again."

The rats relaxed upon hearing this, but the lords were still suspicious. Still, one of them squeaked out orders to the mass of rats, and the rats parted as they had for the Rat King, revealing the entrance.

"Well, that's a good start," said Stephan. "Let's move that way and see what happens."

The rat encirclement opened up further as they moved toward the entrance. But they also closed up behind them, starting with the Rat Lords, who would clearly be following them to ensure the Rat King's safety."

"Well—It's something," said Gareth. "But how are we going to make sure we can leave after we release the Rat King?"

"You leave that to me," said Sorin. "Let's just move over to the entrance. Far away from that mana crystal. Daphne? You had a plan, didn't you?"

"Me?" said Daphne. "What are you—*oh.*"

The atmosphere remained tense as they walked through the rat-packed cave. Though they didn't attack them outright, the rats encircling them made threatening nipping gestures the entire way. The Rat King scolded them, but its scolding seemed to have a limited effect.

"I don't think they're totally under the control of this Rat King," Sorin whispered to Stephan. "Notice that they didn't ask it for orders, and instead, it was the Rat Lords that issued the orders."

Gareth tightened his grip on his bow, and Lawrence took out a second dagger. The lead Rat Lord hissed at them, but Sorin clenched his hand around the tiny Rat King. They pulled back but kept their claws out and teeth bared.

It took them five minutes to finally arrive at the entrance to the cavern. The last of the rats parted, revealing a tunnel just large enough for three people to defend. "Steady," said Stephan as they approached. "Get them to give us a bit of distance, will you?"

The Rat King squeaked hurriedly, and the Rat Lords, still glaring at their group with undisguised hostility, backed up slightly. "Now!" shouted Stephan. A Fireball five times larger than Sorin had ever seen lobbed over the sea of rats and smashed down on the mana crystal, shattering it. The blue mana rushing out of it caught fire, and the room was filled with a dreadful explosion.

Both Sorin's group and the nearest rats were blasted out of the cavern and into the hallway. Sorin nearly lost consciousness, and he imagined everyone else wasn't faring much better.

"Get your bearings!" shouted Stephan. There was blood trickling out of his ears, so his words came out less like orders and more like a feral growl. Two prone rats instantly fell to Stephan's bear paws before the beastshifter launched himself at the nearest Rat Lord and smashed it with a Lunisolar Paw.

Sorin's head was ringing. He looked about, dazed, and saw that the Rat King had flown out of his hands and was trying to nibble his way through the mithril string. "Not on my watch," said Sorin, yanking him back into his hand. He then took out his dagger and proceeded to slit the nearest rat's throat, then he did the same to the other rats he found while making his way toward the Rat Lord he'd previously poisoned.

Lawrence and Gareth had pulled the unconscious Daphne back and away from the rats. Gareth was loosing arrows, and Lawrence had taken out a small crossbow and was hurriedly killing off any rats that recovered enough to stand.

It's just me and Stephan who have enough strength to take out a Rat Lord, thought Sorin as he approached his prey. The Rat Lord on the ground twitched ever so slightly when Sorin's blade came down, injecting a fresh dose of poison, then shivered as Sorin found its heart between its ribs and stabbed it through.

The third Rat Lord got up and launched itself towards Sorin as its companion fell to the ground. Yet as soon as it reached striking distance, Sorin raised the juvenile Rat King as a shield.

The Rat Lord altered its trajectory, allowing Sorin to duck under its sharp claws and stab its side close to where the previous rat's heart had been. Fur fell from the rat's chest, revealing black, poisonous veins on its wrinkly pink skin.

Reeee!

The Rat Lord, finally having had enough, shouted to all the nearby rats. Those that hadn't yet roused from their stupor entered a trancelike state and threw themselves at Sorin.

Sorin raised the small Rat King but was dismayed to discover that they no longer cared about the creature. This was now a life-or-death battle and saving their leader had been punted to the bottom of their priority list.

"Buy me time!" shouted Sorin. Three arrows shot out and killed three rats, and Lawrence appeared behind him and dispatched another. The rats were throwing everything they had at Sorin, all to prevent the unwounded Rat Lord from retreating.

Stephan wasn't much better off. He was in bear form and had entered a berserk rage. Four rats were hanging from his back; their powerful teeth had bitten through portions of his armor, and blood ran down his arms, his legs, and his neck.

The Rat Lord Stephan had wounded was also picking himself up and commanding rats. Under the orders of the two Rat Lords, the horde became completely reckless and ferocious, to the point of suicide. Not all rats had been killed in the explosion. Half-burnt rats rushed into the tunnel from the cavern and launched themselves at their group. And without Daphne to support them, the group was becoming increasingly overwhelmed.

One rat bit deep into Sorin's armor, cutting through leather and flesh and into his bone. Blood gushed out as he stabbed the creature in the neck and pried it off.

These rats are nothing without their Rat Lords. If we're going to survive, we need to kill them. "Lawrence! With me!" Sorin shouted. He used Adder Rush to dodge several rats launching themselves at him and approach the retreating Rat Lord.

Seeing that it couldn't evade Sorin, the Rat Lord jumped forward and bit at Sorin with its oversized teeth. Sorin dodged to the side and intentionally took a claw to the chest, but in exchange, he stabbed the creature in the neck between two vertebrae.

Blood spurted out over Sorin. The rat tried to pull back but found it was impossible; Sorin had already wrapped the back half of his mithril string around its body and pulled back on the fleeing rat using Python Coil. It reflexively tried to bite him, but Sorin stuck his dagger into the hollow beneath its mouth, ruining its attempt to reach over and bite him.

Lawrence appeared behind the rat and struck out at its vitals. Once. Twice. Thrice. Every hit landed on the same point, widening the wound and increasing the damage he caused. But Lawrence was weak in defense and was forced to stop when three rats jumped on him and bit into his arms and legs.

Sorin had also been bitten in the leg, but he forced himself to ignore the pain and blood loss and made his way to Lawrence. Three dagger strikes slew the three rats, and the rogue, now free, picked himself off the floor.

"Well, that's one down," said Lawrence, looking at the dead Rat Lord. "Two if you count the unconscious one you killed." He felt his arm and winced. "Rockgnaw really doesn't do them justice. They should call them *bone gnaw* rats or something."

"Stephan should be about done with his target," said Sorin. Slaying the first Rat Lord had led to a noticeable weakening in the horde. As predicted, a loud screech sounded three seconds later, followed by a communal panicked screech from the remaining rats. They fled into the main cavern and retreated through all its entrances.

Sorin immediately began a mental triage. *Stephan is the most injured and has the most blood loss, but he's also the most durable of the group. Gareth got bit once, but it's only his arm. Nerve damage is unlikely.*

Lawrence had been bitten four times in total and looked to be in good spirits. Which meant that, ironically, *Sorin* was the worst wounded out of the lot. He had suffered several bites to the bone and had also been directly wounded by the Rat Lords' claws.

"Let's lay down and patch ourselves up for a bit," said Stephan, limping over. I'm going to need some of those stitches if you're still offering. How's Daphne?"

"Feigning unconsciousness," said Gareth, dragging her over.

"It's a perfectly legitimate self-defense tactic," grumbled Daphne as Gareth tossed her on the floor next to Sorin. "Ouch. My head hurts. And it's probably going to hurt for the next few days." She took out a mana potion and sipped at it gingerly.

"I'm going to need some stitches myself," said Sorin. "But first, let's decide what to do with this guy." He yanked on the mithril string and pulled back the supposed Rat King. "Call me silly, but I don't think this is actually a Rat King."

"It's probably a mutated rat demon," agreed Gareth. "But since it was helping the other rats grow, the lords treated it like a king. Fortunately, it wasn't a legitimate king. Otherwise, we would never have made it out of this alive."

"We should kill it just in case," said Stephan. "We'll hand over its corpse and its core to the Adventurers Guild and have it identified. Even if it's not a Rat King, it should be worth a pretty penny. Probably a thousand gold for the corpse and the core altogether."

"Fine," said Sorin, pulling the pitiful rat over. "Let's get it over with then." He pulled out his dagger and made to cut its throat. He ignored the rat's teary eyes that begged for life. He had no mercy for demons. And yet... "Hey, Stephan?" A preposterous idea for anyone with a medical background crossed his mind.

"Yes?" asked Stephan.

"Do you..." said Sorin. "Do you think I could *keep* it?"

"Keep it?" shouted Daphne. "It's a rat!"

"So?" said Gareth. "There's nothing wrong with keeping a rat as a familiar. It's quite common, actually."

"Are you sure?" asked Stephan, giving Sorin a strange look.

"I'm sure," said Sorin. "Call me crazy, but I think it's worth it."

Stephan shrugged. "All right. But you'll need to pay for a taming contract and reimburse us for the lost bounty and demon core."

Sorin agreed, then wrapped up the small rat in several wraps of mithril before taking out a needle and thread and getting to work.

REWARDS

"Did our father drop you one too many times, Stephan, or have you been overindulging in mad grass during your time in the forest?" A report folder struck Stephan in the head, and judging by Assessor Haley's fuming expression, she wanted nothing more than to throttle him from across the table.

"Entering the depths of a rat nest with a potential Rat King without calling for reinforcements?" continued Haley. "Not seeing an obvious trap for what it was and nearly getting trapped to death by hundreds of bloody rats? And then bringing said Rat King *into* the outpost, thinking that it *wouldn't* call on all the rats in the city to come and rescue it? I don't even know where to begin."

"With all due respect," started Stephan, but Haley cut him off.

"Sixteen years of premium education were obviously completely wasted on your worthless brain," said Haley. "Did you even *think* about the fact that I'd need to personally quell the panicked non-cultivators and explain the situation to the governor? Not to mention all the medical bills we're going to have to pay to make sure that plague doesn't spread after those hundred guards got bitten?"

Stephan cleared his throat. "Haley, that was hardly a foreseeable consequence. For one, keeping a city clear of demonic rats is common sense. For another, the guards did nothing to stop us."

"Right or wrong has nothing to do with this matter," snapped Haley. "Those were *foreseeable* potential consequences of your actions. A bunch of people got hurt, and the governor can't admit that it was his fault there was a rat infestation. So *now,* he's going to push all the blame onto the Adventurers Guild. And the Adventurers Guild is going to have to push all the blame onto the lot of you."

"That's not fair," Lawrence argued. "They have their responsibilities, and we have ours. My father brought tons of trouble back in his day and never got punished for it."

"That's because your father was smart," said Haley, glaring at Lawrence. "He had enough dirt on everyone that they had no choice but to not punish him for anything he did." She put her face in her hands. "First the Medical Association, and now this."

"What's this about the Medical Association?" asked Sorin.

"They're just being pedantic and trying to extend their control over life mages again," said Haley. "As if the Mages Guild would ever let them get away with it."

"Did my situation have anything to do with this?" asked Sorin.

"Yes and no," said Haley. "They're using you as an excuse to flex their muscles a bit, but it's an old argument. But the result is that we've got a bunch of adventurers going untreated. Our life mages can't keep up. The clinics are saying they're 'overworked' and can't see them right away."

"I could…"

"Absolutely not," Haley said, cutting him off. "I will *not* have you practicing as an unlicensed physician within these walls. What you do out while adventuring is one thing, but if you start treating people openly, this place will be on lockdown because of audits and permitting issues, and we won't be able to get back to business for half a year."

"Isn't a beast tide coming up?" asked Gareth. "They can't just hobble the Adventurer Association when demon activity is at an all-time high."

"Yes, they can," said Sorin. "They do it all the time. It's politics at its finest."

"Sorin is right," said Haley. "Which is why this rat trouble has come at a very unfortunate time."

"About the Medical Association problem," said Sorin. "I *am* someone who cultivates poisons. The application of poisons and the curing of poisons would fall under my domain, would it not? It's just like how life mages can cure however many bleeding wounds they want. Diagnosis and prescriptions are where liability comes in."

"Hm... So you're saying you'll treat poisoned adventurers?" asked Haley.

"And corruption as well," added Sorin. "Because really, isn't demonic corruption just a slow-acting poison, strangling the life out of adventurers as they risk their lives in the wilderness? In fact, I could probably get away with poisoning people to get rid of certain diseases."

"Now you're just pushing it," said Haley. Her eyes looked to Daphne, who'd yet to speak. She was nodding off on Gareth's shoulder. "Mana burn?"

"She launched a legitimate Fireball that blasted 400 rats to bits," said Stephan. "Even with the assistance of a mana crystal, that's got to be tough."

"There's a reason I passed her despite her obliviousness," said Haley. "Next time you get out, you're expanding your party."

"Is that really necessary?" asked Stephan.

"You'll do as I say, or I'll bundle you up and send you back home," said Haley. "As for *you*, Sorin, I'll speak to the guild master about your... expertise. Given the situation and the obvious power moves the Medical Association is pulling, it might not be a bad excuse to escalate this matter. But absolutely none of that until you get the go-ahead. Understood?"

"Yes, ma'am," said Sorin.

"That aside, the report seems to be in order," said Haley. "But due to the size of the nest, we'll be sending a team out to investigate the aftermath of the battle and clear out the remnants. The cores you brought back are, of course, irrefutable proof. You never see three Rat Lords over just 500 rats without some external interference."

She tossed out five light bags at Stephan. "The cores have all been authenticated and stamped. You can do with them as you please. As for the bounty, there was some flexibility on the matter because of scope creep. We're giving you five gold apiece for each of 487 rats, 125 gold apiece for the four Rat Lords, and 300 gold for taking care of this rat 'king'—a discount of 750 gold because the only person on your team who should *know* this is a bad idea decided to keep it as a pet. For reference, its core is probably worth 250 gold."

"Other bounties included 35 Manasurge Persimmons, a Bonecrush Demon Python bounty, 14 miscellaneous one-star demon cores, 45 stalks of Manafuse Grass, 17 Crystal Heart Violets, and 52 units of Bloodstaunch Moss." They'd harvested those while traveling to the rat nest. "There's also the matter of the Steelfeather Sparrow's two-star bounty and its feathers, whole and ruined.

"Your total earnings for this mission are 6,203 gold, excluding the cores, but the guild is deducting 1,000 gold as punishment for bringing that Rat King into the city. Congratulations on a successful first mission. Very few walk out with such a big haul with all their limbs and lives intact."

She then took out ten cards worth 500 gold pieces and a bag containing 203 gold coins. "Split these up however you wish. It's typical to do an equal split after group expenses, like healing and mana potions." In total, they had spent nearly 400 gold on consumables. That meant that each of them would be receiving about 540 gold apiece, excluding whatever rewards they would get from the Temple of Hope.

"Thanks for fighting for us on this, Haley," said Stephan. "I'm sure it wasn't as easy as you make it out to be."

"It wasn't," said Haley. "But I'm happy you all came back in one piece, and I'm thrilled that those rats were taken care of before the demon tide. They would have been a nightmare if allowed to grow for much longer."

Daphne chose this moment to wake up and yawn rather loudly. "Are we done then? Are we rich? Ah!" She wiped a trickle of drool from the corner of her mouth. "Who drooled on me? Who's the pervert who dared drool on me?"

They all burst out laughing and pulled her out of the room before heading out to the Temple of Hope for the second half of their rewards.

The Temple of Hope was crowded, as always. The usual line-up of the poor, the lame, and the dying was unchanged since the last time Sorin had been here, though some of the old faces were gone and had been replaced by new ones.

Unlike last time, they did not beg as Sorin passed them; the kindly physician they knew was no more and had been replaced by a fearsome adventurer.

"This way," said Stephan, pulling them towards a side entrance. "Adventurers don't line up with everyone else."

"And why is that?" asked Sorin.

"Why else?" said Stephan. "It's because we're their biggest customers and the source of pretty much all the demon cores that are offered up here." A special attendant greeted them at a side altar and ushered them into their own personal offering room, complete with altar and kindling and white wish-fire.

"I know it's Sorin's first time—but what about everyone else?" asked Stephan.

"I tagged along with a friend before," said Gareth. "It was quite the experience."

"My dad took me in a few times," said Lawrence. "It's not as great as it's cracked up to be."

Daphne, like Sorin, had never made an adventurer's offering, but she'd heard rumors and was rubbing her hands with anticipation. "Before we offer up anything, I just want to make things clear," said

Stephan to Sorin and Daphne. "This temple is a place for gamblers, and right now, what we're doing is no different than gambling. If both of you would like, you can take a split of the cores and sell them off for a steady income. No one will blame you for doing this. Yes, Daphne?"

"Is the average statistical outcome better than trading them on the market?" asked Daphne.

"The average... *Oh*, you're asking if we're probably better off gambling?" said Stephan. "The answer is yes, by about 10 percent. The only problem is that it's random. If we're lucky, we'll get something useful. If we're unlucky, everything we get will be useless, and we'll have to sell it at a discount."

"Then I support this sort of gambling," said Daphne. "I'll view it as an investment."

"And you, Sorin?" asked Stephan.

"May as well," said Sorin. "It won't make that much of a difference, and maybe we'll get lucky." In truth, he was gambling because he was poor. He'd yet to tame the Rat King, but the impending purchase was weighing on his mind. If all went well, he'd barely have anything left over to fix his armor up with.

Having obtained their confirmation, Stephan upended each of the five bags of demon cores onto the altar in succession and passed a white flame torch to Daphne. "Why don't you do the honors?"

Daphne's eyes lit up. She grabbed the torch and cackled as she lit up the gems. "Fire! Pretty fire!"

The white flames consumed the black gems and summoned forth clouds of black dust. This cloud barely hovered for a few seconds before it was sucked up through the roof of the offering chamber.

There was a flash of light as a chest appeared inside the room, ornate and decorated with a golden fox with nine chain tails. The fox was wearing its usual mischievous grin.

Stephan heaved open the chest and reached inside it. "First up is a bow. Nice!" He tossed it to Gareth, who immediately appraised it.

"This is a blood oak bow made with a one-star demon tendon," said Gareth admiringly. "Wonderful craftsmanship. Not too big, and not too small. Versatile. But... it's much too expensive for the little old me. Something like this would probably run for 1,800 gold."

Stephan rolled his eyes. "You know the unwritten rules, Gareth. Take the bow. The team is better off if you have it, and you'll owe the rest of us the difference next time. Unless one of you disagrees?" None of them did. Gareth's lack of penetrating power had been extremely obvious during their outing.

"Then I won't stand on ceremony," said Gareth, accepting the bow.

"Since Gareth's accepted, he can't claim anything else from this chest," said Stephan. "Next up... is a useless skill book. How wonderful." He tossed it to Lawrence, who groaned.

"Seriously? Shadow steps? That's not even mid-tier," said Lawrence. "I'm not claiming it. We're better off selling it since no one else here can use it. We can probably get 350 gold for it."

They looked on in anticipation as Stephan pulled out another item from the chest. "Nice!" Stephan exclaimed. "A potion set. Three health and three mana."

"Is that good?" Sorin asked Lawrence.

"You win out with potions," answered Lawrence. "Everyone can use them, and you usually get good value for your demon cores. A set like that is good quality—easily worth 600 gold for the entire set."

The next item was something that Daphne could use—a pointy hat. "It increases mana regeneration and intellect," said Daphne. "That's pretty good! Lucky me! I claim it."

"I'd peg it at about 800 gold," said Stephan. "Now let's look at this second skill book and see if it's any good."

Lawrence caught the book. "This one is useful. Triple Stab Execution is easily worth 1,500 gold. I'm claiming it."

"Thought so," said Stephan, rolling his eyes. "Seems it's me and Sorin who are unlucky this time. Oh well. At least we won out in the end. The total value is probably around 5,000 gold."

"I think most of my gold is going to go into paying for this rat," said Sorin. He pulled up a length of mithril string. The Rat King had given up on life and was currently sleeping. With so much mithril wrapped around it, there was no way it would be escaping.

"Then that brings us to the last item on our list: the ceremonial chamber," said Stephan. "We'll pay for taming the Rat King before squaring everything up. Let's see how much these crooks are going to charge us."

21

LORIMER

Demon-taming scrolls were something adventurers used in the wilderness. They were risky items that required complete submission to have even a chance at succeeding.

If one wanted greater assurance at demon taming, the go-to method was performing was, therefore, a ceremony at the Temple of Hope. The cost was much steeper—an entire 500 gold coins for an advertised 50 percent chance at success—but it was much better than 100 gold for a 5 percent chance at gaining a new pet.

"Don't worry, Mr. Kepler," said a cheerful female attendant in ceremonial robes as she accepted his payment. "We will do our best to ensure that this demon aligns its interests with yours and Master Hope's. Now, please place the demon in the circle, and we will take care of the rest."

Sorin tossed the rat wrapped in mithril string into the ritual circle and released its bindings. A bright light flashed when the rat attempted to escape the circle boundary. Undeterred, the rat tried to gnaw on the golden metal of the room's permanent ritual circle, but try as it might, its teeth were no match for Hope's enchanted metal.

"Do you need a drop of blood or something?" asked Sorin, unbothered by the rat's egregious behavior. "A medium of some kind?"

"That won't be necessary," said the attendant. "A good rapport with the demon helps slightly but isn't mandatory."

"Got it," said Sorin. He drew on the snake icon in his body and walked over to the aggrieved rat in the circle, kneeled, and made eye contact. "I'm not going to try to convince you to be my best friend, little Rat King, nor am I going to tell you that everything is going to be all right.

"But I want to make sure that we're clear on something: Playing dead won't help you. Failing this contract won't help you. I can't afford more than one chance at this, and if we fail, I'm extracting your demon core and sending your corpse to the Adventurers Guild for dissection and verification." He then circulated his mana for effect, and the rat shivered and averted its eyes. He was confident it got the message.

Sorin gave the attendant a thumbs-up and backed away from the circle. "Please proceed without worries. Regardless of the result, I won't blame you."

"I will begin the ceremony then," said the attendant. She spread her hands out towards the circle and raised her voice. "Almighty Hope, Greatest of the Evils! Your servant begs you—your servant implores you to show pity upon this lesser demon and bind him to your humble servant, Sorin Abberjay Kepler. Please align their wills so that they may better aid you in your unholy mission."

She then took out a long case containing five crystals. Each one was painted with mysterious golden characters Sorin didn't recognize. She placed each of these crystals on their respective star point on the ritual circle, then walked about with a bowl of incense while murmuring prayers to the almighty Hope.

"The offering has been made," shouted the attendant. "The incense has been burned. May your blessing descend on this corrupt creature and enlightenment!" She then prostrated herself, and the five large crystals on the ritual circle crystals shattered. Their essence poured into the circle, summoning forth a golden chain that tightened around the rat's body.

The rat squirmed under the weight of the chain but quickly freed itself. It was clear that a single chain would not be enough to restrain it. But then, a second golden chain shot out of the circle, and it was quickly followed by a third and a fourth.

Four chains weren't quite enough, so a fifth chain emerged. The attendant on the ground trembled when she saw this. "Forgive this little one for miscalculating the offering!" she pleaded. "Master Hope, please show mercy!"

Darkness descended upon them, and Sorin found himself separated from his friends. A familiar altar appeared before him, as did the familiar looming figure of a fox with nine chains for tails.

"Won't this be fun!" whispered the fox with a grin before vanishing as quickly as he'd come.

Sorin blinked and found himself on the ground, kneeling before the altar. His knees were sore, and he was sweating profusely.

"Squeak! Squeak! Squeak!" Sorin put his hand down instinctively, and a rat crawled up his sleeve and onto his shoulder. It was none other than the mutant rat they'd all mistaken for a Rat King. It had a small fox icon on its forehead along with six golden chains, though the icon was fading with every passing second as it sank into the creature's skeleton.

Success. Sorin let out a sigh of relief. He really couldn't afford to fail the ceremony. "Now the only question is: What *are* you? You're not a Rat King."

The rat naturally couldn't communicate with words, but it could transmit thoughts and images. Most of them were about food or things it had eaten. The creature had eaten many things over its single year of existence.

"So what does it do?" Lawrence, who'd been standing there quietly the whole time, asked. "Does it have super spying abilities? Teleportation abilities? Swarming abilities? A diseased bite?"

"Be polite," scolded Stephan. "It's his pet, not yours."

Sorin's expression turned awkward. "According to the rat, it's really good at eating. That's all it's telling me for now."

"Eating?" said Gareth dubiously. "That's not exactly a supreme ability. Unless it can eat specific things like metal?"

The rat squeaked a few times. "Metal is apparently on the menu," said Sorin. "And books."

"It dares?" said Daphne, snapping her book closed. "Well, if it touches a single one of my books, I'll be burning it alive and feeding it to its relatives." The rat shivered and cuddled up to Sorin when it heard this.

"Congratulations," said the attendant. Her face was flushed, and she was clearly out of breath. "It's my first time witnessing a six-fold chaining, and I'm quite relieved to see that it was successful. This demon will make for an amazing companion."

"More like an amazing glutton," Sorin muttered. According to what the rat described, he'd have a hard time feeding it.

"Well, that's that," said Stephan as their group left the room. "I hope you're satisfied with your new companion, Sorin. Maybe you can get it to bite enemy toes? And now that we have a rat on our team, Lawrence has become a bit redundant. I look forward to seeing how you'll improve to keep your spot, Lawrence."

"Hey!" said Lawrence. "Are you calling me a rat?"

"I believe I implied you were inferior to a rat," said Stephan. "Anyway, it's getting late, and I need to head over to the smith to repair my armor. We'll get everything properly appraised before splitting up the rest tomorrow around noon at the guild. Sounds fair?"

The team scattered. Gareth headed over to the fletcher, and Daphne headed over to the Mages Guild wearing her new hat. Lawrence went straight home.

As for Sorin, he found himself at a loss for what to do. After days of adventuring, home didn't feel like home anymore. "What kind of things *do* you like to eat?" Sorin finally asked the rat. "Nothing too extravagant, I hope?"

The rat replied in a few confident squeaks that he was indeed not difficult to feed. Fine wine and smoked meats would suffice for appetizers. Mana crystals would be a good main course, though he wouldn't say no to some mithril ore now and again.

"Look here, little rodent," said Sorin, tossing him at a wall. The rat peeled off and fell to the ground. "I might have saved you, but that isn't a license to roll all over me.

"I'm broke. I barely have enough money to equip myself, let alone feed a glutton. And who knows when the next time we head out will be? So you're going to need to eat what you're fed, smile happily, and say you're full, even if you're not. Understood?" The rat squeaked an affirmative, and they began discussing names.

It was only when Sorin got home that he remembered an important fact: people *hated* rats.

"I'll kill it! I'll kill it dead!!" A red-faced maid swatted her broom at the lone rat standing imperiously on the dining table. It dodged the broom and taunted the maid, Clarice, who promptly shot a wind dart at it. As for Sorin, he drank a cup of sugar-sweetened tea and was seemingly oblivious to the racket the rat and the maid were causing.

"Please be kind to Lorimer, Clarice," Sorin said after allowing the fight to continue for a while. He put down his teacup and glared at the rat. "He's young and still needs to be house-trained, though I'm sure he'll fix his habits soon. Otherwise, he'll find himself cut up and fed to stray dogs."

"It ate. Our. Dinner!" shouted Clarice. "The entire thing! And you're going to tell me to calm down?"

Sorin's stomach growled, but he kept a straight face. "Then we'll just have to make more food. Or order out if it's too much trouble." He tossed a bag containing twenty gold coins on the table. "Since it's my fault, I'll pay for it. Problem settled."

"There's no need to bring out your personal fortune," said Percival. His words were a refusal, but his hands betrayed him. He picked up the pouch of coins and put it away with a smile. "I'm sure this matter is only temporary. Otherwise, we retired adventurers will need to take out some of our old tricks to keep it in check.

Lorimer placed his paws on his hips and daringly stared at Percival.

The man chuckled and flicked a length of mithril string at it, severing one of the rat's whiskers. Lorimer mocked him as a coward but then retreated to Sorin's slice of cake. Yet before he managed to reach said slice, a kitchen knife came sailing through the air and sliced off a *second* whisker before digging into the table.

"Consider those whiskers a warning," said Percival to the rat. "Clarice and I have been tolerant for the sake of Mr. Kepler but can only be pushed so far." Somewhat intimidated, Lorimer wisely chose to retreat onto Sorin's shoulder.

"I'm sorry about the inconvenience, Clarice," said Sorin. "And you too, Percival. I'll try to remedy the situation as quickly as possible."

The maid let out a loud harumph. "You don't know the half of it, Mr. Kepler. Haven't you noticed how dark it is in here?"

"Now that you mention it... why *have* all the lights gone out?" asked Sorin.

Percival cleared his throat. "It's not so much that the lights have gone out, and more that your new... *pet* decided it wanted to eat all their mana crystals."

Sorin's expression darkened. "It ate *mana crystals*? Wait, you weren't joking?" The rat nodded, then shook its head. "Those are expensive, Lorimer."

"They're on the cheaper side for mana crystals," Percival said to defuse the situation. "Not *that* expensive. But the total adds up to about ten gold coins."

Sorin closed his eyes. "Could we perhaps switch to a different form of lightning in the short term?"

"I've already placed an order for candles and oil lamps," said Percival. "We should be receiving them in the morning. The lightning they'll provide isn't perfect, but still much preferred to having no lighting at all."

"Let's go with low-cost candles," Sorin suggested. "I'm making money now, but not nearly enough to raise our budget. Moreover, this creature is clearly a glutton. I need to figure out how to keep it satiated before it eats us out of house and home."

22

LOOT DISTRIBUTION

"Now, let's get back to the main topic, shall we?" said Sorin, setting Lorimer down on the floor. "You were saying something about Marcus, Percival? How's the clinic going? And how's Gabriella doing?"

"The clinic is developing at a steady pace," said Percival. "Marcus has taken a keen interest in running it and has even brought over some physicians and apprentices from Dustone. As for Gabriella, I'm not too sure. I know the clinic still employs her, but I don't know anything about the details. Physician Marcus has made a point of providing me with as little information as possible."

"What about Marcus himself?" asked Sorin. "A powerful figure like him makes big waves. People would definitely talk."

"He's been making inquiries about you, much like you expected," said Percival. "He's also established contacts in all the guilds. I believe it's only a matter of time until the details of your adventures reach him. Also..." He shook his head. "Never mind."

"Just say it, Percival," said Sorin. "However improper it might seem."

"I'd just like to warn Mr. Kepler not to underestimate Physician Marcus," said Percival. "He was sent here for a reason, and the clinic is not that reason. I'm sure you can understand my meaning."

Sorin nodded. "Don't worry. I fully expect sabotage and spying."

"I wouldn't limit myself to these two things," said Percival, giving Sorin a meaningful look.

"Don't worry," said Sorin. "I'm no longer the naïve boy I used to be." He felt at the lingering scars on his chest that hadn't healed despite his organs recovering. "Do you think he'd act personally, or would he pay someone to do that sort of thing?"

Percival shook his head. "Not likely. A Bone-Forging cultivator using their powers in a backwater place like this would be glaringly obvious. The Adventurers Guild would notice, and all the other guilds and organizations would as well. The Kepler Clan might be ruthless in the way it operates internally, but it still cares a great deal about its image."

"That's good," said Sorin. "If it's Blood-Thickening cultivators, I should be able to manage."

"I recommend maintaining a humble attitude towards this problem, Mr. Kepler," said Percival.

"What do you think, Lorimer?" Sorin asked the rat, who was now nibbling at a wheel of cheese in a corner of the room. "Are you worried about a few human Blood-Thickening cultivators?" Lorimer nodded vigorously, and Sorin rolled his eyes. "Coward."

It took an hour to get a second dinner ready. Lorimer was instructed to wait till they'd all eaten before he was allowed to partake in the feast. Sorin chatted with Percival for a while longer and assured Clarice that he would keep Lorimer in check.

It was only when he retired to his room that his polite demeanor faded. He grabbed Lorimer off his shoulder with lightning hands and held him up to his face.

"So, you like courting death and testing my bottom line, do you?" Sorin said to Lorimer. "Well, here it is, Lorimer: your ability to eat is a *liability*. I tamed you for value, but so far, all you've shown is that you're a cowardly demon that's weaker than a housecat. You might do well as a tiny spy, but you'll need more than that if you want to avoid the chopping block. Do I make myself clear?"

The rat immediately began to explain itself in rat language. Then, seeing that Sorin didn't understand, he demonstrated. Lorimer tumbled across the room in a wonderful display of acrobatics. He climbed up the tallest bookshelf and hopped down with the grace of a swan and the elegance of a peacock.

"Not good enough," said Sorin, not batting an eye. The rat scratched its head, then turned towards Sorin's chair. He pointed at the chair and squeaked at Sorin. "Will I get mad if it disappears? No, not really. I never liked the chair, so I won't get mad."

Lorimer squeaked, ran over to the chair, and began gnawing on it. "Look, showing your wood-eating skills off is…" He didn't even have time to finish before the rat was done. The chair was much larger than Lorimer but had completely vanished within seconds.

"Let me clarify something," said Sorin. "Can you eat through bone like that?" The rat nodded in affirmation. "Stone?" Another nod. "Metal?" An uncertain nod. It depended on the metal. Unenchanted metal was a firm yes.

Sorin pulled out his mithril dagger. "Could you eat through this?" The rat shook its head. Mithril was a no-go. "Okay. Eating fast is actually a good ability. If you can eat a demon's leg while we're fighting, that's a plus. But it's still not enough. What else can you do?"

Lorimer adopted a thinking posture. It thought for several minutes before holding up a finger. It then began to channel its internal mana. *Finally,* thought Sorin. *I knew it was hiding something.*

Yet Sorin's expression fell when all the rat did was glow with a familiar blue light. The rat looked exceedingly pleased with itself, but Sorin was not impressed. "So you can glow like a mana lamp. How wonderful." That level of illumination wasn't even worth mentioning in front of a light stick. "That's still not enough, Lorimer. That much light wouldn't even be a distraction. What else can you do? Don't hold back or…" His voice trailed off as he realized something.

"Lorimer?" said Sorin. "Can you glow this way because you ate those mana lamp crystals?" The rat nodded. "Are you telling me that you can take on the properties of things you eat?" The rat both nodded and shook its head. "What if you ate a demon's core? Would you be able to take on its properties?" Both a nod and a shake. "So it's luck-based?" The rat nodded.

"Interesting," muttered Sorin. "So it's not that you can eat, but that you can eat things and potentially grow." That changed things quite a bit. "What about demon corpses? Can you eat those? Would you gain their abilities?" This time, Lorimer shook his head. Then he gestured to his arm and flexed. "But you'll grow stronger." Another nod.

"Okay," said Sorin. "I've decided to keep feeding you, Lorimer. But you're going to have to be selective about what you eat. Don't eat expensive things without my permission. Understood?" The rat nodded.

Having finished his interrogation, Sorin gave Lorimer strict instructions about sleep time and how he shouldn't eat things while Sorin was asleep in his home, cultivating, or otherwise preoccupied. Only then did he feel comfortable entering a meditative state. Mana entered his body from the outside world and replenished his blood.

Cultivators were people who took in mana from the outside world and stored it inside their bodies. They transformed their bodies little by little, starting with their blood, then moving into their bones, and then their flesh.

Unfortunately, Sorin wasn't a normal cultivator. No matter how much he cultivated, the mana in his blood did not increase. Absorbing poisons was apparently the only way for him to grow. That meant he would need money and a great deal of it. He was far more dependent on money than the average cultivator.

I'll need to see how much money I have leftover before going to the Alchemists Guild, thought Sorin. According to the prices he'd seen last time, he'd be able to purchase one or two premium poisons.

Sorin showed up at the Adventurers Guild just before noon the next day. He wore casual clothing instead of his torn-up leathers but kept a dagger at his belt.

Stephan showed up at precisely noon. He carried a folder full of papers and five small pouches filled with jingling coins.

Like Sorin, Stephan had abandoned his armor in favor of casual wear. He wore a stiff tunic and boiled leather pants. Sorin had met many other geniuses from large families, but it was his first time meeting one who was so unpretentious.

Gareth showed up around the same time, and unsurprisingly, Lawrence showed up late, as did Daphne. The latter yawned deeply and practically fell asleep when she took a seat.

"Since everyone is here, I'll get straight to the point," said Stephan. "I've gotten our gains evaluated by a professional appraiser. Including our initial bounty haul of 5,203 gold, we netted 9,888 gold coins in value, excluding potions, which I added to the group stockpile. I'll go into detail as I hand out everyone's share."

He turned to Sorin first. "We'll get yours out of the way first because it impacts distribution to the other team members. Is that fine?"

"Of course," said Sorin.

"Your share should have been 1,977 gold pieces," continued Stephan. "But you used up 500 gold to perform that ceremony. Keeping the Rat King instead of turning it for its bounty and keeping its core cost the team 1,000 gold coins. That means you owe each member of the team 200 gold. Your share is, therefore, 677 gold." He handed a pouch containing 177 gold and a card worth 500 gold to Sorin. "Other than that, good work. I suggest investing these funds in your growth to prepare for our next outing."

"I'm looking forward to it," said Sorin, accepting the money.

"Next up is Gareth; you should have initially gotten 2,177 gold, but your bow was appraised at 1,875 gold," Stephan continued. "That leaves you with 302 gold." He handed over one of the larger pouches to Gareth.

"Me next!" said Lawrence.

"If you insist," said Stephan with a smirk. "You got unlucky. Your skill, Triple Stab Execution, has increased in price to 1,625 gold."

"What?" said Lawrence. "That's unfair."

"It's reality," said Stephan. "Fortunately, that movement skill book was slightly more expensive at 375 gold. In the end, your share is 552 gold." He handed over the smallest pouch of gold along with a 500-gold card to Lawrence.

"Daphne, your hat was also a little more expensive than we'd thought initially," continued Stephan. "Your share less 860 gold comes to 1,317 gold. But knowing how expensive spell books can be, I'm sure you'll burn through that in no time." Daphne accepted two cards worth 500 gold and a heavy bag containing 317 gold.

"Last comes little old me," said Stephan. "Initially, I should have gotten 2,177 gold. Unfortunately, I had to use group funds to pay for my armor repairs—600 gold in total. So that leaves me with a measly 1,577 gold."

"I'm afraid that leaves you with exactly *zero* gold," came a voice. Stephan panicked and tried picking up his share, but it was too late. Assessor Haley was already holding the small pouch and three small cards. "Actually, keep the pouch since you need to pay for living expenses," said Haley, tossing the bag back to him. "But I'm taking the cards to pay off part of your debt."

Stephan glared at Haley. "How and when I pay my debts is up to me, Haley. Hand those over."

"Make me," said Haley, stuffing the cards in her belt pouch. "And also, you're dead wrong. Your training is to be overseen by yours truly, and that includes your debt repayment. Enjoy being poor for the foreseeable future, Stephan."

Stephan's arms bulged as his temper flared but quickly returned to their original size. "This isn't over, Haley. I'll be speaking to Father about this."

"Knock yourself out," said Haley. "By the way, long-distance communication costs 50 gold per minute. Try to be efficient, or you'll find yourself destitute once again." She looked over the rest of them and nodded to herself. "Not bad. You've all grown considerably since last night. Most of you have reached the eighth stage of Blood-Thickening. Only Stephan hasn't grown in the entire team."

"You know full well why I haven't," Stephan cut in.

"Results, brother dearest," said Haley, wagging her finger. "By the way, I told the master of the Mages Guild about your little experiment in the rat nest. He was quite excited by both the fact that you can cast a legitimate Fireball, Daphne, and the field data surrounding the mana crystal detonation. I don't suppose you kept records?"

Daphne pulled out a sheaf of papers. "I spent all night crunching it and calculating everything. It's good to know my efforts weren't wasted."

"Excellent," said Haley. "I suggest you run over right now and have a chat with the guild master while he's off for lunch. It's a good opportunity to butter him up. Who knows—you might get some freebies or discounts."

Finally, her eyes landed on Sorin. "The rest of you are excused. I need to speak to this troublesome brat for a few minutes." The rest of them cleared out. Gareth and Lawrence took off to go shopping, while Daphne rushed off to the Mages Guild.

Haley took Sorin to her office. It was a small office with barely enough room to stretch one's legs, but it was tidier than Sorin had expected.

"Has the guild master looked into my request?" Sorin asked as he took a seat.

"He has," said Haley. "And he's agreed to have you treat patients, but only on his terms."

"Interesting," said Sorin. "The situation must be worse than I thought."

Haley sighed. "Two of our life mages were especially active in treating patients. The Medical Association claims that their application of life mana outside of adventuring duties infringes upon the basic business agreement between our two guilds."

"That's nonsense," said Sorin. "Physicians in big cities are always overworked, and life mages not on duty always have life mana to spare. In theory, the association is entitled to take legal action against the competitive use of life mana, but in practice, life mages are typically kind and don't charge. They also clean up small cases that are a waste of time for trained physicians. It's a win-win."

"Be that as it may, they are pressing charges," said Haley. "I imagine that your clan's involvement has added fuel to the fire. Our counterplay is to treat the situation as an emergency and expose Marcus's foot-dragging. If you're willing, we'll have you run a temporary clinic. You are to treat poison and corruption only. Moreover, you are to do so near your old clinic.

"Some life mages, including the two that pushed the boundaries, will assist you. We'll give you any consumables you might need, but expensive ingredients will come off the top. You can charge as you see fit, but I suggest being aggressive with your pricing."

Sorin was of the same mind. It was normal practice for physicians to charge higher prices in bigger cities due to higher property prices, and Marcus had brought this practice back with him to the Bloodwood Outpost, much to the annoyance of the Adventurers Guild. But Sorin cared less about the cultivators affected and more about the non-cultivators. They would be the most impacted by this change in cost structure.

"Just so you know, there will be some risks to operating in this fashion," said Haley. "I can't guarantee your safety. We will provide you with some muscle, but if Marcus personally acts, you might be dead before I get there. Understood?"

"Not to worry," said Sorin. "I know my limits. I won't push him to the point that he feels he has to kill me directly to save face. Also, he comes off more as a passive-aggressive individual."

"Then I'm relieved," said Haley. "We'll draft up an official plan and then let you know the details via runner." She picked up a piece of paper off her desk and began to work. She had silently dismissed him. "Unless there's something else you need?" she said, looking up.

"As a matter of fact, there is," said Sorin. "I was looking to get assessed."

Haley frowned. "Talk to the scheduler, and she'll work you in."

"Ah, but that would be an *official* assessment," said Sorin. "What I want is an unofficial one."

"I see," said Haley, pursing her lips. "You don't want your information on the books since your family will get it within the hour."

"Exactly," said Sorin. "Can you make yourself available?"

"Tonight then," said Haley. "Right now, I'm on the clock, and everything I do needs to be recorded. But once I'm off duty, I'm allowed to use the guild's facilities as I see fit. Come back at 7, and we'll see how you unofficially measure up as a cultivator."

23

ASSESSMENT

Sorin returned to the Adventurers Guild shortly before seven. The mission counter was finishing off the last of its paperwork and was about to shut down for the night. The Adventurer's Pub had just served its first few customers of the night, and it wouldn't be long before the place was filled with rowdy, drunk adventurers just back from completing their missions.

Haley's office was tidy as ever, though the papers on her desk had been reorganized over the course of the day. Interestingly enough, a whole pile was dedicated to her brother, Stephan Sebastian York.

"I might seem heartless on the surface, but my family sent Stephan to me for a reason," said Haley, noticing Sorin's gaze. "He learned to fight by killing demons in the arenas. He might think he knows a lot about adventuring because he's studied up on it all his life, but that's all book smarts. It's in the field where you really learn what's important."

Sorin nodded. "I understand. It's the same in the Kepler Clan. You can pass all the exams you want, but it's when you fail to save your first patient that you learn how lacking your skills truly are."

"Hopefully, Stephan won't need to go through such a traumatizing experience to grow up," said Haley. "But as adventurers, it's a given that we'll see some of our comrades die.

"Now give me 300 gold coins so I can explain myself to the Guild Master." Sorin winced, but he handed over a 500-gold card and received two 100-gold cards in exchange. "The tests need mana crystals to operate, so don't think I'm ripping you off."

She led Sorin to the back of the Adventurers Guild, where its training and assessment facilities were kept. The coaches and teachers that normally operated in this space were long gone, giving the two of them free reign over the guild's ample equipment.

"First things first," said Haley. "The brute strength assessment. The average human male can lift around 150 pounds without any training. A cultivator can lift twice that, and the amount normally increases by 10 percent with each cultivation stage in the Blood-Thickening Realm. You can go ahead and show me what you've got."

Haley pointed to a barbell fitted with rune-carved weights. These were variable weights that would adjust depending on the user's strength. Sorin went ahead and lifted the barbell. It was a strenuous lift, but only about 80 percent of his limit, as controlled by the runes on the barbell.

"Okay, 535 pounds," noted Haley. "B-Class strength."

"B-Class?" asked Sorin.

"Less questions and more testing," said Haley. She then brought him over to a series of pulleys and had him test different sorts of strength, including leg strength, arm strength, and even grip strength.

"All right, it's time to explain how the Adventurers Guild evaluates cultivators," said Haley. "It's actually my York Clan who devised the system, and it's very different than your Kepler Clan's system, which only measures soul strength, mana density, and mana capacity and assigns them a score of average, above average, excellent, and genius level."

"So you won't be measuring those?" asked Sorin.

"I will be, but only later," said Haley. "And I'll be using Adventurers Guild notation to do so."

"In short, the C Class is just average among cultivators. B Class is 10 percent stronger, A Class is 30 percent stronger, and S Class is 50 percent stronger and up. You technically fall between B Class and A Class overall in strength. Your grip strength, by the way, is S Class."

"What about someone like Stephan?" asked Sorin.

"S Class, obviously," said Haley. "And we're using his human form, not his shifted form, as the standard. In his shifted form, he's several times stronger than in his unshifted form. It's similar to how a cultivator would channel mana through a technique or use a skill. The downside is that he can't use a lot of skills in that form."

She then led Sorin over to what looked like an iron maiden. "You seriously want me to step inside that thing?" asked Sorin.

"Relax," said Haley. "It won't hurt. *Much.*"

Sorin had his doubts but did as he was told. The spiked coffin shut overtop him, and magical spikes slowly settled onto his skin and pierced it at equal intervals. A mana-based fluid swept through once his wounds were fully healed and repeated the process twice more before he was finally free.

"Your defenses aren't bad," said Haley, looking at the data she'd recorded. "B-Class. You fare much better than Lawrence, who has E-Class defense, or Daphne and Gareth, who have F-Class defense. As for physical regeneration, you're surprisingly S-Class. You're far better than Stephan in that regard since he's only A-Class."

"How do you evaluate regeneration?" asked Sorin.

"We record your healing rate from the spikes and extrapolate," said Haley. "But in general, the difference in regeneration is much more pronounced than the difference in strength for cultivators. Most cultivators have C-Class regeneration, though mages are an exception since their mana regeneration seems to interfere and knock it down to F-Class.

"B-Class physical regeneration means a cultivator can heal muscle damage. Those with A-Class regeneration can heal skeletal damage and some minor nerve damage. As for S-Rank, it's theoretically limitless. Nerve damage and internal organ damage can be healed. Note that I say *healing* and not regeneration—you lose a body part, and it's typically gone for good."

Next, Haley led him to a small, unlit room and closed the door. The floor and walls lit up with targets, and Sorin was told to hit them as quickly as possible to test his reflexes. This was followed up by a rigorous speed examination, which tested not only running speed but also limb speed and climbing as calculated by impact.

"Speed and reflexes are also B-Class," said Haley. "Though arm speed is halfway between A-Class and S-Class." She gave him a strange look. "I've never seen anyone with results like these, but let's continue with the other tests before making a determination."

The physical trials were over, so Haley brought Sorin to the Mages Guild. It was dark out, and they used the back entrance, so Sorin didn't get to take a good look at it. Two hundred gold coins changed hands when they arrived, making it clear that it wasn't the Adventurers Guild's tests that were expensive, but rather the Mages Guild's tests.

It was common knowledge that mages burned through money. Proper training in their arts required wands and spell books, and most importantly, repetition. The amount of repetition one was capable of was directly correlated to the amount of mana potions one could purchase and imbibe.

"You must be familiar with this test," said Haley as she led Sorin to a rune-covered orb. "But I'll refresh your memory just in case. We'll use this orb to measure your mana parameters. You'll pour mana into it from your body and won't stop until you run out. I'll feed you a mana potion, and then you'll do it again two more times."

Sorin nodded and stepped up to the orb. Poisonous mana moved into his hands and rapidly entered the orb. He continued squeezing mana out of his blood and into the orb until, finally, his blood went dormant.

"Drink," said Haley, pushing a potion into his hands. Sorin did as he was told and recovered to a full state before pouring mana into the orb two more times.

"Now, *this* is interesting. Mana storage, S-Class. Mana density, A-Class. Mana regeneration, B-Class."

"Why is that interesting?" asked Sorin. "I always outperformed my peers on mana parameters."

"Your mana regeneration and mana density aren't that impressive," said Haley.

"We assessed a physician, not a mage," Sorin pointed out.

"Just so," said Haley. "The mark of a good mage is S-Class mana density, so you don't stand out in that regard. But what *really* surprises me is your mana storage." She showed him a figure on her assessment sheet and a note beside the entry. It was five *times* higher than the average amount for his cultivation stage. "Basically, the amount of mana you have is monstrous. It's not even on the same level as other people's. You can't recover it quickly and have a lot more to recover, but even so, this is a very good result. I'm beginning to see why you wanted this off the books. The Mages Guild would be all over you, by the way. In fact, I recommend you join them when you have the coin."

Sorin shook his head. "I'm rubbish on mage potential."

"Even so, the sheer quantity of mana you have is enough to make a Bone-Forging mage jealous," said Haley. "And that's when you're only in the Blood-Thickening Realm. Now, let's go through a few formalities before I finalize my assessment."

Haley first had him juggle crystal balls with his mana and manipulate them. In terms of mana manipulation, he was A-Class due to the sheer amount of practice he had. In terms of mana flow, however, he was only B-Class. This was because mana flow was evaluated based on the number of open meridians in one's body. While Sorin had opened his main meridians, his extraordinary meridians were still shut.

Finally, they performed the mage potential and soul test. "I told you, my soul is strong, but my mage potential is rubbish," said Sorin. "There's no need to waste good coin on this."

"Less talking, more doing," said Haley, shoving him into a coffin-like box.

Sorin was familiar with this test. He engaged his spiritual senses and blasted past the initial layer of resistance. He then did his best to feel out at the 'stars' that had appeared in his periphery.

He started with the nearby stars, as this was the limit of the runes he had sensed during his examination of the Kepler Clan's faculties.

To his surprise, sensing these runes was quite easy. *Did the Ten Thousand Poison Canon even transform my soul?* thought Sorin as he expanded his search range. He identified many unfamiliar runes and marked them until he could no longer find any more runes to identify.

"Soul potential: S-Class, as expected," said Haley, reading from her report as he emerged from the box. "Mage potential: B-Class. *Not* as expected. What level were you in the Kepler Clan's assessment?"

"Average," said Sorin. "I barely managed to sense anything."

"Then something's changed," said Haley, slapping down her assessment. "Something big. Because B-Class is the cutoff to become a mage.

"Moreover, your results are—quite frankly—anomalous. You're good at quite a few things, but you're not bad at *anything*. You should know that there's an old saying from the ancient world: the heavens give as much as they take. Mages are well off in terms of mana, but physically, they're garbage. It's the same for warriors. My brother, a genius beastshift warrior, is no exception.

"In fact, in all my years as an assessor, I've never seen anyone with all their scores at B-Class or higher. I've seen people that have around D-Class stats, but never someone like you. You're basically a monster, Sorin. It's something you want to keep close to your chest going forward.

Sorin licked his lips. "It seems I gained a lot more from my wish than I expected. I hope you'll keep this secret for me."

"My lips are sealed," said Haley. "It's very beneficial for my brother to have such a versatile teammate. We'll now move on to the next part of the assessment: career recommendations. I'm sorry to say that I can't recommend anything to you. You're more than capable of filling any role, and that includes the role of a warrior.

"That being said, I have some general advice for you: if you start wearing anything heavier than leather armor, you won't be able to cast any spells you learn or use your speed properly. Your mana flow will become inhibited. It's the same with your hand speed—don't use anything heavier and longer than a short sword because your hand speed score is much higher than your strength score."

"Understood," said Sorin.

"The most important advice I have for you is this: you might not be bad at anything, but you can't dabble in everything either. Choose a path and commit. Also, remember that your element is poison; you can technically become a mage with your parameters, but you need to decide if that's really the best use of your talents."

"I understand," said Sorin. "And thank you for the assessment and the advice."

"The pleasure is all mine," said Haley. "By the way, are you interested in getting adopted into my York Clan? It might be politically difficult to pull off, but I think the rewards will be well worth it."

Sorin shook his head. "I'd rather not trouble anyone over my personal matters. It makes more sense for me to keep my original name and not rock the boat too much."

"Suit yourself," said Haley. "And another thing: the guild master sent me a message while we were performing your assessment. Are you willing to start causing trouble for the Medical Association tomorrow?"

Sorin raised an eyebrow. "That was fast. What did Marcus do to provoke the guild this time?"

"He sent a rat to sneak a peek at your personnel files, which is unacceptable," said Haley. "We fired the employee but can't directly retaliate. Therefore, indirect retaliation is the best we can do."

"Then count me in. Marcus has been a pain in my ass ever since he arrived. But I wouldn't get my hopes up quite yet. He strikes me as a difficult person to bait."

24

NOSTALGIA

Sorin woke up bright and early the morning after his assessment. His body was full of mana, and his limbs were filled with strength. He had a quick breakfast with Percival before heading out to the Kepler Clan's clinic, where the Adventurers Guild was busy assembling a tent structure for their temporary medical clinic.

Most of the patients present were cultivators. Due to the proximity of the outpost to Bloodwood Forest, absorbing corruption into one's body was inevitable. There was also a small portion of non-cultivators suffering from similar symptoms. In their case, the absorption was due to physical contact with objects charged with demonic energy.

The medical tent was fully assembled by 7 o'clock. Its material, beds, and cupboards were fully sterilized, and there were cupboards full of medicinal ingredients, syringes, and mithril medical equipment.

Three individuals in mage robes greeted Sorin as he entered the tent. "Greetings, Sorin Kepler," said the lead mage. "We're one-star life mages hired jointly by the Adventurers Guild and the Mages Guild to assist you today. My name is Leffen, and these two are my associates, Elise and Marlyn." Those two were the ones being charged by the medical association.

There were also a handful of assistants in the tent. Of note was Janice, who wasn't a qualified life mage or adventurer. Regardless of their talent, however, they all had something in common: life mana. Life mana was useful, even if the wielder was dumb as rocks and couldn't control their mana flow.

"It seems Assessor Haley wasn't exaggerating when she mentioned the Medical Association was making it hard on life mages, given the size of this clinic," Sorin said to Leffen.

"They're despicable scum who make it difficult for people to save lives," said a clearly prejudiced Leffen. "While I have great respect for individual physicians like yourself and Physician Lim, a few greedy individuals and their cliques have basically taken over the Medical Association and have made it difficult for us life mages to make a difference."

Sorin had met many physicians and interacted with the Medical Association several times, so he disagreed with that assessment. But he understood that his perspective was limited, so he simply smiled and moved the conversation along.

"I'm not a physician," Sorin corrected. "In fact, you could argue that I'm the opposite of a physician."

"Words are words, and actions are actions," said Leffen.

"Just so," said Sorin. "Does the Adventurers Guild have anything else to prepare?"

"There's just one last thing," said Leffen. "Marlyn? The sign?"

"Right!" said Marlyn. She rushed out and pulled out a large white-board. It bore the words:

Temporary Medical Relief Center: Courtesy of the Adventurers Guild and the Mages Guild
Commoners receive free treatment!
Reasonable rates for cultivators of all backgrounds!
Staff on Duty:
Sorin Kepler, Anti-Poison and Anti-Corruption Specialist, one-star

Leffen Woodrow, Senior Life Mage, one-star
Elise Firebringer, Intermediate Life Mage, one-star
Marlyn Watchmaker, Junior Life Mage, one-star

Disclaimer: The Temporary Medical Relief Center operates with a staff of adventurers and mages and, as a result, cannot provide official prescriptions or a professional diagnosis. Treatment will be provided to the best of their limited capabilities. The Temporary Medical Relief Center is intended to provide emergency medical services in response to the overwhelming demand for medical services and the inability of local physicians to cope with this demand.

"They're being very cagey about all this," said Leffen. "We've provided emergency relief before, but never with such pageantry and legal disclaimers."

"That's politics for you," said Sorin. "It changes everything it touches. But let's not concern ourselves with that and provide whatever services are within our capabilities. We'll charge reasonable rates for our services, and by reasonable, I mean lower than the current rates set by the Medical Association for rural patients.

It was also important to remember that their goal was to fight back against the Medical Association's encroachment in a tit-for-tat manner. They wanted to be territorial with life mages and withhold services to retaliate once that didn't go well? Fine. The Adventurers Guild and Mages Guild would eat their dinner. Exactly how the local physicians would react was up in the air. But one thing was clear: This was a provocation they couldn't ignore for very long.

"Looks good," said Sorin, giving Marlyn a thumbs up. "Put up the sign, and let's have our security team shout it out periodically for advertisement."

"You want them to shout?" asked Leffen. "In front of a clinic? Isn't that a bit rude?"

Sorin shrugged. "How else are we going to get their attention?" With that, he retreated to a desk in the corner of the room and started brain-storming options for his next poison.

It was several hours later when Sorin received his first patient. A tall man coughed as he stumbled towards Sorin's desk, looking pale and gaunt.

"They say you're a Poison Master?" said the simply dressed man, taking a seat at Sorin's desk. His hands trembled as he wiped away a trace of white phlegm from his mouth.

"I believe the words used on the sign are anti-poison and anti-corruption specialist," said Sorin. "But Poison Master has a nice ring to it, so I'll allow it."

"Well, I've been poisoned," said the man. "And no one will believe me. They say I have a cold, but... colds don't last that long. And every doctor I've been to says there's no infection. Poison's the only thing it can be."

Sorin put away the stack of calculations he'd been working on and observed the man. His skin was pale, and light spots could also be seen on his sleeveless arms. Moreover, the skin on his arms was wrinkled, a symptom of atrophy.

"You were once a strong man, weren't you?" asked Sorin, nodding towards his arms. "The calluses on your hands and the powerful veins on your wrists and forearms indicate previously impressive musculature. You're not just sick—you've been wasting away for several months without knowing what's ailing you."

He cut off as the man started coughing. The coughing continued until the man spat out blood. "I just don't know what to do," the man said. "The doctors say it's not an infection, that there's nothing they can do."

"Let me have a look and see if there's anything to be done," Sorin reassured. He led the patient over to a bed and closed the privacy screen.

"Shirt and pants off. You can keep your underwear. I want to see if there's any other wounds or symptoms I might be missing."

The man did as instructed and sat on the bed. Sorin placed a hand on his chest and used his spiritual strength to test his breathing. "Breathing is normal. Heart function is good. Mana flow is blocked, but you're not a cultivator, so that's normal. Are you a farmer, then? Why the mismatched clothes?"

The man winced. "Farmers have a harder time getting seen at a clinic, I've been told. So every time I go to the doctor's, I dress up as a town worker."

"I don't ever recall seeing you at my clinic," said Sorin.

"I always went to Physician Lim's clinic," said the man. "Most of us farmers go see him since he'll see a certain number of non-cultivators every day for a low price. It's been the same for the past thirty years."

"But now you don't have the coin," said Sorin. "So here you are."

"It's not so much that I don't have the coin but that Physician Lim doesn't have the time," said the farmer. "Physician Lim is understanding. He won't charge someone if they can't afford it. But the problem is that there are too many people lined up every day. And ever since you stopped your practice, it's only gotten worse."

"Hm…" said Sorin, taking his hand off the man's chest. "You must have been working at the fringes of the bloodwood. There's nothing wrong with your internal organs, strictly speaking, but your hands are so heavily corrupted that it's starting to affect your other organs. Your heart and lungs *sound* fine, but they're actually all underperforming. And I know the corruption is localized in your hands because your legs are still quite strong."

"Then… you don't need to *amputate* them, do you?" said the man, frightened at the prospect. "Those are my *hands*. They're how I make a living!"

"There's no need to amputate," said Sorin. "Just wait here, and you'll see improvement shortly." He went to fetch a set of crystal needles, a cup of water, and a pack of white powder. "It's cowbane grass seed, ground up," Sorin said to the man as he poured the white powder into the water. "It's poisonous to most animals and humans. Very poisonous against lesser demons. And no, you're not drinking it. I am."

To the man's horror, Sorin downed the cup of poison and winced as it worked its way down his throat. The five poisons in his body immediately came to his defense.

Unfortunately, imbibing the poison didn't greatly enhance the quality of his mana, nor did it increase his cultivation. But by assimilating the poison, he was now able to generate it on demand. Sickly green mana appeared on his hands and poured into a crystal needle, which he then inserted into the farmer's leg.

"Unfortunately, this is going to sting quite a bit," explained Sorin as he continued inserting needle after needle into the man's thigh, then into his torso, and finally into his arms. "The corruption is set in deep, and we need to chase it out of the rest of your body and into your arms before pulling it out of your hands, one of the most sensitive parts of your body."

He pricked the man's finger, drawing a trickle of blood into an empty pan. At first, it was only red blood, but as Sorin placed more needles, the blood gradually turned black.

He repeated the process with all the meridians connected to the man's arms until, finally, only red blood flowed. By then, the man was even paler than before and on the verge of fainting.

"Blood-Replenishing Potion," called out Sorin, holding out a hand. One of the assistants came over and gave it to him. "Drink this. Anyone can get a Blood-Replenishing Potion at the Alchemists Guild without a prescription, so if you find you need another, you can buy one. Mortal-grade potions are cheap." The man drank the potion, and his face flushed red as new blood was created.

"My hands..." said the man as he placed the vial down. "They're not shaking!"

"And they won't for a while, assuming you take the right precautions," said Sorin. "Wear the demonbane gloves the outpost provides next time you do fieldwork. Not only do they not make you any less of a man, but they'll also stop such a problem from reoccurring in the future."

"Thank you, Physician Sorin!" said the farmer.

"I'm no physician," said Sorin, shaking his head. "I'm just a man who's good at treating poisons." By the time he escorted the man to the entrance, another patient was ready and waiting.

AN ENCOUNTER WITH GABRIELLA

The farmer Sorin treated returned to his home, but not before spreading the news of his treatment across the outpost. From then on, all sorts of people flocked over to the Temporary Medical Relief Center. This was especially the case for non-cultivators. Physicians typically saw quite a few non-cultivators as part of their practice, but it was inevitable that many would be turned away.

While the temporary center couldn't treat all cases, life mages were proficient in healing physical trauma injuries to bones, skin, and tissue. As for Sorin, he could treat cases of corruption in both cultivators and non-cultivators, as well as the many cases of poisoning suffered by adventurers who patrolled Bloodwood Forest.

It was at the end of the day, when the clinic was closing up, that Sorin received an unexpected visitor. "Is Physician Sorin—I mean, is Mr. Kepler in right now?" came a woman's voice. Sorin looked up to see Gabriella, his former apprentice.

"Gabriella," greeted Sorin. "Why don't we step over to a treatment bed?"

"I'm not sure—" she started, but Sorin didn't give her a chance and led her behind a sound-isolated curtain.

Gabriella took a seat on the bed, and Sorin sat down on the table in the treatment room. For a moment, neither of them spoke. "You seem to be doing well," Sorin finally said after some time. He frowned slightly when he saw that her hands were red and calloused and her eyes were tired and sleep-deprived but schooled his expression.

"I'm doing fine," said Gabriella. "Studying mostly. Keeping busy at the clinic. There's always lots to be done."

"That's good," said Sorin, nodding. "I suppose that as a two-star doctor, Marcus would know how to guide an apprentice physician."

Gabriella shifted uncomfortably. "It's more self-driven studies under the guidance of Physician Marcus. He's not nearly as involved as you were. Lots of one-star physicians. Lots of apprentices from his old clinic."

Sorin groaned. "Do you want some unofficial guidance? Medical texts can be extremely obscure to the untrained."

"I wouldn't want to get you in trouble," said Gabriella. "Also, I'd rather we not go back to a physician-apprentice relationship. It was quite awkward, given that we're around the same age."

Sorin nodded. "If that's what you want. And… I'm sorry, Gabriella."

"Sorry, for what?" asked Gabriella.

"For not coming to see you, of course," said Sorin. "I thought… I thought you'd be better off without my attention, given how aggressive my family is being."

"That's probably true," said Gabriella. "Even so, I didn't know if you were all right. They said… They said you've become an adventurer. A wielder of poisons."

"I believe poisoner, charlatan, and snake are the common derogatory terms," said Sorin. "And the answer is yes. My team and I just returned from clearing out a nest of Rockgnaw Rats. There were hundreds of them." Sorin cut his explanation short when he saw Gabriella's smile fading a bit. "I'm sorry. You were never much of a fighter. Kind to a fault."

"I know it needs to be done," said Gabriella. "If adventurers never went out to kill demons, they'd quickly overrun us. It's just… me. *I* can't do it. Killing is not something physicians should be doing."

"You're probably right," said Sorin. "It would shake up the physician's priorities. Make death more palatable or acceptable. But remember that death is inevitable in your chosen profession. Eventually, one of your patients *will* die. And you'll have to come to terms with that."

Gabriella sighed. "This is exactly the kind of advice I'm not getting. Information is easy to remember, but lessons like this can only come from experience. I can't wait to finish up studying and head over to a big city for the physician's examination."

"You could probably pass with your current knowledge," said Sorin.

"But I wouldn't have a recommendation letter, now, would I?" said Gabriella.

Sorin now saw the crux of the issue. "Is he withholding his recommendation unduly?"

"The way Physician Marcus put it, all your teachings are suspect," said Gabriella. "My skills and knowledge must therefore be re-evaluated. Of course, the review keeps getting pushed back. It's only been made worse with all the busy work he's having his clinic do."

"Sounds troublesome," said Sorin. "I know you don't want to inconvenience me, but I can still see if there's anyone in my family willing to do me a favor. And don't refuse just yet. Let's see how Marcus treats you. If he still doesn't move on it after a few months, come talk to me."

"I'm sure it won't come to that," said Gabriella. Her eyes flickered to the entrance to the treatment room. "I should really get going, Sorin. I wouldn't want to be seen hanging about around here. No offense."

"None taken," said Sorin.

Gabriella moved to leave the treatment area but turned around before opening the curtain. "By the way. I missed you, Sorin."

"I missed you too," said Sorin. Alas, unless Marcus packed up his bags, they wouldn't be able to see each other much going forward.

Sorin watched as she left the room, and it was only when she was well and truly out of the tent clinic that he shot two poison-infused needles through the tent's canvas material. He then lifted the canvas and pulled in two bodies—that of a human and that of a rat.

"Lorimer, what did I tell you about skulking around the tent?" said Sorin. "You can't be seen with me. At least around patients. Also, I gave you an important task." Lorimer squeaked in protest, but Sorin cut him off. "I *know* you didn't get any opportunities, but what about tomorrow or the day after? I guarantee they won't be able to swallow this insult and will do something to recover their image.

Lorimer grumbled and ran out of the tent. Lawrence tried to do the same, but Sorin grabbed him by the collar. "I see your peeping ways haven't gone anywhere," he said to Lawrence. "Speak. How much did you overhear?"

"Nothing at all," said Lawrence. "I specifically didn't hear anything from Gabriella about self-study and the like."

Sorin sighed. "I really did her a disservice."

"Don't say that," said Lawrence. "It's your family that's being mean."

"So you *were* listening," said Sorin, throwing a few more needles at Lawrence.

This time, however, the rogue was prepared. He caught the needles with gloved hands and placed them on the small table in the treatment room. "You'll never catch me with the same trick twice. I... yikes!" He pulled his leg back, but too late. A paralytic poison had already crept up the mithril string and onto his leg.

"Eavesdropping is a grave offense, Lawrence," Sorin said. "But I can forgive you if you're willing to do something for me."

"Oh-Oh yeah?" said a sweaty-faced Lawrence, massaging his numb leg. "And what might that be? Do you need money? I can lend you money!"

"I don't need your money," said Sorin. "I need your expert peeping skills instead."

"Who do you want me to spy on?" asked Lawrence. "And I'll tell you now, I'd rather cut off this paralyzed leg than spy on Marcus."

"I'd never ask you to spy on a Bone-Forging cultivator," said Sorin. "I just want you to spy on Gabriella and find out more about her situation. I think she was sugarcoating her situation, and I want the details."

Lawrence's eyes brightened. "Spying on a damsel in distress to save her? This is it—my noble calling! The mission of my life!"

"Not so fast," said Sorin, catching Lawrence before he could leave. "I also want you to investigate my old clinic. See how many physicians there are and how they've changed the way they operate lately. A crafty rogue like you should be able to do that, right?"

"Absolutely," said Lawrence. "I'll find out everything there is to know about them, including Physician Marcus's underwear color. Actually, scratch that. That's way too risky. But I could *maybe* pull it off?"

Sorin left after Lawrence assured him he'd take the matter seriously and returned to count supplies and coordinate with the life mages. "The day went by with surprisingly few interruptions," said Leffen. "I expected some sort of confrontation."

"They're assessing us," said Sorin. "But don't worry. A confrontation is inevitable. Otherwise, we'll run them out of business."

"So we're coming back tomorrow?" asked Leffen.

"And the day after that and all week if we have to," said Sorin. "People being refused treatment for petty reasons is unacceptable. It affects not just the Adventurers Guild but also every person in the outpost. The Adventurers Guild's position is that adventurers being refused medical treatment and life mages getting harassed is unacceptable. The Medical Association's position is that others shouldn't mess with their business. The way I see it, the Adventurers Guild's position is stronger, so it'll eventually win out."

Sorin packed up a few more things before returning home. He had a quiet dinner, then returned to his study to work late into the night on his poison formulations. It was just past midnight when he heard a sudden crash.

Sorin bolted down the stairs using Adder Rush yet wasn't able to make it on time. A cloaked cultivator blended into the night's darkness and would be impossible to track down.

"Those bastards," said Percival, still in his nightshirt. He looked at the wall in disgust. "Can't they leave a person trying to do good things alone?"

"I expect as much," said Sorin, shaking his head. "And so did the Adventurers Guild. Take some mana pictures and send them to Assessor Haley and see how much they can give us for damages." He then walked over the broken glass to the cleared-out section of wall where words had been written in red over the expensive wallpaper.

Leave the outpost, filthy poisoner.

Don't hide behind innocent commoners, cowardly snake.

"It seems the usual insults haven't changed much over the years," observed Percival.

"Indeed, they haven't," said Sorin.

"Don't worry about any of this, Mr. Kepler," said Percival. "Clarice and I will have it cleaned up in no time at all."

With a sigh, Sorin returned to his office and picked up where he'd left off.

26

GROWING BRANCHES

Sorin spent the next three days treating patients during the day and calculating potential poisons at night. Having already ingested five poisons, it was difficult to find one-star poisons that weren't at least partially replicated by those five.

After the initial vandalism incident, there were no further attacks on Sorin's character. Marcus's clinic remained silent as ever, and the Temporary Medical Relief Center operated with no interruption from either Marcus or Physician Lim, the only other physician in the outpost.

"He can't stay silent forever," Sorin grumbled to Henry as they talked in the Alchemists Guild. "A clinic needs to turn in a profit of some kind, and the Kepler Clan will only allow him to waste money and tarnish their image for so long."

"I have no idea what you're talking about," said Henry, walking out from the back. "And *yes*, I really did check everywhere this time. There are no violet salamander skins or rainbow toad warts, either. We're fresh out of everything poison related thanks to an order from Marcus's clinic. I believe something was said about medical research."

"How could it be for anything *but* medical research?" grumbled Sorin. "Half of what he ordered is useless for all but the rarest medical treatments!"

"Look, Sorin," said Henry apologetically. "I like you. I really do. But this is a business, and Physician Marcus spent an extra 30 percent to clear out all our stock of one-star poisons. And two-star poisons, for that matter."

"How wonderful," said Sorin. "Since demand is so high, you'll surely be restocking these items promptly."

Sorin was irritated by Marcus's actions. There was no way for the physician to know that Sorin needed to imbibe poisons to increase his cultivation, but it remained that poison users needed poisons for their abilities. The only ones left in the shop were those that the alchemists of the guild had reserved for their own potion-making.

"Fine," said Sorin, accepting the situation. "Then I'll need to rent a one-star workshop. Sometime next week, if possible."

"About that…" said Henry.

"You've got to be kidding me," said Sorin. "What did Marcus do? Rented all your spare one-star workshops?"

"Not exactly," said Henry. "It's more like he looted them. He used his connections to rent all the unused earth flames in our guild for an unspecified amount of time. I can rent you one-star glassware and spell circles, but in the end, I can't rent you a full one-star workshop. Without a one-star earth flame, it just wouldn't qualify."

Sorin's expression darkened. "Is he not afraid that by throwing his weight around so much, someone will get fed up with him?"

"He *is* a two-star physician, Sorin," said Henry. "In a place like this, that's practically royalty." Not that Pandora had royals. Those had been done away with shortly after the Cataclysmic Emergence.

An earth flame was truly too important. Even Sorin, who was dabbling in alchemy to pursue poison concoction, wouldn't be able to properly concentrate or fuse higher-level one-star poisons without one. By taking all the earth flames, Marcus had effectively sealed off all of Sorin's avenues for growth short of Sorin risking his life in the wilderness.

When Sorin returned to the temporary clinic the next day, he found

Lawrence waiting for him at his desk. "What did you discover?" he asked Lawrence. "Anything sinister?"

"No," said Lawrence. "Not really. I confirmed your suspicions that they're basically wasting time in that clinic. But they have an excuse—Marcus is training his apprentices and the one-star physicians in the clinic in rudimentary alchemy. To better understand medicines and mix them themselves if required. That way, they'll better be able to respond to critical shortages during the demon tide."

"Of course," said Sorin, rolling his eyes. "I should have known their barking and arguing with the Adventurers Guild and the Mages Guild was all a front. What about the other thing I asked you to look into?"

"Marcus isn't making things *that* difficult for Gabriella," said Lawrence. "He's not teaching her anything. In fact, he's not paying much attention to her at all. He's stated in no uncertain terms that she'd need to study on her own time and perform menial work to retain access to study materials."

Sorin frowned. "How isn't that making things difficult for her? If he's not giving her opportunities to practice or guiding her, isn't he just extorting her?"

"Apparently, it's how they do it in the big cities," said Lawrence with a shrug. "According to what I've discovered, you wouldn't really have a case if you made a complaint. If anything, you'd just hurt Gabriella." Sorin could only swallow his anger and hope things would improve for her.

The temporary medical clinic continued treating patients for a full week until, finally, Lawrence returned with some news. "My sources say that Marcus has finally realized how committed the Adventurers Guild is to retaliating. As a result, he'll be reopening his clinic soon."

"Will he be confronting us while he's at it?" asked Sorin.

"I didn't hear anything about *that*," said Lawrence.

"Damn," said Sorin. "I guess Marcus is even more of a snake than I realized."

It was around noon the next day when Sorin heard a commotion outside the clinic. "Are you ready?" he asked Leffen and the adventurers posted at the temporary clinic.

"Ready for anything," said Leffen. "Just take the lead, and we'll support you as we can."

Sorin wasn't so sure that the confrontation he wanted would take place, but he had memorized his lines. He was familiar with any attacks that could be made against poison users, and it was the same for life mages and their parallel practice in free cities.

Sorin walked out of the clinic to see that a crowd had gathered. There were both cultivators and commoners in the crowd. They had not gathered because the clinic was opening; instead, they were there because there was a tent, and that tent was serving free food. A podium had been erected just outside Sorin's old clinic. The sign was covered up with white fabric, which meant that Marcus was rebranding.

I see. Training his physicians might be a passable excuse to make official, but his actions greatly hurt the clinic's public image. As a result, he can't just write a formal explanation—he needs to make a big deal of why exactly he spent so much time treating so few patients in a way that will look good to the farmers and non-cultivating workers.

The timing was, naturally, very harmful to Sorin. Instead of quickly gathering the poisons he'd needed and cultivating, Sorin had gotten dragged into operating the temporary clinic. As such, he had been too slow to react when Marcus snatched all the one-star poisons and earth flames.

Physician Marcus stepped out shortly after the food tent opened. Alongside him were three one-star physicians and a host of apprentices and nurses, including Gabriella. Marcus cleared his throat before speaking.

"I would like to thank everyone for attending our clinic's grand opening," said Physician Marcus, projecting his voice as only a Bone-Forging cultivator could. "It warms my heart to see such a supportive community in the outpost. We look forward to serving you with our hearts and all our souls.

"But first: a name. A clinic needs to have a distinctive name. Gabriella? If you will?"

Gabriella wasn't looking too happy to be singled out, but she did as she was told and pulled on the white cloth, revealing a name in bold golden lettering: The Growing Branches Community Clinic. Two bright stars could be seen beside the name, just before the two coiled serpents symbolizing the Pandora Medical Association.

"At the Growing Branches Community Clinic, we firmly believe in not only treating members of our community but also being involved in their wellbeing," said Marcus. "Our mission here at the outpost is to reclaim land for humanity. We at the Growing Branches Community Clinic will do our utmost to support the brave adventurers and farmers who make this happen. Yes? I see there's a question back there?"

"Why does there need to be a name change?" asked a man in farmer's clothes. "Aren't you a Kepler, just like Physician Sorin is?"

"That's a very good question," said Marcus.

And probably a planted question, thought Sorin.

"In truth, each clinic's name is left to the discretion of their manager," said Marcus. "The previous manager might have been too attached to his family name, which was why he kept it. Other than that, I need to clarify that Mr. Sorin Kepler was not a normal physician. He was an honorary physician due to his previous accomplishments prior to suffering a grievous injury. But when he regained his ability to cultivate in recent days, his designation was revoked due to mana compatibility issues. He is, of course, more than welcome to try reclaiming his credentials."

Unlikely. Given how badly biased the Medical Association is towards poison users.

"Now that introductions are out of the way, I'd like to thank you all for being patient while our staff underwent group training," continued Marcus. "The first week is always very sensitive for a clinic, and I wanted to make sure we got off on the right foot.

"This training was done in collaboration with the Alchemists Guild, and we will be working closely with them in the future. Not only will our physicians be cross-training, but their alchemists will also be cross-training as physicians. We hope to see the results soon. "Ah, I see there's another question."

Once again, he pointed to someone in the crowd. Sorin recognized the man as Edward Marsh, the governor's youngest son. "I heard you're a two-star physician," said Edward. "Does that mean we'll finally have a doctor that can treat our Bone-Forging experts?"

"That's correct," said Marcus, looking extremely satisfied with himself. "In fact, I've already talked to your father, the governor, about potentially expanding the operations of our Bone-Forging experts. With me here to support them, they'll be able to more safely contribute to clearing Bloodwood Forest."

It was a two-pronged attack, as Sorin saw it. For one, he was showing off his importance to the local powerhouses and increasing his status in everyone's eyes. For another, he was half-accusing the Bone-Forging powerhouses, specifically those at the Adventurers Guild and Mages Guild, of cowardice.

I can't allow him to control the narrative, thought Sorin, so he raised his hand once Edward had finished.

"Now let's continue with the next improvement, holistic—"

"Excuse me, I have a question," said Sorin loudly.

"Of course," said Marcus. "There'll be chances for questions later. Now holistic services are—"

"I'm sorry, but it just seems to me like you're answering pre-prepared questions to make it look like you're answering questions," said Sorin, cutting him off once again. "But I'm sure that's not the case and that you'd be more than happy to answer unscripted questions."

Marcus's eye twitched, but he smiled at Sorin and nodded. "Of course, Poison Master Sorin—assuming that's what you like to call yourself these days."

27

SLIPPERY SNAKE

The audience began muttering loudly at Marcus's mention of Sorin's occupational change. The change had not been well-received by the populace. It seemed a pity for a perfectly good physician to change his career and become an adventurer—ignoring, of course, how the situation had practically been forced.

"How you choose to address me doesn't really matter," Sorin said to Marcus. "Instead, what matters is the clinic and how you intend to run it. I noticed that you were talking about improvements to your facilities and your ability to treat higher-stage cultivators. But you made no mention of the current undertreatment of non-cultivators, specifically as it relates to corruption."

"Ah," said Marcus. "We will, of course, be providing services to these individuals at an increased capacity."

"At a steeply discounted price, I hope?" said Sorin. "Because as I understand it, clinics tend to receive a stipend from the governors. A per capita amount that is in turn subsidized by the state government and intended to cover the full costs of treatment.

"I ask this because while we were operating this Temporary Medical Relief Center to accommodate the 'cross training' of your staff and preparation for your grand reopening, many clients stated that they were turned away for lack of funds—something I find grossly disturbing and in contravention of the physician's code of ethics."

Marcus's expression fell. "Turned away? Not on my watch!" There was no way he could admit to such a thing in front of a large crowd. "As for charging, it is in my understanding that physicians have always charged for such services in the Bloodwood Outpost. Physician Lim does, at least."

"It's only a nominal fee," said Sorin. "Very different than the fees in a big city. And back when I ran this clinic, as I'm sure many remember, I always matched the stipend amount or charged less if I could. I also happened to know that Physician Lim won't charge if his customers can't afford it, and I didn't either. At least as it concerns non-cultivators."

"On that note, I notice that you've brought in three one-star physicians and a few apprentices with you. I must say that I am relieved. I'm sure that with a two-star physician and three more one-star physicians to help out Physician Lim, there will be no need for the Adventurers Guild and Mages Guild to set up temporary clinics in the future. I'm sure everyone who requires prompt medical treatment will receive it."

"It is as you say," said Marcus, smiling brightly. "We're here to grow together with our community and hope to see everyone live bright lives to their full potential."

He continued his speech, but Sorin didn't bother listening to the rest of it. Marcus was much craftier than he'd suspected and wouldn't give him much of an opening. In the end, the entire conflict between the Medical Association and the Adventurers Guild had all been a clever cover for his greater scheme: sabotaging Sorin at every opportunity, just like the Kepler Clan intended.

"Pack it up," Sorin said to Leffen as he arrived at the temporary clinic. "We're done here."

"That's it?" said Leffen, looking confused. "Wasn't there supposed to be some sort of epic showdown or physician standoff?"

Sorin shrugged. "Marcus is a two-star physician, Leffen. He doesn't need to prove anything. He's also clearly collaborating with the

Governor and the Alchemists Guild. By opening the temporary clinic, we brought attention to the Growing Branches Clinic. It looks like we won, but in the end, it was Marcus who did.

"But we forced him to open up again and treat our people," said Leffen. "I also heard from the vice guild master that the Medical Association, having 'realized the severity of the situation,' is no longer pressing charges.

"That's all we could do with what we were given, Leffen," said Sorin. "We forced him to act and start treating our adventurers again, but in the end, he's making it sound like *he's* the good guy." As a bonus, they'd advertised life mages as an alternative to healing potions for nonserious injuries. Combined with their low treatment costs, they'd fixed a low price in everyone's mind. A win, in Sorin's opinion.

"Well done," said Haley, outside the tent, just as Sorin was leaving. "You did a good job out there, Sorin, no matter what you might think."

"I hope the guild master didn't have sky-high expectations," said Sorin. "Looking at your attire, you weren't exactly expecting a fight?" Haley was wearing casual clothes, but a careful inspection would reveal an array of weapons tucked into her clothing and undergarments.

"Unfortunately, there's only so much that can be done when the governor, the highest-ranking physician in the outpost, and the Alchemists Guild are in bed with each other," said Haley. "To get them to give up on their aggression and to provide normal, non-discriminatory care to our members again was the realistic outcome.

"As for a *fight*—well, I'm sure you know that Marcus has much better ways of targeting you. Don't be too surprised if the Alchemists Guild finds itself too busy for custom orders in the foreseeable future."

Sorin sighed. "I don't suppose you have back-channel access to key resources?"

"I do, but that service comes at a premium," said Haley. "What are your plans going forward?"

"I'm not quite sure," said Sorin. "Marcus has done a really good job in strangling my growth opportunities. Are there any good missions to be had?"

"Maybe in a week," said Haley. "But you should visit the guild on a daily basis just to be sure."

Sorin said goodbye to Haley and continued toward the Adventurers Guild. It was just after noon, so there were many people outside for lunch, enjoying the last warm days of fall.

But Sorin wasn't in the mood for lunch, and neither was he in the mood for people. He settled for a cup of coffee at a rundown café in an alley a few blocks away from the main street, and then he slowly sipped on his cup of coffee as he waited for news from his accomplice.

A half-hour later, he heard a familiar squeak. Lorimer scurried down the alley and climbed onto Sorin's table, then started lapping at an extra coffee he'd placed there. "Hey! No pets on the tables!" shouted the owner.

"Sorry about that," said Sorin. He placed the coffee cup on the ground and petted Lorimer as he drank. "How was it? Was Lawrence's map accurate?"

Lorimer squeaked that the map was completely useless, as expected. But Lorimer was a smart mouse and knew what to look for. He'd eaten many delicious things. In fact, he'd broken through to the fourth stage of Blood-Thickening!

"Excellent," said Sorin. "It's not quite peeing in his coffee cup, but it'll have to do." Then Sorin sighed. "It's too bad you're so small. Otherwise, you might have been able to steal me earth flame crystal." Lorimer froze when he heard this and transmitted a thought. "You're asking what those crystals look like? I'm not sure—orange and red? The size of a fist? They're a kind of variant mana crystal. Very useful for alchemists. You... you're saying you *ate* one?"

Lorimer shook his head. "You didn't eat one?" asked Sorin. The rat shook his head once more. "You mean you ate *more* than one? How many did you eat exactly?" To answer, Lorimer drained the coffee cup. "*All* of them? Are you insane?" Lorimer licked his lips as if asking for more. "You're insatiably greedy, Lorimer. If you keep this up, I won't be able to afford to feed you."

Fortunately, it wasn't him who paid for the food, but Marcus. Moreover, Marcus wouldn't be able to admit to the Alchemists Guild that the earth flames had gone missing. For someone of his stature, it made much more sense to order some from Dustone to replace them. He would also never suspect Sorin because Sorin had been right there in front of him. He had a perfect alibi.

Sorin ordered two more coffees, one for him and one for Lorimer. Today was a wonderful day. A fruitful day. He wished he could have goaded Marcus into attacking him in public, but there was nothing to be done about it.

If only Lorimer were bigger, thought Sorin. *Maybe I could get him to wear a satchel?* No, that would be too conspicuous. A rat with a satchel would be immediately noticed.

He was about to take another sip of his coffee when a thought suddenly occurred to him. "Lorimer? Do you remember that trick you did with the mana lamp crystals?" Lorimer looked up from his coffee and nodded. "Do you... Do you think you could warm up my coffee?" He held out his cup to Lorimer expectantly.

Lorimer was quite smart and immediately knew what to do. He began to glow orange-red, and Sorin's coffee cup, which was only made of cheap ceramics, exploded from the sheer amount of heat injected.

"Hey! Watch it!" said the owner of the café. "And don't think I didn't see that. I'm adding that cup to your tab."

Sorin slapped a couple of gold coins on the table. "I'm in a good mood today," he said to the owner. "Thanks for putting up with Lorimer. Keep the change."

"Any time!" shouted the owner, one of the few who would tolerate a pet rat in his establishment.

Having confirmed that Lorimer was now essentially a living earth flame, he stepped out of the alley and made his way to Main Street. His next destination? The Alchemists Guild.

EARTH FLAME POISON REFINEMENT

The Alchemists Guild was unusually quiet when Sorin arrived. The ingredient shop's regulars, whether it be alchemists or adventurers, were nowhere to be found. As for the workshops at the back, it was clear from the chimneys belching out black smoke that every available earth flame in the guild was currently in use.

"Sorin!" welcomed Henry. "Who would have thought you'd be back so soon? Did you change your mind on the minor poisons? Or perhaps you'd like to rent a flameless room?" He didn't seem so optimistic about either offer, but Henry was a professional and wouldn't allow the simple drying up of business to dampen his mood.

"I really wonder how the traveling alchemists will survive without earth flames to rent," Sorin said to Henry. "And without the traveling alchemists, I can't see how the outpost will be able to stockpile potions before the demon tide."

Henry's smile faded somewhat. "That's life, Sorin. And business, for that matter. No earth flames mean that what few traveling alchemists we did have moved on to another outpost. It's only regulars with their own flames and long-term rentals now."

Marcus's pilfering of the earth flames was a vicious move that didn't just hit Sorin but the entire outpost. There was no telling how many more casualties they would be taking as a result.

"Anyway, there won't be a shortage," assured Henry. "The guild has somehow gotten into a lot of money, if you get my drift, and will be importing the difference from Dustone. All our alchemists are also on contract to make as many healing and mana potions as possible. They're contractually not allowed to make anything else."

Sorin had been wondering how Marcus would prevent him from hiring an alchemist to concoct his poisons, so the news came as no surprise to him. "What about Blood-Thickening Potions?" asked Sorin. "If they don't make them, how will people advance? Actually, can I buy some right now? I'm worried about inflation."

"No can do," said Henry, raising his hands. "Everything I've got is sold out, and whatever is coming in next week is already paid for. Double, sometimes triple the usual price."

What a good-for-nothing, short-sighted move, thought Sorin. *All because a two-star physician decided they wanted to throw their weight around.*

There was a silver lining to the shortage of potions, however. It confirmed for Sorin that while Marcus had struck his weakness, it was more incidental than on purpose. The shortage of Blood-Thickening Potions—aids to increase one's cultivation in the Blood-Thickening Realm—had likely been orchestrated by Marcus as well. Fortunately, what Sorin was *actually* lacking was poisons, a problem he would be remedying shortly.

"If a flameless workshop is all you've got, I'll have to try my luck and see what I can pull off," Sorin said to Henry. "I'll need the following ingredients. What do you have in stock?" He wrote down a list of fifty or so common ingredients and passed it to Henry.

"I can give you most of these, but not the Blood-Thickening Lichen," said Henry after perusing the list. "And I can't give you the Fleshknit Grass or the Manabrew Root. My entire supply's been taken away by the guild master. Nothing I can do about it."

Once again, Sorin had to praise Marcus's ingenuity. Others might not see it, but to Sorin, it was clear as day. The requirement to become a one-star alchemist was to be able to brew both a mana potion and a healing potion one time out of four. Yet without these ingredients, it would be impossible to practice this crucial bit of alchemy, let alone take the examination. Sorin would, therefore, not be able to become an alchemist and join the guild and would, therefore, be helpless to prevent Marcus's tampering.

"I guess I'll have to be happy with what you've got," said Sorin to Henry. "Bring them all up to the workshop you're giving me, and we'll see if I can come up with something new and innovative.

Before long, Sorin was standing in one of the looted one-star workshops. Official alchemists were a tidy lot, so he didn't have to scrub it down like the one before.

He first went through the glassware and the heating, isolation, and ventilation arrays and confirmed that, save for the heating array, they were all functional. As for the heating array, the spell circle was only missing an earth flame to serve as its core.

"All right, Lorimer," said Sorin. "Time to show me what you've got." The rat hopped into the spell circle and began to glow with red and orange earth flames. The spell circle lit up, and Sorin let out a sigh of relief.

He then spent the next half-hour organizing the medicinal ingredients he'd purchased. In all, it had cost him an entire 405 gold pieces. As for the room itself, it cost twenty gold per day—he'd paid for five consecutive days to avoid potential sabotage by Marcus.

It's a good thing that the Ten Thousand Poison Canon contains methods on potency enhancement. But still, how many of these poisons will end up working?

The Ten Thousand Poison Canon was an encyclopedia of poisons and naturally contained recipes for all manner of poisons. Concocting these low-level poisons also didn't require much skill. The temperature control and ingredient nurturing skills often used by alchemists didn't matter as much when one was hyper-concentrating ingredients and blending them in the simplest of fashions.

In all, Sorin had enough ingredients to make fourteen intermediate one-star poisons. The first step to refining these poisons was extraction and preliminary enhancement. Sorin used his experience with the Cockatrice Grass extract and expanded it to the forty-seven reagents he'd acquired.

There were only ten beakers and ten regular heating stations. Since the purity and potency requirements for these poisons were high, Sorin spent a whole sleepless day producing 156 tubes of reagents that had undergone preliminary enhancement.

He then rested for half a day before moving on to the next phase: merging and enhancement. Sorin took two vials, one violet and one blue, and brought them over to the rat-powered heating array. He placed a small alchemical cauldron atop the stand and poured in one vial, then used his spiritual force to command the spell circle to increase the temperature to 365 degrees.

The violet ingredient was called Thistlehorn Paralytic extract, and its boiling point was just above 365 degrees. Sorin maintained the temperature for twenty minutes, giving the mixture just enough time to nourish itself with the rat flame. He then poured the other vial of poison into a small dropping funnel and began adding in the Blue Demonic Mayflower extract drop by drop, carefully adjusting the flame as a sickly yellow poison formed on the bottom of the cauldron.

Thirty minutes later, Sorin was left with one ten-milliliter vial of Coldblood Poison. It was a bright yellow poison that would turn clear and odorless when mixed with water but sweet and tangy when mixed with something caffeinated, like tea or coffee.

"One down, thirteen to go," muttered Sorin, setting the vial on an empty rack.

Sorin spent the next two days mixing and blending poisons. His days were so busy that he ate only field rations and slept in the workshop cot.

In the end, he failed to mix three of the poisons, leaving him with only eleven vials of deadly one-star toxins. Some could be added to weapons like daggers or arrows, while others had to be slipped into food or drink. Two of these poisons were even contact poisons that could put a person into anaphylactic shock with only the slightest skin contact.

Sorin stared at the eleven vials with trepidation. As a physician, he knew all too well how terrible one's fate would be if one ingested any single one of these poisons. *But here I am, prepared to drink all of them.*

There was still a day and a half left on his rental contract, and Sorin, still unsure of how Marcus would react to the disappearance of his medicinal reagents and his earth flames, decided to cultivate in the workshop for the remaining time.

"Well," Sorin said to Lorimer. "If I die, don't you dare eat my body. Bottom's up!" He broke the cork on the vial of Coldblood Poison and downed the entire contents. It went down his throat like a glass full of razor-sharp ice shards and slowed his heartbeat down to a crawl. Sorin's body temperature plummeted, and within seconds, he entered a near-death state.

This state of suspended animation continued for several hours. Then... warmth. Just enough to grab the second vial of poison called Innard-Scorching Life Syrup. Ironically, it was a medicine that could be used in small amounts to kill parasites in the intestinal tract and stomach.

The second poison infused Sorin with a current of energy. He used the sudden burst of life to drink the third vial containing Living Dead Serum, a strange poison that was sometimes used in underground gambling dens and would give the drinker a 50 percent chance at life and a 50 percent chance at death.

The addition of the third poison brought the first two poisons into equilibrium. With the three poisons somewhat under control, Sorin was able to mobilize his five poisons to devour them bit by bit.

The five poisons grew stronger, and a sixth poison lacking any of their properties appeared in their midst. It rapidly grew as the remainder of the three poisons was devoured until, finally, the poison established itself as an equal partner in Sorin's body.

Sorin's blood surged. His primary meridians circulated aggressively to provide the massive amounts of mana the poison required. And when there wasn't enough, Sorin was forced to crack open a fourth vial containing Bloodberry Tongue-Exploding Poison; it didn't even get a chance to act on him before the sixth poison pounced on it and assimilated it.

This final dose was exactly what Sorin needed to break through. His body transformed, and his ten primary organs were strengthened. As for the four hidden meridians that Sorin had previously unblocked, their bottlenecks loosened slightly.

Invigorated by his success and knowing that time was not his friend, Sorin directly took in two more vials of poison. It took an hour for them to reach equilibrium, after which he directly drank the remaining poisons, pushing himself once again to the brink of death.

There were two ways to break through quickly in the cultivation world—one was combat, which poked at death like one might poke at a sleeping bear with a stick, while the other was putting oneself in a true life-and-death situation.

According to Sorin's calculations, he had a 90 percent chance to live and a 10 percent chance to die. A 10 percent chance might seem small, but it wore away at his limitations like a grindstone and forced his body to either accept the poisons or perish.

Unfortunately, the six poisons in his body were unable to react quickly enough to subdue the seven poisons Sorin pitted them against. His body became a warzone. His flesh necrotized, and his internal organs teetered on the brink of failure. Neither side wanted to give in, and it was his body that paid the price.

Did I move too quickly? Should I have waited a little longer before pushing forward?

No, he decided. The others had broken through to the eighth stage of Blood-Thickening after their return. The eighth stage was a dividing line that would greatly strengthen one's abilities. The only way to not get left behind was to break through quickly. *But if these poisons don't behave, I'm really going to end up dying.*

Sorin opened his bloodshot eyes and focused on Lorimer, who was nibbling at a flask in the corner of the room. "Lorimer!" Sorin whispered to the rat in a ragged voice. "Get over here and roast me!" The rat squeaked and ran over, and to Sorin's surprise, it began sending a stream of what appeared to be insults and expletives. "No, you idiot! I want you to use your earth flame to scorch my mana!"

A ball of poison appeared in Sorin's hand. It contained his original six poisons and seven other streams of energy that were slowly devouring them. Neither side wanted to concede, making Sorin the greatest loser in the exchange.

"Quickly!" he whispered. Lorimer, bound by his slave seal, could only comply.

A gentle stream of earth flame floated toward the ball of poison and attacked it. It could not differentiate between the six original poisons and seven new poisons, so most of either group was annihilated.

"Again!" called out Sorin.

He pulled mana from his blood to increase the size of the mana blob. All thirteen poisons were reinforced by the infusion, enabling them to resist the earth flame once again. The flame came in waves that repeatedly tempered Sorin's mana, increasing its quality.

As for the thirteen poisons, they began to show signs of reconciliation. They began cooperating to fight against Lorimer's earth flames. Eventually, they reached a tipping point where one of the poisons defected and joined the original group of six. Then, using the earth flame as an external stimulant, they devoured the remaining six poisons and used them to temper and strengthen themselves.

"Stop!" a half-dead Sorin finally said. Lorimer grumbled as he pulled back his earth flame and returned to the half-eaten beaker. As for Sorin, he didn't bother stopping the rat and instead focused on his internal condition.

His blood broke through and thickened once again, bringing him to the seventh stage of Blood-Thickening. His poison became a seven-poison fusion that was not only much stronger than the original six-poison blend but also attacked the mana blockages in his extraordinary meridians.

MYSTERIOUS MARKINGS

Four dams simultaneously burst open inside Sorin's body, almost doubling the speed of mana circulation. The four extraordinary meridians Sorin had opened before his cultivation was crippled were instantly restored.

Strictly speaking, these meridians didn't occupy any individual acupoints. Instead, they were new circulation paths between existing points. They were, therefore, called vessels and served to store and circulate mana, among other things.

The four pathways were respectively called the Yin Link Vessel, the Yang Link Vessel, the Yin Heel Vessel, and the Yang Heel Vessel. The Yin and Yang Heel Vessels governed the legs and would increase Sorin's explosive speed by nearly twofold. It was a useless ability for a physician, but for an adventurer, it was crucial. Thanks to these unblocked vessels, his movement speed might even exceed Lawrence's if he didn't use techniques.

The Yin and Yang Link Vessels were much more subtle in their application. They didn't directly improve Sorin's mana flow but instead allowed his mana, spiritual strength, and physical strength to join together and harmonize. This ability had been his bread and butter back when he was a physician and would now allow him to apply his abnormally high spiritual strength in battle.

Sorin spent the next few hours acclimatizing himself to his new condition. His roiling blood calmed down, and the mana circulating in his body changed several times. Soon enough, all the weaker mana in his body was forced out to make room for denser mana, which he stored in his abnormally thick blood.

He'd just broken through two middle stages of the Blood-Thickening Realm in quick succession, yet his foundation was just as stable as ever. This was because his body had originally reached the tenth stage of Blood-Thickening. Yet, thanks to the Ten Thousand Poison Canon, the degree of transformation his body experienced in the Blood-Thickening Realm was much greater. Whether it be in strength, speed, regeneration, or mana abilities, he was superior in every way to his past self.

It was only once his body calmed down that Sorin took stock of his current cultivation. He formed spheres of mana that he manipulated with his fingers and much larger mana needles than before. Previously, Sorin had needed a physical medium like a crystal needle to force his poisonous mana into a usable form. Now, he would be able to throw out poison needles all day long, as long as he didn't over-exert himself.

After the mana manipulation tests came a thorough inspection of his body. His mana quality was much higher than it had been the last time he cultivated to this realm. Thanks to the corrosive nature of his mana, it flowed without restriction. As a result, he could inspect every inch of flesh in his body, including the various blood vessels in his internal organs.

Yin organs are clear and functional, thought Sorin, working his way through a mental list. *Yang organs are clean and functional. Arm, leg, and torso blood vessels are unimpeded. Minor clots have been rectified. Blood flow in the neck and skull is unimpeded.*

Normally, the process would stop here, but thanks to the increase in Sorin's mana quality, he was able to see the surface of his bones, along with several 'nodes' that would become clearer as his cultivation increased. Sorin had no interest in these nodes since they would only be useful in the Bone-Forging Realm, but as he quickly inspected them, he noticed something strange on the bone in his ribcage.

What the... Sorin's spiritual senses fused with his mana and rubbed against the bone, 'cleaning' it in such a way that he could more clearly see it. And what he saw caused his jaw to drop. *Is that... writing?* He'd never seen anything so strange on a skeleton in his life. Golden lettering, metallic in appearance but completely fused with his bone matter, had appeared on his ribcage.

What's more, the writing made sense to him. He'd seen the style before, inside the Kepler Clan's Divine Medical Codex.

If Sorin could choose a single thing to have an abundance of, it would be knowledge. Knowledge was the gift that kept on giving and the resource that would never betray you or diminish in value. He, therefore, got straight to work and cleaned off his bones to expose the text in full.

Only his rib cage had been imprinted with golden lettering, but thanks to the dense information conveyance methods of the Kepler Clan, such a small amount of text was enough to deliver monstrous amounts of information.

At first, the information made no sense to Sorin. Most of it came in the form of numbers and included tables and category references. Yet Sorin soon realized that these weren't just tables of numbers but actual research data, codified and organized according to the Kepler Clan's strict conventions.

Moreover, their originator was shocking. It was the ancestor of the Kepler Clan, Sirius Abberjay Kepler, who had compiled these tables. He had also included extensive notes as to their collection and contents.

Unfortunately, Sorin's joy was short-lived because he soon realized that this data had to come from somewhere. His gaze turned frosty as he realized that the taboo of all taboos for medical practitioners had been inscribed on his very bones. Human experiments, tens of thousands of them, had been required for their completion.

Sorin wanted to look away, but he was unable to keep his eyes from the glowing text. And the more he read, the more horrified he became. *So the Kepler Clan's top-secret meridian clearing method came from here,* thought Sorin as he memorized the text. A method was inscribed for all twelve primary meridians and seven of the eight extraordinary meridians.

A memory came to Sorin unbidden. It was a memory filled with unbearable pain and medical reagents specially administered by his father as he lay strapped down on an operating table. Sorin had been born with twelve naturally unblocked primary meridians and two unblocked extraordinary meridians, but thanks to his father's tender 'care,' witnessed entirely by his lucid self, Sorin had been able to open two more.

One reason Sorin hadn't broken through to the Bone-Forging Realm all those years before was that he'd been waiting for his father to open more of his extraordinary meridians. Unfortunately, his father's death had upset these plans, and his cultivation had been destroyed in the aftermath.

Unblocking the twelve main meridians isn't difficult using these methods, thought Sorin. *But the seven extraordinary meridians all require a special concoction. The primary ingredient is difficult to find and must be used in all seven concoctions.*

Another thing that shocked Sorin was that these clearly weren't medicinal concoctions. They were all violent poisons that would kill a cultivator with the slightest mistake in their application. And the worst part yet, he knew exactly how many people had died to deliver these results: 23,506.

He wanted to throw these results away. He wanted them gone. Yet try as he might, he couldn't put them out of his head. Like much of the medical practices developed over the years, these things built upon atrocities were not inherently evil. It was the methods that were awful and that Sorin could never, in good conscience, partake in.

Sirius Abberjay Kepler's research was built on a mountain of corpses, and yet the Kepler Clan never disseminated it to the public. In that case, it falls to me to rectify this mistake. I'll get to the bottom of these experiments and exactly why they were engraved on my bones. If the Kepler Clan is destroyed as a result, so be it.

So many people had died to develop a potential unlocking method that the Kepler Clan had then locked down. It was this lockdown that allowed the Kepler Clan to wield oversized influence over the Medical Association and all the noble families that relied on it.

Having made his decision, Sorin turned his attention back to the meridian-opening method. Many of the ingredients he saw were things that had gone extinct following the Cataclysmic Emergence of the Eight Evils and the demise of the gods of Mount Olympus.

But the main ingredient still existed. Sorin had seen it in the Divine Medical Codex and the Ten Thousand Poison Canon. It wasn't so uncommon and could actually be found in Bloodwood Forest if one were lucky to find it.

Manabane Poison. A poison that, if ingested or injected into a Blood-Thickening cultivator's body, would make its way into their mana sea and cripple their cultivation. Ironically, it was this same poison that had crippled his cultivation following the death of his parents.

Manabane Poison was also a one-star poison and was technically compatible with the Ten Thousand Poison Canon. If he could channel its properties, it could unlock up to three more of his extraordinary meridians. He might even be able to do the same for others.

Noticing that the number seven was mentioned once again, Sorin looked for any references on unblocking the eighth meridian. But all that he found was a note at the end of the text. The eighth extraordinary meridian was impossible to unblock. The exact reasons for this were unknown. According to Sirius Abberjay Kepler, research into the 'divine lock' restricting human potential had been forbidden by the now-dead gods.

It wasn't until several hours later that Sorin finally calmed down. Dawn arrived at the Bloodwood Outpost, and with the familiar change in humidity that accompanied the rising sun came a knock on the door and a jingling of keys.

"You can come in," said Sorin, picking himself off the ground.

"Everything is clean and in good order. I…" His voice trailed off as he saw that the laboratory was a mess of chewed-up and broken glassware.

"Great," said Henry, opening the door. "And here I was afraid you'd lost track of the time." His eyes bulged when he saw the carnage in the lab. "*This* is what you call clean and in good order?"

Sorin cleared his throat. "I don't suppose you'll need the whole 100 gold damage deposit to fix this, would you?"

"Out!" shouted a red-faced Henry. "Get out! You're banned! Never step foot in this guild again!"

CLUE

It took the better part of an hour for Sorin to convince Henry *not* to ban him for life. "I'm really sorry about this, Henry," Sorin reiterated as he added twenty more gold coins onto the counter. "It won't happen again. I promise."

"You're lucky there was no earth flame in the room and that all the spell circles were intact," said Henry with a growl. "Otherwise, you wouldn't be able to pay for these damages even if you sold yourself!"

In the end, Sorin was left with less than thirty gold coins to his name. Most of that was needed to fix his slashed-up leather armor and to purchase rations. On the bright side, Lorimer was somewhat satiated from eating the expensive glassware. He expressed that he wouldn't need to eat for the next twenty-four hours.

"What am I going to do with you?" muttered Sorin as he petted the rat on his shoulder. "You're not just a glutton—you're a worse trouble-maker than I am."

"Rats," said Henry, shuddering. "Well, it's not the first rat familiar I've seen. At least tell me you ended up concocting something that works?"

"Unfortunately not," answered Sorin. "I might specialize in poison, but it's just as difficult a field as alchemy in some respects."

"Especially without an earth flame," said Henry with a nod. "It's just not possible to infuse enough mana into reagents without one or to catalyze many of the reactions." Sorin grimaced but said nothing to contradict him.

Having spent so long in seclusion, Sorin paid a quick visit to the Kepler Manor and assured Percival and Clarice that he was all right. He also popped by the Adventurers Guild and was told he should come by the next morning for news on a potentially lucrative mission.

That didn't leave much time for repairing his armor, so Sorin was forced to cough up eighteen of his gold coins for a rush job and to replace the belt loops with more durable mithril ones. His funds shrank down to a sad ten gold coins, two of which he used to buy rations.

It was just after sundown when Sorin's armor was completed. After inspecting the leatherworker's craftsmanship and confirming that everything was fine, he packed up the armor and made his way toward the outskirts of the outpost where the Kepler Manor was located.

It was dark out, and the air was getting chillier. Winter would be coming earlier this year, or so the weather mages said.

Sorin was only a dozen blocks away from the manor when he felt a flash of killing intent. He looked around with his peripheral vision and saw that there were five other people in the street aside from himself. Most of the storefronts had already closed for the day.

Yet despite the lack of traffic, these five slowly got up and walked up beside him. A streetlamp fizzled and dimmed overhead, followed closely by a second, then a third.

Sorin bolted the moment the hooded figure closest to him swung his arm. He barely avoided the man's dagger, only to come face to face with another assailant's sword. Sorin used Adder Rush and his unblocked Yin and Yang Heel Vessels to avoid the blade, then grabbed the cultivator's wrist and slammed a palm into his chest, infusing it with poison.

He then threw the cultivator over his head at the other four, who were attacking him with bladed weapons. They caught their companion and quickly encircled Sorin once again. Their auras were tightly concealed, and their faces were masked, but Sorin knew exactly who had sent them.

"How much does it cost to pay a bunch of rogue cultivators like you to kill physicians anyway?" said Sorin, hoping to stall for time. "Fifty gold apiece? A hundred? Three hundred? Bad deal, if you ask me. Your life is much more precious."

"If you think help is coming, you're dead wrong," said what appeared to be the leader of the group with a garbled voice. "Throw down your dagger and come with us, and I promise that you will not be harmed."

Sorin laughed. "Sorry, I've already fallen for that one already."

"Then you can die," said the speaker calmly. Shadows stretched out from around the man and covered his four black-cloaked accomplices. They covered the street in darkness and blotted out all sources of lamplight and moonlight.

Suddenly, Sorin was fighting blind. The only way he had to track their movements was through their padded footsteps and the whistles of air that accompanied their swords and daggers. Sorin used Adder Rush to evade their attacks, but their blades still caught flesh. It wasn't long before his clothing was soaked in blood.

I need to keep moving, thought Sorin as he dashed about and twisted, only to take a dagger cut to the rib cage. He struck back with a poisoned dagger, only to discover that his foe was long gone.

I need to wait, thought Sorin as damage continued to pile up. *I'll only get one chance at surprising them with this.* His posture gradually deteriorated until, finally, his spiritual senses picked up a murderous intent from behind him. *Now!*

Sorin fell to the ground and used his powerful legs to launch himself in that same direction. His body collided with a surprised assassin, and his lightning-fast hands stabbed a mithril dagger into the man's torso and infused it with poison.

Flesh melted around the wound. The man's internal organs seized up. His body twitched three times before he fell to the ground, dead.

Sorin put his hand to his side as he readied himself for their follow-up. He'd taken out his opponent, but another assassin had knifed him in the process. He slowly pulled a dagger out of his intestines and used a dose of Flesh-Melt Poison to glue the wound closed and staple the cut on his torso shut.

He'd just staunched the bleeding when three more sources of killing intent fired off from three different directions. Sorin bolted between these sources and threw out a mithril string with paralytic poison at one of them. An assassin yelled as he fell to the ground, but the two remaining assassins were joined by a third, much slower opponent. It would be impossible to evade them.

"Lorimer! Light!" Sorin yelled. A glowing rat appeared on his shoulder and illuminated the nearest ten feet. He quickly located the originator of the shadow technique and launched himself at him using Adder Rush.

The man reacted, interposing his sword between himself and Sorin. Yet, to his horror, Sorin only slightly adjusted his trajectory and took a sword through his liver. In exchange, he stuck a dagger into the man's heart and took his life.

"Lorimer, get them!" shouted Sorin as he pulled away from the man. The rat shot out at the nearest assassin without hesitation and, to the assassin's horror, bit a large chunk out of his throat.

The last assassin, seeing that he was clearly outmatched, tried to make a run for it. But Lorimer was fast and took a bite out of his leg. The assassin tripped, and Lorimer took a bite out of his throat, slaying the fourth assassin in three seconds flat.

"Keep him alive," Sorin said when Lorimer went to finish off the paralyzed assassin tangled up in mithril string. "No, wait. It's too late." The assassin, realizing that the situation was bad for him, had somehow taken a dose of poison despite his paralyzed state. Blood was leaking out of his eyes and nose.

They were dead. Five humans who had tried to kill him had died. It was only when the moment was over that Sorin realized he'd fully crossed the line between physician and adventurer. To slay demons was understandable, even *commendable.* But to slay humans, even if they *were* trying to kill you… it was something you didn't forget.

Sorin felt both loathsome and indignant. He hadn't been going out of his way to take the lives of people, but people had thrown themselves at him. Whoever had sent them was extremely sinister. Even failing would affect Sorin's disposition and reputation as a physician.

"Lorimer, stand guard," Sorin instructed. Life preservation came first. He gritted his teeth and pulled out the sword in his liver. He groaned as the sword inevitably cut through extra flesh on its way out but relied on his powerful spirit to remain conscious as the sword came free and clattered to the ground.

Sorin's vision swam from the blood loss. He reached his fingers inside his body, found the major blood vessels that had been severed, and once again melted them together. Several minutes passed as he carefully sewed the remaining wounds. A healing potion would have greatly helped, but Sorin didn't have one.

It was only when he finished the last of his stitching that he heard armored footsteps. "Lorimer, return," croaked Sorin. He then stood up and looked at the group of guards who'd just arrived. His expression fell when he saw that these guards had their weapons drawn, and their eyes were filled with malice.

"Sorin Kepler, you are under arrest for the murder of these five people!" yelled their captain.

"Are you insane?" said Sorin coldly. "I was attacked by five cloaked people with masks in broad daylight, and you're saying I murdered them?"

"What you say doesn't matter," said the leader of the guards. "You will come with us, and we will perform our own investigation. If you are guilt-free as you claim, we will naturally free you."

He moved to arrest Sorin, but the man held up his poisoned dagger and glared at the guard. "I'm afraid I won't be going with you. In fact, I suspect you've been paid to collaborate with these assassins."

"You dare accuse us of something so treacherous?" yelled the guard. "Kill him! That's poison! He's resisting arrest with lethal force!"

Sorin sent a mental message to Lorimer and told him to prepare for battle. His instincts told him that should he land in their hands, he'd be as good as dead.

The guards spread around him and then tightened their encirclement. They were much better armed than the assassins and also wore armor. Killing them all in his wounded state would be impossible.

"You guys keep him busy, and I'll go in for the kill," instructed the captain. He raised his sword and was about to charge when suddenly, a dagger flew through the air and stabbed him in the hand.

The guard captain screamed. His sword dropped to the floor as he fell to his knees, clutching his bloody hand. "What are you all waiting for?!" he yelled. "Kill him!"

The guards prepared to attack Sorin, but it was then that footstep sounded out from a nearby alley. Every step was filled with an unfathomable pressure that froze the guards in their tracks. "By all means, *try* and kill him. Don't let little old me stop you." It was the most wonderful voice Sorin had ever heard in his life. Haley York's. "Anyone who wants a dagger to the hand can go ahead and attack him. I won't discriminate."

Assessor Haley made her way out of the shadows and stood by Sorin. "You look dreadful, Sorin. Why in Hope's name would you take a sword to the gut with your speed?"

"To kill my enemies faster and hedge against unknown variables," answered Sorin, still clutching his gut. "Like these guys." He looked around worriedly. "Is this going to escalate?"

"Most definitely," said Haley. "But the Adventurers Guild doesn't let its people get pushed around. By the way, drink this."

Sorin accepted a healing potion from Haley and drank it without hesitation. It was a high-grade potion that immediately got to work, healing the damage to his internal organs. Normally, potions wouldn't be able to heal such injuries, but Sorin was more python than human in that regard. By the time the potion was fully spent, all but the shallowest cuts on his body were fully healed.

They didn't need to wait long before a group of twenty guards came pouring into the street. They circled Sorin and Haley with weapons drawn and parted for their commander. A dreadful pressure weighed down on Sorin, but it only lasted a split second before a similar pressure came oozing out of Haley and pushed it back.

"Haley York," said the tall and imposing guard commander. "You've got a lot of guts."

"It seems my guts are lacking compared to yours," said Haley. "Now tell me how you want to die, or I'll pick for you."

31

KNIVES IN THE DARK

"You're saying I should tell *you* how *I* want to die?" mocked the guard commander. "Look at where you are, Miss York. This is the Bloodwood Outpost, not Ephesus."

"If this were Ephesus, you wouldn't so much as look at me the wrong way," answered Haley. "But you're right. I *am* far away from home. But that also means I don't need to be so inhibited when I pull out your guts and cut up your bones."

"Who will be cutting up whom remains to be seen," said the guard commander. "Your man killed five innocent people and resisted arrest. That's a grave offense."

"One of our guild members gets attacked in the street by a group of assassins, your guards call him a criminal without an investigation and try to kill him, and it's called resisting arrest?" retorted Haley. "What sort of bird-shit logic is that?"

"All I know is that my guards are all carefully screened cultivators under the direction of the governor," said the guard commander. "To question them is to question the governor."

"If you want to go tell the governor about this, Zenol, be my guest," Haley said sarcastically.

"Are you making light of the governor?" asked Commander Zenol. "Because that's a worse offense than resisting arrest."

"You know that I would never dare do such a thing," said Haley. "But to be clear, my man did nothing wrong. The fact that these five are wearing cloaks and masks and attacked him when there was no one around is ample evidence. Unless you're going to tell me that he happened to attack five cloaked and masked men of his own initiative."

Commander Zenol grunted. "Even if that's the case, he should have gone with the guards so they could perform an investigation."

"He was simply waiting for a guild representative to accompany him," said Haley. "It was *your* people who decided to force the matter and attack him."

"He didn't mention anything about the Adventurers Guild when we attacked him!" shouted the man with the dagger in his hand, only to realize he'd misspoken.

"So you *did* attack him," said Haley. "Well, that's a problem, see. The correct course of action would have been to surround him and call on the Adventurers Guild to mediate."

A loud snort sounded out from a neighboring street. A group of cultivators in alchemist robes emerged. "How typical of your Adventurers Guild," said a man who, just like Haley and Zenol, had reached the Bone-Forging Realm. His robes were embroidered with the symbol of the Alchemists Guild, along with two golden stars. "I'm not surprised. It doesn't change wherever I go. Your lot thinks you can get away with anything and use martial might to suppress the local law enforcement teams."

"Oh? And what brings you here, Alchemist Avery?" asked Haley. "What a small place this outpost is. I suppose you were just out on a walk with most of your senior guild members?"

"Don't speak nonsense, Haley," said Avery. "How could us old timers *not* sense it when Bone-Forging auras clash?"

"I couldn't agree more," said another voice. Unlike the ones who'd arrived before, the speaker's arrival caused the mana in the air to ripple. The speaker was a lone man in simple mage's robes. He walked up to

Haley and stood beside her. "Pardon for arriving so late and so alone, but this scuffle took me a bit by surprise. Otherwise, I would have emptied the guild to cause an even uproar."

"Why don't we all take a step back?" came the voice of a fifth Bone-Forging cultivator. A handsome, caped man in gold and silver armor came walking down the street. He wore a gleaming golden sword at his side but didn't bother unsheathing it. Out of all those present, he was clearly the strongest.

"A step back?" asked Haley flatly. "A bunch of people tried to kill one of my members, but the outpost guard—the *governor's* people—didn't try to find justice for him and instead tried to silence him. To ask us to take a step back shows how lacking your entire team is, Allan."

The man's smile twitched slightly, but he maintained his friendly demeanor. "Shouldn't you address me as Vice Governor, Miss York?"

"No, I don't think I will," said Haley. "Don't take it personally; I just can't respect a man who relies on his father to obtain his position." Her words wiped the smile off the vice governor's face.

"Then let's get down to business, shall we?" said the vice governor. He looked at the dead assassins and snorted. "These are clearly hired killers. Have your guards no shame?"

Sorin's eyes narrowed. It seemed they'd really come prepared if they were going to give up on the assassins and the guards immediately.

"Apologies, Vice Governor Marsh," said Commander Zenol. "I will strictly discipline my people on this matter and will not pursue the matter of Miss York assaulting my men."

Haley snorted. "You think they can try killing my person and get off with a slap on the wrist?"

"With all due respect, Miss York, this matter is unclear," said Vice Governor Marsh. "Moreover, a knife to the hand is hardly a slap on the wrist."

"Fine," said Haley. "If that's how you want to play it, let's play. Come along, Sorin."

"Not so fast," said Commander Zenol. "There is a separate matter that needs investigating. Physician Marcus recently reported that an earth flame was stolen and listed Sorin Kepler as the prime suspect."

"How surprising," said Sorin to the commander. "Marcus's grudge against me is well known, as is the conflict with my family. Am I to become a suspect just because he throws my name out? Tell me, did you see me anywhere near his clinic when the theft occurred?"

The commander's expression turned icy. "This isn't the place for a Blood-Thickening whelp to speak."

"So, by your logic, the accused can't even defend themselves?" retorted Haley. "This is exactly why our guild insists on representation before law enforcement."

To Sorin's surprise, the vice governor nodded. "Indeed, it is," he said. "And we're thankful for your presence. I think such an accusation is dubious at best."

"Nonsense!" yelled Alchemist Avery. "He clearly has an earth flame!"

"Oh?" said Vice Governor Marsh. "And how would you know that?"

"Because this man rented a flameless one-star workshop from my guild and caused a ruckus!" said Alchemist Avery. "I received a report earlier this morning and rushed over to investigate. To my surprise, I discovered the aura of an earth flame. I put it out of my mind because it didn't seem to matter, but given this surprising report of earth flame thefts from Physician Marcus, I can't, in good conscience, *not* speak up."

Haley eyed Sorin. "Is this true, Sorin?"

"I'm afraid this is all a big misunderstanding," replied Sorin.

"What do you mean, a misunderstanding?" pressed Alchemist Avery. "I am a two-star alchemist and couldn't possibly be mistaken about the aura of an earth flame."

"That's not what I was talking about," said Sorin. "I *do* have an earth flame." Then, seeing Haley's expression fall, he amended his statement. "But it's actually a *beast* flame, not a proper earth flame you were speaking of."

"A beast flame," said the alchemist flatly. "I find that very hard to believe. Beast flames are extremely rare and difficult to harvest."

Haley, however, suddenly seemed to realize something. "Are you saying the Rat King you tamed, the one the guards saw you bring back, the one you tamed in the Temple of Hope recently, can actually produce a beast flame?"

"Indeed it can," said Sorin. "Lorimer, show them." A rat crawled out of Sorin's ruined coat and jumped onto the paving stones. His entire body lit up with orange-red flames. "While it's not strictly an earth flame, its properties are nearly identical. So I can see why this would cause confusion."

The alchemist was dumbfounded, and so was the vice governor. As for Haley, she could hardly suppress a laugh and patted Sorin on the shoulder. "How lucky you are, finding something even alchemists dream they had. A living earth flame!"

"I personally find it extremely suspicious," said Commander Zenol. "Why did he not reveal this earth flame when he discovered it?"

"Yes, because every cultivator reveals all their secrets," said Haley, rolling her eyes. "So what do you say? Are you going to continue insisting on this dubious charge or drop it?"

"There's still the matter of practicing medicine without a license!" started Commander Zenol, but the vice governor cut him off.

"The guild responded to an emergency shortage out of their own pocket, and by not speaking on the matter, the Governor's Manor implicitly approved of their actions," said Vice Governor Marsh. "So yes, Assessor Haley, this matter ends here. You can all scatter and return to where you came from."

With that, he turned around and walked off. The remaining guards dragged away the wounded guard and the assassins' bodies. Doubtless, their investigation into these people would yield no results.

"Thank you for your support, Vice Guild Master Thomas," Haley said to the friendly mage who'd come to support them.

"It's no problem, Assessor Haley," said the vice master of the Mages Guild. "Those fellows are always so overbearing. Us reasonable people need to have each other's backs. "He eyed Sorin's rat, then looked at Sorin with an expression of surprise. "You should send that lad over to study with us sometime. He's quite the oddity, mana-wise, don't you think?"

"Don't you dare steal him from me," said Haley. "He belongs to our guild, not yours."

"There are no conflicts between our guilds, and people are often members of both guilds at the same time. Anyone who wishes to learn spellcraft is welcome within our halls."

Sorin coughed lightly. "I'll pay a visit when I have time," he said diplomatically.

"Then I'll be looking forward to your visit," said the vice guild leader. "Since that's everything, Haley, I'll be off. Be sure to keep your guard up. The Kepler Clan's really kicked the hornet's nest this time around."

"You have a lot of guts renting a workshop in the Alchemists Guild, given your current situation," said Haley to Sorin when the vice guild leader was gone. "I have to wonder—are you an idiot or just desperate? You should know that the Alchemists Guild and the Medical Association are in bed with each other on every level."

"I guess I underestimated how deeply the connection ran," said Sorin, shaking his head. "I assumed it was a business alliance. But it seems it's closer to marriage instead."

"Business and politics are inseparable in this world, Sorin," said Haley. "As you can see, even the supposedly neutral governor has conflicting interests with the various organizations."

"It seems I was still a bit too naive," said Sorin. "Many thanks for your help, Assessor Haley. I would have died without your intervention."

"I didn't step in because it was you," said Haley. "I'd stand up for any one of our members in this situation. Alchemists and physicians can be insufferably arrogant at times, and the local governor's disposition has only made things worse."

"Still, I appreciate it," said Sorin. "And you can rest assured about my condition. I'll be sure to come by in the morning."

"Don't even think about taking off," said Haley. "Come over to the guild and sleep there. There are beds aplenty, and they're much safer than the ones in your manor."

Sorin's heart warmed at the consideration. "Then I'll be troubling you, Assessor Haley."

"It's like I said," said Haley. "Don't worry about it. The Adventurers Guild looks after their own."

32

'ARCHEOLOGY'

Sorin woke the following day to the ticking of an old clock. The room smelled like a wet bar rag, and the bed he'd slept on had squeaked all night. He groaned as he picked himself up and felt the wound on his torso. Only a thin scar remained of the stab wound he'd taken to the liver a half-day prior.

I killed five people yesterday, thought Sorin as he traced the wound and pieced together his memories from the night before. Though his heart was in turmoil, Sorin's practiced mind slipped back into his usual thought patterns. No matter what the Medical Association said, no matter how much blood he had on his hands, he *was* a physician. Physicians had to be cold and objective when assessing patients.

Internal organs are completely healed and in good repair, thought Sorin as he worked through a mental checklist. *Mana circulation is unimpeded. All sixteen unblocked meridians are functioning as normal. Muscle tissue is slightly stiff and in need of stretching and exercise. Skin is scarred over, but interference with day-to-day movements will be minimal. Recommendations: soft tissue massage hourly for the next half-day and moderate exercise until full function is restored.*

Sorin performed said massage, then got out of bed to perform a series of movements designed to limber up old and atrophied patients.

Multiple cycles of stretching and compression released any residual stiffness from his injuries, restored his strength, and loosened up his internal organs so that they could resume normal functioning.

By the time he was done, it was 8:21 in the morning. According to Haley, the guild announcement was at nine, giving him plenty of time to meet up with his companions and have a quick breakfast.

The Adventurer's Pub was packed full of people when Sorin arrived. The bartender was off duty, but the cooks were busy in the back preparing a generous breakfast for the many adventurers awaiting the announcement. Sorin's teammates were munching on their respective breakfasts when he arrived.

"I heard about what happened last night," said Stephan as Sorin pulled up a chair. "Getting mugged isn't pleasant. Clashing with the guard afterward isn't great either."

"It sounds like you have experience with this sort of thing," said Sorin, grabbing a menu.

"All the factions like throwing around their weight in my hometown. Brawls aren't uncommon, and many of them are instigated. There's also sham adventurers, crooked magistrates, and assassins aplenty."

"Where's Lorimer?" asked Lawrence, shoving a piece of ham into his mouth. "I hear he's the rat of the hour. Took out two muggers by himself."

"Unfortunately, rats are not welcome inside the Adventurers Guild," said Sorin. "I told him to go scrounging if he wanted something to eat. Speaking of which, I'll have the Super Adventurers Breakfast. Triple Hungry Edition."

"You sure?" asked the waitress, accepting his menu. "No offense, Mr. Kepler, but you don't *quite* look like you can put it away."

"I'm sure," said Sorin, slapping fifteen silvers on the table. "A coffee, too, if you don't mind. From the bottom of the pot if possible."

Several minutes later, Sorin's pale complexion had recovered its original rosiness. His digestive system was working at full capacity, and Sorin could literally feel extra blood being generated inside his body to replenish what had been lost before.

"That hit the spot," said Sorin, looking up to find four adventurers watching him with concern in their eyes. "What? Did I do something wrong?"

"I mean... physically, it should be impossible for you to put away that much food in so little time," said Gareth. "Also, I think we saw your jaw dislocate and your throat bulge as you ate nearly an entire ham without chewing it. Tell me, should we be relieved or have the guild confirm that you're still human?"

"Huh," said Sorin. "Must be my snake aspect. Looks like there are more benefits than I expected. Daphne, are you writing down story ideas again?"

"You can ignore what doesn't hurt you," said Daphne, putting away a pen and notepad. "Also, that was disgusting. Half the bar was looking at you when it happened."

Sorin looked around to see that many people were indeed giving him strange looks. But Sorin was used to that kind of thing, so he put it out of his mind and sipped on his coffee, still piping hot. His mind sharpened, and what remained of the pain in his body faded into the background.

"Now that Sorin's done turning our stomachs, let's get back to the main topic," said Stephan. "I don't know much about the announcement, but rumor has it that a new ruin has been discovered."

"A ruin?" asked Daphne, looking up from her scribbling. "Pre-Emergence or Post-Emergence?"

"Pre-Emergence," said Stephan. "Which means that most of what we find will be useless, time-rotted garbage. That being said, the good things we *do* manage to find might be priceless artifacts."

"I didn't expect wishful thinking from you of all people," said Lawrence. Stephan scowled, but the man didn't back down. "What? Do you really think they'd release something with priceless treasures to one-star adventurers? New ruins always get assessed by the Temple of Hope before the Adventurers Guild gets called in. They'll assess the treasure level and difficulty level. You, of all people, should know that."

"By priceless treasures, I meant things that are currently not for sale," backpedaled Stephan. "I meant relics from the time before the Seven Evils almost destroyed humanity. There could even be long-lost spells and archaic skills." Daphne's eyes brightened at that. "According to my teachers, not even ten percent of humanity's cultivation methods survived the Cataclysmic Emergence. The only reason we managed to keep so many of these inheritances is because the Temple of Hope occasionally churns them out as prizes for adventurers. There are also the ruins that we occasionally discover and raid, such as the one they'll be announcing."

"If you're saying it'll be lucrative, I'm in," said Sorin. "I'm broke and have no better way to make money."

"If there's fun to be had, I'm game too," said Lawrence. "I'm a fan of grave robbing—I mean, *archeology*."

"Graverobbing is actually pretty accurate," said a voice, interrupting their conversation. It was a rough voice filled with authority that instantly hushed the handful of adventurers. A middle-aged man in light snakeskin leather walked into the room. At his side were Haley and a sharp-nosed man with golden eyes.

"They're all Bone-Forging experts," whispered Sorin.

"Two of them are, at least," muttered Stephan. Sorin's eyes narrowed as he realized that the one at the center, Guild Master Roy, had a much more subdued aura than the others. Sorin hadn't managed to sense this his last time meeting the guild master. Still, now that his extraordinary meridians had fully recovered, he could sense a faint pressure coming off the man that exceeded those of his assistants.

"I normally don't come out for these sorts of announcements," continued the guild master. "But graverobbing—or archeology, as our young friend Lawrence put it—is something our guild hasn't gotten to do in quite some time. I'm here to tell you that it's true. Ruins were discovered by a one-star adventuring team two weeks back; only one person returned alive, so Vice Guild Master Victor was dispatched to investigate along with a priest from the Temple of Hope.

"I'm pleased to announce that this ruin has been classified as a one-star ruin, a good level considering the cultivators our outpost produces.

The coordinates are available for purchase for a 500-gold fee per team, payable upon return of the expedition, a small price compared to each group's potential earnings. Yes, Silphia?"

"Will the ruin be protected by spell formations or trapped in any way?" asked a mage in bright green robes.

Guild Master Roy chuckled. "I actually have no idea. This is an unspoiled ruin, you see. Vice Guild Master Victor was only responsible for escorting the Priest of Hope. Only its difficulty level and treasure levels were determined. Yes, Mr. Wexler?"

A tall, burly man with a shield strapped to his back stood up. "Pardon, Guild Master, but I wanted to clarify: is the difficulty upper one star or lower one star?"

"Definitely upper," said the guild master. "Almost pushing in on the two-star level, which is why we recommend a large team raid it. Any other questions? Excellent. Then let the—"

The guild master's voice trailed off as he looked towards the entrance of the Adventurers Guild. The door creaked open, revealing a pleasant-looking man in physician robes. Sorin immediately recognized the man as Physician Marcus.

What's he doing here? thought Sorin.

"Physician Marcus," said Guild Master Roy with an obviously fake smile. "I don't recall inviting you to this announcement. To what do we owe the honor of your presence?"

"It's me who is honored by *your* presence, Guild Master," said Physician Marcus, looking about the room with a smile. His gaze lingered on Sorin for a few seconds before moving over the rest of the crowd and settling back onto the guild master. "I just thought I'd pay a visit, given the recent misunderstanding between the Medical Association and the Adventurers Guild."

"I'm not sure exactly what you mean," said Guild Master Roy. "The Adventurers Guild and the Medical Association have always had a positive and cooperative relationship."

"And that is exactly what I wish to re-iterate," said Physician Marcus. "Your guild has my personal assurance that regardless of the injuries or setbacks anyone suffers, the Growing Branches Clinic will not turn anyone down. Adventurers are the lifeblood of this outpost. Heroes who defend our growing civilization."

Guild Master Roy's smile slipped for a moment but recovered quickly. "I'm happy to hear you make such a guarantee. But I also hope that our adventurers will be more cautious and remember that while fighting demons is allowed, fighting amongst themselves is strictly prohibited."

"I meant no harm with my words," said Physician Marcus. "It is my humble wish that all our adventurers return in good health and good spirits."

"Of that, I have no doubt, Physician Marcus," said Guild Master Roy. "Will that be everything, or will you be taking a seat?"

"I won't take up your valuable time, Guild Master Roy," said Marcus. "If you or your adventurers require anything, please don't hesitate to ask." His gaze settled on Sorin one last time before he turned around and left the guild.

Guild Master Roy said a few more words before announcing the official release of the 'archeological mission.' All loot from the raid is the finders to keep, but everything will need to be assessed before being exchanged for rewards. Do note, however, that ample rewards have been posted for lost techniques, medicinal seeds, alchemical potions, and spell books, among other things. It is in everyone's best interest to have their loot appraised upon returning to the outpost."

"What a snake," said Sorin as the guild master left.

"Who? The Guild Master?" asked Lawrence.

"Physician Marcus, obviously," said Sorin. "The man basically begged everyone here to be reckless on this expedition."

"That's the Kepler Clan for you," said Stephan. "And most of the big clans, for that matter. Scheming and intraguild conflicts aside, is everyone for?" No one dissented, so Stephan went to register their team and obtained a map of the location of the ruins.

"That's a long way out," said Gareth, inspecting the map. "We'll need to carry weeks of provisions with us. Actually, fasting potions are probably the better option, considering weight limitations."

"I'm of the same mind," said Stephan. "Thoughts, anyone?"

"I'm fine with going directly to the ruin, but I was wondering if we could make a small detour," said Sorin. "There are poisons I'm looking to acquire, and there's a location where they can be found along the way, assuming we're going by boat. I'm sure that we'll find demon cores and other medicinal ingredients while we're at it."

"I'm pro diversifying our activities," said Gareth. "But it really depends on location."

Sorin placed a finger on the map, and Daphne groaned. "Really? Manabane Swamp?" she said. "You want to go there of all places?"

"It's the most likely place for me to find the poison I'm looking for," said Sorin. "Though I understand if you all don't want to go. Daphne's abilities would be of limited use in such a location."

"Who needs to blow things up when we can just sneak around and steal things?" said Lawrence. "I'm sure Sorin isn't suggesting we exterminate everything in the swamp for bounties. In and out, then onto the dungeon, right Sorin?"

"My thoughts exactly," answered Sorin.

"Manabane Swamp..." said Stephan, wincing. "It's not the best place to go, but if there's money to be made and demons to kill... All in favor?" Sorin, Gareth, and Lawrence raised their hands, but Stephan and Daphne did not. "Looks like the motion passes. But I agree with Lawrence. If we're going, we're not going to fight. There's no winning a war of attrition in a swamp."

"That's not a problem," said Sorin. "We can poke our nose in, and if we don't like what we're seeing, we'll turn the boat around."

"Then it's settled," said Stephan. "We'll spend a day making preparations. Gareth and Daphne, sort the boat out. Lawrence, you're with me on supply-gathering duty."

"What about me?" asked Sorin.

"You?" said Stephan. "You're wounded, Sorin, and there are people out there that want your life. And don't think I didn't see you wince when you sat down. You're on bed rest for the entire day, and if I hear anything about you causing trouble, I'm kicking you out of the group and finding someone else to fill your shoes."

Sorin groaned. "This place is *terrible*. Why can't I go back to my place to rest?"

"If you're sure your butler and maid can keep you safe, then go right ahead," said Stephan. "Now—Lawrence? Where did Lawrence go?"

"He slipped out back," said Gareth. "Said something about having better things to do than following a bear around the outpost."

Stephan didn't seem surprised by the revelation. In fact, he was pleased by this result. "And here I thought he wouldn't give me a chance to retaliate. Know any trustworthy alchemists, Gareth?"

"I happen to know a few female alchemists who have it out for Lawrence," said Gareth. "I'll ask around to see what kind of ideas they have."

33

MANABANE SWAMP

Manabane Swamp was one of the few large water bodies in Bloodwood Forest. As a result, much of the forest's energy was concentrated within its putrid and corpse-infested waters. The demons inhabiting it favored Death and Disease instead of the dominant Evils of Bloodwood Forest, Madness and Violence.

The swamp was a shallow one. Brave adventurer could theoretically cross it on foot if they were careful. In practice, however, these fools would die a gruesome death via the leeches, mosquitoes, and venomous insects infesting the swamp, not to mention the high population of crocodile and turtle demons that called it home. A tight canopy of interlocking branches blocked out all but a tiny amount of sunlight, making it difficult to spot these threats before they were lethal.

"Demonic mosquitoes are the *worst*," said Lawrence, slapping a fat, thumb-sized one and wiping its blood off on his tunic. "Even one-star mosquito repellent can't scare them off. And they always hit you where it hurts most—your ankles and your wrists."

"Stop exaggerating," scolded Gareth, the sole rower on their boat. "We've got bug-repelling smoke filling up a cloud around the entire ship. If that mosquito managed to land on you, it's because you let it."

"Did not!" said Lawrence. "They happen to like my blood. There's nothing I can do about it!"

"They like Daphne's blood too, but you don't see her complaining," said Stephan.

"She's literally using a shield of fire mana to scare them off!" said Lawrence.

"You want a fire shield?" asked Daphne, finally looking up from her book. "Then pay up. I told you, it's only a hundred gold for twenty-four hours of protection."

"That's highway robbery," muttered Lawrence. "I'd rather be eaten alive."

"Suit yourself," said Daphne with a shrug.

"Don't you cultivate the shadow element?" asked Sorin. "All you need to do is circulate your mana, and the mosquitoes won't even be able to see you."

"Says the poison cultivator," grumbled Stephan. Painful mosquito bites could be seen on his hands, neck, and ears. "I think my repellant is wearing off. Care to give me another dose?"

"Of course," said Sorin. He flicked a glob of poisonous mana over to Stephan, who then smeared it on every inch of his exposed skin. The mosquitoes hovering around him sensed the difference and immediately retreated.

"Why don't I get poison repellent?" asked Lawrence.

"A hundred gold," said Sorin, holding out his hand. "I can't, in good conscience, undercut my companion's business."

Sorin then circulated his mana to replenish his stores. It was necessary to be frugal with mana in Manabane Swamp. Still, Sorin had discovered himself relatively immune to the swamp's constant mana-leeching effects.

"How is everyone holding up?" asked Sorin.

"I'm at about 80 percent," answered Daphne. "But I can feel my mana stores depleting themselves at an alarming pace."

"Let me take a look," said Sorin. He put a hand on Daphne's neck and felt her pulse.

Meanwhile, his spiritual force and mana sank into her body and observed her meridians. Mana was circulating healthily within them, but tiny blue strands were worming their way through her skin and flesh and entering her bloodstream, where they vanished along with a small amount of her mana. Sorin tried to suck them up but was unable to do so before his poisonous mana dispersed.

"I'm sorry," said Sorin. "I thought I could do something about this miasma, but it seems I was mistaken. At most, I can somewhat resist the erosion."

"Then what do you recommend?" asked Stephan.

"The only way is to keep sipping mana potions to keep up our reserves," said Sorin.

"But you've confirmed it's a poison?" asked Stephan.

"If it weren't, I wouldn't be so resistant," said Sorin. "Truth be told, I'm thrilled to have made the discovery. It means the poison I'm looking for is definitely here in this swamp. Only the one-star poison, Manabane Chrysanthemum, can achieve this effect."

"I've never heard of such a flower," said Gareth. "And I make it my business to study plants, medicinal and otherwise. What are its properties? How does one find it?"

"Manabane Chrysanthemums are white flowers roughly the size of one's fist," answered Sorin. "When concentrated and injected into a person's bloodstream via stab wound, it will cripple their cultivation by destroying their mana sea."

"That's terrible!" said Lawrence. "You might as well kill the person!" Then, realizing whom he was speaking to, he laughed awkwardly. "Just ignore me. I can be a little silly sometimes."

"You're not wrong," said Sorin, grimacing as he remembered the experience. "In fact, you might not know this, but my cultivation was crippled specifically by said poison. So, I know more than most how devastating its effects can be.

"Getting back to your question, the flowers produce a poison mist. It has no direct effect on mana, but when absorbed via skin contact or respiration, it will worm its way into a human or demon's meridian system and destroy their mana reserves. The miasma in this swamp can only be explained by a large quantity of Manabane Chrysanthemums."

"How exactly do we fight this poison if the concentration increases?" asked Gareth. "Is there an antidote to this poison?"

Sorin shook his head. "No antidote, so be careful of any flowers you see. If there's anything that I can recommend, it's water. The poison loses effectiveness in water, which is why the most powerful life forms in this swamp are aquatic. There are no avian demons to speak of, and all insects you see are resistant to poison."

"What about Lorimer?" continued Gareth. "Why is he fine?"

"I actually have no idea," said Sorin. "But I won't look a gift horse in the mouth. Keep up the good work, Lorimer."

In fact, Lorimer was better than satisfactory. The toxic miasma in the swamp was allowing him to steadily grow in strength. The swamp was also full of lifeforms that offered themselves up as snacks.

"Crocodile," said Gareth lazily. A massive set of jaws burst out of the water and tried to devour their rune-covered canoe.

"Reeee!" Before anyone else could react, Lorimer jumped out of the boat and into the crocodile demon's mouth. The crocodile wailed and thrashed as Lorimer dug his way out through the back of the creature's mouth and into its skull. It then tunneled its way out of the crocodile's eye and jumped back onto the ship as the creature sank back into the swamp's murky waters.

Sorin held out his hand. "You had the last one, Lorimer. This one's ours." Lorimer glared at him and bit down on the crystal, but Sorin glared back. "We agreed on a fifty-fifty split, Lorimer. Don't think I'm a pushover."

The rat snorted and tossed the crystal into Sorin's hand, who then tossed it over to Stephan. "It's amazing that he can eat those things," said Stephan. "Usually, demons eat the corpse but not the core."

"He's a special one, all right," Sorin agreed. In fact, he was pleased with this arrangement. The half they'd agreed on was directly strengthening Lorimer. Though Sorin wouldn't be getting a share, he had no regrets because a stronger Lorimer would only benefit him. Over thirty one-star demons had already fallen to the vicious rat. Thanks to their cores, Lorimer's power had already reached the sixth stage of Blood-Thickening. It was only now showing signs of slowing down.

They continued traveling through the swamp in a straight line, only stopping to wait for larger groups of demons to pass. Thanks to the runes on their boat, the aquatic demons had a hard time spotting them. Only a few stragglers managed to pierce their veils and cause them problems.

"There's an island up ahead," said Gareth. "We've also reached the five-hour mark, which is three hours from our point of no return." In the end, it was necessary to maintain full mana reserves for safety reasons. Based on their current stock of mana potions, they would only be able to remain in the swamp for twenty-four hours. Sixteen hours was the limit they set to maintain a buffer of safety.

"Then let's see if this island has anything good," said Stephan. "Everyone, battle positions. Conserve your mana, if possible. Especially Daphne."

Their boat slowly approached a mass of mists. It was only thanks to a small gravel beach jutting out from the mass that they could confirm it was indeed an island. As they drew closer, the mists thinned, revealing a pile of bones on the gravel beach, along with the wrecked remains of canoes. Each of these runic boats bore the mark of the Bloodwood Outpost.

They were barely thirty feet from the island when, suddenly, the entire group stiffened. Stephan growled and half-shifted into bear form. "Something's wrong," said Stephan.

"You've got that right," said Gareth. "We're surrounded."

Lorimer was squeaking anxiously and pointing into the water from the side of the boat. "He's saying we should get out of the water and get onto the island," Sorin translated. "He says whatever's on the island is much less dangerous than what's underwater."

"I can only row so fast," said Gareth, doing his best to steer the boat through what appeared to be a swarm of tiny turtles. Their shells knocked on the ship, threatening to capsize it. "That's it. All oars on deck, including Lawrence." The mosquito-bitten Stephan moved to one side of the boat. Sorin and Lawrence joined Gareth to balance out the ship and barely maintain its course.

"Are those bubbles?" Daphne suddenly exclaimed.

"Those appear to be bubbles, yes," said Gareth. "Wait. That's bad, isn't it?"

"Very bad," confirmed Daphne.

"Why is that bad?" said Lawrence. "Don't bubbles push us up?"

"Bubbles are bad," said Daphne. "There's math involved, but I don't think you'd understand it."

"Stop arguing and prepare to evacuate!" snapped Stephan. "Gareth, cover us! Sorin, grab Daphne!"

Gareth jumped out of the boat and fired three arrows into the mouth of a giant turtle as it emerged from the water. He then stepped onto its shell and hopped onto the next turtle in sequence, all the while keeping his bow out to cover their group's retreat.

Stephan was the least nimble of their group. He directly shifted into bear form and jumped into the swampy waters before they reached the bubbles. He was immediately beset by demonic turtles that tore out chunks of his flesh. Yet he could only grit his sharp teeth as he paddled toward the shoreline.

"You going to be all right?" Lawrence asked Sorin.

"I'll be fine," said Sorin. "Are your spells ready? Are you mentally prepared?"

"Just watch your hands," Daphne said coldly. "I value my life, but I'm not against mutual destruction."

Sorin grabbed his pack and slung Daphne over his shoulder. He then jumped off the boat and onto a turtle shell like Gareth and Lawrence did.

Because of their combined weight, the turtle immediately began to sink. Sorin used Adder Rush to hop to the next turtle, but he fell just short of it. Fortunately, Daphne was ready for such an occurrence. She blasted flames towards their backs, pushing them forward by a foot, enabling Sorin to secure their perch. "Duck!" Daphne yelled. Sorin fell on all fours as the turtle came flying out of the water, missing him by less than three inches.

"Lorimer!" Sorin shouted. "Do your job and keep these things away from us." The rat squeaked and jumped off Sorin's shoulder, intercepting another flying turtle and biting off its head in a single gulp before diving into the water.

"Will he be okay?" asked Daphne.

"I'm not worried about him one bit," said Sorin. He looked around and saw that the turtles had spread out. Aside from the frustrated demon he was standing on, the others had all retreated twenty feet in every direction. "I don't suppose mages can fly, can they?"

"I can lighten us if that helps," said Daphne.

"Do it," said Sorin.

"Sustain - Feather Fall!" shouted Daphne. Sorin immediately felt lighter. Not light enough to jump onto the next turtle, but light enough for his next best idea.

"Hold on tight," said Sorin, jumping. They flew ten feet into the air, crossing half the remaining distance to shore in a single leap.

"We're not going to make it!" yelled Daphne.

"Shut up and hold on!" snapped Sorin. They were about to hit the water when they suddenly stopped falling and flew towards the beach. Blood leaked down Sorin's hand as his trusty mithril string bit into his flesh due to their combined weight. "Pull us in!" he shouted to the bloodied Stephan before falling into the water.

Stephan smashed a turtle off his shoulder and wrapped the mithril string Sorin had thrown him around both his arms before pulling with all his strength. Sorin held onto Daphne with one arm as Stephan yanked them through the water before a turtle could so much as take a bite out of either of them.

Seconds later, they dragged themselves up onto the gravel beach, coughing. "This... isn't... sanitary," said Sorin, shuddering. "I think... I think I'm going to throw up."

"Then it's a good thing I bought some of these," said Lawrence, dumping a potion over both of their heads. A clear mist washed over their bodies and pulled away the dirty and bacteria-laden water, leaving them fresher than if they'd gone to a bathhouse and gotten a professional scrub-down.

"Good call," said Daphne, giving Lawrence a thumbs-up.

"Just give me a hundred gold, and we'll call it even," said Lawrence with a grin.

"These aren't even worth three silver," said Daphne. She opened her pack and was relieved to discover that its waterproof feature was not without merit. Her books, non-magical ones included, had all survived their dunk in the water.

"I don't want to be a pessimist, but it looks to me like we're trapped," said Sorin.

"For a short while at least," agreed Gareth. "I did a bit of scouting once you were safe and sound and found a washed-up rune boat. The runes are a little worn out, but we could touch them up. Thoughts, Daphne?"

"Maybe?" said Daphne. "I'd have to take a look."

Sorin picked himself up after throwing up the last of his breakfast. "Stephan, you look terrible. Are those turtle bites as deep as they look?"

"I'm just thinking about the penalty we'll have to pay for failing to return the rune boat," said Stephan. "That's 2,000 gold, straight off the top."

"I told you we should have taken the insurance," said Gareth.

Stephan sighed. "Then we can only hope what's on this island is enough to make up for the loss. Sorin, what are you doing?"

"Just collecting valuable weeds," said Sorin, taking out a low-grade medicine storage box. He used a gold knife to cut a stalk of purple grass just above the roots. "Purple Butterfly Grass is a one-star ingredient that goes for 15 gold a stalk. And there's ten whole stalks just growing here without anyone picking them up."

"I'm glad to know this wasn't a total waste of time," said Stephan. "Now let's just hope Gareth and Daphne can find us a way out of here."

RED-EYED SILVERBACK APE

Sorin's party spent the next two hours recovering. Only Stephan had suffered any injuries from the turtles, and Sorin was able to handle most of them with a few drops of healing potion and targeted stitches.

"They really need to figure out a better flavor for these fasting potions," said Lawrence, chugging back a small yellow vial. "Sour lemon gets old after a few days on the trail. How are we supposed to survive the next few weeks on this awful stuff?"

"Sour lemon?" asked Gareth. He was currently painting a concoction of crushed demon cores and liquified mana extract on the damaged rune boat with Daphne's help. "It tastes like an apple to me—apple pie. Maybe you're reacting to something in the potion? Ahah! Found it!" Several runes activated and drank in the paint on the boat. The network of runes covering the boat remained dim but appeared to be gaining function.

"Move over and let me fix this shoddy job," said Daphne, pushing him to the side. She painted supplementary runes in vibrant green ink, then connected these lit-up runes to the others they'd activated during their two-hour rest.

"I have good news and bad news," said Daphne after painting the finishing touches. "The good news is that I'm officially 90 percent confident that we can fix this boat. Moreover, it's a high-class rune boat. It will be instrumental in avoiding those demonic turtles that are guarding the island."

"What's the bad news?" asked Stephan.

"The bad news is that activating the runes will destroy the boat," said Daphne. "If we use them, we'd better be sure we get to shore." She sighed and took a swig of her fasting potion. "Mmm. Falafel. Yummy."

"Why is it that you guys all have good flavors while I'm the only one stuck with lemon?" Lawrence complained.

"You want this?" asked Daphne, looking at her half-empty vial. "Enjoy." She tossed it to Lawrence, who chugged it down.

"Urgh!" said Lawrence, spitting it out. "That one's even worse! It tastes like vomit!"

"Lawrence, stop wasting fasting potions," scolded Stephan. "We only have a limited amount."

"But it tastes like vomit," said Lawrence, gingerly sipping the rest. Sorin stifled a chuckle, as did everyone else in the group. It was an open secret that Stephan had tainted the first fasting potion he'd fed him, modifying the otherwise tasty fasting potions to have flavors he didn't like.

"Haley once told me that fasting potions taste like the user doesn't want them to taste," said Stephan, drinking down a potion of his own. "For me, that's chicken breast."

"Chicken breast?" asked Sorin. "Why would anyone hate chicken breast?"

"You would too if your parents forced you to go to the gym four hours a day and eat ten servings of chicken breast every day as part of your education," said Stephan. "To be honest, it's not just chicken breast. I can't stand the taste of chicken. Or turkey, for the matter." He shuddered as he put away the empty vial.

A half-hour later, the entire rune boat glowed with a faint blue light. "Victory!" said Daphne, holding up her arms like the winner of a sporting event. "The spell matrix is now functional. All that's left now is to patch up these holes and stop water from getting in, and we'll have ourselves an escape route."

"Patching up the holes won't be a problem," said Gareth, the group's survival expert. "There's a fair number of bloodwood trees. Their bark is easy to peel, and their sap turns to glue if we mix it with mashed fern root.

"After that, we'll only need oars. It'll take me about twenty minutes to carve out oars from these dead trees. That gives us enough of a buffer. You guys can go ahead and begin your exploration."

"I'll stay with Gareth and Daphne," said Stephan to Sorin and Lawrence.

"Relax and let us do our thing," said Lawrence. He tossed a crossbow to Sorin and shot off into the woods, taking special care not to disturb the wilderness too much.

"You're up, Lorimer," Sorin mentally said to his trusty rat companion. The rat grumbled but scurried into the underbrush, giving Sorin a fuzzy map of what lay ahead and warning him of potential threats and things Lorimer identified as tasty treats.

They traveled for fifteen minutes before Lorimer stopped him. Lawrence appeared beside Sorin and tugged him into a bush. "There's a group of Bronze-Tusked Demon Boars over there," said Lawrence. "We're going to bypass them since we don't want to cause a fuss. They're very territorial and will even fight two-star demons when provoked."

There were many more such instances. They encountered chameleons, salamanders, and vipers, as well as vampiric creatures like musk deer and five-line demon raccoons. Each creature had its own habitat and mannerisms, and disturbing them wasn't worth the effort, given the better prizes awaiting them elsewhere.

Twenty minutes later, they arrived at a small clearing, seemingly empty of demons. It was only when three vicious-looking monkeys fell out of the sky, dead, and Lawrence jumped down after them that Sorin realized his error.

"All the other demons are gone," said Lawrence. "There seems to be a lot of nice stuff around here. Why don't you harvest them while I keep watching?"

Sorin looked around and spotted at least five types of medicinal herbs and two types of medicinal roots, all growing in the same area. *Strange. This isn't a place that's particularly rich in natural energy.* But money was money, so Sorin got digging.

It was when he was excavating the roots that he realized why so many plants had grown in this place; the monkey demons Lawrence had killed had dragged countless decomposing carcasses into the clearing to nourish the soil with their energy.

Sorin and Lawrence had no use for these bones, but to Lorimer, they were a delicacy. While Sorin harvested precious medicinal ingredients, Lorimer gobbled up bones and half-rotted carcasses, as well as low-value herbs that Sorin didn't bother picking up.

"Bad news," said Lawrence when Sorin finished gathering the last herbs. He was panting heavily, and his face was unusually pale. "You were right. There's a two-star demon guarding this place."

"Any sign of the Manabane Chrysanthemums I mentioned?" asked Sorin.

Lawrence shook his head. "I didn't get past the guardian, but my mana started to erode quickly when I got close to its territory." He led Sorin and Lorimer down a winding trail to a small valley at the center of the island. Dirty swamp water trickled into the valley from all sides. Still, as it ran down the valley slopes, it turned increasingly clear before eventually settling into a pristine pool at its center.

"This is definitely the place," said Sorin. He could feel his mana eroding with every breath he took. "There's one over there. Also there, there, and there." Over twenty crystal-blue chrysanthemums were growing on the outskirts of the valley. "I think these chrysanthemums are what's purifying the water pouring into the valley."

"Then we can't take too many," said Lawrence. "The same goes for all the plants growing here. Their guardian will be upset if we take a few, but it'll lose its mind if we take everything."

Sorin agreed with Lawrence and edged in to take a closer look. He was about to reach a Manabane Chrysanthemum when he suddenly felt a dreadful pressure weighing down on him.

A gust of wind blasted Sorin backward and onto the ground. He stood up, ears ringing, and looked at the canopy, where an ape demon was hopping from branch to branch. "Is that the guardian?" asked Sorin, trembling. The creature had conspicuous silver fur on its humped back and smoldering red eyes.

"That, my friend, is a Red-Eyed Silverback Ape, a two-star demon," said Lawrence.

"That's a very long-winded name," said Sorin.

"But a very descriptive one," said Lawrence. "That thing's a brute. All it has going for it is pure physical strength. But it has a lot of it compared to most two-star demons, so it's usually more than enough. Even Stephan wouldn't last half a minute against it."

"Then what can we do?" asked Sorin. Even if they *could* beat it in a fight, they'd alert all the creatures on the island once the battle started."

"I guess there's no helping it," said Lawrence dramatically. "It falls to little old me to play the hero. I'll distract the brute while you go in and rob it. I have only one request. Take care of my women and my children if I don't make it."

Sorin rolled his eyes. "Godspeed." It wouldn't be easy distracting a two-star demon with a Blood-Thickening cultivation base. "Leave the looting to me and Lorimer. We'll make sure to get our money's worth."

"Sure thing, boss," said Lawrence. He blended into the shadows and appeared behind the ape moments later. The creature had yet to spot them and was munching on spirit fruits growing on a large tree near the center of the valley.

Crystal Demon Fruits. Utterly useless to cultivators, but priceless treasures for demons. Wait... Why would he...? His jaw dropped as Lawrence grabbed one of the crystalline fruits and took a bite out of it before tossing it hard between the ape's legs. The creature howled in rage and spun around to face Lawrence.

"Urgh! This stuff tastes awful!" said Lawrence in an exaggerated manner. "Do you have anything better-tasting around here?"

Not good! thought Sorin as the ape's eyes turned red. It sent a violent fist crashing down toward the branch Lawrence stood on.

Fortunately, this action was well within Lawrence's ability to deal with. He appeared on another branch fifteen feet away, holding three more fruits. These were Blue-Gold Wind Pears, top-grade one-star ingredients worth a hundred gold each.

The ape let out an angry roar and threw itself at Lawrence. But just like before, it smashed into an empty branch. Lawrence appeared not far away, with even *more* fruit in his hands, looking completely unharmed and undisturbed.

The rogue retreated out of the clearing branch by branch, but not before taking a few other expensive fruits with him. They were the kind that didn't need any special precautions to collect—Sorin had to admit that Lawrence had common sense when it came to this.

Three minutes later, when the ape's raging no longer caused his surroundings to tremble, Sorin picked himself up and ran over to the nearest Manabane Chrysanthemum. All soil within three feet of the flower was infertile and devoid of mana, and Sorin, who had the protection of his poisons, was unable to resist its erosion fully.

Fortunately, he had come prepared to harvest such a plant. It was strong against mana-infused containers but weak against gold. Sorin scooped up the plant, root and all, and placed it in a gold-lined box before sealing it. Only then did his mana stop burning away.

Sorin took a sip of mana potion and made his way over to the next chrysanthemum. He repeated the process until he had a total of four flowers, more than enough to cultivate the Ten Thousand Poison Canon. Though more would be helpful to him, he was concerned about disrupting the ecology of the valley. Wanton destruction went against the principles of both adventurers and physicians.

Lorimer didn't have such compulsions, however, and ate everything in sight. It was only due to Sorin's strict directions that he left behind seeds and duplicates of every plant. His aura increased sharply with every plant consumed, and it wasn't long before he broke through to the seventh stage of Blood-Thickening.

Several minutes swiftly passed. The Red-Eyed Silverback Ape smashed apart trees and dug up the land to find the elusive cockroach, Lawrence, while Sorin and Lorimer made out like bandits. There were thousands of herbs and roots in the valley, far too many for Sorin to take away. He only had twenty boxes he could use to store ingredients, so he made sure to select only those worth 50 gold or more.

By the time Sorin arrived at the pool in the center of the valley, his pack was stuffed full of medicinal ingredients. Logically, it was time to return, yet looking at the island at the center of the pristine pool, he felt an itch that he couldn't help but scratch; there was no way he could leave without seeing what lay in the middle of such a rich garden.

Sorin was surprised to discover that the clear water at the center of the valley was only two inches deep. It was covered in lily pads and filled with non-demonic animal life. *How can nothing be growing here?* thought Sorin as he crossed the shallow pool and arrived at the secondary island. The air on the island was utterly devoid of ambient mana. Even the trees were mortal trees instead of the demonic trees infesting Bloodwood Forest.

He soon found the culprit of this strange mana-deficient atmosphere: a single demonic tree, short and squat, bearing jade-colored fruits. Sorin was about to approach the tree when Lorimer stopped him. "You're saying there's a second guardian? And it's easy to see?" Sorin squinted but was unable to locate said guardian. "What do you mean, it's sitting right there?"

His eyes widened when he finally saw tufts of green fur hidden amongst the tree's jade-green leaves. A giant ape demon, much bigger than the Red-Eyed Silverback Ape, lay sleeping on the tree's largest branch. And on that branch, he saw twenty emerald-colored fruits that gave off an unmistakable two-star aura.

35

JASMINE BONE FRUIT

Sorin immediately recognized the squat demonic tree as a Jasmine Bone Tree. The emerald fruit it produced was called Jasmine Bone Fruit, and this fruit was the main ingredient in Bone-Forging Pills, which Blood-Thickening cultivators used to break through to the Bone-Forging Realm. Such things always traded for sky-high prices and were easily worth at least 500 gold apiece.

Despite the high value of the fruits, Sorin eyed the tree with dread. The ape demon guarding the tree was an unknown quantity to Sorin, and collecting the fruits would definitely awaken it.

"So here's the plan," Sorin said to Lorimer. "You're going to run up to that thing and provoke it, just like Lawrence did." To his surprise, Lorimer refused. "I'm your master, Lorimer. You're supposed to listen to me unconditionally." Once again, Lorimer replied, and Sorin realized that there were limits to the slave mark binding it. "Fine. I'll think of something. But we need to hurry and do this before Lawrence runs out of energy." A smashing sound echoed through the wilderness, confirming that the silverback ape was still very much distracted and very much upset at the clever rogue.

Sorin looked around and identified a few more two-star ingredients.

Unfortunately, they weren't like the Jasmine Bone Fruits and required special storage methods he didn't have access to.

But I don't necessarily need to keep them, do I? Maybe I could mix up a simple poison? He didn't have a cauldron or liquified mana essence. Still, even a simple medicinal powder or paste could work wonders if used correctly.

Time was of the essence, so Sorin quickly settled on a main ingredient: Mind Draft Daffodil. He picked a cluster of said two-star flowers and took out a simple mortar and pestle, then ground the petals and the roots into a paste.

Sorin then broke open four boxes of medicinal ingredients he'd collected and added them in. *Lavender Dream Root, Cinnabar Rain Flower, Star Skin Mint, and Red Devil Ivy should all promote contact infusion. That way, I won't need to pierce the demon's thick skin.*

"Lorimer, you're up. Use low heat, and we'll gradually increase it." Lorimer squeaked in an aggrieved fashion, and Sorin petted him on the head. "Yes, I *know* you did good work back in the laboratory. It was hard on you, sitting in that circle for days."

Relieved that Sorin knew what he was talking about, Lorimer adopted his earth flame form and transferred a bit of his energy into the mortar and pestle. "Easy. *Easy!*" said Sorin. He mashed the paste in the mortar and pestle as it dried up, making sure not to inhale any of the silver-violet smoke that was produced.

Once most of the liquid had evaporated, Sorin had Lorimer increase the intensity of his earth flames. They performed seven more rounds of evaporation and mashing until, finally, the resulting powder began to glow.

"One last burst of energy," Sorin instructed. "Double your output and hold." The heat rose sharply, causing the mortar to crack. The silver-violet powder glittered violently before finally adopting a stable form. The refinement was a success.

The tricky part will be applying the medicine. There aren't any high points, and I can't precisely manipulate the wind. Wait a minute—there's that crossbow Lawrence passed to me on our way here! According to Lawrence, a crossbow was a necessary tool for any heist. It could be used to distract, kill, and pull attention. In this case, Sorin fastened a pouch full of medicinal powder to one of the three bolts he'd been given. He then aimed the foolproof device at the giant green ape and let loose.

There was a chance that his attack would provoke the creature, so Sorin and Lorimer bolted in separate directions. A tense minute passed as a cloud of silver-violet powder drizzled over the creature's fur and worked its way into its flesh. As for the bolt, it was insignificant and had lodged itself into a large tuft of fur on the creature's chest.

"He should be out cold, but we need to be careful," said Sorin. "I'll go take the fruits. As for the other stuff, go wild."

He then used Adder Rush and dashed over to the tree. The Jasmine Bone Fruits were over twenty feet up in the air and climbing the tree would take too much time. Fortunately, Sorin had his trusty mithril string, which he used to coil around the fruits and pull them down.

They're heavy, thought Sorin as he placed some fruit in his back-pack. A single fruit weighed three pounds. That wasn't much on its own, but combined with the rest of Sorin's pack, the twenty-three fruits in the tree would make it challenging to run.

Even so, Sorin didn't hesitate to pick all the fruits on the tree. If he were going to offend this creature, he would offend it thoroughly. Lorimer seemed to be of the same opinion as Sorin because he didn't hesitate to gobble up even two-star ingredients, causing his blood to surge and his body to transform.

Lorimer immediately broke through to the eighth stage of Blood-Thickening and quickly broke through to the ninth stage after that. Sorin felt a tugging on the golden chains binding Lorimer, warning him that the rat would go out of control if it became much stronger than this.

"You can have a bit more, but if you try to break through, I'll end you," Sorin transmitted to Lorimer. The rat squealed an affirmative and devoured a two-star herb called Life Soaring Sage Grass. He instantly

reached the peak of the ninth stage of Blood-Thickening, causing an even greater tug on his binding chains.

"Enough!" Sorin snapped as Lorimer defied him and tried to eat another precious plant. "Don't think you can sneak out of your bindings on my watch." The golden chains tightened, and the aggrieved rat could only give up on the tasty treat.

Sorin's pack was now cumbersome from all the boxes in it and the fruit he'd gathered. He'd even been forced to throw away less valuable boxes of medicinal ingredients. He was about to leave when suddenly, a shiver ran across his entire body. His bones shook, and his blood ran cold as the giant ape presiding over the tree shifted in its sleep.

Both Sorin and Lorimer stood dead still, praying, *hoping* that the creature was having a bad dream. Seconds later, the pressure lifted, and Sorin and Lorimer bolted away from the tree with their ill-gotten gains.

The man and his rat ran through the water, isolating the secondary island from the primary island, and entered the domain of the Red-Eyed Silverback Ape. Judging by the clashing sounds occasionally heard in the distance, the ape was still busy with Lawrence.

Yet the moment this thought ran through Sorin's head, he saw the barest flicker of a flare through the dense canopy. The raging and thrashing of the ape stopped, and a dreadful roar sounded out from the direction of the jasmine bone tree.

"Run!" Sorin shouted to Lorimer. They threw caution to the wind and dashed through the wilderness, shocking sleeping demons awake and provoking the region's guardians. Sorin used Adder Rush to avoid some of these threats. In contrast, Lorimer directly took a bite out of the stronger ones, frightening off any lesser demons.

The earth trembled as a giant creature entered the outer forest from the valley, frightening off demons and tearing down 100-year-old trees. "Holy hell, what did you *do*?" said Lawrence, appearing beside Sorin.

"I robbed over 10,000 gold worth of fruit from a very angry, very green ape," answered Sorin.

"A green-furred ape?" exclaimed Lawrence. "You mean that star-eyed green-furred demon ape?"

"I didn't take a look at its eyes," snapped Sorin. "All I know is that it's *huge.*"

"This is bad, bad, bad," said Lawrence. "Quick, this way. We can't draw a straight line back to the boat, or it'll kill us all." He pulled Sorin past a herd of bristle-furred demon boars and led him over a trip wire. The boars were infuriated by the trap and immediately attacked the nearest target—an ape with green fur that was hot on their tail.

Lorimer hopped onto Sorin's shoulder and squeaked anxiously. "How far are we from the boat?" asked Sorin.

"I don't know, about three minutes?" said Lawrence. "Quick, poison my dagger. Make it painful."

"I don't have painful, but I can do flesh-melting," said Sorin, cutting his arm and coating Lawrence's mithril dagger with his blood.

"You go to the boat and get them to set off," said Lawrence. "I'll distract them."

"Squeak! Squeak! Squeak!" shouted Lorimer. He dashed off with Lawrence and headed into the forest. Sorin could only grit his teeth and run full tilt.

It was two minutes later when he heard two dreadful roars that shook the forest. *What exactly did they do to piss them off so badly?* thought Sorin.

"We need to go!" Sorin shouted as he exited the woods and onto the beach. "Now!"

Stephan and the others had been enjoying a short break, but at Sorin's urging, they tossed their belongings into the boat and prepared to set off. "In how much danger are we exactly?" asked Stephan. "And is it just me, or is the earth shaking?"

"What in Hope's name did you two troublemakers provoke?" asked Gareth, hopping into the boat. "Should I even bother taking out my weapon? And where are Lawrence and Lorimer?" He tossed an oar out to Stephan and prepared to set off.

"Arrows won't do us much good, and neither will Stephan's bear form," said Sorin. "Unless you're confident in being able to hurt the Red-Eyed Silverback Ape and some green-furred demon ape."

"You two provoked not one but *two* two-star demons?" said Daphne, hopping into the boat. "Let me activate the flight runes in advance. If those things catch up, we're dead."

"What are you guys waiting for!" came a shout from the woods. Lawrence burst out with Lorimer at his side. Moments later, the two giant apes appeared behind them, looking murderous.

Lawrence hopped into the boat, but to Sorin's surprise, Lorimer squeaked and remained behind. They pushed out onto the water as the apes, clearly furious at the rat, pounded the beach with massive fists and giant feet.

"What exactly did Lorimer do to them?" asked Sorin curiously.

"That... well, we both did awful things to them," said Lawrence. "For starters, I poked one in the toe just beneath its toenail. It hurt it quite a bit. But then Lorimer didn't seem satisfied with biting toes and went for what I can only describe as a critical weakness common in both males and females. He turned orange-red and then flew straight into their unmentionables."

Sorin's expression darkened. "So they won't let him leave no matter what, is what you're saying. That's too bad. He was a good rat if disobedient."

"I think he might have a plan," said Lawrence. "It's tough communicating with a rat. I don't know how you do it."

They were a hundred feet out from the island when Lorimer, having had enough fun with the apes, ran off in their direction. He hopped into the water and, to everyone's surprise, moved through it with the grace and agility of a crocodile.

"I'm going to have to teach that rat a lesson," muttered Sorin. "It dares keep secrets from me?" It had clearly gained the demon crocodiles' abilities after devouring so many cores yet hadn't mentioned such an essential thing to Sorin.

Turtle's jaws snapped at Lorimer as he made his way to the boat. But these creatures were slow, and Lorimer was their natural predator. He snapped off ten of their heads before they backed off and cleared a path for him.

Yet before their team could rejoice, the green-furred ape with scorch marks between its legs launched itself into the air and landed in the water. The impact sent a twenty-foot wave their way that threatened to capsize their salvaged rune boat.

"Shield!" shouted Daphne, activating one of the boat's functions. The wave sent them flying but didn't otherwise harm the boat. "Lorimer, get on here, or I'm leaving you behind!"

Lorimer was currently swimming for his life. He was less than thirty feet away from the boat, but the ape was gaining on him.

"Sorry, Sorin," said Stephan. "Your rat saved us all, but we're going to have to take off."

"Just wait a second longer," said Sorin. "Lorimer has a plan. He's a smart rat and wouldn't do anything stupid. How long can we delay, Daphne?"

"Five more seconds," said Daphne. "Four. Three. Two." She was about to activate the rune when suddenly, a pressure that exceeded that of both apes filled their surroundings. The mists around the island parted, and the murky waters suddenly grew bright yellow.

"That's not water," muttered Stephan. "It's…"

"An eye!" shouted Daphne. What remained of her mana could no longer circulate.

"It looks like whatever it is, the ape's afraid of it," said Gareth. The green-furred creature was already doubling back, giving Lorimer precious time to hop onto the boat and squeak for them to take off.

The yellow eye beneath the depths closed when the demon ape left the swamp, releasing its dreadful pressure from their surroundings. They were about to set off when Lorimer suddenly squeaked in a panic. "What's that Lorimer?" asked Sorin. "You're saying that the eye was the turtle boss and turtle minions are on their way?"

"There's a swarm of demon turtles up ahead!" shouted Gareth. "Activate the flight rune!"

"We only get one shot at this," Daphne warned.

"If we don't activate it now, we're dead!" snapped Gareth.

Shots were called by either the party leader or the party archer, so

Daphne pressed her hand on the rune and poured her remaining mana into it. The entire boat jolted and shot them through the air as they ricocheted off a demon turtle's shell.

"I can barely steer this thing," said Daphne through gritted teeth. "Also, the shield is failing. Prepare to abandon ship." They hit an open-mouthed crocodile demon as the shield faded. The boat's wood splintered, sending them flying into the marsh.

"This way!" said Stephan, shifting into a bear form and grabbing Daphne by the collar. Sorin's dagger struck out on reflex, stabbing a turtle demon through the head as another bit him on the leg.

"Protect Daphne!" shouted Stephan. Sorin ignored his wounds and plunged beneath the water, spotting no less than three turtle demons heading her way. He shot out a poisoned mana needle in one's eye and smacked the other with a poison palm. As for the third, Stephan blocked it with his arm, suffering a deep bite but protecting the fragile Daphne.

Finally, solid ground. Air. Sorin pulled himself and Daphne onto a rocky beach swarming with turtle demons. Yet before they could even think of attacking their group, three arrows shot out from the trees, directly blowing off their heads, and a burning rat bit off two more heads, frightening the remaining turtles into submission.

A bear-shifted Stephan, pulling himself onto shore, was the straw that broke the camel's back. The turtles retreated, much to Lorimer's chagrin, leaving behind only the corpses of their dead comrades for their group to harvest.

"So," said Lawrence, grinning from ear to ear. "How was the haul?"

"Pretty good," said Sorin. "Definitely worth it." He kicked a turtle shell and looked at Gareth and Stephan. "Is this thing edible?"

"If Lorimer's up to making turtle soup, I don't see why not," said Stephan. "In fact, such a thing would be considered a delicacy in the cities."

"I'm game for anything that's *not* a fasting potion," said Lawrence.

"Same," said Daphne weakly. "I requested stale bread flavor since I really like stale bread, but it's getting old." They all looked at her strangely. "What? I'm a woman of simple taste. Extremely low main-tenance."

Having confirmed that the turtles were, in fact, edible when cooked with an earth flame, Sorin and Lawrence got busy cutting them apart and turning their shells into bowls.

36

THE SEALED RUIN

It was three days later when Sorin's party arrived at the designated ruin site. Dozens of campfires were bunched up in a defensive perimeter, guarded by vigilant adventurers who verified their identities before letting them through.

"And I was worried that we'd be late," said Gareth. "Especially with all the demon attacks we suffered."

"I think we lucked out going through Manabane Swamp," said Sorin, eyeing the deep, infected cuts and corrupted injuries these adventurers had suffered.

"Speak for yourself," said Lawrence. "It was Lorimer and I who distracted those two-star apes. They nearly squished us into pancakes." Lorimer squeaked, and Lawrence nodded. "That's right. You tell them, Lorimer."

"Calm down, Lawrence," said Stephan. "It's clear that the situation isn't what we expected. I'm going to go find out what's going on with the other party leaders. You four should find yourselves a spot to relax and eat. Oh, and take a trip to the Adventurers Guild stall. Let's offload everything we don't need for credit while we still can."

Sorin's pack was bulging full, and so were the others after their three-day trek through the wilderness. Thanks to the continuous waves of one-star demons, they'd amassed over 200 one-star cores and many useful medicinal ingredients and poisons. The poisons, Sorin kept, but the cores were group loot and far too valuable for Lorimer to use as rations.

It took them only a short time to familiarize themselves with the camp. There were over twenty groups of adventurers present, as well as a smattering of loose adventurers who'd made their way there alone. The Adventurers Guild, Alchemists Guild, the Mages Guild, and even the Blacksmiths Guild had set up shop near the center of the encampment to supply much-needed services to all the adventurers participating in the raid.

"These prices are ridiculous," said Lawrence, gesturing to a sign. "Two hundred gold for a potion? Ten gold for repairing standard leather armor? Five gold for sharpening a simple steel short sword?"

"I'm pretty sure they've got a captive audience," said Sorin. "It'd probably be much worse if we bought extras from adventurers who brought them. By the way, how's your recovery going, Daphne?"

"I'm fine," said Daphne. "I just overdrafted myself over the past few days. I'll be fine once we buy some mana potions to replenish our stock."

The prices were atrocious, but their team, like others, had no other choice but to buy. After turning in their cores for credit notes and the bulk of their medicinal ingredients, their team purchased five mana potions and three healing potions, bringing their total up to five of each type.

"Why didn't we trade in those fruits?" asked Daphne. "If we did, we'd be able to buy better weapons or spells before heading into the dungeon."

"Those ingredients are always in short supply in our outpost," said Stephan. "It's better to save the ingredients and directly commission Bone-Forging Pills, then sell any extras we get to the Adventurers guild or the Mages Guild. Now, if you'll excuse me, I have a bunch of pretentious team leaders to go meet."

Stephan split off from their group and joined a small group of adventurers with much better gear than average. Sorin was knew to the adventuring scene, so he didn't recognize any of them, but Gareth and Lawrence were familiar with a few of the more famous faces.

Twenty minutes later, Stephan returned looking none too pleased at the exchange. "What did you find out?" asked Gareth. "We made our own inquiries, but no one seems to know anything. And what's with all these wounded adventurers? Not all of their wounds look like the kind inflicted by demons."

"I'll answer the second question first," said Stephan. "Most of the wounds come from defending against demons that have been attacking this encampment just like they attacked us in the wilderness. There were also some adventurers that had 'disagreements' on their way here. It's unfortunately impossible to tell who instigated these matters, so everyone is on edge and not trusting anyone."

"You're saying adventurers fought adventurers on the way here?" asked Sorin.

Stephan shook his head with disgust. "Suffice it to say that many adventuring groups that set out didn't make it here. That daft physician Marcus didn't do anyone a favor by telling everyone they didn't have to worry about getting hurt."

"How the deciphering of the runes coming along?" asked Daphne.

"How did you know about the runes?" asked Stephan.

"Because if it were anything other than barrier runes, there wouldn't be a dozen mages arguing in front of the tomb's closed door," said Daphne. "I imagine they've made no progress during this time?"

"They're making progress, so I've been told," said Stephan.

"*Right*," said Daphne, rolling her eyes. "I think I'll just go talk to them directly. Odds are, they've made absolute zero progress."

"While she's doing that, I think we should discuss an oddity," said Gareth. "What's with the waves of demons?"

"Apparently, it relates to residual holy mana oozing out from inside the tomb," said Stephan. "You all can't see it, but apparently, the mages and the Priest of Hope who came to assess the tomb could."

"Holy-element mana?" asked Lawrence. "You mean the mana priests used to use during the Divine Era?"

"That's the one," said Stephan. "It's thanks to this holy mana that we know this tomb was built prior to the Cataclysmic Emergence."

"But what does that have to do with the demons?" asked Gareth. "Shouldn't demons hate holy mana?"

"Apparently, it operates on a different frequency," said Stephan. "It wasn't built to scare away such weak creatures since they can't break through the barrier. It's only two-star demons and above that can't stand the aura.

"As for one-star demons, it confuses them. That's why they're so aggressive instead of defensive, as they'd usually be."

"I think something's happening," said Sorin, interrupting their conversation. A wall of golden glyphs had appeared on the door to the tomb, and it was now covered in a counter-arrangement of burning red glyphs. Daphne was the one adding the glyphs to the wall, and the more she added, the more unstable the wall became.

"Watch out, it's going to blow!" Stephan suddenly yelled and pulled their group to the ground. All adventurers in earshot followed his lead. Those unlucky enough not to hear him were struck by a wave of force that led to bloody noses and a few broken bones.

"What happened?" asked Stephan when Daphne walked back to their group.

"What happened is that they're all idiots, and *I'm* a genius," said Daphne, flipping her hair. "Honestly, why would anyone bother solving a stupid puzzle when they can just burn it to the ground? It's beyond me how they even became mages in the first place."

"I'm new to this whole ruin exploration thing," said Sorin. "What happens next? Who enters first?"

Stephan snorted. "I made some suggestions, but they ignored me. The common convention is that lone adventurers go in first to sound things out—something that's completely idiotic in this case, I should add." As he spoke, a stream of cultivators shot into the tomb's open door. None of the teams made a move.

Not long after, they heard horrendous screaming and shouting from the entrance. A handful of adventurers from the original group of twenty ran out of the tomb with fearful expressions. One of the captains Stephan had met approached them to ask questions, but the least wounded among them spat at him and walked off.

"I warned them," said Stephan with a sigh. "But they wouldn't listen. It's traditional to let individual adventurers through to try their luck. But with such a powerful protective field, I felt that was ill-advised. Out of the twenty team captains, only three of them agreed with me. The rest egged on the remaining individual adventurers, and there was nothing else I could say. Now watch. They're going to send someone our way."

As Stephan predicted, an adventurer peeled off from the group of captains and greeted Stephan. "Mister York. The team leaders see the merit in your words and would like your input on how to proceed next."

"So now that fifteen or so adventurers died needlessly, you want my input?" Stephan questioned sharply. "Tell them to get lost."

"That… you were right, of course," said the adventurer apologetically. "But the past is in the past, and the adventurers here are all living, breathing people. Surely you have some advice that you could share to reduce casualties?"

"Hypocrites," Gareth said under his breath. The adventurer heard him but maintained his false smile.

"Fine," said Stephan, his expression softening. "I can't make you horses drink, but I can at least lead you to water. Gather your people, and I'll tell you what I know. It's more than you deserve, but I'm not a callous man."

"Surely you don't mean to involve everyone here in a big discussion?" asked the adventurer nervously.

"What is there to discuss?" asked Stephan. "You want my family's information, not my advice. You won't listen to me no matter what advice I give."

"If you'd nominate yourself as raid leader, you'd surely have an oversized impact on the discussion," suggested the adventurer.

"I have no interest in leading anyone but those in my party," said Stephan, shaking his head.

The adventurer retreated from their group and went to speak with the group of twenty leaders. There was a bit of shouting, and some cold eyes glared at their team, but Sorin's group was filled with oddballs that had thick skin. They waited patiently for the adventurer to come back.

"The group leaders are very pleased with your decision to hold a group discussion," said the adventurer with a smile. "They'd like you to pardon their rudeness; things have been tense, given recent demon attacks and troubles with the ruin's door."

"*Right,*" said Stephan. "Please tell them to bring their teams, and I'll tell them what I know." He then put down his pack to retrieve a small, foldable chair from it and took a seat. "Sorry, everyone," he said to the rest of their group. "I won't be able to posture effectively if we sit as a group. How about you all take a seat at the front?"

37

THE THREE TYPES OF DUNGEONS

Twenty minutes later, all the adventurers raiding the tomb were sitting near Stephan. His chair was quite conspicuous since none of the other party leaders had brought one. Moreover, he was in no hurry to speak and had evidently practiced for this sort of thing.

"Hello, everyone," said Stephan after the last of the adventurers not on guard duty were seated. "My name is Stephan. But many of you know me as Mr. York, Stephan York, or any of the many variations. The main thing is obviously my family name, which is quite famous in adventurer circles.

"I don't have much personal fame to draw on or any personal experience to share. Instead, I have lessons that I've been receiving from my family since I was a child.

"I would first and foremost like to say that I was against letting loose adventurers—or independent adventures, as I like to call them—into the ruins first. My reasoning was quite simple: We don't know what kind of tomb this is. Or, to be more technical about it, we don't know what kind of dungeon this is. All tombs worth exploring are dungeons, in the end, and should be treated with reverence instead of disdain. When dealing with unknowns, it is best to be prudent."

"I'm sorry, but could we discuss that part first?" said a tall, silver-armored woman with golden hair. She had a dignified and professional look about her. It was clear that she was every bit as noble as Stephan was. "Common convention is to let loose adventurers in first. This is because the outskirts of a ruin typically have the least amount of danger. Loose adventurers don't have teams to rely on, and this is the only way they'll be able to gain anything from this expedition."

Stephan smiled. "I don't doubt your pure intentions, Barbara. Your reputation precedes you, and if my sources are correct, you also started as an independent adventurer after refusing the arrangements of your family."

"That is correct," said Barbara. "So you'll have to forgive me for keeping their best interests in mind."

"What is there to forgive?" asked Stephan. "I am also a big supporter of independent adventurers, which is why I didn't want those with ulterior motives sending them to their deaths. It should be known that there is a significant risk in sending independent adventurers first. It is only thanks to those risks being quantified ahead of time that the convention works. But what if these assumptions fall apart? Isn't that just the equivalent of gambling with human lives?"

"And how exactly are we meant to know anything about this place?" asked a tall, slovenly man with thick sideburns. Judging by his red face and cheerful disposition, he was clearly drunk. "No one's ever been in there before. And if they had been, why bother with conventions?" He then looked around uncertainly. "If what I say doesn't make sense, please feel free to ignore me. I've been known to drink a tad too much."

"That is an excellent question, Haster," said Stephan. "And the answer is that it's impossible to know anything about this place, which makes conventions rather useless. In fact, the convention was implemented and supervised by my York Clan as a risk mitigation strategy designed to avoid a total wipeout when exploring quantified variable dungeons. The key here is 'quantified.' The risks are known ahead of time."

"Quantified variable dungeons?" asked another captain. "What's that supposed to mean?"

"He means one of the dungeons in the big cities," said a handsome man with sword-like eyebrows. He was the leader of the assembled captains and the one who had been most against being cautious while entering. "You're talking about the repopulating dungeons whose layouts change every time they open, aren't you, *Mr. York*?"

Stephan nodded. "That is correct, Orpheus. The dungeons are always different, which means that they have a slight chance of spawning a catastrophically one-sided map. The chance is about one percent, but the consequences of such an occurrence are dire.

"After many complete team wipes, the Adventurers Guild and their concerned parties discussed the matter. It was the representative of independent adventurers who suggested allocating spots to independent adventurers in each raid to scout ahead.

"It was a win-win proposal. These people normally wouldn't be allowed to enter the dungeon, and there was a 99 percent chance of safely acquiring some of the dungeon's wealth. The major powers and teams that normally raided these dungeons would lose a bit of profit every time but would be able to avoid a total team wipe in the event of a one-sided map."

"Which is exactly what happened in this case," said Orpheus. "But just because the result wasn't good, it doesn't mean our approach was wrong. The loose adventurers served their purpose, in the end." His words were quite callous and drew sharp looks from Barbara, Haster, and over half of the remaining captains."

"If that's the way you want to put it, I can't convince you," said Stephan. "But I'd like to point out that the convention was invented based on a 1 percent chance of a total team wipe in a repopulating dungeon. The risks were known. But what if these odds *didn't* apply? What if the odds are closer to 35 percent for a small group of unorganized adventurers?"

"Pardon, Stephan, but I don't see why there would be such a huge difference," said Barbara.

"The difference largely stems from the different types of dungeons known to exist," said Stephan. "Dungeons are mainly classified as memorial dungeons, inheritance or trial dungeons, and sealing dungeons.

"Memorial dungeons are the least threatening—they are usually tombs erected for rich cultivators that contain a portion of their wealth and teachings. They typically contain ample traps, and due to contamination from the Seven Evils, they also contain demonic life."

"Is this not a memorial dungeon?" asked Barbara. "The decorative columns and artwork all indicate that this is some sort of tomb." Other experts in the crowd voiced their agreement.

"This much is true," said Stephan. "Tombs are *often* memorials, but not always. This brings us to the second type of dungeon: the inheritance dungeon. These either contain recurring trials or one-off trials to pass on the inheritance of a sect, organization, or religion.

"Traditionally, they were erected prior to great wars between countries by the edict of the gods. They're still tombs, but for organizations instead of the deceased. These types of dungeons are the least risky, and most of them were erected at the direction of the gods prior to the great war that accompanied the Cataclysmic Emergence. Surviving historical records indicate that they anticipated their fall and had all major powers leave behind seeds for future generations of humanity."

"Well, this clearly isn't one of *those*," said Orpheus. "An inheritance dungeon would normally have a welcome room or an explanation beforehand, not a nameless seal."

"It seems to me like you're familiar with these matters, then," said Stephan with a smile that was not a smile. "So you should also know that the reason I warned everyone wasn't because of these first two dungeons. Their potential threats are minimal, and even if individual adventurers suffered losses, they wouldn't be catastrophic. Instead, the reason I warned you all was because of the third type of dungeon: sealing dungeons."

"Sealing dungeons?" said Lawrence, who'd remained silent the entire time. "I've heard of those. My dad raided one once. Wiped out most of his party."

"Yes, you *would* know about sealing dungeons, wouldn't you?" said

Stephan. "There was once a sealing dungeon near the Bloodwood Outpost. In that dungeon's case, it wasn't cleared for many decades, and the seal suffered irreparable harm. When the adventurers failed to clear it, the seal ruptured and released demons upon the outpost when it was unprepared. The outpost lost over 50 percent of its population in two weeks, and it wasn't until recently that these losses were made up for. Any survivors of that raid were so traumatized and guilt-ridden that they could only retire from adventuring."

"What *is* a sealing dungeon?" asked the red-faced Haster. "Please. We just want to know why so many of our fellow adventurers died. Otherwise, I won't be able to face their ghosts in the afterlife."

"Sealing dungeons are built to keep something suppressed," said Stephan. "Some evils are so potent that they can't be entirely eliminated. The seals are there to gradually wear them down. A prime example would be the recurring dungeons in each major city. A fragment of evil was sealed beneath each dungeon by the Temple of Hope, and every day, a certain amount of energy was extracted in the form of demons and a temporary dungeon.

"These dungeons are stable when cleared regularly, but when they *aren't* cleared for a while, their energy accumulates. Threats multiply until they become unmanageable, except by large groups of organized adventurers.

"Judging by the casualties, this dungeon is a sealing dungeon. Not the type you find in cities, but a historical type. Some evil entity from the time of the gods was sealed away, and mana contamination has likely animated any corpses or threats inside the dungeon."

"What about the original sealed entity?" asked Barbara. "Is it a threat to us?"

"It's difficult to say," answered Stephan. "It may or may not have returned. The Evils of Death, Violence, and Madness complicate things. We might find a powerful boss-type demon inside, or we might only find a large number of aggressive demons. The only way to confirm this is via careful exploration."

Orpheus snorted loudly. "So you don't know anything. All you can do is speculate."

"That's right," confirmed Stephan. "I confirm that I have no idea what's going on. The Temple of Hope has assessed this as a one-star dungeon, so we should theoretically be able to clear it with the people assembled. But we *must* be prepared for anything. Rogues, rune-breakers, and life mages—each group needs at least one of these. Each team should also have at least two tanks per team, one primary and one secondary."

"An ambitious quota, one that your team doesn't seem to meet," said Orpheus.

"Once again, you are correct," said Stephan. "Which is why we won't enter the dungeon until we join up with another party with a life mage and a tank. And if there is an extreme shortage, we will join up with *two* teams. Otherwise, we won't be entering this dungeon."

"And that is where I end my talk. I've given you all the information I can, and it's up to you all to make your decisions. I welcome any teams with a life mage to approach me and discuss a collaboration. My team is amiable, and we already have a rune-breaker, a rogue, and a tank in our party composition."

Stephan then stood up and folded up his chair before sitting down beside the rest of his team. "How was I, Lawrence? Did I come off as too arrogant?"

"I had no idea you could be such a poser," replied Lawrence. "Though it doesn't seem like there are any teams interested in joining up with us."

"We won't get matched up right away," said Stephan, shaking his head. "The best teams will approach weaker teams, and stronger teams like ours, Haster's, Barbara's, and Orpheus's will get the dregs. I'd wager some weaker teams with life mages will seek us out after they get refused too many times. We'll offer them an even share, and they'll take it."

Things developed exactly as Stephan predicted. The more successful teams with life mages banded together with one or two lesser teams. As for the three leading captains and Stephan, they received multiple offers from some weaker teams. After a round of intense and secretive discussions, Stephan led five individuals back to their group.

"This is Team Oasis," said Stephan to the team. "Their party consists of a tank, a swordsman, a life mage, a rogue, and an archer. We'll be collaborating with them for this raid."

"We're happy to have the opportunity to work with you," said their leader, a swordsman in ragged chainmail and mismatched boots. "I'm Nale, a swordsman, and this is our life mage, Hellen."

The teams exchanged greetings and familiarized themselves with their respective abilities. They ignored the few teams rushing into the dungeon and practiced together instead. Two hours later, their combined team and that of the three captains entered the dungeon together.

EXPLORING THE TOMB

The entrance to the tomb was made of fine marble and carved with wavy blue-green patterns. Looking upon it was akin to gazing into an endless ocean, one absent of life and bereft of mercy.

Sorin was struck by a suffocating sensation as soon as he entered the ruin. The feeling faded after a few seconds, but the dread of almost drowning and the reverence it instilled left Sorin on edge and prepared for anything.

"What a massive tomb," Lawrence said as he and his companion rogue, Warren, led their group into the tomb. "There's about fifty of us entering all at once, but we're still not cramped for space. Gareth might even get to shoot arrows this time! Whoever made this place was *rich*."

"More like influential," said Sorin as his eyes wandered over the carved patterns on the walls. "These patterns are usually seen on tombs of great religious significance. Specifically, whoever commissioned the tomb must have been a descendent of the ancient god, Poseidon."

Stephan gave Sorin a sidelong glance. "I'd expect this much from a member of my family or from Daphne, but not from someone from the Kepler Clan."

Sorin shrugged. "I've always found history to be interesting. I made a point of reading up on any scraps of pre-Cataclysmic Emergence history I could find during my spare time."

Records of the Divine Era were rare. Only a few scattered texts remained as proof of godly existences. The countless myths they had sired or encouraged were lost to time, with only a handful of prominent names remaining.

"I never paid attention in ancient history class," said Stephan. "Was Poseidon the leader, or was he the promiscuous one?"

"I think they were *all* promiscuous," Daphne cut in. "So much so that it's leaked over into modern literature." She cleared her throat. "Not that I read too much of that sort of nonsense."

Sorin gave her a strange look but nodded. "Word has it that Poseidon had over a hundred mortal offspring. As a result, modern fiction tends to invent characters and claim they're Poseidon's descendants. Or the product of humans and animals after divine intervention. Regardless, it remains that tombs with Poseidon's blessing are the most common, thereby solidifying Poseidon's reputation as a divine breeding horse." Sacrilegious words, Sorin was sure, if uttered a few centuries prior.

"There are corpses up ahead," said Lawrence. "We'll go check them out." He and Warren joined up with the other rogues, who were equally interested in the matter. They returned a minute later with additional information. "They're undead, by the looks of it. The teams that went in before us made quick work of them. Oh, and we found about five of the adventurers that were killed upon entering. Their belongings have already been looted."

"Have they?" Stephan said coldly. "It seems *some* people aren't respecting the rules when it comes to slain adventurers' belongings. We'll see if they keep up this foolishness when I make my report to the guild." A group of ten adventurers approached from the side just then. "Hello, Barbara. How can I be of assistance?"

"No need to be so distant, Stephan," said Barbara. "The other captains and I were just discussing potentially increasing our pace. Since other teams have already gone ahead, most of the dangers in the tomb would have already been tripped by them."

"Increase the pace if you wish," said Stephan indifferently. "We'll maintain our current speed. You never know what kind of traps might have been—"A sharp scream suddenly cut through the tunnels, interrupting him. "As I was saying, you never know what traps might have been missed. Lawrence? Warren?"

"We'll go check it out," said Lawrence with a sigh.

Their team and the other five teams that had entered with them gathered before a large pit that had collapsed just ahead. "Two rogues died in that pit," said Nale. "They were obviously not very good at their jobs. How exactly did they even pass the guild's assessment if they couldn't sense a simple pit trap?" The swordsman was a very cynical person, as Sorin had discovered during their few interactions. He didn't like him but tolerated him since they were going to be teammates for some time.

"There's no need for such sharp words, Nale," said Hellen, their life mage, before Stephan could scold him. "This place is *old*. There were probably issues with the traps. Things that made them difficult to spot."

Indeed, it took a team of nearly fifteen rogues around twenty minutes to finally figure out the mechanism for the trap. It was so badly corroded that the first few people who'd traveled over it had broken off layers of rust instead of activating it.

"Us rogues have all agreed that we can probably expect more things like this going forward," said Lawrence upon his return. "No one wants to take the lead, so we've agreed to a rotation between traps. The frontmost teams will be migrating to the back after every exposure. This corridor is quite wide, so we'll travel in groups of two teams wide to make sure nothing is missed."

The deaths of two rogues increased the vigilance of the entire raiding party. Sorin's team was placed in the middle alongside Barbara's team, while Orpheus's team took point along with one of the lesser-known teams.

Five minutes later, Orpheus's team discovered a group of corpses along with a trap. After deactivating the trap, it was up to Sorin's team and Barabara's team to take point.

"Everyone, be vigilant," said Stephan, shifting into bear form.

"Collin, you're the secondary tank, so take the rear. Nale and Sorin, attack anything that gets past me. Daphne, keep fire in your hands. Lise and Gareth, get ready to shoot when you get a chance.

"As for Hellen, conserve your energy for critical cases. Sorin will collaborate with you after combat if there are significant injuries."

"With all due respect, Stephan, there are about eight teams worth of adventurers that have already gone through this place before us," said Nale. "There's no need for such caution."

"It seems we've gotten off to a bad start, Nale," said Stephan.

"How so?" asked Nale.

"For starters, when we agreed to team up, we also agreed that I would be in command," said Stephan. "But we've been here less than an hour, and you're already resisting my very reasonable commands. Should we just turn back now and call our alliance a mistake?"

"I meant no disrespect," Nale said stiffly. He drew his sword and adopted a two-handed fighting stance. "Let's hope all these preparations are a waste of time."

"That would be for the best," said Stephan. "Lawrence? Warren? Sweep the area ahead and keep an eye on the walls. Don't assume Barbara's rogues are going to find everything on their side."

Sorin continued to inspect the walls as they advanced. There were depictions of heroic figures lost to time and memory, as well as vicious monsters that had lost their luster with the emergence of the Seven Evils and their demons.

He paid special attention to the guardian gods of Pandora. Each god had a domain they governed, and these domains were far more complex than those controlled by the Seven Evils and their nemesis, Hope.

These gods also had complex relations with mortals, monsters, and beasts, giving rise to countless myths, of which only a minority had been recovered to date. Of these gods, Sorin only recognized a dozen and a half, despite his well-read and studious nature.

There were Zeus and the other Twelve Olympians. There was Hades, King of the Underworld, and his queen, Persephone. There was Gaia,

Goddess of the Earth, and Helios, God of the Sun. And finally, there was Asclepius, the God of Medicine.

To Sorin's knowledge, his family had once been proud followers of Asclepius. They'd wielded poisons in the name of healing and medicine and had been one of the most influential families after the Cataclysmic Emergence. But at some point, they'd stopped cultivating poison in favor of cultivating life mana, which they were also gifted with.

Sorin was unsure of what exactly had transpired and had honestly not been too interested in the topic. It was only now that he too cultivated poison that he was curious about his family's past and the reasons for their sudden loss of power and change in philosophy.

It was several minutes later when Lawrence and Warren stopped in front of a stretch of empty corridor.

"What's the matter?" Stephan asked the two rogues.

"We're not sure," said Lawrence. "Something feels off, but we don't know what."

"It's like there's danger everywhere," Warren added. "We started feeling it a few seconds ago."

"Come to think of it, I've been feeling a little uneasy as well," said Stephan. "Daphne?" The mage pulsed with mana as she performed a scan of the passage.

"It's not magical," said Daphne once the glow faded. "What about you, Seffias?"

"Nothing on my end!" called out a mage on Barbara's team.

"Is there a problem?" Barbara asked, walking over.

"We're not sure," said Stephan. "But our rogues think something is up, and my instincts are telling me to get ready for something."

"Our rogue has also been feeling uneasy," said Barabara. "But he doesn't think it's a trap."

"Then let's stop and try to figure this out," said Stephan. "Why don't we take a break while all the rogues look around?"

"Get off your high horse, Stephan," said Orpheus, stomping over. "We already took risks identifying a trap, and now that you've gotten to your first trap, you want to stop?"

"I'm not going to risk my team's lives just because you're getting antsy," Stephan snapped.

"What's the risk?" said Orpheus. "Worst case, it's a pit trap. If they're quick enough, they aren't a problem. Here, I'll show you."

"Don't!" said Stephan, but it was too late. Orpheus had already run forward. He passed the supposed danger zone without a hitch, then turned around and grinned. "See? Nothing to worry about." It was then that the floor rumbled. The ground beneath Lawrence and Warren burst open, along with the wall just beside Sorin. Corpses emerged from these entrances, putrid and hungry, and attacked their six groups from all sides.

"Zombies!" shouted Stephan, who was still in his bear form. "Sorin and Nale, protect the others. Collin, stand your ground in case any of them circle past us!" He then roared and smashed two corpses apart with a Lunisolar Paw before biting down on another corpse with his sharp bear teeth.

39

THE BURIAL CHAMBER

Sorin had never seen a zombie in person, or at least one with its head still attached. He'd handled human cadavers and had slain many demons and even a few humans, but nothing could compare to the sheer *wrongness* of the animated dead.

It wasn't just their group that fell under attack, but all six groups in the tunnel. Doors opened in every direction, pouring endless amounts of rag-covered, disease-ridden abominations empowered by death mana.

While Stephan held the front, Lawrence and Warren retreated to cover their flanks. Nale cut down two corpses with his sword, leaving the other two that had emerged from the wall to Sorin.

Even powered by death mana, they still need to follow basic anatomy, thought Sorin. He didn't even bother with poison and used Viper Strike to stab a zombie in the neck directly between its vertebrae. He then retreated using Adder Rush and stabbed the second corpse in the neck as it tried to bite him.

"How many of these things are there?" complained Nale, impaling another zombie with his sword. This one didn't collapse immediately but pulled itself forward. A wind-powered arrow, courtesy of Gareth, blew its head off before it could reach the swordsman.

"Either cut off their heads or don't bother," Gareth shouted. "Don't you know the basics?"

"I know what I'm doing, thank you very much," growled Nale. He then charged at one of the three undead coming out from the wall, leaving their flank open to attack. Sorin was forced to maintain his position and block the two zombies, but he suffered a plague-filled scratch to his arm in the process.

Disease entered his body from the open wound and immediately began contaminating his mana and thickening the blood. Sorin instinctually mobilized the poisons in his body to attack this foreign invader—typically a poor move that would nourish the disease and corruption. But to his surprise, it worked extremely well and completely eradicated the contaminants. *It seems it's not just poisons and corruption I'm resistant to, but disease as well.*

Sorin was encouraged by the discovery and fought even more viciously than before. Scratches and shallow cuts were fine for him, given his rate of regeneration. Adventurers didn't fear zombies because they were strong, but because they feared getting infected by them. Curing such infections cost life mages valuable energy.

"Sorin, our back's under attack!" shouted Gareth. He and his fellow archer, Lise, were busy sniping off zombies that threatened their neighboring groups. Both archers were poorly equipped to resist a flood of zombies and required steady protection.

Collin was doing his best to repel the zombies with his sword and shield but could only do so much, given that they were under attack from all sides. "Lorimer, guard this place," said Sorin, grabbing the rat out of his pocket and tossing it to another approaching zombie. The rat burst into flames and launched himself at the zombie's head. Then, to everyone's horror, he dug into its brain and chomped down on the black crystal core within.

"Sorin!" shouted Gareth again.

"Coming!" said Sorin. He used Adder Rush to weave between both archers and meet the first of three zombies in battle. He kicked the first zombie back, stabbed the second in the throat, and took a bite from the third just before an arrow took its head.

"They're endless!" shouted another adventurer not far away. Their flank was getting overrun. They weren't part of Sorin's team, but letting them fall would endanger the entire formation. Sorin tossed out his mithril string and used Python Coil to tie up unstable zombie legs. The zombies stumbled, opening them up to an attack from the wine-drinking swordsman, Haster.

"Many thanks!" said Haster as he hacked off the last zombie's head.

Crisis averted, Sorin examined the battlefield. The zombies were no longer pouring out from the sides and were instead most concentrated at their front and rear. Orpheus was fighting alongside Stephan, but both of them had suffered several wounds. They were starting to show signs of fatigue.

"Sorin!" shouted Daphne. "I want to burn some of these down, but I need protection."

"Can't you just lob a Fireball over their heads?" asked Sorin, running up beside her.

"Don't argue and just help me," said Daphne.

Sorin quickly ran over to her side and blocked a zombie as she charged her spell. "Stephan! Fireball!" The bear threw himself to the side just in time to avoid a blast of flame that downed eight zombies. "Fireball! Fireball! Fireball!" Twenty more zombies fell, buying Stephan and Orpheus along with their groups time to form a new defensive line.

The tanks in each group formed a circle, blocking out most of the zombies and preventing them from pushing in. The remaining melee fighters killed those that slipped through the cracks. Archers and mages then took up positions at the center and fired between natural openings as convenient.

Finally, as quickly as it had arrived, the tide of the undead dried up. All that remained were hundreds of diseased corpses, complete with useless, rusted equipment and rotted clothing.

"All wounded, convene with your life mages to receive treatment!"

shouted Orpheus, spitting blood. "Unless you're opposed to that as well, Stephan?"

"Don't create conflict where it doesn't exist," said Stephan, shifting out of bear form. He winced as he rolled his shoulder and stumbled over to Hellen, their group's life mage, who was currently treating Nale's injuries.

"Hold still," said Hellen, applying a healthy but controlled dose of life mana. It poured into Nale's flesh and blood, invigorating it so it could fight off infection.

I wonder, thought Sorin as he inspected Stephan's injuries. "Stephan, come over here and let me take a look at you."

Stephan had grown used to receiving treatment from Sorin and took a seat. Sorin knelt beside him and looked him over in his usual manner. He poured a small amount of poison mana into one of Stephan's more shallow wounds, destroying a bit of flesh but also eliminating the disease.

"Looks like my theory was correct," said Sorin. "Give me a few minutes to treat you, and you'll be good to go." He looked over Stephan's body and identified no less than fourteen cuts and bite wounds. By the time Hellen was finished, Stephan's treatment was complete.

"Let me take a look at you," said Hellen, holding Stephan back.

"He's fine," said Sorin. "I eliminated the disease, and his natural recovery is high. He's perfectly capable of fighting."

Hellen frowned. "And what about you? I see no less than ten wounds on your body."

"I'm immune to such weak diseases," said Sorin. "And these wounds are all shallow. But go ahead and examine us if you feel strongly about it."

"Pardon my rudeness, but this *is* my job," said Hellen, inspecting Stephan's wounds. Her eyes widened when she realized Sorin was correct. "Impressive. You damaged him slightly in the process, but the disease was expelled. How taxing was it on your mana?"

"It didn't require much effort," Sorin admitted. "I can't heal tissue damage like you can, but when it comes to killing things, I'm not half bad. I guess I can add killing disease to my list of specialties."

"It's unconventional on the battlefield, but I'm happy to save my mana," said Hellen. "I'll be sure to leave cases like this for you in the future. But please, see me for more serious injuries. I see the reason why you'd try such a treatment, but in the end, it's a barbaric way to treat wounds that can potentially kill someone with the slightest misstep."

"I'll keep that in mind," said Sorin. He knew perfectly well the disadvantages of using poison to fight disease. The Medical Association had used that same argument to oust poison users from their ranks over a century ago.

Only a few adventurers were gravely wounded by the zombie attack. One of them was too injured to continue and had to be escorted to the entrance. Those that remained quickly looted the battlefield by extracting black crystals from the zombies they'd slain.

"Are these demon cores?" asked Sorin, holding up a crystal. The demon cores he'd seen before were all vibrant in color, not pitch black like those they found in the undead.

"They're about the same," answered Stephan. "The demons we hunt in the forest are aligned with Violence or Madness. These, however, are aligned with Death."

"They're worth about the same at the Temple of Hope," added Lawrence, tossing a pouch of them to Stephan. "How are we going to split this mess? Group loot?"

"Group loot," Stephan confirmed. "We captains already discussed it before entering. Whatever we find as a super-group will get split evenly. It's only when we split up that everything reverts to finders keepers. Now quiet down—I think I hear something." Sorin looked around to see that other groups were hushing their companions. The rogues and archers were frowning while looking down the dark corridor.

"I think there's fighting up ahead," said one of the more powerful archers with mana glowing in her eyes. "I think... I think I see adventurers fighting zombies!"

"Then what are we waiting for?" shouted Orpheus. "Let's go help our fellow adventurers! Unless a certain coward doesn't want to rush in alongside me?"

"Don't insult me," said Stephan. "It's worth the risk if they're in danger. Everyone—move!"

They advanced at a brisk pace while maintaining their previous formation. The remaining rogues fanned out ahead, spotting traps that they walked around instead of disabling. Fortunately, there weren't too many traps, and they arrived inside a large ceremonial chamber in less than a minute.

"Reinforce our brothers and sisters!" shouted Orpheus. "I'll take front!"

"I'll take left!" shouted Stephan.

"I'll take right!" shouted the greatsword wielder, Haster.

"Keeper!" answered Barbara, leading a group to the middle of the room, where they cleared out immediate threats.

The ceremonial chamber was a mess. Out of the eighty or so adventurers who'd gone ahead, twenty were already dead, and ten were severely wounded. They, too, were under attack from the undead. Unlike the rag-wearing weaklings they'd fought before, these undead were deadly and even wore armor and only partially corroded weapons.

Sorin's group arrived just in time to fight off two greatsword-wielding zombies before they could cut down a bloodied bard. Her companions had already fallen, and her mana was completely exhausted.

"Daphne, take out that bigger zombie in the corner!" shouted Stephan.

Daphne immediately smashed apart an armored halberd-wielding zombie with a Fireball, slaying it before it could kill a retreating archer.

Sorin and Lorimer launched themselves into battle. Sorin's poison wasn't especially useful against the undead, but his knowledge of anatomy and his practiced hands more than made up for it. Every slash and stab of his dagger took down an empowered zombie.

As for Lorimer, he was a menace on the battlefield. Whatever he saw, he ate. That included rusted armor, zombie bones, and zombie flesh and cores. It wasn't long before he began to glow with a diseased light, indicating that he'd successfully absorbed their plague-bearing properties.

Great, thought Sorin, using his mithril string to pull back a zombie's sword long enough for an axe-wielding warrior to cut it down. *I'm now the proud owner of a disease-ridden rat.* He had no plans on coming forward with Lorimer's latest ability.

With their arrival, the battle ended quickly. There were no further casualties on the adventurers' side. Sorin immediately got busy treating the lightly wounded with poison. He left the more gravely wounded for the life mages to handle.

As for Stephan and the other party leaders, they approached the survivors to determine what had happened while the rogues looted. "Apparently, it wasn't Orpheus who triggered the trap," said Stephan when he returned. "Our rogues were feeling uneasy because of impending danger. Someone—they're dead now—was stupid enough to touch a statue. The statue was apparently a switch to open all the side doors where dead soldiers and servants had been buried to hold eternal vigil.

"Didn't you say this was supposed to be a sealing tomb?" asked Sorin. "These things were clearly animated with death mana. Why would that be worked into their traps when this place was built prior to Cataclysmic Emergence?"

"I didn't say it was a trap; I said it was a construction feature," said Stephan, shaking his head. "As for the zombies, that's just Death's influence that infiltrated the tomb."

"So what now?" asked Lawrence, returning with a gory bag of crystal cores. "Everyone's exhausted, including the life mages."

"Everyone's agreed to a two-hour rest," said Stephan. "Try and recover as much mana and energy as you can. Those who wish to retreat can go back to the camp. I doubt that the survivors of those groups that were destroyed will want to stay much longer."

40

DAEDALUS'S LABYRINTH

The battle with the zombies was the first extended battle for their combined adventuring teams. Each team, therefore, took time to adjust their formations and discuss improvements. "So what's your opinion on what our core team lacks, Sorin?" Lawrence asked when he finished recovering his mana. Hellen had healed a brutal cut on his arm, and only a thin scar remained.

"I'm not sure," said Sorin. "Maybe more bodies to protect our squishier members? A swordsman like Nale? Even if they aren't a tank, it would take a lot of pressure off of you and me."

"Agreed," said Lawrence. "And I think Stephan does as well. It's just that good warriors are often team captains, so it's tough to find someone reliable."

Anyone else would be more reliable than Nale. Then again, this was a temporary alliance. "Why don't you want a life mage?" asked Sorin.

"Why do we need a life mage when we have you?" asked Lawrence. "Whatever you can't fix can be solved with healing potions. No point in splitting loot an extra way for that." A fair point that Sorin hadn't considered.

Two hours had already passed, so the adventurers began to pick up their belongings and group up. Demon crystals had been looted and delivered to the Adventurers Guild station outside the ruin. As a result, there was no need to carry everything they'd gained deeper into the ruin.

"It's about time we head out," said Stephan, slinging his pack over his shoulders. "Is everyone else good to go?"

"Ready when you are, *boss*," said Nale, drawing his sword.

Having learned their lesson earlier, the teams moved forward as a single pack, making sure to rotate periodically to remain fresh. Mages had spells at the ready, while archers kept arrows nocked. Everyone kept their weapons drawn in case of a surprise attack.

Surprisingly, the corridor out of this welcoming chamber was unob-structed. There were no traps, and no zombies rushed out to fight them. According to the mages, this was due to a sacred aura coming from the end of the corridor that prevented the reanimation of corpses.

The corridor eventually opened into a room just as large as the first ceremonial chamber. It contained coffins and statues of various gods, all cast in marble and still in one piece despite the centuries that had passed. Stephan informed everyone that the Adventurers Guild would recover such things, and they would only get a share of the profit after the pieces were appraised and auctioned to curious collectors.

"Now, *this* is what we're here for," said Orpheus, stepping up to two large tables set up before a marble slab. "Loot, for those brave enough to obtain it." There was a trident, a longsword, a bow, and a helmet. "Mages? Rogues? What are you all waiting for?"

Daphne, Lawrence, and Warren joined a larger group of rogues and mages in sweeping the area for traps and enchantments. The stone slab was immediately confirmed to be enchanted with powerful barrier magic. As for the items, they were all enchanted items without curses.

Since they were all in a safe place, they relaxed and rested as they waited for representatives from the Mages Guild and the Adventurers Guild. "I can't assess their exact value, but these are clearly historical relics," said an older mage with a white beard. "I'd peg them at 5,000 gold apiece just based on the power of their enchantments. Of course, their historical value might mean they're worth far more."

"They're one-star items, aren't they?" asked Stephan. The mage confirmed this, and so did the Adventurers Guild representative. "Then anyone here can claim them, and the Adventurers Guild will record the debt to the expedition. Is anyone in my party interested?" Sorin shook his head, and so did everyone but Nale, though in the end, he, too, decided against claiming them. "Very good. We renounce any claim to these items."

"How generous of you," said Orpheus, picking up the longsword. "I'll take this one then. Unless you want it, Barbara?"

"I'm a weapons master, not a sword specialist," said Barbara. "I can take either the trident or the bow. I'm not too picky. How about you, Haster?"

"I already have a good sword and good wine," said Haster. "My team is also well-equipped. But I think that chap over there wants the helmet. Can I use my pick from him?" He was the most easygoing of the captains.

"If that's what you want," said Barbara. "What about this bow and trident?"

"If no one else wants it, I'll take the trident," said one adventurer.

"Then I'll take the bow," said Barbara. "Very good. Now I have another good weapon to rely on."

"Then that just leaves what to do about this door," said Orpheus. "I say we break it open and keep going."

"I think the *prudent* course of action would be to ask the guilds for their opinion, Orpheus," said Barbara. "What do you think, esteemed appraiser?"

"I'm afraid this old man doesn't have one," said the appraiser. "I appraise items, not barriers. And frankly, Miss Daphne is my superior when it comes to this kind of thing."

All eyes focused on Daphne. "I'm just good at breaking things," said the mage. "And the answer is yes. If you want me to break it, I'll do it."

They turned their attention to the representative from the Adventurers Guild, who'd placed a pair of golden spectacles on her face. She jotted down notes on a pad of paper as she read the stone slab. Fifteen minutes later, she took off her glasses and wiped the sweat from her forehead. Using the glasses was obviously taxing.

"Adventurer Stephan was correct," said the representative. "This is a sealing tomb. An old one at that. I'd peg it at 600 years old, given the syntax on the slab."

"What does it say?" asked Barbara.

"Herein lies the corpse of an abomination," read the representative. "A cruel curse upon humanity. I leave my seal upon Daedalus's Labyrinth, knowing that Death makes a mockery of us all. It's signed by someone called Theseus, whoever that was. Probably a hero of his time." Sorin had never heard of him either, but that was normal. Only a handful of heroes from the Divine Era were remembered.

"I believe Barbara was asking more about the guild's opinion on continuing the raid," said Orpheus. "A sealed dungeon that hasn't been opened in a long time; is the guild against us unsealing it?"

The representative shrugged. "I have no opinion on the matter. The dungeon was assessed as a one-star threat, and with so many one-star teams, raiding it should be achievable. If you wish to proceed with raiding the dungeon, you may do so. I will wait outside the dungeon for three days with the representatives of the other guilds before returning, regardless of your success or failure.

"That being said, you may choose to report your findings to the guild and stop here. I can guarantee a 20,000-gold reward for what's been found so far, to be split amongst all concerned parties according to our guild's rules."

The captains all exchanged looks with their teammates before voicing their opinions. "Let's do it," said Orpheus. The other captains echoed his sentiment.

"I'd like to give this dungeon a try, assuming enough of us join in," said Barbara.

"My party is full of hot-blooded men that don't back down," said Haster. "Also, I'm drunk. So I'm in."

The remaining parties agreed to proceed, leaving only Sorin's party. "If everyone else is game, how could we say no?" said Stephan. "Daphne, will you do the honors?"

"Piece of cake," said Daphne, cracking her knuckles. She moved up to the barrier and began drawing red sigils upon the blue forcefield that appeared. They formed a resonance with the field and caused it to vibrate until, finally, the field shattered, releasing the seal.

She stepped back as the door slid open. Fierce mana oozed out of the door and attacked everyone present. For a moment, Sorin was overwhelmed with white-hot rage. It was only thanks to a gentle flute melody from the only bard in their supergroup that he was able to bottle up his anger once again.

"The aura of Violence is extremely thick," warned Stephan as Orpheus brought his party up to the open door. "Expect powerful one-star demons. Two-star demons aren't out of the question either."

"I'm not new at this, you arrogant twit," said Orpheus, swishing his cloak and entering the doorway.

"Do I come off as arrogant?" Stephan asked the rest of the party.

"Sometimes," said Lawrence, holding up his thumb and index finger. "Just a little bit."

"I'll go next," said Barbara, entering the doorway. Her group vanished just like Orpheus's just after they entered. The teams slowly trickled in after them, with Sorin's team taking up the rear.

A golden light washed over them as they passed through the door, transforming their surroundings. Walls stretching a hundred feet into the air appeared on either side of them. They were ancient things made from ordinary stone. Reinforcement runes had been affixed every thirty feet.

"Everyone be careful," said Stephan. "We've clearly been split up into different parts of the dungeon. The golden circle here is our starting point. No matter what we do, we need to remember the way back."

Their team walked down what appeared to be a hallway, only to reach a sharp corner that split into two separate directions a few seconds later. By the second split, they confirmed that it was indeed a maze, like they'd initially suspected.

"How exactly are we going to find our way back?" asked Sorin. "I doubt whatever map we draw will be accurate."

"Oh, I know!" said Lawrence. "It reminds me of that story with the ball of yarn to find the way back. All we need now is a *really* big ball of yarn. Maybe we unravel someone's cloak?"

"I'm starting to get second thoughts about working together, Stephan, if this is all your team can come up with," said Nale.

"Do you have any better suggestions?" asked Stephan.

"I don't," said Nale. "But it's better than spitting out children's tales and making light of the situation."

"Poison," Sorin said suddenly. "We'll use poison to find our way back."

"Poison?" said Hellen, the life mage. "How does poison let us return to the entry circle?"

"Like this," said Sorin, flicking a drop of his blood onto the labyrinth wall. It ate a small hole in the stone and caused them all to wrinkle their noses.

"Is that really your blood?" said Nale. "Disgusting."

"Hey!" said Lawrence. "That's our teammate's blood. You can't talk trash about it. Only we can."

"Actually, I think he's onto something," said Warren, Team Oasis's rogue. "You guys can all smell that, right? How long does the smell last?"

"Days? Maybe a week if we're lucky?" said Sorin. "I'm honestly not sure. I haven't had long to test it. All I know is that whatever I bleed on doesn't stop smelling. I need to use clearmist vials to wash away the smell."

"It *does* have the advantage of not giving off a mana signature," said Gareth, smelling a spot of corrosion. "Also, it's not a loose item that can just be picked up. It has advantages over paint in that it might not be obvious to others not part of our group."

"Then it's decided," said Stephan. "We'll use smell to track our way back, but we'll also use maps as a backup. Gareth? Lise? Are you comfortable writing all this down?" They nodded and took out a pen and paper. "Great. Then, let's have Lawrence and Warren scout the way forward. Sorin, try not to bleed yourself dry." Their team then warily entered the labyrinth, completely unaware that five minutes after their departure, the walls at the entrance shifted, cutting off their escape path.

41

TEAM 'WE DON'T NEED A LIFE MAGE'

Having experienced the horrors of the sealing tomb leading up to the labyrinth's entrance, Sorin's team and Team Oasis adopted a tight formation, with Lawrence and Warren taking turns scouting up ahead. The rest of them pressed together behind Stephan and Collin, who would buy them precious seconds to react should enemies arrive.

There were advantages and disadvantages to this arrangement. For example: both the absence and presence of Lawrence in their formation.

"Look, Stephan," said Lawrence, nudging up beside him and pushing everyone out of position. "I know we're in the middle of the dungeon and all, but there's something very important I think we need to address."

"Stop blabbering and focus on our surroundings," said Stephan, who was half-shifted in case of a surprise enemy attack. "You never know what you'll find in old dungeons like these, Lawrence. Best be careful in case your whining accidentally triggers a curse or something."

"I'll take that with the mountain of salt it deserves," said Lawrence, "and I'll also choose to ignore your suggestion. Some things are more important than surviving an ambush. You know what I'm talking about, don't you, Sorin?"

Sorin shook his head. "I have no idea, Lawrence. But if it's that important, get it off your chest. For all our sakes." It was something both teams could agree on.

"Then I won't hold back," said Lawrence. "Both our teams are wonderful and filled with strong and memorable adventurers. Stephan, the angry bear, and Lawrence, the handsome. Let's not forget Nale, the edgy swordsman, and Helen, the pedantic healer.

"Unfortunately, there's an imbalance between our two teams. I'm not talking in terms of strength, but in terms of style. Team Oasis has something we are sorely lacking, and you should know by now where this is going."

"Are you complaining about us lacking a life mage?" asked Stephan.

"Seriously?" said Lawrence. "After I took great pains to make it obvious? I'm talking about a name, you brainless bear."

"You can't be serious," said Gareth, finally unable to take it any longer. "Here I am, tiring my eyes out scouting for danger, and you're wasting brainpower thinking about a team name?"

"Is that so wrong of me?" asked Lawrence. "A name is a powerful thing. It describes. It inspires. It intimidates our enemies every time we yell it out."

"I can't say I speak for the entire team, but I believe most of us see a name as a low priority," said Stephan. "Also, we've been holding back on a team name because we weren't sure if the team would remain the same after returning from our last mission. The paperwork for setting up an official team is also horrendous, so I haven't gotten to the part about our name and sigil."

"That hurts, Stephan," said Lawrence. "We've been through life and death together, you and me. This entire team has. It, therefore, only makes sense to have a team name celebrating that accomplishment, one expressing our unity and will to stay together for time eternal. Nale, how did you guys come up with the team name 'Oasis'?"

"Uh... I think I just left it to Hellen," said Nale. "We're not very good at naming things. How *did* you come up with it, Hellen?"

"I believe I just tossed a dictionary up in the air and then chose a word in it," said Hellen. "Can you please try to be more serious, Lawrence? You might be out of rotation, but you might be able to spot something Warren doesn't if you're paying attention."

"I, for one, think a name is very important," said Daphne, interrupting her continuous chanting as she scried the walls and floor for runes and magical traps. "For one, it's good for morale. For another, I'll need it to write my nov... my *report* when everything is said and done."

"Maybe instead of focusing on a name, your team should focus on fixing up its deficiencies," said Hellen. "For example, a life mage. Any proper team has one. The other three main captains did, at least." Stephan snorted loudly when she said this. "What? You're the one who said so at the team gathering. Am I wrong?"

"You're not wrong," said Stephan. "For the most part. Most teams *do* need a life mage. But some teams can do without one. Teams with druids. Teams based on a theme, like an all-archer or all-mage team. Sorin, do you think we need a life mage?"

Sorin frowned at being put on the spot but gave the matter some thought. "In truth, as long as we have healing potions, I can take care of any injuries that come up."

"Are you sure you're not being a little too arrogant?" asked Hellen.

"I'm fully aware of my capabilities, thank you very much," said Sorin icily. "I *was* trained as a physician. More to the point, poison, disease, and corruption aren't issues for me, and potions and surgery can heal most wounds. As for broken bones, once you set them right, a healing potion will work just fine. Am I missing anything, or can you somehow regenerate entire arms without my knowledge?"

Hellen sniffed. "Your treatment takes too much time."

"And *yours* takes too much mana," countered Stephan. "Moreover, other than healing, you can't do anything else. On the other hand, Sorin can kill things quite quickly, thereby *preventing* injuries. Lawrence, I see Warren. It's almost your turn."

"I feel strongly about this name thing," said Lawrence. "And I'd feel much more comfortable doing my job if we had one."

Stephan rolled his eyes. "Gareth, do you care about our team name?"

"Nope," said Gareth.

"How about you, Sorin?" asked Stephan.

"Not in the slightest," said Sorin.

"Daphne, do you have specific opinions on what a good name should sound like?" asked Stephan.

"Hm, well, I was thinking that if we incorporate the names of ancient—"

"Excellent," said Stephan, cutting her off. "Then, if there's no opinion to the contrary, we'll go with team 'We Don't Need a Life Mage'. Sound good?"

"I like it!" said Daphne, sticking out her thumb.

"If that's settled, I think we should adopt battle positions," said Gareth, drawing an arrow. Lise, Team Oasis's archer, was just a step behind him. Warren rounded a corner seconds later. Chasing after him was a group of large beetles.

"The labyrinth!" yelled Warren as he ran. "It's changing!"

"Changing?" asked Stephan. "What do you mean, it's changing? Prepare to receive their charge! Collin, with me! Archers, shoot on my mark. Ready? Loose!"

Two arrows, one of wind and one of lightning, tore through the large group of advancing beetles, blasting off legs and piercing carapaces but not slaying any of them. Stephan, the armored bear, and the shield and sword-wielding Collin crashed into the three-foot-tall beetles, knocking them back and buying precious time for Daphne to throw a Fireball into their rear ranks.

Over a dozen beetles fell to the floor, writhing with pain as their innards boiled. Except the stone floor didn't *remain* stone. The labyrinth began to transform.

The stone floor became a dirt path through the woods. Walls opened up, making it so that the swarming beetles no longer had to climb over themselves to attack them. A portion of them dug into the loam and added a third dimension to their attacks.

Daphne was about to launch another spell when Sorin felt vibrations underground. "Careful!" he said, shoving her toward Gareth. A beetle burst out of the ground and knocked Sorin prone. But he quickly recovered and twisted in a snakelike fashion before stabbing at the beetle, only for his mithril knife to bounce off its hard shell.

"It's mana-sensitive!" shouted Gareth. "Sorin, keep it away from Daphne!" He shot an arrow at the creature, but it once again used its tough shell to block. Another two beetles poked their heads out of the ground. Sorin, having learned the basics of their anatomy from his last attack, struck a weak point in their exoskeletons with his dagger. Both beetles writhed in pain as the poison he injected melted the flesh locked inside their shells.

Sorin was about to handle the third beetle when a Fire Bolt shot through its shell and blasted it apart. "Huh," said Daphne, blowing on her wand. "Weak to fire mana. No wonder they hate me." At the sight of their companion burning alive, the beetles shivered with rage. They pushed past Stephan and Collin, ignoring their deadly attacks.

"If you're done clearing up the rear, would you mind helping out here?" asked Nale, slicing a beetle in half with his obviously enchanted longsword. "They're getting a little overwhelming."

"Handle it yourself," snapped Sorin. "I have better things to do than listen to your orders. Lawrence, cover Daphne!"

"Yes, sir!" said Lawrence.

On the surface, these beetles are endless and durable, thought Sorin. *But in practice, they're very weak. It's only their exoskeleton that's a problem. A single dose of poison is enough to melt one alive, as opposed to crushing and slicing them over and over until they stop coming.*

Having figured out the crux of the issue, Sorin used Adder Rush to squeeze past Stephan and Collin and into the bulk of the beetles. His dagger struck repeatedly like a snake's fang, and each time it struck, a beetle fell to the ground, not dead but dying.

In medicine, using poison is about knowing how much to use and when. It's the same in battle as well. Overusing poison on an enemy is a waste. Wasting time is a cardinal sin that might lead to the death of my companions.

He struck one more time, taking a beetle in the neck, but when he tried to remove his dagger, he discovered that it was stuck. He, therefore, decisively abandoned it and shot a poison needle into a beetle's eye. It struck the beetle's brain and killed it all the same. He didn't *need* a dagger. A dagger was just a convenient tool to accomplish his end goal: slaying his enemies.

Seeing Sorin so effectively kill members of their species, the demonic beetles changed their target from Daphne to Sorin. He found himself under attack from all sides. Thanks to Adder Rush, he was able to avoid most nips from their deadly pincers, but it wasn't long before his arms and legs were covered in deep cuts.

Poison needles are useful, but they're difficult to aim in close combat, analyzed Sorin. He slammed a beetle with a poisonous palm, injecting it with a heavy dose of Flesh-Melt Poison. It fell to the ground just like the others, but the cost in mana was much greater than when he'd used his dagger. *This poison palm is garbage. I can't spread out my power like Stephan does. I need to focus on a single point.*

Stephan and Collin were needed to defend their weaker members, so Sorin could only make the best of the situation. He continued to ignore sharp beetle bites in favor of improving his palm arts. *Too focused. The dose isn't lethal. Too spread out. The dose is lethal, but penetrating power is insufficient.* He repeatedly iterated his attack while dispatching the nearest beetles, using their bodies as shields as he prepared himself for the next in line.

Sorin's palm skill was, in fact, a paw skill based on Stephan's Lunisolar Paw. What Sorin discovered as he modified the attack was that he didn't *need* heaviness. He needed sharp piercing power and consistent dose delivery.

My attacks need to be more snakelike, Sorin finally decided. Something clicked in his mind when he thought this. His palm shot out like a viper, summoning a mana projection of two fangs that pierced through a beetle's shell and delivered a fatal dose of flesh melt poison.

He repeated the attack twice more before retreating and pulling his dagger out of a beetle's corroded exoskeleton. A green mana projection appeared around his dagger as he channeled the same attack into a beetle's hard shell. This time, the dagger didn't bounce but directly pierced its defenses.

My understanding of Viper Strike was shallow, thought Sorin, dispatching beetles at a rate that was three times greater than before. *If my fangs are sharp enough, I don't need to consider weak points. If my poison is vicious enough, I don't need to strike vitals.*

The new and improved Viper Strike consumed twice as much mana, but Sorin didn't need to care about such things. The attack already had low mana consumption, and his mana reserves were several times that of a normal cultivator.

Sorin fought for several minutes straight before the tide of beetles finally receded. He slew one last beetle before the beetles decided to retreat. They tried to hurry off, but Lawrence and Warren took care of them before they made it very far.

"Rogues, loot," said Stephan. "Wounds, everyone?"

"I'm fine," said Sorin, applying a dose of Flesh-Melt Poison to his cuts and sealing them off. "You?"

"Flesh wounds," said Stephan, reverting to his human form. "Though I could use some stitches on my shoulder."

"*I* could take a look at that," volunteered Hellen.

"That's all right," said Stephan, brushing her off. "Team 'We Don't Need a Life Mage' is self-sufficient. These wounds aren't worth wasting valuable mana on."

Hellen gritted her teeth before turning her attention to Nale. He'd slain no small number of beetles. Given the mismatched state of his armor, it was only natural that he suffered a few deep wounds, which she treated.

With the beetles slain, the labyrinth returned to its original state. The dirt path and woods faded into the labyrinth's stone walls, revealing a pile of decayed corpses in a dead end. "How old *are* these things?" said Lawrence, picking through them. "Hey, wait—this corpse is fresh. Maybe a year old, tops. Didn't we just open this place?"

THE SHIFTING LABYRINTH

"How is this possible?" asked Nale, kicking a skeleton whose flesh had been picked clean by beetles. It was as Lawrence said: the corpse was maybe a year old, and the bones hadn't yet had time to dry properly. "Didn't we just unseal this dungeon? I was there. I saw it."

Stephan snorted. "Just because we unsealed *this* entrance, that doesn't mean it was the *only* entrance."

"Didn't the tomb imply only a single entrance?" asked Lise, Team Oasis's archer. "Pardon, but if we can't explain this phenomenon, we might all be in danger."

"I think the answer is self-evident, yes?" said Daphne. "This place was contaminated when we arrived, but the seal was intact. It stands to reason that the contamination came from *somewhere*."

"In other words, there was at least one extra entrance to this dungeon before we even arrived," muttered Sorin. "A point of infection not necessarily related to the obvious gaping wound."

"There could have easily been multiple entrances," said Daphne. "It's a well-known fact that dungeons are dimensional anomalies that actively seek to connect to the mortal world."

"Daphne is correct," said Stephan. "It's not unusual for there to be separate entrances to a dungeon. In fact, the main entrance to a dungeon, like the one we found, is seldom used, and we typically discover it after the fact. Lawrence? Warren? What's the count?" The two rogues dumped a pile of one-star demon cores onto the ground, along with a short sword, a wand, and a pile of outdated old coins.

"I think some of these coins might be collectors' items," said Lawrence. "Look at this one! A hundred and fifty years old!"

"I think the more important things here are the two enchanted items," said Nale. "The wand. We want it."

"Hey!" said Daphne, putting her hands on her hips. "I'm a mage too, you know."

"But you're not a life mage," Hellen pointed out. "And that's clearly a life wand."

"You technically have priority since it *is* a life wand," said Stephan. "But I hope you realize life wands are expensive."

"Of course, I know that," said Nale. "But Hellen is a valuable part of our team, so we must have it. Also, you don't have a life mage, so priority goes to us."

"These wands are expensive because they allow non-life mages to heal others to some extent," said Stephan. "But you're right. It'll also make Hellen that much more effective, so I won't quibble with you. Most importantly, our team name stands. As for the difference between this short sword and this wand... these cores will do nicely. *And* the gold."

"Don't you think you're going a bit too far?" asked Nale stiffly. "You're also benefiting from Hellen's magic."

"Not at all," said Stephan. "Life wands are valuable items, but they're still individual equipment. Moreover, we're two separate teams. I need to look out for my team, just like you need to look out for yours."

"Fine," said Nale. "You win this one." He snatched the wand and handed it to a very pleased Hellen. As for the short sword, Sorin's group had a quick discussion and decided that Lawrence was in dire need of a better weapon. Sorin would get priority on the next short weapon they got their hands on.

"If that's everything, then let's be on our way," said Stephan. They traced their steps back, only to discover that the way they'd come was now an unfamiliar branching corridor that didn't match the maps they'd been taking.

"I'm honestly very confused," said Gareth. "And I wrote this map. See that mark over there? Can you smell it? That's Sorin's mark. Except that mark he left was just inside the wall of a corridor. Now it isn't."

"I can confirm that," said Sorin. He'd been dutifully marking every corridor they'd come out of.

"Then I have some bad news for you all," said Stephan. "It appears that we've stumbled onto an autonomously mobile puzzle dungeon." Seeing their confusion, he clarified. "A shifting labyrinth, if you will."

"And why is that bad news, exactly?" asked Nale.

"Aside from the notorious level of difficulty such dungeons offer, I think the main reason is the lack of a way back," said Stephan. "Unless you have a three-star escape spell or a family heirloom on your person?" His next words immediately sobered up the entire group. "Why don't we all take a quick five-minute break and do a ration count?"

They proceeded to unpack any food items, water, or fasting potions on their persons. Sorin's team had thankfully packed plenty, enough to last three weeks. Nale's team, on the other hand, only had a week's worth of fasting potions, along with some waterskins enchanted with minor magics and dry rations that might last a few more days.

"This is going to be a problem," said Stephan, eyeing the rations grimly. "From now on, everyone is on half rations."

"What do you mean, half rations?" snapped Nale. "A week is more than enough time to escape this stupid dungeon."

"Question?" said Sorin, raising his hand.

"We're not students here; ask away," said Stephan.

"To get out of this dungeon, do we simply need to find the exit, or do we need to clear the dungeon?" asked Sorin. "Because that's a pretty big distinction, isn't it?" Though he was new to adventuring, he'd been gaining snippets of knowledge here and there. From what he'd heard, clearing a dungeon in the big cities would automatically send everyone out of the dungeon.

"In theory, we can do either," said Stephan. "But in practice, it's much easier to clear the dungeon than to find a specific exit. This is because dungeons all obey specific rules. I'm sure Daphne has noticed a certain phenomenon by now?"

Daphne had been scribbling on a notepad while they'd been counting rations. Sorin had assumed she was jotting down story ideas or working on a spell, but to his surprise, her scribbles turned out to be a simple map covered in strange symbols.

"I'm sorry, Daphne, but your map skills are even worse than Lawrence's," said Stephan. "Could you please translate this technically accurate monstrosity?"

"The mana density has been getting progressively thicker," replied Daphne. "I assume one of the rules you mentioned relates to mana density? Perhaps the endpoint or core of the dungeon is typically located where the mana density is highest?"

"That is correct," said Stephan. "Danger also scales with mana density. More powerful demons will gather where the mana is denser. The strongest demon in the dungeon will likely occupy the center, and only by defeating it will we count as clearing the dungeon."

"Well then. This greatly simplifies things," said Daphne. "I have a few more things I need to research. You can all lead the way while I figure out how to get us out of this mess."

"Then, if it's too much of a bother, I suppose little old me will take charge of tracking mana density," said Hellen, eager to point out her advantages.

"Suit yourself," said Daphne, taking out a new notepad. Sorin tried to decipher the writing, but his head started hurting. Magical theory was beyond him.

The next few encounters following the beetles were easy to clear, requiring only two or three of their members to participate. The others stood guard or rested. Conserving stamina was important now that they were on half rations. Team members were only permitted to use mana they could recover passively.

Before long, a day had passed. Their teams set up two camps for eight hours, during which the labyrinth mysteriously went dark and projected a starry sky above their heads. And when they woke, the walls grew lighter and gave off a rosy hue like a sunrise.

They wandered this way for three days before Hellen finally realized the crux of the problem. "What's *with* this labyrinth?" she muttered. "The density was increasing fine over the past day, but now it's shot down almost to its original levels."

"That's why I had everyone count their rations," said Stephan. "Mana density is only an indication of proximity to the center. But proximity to the center doesn't necessarily mean we're anywhere near the exit. Now quiet; I think Lawrence found something."

"Stop *doing* that!" said Lawrence, stepping out from behind a wall. "You keep ruining my dramatic entrances."

A smile tugged at the corner of Stephan's mouth. "You'd better work on your stealth skills then. Maybe doing some exercises in the morning would help?"

Sorin suppressed a laugh. It was an open secret in the group that Stephan was using underhanded means to trace Lawrence. At first, it was a fun, practical joke—at least, until Lawrence's stealth skills began to improve by leaps and bounds. After that, it became a core training exercise for the lazy rogue; in fact, Stephan had gone so far as to pay off Team Oasis in exchange for not mentioning it.

"*Anyway*, as I was about to say, there's a group of strange creatures up ahead," said Lawrence. "I'd call them demons, but…"

Stephan seemed to understand something. "Are they humanoid?"

"They are," confirmed Lawrence. "I'm just not sure if those are corrupted humans or spawned demons."

"Why don't we take a look?" said Stephan. "Gareth, Lise. Why don't you two take the lead and make sure we get a good vantage point?"

It wasn't long before the scenery changed in its usual fashion. Stone hallways gave way to a rock-covered island littered with caves. The endless darkness of the ceiling transformed into a clear blue sky, with not a cloud to be seen in every direction.

Gareth and Lise motioned for the team to come forward and only stopped them once they reached the edge of a cliff.

"Incredible!" Hellen was the first to comment on the 'demonic life forms' they saw. "Looking at them, it's like seeing a primitive human settlement."

"With a few *big* differences," said Lawrence. "If you'll notice their size."

"It was the eye that stood out to me more than anything," said Sorin. "These aren't humans, Stephan. These are ancient mythical creatures. I've seen fragmented pictures of them before in the Kepler Clan's library."

"I also recognize them," said Stephan. "In the Adventurers Guild's records, they're called cyclopes."

Stephan proceeded to explain the characteristics of cyclopes. They were humanoid and had a similar anatomy to humans. The main differences were that they were much larger, had a single eye, and had two hearts. They were also carnivorous. Their power scaled to size. Ten feet or less was the equivalent of a one-star demon. Larger cyclopes could be considered two-star demons.

Gareth was already familiar with this knowledge and added his commentary while scanning the enemy camp. At first, he was relaxed about it, but suddenly, his expression changed. "Lise, could I bother you to inspect the area beside the small fire over there?"

"I think it's… No, it couldn't be," said Lise.

"It could," said Gareth with a grimace. "That confirms it. They're monsters, all right. Permission to draw closer and show everyone something?"

"You two are in charge here," said Stephan.

"Then let's see how close we can get to those abominations," said Gareth.

The two archers cautiously brought their group through the mountainous terrain, making sure to avoid any cyclopes that were busy hunting, gathering, and fishing. The creatures lived in small grass huts and seemed to have a primitive language that relied on grunting and gestures. They were aggressive, but team-oriented.

"What's that wonderful smell?" asked Lawrence when they drew nearer. "Smells like pork."

Stephan's nose wrinkled. "It most definitely does *not* smell like pork, Lawrence. In fact, I strongly advise you to associate that smell with terrible things instead of salivating." He sighed. "Gareth? Lise? Is it confirmed?"

"Is what confirmed?" asked Nale.

"He... he means that... well..." Warren said, only to throw up suddenly.

Only then did it dawn on Sorin that he had encountered this smell many times before in burn patients. "Are you saying that in that camp, they're cooking humans?"

43

WHERE ARCHERS EXCEL

Stephan ignored the looks of horror and allowed Gareth and Lise time to inspect the camp from up close. "Well?" he said a few minutes later. "Did you find any signs that we might know these humans?"

"We spotted adventurers gear off to the side," said Gareth as mana faded from his eyes. "What you're smelling is stew. There's a large pot, about thirty feet wide, at the center of this encampment. By the looks of it, an entire team of adventurers was captured and chopped up into that pot. I see no cages and no survivors."

"There you have it," said Stephan. "Cyclopes are dreadful creatures, everyone. They're tribal, cannibalistic, and will eat anything with meat on them, including humans. Raw, if they don't have access to fire yet.

"Normally, I'd advise sneaking past them, but in this case, we have a duty to our fellow adventurers. Unless anyone objects?" Not even Nale was against teaching these creatures a lesson. "Then I suggest we return to the outskirts and pick off any members we find in the caves. We can hide the corpses as we kill them. See if we can whittle down their numbers. Alternatively, we could throw a Fireball into their camp and see what damage we can cause?"

"No need to waste Daphne's mana," said Lise. "I finished surveying the camp. They're too spread out for area-of-effect spells."

"Gareth, I have a suggestion," Sorin interrupted.

"Go ahead," said Gareth.

"Since we're already here, I was wondering if I could have Lorimer deliver a present."

"A present?" asked Gareth. "Are you thinking poison?"

"I *am* a poison user," said Sorin. "And I happen to have been bleeding myself every day for the past five days, just in case."

"If you have an idea that can neutralize a portion of their threat, go ahead," said Gareth.

Sorin smiled as he pulled out an enchanted waterskin and took a squeaking Lorimer out of his pocket. "Shut up, you lazy mouse," he said, strapping the waterskin on his back. "It's time to earn your keep."

"Ree!" Lorimer complained.

"This poison is no threat to you, Lorimer," scolded Sorin. "You've drunk enough of my blood to gain immunity. What I want you to do is sneak into their camp and start burning with low-intensity flames. The herbs I mixed into my blood will cause it to smoke up when heated. Have them chase after you until all the blood evaporates, then hide until I provide further instructions."

The rat squeaked in protest but ultimately lowered his head in submission. He then wobbled off into the wilderness with the enchanted waterskin.

"Let's not stick around for the show," said Gareth. "Since we'll be provoking them early, I suggest we strike a few of their bigger groups before they assemble. Unless Team Oasis opposes?" No one did. "Then let's move out."

Gareth and Lise split up their groups and led their two teams in separate directions. Barely two minutes passed before Sorin's team arrived at a cave. To Sorin's surprise, Gareth directly shot an arrow imbued with wind mana into the darkness. A group of six angry cyclopes rushed out of the cave and, upon seeing them, charged.

Stephan launched himself at the largest target, while Gareth shot the second largest in the eye. Sorin used Adder Rush to close in on the third largest. At the same time, Lawrence appeared behind the weakest of the cyclopes and used Triple Stab Execution. Three bloody holes appeared on the cyclops's chest, and it fell to the ground, dead.

If I hadn't broken through with Viper Strike, dealing with these cyclopes would prove tricky, thought Sorin. His opponent was nine feet tall, making vital points difficult to access. He dodged the cyclops's heavy club and stabbed a dagger into its thigh, piercing its bone. It roared in pain and fell to one knee, exposing its head to a second Viper Strike, which turned its brain to mush.

The two remaining cyclopes were horrified and tried to retreat, but Lawrence appeared behind one and used Triple Stab Execution to eliminate it. As for the last one, it was intercepted by a single paw from Stephan that smashed its brain out of its head.

"No time to loot," said Gareth when the last of them fell. "Lawrence, sweep the cave and check for survivors while I scout out the next batch."

Sorin's party was, for the most part, a team of oddballs. Stephan was a beastshift warrior, and Daphne was a hyper-distracted and hyper-energetic mage. Lawrence was slippery and immature, and Sorin stuck out like a sore thumb because both physicians and poison users tended to keep their distance from the general public.

Only Gareth had seemed somewhat normal, but it was in this situation that Sorin realized he'd been holding back. In this place where mobility, arrows, and camouflage were essential, he was practically a god of war. Gareth had gone from boring to amazing in the span of a few minutes.

Under Gareth's direction, they repeatedly struck at small groups and managed to take out five of them before leading them back to their original position half an hour later. They met up with Lise's group, who'd just finished a similar sortie.

"I count fifty-five cyclopes remaining," said Gareth.

"Fifty-five cyclopes," confirmed Lise. "No prisoners."

"No prisoners," confirmed Gareth. "About half appear ill."

"I count 60 percent, but let's be conservative," said Lise. "Smash and break before they organize?"

"Smash and break," confirm Gareth. "Unless you two are opposed?" Stephan shook his head, and so did Nale. "Great. Since they're all clustered up, how about you throw your strongest spell at them, Daphne? And Hellen, do you know regeneration-style life magic?"

"I know spell, but none of us are wounded quite yet," said Hellen.

"Cast it on Stephan, Sorin, Collin, and Nale," said Gareth. "Quickly!" Seeing that Nale wasn't going to argue with him, she muttered darkly and proceeded to cast her spells. "Daphne, why aren't you charging up a Fireball yet?"

"Shut up, I'm concentrating!" said Daphne. "Stupid archer, interrupting me while I'm just about to figure out something big." The mage began chanting in a medium-loud voice that caused Sorin's hair to stand on end. A spell circle appeared around her, and a Fireball much larger than the one he'd seen in the rat cave appeared above her head.

As expected, there's a huge difference when she has time to chant, thought Sorin. The Fireball accumulated mana until Daphne could no longer hold it and shot it at the cyclopes that had gathered around the cooking pot.

There was a large explosion. Twenty of the fifty-five cyclopes were burned down, and fire spread out to half the buildings in the village. "Daphne's out of mana, so she's out of this fight," said Gareth. "Stephan and Collin, you're the vanguard. Sorin and Nale, you're up next. Lawrence and Warren, take any opportunity you find to eliminate targets, but stay at the edge to prevent any of them from escaping."

The momentum of the battle did not allow Sorin time to think or rest. He gripped his mithril dagger with his right hand and summoned a handful of poison needles in his left hand while he ran behind their armored bear and steel-covered tank. The two warriors smashed into the nearest cyclopes, with Stephan using Lunisolar Paw to smash one apart as an intimidation tactic, while Collin used a taunt skill to draw the nearest five cyclopes over.

The cyclopes were tall, making it so that Sorin could only target their legs and torsos directly. But the places he *did* strike melted away in an instant. Organs were destroyed, and leg muscles dissolved. He quickly found himself surrounded, but fortunately, they were slower than the beetles and could barely land glancing blows as he used Adder Rush to dance between them.

It wasn't long before Sorin was surrounded by cyclops corpses. Moving became tricky, and Sorin, now trapped behind a wall of corpses, could only passively dodge the cyclopes and their clubs.

But the ground was rocky and uneven, and evading was difficult. Sorin soon slipped on the blood-covered ground, and a club came down and caught him in the chest, breaking one of his ribs and tearing open his flesh. Fortunately, Hellen's regeneration spell kicked in, allowing him to push through the dizzy spell that accompanied the traumatic blow and throw a poison needle in its eye.

"So much for Team 'We Don't Need a Life Mage,'" Sorin muttered, jumping out from the wall of corpses.

He emerged to find the cyclopes in disarray. One cyclops was trying to rally its species at the rear, and those not immersed in battle began retreating from the battlefield. "Lorimer, stop lazing around and kill them!" he shouted.

"Reeee!" A rat suddenly jumped out of a pile of charred corpses the cyclopes were retreating past and dug through one of their eyes like it was cottage cheese. He then nipped at another cyclops's heels, bringing it down just before it reached the safety of its new group.

Arrows took down a few of the remaining cyclops, leaving only a group of ten cyclopes near a strange stone object at the back of the camp. Sorin's eyes narrowed when he felt powerful mana erupt from the object and infuse itself into the leader of these cyclopes, who was a full head taller than the rest.

"It's a sacrificial ceremony!" shouted Stephan. "Gareth! Lise! Interrupt it!" Both archers wasted no time in aiming their bows at the rapidly growing creature. Wind and lightning blasted its head, only to diffuse as they struck a thick shield of mana that had appeared on its skin. "Shit! What a wasted effort. Prepare for battle. This opponent won't be an easy one!"

"What's going on?" asked Nale, running up beside Stephan. "What's it doing?"

"What does it look like it's doing?" snapped Stephan. "That red spell circle is collecting their blood and their lives. It's sacrificing all the remaining cyclopes and the essence of these dead cyclopes and pouring them into their leader!"

The cyclops was brimming with energy. Its arms and legs were twice as thick as before, though it was still only ten feet tall. Then, suddenly, it sprang up like grass in the spring . It didn't stop until it was sixteen feet tall and gave off a pressure that wasn't lacking compared to a Bone-Forging cultivator's.

"A two-star demon," muttered Nale. "Damn. Should we retreat? This isn't a good match-up."

"We'll be fine," Stephan assured. "We just need to be systematic about this."

"Fine," said Nale, wiping cyclops blood off his blade. "I've always wanted to fight a two-star demon. Let's see what they're made of."

44

SLAYING THE TWO-STAR CYCLOPS

"There's not much time until the sacrificial ritual is over, so I'll make this quick," said Stephan as everyone gathered around him. "By all rights, we shouldn't be fighting an oversized creature like this. We don't have the toughness of Bone-Forging cultivators, nor do we have the right spells or the right weapons." He pointed to Collin. "You can't fight this thing directly. It'll kill you in three blows."

"That doesn't mean I can't try," Collin, who rarely spoke, said. "I should be able to take a few hits."

"I'm not saying you can't take a few hits; I'm saying you can't be the main tank," said Stephan. "I need you to stay in reserve until you're needed. Maybe you'll be able to save one or two of us or let us land a direct hit or something. Unless you've got an enchanted sword stashed somewhere on your body?"

His gaze then settled on Gareth next. "You archers don't need to be told what to do, right?"

"We'll hit it in the eye with everything we have," said Gareth, giving him a thumbs-up. "We'll use the poison blood Sorin gave us. Our normal attacks might not be able to hurt it much, but our powered-up shots should be able to since our bows are enchanted."

"Lawrence? Warren?" said Stephan.

"We'll keep stabbing him till he drops," said Lawrence. "Unless you're partial to cutting?"

"I'm a fan of stabbing," said Warren. "Just don't get in my way."

"Then that leaves Sorin," said Stephan. "Try your best to pierce its defenses and poison it. You'll find two-star creatures are very resistant to one-star poison, and large creatures are extra difficult to deal with. Even so, you have the best damage potential on the entire team against this thing, assuming you can land enough hits. Our main job will be distracting it so that you can hit it."

"What about me?" asked Nale. "Any advice for a swordsman?"

"As if you'd take it," said Stephan, rolling his eyes. "Just try to cut pieces out of it, Nale; it's not complicated. Don't get hit. There's only one person here tough enough to take hits from that thing, and it's me." Finally, he turned to Hellen. "I hope our rocky start won't hurt our collaboration because this time, my little life really *does* depend on you."

Hellen smiled. "So you *do* need a life mage. I'll keep regeneration spells on you at all times, but if you want more healing, either chug a potion or retreat from combat. That thing will smash me in a single hit."

"I'm... I'm awake!" Daphne, who'd been sitting down to recover, finally stood up. Her eyes were bloodshot, and she couldn't even stand properly. "I have a spell, and it's a good one!"

Stephan shook his head. "Don't bother. You can barely stand, and this thing is magic-resistant. You're far better off drinking a mana potion and conserving your strength." His eyes narrowed as the bloody ritual circle began to shrink and retreated into the altar, which then broke as the cyclops opened its single eye. A wave of paralysis washed over them, dulling their senses. "It's got an eye technique, so watch out for that. Everyone, stick with the plan. Go!"

Gareth and Lise immediately began firing arrows at the creature as it walked toward their group with the steady certainty of an apex predator. The arrows struck its eye without issue, only to rattle off harmlessly as they struck a thin shield of mana that seemed to cover every inch of its body.

"Kill!" shouted Stephan as he morphed back into bear form. He was only ten feet tall to the cyclops's 16 feet, but his powerful claws met the cyclops's large hands and even caused it to stumble backward.

Sensing an opportunity, Sorin used Adder Rush to close the gap and Viper Strike to attack the creature's knee. To his surprise, the cyclops moved its leg slightly at the last minute, such that his dagger hit its knee cap. Sparks flew as his mana blade and the cyclops's hard bones collided, neutralizing his attack in the process.

"Dodge!" yelled Stephan, but too late. The cyclops's leg whipped out at Sorin and caught him in the chest, sending him flying twenty feet before he struck a piece of half-burnt timber. Three of Sorin's ribs cracked, and his internal organs were wrenched out of place. His vision blackened for three whole seconds before he picked himself up off the ground, groaning in pain.

Sorin winced as he popped his shoulder back into place and surveyed the situation. His regeneration powers were already quite strong, but given the severity of his injuries, he had no choice but to gulp down half a healing potion.

His body kicked into overdrive and began healing his ligaments first, followed by his muscles. He watched as Lawrence and Warren launched sneak attacks that barely penetrated the creature's skin through its mana shield. Stephan had clearly underestimated the creature.

Though new to its powers, the cyclops quickly adapted to its body and began to overpower Stephan, pushing him back. The bloodthirsty cyclops then began hammering onto Stephan's armored bear hide with its fists, with no regard for the sharp bear teeth biting into its torso.

"What are you all waiting for?" shouted Stephan, blood pouring out of his mouth. "Deal damage to the damn thing! It's not easy taking a beating!"

Sorin was still reeling from getting smashed by the creature's leg, but he gritted his teeth and prepared for another attempt. *That thing is huge and shouldn't have been able to dodge in time to avoid my knife,* thought Sorin. *Something must have caused me to miss it.*

"Cover me!" shouted Sorin as he rushed in. Stephan immediately grabbed the cyclops's arm and bit down with his sharp bear teeth. It howled with rage and redoubled its hammering, giving Sorin yet another opening. This time, he stabbed its thigh where a human acupuncture point would normally be located.

One. Poison broke through the creature's mana shield, directly attacking the muscle. *Two.* The second strike hit a nerve, and Sorin got a better feel for the creature's anatomy. *Three.* Sorin could feel the poison melting away at the creature's tough muscles. Its bones were unimaginably hard, but its flesh, not so much. *Four.*

The moment he landed the fourth strike, a heart-palpitating feeling gripped Sorin. The creature flung Stephan into a burning building and moved in to kill Sorin with a single blow. Sorin tried to dodge but discovered, to his horror, that he was paralyzed. *What's... What's going on?*

And that was when he saw it—the glowing mana signature in the cyclops's single eye, freezing him in place. The same technique it had used at the beginning of the battle to land its deadly kick.

"Wake up, sleepy head!" Sorin snapped out of his trance thanks to Lawrence's voice and kicked back just in time to avoid the creature's fist. Wind and mana pelted Sorin's body, stunning him just long enough for the cyclops to swat him with its offhand.

Sorin's head spun as he tumbled down a small hill. *Serious crush injuries and bruising,* he calmly analyzed. *Unable to mobilize 20 percent of strength. Blood clotting. Recommendation: Clear out the clot before continuing the battle.*

Sorin picked himself up, inserted crystal needles in seven different acupoints, and used his poison mana to dissolve the clot that formed. He then stabbed needles into twelve different points and unstiffened the bruised and crushed muscles, inhibiting his movements as what remained of the healing potion he'd drunk worked its magic.

With Stephan and Sorin down, Collin jumped in and confronted the cyclops. The battle was completely one-sided, but he bought ten precious seconds for Hellen to cast all the healing spells she could on the wounded bear before it jumped back into battle.

Holding back such a large creature was difficult for Collin, but fortunately, Nale, Lawrence, and Warren were doing a good job chipping away at the creature's defenses. Most of their attacks were absorbed by the cyclops's mana shields, but some managed to sneak through and draw blood. Sorin noted a conspicuous black trail leaking out of the creature's leg.

It's working, Sorin realized. Unlike his companions, his poisons penetrate the creature's mana shields and directly affect it. It was clear now why Stephan had so much confidence in his damage potential.

Sorin ignored the stinging in his eyes from the clash with the cyclops and coldly analyzed the situation. *The key to this fight will be taking out its weak leg. It's trying to hide it, but the leg I struck has weakened significantly.*

By now, Stephan had thrown himself back into combat, and Gareth and Lise were attacking with special arrows imbued with wind and lightning, bruising the creature's singular eye.

Sorin used Adder Rush as an opening revealed itself, only to pull back at the last second as the cyclops's body twisted. He circled it and attempted another rapid strike, only to find himself confronted by the creature's wary eye.

Another wave of paralysis struck Sorin, but this time, the serpent within him awakened. A phantom cobra appeared behind Sorin and dispelled the creature's paralysis spell. Then, to Sorin's surprise, it channeled Sorin's spiritual energy and sent an attack right back at it.

"Keep it up!" shouted Gareth from the back. "You're drawing all its attention, Sorin!"

Thanks to Gareth's reminder, Sorin realized the crux of the matter—he didn't need to deal extra damage to it. He'd already poisoned it, and the poison was gradually taking effect. His threatening presence was enough to conserve their formation.

He, therefore, picked up his speed and focused on dodging and avoiding, all the while remaining in the cyclops's threat zone. Adder Rush was a versatile technique that incorporated a serpent's weaving and the explosive might of a serpent's bite. It allowed Sorin to pop in and out of the creature's threat range with minimal risk.

Enraged at the provocation, the cyclops gave up on facing the other party members and tried to engage Sorin directly, but the poison specialist refused and repeatedly dodged, slipping back just in time to avoid getting crushed by the creature's fists.

It's getting faster, thought Sorin as he fought. *Its entire body is turning red. Its heart is speeding up, and its strength is up by 20 percent. What's going on?*

"It's going berserk!" shouted Gareth suddenly. "Sorin, run!" The cyclops exploded with power and attempted to grab its opponent.

Sorin didn't even think. His footwork changed in reaction to the threat, and he directly squeezed between the creature's legs. *One. Two. Three.* Sorin stabbed it three times as he passed. The cyclops whirled around to face him, only to discover that Sorin had already slipped around the other side.

So this is the essence of Adder Rush, Sorin realized. *It's not about just weaving and darting but also circling one's prey.*

"Its leg is critically weak!" shouted Sorin as he dodged and struck again. "A high-impact attack will make it give out!"

"Got it!" shouted Stephan. "Lunisolar Paw!"

"Silverblade Cleave!" shouted Nale.

Both Lise and Gareth drew back their arrows and poured wind and lightning into their shots, blasting the creature's shielded leg just before Stephan and Nale struck it.

A Bone-Forging cultivator's mana shields were difficult to pierce by Blood-Thickening cultivators, but with their combined efforts, they finally managed to shatter the protective covering and directly attack its flesh. Nale's sword cut apart its thigh and dug into the bone, while Stephan's paw smashed apart what remained and caused the creature to collapse to one side.

"Retreat!" Gareth called, and everyone, including Stephan, pulled back.

"Is it over?" asked Sorin as he observed the cyclops. "Can it recover?"

"Its regeneration is strong, but not strong enough to overcome the residual poison," said Stephan, shaking his head. "You're the physician. With one leg down and thus interrupted blood flow, even a demon won't last long in this state."

The creature struggled at death's door for another two minutes before the last of its life left it. Its mana shields dimmed, and its surroundings faded. They found themselves inside a hallway filled with cyclops corpses.

"Everyone, rest up while you can," said Stephan, reverting to human form. He was covered in bruises from head to toe, and Sorin didn't dare imagine what kind of pain he was in.

"I'll go get its core," said Lawrence, hopping up on the creature's corpse. He cut into its eye and retrieved a large crystal. "Nice! It's a big one."

"I suggest you drop that core and leave the rest of this battlefield to us," a voice suddenly sounded. Footsteps clanked in the hallway, revealing a group of ten adventurers led by none other than Orpheus.

"What's the meaning of this, Orpheus?" asked Stephan warily.

"It means what you think it means," said Orpheus. "You're all wounded and won't be able to put up much of a fight. I therefore suggest that you retreat while we clear up the battlefield. Don't worry; we'll give you a fair share of the spoils after we exit the ruins."

45

THEORY VS PRACTICE

Orpheus's arrival put an immediate damper on the team's festive mood. Stephan, who'd been receiving treatment for his bruises, stood up abruptly and half-shifted into bear form. Lawrence and Warren took out their daggers, while Gareth and Lise each nocked an arrow.

Unsurprisingly, Daphne didn't even seem to notice the altercation. She'd been recovering during their battle and trying to figure something out while scribbling on a piece of paper. It was only when Sorin flicked a rock at her that she blinked and realized their current predicament.

"Has my behavior so far led you to think me a pushover?" Stephan asked Orpheus. "Because you know full well that fighting amongst adventurers is against the rules. What will you do if we don't vacate? Would you dare kill us for treasure?"

Orpheus shrugged. "Who's to say you didn't die to monsters? In fact, how dare you try to steal our loot? We worked hard to slay those cyclopes, and here you come in, trying to steal from us? That's a capital offense."

"Hahaha." Lawrence burst out laughing. "And here I thought *I* was shameless. Are you taking students by any chance? It's my first time meeting a master of the craft."

"You think I'm joking?" asked Orpheus, smile fading. "Raneev, shoot him." Lawrence jumped back just as an arrow shot into the corpse he was standing on.

"Hey!" said Lawrence. "Weren't we talking? Why escalate when we can smoothly resolve this without violence?"

"You can't fight us without taking losses," Stephan said to Orpheus. "We might be tired from that battle, but we can at least take half of you down with us. It's not worth it to risk losing half your team to get a few demon cores."

"Likewise, it's not worth it for your team to fight us over a few demon cores," Orpheus countered. "Especially since you stand to lose your entire team. A pretty boy like you, from a big family—money is meaningless to you. Your life is everything. I've seen your type before, Stephan, so I know you'll back down now and try to escalate this when we get back."

"You confuse concern for one's companions with cowardice," said Stephan. "Don't push me, Orpheus. You'll regret it."

"Your attempt at buying time for you all to recover is pathetic," said Orpheus. "You have ten seconds to get the hell out of here. Nine. Eight."

Sorin frowned and looked over at his companion. They were all ragged from the battle, even those who hadn't taken any direct hits. At the same time, Sorin was indignant. Ever since the death of his parents, people had been pushing him around and restricting him. This was just one more iteration of the same old pattern.

"I'm tired," Sorin finally said. He pulled a box from his pack and opened it. The labyrinth shivered as Manabane Poison entered the ruins and began sapping away at everyone's strength. "I'm tired of getting pushed around, Orpheus. I thought the Adventurers Guild was different, but it seems that everywhere you go, there's always people like you trying to take what's not theirs."

Orpheus eyed the box warily. "What exactly is this treasure, Sorin? Are you offering it up to us so we'll let you leave in peace?"

Sorin laughed. "In a sense. But first, let me introduce the contents of this box. It's a flower called Manabane Chrysanthemum. It's not a lethal poison, but if received in high enough doses, it will cripple one's cultivation and rupture one's mana sea. Even breathing in its fumes would wipe out one's mana and leave one crippled with agony."

"So you're threatening me," said Orpheus. "Reasonable. But if you crush that flower, won't you cripple everyone in your party? It hardly seems worth it."

"Isn't that better than dying?" asked Sorin. "My party members will suffer, but as a poison cultivator, I'll be able to resist the effects somewhat—long enough to kill everyone on your team, at least. And even if you do manage to stop me, your entire party won't survive the labyrinth without mana. So tell me, Orpheus, do you still want to attack us for our things? Are you willing to gamble with your life on the line?"

"You wouldn't," Orpheus sneered.

"Actually, I would," said Sorin. "Do you think I wouldn't dare risk crippling my cultivation? You should have heard stories about the crippled physician who became an adventurer. That's me. I've been there, and I know exactly what it feels like.

"You're putting on a strong front and abusing the knowledge that if we fight, we'll die, and at least half of you will live. Well, I'm throwing that right back at you. Will you really attack us if your chances of survival are nil? I don't think you will because I've seen your type before; you're a coward, through and through."

Cultivators weren't equally knowledgeable, but they *did* have sharp instincts. And everyone in the room's instincts were screaming at them that this flower was bad news, including Sorin's.

Orpheus stared Sorin down for a few long seconds before spitting on the ground. "You win this one, Sorin Kepler. Let's hope you continue to be as lucky in your future encounters."

Sorin didn't immediately put away the flower but held onto it for five minutes before placing it back in the box. His teammates let out a sigh of relief once it was safely packed away and resumed their looting and healing.

"That was quick thinking, Sorin," said Stephan, walking over. "But would you really have destroyed that chrysanthemum?"

"Of course I would have," said Sorin. "Otherwise, why would someone like Orpheus have retreated?"

"Well, you've got balls," said Nale, walking up to him. He winced as he rolled his shoulder, which had been dislocated during the fight. "I can't believe a guy like him managed to become such a high-ranking adventurer."

"He's a bully," said Stephan. "He makes it his business to roll over weaker adventurers. He has a gift for knowing what people want to avoid as well. Warren. Lawrence. Did you find it?"

"They put it all in one big pile," said Warren, dragging over a grass net piled up with adventurers' gear, including armor and weapons.

"Rules are rules, but living people are living people," said Stephan. "Inventory everything and split the rations amongst everyone present. We'll split potions half and half and then decide what to do with the rest of the gear." He then walked over to the pile and picked out a dagger. "We're taking first pick, if you don't mind. Sorin needs a sharper weapon." He handed the dagger over to Sorin before walking over to Hellen, who'd yet to finish administering his treatment.

Sorin looked over the dagger and marveled at its sharpness. He set its blade against the mithril dagger's and stopped once he cut a nick in it. *With this dagger, I could cut through one-star bones like I'm cutting through flesh,* thought Sorin. *I also wouldn't need to spend so much mana piercing a two-star demon's mana shields.* He also faintly felt that the dagger had another ability, but without identifying it, he had no way to discover what exactly this ability was.

Speaking of abilities, Sorin reflected on the change that had occurred when the cyclops had tried paralyzing him with an eye technique. At first, he'd thought the serpent was just passively helping him resist paralysis. It was only now that he was out of combat that he could further assess the situation.

Instead of resisting the paralysis, it's more like my technique fought against the cyclops's technique and canceled out most of it, thought Sorin. During combat, he'd unconsciously uncovered yet another ability from the Ten Thousand Poison Canon, Cobra's Gaze. It was an eye technique that could mesmerize or paralyze an opponent. It was heavily reliant on his spiritual strength, which was abnormally high to begin with.

Sorin spent the next six hours studying the technique as he recovered. During this time, Hellen treated all their wounds, and Lawrence and Warren finished collecting the demon cores from nearly a hundred cyclopes. There was only one two-star core, but Nale bargained for additional one-star cores instead, as well as the second and third pick of the adventurers' magical items.

When Sorin asked about getting a bounty for the cores, Stephan informed him that they wouldn't be getting one. "Creatures in dungeons normally don't wander out of said dungeons, so there's no point in offering a bounty for them," said Stephan. "All we get are their cores, which are larger than usual. We'll either trade them or gamble them at the Temple of Hope."

Bruises were tough to heal, but Sorin knew some acupuncture techniques that could mobilize a person's blood and increase recovery. By the end of their extended rest, even the badly battered Stephan was fully functional. His armor was ironically in better shape than after facing the Rockgnaw Rats.

Speaking of Rockgnaw Rats, it was Lawrence who finally found Lorimer after the dust settled. Apparently, a cyclops had fallen on top of him, and he'd used this opportunity to rest and avoid combat. Sorin scolded the rat and prohibited it from eating further demon cores. If it wanted to eat, it would need to participate in combat in the future.

Since Sorin had gotten his mysterious gem-studded dagger, there were still three enchanted items left from the adventuring team's gear. Stephan claimed a pair of boots that increased his strength and footing, while the remaining two items, agility-increasing bracers and a set of enchanted leather armor, went to Nale and Warren.

"Yes, yes, yes!" Daphne cried out when they finished dividing the loot. "I did it! I'm a genius!"

"What is it this time?" asked Stephan. "Was it worth getting distracted while we were facing off against Orpheus and his gang?"

"Of course it was," said Daphne excitedly. "I can't *wait* to test this out. Which way does the mana density increase again?"

"That way," said a confused Hellen, pointing towards a wall.

Daphne whistled joyfully as she walked over to the wall and ran her hand along it. She traveled roughly a hundred feet before stopping and tracing symbols onto the wall.

"Did you find a secret door or something?" asked Gareth, walking over. "I thought it might be something there, but I didn't look too much into it."

"Yes, yes, stand back a bit, will you?" said Daphne. She summoned a shield as the wall exploded, revealing a passage on the other side leading deeper into the maze than they'd ever gone before. Their team cautiously entered the gap and inspected the situation. There were no demons or traps, and the labyrinth didn't seem to mind them taking such a shortcut.

"Couldn't you just open the door?" asked Lawrence, looking back at the hole in the wall. "Maybe only break down the door as a last resort?"

"In some cases, yes," said Daphne. "But in this case, the door was already broken. Its runes were ill-maintained and couldn't be revitalized. If I find some in better condition, I could probably open them. But... why bother?"

Indeed, why bother? thought Sorin. The only advantage to keeping the maze compartmentalized was keeping groups of demons separate. Aside from people like Orpheus, gathering with other adventurers would only be an advantage given the difficulty of the labyrinth.

"I'm personally a fan of having an escape route we can open and close," said Nale.

"It would be a good tactical option," said Gareth in agreement.

"Oh," said Daphne. "I never considered retreating. Hm... let me think about this." She took out her paper and began jotting down more notes.

"Since we've recovered, we should probably get going," said Stephan. "We don't want Orpheus getting too much of a head start on us."

"I don't think we have to worry about time anymore," Sorin pointed out. "Since we can just go directly to the center of the labyrinth. Though, I must wonder—if whatever is at the center is worse than the two-star cyclops, are we biting off more than we can chew?"

"Hm… that is a good question," said Stephan. "But we can't know the answer unless we see what's there, can we? If we find a threat that's too difficult to tackle, can't we just retreat and find reinforcements?"

"Agreed," said Nale. "If it's something we can handle on our own, there's also no point in sharing. No danger, no glory, am I right?"

"I think I've figured out how to open doors without breaking them down," said Daphne, putting down her notepad. "It's not as fun, and it *might* break the door, but I can see the tactical applications. I'll have to be pickier about the doors we use, though."

"I think we can spare the time if it means retaining a way out," said Stephan. "Everyone in agreement? Great. Then let's go hit Orpheus where it hurts most: his ego."

THE CENTER OF THE LABYRINTH

With Daphne's new ability to open doors in walls, their group made good time travelling through the labyrinth. They only occasionally encountered trouble when demons happened to be located on the other side of a wall, but for the most part, they were able to bypass threats without needing to fight them.

The labyrinth gave way to an open area. A small temple-like building occupied most of the space, which formed a complete circle only broken up by six passageways heading into different parts of the maze.

"Do either of you see anything?" Stephan asked both archers.

"I don't sense any mana fluctuations or vibrations," said Gareth, shaking his head. "Whatever boss monster calls this place home, it's not here."

"Maybe it's wandering the labyrinth, chasing down adventurers," Sorin suggested. "I think I read a story about a creature like this once. They called it the Minotaur."

"Wandering boss monsters are rare but not unheard of," muttered Stephan. "Fine. Then let's check this place out and see if we can get some of its treasures before it gets back."

"How do we know there's *any* treasure?" asked Gareth. "Let's not get carried away with wishful thinking."

"Guys!" said Lawrence and Warren, who'd gone ahead to scout. "This place isn't trapped at all, and it's *loaded* with treasure!"

"You were saying?" said Stephan.

"I'm not *against* treasure," said Gareth. "I just don't want anyone getting upset if we don't find some."

The rogues led them through the front entrance and into the temple's single room. It featured tinted windows that told a story so old no one in the room could interpret it. There was a white bull, an ancient king, and a heavily muscled god that commanded the wind and waves.

"That one's Poseidon," said Sorin, pointing to the powerful trident-wielding figure. "As for the city it's depicting, I believe I recognize the symbol on the gates. It used to be the capital of an island prior to the Cataclysmic Emergence. A famous island called Crete."

"I'm not going to lie," said Nale, cutting him off. "Your story isn't very interesting, and those treasures *are.*"

"Agreed," said Stephan. "We also don't know how much time we have, but I think the center of the room deserves some attention."

"The center of the room?" said Nale. His eyes narrowed when he saw what the rest of the party was staring at: the half-eaten corpse of an adventurer and the dry bones of many others. It lay there, fully naked, beside what appeared to be a bed of rags, furs, leathers, and any other soft items that could be found in the labyrinth.

"There are scars on the walls," observed Gareth. "Most of them are between nine and ten feet high. Otherwise, this place is well preserved."

"Well-preserved, my butt," said Lawrence. "Look at that big scratch running down the floor. And the bloody hoofprints."

"More like tens of thousands of scratches that have merged into one," muttered Gareth, inspecting the mark. "How heavy would a weapon need to be to leave such a mark when dragged? How strong *is* this creature?"

"I'm not sure if I'm the qualified person to say this, but shouldn't we be taking things and running?" pointed out Hellen.

"Agreed," said Stephan. "And let's be quick about it. Gold is useless —prioritize gems and magical items. The ones that *haven't* rotted away."

The team immediately split up to fill their packs. Sorin found a pile of rubies and shoved them into his bag before looking over the other items to see anything he fancied.

Many tables, cases, and mannequins were arranged inside the temple. Whatever this thing was, it enjoyed collecting things and showing them off. There were suits of armor that had long since rotted, but a few suits had resisted the test of time, as had some swords and spears and other quality goods.

Stephan donned a pair of gauntlets. They were silver, covered in blue runes, and ended in sharp claws that complemented his bear-shifted form. Daphne, on the other hand, was inspecting a staff with a ruby the size of a baby's fist atop it, muttering something about ancient runes and incompatibility with the current magical zeitgeist.

Sorin soon found something that caught his eye—a ring bearing the symbol of twin serpents. He immediately put it on his finger and felt that it would likely complement his abilities nicely once he figured out how to use it.

"What's this?" muttered Sorin, pushing off rusted junk from a table and revealing a ball of silver string. It wasn't metal like his own mithril string but seemed to be composed entirely of enchanted human hair.

He picked up the ball of hair and was about to try peeling a suit of leather armor from a mannequin when suddenly, the mana in the room went still, and his breath caught in his throat. Everyone, including the hungry Lorimer who'd been gobbling up gems, stopped what they were doing and pulled out their weapons.

A dragging sound could be heard outside the temple, along with heavy hoof beats that caused the building to shake and the windows to tremble.

It was then that they saw it: the Minotaur. It had a thick, muscular human body with giant hooves for feet. Its head was a bull's head, with red eyes and sharp horns covered in golden wave patterns.

"You lot dare defile this Minotaur's home?" it spoke in a chilling voice. "You all deserve to die!" A two-star pressure far greater than the cyclops's they'd faced pressed down on the entire room, sealing away most of Sorin's mana and likely doing the same to his companions.

"Retreat!" shouted Stephan, launching himself at the creature. He morphed into bear form, including new metal gauntlets that covered his original claws and a helmet that allowed his muzzle free movement.

He was quick, but the Minotaur was faster. It picked up the axe it had been dragging and brought it up in a sideward arc. Stephan nimbly dodged the axe before tackling the Minotaur. "Run!" he shouted a second time. "Out the windows, fools!"

Sorin wasted no time throwing a table at a nearby tinted window. He grieved the loss of precious knowledge as the glass shattered but quickly found Daphne and helped her jump through the opening.

Nale and his companions similarly left the temple. The two teams converged at the original entrance and got there just in time to find Stephan rolling out of the entrance. The bear narrowly avoided a thrown great axe that sank halfway into the dry, desolate ground.

"Into the labyrinth!" shouted Stephan. "And find us a door that Daphne can use. Nale, you lead the way!"

Their group of ten ran through the entrance to the labyrinth and immediately encountered a different set of hallways than they'd encountered before. "Which way now?" asked Nale, stopping.

"Just pick a direction," said Stephan, bringing up the rear. The Minotaur's hoof beats were drawing frighteningly close. The bull-headed creature had just rounded the corner and would be catching up in less than twenty seconds.

"Sorry about this," said Nale. "No hard feelings."

"Sorry about what?" asked Stephan.

"*This,*" said Nale, suddenly ripping a scroll. A web shot out at Sorin's group of five, centered around Stephan. The scroll had targeted none of Nale's group, and his group took the left fork, leaving them in the middle of the crossroads as bait for the boss monster.

"Bastard!" shouted Stephan. "Lawrence, get us free!" Lawrence was the only one who had managed to dodge the sticky webs in time. He busied himself with his dagger, and so did Sorin. They had barely finished cutting through the sticky webs when the axe-wielding Minotaur arrived. Stephan jumped out to meet it, and this time, the axe tore through his armor, and he suffered a heavy gash along his back.

"Daphne, go find us an exit," commanded Gareth. "Lawrence, escort her. Sorin, see if you can do anything about that thing."

Sorin rushed in just as the Minotaur's axe struck down a second time. Stephan dodged and bit at the Minotaur's bare chest but was repelled by its mana shield. Still, the sudden move caused the Minotaur to drop his axe, giving Sorin the opening he needed.

It's humanoid, so vitals should be about the same, thought Sorin, stabbing out with his new enchanted dagger. It directly pierced through the Minotaur's mana shield but only stuck three inches into its skin before stopping.

The Minotaur growled when Sorin stabbed him a second time and moved to swat him like a fly. But Sorin was a nimble serpent. He appeared at the monster's other side and stabbed it between two of its ribs, this time drawing a slight trail of blood.

"Its defenses are ridiculous," yelled Sorin. "I can pierce through its mana shield, but then its hide takes up most of my blade's power. My poison isn't taking root, either. It's clearly either poison-resistant or mana-resistant."

The Minotaur, annoyed at Sorin's antics, kicked Stephan out of the way and charged towards him. It was about to reach him when an arrow pierced its eye, forcing it to defend with its hands. Sorin dodged to the side and retreated towards his party.

"Over here!" shouted Daphne. "Found one!"

"Let's go!" said Stephan, running towards the rogue and the mage.

"We won't make it on time," said Gareth as he fell in beside Sorin.

"Yes, we will," said Sorin. "It's resistant but not immune. Python Coil!" Sorin tossed out his trusty mithril string just as the Minotaur was about to arrive. The mana-infused string coiled around its skinny lower legs and pulled. The string snapped, but the Minotaur also lost its footing and crashed down onto the ground.

Sorin continued his retreat. They weren't far from the door now. But the Minotaur was strong and quick and had already gotten back up. Stephan charged at the creature, and Sorin, knowing full well that doing so would incur backlash, decided to activate his newest technique. "Cobra's Gaze!"

A trickle of blood ran down Sorin's eyes, and a splitting headache struck him as the Minotaur, bracing himself to receive Stephan's charge, suddenly froze. As a result, it was unable to stand its ground when the bear pushed it down and ran toward the open doorway.

"Now!" shouted Gareth as Stephan entered. The door slammed shut, separating them from the Minotaur.

"Wait, how do we know it can't open the door itself?" asked Lawrence.

"We don't," said Daphne, smashing a red glyph into the stone wall and disabling the mechanism. "That's why we need to get as far from this place as possible."

They traveled deeper into the labyrinth, using and disabling multiple stone doors in the process. It was only once they'd disabled the fifth stone door that they finally took the chance to rest.

"Those double-crossing bastards," spat Lawrence. "They tripped us up as a distraction, and they did it after Stephan blocked that thing for them!"

"Let it be," said Stephan, shaking his head. "We can't do anything about it. It's when life and death are up in the air that people reveal their true character."

"That thing—it was *strong* for a two-star demon," said Gareth.

"That's because it's a boss monster," said Stephan. "Most of the demonic energy in this dungeon is concentrated on it. What's worse, it's clearly intelligent and has retained some of that intelligence despite being so thoroughly corrupted."

"Correct me if I'm wrong, but we need to kill that thing if we want to leave, don't we?" asked Sorin.

Stephan nodded slowly. "That's typically how it goes. Treasures mean nothing when clearing a dungeon. Only by killing the boss monster and claiming its core will we be sent out by whatever laws govern this place."

Sorin thought back to their encounter and determined that he would be useless in a battle against this creature in his current state, even *with* the enchanted blade.

He needed to get stronger to contribute. He needed a stronger poison.

Having made his decision, Sorin approached Stephan about potentially resting for a longer period. "I need to cultivate," he explained to Stephan. "We're not strong enough as it is, and our best chance is for individuals to make a breakthrough."

Stephan frowned. "Now isn't exactly the best time for a breakthrough, Sorin. That Minotaur could find us at any time."

"Which is why we need to take some risks," Sorin insisted. "I can get stronger, fast. My cultivation method... it's different from others. I cultivate by absorbing poisons, which is why we took that trip through Manabane Swamp."

Stephan's eyes widened. "You mean..."

"That's right," said Sorin. "I'm going to absorb the Manabane Poison we harvested and hope it doesn't kill me."

THE THRESHOLD

"Isn't absorbing Manabane Poison a little to risky?" Gareth interjected. "I mean, you *are* the team's physician, but…"

"You're right," Sorin admitted. "Manabane Poison is definitely lethal to cultivators in high doses. Even lower doses will cripple a cultivator."

"Then why are you going to try something so suicidal as using it to cultivate?" asked Stephan. "I don't mean to pry, but given the situation, it's not unusual for people to want to take extreme risks in situations like these."

"It's something I calculated long ago," said Sorin. "In theory, with my tolerance to poison, I should be fine as long as I take it slow. Moreover, I'm different from you all. I don't have a mana sea as a result of being crippled by this poison in the past."

"Hm…" Stephan shook his head. "I don't like it."

"You don't like it, but do we have any better options?" asked Sorin. "With Manabane Poison, I might be able to neutralize some of its ridiculous defenses."

Stephan looked at his exhausted teammates and threw up his hands. "Fine. Whatever. Do what you want, and we'll cover you."

Sorin proceeded to take out four boxes. Each one contained an intact

Manabane Chrysanthemum. The mana in their surroundings rippled and began to slowly drain away when he opened one of them. He hastily cut off the flower and crushed the root where most of the Manabane Poison was located.

"Get out here, you lazy rat," said Sorin. Lorimer crawled out of his pocket and obediently began heating Sorin's cracked mortar and pestle. The vapors alone forced the entire team to relocate a hundred feet away.

It was impossible to properly refine poisons in the labyrinth. Fortunately, Sorin discovered that he had one more tool to draw on: the coiling serpent ring he'd swiped from the Minotaur's collection. The ring was apparently made to manipulate poisons, and this included both raw poisons and poisonous mana.

Soon, Sorin was done refining all four chrysanthemums with earth flames. He stored their concentrated black tarry juices in four vials. As for the dregs, he had no way to store them, so he had Lorimer directly immolate them.

Manabane Poison spreads as a vapor, but it will only cripple you when applied as a liquid, thought Sorin, looking through the Ten Thousand Poison Canon. *The lethal human dose is ten drops. Three is enough to rupture a mana sea. I'll take it one drop at a time and see what happens.*

Sorin used a crystal needle to retrieve a drop from a flask and dripped it on his skin, where it wormed its way into his body like a parasite.

His poisonous blood and mana instinctually attacked the Manabane Poison and attempted to consume it. When the drop was almost completely exhausted, he repeated the process, thereby gradually increasing the concentration of poison in his body.

He imbibed drop after drop until, finally, the mana stored in his blood started burning away. The Manabane Poison was now strong enough to overwhelm his seven-poison body. It was a tense balance, however, as attacking him would consume its source poison. It wasn't long before both his poisons and the Manabane Poison were almost completely depleted.

This was the critical moment for Sorin. As a cultivator, his internal organs and vital processes were all dependent on mana. His complexion turned blue as his lung function slowed to a crawl. His blood stopped taking in enough oxygen to support him, thereby starting a chain reaction that would eventually lead to his death.

"Sorin, are you all right?" called out Gareth from a distance.

"I'm... fine..." croaked Sorin. He sucked in a tiny bit of mana potion to restore the balance.

Like this, a full day passed. Sorin's body entered a state of partial hibernation, reducing the amount of mana it required to operate. First, it was his lungs that slowed, but this was quickly followed by his kidney, his liver, and his large intestine until all ten of his yin and yang organs, including his heart, went dormant.

Sorin felt an ache where his mana sea had once been. It was where all the mana in a cultivator's body was typically stored. Manabane Poison was accumulating in that empty space—the same space that the phantom viper in his body occupied.

The poison continued to build up until suddenly, the viper's eyes opened. The poison, horrified by this development, attempted to flee.

But the viper was too quick. It snapped its mouth shut around the glob of poison and took a bite out of it. An eighth color joined the phantom viper's original seven colors.

The eighth streak then began to grow larger as Sorin's poisons gained the upper hand in their conflict and consumed what remained in the poison to replenish themselves. The poison was soon neutralized, prompting Sorin to add one more drop, then a third, then a fourth.

Finally, Sorin's entire body shook. The poisons completed their fusion, and Sorin's blood broke through to the eighth stage of Blood-Thickening. His mana grew thicker alongside his blood, and both began nourishing his dormant internal organs, his muscles, and his tendons.

Sorin rested for several hours after completing his breakthrough before moving on to the next step. He took out crystal needles from their protective case, using them to alter the flow of mana in his body, and attacked key points in his meridian system—points that had always been sealed and could theoretically only be unsealed using the method inscribed on his bones.

A full quarter of the ingredients for the tincture are extinct. Most of them operate on principles of dissolution, so I can only use the acidic part of my personal poisons to make up for it. The critical ingredient is Manabane Poison, which I have. It should be theoretically possible to unlock additional meridians.

Having made his decision, he continued impacting the meridian-opening corresponding to the Thrust Vessel. The membrane from the Belt Vessel and Thrust Vessel were around the same thickness. Still, compared to the balance attribute the Belt Vessel provided, Sorin valued the additional power the Thrust Vessel would provide more highly.

The eight fused poisons wormed into the barrier like a drill, first creating a tiny hole and prying it open little by little. It took a full hour before the hole was big enough to accommodate a small stream of mana, after which natural erosion gradually expanded the new meridian pathway until it was fully opened.

Sorin's mana did not thicken, but it grew exceptionally lively with the opening of the Thrust Vessel. The extra circulation pathway was like an extra stretch of road his mana could use to accelerate, thereby increasing its lethality and the explosiveness of his body. He had not gained any physical strength but had instead gained the ability to better use the existing power in his body.

Thanks to the increased thickness of his mana from breaking through to the eighth stage of Blood-Thickening, Sorin's awareness of his own body increased by leaps and bounds. His entire mana circulation system could now be mapped out in his mind, and he could feel the slightest changes in flow and even alter it as he wished.

Most importantly, unlocking the fifth extraordinary meridian illuminated the last three extraordinary meridians. The sixth meridian, the Belt Vessel, was still protected by a thick membrane.

But it wasn't this meridian Sorin concerned himself with. Instead, he paid close attention to the Conception Vessel and the Governing Vessel.

Both meridians had acupoints—they just happened to be inactive in most humans.

Strangest to Sorin was the appearance of both meridians. They *looked* like standard meridians, but the Conception Vessel's acupoints were covered in a silver sheen. In contrast, the Governing Vessel's acupoints were covered in a gold sheen. Theoretically, the Conception Vessel's acupoints could be opened with the right tincture, but opening the Governing Vessel's acupoints was impossible.

Sorin had wondered why this meridian was forbidden, but it was only now that he could sense it within his own body that he realized why that was. The golden sheen covering its acupoints gave off frightening divine fluctuations, not unlike those he'd sensed at the entrance of the ruin.

Is this what Sirius Abberjay Kepler meant by divine locks? Theoretically, the Governing Vessel is a part of the human body and should have a use. Still, it's clear that research into this meridian wasn't just forbidden—the gods clearly sealed it off. Studying it was nothing short of impossible.

Sorin had no idea why the gods would do this, especially considering their eventual fate. Wouldn't it have made sense to remove this seal and obtain better help from humankind during the Cataclysmic Emergence?

As a formality, Sorin tried attacking all three meridians with his mana. Unsurprisingly, these blockages were impossible to undo with his current strength. This was especially so for the seventh and eighth extraordinary meridians. Which was a pity because, according to his knowledge, the main ingredient in the tincture that could unlock this seventh extraordinary meridian, Seven Star Underworld Flower, had gone extinct. There were no records of this flower in the Alchemists Guild.

Having determined that further advancement was impossible, Sorin opened his eyes and stood up. He stretched out his limbs and shadow-boxed. His movements were at least 50 percent quicker and much more powerful.

"Congratulations!" said Lawrence, clapping from a distance. "Is it safe to come over now?"

"Give me a second," said Sorin, sweeping up the remaining two vials of unused Manabane Poison and drawing in the poisonous spores in the air into his body. "Yes, it's safe now."

"Excellent," said Stephan. "Exactly a day has passed, so we should get going."

"Get going?" asked Sorin. "But I still wanted to experiment with something. Can I borrow Lawrence for a minute?"

"What do you want to borrow Lawrence for?" asked Stephan. "Actually, you know what? Do whatever you want to him. He's been getting on my nerves." He decisively picked up the rogue by the collar and tossed him over.

Sorin stepped up to Lawrence faster than he could react and pinned him to the ground. "Mercy! Mercy, Sorin! You're a physician, remember?"

"Hold still," said Sorin, tapping on a few of his acupoints. A mental map of Lawrence's mana circulation system lit up in Sorin's mind. "Eight naturally unblocked meridians. Not bad, but not great. Two of them are actually extraordinary meridians. Let me see if I can take care of that."

Sorin pressed a finger to Lawrence's leg and injected a stream of Manabane Poison mixed with acidic poisons and carefully controlled it to minimize damage to Lawrence's flesh. Like Sorin's own blocked meridians, Lawrence's were chock full of a mix of flesh, corruption, and crystalized mana, as was typical for congenital blockages.

Using the ring he found in the Minotaur's home, he was able to slowly erode at the blockages neighboring each of the acupoints on a single meridian. It took half an hour to fully open the meridian in question, at which point mana rushed through and cleared out the remainder, then proceeded to join Lawrence's original mana circulation pathway to create a new one.

"Do you want me to continue?" Sorin asked the wide-eyed Lawrence.

"Continue! Continue!"

Having obtained his permission, Sorin continued to clear Lawrence's meridians. He started with his primary meridians since unblocking extraordinary meridians would only be possible after the whole set was unblocked.

The process became increasingly difficult as he proceeded. One hour became three, and only after an intense struggle was Sorin able to unblock Lawrence's twelfth primary meridian, granting him a total of fourteen unblocked meridians.

"I feel... I feel amazing!" said Lawrence as his body crackled. Unblocking the twelve primary meridians was akin to completing the human body's mana circulation system. It not only improved one's control but also significantly increased one's mana density. It further refined the body and thickened the blood by a whole stage, independent of one's cultivation.

Lawrence was still a cultivator at the eighth stage of Blood-Thickening. But having unlocked six additional primary meridians, it was like he was reborn. His physical strength and the thickness of his mana saw an especially stark improvement.

"It seems unblocking your primary meridians is the limit of my abilities," said Sorin. "Perhaps I can unblock extraordinary meridians with my mana, but I lack the technique to fully pierce the blockages between your existing meridian pathways. But we can continue exploring this option if that's what you wish."

He then looked to his remaining party members. "Who else would like to have their primary meridians unblocked?"

Sorin was reluctant to use the forbidden knowledge inscribed on his bones. It had been built on a mountain of corpses and could, in no way, be morally justified. But this was also the case for much of the medical knowledge in his possession. Knowledge of poisons, diseases, and how to treat them. Even basic human anatomy.

Yet what was done was done, and strengthening their party was difficult to rationalize as a bad thing, especially when no additional harm was done. Moreover, he was already relying on the method to increase his personal strength. Since that was the case, why *shouldn't* he try to improve his comrades' capabilities?

"Me! Try me next!" shouted Daphne.

"I wouldn't say no to going next," said Gareth.

"It might be best to alternate between patients," said Sorin. "Why don't I gradually work on you both so that you have time to adjust?"

Both Gareth and Daphne sat down and prepared themselves to accept treatment, and Sorin analyzed both their conditions. Gareth was exceptionally talented and had eight naturally unblocked meridians, including the Yang Link Vessel. Daphne, on the other hand, was as talented as Lawrence. She had six naturally opened primary meridians and two naturally opened extraordinary meridians. Except instead of Yin Heel and Yang Heel Vessels like Lawrence, she had been born with an unlocked Belt Vessel and Thrust Vessel. It was for this reason that she could cast spells with high mana requirements.

It took Sorin the better part of four hours to complete the meridian-opening process. Their bodies shook as the last meridians were cleared, and their mana circulation patterns became complete. Gareth's mana density increased the most of the two, while Daphne's mana capacity received the most significant benefit.

"What about you, Stephan?" asked Sorin. "Do you mind if I conduct an examination?"

"If you insist," said Stephan, allowing Sorin to place his hand on his back.

But Sorin almost immediately pulled his hand back. "Are you serious, Stephan? Fully unblocked primary meridians? And five unblocked extraordinary meridians?"

Stephan grinned. "The York Clan has its way to unblock meridians. Apologies for being unable to share it. It's difficult to get as far as I have without enough naturally unblocked meridians, but here I am."

"Do you mind if I take a second look?" asked Sorin.

"Go right ahead," said Stephan. He placed his hand on the large man's back once again, taking note of the high strength and defensive characteristics his body and mana possessed.

Sorin ignored the single blocked Yin Heel Vessel and instead focused on the silver and gold-covered meridians. *Interesting,* thought Sorin as he inspected his Conception Vessel. He only had six blocked acupoints instead of the full twenty-four. Eighteen of them had somehow been unblocked.

"I don't suppose you can share your method for unblocking your Conception Vessel?" asked Sorin.

"I don't know what you're talking about," said Stephan with a grin. "But feel free to give me a checkup on a regular basis. Adventurers need to maintain healthy bodies, after all."

There was no additional information to be gained, so Sorin sat down and recovered his mana. It wasn't long before Lawrence, Daphne, and Gareth finished adapting to their newly opened meridians.

"This is *unreal*," said Lawrence, hopping in and out of his companions' shadows. His speed had increased by 30 percent following Sorin's treatment. "I've always been taught that everyone has a different level of talent and that you couldn't just drink a miracle potion to change it. But here we are."

"Cultivation talent and natural endowments are two separate things," warned Sorin. "Your abilities will also be influenced by your cultivation method. By opening your primary meridians, some of your flaws will have been eliminated. Still, you'll definitely see the greatest improvements where you are strongest."

"I think this should be obvious to everyone present, but I'd like to make it clear that no one can speak of this," Stephan added. "If anyone asks, consecutive life-and-death battles, along with some strange things you ate in the labyrinth, unearthed some of your hidden potential. Is that clear?"

"Crystal clear!" said Lawrence, practically hopping with joy. Sorin was moved by Stephan's caution and agreed that keeping things quiet would be for the best.

"Excellent," said Stephan. "Now, all we need is a few fights for you all to get used to your new mana flow. You'll find that your techniques will be much stronger and operate on different principles. That's especially the case for you, Daphne. You're probably going to have to revise all your spell models."

"I'm looking forward to it!" said Daphne with a grin.

"In that case, let's set out right away," said Stephan. "Lawrence, scout ahead. Gareth, call the shots. I'll play keeper for the time being. You guys have fun while you still can."

48

CONVERGING

Sorin's unblocking of his teammate's primary meridians led to a sharp increase in combat prowess. Their team easily swept through any obstacles they found in the labyrinth, even going so far as to take turns single-handedly holding off swarms of weaker demons.

They soon doubled their stash of demon cores. While they did not discover any more adventurer remains and the corresponding equipment, Sorin and the others considered this a blessing and hoped that more of their companions would make it out alive.

It was difficult to immediately adjust to such a huge change in cultivation quality. They, therefore, made a point of meditating after every fight to reflect. It took three days to fully accustom themselves to their new abilities and the equipment they'd found in the center of the labyrinth.

Daphne's staff was the most straightforward as an artifact that could amplify raw power and increase the area of effect. As for Sorin's dagger, it had a built-in one-star curse that would weaken any enemy he cut.

"This is the last identification of the lot," said Daphne, muttering under her breath. "I should have forced you all to wait until we got back. I *hate* identifying."

"We can always wait if it makes you feel more at ease," suggested

Sorin. "Armor and weapons are one thing, but this piece of string is by far the most useless item of the lot. It can't even tangle enemies properly."

Daphne ignored Sorin and chanted as she drew a ritual circle with her mana and demon core dust. A symbol appeared above the ball of thread as it had for all eight previous identifications, revealing the school of enchantment imbued into the thread.

"Damn it," Daphne cursed under her breath. "It's a divination school item." I won't be able to determine its abilities with my limited talents. This needs an appraiser."

"What do you think it's made to divine?" asked Sorin, picking up the ball of thread. "Wait a minute. Lawrence, didn't you mention a ball of yarn when we entered the labyrinth?"

"Oh, that," said Lawrence. "I mean, it's not even a story. More of a folk song."

"Well, I'd like to hear it if you don't mind singing it," said Sorin.

"You sure?" asked Lawrence. "It's something I heard while investigating a certain charming young lady with the most startling green eyes I've ever chanced upon."

"Please spare me the details and just share the song," said Sorin.

"*All right* then," said Lawrence. "Here goes." He cleared his throat and began singing in the most tone-deaf voice Sorin had ever heard.

"Dancing in the corn maze,
"We seek a special light.
"A fire to illuminate,
"And find our Mr. Right.

"A special meeting unforetold,
"A morning of adventure.
"And if the day would turn to night,
"Re-spool and find the center.

"Dancing in the corn maze,

"We seek a special—"

"Okay, okay," Stephan said, cutting in. "You could make milk curdle with that voice."

"You think so?" said Lawrence, lighting up.

"That wasn't a compliment," said Sorin. "Anyway, I think I get the gist of it. They use a spool of yarn to wander from the center of the corn maze and have some fun for a day, and when it starts getting dark, they can find their way back. Hm... Does anyone know how to use divining artifacts?"

"I mean, they're pretty straightforward," said Stephan. "Most look like compasses. You roll a hair around a needle or something, and it always points to the owner of the hair."

"I don't think this ball of thread will work that way," said Sorin. "It's all spooled up already. Unless..." He held the ball of thread before his face and spoke to it. "Take me to the center." He then tossed out the ball of thread. To everyone's surprise, the ball kept rolling even after a hundred feet and even rounded the corner sharply.

"We should probably follow it before it runs out of thread," said Gareth. "Unless there's a way to stop it?"

"Only one way to find out," said Sorin. "Stop," he commanded. "Return." He felt a tugging from the thread in his hand, and several seconds later, the ball of thread rounded the corner, then jumped into his outstretched hand.

"Well, at least we know it can find the center," said Stephan. "Probably."

"Shouldn't we try finding the others instead?" said Gareth.

"Indeed," said Stephan. "Do you think it can find other people in the maze?"

"Let's find out," said Sorin. "Take me to the living people inside the maze," he commanded, then tossed out the ball. This time, it traveled in the opposite direction. After retrieving the ball, he issued a few other test commands, including 'Take me to the Minotaur' and 'Take me to Adventurer Barbara.' Of note, 'take me to the maze's exit' yielded no result, and neither did the request to find a good half of those who'd entered the maze."

"What a disaster," said Stephan. "Over seventy adventurers have died so far exploring this place."

"Is that going to be a problem for the outpost?" asked Sorin.

Stephan shook his head. "In truth, the outpost doesn't need so many adventurers. The Bone-Forging cultivators in the outpost are its true defenders. The rest of us are just here to make up the numbers and block low-level bodies during demon tides. As for us low-level adventurers, our job is to clear out as many demons as we can before the demon tide hits. That way, the city won't be under as much pressure."

"There are also more adventurers than you might think," added Gareth. "I asked around in my spare time. The outpost's population is small, but many adventurers come here from the cities. In all, I think the total population of registered adventurers is about 500. The Governor's Manor also employs 200 cultivators. The other organizations in the city employ about 300 combat-ready cultivators, for a total standing force of about a thousand, not counting non-combat cultivators."

This made sense to Sorin, who'd treated at least a few hundred cultivators during his time as a physician. There were few repeat customers like Lawrence. "Even so, there's no telling if the others were killed by monsters or teams like Orpheus's," said Sorin. "Shouldn't we converge with other teams?"

"Agreed," said Stephan. "Why don't we find Barbara first? Her team will make up for some of our major deficiencies." The rest of the team agreed, and Sorin, the controller of the ball of thread, activated the item. The ball led them further into the maze, never straying further than a half mile in any direction.

It was a half-day later when they finally encountered signs of struggle. Their surroundings changed, revealing a rocky cliff face and a group of ten strange demons made of stone. "This place even has gargoyles in it," muttered Stephan. "I've never heard of such a varied dungeon."

"Should we go help them?" asked Sorin, nodding towards the group of six women who were fighting the stone creatures. Their leader,

Barbara, stood at the back of her group and picked off gargoyles with the bow she'd obtained in the labyrinth. Overall, her team was well-armed and well-armored. Sorin shuddered to imagine how much all that equipment cost.

"It's best to avoid interfering with an adventuring team mid-combat," said Gareth. "Even getting this close could be considered mildly threatening."

"Then let's back off to make our intentions clear," agreed Stephan. "Daphne, blow that Fireball out, will you? We wouldn't want any misunderstandings."

They waited ten minutes for Barbara's team to finish off the gargoyles. While not very threatening, gargoyles had tough, stone-like skin and could regenerate their flesh exceptionally quickly. It was a battle of attrition in the best of cases. Combined with Sorin's group's arrival, it wasn't surprising that Barbara's team took a long time to wear them down.

Barbara then instructed her team to rest for ten minutes before making their way over. The cliff face had vanished with the last of the gargoyles, significantly shrinking the distance between both teams.

"I'm glad to see that you're all still alive," Barbara greeted. "Though I notice that your team has split up with Team Oasis. Did you have a disagreement of some kind, or did you encounter trouble like we did?"

"If it was trouble, there's no way the five of us would be standing while Team Oasis fell," replied Stephan. "No, we just had a... *disagreement* while fighting a powerful enemy. A bull-headed creature with an abnormally large axe."

"That you were able to face that creature and escape unscathed is a miracle in and of itself," said Barbara. "We lost four sisters to the creature before managing to retreat."

"We wouldn't have lost anyone if that bastard Orpheus hadn't run off," cut in the spear-wielding member of their team.

"Seriously?" said Lawrence. "Orpheus again? Shouldn't he be afraid of people teaming up on him, given how many people he's upset?"

"We had an unfortunate encounter with Orpheus as well," Stephan confessed to Barbara. "As for the Minotaur, our parting with Team Oasis was related to it. As for the reason we could reunite with you, it's far from coincidental. We encountered a treasure in this Labyrinth that allows us to find both its center and others within the maze."

"Are you suggesting that we band together to take care of the creature?" asked Barbara. "Not a bad idea, given its power. Unfortunately, I don't think our teams alone will be able to take care of the thing."

"Which is why I suggest we find Haster's team," said Stephan. "As the drunken swordsman, his attack power is amongst the highest of all the adventurers gathered."

"No need to come looking for us," a voice suddenly sounded. A group of five adventurers rounded the corner. It was none other than Haster's team, and they looked much worse for wear than Sorin's or Barbara's team.

"What happened to you guys?" asked Barbara. "And where's Team Midnight?"

"Dead," said Haster, spitting. "They tried to stab us in the back when we found a couple of corpses with magical equipment. They thought a drunk like me would be easy prey."

"Rogues," muttered Barbara. "They're always shifty creatures. And yes, that does include you, Lawrence. Don't think we've forgotten our close encounters."

"I heard you mention my team by name as I was rounding the corner," said Haster. "What are your intentions?" Stephan summarized their findings and the existence of the Minotaur. The honest swordsman immediately accepted their proposal to take it down together.

"That leaves us with two choices," said Stephan. "The first choice is to locate the creature and kill it. The second choice is to return to the center of the maze and try to find ourselves suitable weapons, knowing that should we get caught, we'll be at a terrain disadvantage."

Haster and Barbara exchanged looks. "By the looks of it, you've all had a chance to upgrade your equipment while we haven't," said Haster. "That's hardly fair, and we probably need all the help, given how strong you describe this creature to have been. Also, we wouldn't want that idiot Orpheus looting the place while we're fighting."

"That's my sentiment exactly," said Barbara. "Pardon me for being blunt, but we also need to benefit from this raid.

"Hey, we found the center fair and square!" said Lawrence. "It's not our fault you guys didn't find it."

"We're not saying we want a share of what you took," Haster assured them. "We just want a chance at the loot. Otherwise, we might as well go our separate ways."

Stephan exchanged looks with his teammates before nodding. "Fine. Fair is fair. But we'll raid the center at the same time. If the coast is clear, we'll each rely on our luck and grab what we can to prepare for when the Minotaur returns. But if the Minotaur decides to wait for us at the center, we can only go all out. With any luck, we'll still have time to collect loose once we kill this abnormally strong boss monster."

Haster and Barabara agreed that these were fair terms. They formalized their agreement on paper and prepared to move out.

In terms of firepower, both teams were quite strong. Haster's team had a powerful ice mage, while Barbara's team had one of the better life mages in the raiding party. There were also Haster and Barabara themselves, who were only slightly inferior to Stephan in terms of combat capability.

Sorin, however, wasn't convinced that this would be enough. After discussing with Stephan, he split his remaining Manabane Poison between himself, Lawrence, Gareth, and Barbara. Only those with superior mastery over their weapons or with excellent dexterity, like Lawrence, would be able to ensure that the substance harmed none of their teammates.

"Sorin, Gareth, Lawrence, and Barbara—your roles are the most crucial," said Stephan. "The Minotaur isn't a standard boss monster. Its skin is tougher than normal, and its flesh isn't much weaker. Our weaker party members won't even be able to scratch it."

"So, out of curiosity, what happens if I get this stuff on my skin?" asked Lawrence. "By accident, of course."

"Your mana sea will explode, and without a three-star physician to save you, you'll be dead," replied Sorin. "Having said that, it's not too late to give me back the vial. I'm somewhat immune to the stuff, so I don't need to worry about accidentally offing myself."

"I'll just be *cautious*," said Lawrence, gingerly putting away the vial.

"If that's everything, let's move out," said Stephan. "Sorin, do the thing."

"Take us to the center of the labyrinth," Sorin commanded. The ball of silver string unfurled, and their three combined teams took off after it.

49

THE BATTLE AT THE TEMPLE

With the addition of Haster and Barbara's teams, their speed through the labyrinth increased severalfold. They encountered four groups of demonic creatures that took a total of a minute each to dispatch before arriving at a different entrance to the Minotaur's residence.

"I hear sounds of battle," said Gareth as they approached the temple-like structure. "Sounds of steel and magic and bows."

"Looks like someone made it here before us," said Stephan. "Let's see exactly who we're up against before making a decision."

The entrance led to the side of the temple. Tinted glass from where they'd broken out to escape still littered the ground. Not far away, sixteen adventurers were engaged in battle against the mighty Minotaur. "I see Orpheus, Nale, and Mercella's teams," said Gareth. "Permission to shoot them in the back?"

"Permission denied," said Stephan. "We're better than that."

"How much better, exactly?" asked Barbara. "Because I'm not fond of any of those teams. Judging by your story earlier, you have cause to hit back at both Orpheus *and* Nale."

"There's a big difference between a frontal clash and stabbing someone in the back," said Stephan. "Also, they'll tire the beast out, and we can use the distraction to sneak into the temple. Lawrence?"

"Way ahead of you," said Lawrence, sprinting towards the temple. He was about to reach the window when he suddenly stopped. "Damn it!" the rogue cursed and picked up a broken shard of glass. He tossed it towards the temple, causing a reaction from a golden shield that now isolated the temple from the rest of the labyrinth.

"You idiot!" cursed Stephan. "You ruined our element of surprise!"

Sorin looked over to the Minotaur and noticed that its bull head was staring straight at them. Orpheus had also noticed them, and their teams were now adjusting their positions in case of potential treachery. In addition, he felt a cold sensation sweep through his body. Their three teams stiffened as sounds of grinding stone drowned out those of the ongoing battle.

"The labyrinth!" said Gareth. "It's shifting!"

"Thank you very much for pointing out the obvious," said Stephan. "Everyone, prepare for battle!"

The grinding sounds only lasted thirty seconds, but they were immediately followed up by bestial roars from the same passageways. Demons began pouring out from all eight entrances to the center of the labyrinth.

"Defensive formation!" Barbara called out. Her team members immediately adjusted their positions.

"Get ready to cut a wedge towards the boss," Haster commanded his team. Then, to Sorin's surprise, he pulled out a large waterskin and took a deep drink.

Wine? thought Sorin as he pulled out his dagger and summoned a handful of poison needles. He then carefully inspected the eight different varieties of demons that emerged all at once. There were lizards and serpents and all manner of furred animals. There was even a group of cyclopes like the ones they'd killed earlier.

"Steady!" shouted Stephan as he assumed his bear form and received the charge of a group of demonic boars. "Their numbers are great, but their strengths are weak. Let's push forward towards the Minotaur!"

Sorin and Lawrence pulled back and guarded Daphne as she chanted a spell. Thanks to her new staff, a Fireball that was 50 percent larger than normal and formed in record time. It blasted the group of thirty charging boars, directly eliminating half of them. As for the other half, Stephan swatted two to death, and Barbara's team used swords and spears to finish them off.

Having received the initial charge, their group sped toward a group of forty lizards that had surrounded Orpheus's team. While Sorin believed they should let them deal with that themselves, fighting so many one-star demons while also handling the Minotaur likely wouldn't end well for either group.

The lizards only realized their predicament seconds before they clashed. Sorin used Adder Rush and Viper Strike to dispatch a few that came at him and threw out a handful of poison needles, killing another two.

"I don't suppose you're open to cooperating against this thing before we all die?" Stephan asked Orpheus as he smashed a pair of lizards to a pulp.

"You're just here because you have no choice," Orpheus snapped back. "And the answer is *yes*, obviously. Get your elites in here so we can deal with this monstrosity. We'll each peel off a portion of our members to hold back the lesser demons."

"Barbara, Haster, Sorin, and Lawrence, you're with me," commanded Stephan. "Gareth, help us out with a few well-timed arrows. Spend the rest of your time with Daphne and Sypher and pick off those they can't eliminate with their area of effect spells."

Having already discussed their strategy against the Minotaur, their teams were fine with these arrangements. Barbara's team was well-balanced and had a proper life mage. In contrast, Haster's team consisted of swordsmen and a single frost mage, Sypher, who quickly teamed up with Daphne to eliminate a large group of cyclopes as they emerged.

Orpheus and Nale's teams each had their respective tanks and life mages, but it was clear that they were having trouble holding their own against the Minotaur. Stephan directly launched himself at the creature and attacked with a Lunisolar Paw, drawing its attention. This bought time for Sorin to close the gap with Adder Rush and stab the Minotaur in the side.

Sorin's enchanted dagger punched through the creature's thick mana shield and hide, injecting a hefty dose of Flesh-Melt Poison. He was now able to inject twice as much poison as usual. While it wasn't very effective, it helped to disperse the Manabane Poison he'd coated onto his dagger before charging in.

Violet tendrils spread out from the point of entry, severely weakening the Minotaur's flesh and creating disruptive ripples in its mana shield. The Minotaur responded violently to Sorin's attack. It chopped down with its axe, and Sorin, not nearly as agile as Lawrence was, barely avoided the attack and suffered a six-inch cut to his shoulder.

Lawrence took the opportunity to take the Minotaur's back. He used triple stab execution with his enchanted sword to apply another dose of Manabane Poison, further disrupting its shielding. Gareth and Barbara followed shortly after. An arrow struck the creature's dominant arm, while a sword plunged into one of its legs. The combined poison of all four attacks peeled away its most potent defense, making it possible for the melee combatants to whittle away at its health pool.

"Gareth, pull back! Barbara, switch to your spear!" commanded Stephan. "Haster, attack it before it recovers its shields!" The drunken swordsman stumbled forward and swept out awkwardly with his sword, cutting a gash six inches deep into its hide, far deeper than anyone else had so far.

Unfortunately, Haster's efforts seemed in vain because the wound immediately began to close over. Violet and black streams leaked out from the wound, indicating that the poison was now spread out all over the Minotaur's body.

The Minotaur, enraged by the sudden development, grabbed his axe with both its hands and chopped down toward Barbara. Reacting quickly, Collin activated a taunting ability and received the blow. The power of the attack took him entirely by surprise and sundered his shield in half, taking Collin's arm out along with it.

"Damn it!" shouted Nale, pulling a bleeding Collin out. "Hellen, apply a healing potion and stop the bleeding before coming back to help us. Collin, you're useless now. Make sure to pull back away from the fighting."

Sorin was in no rush to attack a second time. As he was the only team member with leftover Manabane Poison to coat his blade, the Minotaur had grown wary of him. This was the final dose of Manabane Poison that could disrupt its heavy shielding and mana-reinforced muscles. Failure was not an option.

With Gareth picking off those Daphne and Sypher don't eliminate, we don't have to worry about outside interference. But whenever I get close to the Minotaur, I immediately draw its attention. I need a better opening. Otherwise, I'll end up just like Collin.

"Sorin, get ready!" shouted Stephan. "Orpheus, use a powerful attack to draw its attention! Lunisolar Paw!"

"Nether Blade!" shouted Orpheus as he attacked with a sword encased in sinister energy.

"Drunken Sword!"

"Masterful Stab!"

The Minotaur, overwhelmed by the sudden onslaught, erupted with dense mana fluctuations. Golden axe blades erupted from it, forcing back all four attackers.

Sorin used Adder Rush on instinct, avoiding the heaviest part of the Minotaur's burst attack. He suffered a few cuts on his chest. In exchange, he stabbed the Minotaur's arm, injecting another heavy dose of external Manabane Poison and further disrupting its mana shield.

Despite its predicament, the Minotaur was ready for Sorin. It swept out with its arm and moved to swat him like a bug. But Sorin already knew how heavy-handed it could be and immediately used Python Coil to wrap around its arm and adjust his position. He held on for dear life and stabbed it several times with Viper Strike before the Minotaur managed to fling him off towards a group of demonic lizards.

Sorin rolled away just in time to avoid a burning claw to the chest. An arrow struck another lizard in the head, buying Sorin the time he needed to pull back to where Daphne, Gareth, and Sypher were located.

"You all right?" asked Gareth.

"I'm fine," said Sorin, wincing as he rolled his shoulder. "It's not worth wasting what's left of my healing potion on it."

"You're the physician," said Gareth, nocking three arrows and shooting down three bat demons that had just emerged from the tunnel with Split Shot.

The Manabane Poison they'd applied to the Minotaur was only a one-star poison, but it was a potent one that had been applied in large quantities. Thanks to its effects, Haster, Orpheus, Stephan, and Barbara were able to execute their attacks against the Minotaur effectively.

But it's still not enough, thought Sorin, noting how quickly its wounds were closing. Having struck it twice, he was familiar with its anatomy and knew that these attacks were just flesh wounds.

Having no more external Manabane Poison to supplement his attacks, Sorin could only rely on his personal poisons. He chose a moment when the Minotaur was attacking Orpheus to dart in and out and apply a few more viper strikes. He was wary about retaliation but discovered that this time, the Minotaur didn't pay much attention to him.

It must have powerful instincts that could sense the threat of poison on our blades, thought Sorin. But that suited him perfectly. His personal poison might not be as effective as the external poison, but it would continue to build up in the Minotaur's system and cause him damage over time.

Sorin continued in this fashion, landing one Viper Strike after another, steadily increasing the dose of poison in the Minotaur's body. At the same time, he applied the curse from his dagger, which seemed to weaken the Minotaur's offensive prowess with each application.

"I sense sharp mana fluctuations," Orpheus suddenly shouted. "We've reached the halfway point. Prepare for the next phase!" The Minotaur let out a loud bellow as it suddenly grew to a height of thirteen feet, with arms and legs the thickness of Sorin's torso.

Sorin felt a cold chill as his spiritual senses were forced back. The Minotaur's wounds closed, and its mana shields lit up with a golden light, seemingly erasing all their progress.

50

SLAYING THE MINOTAUR

The Minotaur cleaved down with its axe, catching Stephan by surprise and giving him no chance to retreat from its attack range. Sparks flew as the axe blade bit into the bear's half-plate armor, splashing blood over the labyrinth's stone floor.

"I've taken its berserk attack!" shouted Stephan. "Its essence is confirmed to be Violence! Watch out for the minions, as they'll likely grow stronger!"

The demons that both their teams were holding back suddenly pulsed with aggressive mana and increased in size and strength. Their defensive lines collapsed, and one of Barbara's teammates, Sarah, was overwhelmed by a demonic panther that bit out her throat before making its way toward Daphne.

"Lorimer, it's up to you," said Sorin, throwing the rat out like a dart.

"Reeeeeee!" Lorimer skipped on the dungeon's stone floor and launched itself at the demonic panther, tackling it just before it reached Daphne and tearing out its throat. It then threw itself at the remaining demons, alleviating much of the pressure on Daphne's end.

Having taken care of the urgent situation, Sorin increased the rate at which he picked his openings. Though the Minotaur was indeed stronger and more muscular than before, and its defenses had also increased, its speed had slowed significantly. Moreover, its essence was confirmed to be Violence, which meant that it wouldn't have any strange attacks for them to cope with.

Sorin focused on speed and efficiency instead of hitting the Minotaur's vitals. The Minotaur tended to react strongly to more potent attacks, and it didn't seem to care as much about cuts and stabs on its arms and legs.

It wasn't long before Sorin landed twenty more attacks, all on crucial acupoints. Once the last dose was applied, the poison in the Minotaur's body flared up and reached a critical level. Hair began falling out of its tough hide, exposing black, puss-filled veins and gashes where the poison had finally dissolved enough flesh to reach the surface.

"Keep at it!" shouted Stephan. "It's almost done for. Watch out for its final rampage. Sorin, I'll hold it down for you!"

Stephan let out an angry roar as he leaped onto the Minotaur and gave it a vicious bear hug. The Minotaur was interrupted halfway through attacking Orpheus's tank and could only drop its heavy weapon and attempt to wrestle Stephan off itself using its muscular arms.

Sorin would find no better opportunity. He rushed in and stabbed the Minotaur between its back ribs, injecting a dose of paralytic poison into its heart, disrupting its attempt to throw off Stephan. He then repeatedly stabbed it while injecting Flesh-Melt Poison, only pulling back once its skin suddenly became incomparably tough, trapping his dagger within its armor-like flesh.

"It's rampaging!" shouted Sorin. He abandoned his dagger and pulled back just in time to avoid a lethal palm strike. Stephan, who'd been hugging it, wasn't so fortunate. The Minotaur bit him, and Stephan, stubborn as always, bit it back.

The Minotaur, in its rage, tried to throw him off, but Stephan clamped on tightly. The Minotaur tossed him about like a limp rag until Stephan's teeth were knocked out, then threw him away before turning its attention to the remaining adventurers.

"The rampage shouldn't last more than ten seconds," said Orpheus. "Let's disperse and not give it a chance to attack us as a group." He pulled back just as the Minotaur picked up its axe, and both the weapon and the creature grew to 50 percent of their already inflated sizes.

Seeing that Stephan was no longer able to fight, the Minotaur picked Haster out as its next target. The drunken swordsman used his sword to somehow parry the axe two times. But his sword, clearly enchanted, broke after deflecting a third attack.

Haster stumbled back like a drunken idiot when the fourth attack came, conveniently gaining the protection of Barabara, who was now wielding a heavy spear. *Where did she get that spear from?* thought Sorin as he rushed in to pull away Haster. He didn't remember seeing it earlier. As for Haster, the man was heavier than he looked, and due to his drunkenness, he was difficult to get a grip on.

As strong as Barbara was, she was only able to buy them three precious seconds before retreating. The Minotaur, upon seeing Sorin, who'd dealt so much damage to it, gave up on pursuing her and tried to cut him down.

But before it could swing its axe, a startling roar erupted, and a bear, now significantly larger than before and with white fur covered in silver runes, bit into its chest and hugged its body. The Minotaur's impervious state faded then, but its enlarged body and toughened skin remained.

Haster, who'd seemingly passed out, rose from the ground and tossed out his broken sword. It traveled at an awkward angle that missed Stephan but struck the Minotaur straight in the eye. A golden spear then pierced its side, drawing out a massive amount of black blood.

Sorin took the opportunity to approach the Minotaur and slapped its leg to evaluate its body. Its organs were on the verge of failure, and this was especially the case for its livers, of which it had four. "Lorimer, help out!" The rat launched itself at the Minotaur's head and began tunneling into its remaining eye. The Minotaur tried to slap him away but was unable to free itself from Stephan's deadly bear hug.

One. Taking advantage of the Minotaur's distracted state, Sorin grabbed his dagger out of the Minotaur's back and struck out with Viper Strike, destroying one of its failing livers. *Two.* He struck the Minotaur's second failing liver, which led to a chain reaction that caused its heart to seize up. *Three.* The Minotaur's legs gave out when he attacked the third liver. This brought its fourth liver into Sorin's attack range; he immediately destroyed it, taking away its last shred of resistance to the poisons coursing through its body.

Having lost its final liver, the Minotaur's strength rapidly drained away. Stephan, who was still holding on for dear life, was able to wrestle it to the ground and protect the others from its final thrashing.

Seconds later, the Minotaur's body fell limp, and the labyrinth, having fulfilled its purpose, began to shake violently.

"The dungeon is collapsing!" shouted Stephan. "Prepare for teleportation!"

"The shield is gone!" said Lawrence. "Nale and Orpheus are already heading straight for the temple!"

"We have a minute at most," said Barbara. "We're going to run in and grab what we can. We'll talk about splitting things up later."

"Agreed," said Stephan, his mouth still a bloody mess.

"Agreed," said Haster.

With the death of the boss monster, the remaining demons in the dungeon had no more interest in fighting. They retreated into the labyrinth, freeing up Daphne, Gareth, and their other teammates, who immediately ran into the temple.

"Lawrence, stay here with me," said Sorin. "Start skinning the most intact piece of hide you find. I'll chop off anything valuable."

"Good thinking!" said Lawrence. He took out his short sword and immediately got to work. The Minotaur's hide was tough, and some parts were porous because of Sorin's poison, but he was still able to find several pieces of tough hide to start peeling away.

As for Sorin, he was already familiar with the Minotaur's anatomy and, therefore, knew precisely where to find its core. He directly cut into its ribs, where its heart was located, and exposed the tainted organ, then sliced the organ open, revealing a dark, pulsing mass.

"As if I'd let you eat this," said Sorin, catching Lorimer by the tail as he attempted to devour the core. He reached out and grabbed it, but was surprised to see it solidify into a gem. The labyrinth began to shake even more violently the moment he retrieved it.

"Eat what you can!" Sorin snapped at Lorimer. He used his knife to cut off the Minotaur's horns, which seemed to be made from some sort of metallic substance, as well as its hooves. He then joined Lawrence in peeling away additional pieces of hide. At the same time, Lorimer gorged himself on Minotaur flesh, heedless of the deadly poison it contained.

Seconds after they peeled away a large chunk of skin from its back, a golden light enveloped the trio. A wave of energy, not unlike the crashing of waves at sea, carried them off. Seconds later, Sorin slammed into the ground and found himself just outside the ruin's original gate. His entire team was there, as were Haster's, Barbara's, Orpheus's, Nale's, and Mercella's teams. Two more teams that hadn't taken part in the final battle also appeared. They still had their original ten members and had clearly limited themselves to the outskirts of the labyrinth.

The adventurers immediately picked themselves off the ground and separated into groups. Orpheus's companions retreated a safe distance, as did Stephan's team. Neither side was willing to put their weapons down.

"How dare you attack us to steal our treasure after we fought the boss monster for so long!" Orpheus shouted suddenly.

"You shameless bastard, we clearly fought that thing together!" Lawrence shouted back.

"At ease," said Stephan, who'd reverted to his bear form. His teeth had regrown after transforming, but he was pale and clearly out of energy. "Orpheus, you know perfectly well that in situations like these, no one has sufficient proof of anything. So, stop it with your games and back off while you still can."

"Are you trying to slander me?" said Orpheus. "We'll see what the guild says about that."

"Indeed, we will," said Stephan. He then looked to the two remaining teams, who needed clarification about the situation. "I recommend you don't get sucked in with Orpheus and his ilk. They're a nest of vipers, the whole lot of them."

"A nest of vipers?" said Orpheus, drawing his sword. "Do you dare repeat that? You think I don't know that your mages are all out of mana, and you're a step into the grave yourself?"

"Are you sure you want to try me?" asked Stephan, looking not at all worried. Sorin had no idea where he got his confidence from and was now very regretful for having used up all the Manabane Poison.

"I think we can stop things here before they get too messy," a voice suddenly called out. A man leaped down from atop the ruin's entrance. He had a sharp nose and golden eyes, and Sorin immediately recognized him as Vice Guild Master Victor.

Stephan didn't seem surprised at all by his appearance. "Many thanks for your intervention, Vice Guild Master. Enough lives were lost inside that bloody labyrinth. There's no need to add to the body count."

"A labyrinth, was it?" asked Guild Master Victor. "Unfortunate. But by the looks of it, you all had a good haul?" Indeed, everyone's packs were bulging, and many of the adventurers present had yet to put away the things they'd looted from the temple. "Seeing as there seem to be some disagreements between the returnees, we'll be returning to the outpost as a group. Raids like these are messy, and it's necessary to record what transpired in case it becomes a recurring dungeon. As for any grievances you might have, we'll address them after we've taken down everyone's testimony. I'll note that this is *not* optional. You'll each have one chance to make your voice heard."

"But we weren't involved in their dispute!" said the leader of one of the two adventuring teams who'd stuck to the outskirts. His courage lasted roughly two seconds, however, as the vice guild master released a hint of Bone-Forging pressure that forced him into submission.

"We'll happily cooperate with the vice guild master's investigation," said Orpheus. "My only request is that you give us justice against these thieves who pose as knights instead of the knaves they are."

"Everyone, take two hours to rest," instructed Vice Guild Master Victory, ignoring Orpheus. "The demons that were drawn to the tomb have scattered, and it will be much easier to return home. I also ask that you keep to your separate camps to prevent conflicts. Any mediation or arbitration can wait until our return."

Having obtained permission, Sorin walked over to Stephan and supported him. *Seven bone fractures. Internal organs are in disarray. Muscles have ruptured in several locations.*

"I'm going to have to cut you open and apply healing potions directly to your muscles to prevent trauma," Sorin said to Stephan. "I'd normally recommend a life mage heal you, but those seem to be in short supply right now."

Stephan chuckled. "There's also our team name to consider. By the way, are you sure you shouldn't be helping out Gareth and Lawrence? They seem to have taken a few serious injuries."

"They're just flesh wounds," said Sorin, shaking his head. "Nothing they can't tough out for thirty minutes while I stitch you up." He then took out a needle and thread and cut open Stephan's biceps, revealing a lump of crushed flesh. "You *might* want to get a leather belt or a rag or something. This is *really* going to hurt."

JUDGMENT

The Adventurers Guild was unusually silent, given the time of day. The mission counter was closed, as was the materials exchange center. Only the Adventurer's Pub was doing steady business, but only because of the thirty-five adventurers that were kept from leaving the premises and had been loitering there since mid-morning.

Sorin and his team were naturally part of this large group, and unlike the other eight teams that had joined forces in the labyrinth, they were healthy and whole.

"Stephan York!" a voice called from the guild master's office.

"Wish me luck," said Stephan, pushing up his large body.

He's gotten taller and physically stronger since our fight against the Minotaur, thought Sorin as he watched the man duck to enter the office. *I'll need to get his permission to perform an in-depth investigation of the changes.* The past five days of arduous traveling had been neither the time nor the place for such a thing.

Stephan returned after twenty minutes. Sorin, Gareth, Lawrence, and Daphne had already been called up, and only Orpheus and Barbara's statements remained.

"How did it go?" asked Lawrence. "Did Haley cross-examine you? Or did the guild master tear you a new one like he did me?"

"Maybe he'd have kinder words for you if he didn't catch you peeping on his daughter three months back," said Stephan. "And no, this is just a routine interview. I submitted my statement, and they cross-examined me to ascertain the veracity of my report. They'll do the same to Barbara now. Last will be Orpheus, the most heavily accused party in this entire affair. Now, what's for dinner?"

"Dinner?" groaned Lawrence. "You mean we have to eat *dinner* here too? What happened to freedom and not eating deep-fried food?"

"I believe you can order a steak if you want something different," said Sorin. "There's also grilled haddock and stewed beef. Lots of options. All pretty low on grease."

"It shouldn't take more than a couple hours after the last statements are issued," said Gareth. "What? I asked one of the guild's employees while you were all busy playing table games and sneaking food into your front pockets to feed your illegal rat. By the way, they know about Lorimer but are forcing you to hide him so as to not encourage the practice of rat taming."

Sorin shrugged and pulled a leftover chicken leg from their afternoon snack off the table and into his front pocket. Lorimer devoured it, bone and all, and issued silent squeaks of approval and compliments to the chef.

"I'll have the stewed beef. Quadruple portion," Sorin called out to the waitress. "Also, two more coffees." A good half of the food would go to Lorimer. The rodent had also developed a taste for coffee over the past day and would get cranky if Sorin didn't share.

"I'll take the roast chicken," said Gareth when the waitress came over with a notepad.

"Spiced lamb skewers," said Daphne, raising her hand. Her head was buried in the notes she'd been taking since returning.

"Why is everything good on the menu deep-fried..." muttered Lawrence. "Fine. I'll take the fried haddock."

"You don't *have* to order fried food every time," said the waitress. "We can probably steam it if you like."

"But then it wouldn't be as tasty," complained Lawrence. "Batter it and fry it. Extra batter. Extra spice. Yes, I know you normally don't add spice."

A half-hour later, they were all tucking into a hearty meal. Unlike the other teams, who'd lost members, they all had a healthy appetite. The team who'd suffered the worst was Barbara's. Her original team was down to three members, while her accompanying team was down to two. According to Gareth, there were talks of merging both teams after their successful cooperation.

Nale's team had suffered the second most casualties. Warren was dead, and Lise and Collin had suffered crippling injuries. Collin had lost an arm, while Lise's leg had to be amputated due to an untreated snake bite. It had taken her over an hour to thicken her skin and ask Sorin for treatment after Hellen's mana failed to accomplish good results. By then, Sorin could only save her life, not her limb.

"The food here isn't bad, but it's not excellent," said Sorin. "Clarice and Percival are excellent cooks. Maybe I could have you all over for a meal once things settle down?"

"I'll have to shamelessly accept," said Stephan. "I don't have a permanent residence and keep having to eat out. I haven't had any good food since coming here."

"That's because you refused the family's arrangements to live with *me*," came a voice. Stephan flinched as Haley sat beside him, set her own plate of food down, and began eating.

"Shouldn't you not sit by me in case people think there's favoritism?" asked Stephan stiffly.

"What favoritism?" said Haley, cutting into her steak and sticking a medium rare piece into her mouth. "I'm not actually part of the investigation. All I did was cross-examine people along with the guild master and vice guild master. It's *them* who are going to decide what happens next. Although... I wouldn't expect too with respect to the Orpheus situation."

"Don't worry," said Stephan. "I already told the team as much."

"Isn't the situation pretty clear cut, though?" asked Lawrence. "With so many people complaining, shouldn't Orpheus get the boot?"

"Haven't you heard of plot armor?" asked Daphne, not raising her head as she picked up a lamb skewer and lazily bit off a piece. "The bad guys never get punished in stories. It's always the good guys who suffer."

"I don't think that's how plot armor works," said Gareth. "Anyway, the result is obvious, given who the other party is loitering around. With Vice Governor Marsh and a high-level member of the Alchemists Guild here, I can't see any extreme actions being taken." The two people in question were also seated at a table at the Adventurer's Pub since the raiding party's arrival.

It took roughly an hour after Orpheus's testimony for the vice guild master to emerge. He looked over the assembled adventurers coldly before looking straight at the vice governor. "I don't remember inviting the Governor's Manor or the Alchemists Guild for a consultation regarding our internal affairs," said Vice Guild Master Victor.

"I wouldn't dare interfere in the guild's operations," replied Vice Governor Marsh. "*Unless,* of course, the judgment showed evidence of nepotism. Internal guild matters are one thing, but the Governor's Manor reserves the right to contest unfair verdicts and submit them for arbitration."

The vice guild master's lips pulled into a thin line. "And what about you, Mr. Primrose?" he asked the representative from the Alchemists Guild. "Unlike the Governor's Manor, you have no official sway in this matter."

"I'm just here as a spectator," said a pale man with long black hair tied back in a ponytail. He didn't at all look like an alchemist. His alchemist's emblem also had a slightly green tinge and a serpent coiled around the cauldron. "Don't mind me. All I need to do tonight is write a report, and it will fall to the guild master to decide on our official stance."

It's a good thing Marcus isn't here to mess things up, thought Sorin.

He frowned as he thought of Marcus's relatively light hand over the past while. *What is he up to exactly? He's only interfered directly in my matters once. Though his second visit to the Adventurers Guild was damaging, he didn't directly attack me.*

"I'm sure the Alchemists Guild will be satisfied with how we resolve things," said the vice guild master. "The judgment is as follows: no one will be held culpable for any losses or casualties inflicted during the raid."

"*What?*" shouted Barbara. She stood up from her seat and glared at the vice guild master. "I'd better get a good explanation for this. Four of my sisters died because of Orpheus's games."

"Please *refrain* from inappropriate actions," snapped the vice guild master, releasing a small burst of Bone-Forging pressure. "We've given a great deal of thought to this judgment and will *not* have our members second-guessing our decision."

"I'm concerned about the validity of this judgment, Vice Guild Master," said Vice Governor Marsh. "I've spoken to a fair number of people, and there are concerns that Mr. York's team, which suffered the least casualties, was an opportunist in the battle. They ambushed Orpheus's team as they landed the final blow on the Minotaur and stole its core while taking advantage of their wounded state."

"You son of a—"

"Calm yourself, Miss Strider," Victor said, cutting off Barbara before she could directly insult the vice governor. "Vice Governor Marsh, you know full well that this is, at best, a one-sided story. Our guild has taken great pains to collect and collate each person's narrative before coming to a judgment.

"While most of the testimony incriminates Orpheus's team, and only a fraction of the adventurers positively speak of their actions, there is a lack of overall evidence. Orpheus's team will, therefore, *not* be issued fines or corporal punishment for what the guild sees as horrendous and underhanded behavior.

"*However,*" continued Victor, noting Orpheus's smirk. "A decision has been made to strip Orpheus and his remaining three team members of their guild membership. As for Nale's team, they will be issued a thousand gold fine each for voluntarily disclosing their inappropriate actions."

"I object," said Vice Governor Marsh, whose expression had grown increasingly cold during the announcement. "You say that teams involved will not be punished. But isn't stripping them of their guild membership considered a punishment? And why is Nale's team being punished with a fine?"

"Orpheus's team is being stripped of its membership for reasons of character and trust," replied Victor evenly. "It relates to prior offenses and their terrible reputation in the guild. The guild feels uncomfortable associating with these individuals, given the friction they cause. We are well within our rights to do so."

"As for Nale's team, they confessed to sabotaging the retreat of a partner team, a crime normally punishable by expulsion but lessened due to them voluntarily bringing up the matter. I'll note that they *also* testified against Orpheus's team about an incident involving kill stealing. Still, given the minor nature of the offense and their credibility given the matters they admitted to, these charges will not be pursued."

Vice Governor Marsh snorted loudly. "So much for the reputation of the Adventurers Guild. All they can do is bully with numbers instead of investigating the *actual* truth."

"You can believe what you will," said Victor with a smile. "In fact, if you trust in this judgment so much, why don't you hire these wonderful individuals to work for your Governor's Manor?"

Vice Governor Marsh's smile froze as he realized he'd been trapped by his counterpart. "Perhaps I will. The Governor's Manor is always looking for premium talents of good character. What say you, Orpheus? Are you willing to accept my offer of employment?"

"Of course," said Orpheus, quickly grabbing onto the offered life raft. He looked surprised, but Sorin felt this was his intended result, given his behavior. "What are you three doing? Thank the vice governor for supporting the side of justice." His three minions stood up and thanked the vice governor, though it was clear that the vice governor wasn't too pleased by this development.

"That about covers it, then," said Vice Guild Master Victor. "Does the Alchemists Guild have any problem with how we managed this issue?"

"It's like I said, I'm just a spectator," said the man from the Alchemists Guild. "I try not to involve myself too deeply in politics."

"Very good," said Vice Guild Master Victor. "That's the worst of it then. Earnings and costs will be split as normal, including Orpheus's team. Since it's too difficult to split loot given disagreements between parties, everyone will keep what they managed to retrieve from the labyrinth, *including* the Minotaur's core retrieved by Team 'We Don't Need a Life Mage.' An exciting choice of team name, by the way. I wonder how long it'll take for you to change it."

"We stand by our name," said Stephan, looking up from his fourth plate of food.

The vice guild master then retreated to the back. Orpheus, who was no longer welcome, followed the vice governor out of the Adventurers Guild.

Though the exchange counter was closed, Stephan used his connections to convert gems to their equivalent in gold coins. Each of them walked out with 500 gold apiece, more than enough to get by in the short term.

Sorin returned to the Kepler Manor and was warmly received by Percival and Clarice. The manor was dimly lit and cold, but Percival threw a few pieces of coal into the fireplace and fetched Clarice. Together, they quickly prepared tea and snacks and patiently waited for Sorin to retell his adventure.

"That Orpheus is a bad apple," said Percival when Sorin finished. "Though he's transferred over to the Governor's Manor, you'll want to be cautious of him going forward."

"He seems like the vengeful type," Sorin agreed. "He's also a schemer. My intuition is that he purposefully caused conflict to join the Governor's Manor."

"Orpheus's Valmer family used to be quite the reputable family," said Percival after some thought. "They were once supporters of the former governor but were purged when Governor Marsh took over. This must be their attempt at reclaiming some political power. Though I wish them luck, given the state of their finances."

"That's good to know," said Sorin. He placed three cards worth a hundred gold each on the coffee table. "I noticed you've been skimping on coal. As the master of the house, I regret leaving our finances in such a state."

"It's no problem at all," said Clarice, though Sorin noted that she didn't hesitate to pick up the cards. "We'll keep the place lit by candlelight until you've finished training Lorimer, but with this amount of coin, we'll be able to appropriately host others. For example, the friends you mentioned. Have you thought of a date yet?"

"Will three days from now work?" asked Sorin.

"We'll make it happen, dear," said Clarice. "Percival, weren't you talking to the grocer this morning? Why don't you take him up on his offer to deliver food periodically?"

"I think I'll do just that," said Percival. "Mister Kepler, pardon my rudeness, but you look utterly exhausted. Might I interest you in a hot bath before a well-earned early rest?"

"That sounds wonderful, Percival," said Sorin. He'd accumulated far too much tension over the past couple of weeks. "Please leave some bath salts on the side and a bucket of boiling water."

"As you wish, Mister Kepler," said Percival.

A half-hour later, Sorin slipped into the tub and allowed himself to relax. Though he was still worried about potential assassins, Lorimer was currently hunting stray cats and crows outside and would warn him if any intruders came wandering by.

"Adventures," muttered Sorin as he dosed off. "They're dangerous but rewarding. Stressful but exciting." The last of his reservations towards his new profession faded with the revelation that despite the dangers involved, he'd had fun. Most importantly, he'd gained something he'd never had: Friends. The kind he could trust his back to.

"I'll have to inspect their meridians once I get a chance to read up on the subject," muttered Sorin. "I refuse to believe their extraordinary meridians can't be opened." This was his next target, along with finding two more appropriate poisons to reach the peak of Blood-Thickening. He would need to reach the Bone-Forging Realm before he could even think of looking into his parents' death.

52

ANALYSIS

Sorin ate a hearty breakfast the following day. There was toast, ham, and a poached egg covered in a creamy sauce, with more than enough for even Lorimer to partake.

When Sorin asked about this new dish, Percival confessed that he'd been learning from a chef in town in his spare time. "He was short on staff, and I had not much to do in your absence," said Percival. "I learned a lot, and I'm looking forward to showcasing the other dishes I added to our weekly rotation."

Having had his fill, Sorin secluded himself in his office. Due to the infusion of gold into the household, there was now ample paper and manafuse pens. Lorimer was especially fond of these pens, but after a few rounds of scolding, he stopped eating their tips and focused instead on patrolling the streets for food sources.

It was early in the afternoon when Sorin felt well-rested enough to analyze his physical condition. He combed through his meridians, blood vessels, and muscles, taking extra care to look out for signs of corruption. As usual, he found none; the Ten Thousand Poison Canon was highly potent in cleansing corruption and had yet to show any side effects.

Sorin now had twelve unblocked primary meridians and five

unblocked extraordinary meridians. Theoretically, only two extraordinary meridians could still be opened. Namely, the Belt Vessel and the Conception Vessel.

I'm still not convinced that it's impossible to unlock the Governing Vessel, thought Sorin as he tapped his pen on the piece of paper he'd used to map out his meridians and acupoints. The source of his confidence lay in the condition of his acupoints.

I have no idea how it happened, but six of the silver seals on my Conception Vessel have vanished, thought Sorin. *The meridian is still clogged and won't function until the remaining seals are undone. But how did it happen? What prompted this?* He hadn't consumed any cultivation supplements or additional poisons since his last inspection. Sirius's research notes didn't mention such occurrences either.

Another critical factor was that only a physician could discover the strange silver seals. He very much doubted that Stephan was aware of them. At most, he knew of the seals loosening on an instinctual level.

Then there's Stephan's twenty unblocked silver seals. There's also his strange mutation during combat. Why did his bear form suddenly change? Why did he suddenly grow more powerful? Typically, such things would only happen due to a mid-combat breakthrough, but even then, such a drastic change was impossible.

His suspicion was that Stephan's transformation was connected to his Conception Vessel. Unfortunately, he would need to wait for a more private setting to verify his hypothesis. He also needed to finish verifying his condition before doing anything else.

Conveniently, Percival arrived and knocked on his door. "I made the trip to the Alchemists Association as you instructed."

"And?" asked Sorin. "Did they cause you any problems?"

"No, they did not," said Percival. "I was able to successfully obtain the things you requested. Shall I take them down to the laboratory?"

"Please do, Percival," said Sorin. "I'll be right down." He scribbled a few more ideas down before going to the basement.

Sorin had yet to go to the basement since the Kepler Clan's ransacking. Percival had long since cleaned up the mess and rearranged the furniture in case Sorin wanted to use the room. His original glassware was long gone, but thanks to Percival's recent trip, he now had a set of beakers, test tubes, and separatory funnels. Not enough to be called a legitimate alchemical laboratory, but enough for him to mix and heat ingredients without contaminating them.

"I don't have the funds to repair the ventilation formation yet, so you and Clarice must avoid the area," Sorin instructed.

"Perhaps you should also wait until these arrangements are made?" suggested Percival.

Sorin shook his head. "I'm mostly immune to these poisons and won't be working with large quantities. Don't worry about it. I'll be fine."

Sorin proceeded to unpack the ingredients Percival had purchased. The main ingredients were veridian chalkstone, amethyst thistle, death-ward sap, and three lesser-known neutralizers and anti-venoms. He mixed these into an all-purpose anti-poison solution and diluted it with liquified mana extract.

Let's see how potent my mana has gotten now that I've increased my strength to the eighth stage of Blood-Thickening, thought Sorin. He measured a set quantity of neutralizers and channeled a small quantity of mana into a mana crystal. The crystal would only accept a certain quantity of mana, regardless of density.

He then repeated the same experiment with ten milliliters of his blood. By back-calculating the volume and the remaining potency of the neutralizer, he was able to roughly gauge the effectiveness of his poison.

The results ended up surprising Sorin. Not only were his poisons resistant to neutralization, taking a long time to react with the reagents, but they also slightly exceeded the scope of one-star strength.

But it isn't enough for me to pierce through the membrane blocking my Belt Vessel, Sorin thought. *I lack the mana volume to clear it out and will have to wait until my next breakthrough.*

This highlighted Sorin's other problem: opening his companions' extraordinary meridians. Opening his own meridians required his mana to have a specific volume and available potency, which he suspected would happen automatically after his next breakthrough. Unblocking the meridians of others, on the other hand, relied more on the potency of his mana and his application of it. Either that or the strength of tinctures, which could also lead to severe injuries or even death of those receiving the treatment.

Sorin's treatment was more reliable and safer than the traditional tincture method. But in his initial experiment with Lawrence, he quickly realized that Lawrence's mana was fighting against the treatment. Moreover, Lawrence's meridians weren't very resistant to foreign mana. This was especially the case for poison mana, which could easily damage meridians if not adequately controlled.

Sirius's research notes also address this topic, thought Sorin. *The fatality rate for unlocking extraordinary meridians is much higher than for unlocking primary meridians. There are strengthening potions and advanced poison mana application methods to fix this, but I've never read anything about these in my medical textbooks. Either these methods have been lost, or they are also secret arts labeled as restricted by the family head.*

To proceed with his plan for unlocking his companions' extraordinary meridians, he would need to either find a way to reinforce their meridians or apply his mana differently. He had *some* ideas on how to accomplish this, but it would require a lot of experimentation. He wrote down several ideas and potential solutions; none of them addressed the root of the problem.

Knowing that research was a marathon and not a race, he went upstairs for a cup of tea. Percival happily poured him a cup. Sorin added sugar and was about to take a sip when suddenly, the doorbell rang.

"Shall I tell whoever it is to return later?" asked Percival.

Unfortunately, Sorin's spiritual senses were strong enough that he could tell that the person at the door was someone he couldn't reject. "Please take our guests to the sitting room so that I can properly receive them," said Sorin. He was still tired from adventuring, but a weakling like him was in no position to reject a Bone-Forging cultivator visiting in person.

"Oh—hello there, Mister Kepler," said Percival in a voice that quickly traveled to the coffee room. "To what do we owe the pleasure?"

"I'm just here to see my dear cousin, Sorin," came a familiar voice from the entrance. It was none other than Marcus Sovinger Kepler. "There's no need to pretend he's not there. I can sense him from where I stand."

"Mister Sorin has already instructed that you be brought into the sitting room," said Percival. "Would you like a cup of tea? Or coffee, perhaps?"

"I'll take black Inglewood tea if you would be so kind," said Marcus. "Sugar, but no milk. I can't stand the stuff."

It wasn't long before he saw Percival preparing tea. They exchanged a few silent gestures to confirm that Marcus was welcome. Sorin sighed as he finished his cup of tea. Marcus could wait five minutes.

After stretching the bounds of propriety as far as he dared, Sorin entered the sitting room. Marcus was seated on a plush leather couch, a porcelain teacup in hand. He quietly took a seat and waited for Marcus to speak first.

"I sense a lot of hostility in your posture," the man finally said with a smile. "Perhaps there's been some sort of misunderstanding between us."

Sorin crossed his arms and sat back in his chair. "I don't personally see any misunderstandings, as your actions have all been blatantly obvious. You came here at the direction of the Kepler Clan and used your authority to suppress me. You then proceeded to make my life extremely difficult and even bullied the people I employed.

Marcus frowned. "I admit to slightly suppressing you, Sorin, but that was all in due course. The family's position is that you *cannot* be a physician, Sorin. And neither can you be an alchemist. Either profession —or preferably both—is enough to vie for the position of family head in the future."

"I'm not an idiot," said Sorin. "As a cripple, I was no threat. As a cultivator, I'm a moderate threat but not a significant threat since I cultivate poison. The Medical Association will disqualify me from taking any examinations upfront. They and the clan can also veto my application to the Alchemists Guild.

"I'm glad there's no need to spell it out for you," said Marcus, taking a sip of his tea. "But apart from these major things, I can't see myself having done anything else to interfere with you."

"Really now," said Sorin. "Am I just supposed to forget that assassination attempt and the meddling of the Governor's Manor and the Alchemists Association in the case?"

"This…" Marcus winced. "I suppose that requires some explaining."

"Indeed, it does," said Sorin. "Because the way I see it, you're a thorn in my side that needs to be plucked as soon as possible."

Marcus chuckled. "That could be construed as a threat, Sorin. If I were another Bone-Forging cultivator, no one would blame me for crippling you a second time."

"But you're *not* another Bone-Forging cultivator," said Sorin. "You must abide by the arrangements of the family. And given our disagreements, I see no reason to be polite."

"Given our *misunderstandings,* you mean," said Marcus. "Because this is indeed a misunderstanding. In case you've forgotten, I'm from the *Sovinger* branch of the family."

53

FAMILY POLITICS

It took a short while for Sorin to process Marcus's words. *Marcus is indeed from the Sovinger branch. He's not from the Mockingjay branch under my uncle's control, and neither is he part of the Lucian branch that supports the Mockingjay branch.* Marcus's words implied that there was some disagreement on how to handle his situation.

"Your branch is historically a neutral branch," Sorin said after a time. "Among the neutral branches, there's the Sovinger branch, in charge of logistics; the Defensor branch, in charge of protection and security; and the Rosair branch, in charge of records."

"Indeed," said Marcus. "Hiring assassins is something the information branch, the *Lucian* branch, would do. As for the Mockingjay branch, they would directly dispatch a punishment squad and have you eliminated. Of course, they'd need to think up a good excuse to do so, as the Council of Elders reviews all high-level punishment matters.

"As for your Abberjay branch... well, it was never a big branch, to begin with, since your ancestors never tried to actively grow it in favor of maintaining the purity of the Kepler bloodline. Aside from the Grand Elder, there are maybe a hundred members left, and none of them are in important positions."

"Your point is made with respect to the assassination attempt," Sorin admitted. "But you've still grossly interfered with my matters. There's also the issue of you indirectly restricting my access to laboratory space in the Alchemists Guild, as well as the mass-buying of all one-star poisons in the outpost."

To Sorin's surprise, Marcus was taken aback by the accusation. "This is actually more a coincidence than anything else," said Marcus. "Believe it or not, we desperately needed these ingredients. This relates to some family activities that I cannot divulge."

"Really," said Sorin, not believing a single word Marcus was saying.

"In fact, we just received our order from Dustone after two long weeks of waiting," continued Marcus. "We've found replacements for the one-star earth flames that have gone missing of late and have restocked the Alchemists Guild as per our agreement with them. We'll now be obtaining all our supplies directly from Dustone."

"I'll believe it when I see it," said Sorin.

"It's an easily verified matter," said Marcus. "As for the issue with employees you mentioned earlier, I believe you're talking about the situation with Gabriella.

"I'm sure you are aware of the tradition of testing the resolve of all apprentices. Due to certain family politics, it was necessary to apply the test a second time. But I would *never* reject such a talented future physician. You'll be happy to know that Gabriella is now actively studying and will be qualified to take the physician's examination in two months if all goes as planned."

This only further confused Sorin. *Was I mistaken in my assessment of Marcus?* he thought, looking the man over. *He's always come across as a snake to me. But then again, most people in the Kepler Clan are that way.* He was pleased by this development but opted to remain cautious.

"If things are as you say, then I apologize for taking offense at your actions," said Sorin. "I understand the family's position and its need for stability. I don't blame you for restricting my access to the physician and alchemist occupations.

"With that out of the way, I'll have to ask your reason for coming here. I doubt you'd come personally for something easily addressed in a letter."

"Honestly, it's a little embarrassing," said Marcus, scratching his head. "A two-star physician like me should have no problem dealing with cases that come up in a small town like this. But just the other day, I encountered an issue where I almost lost a patient, and it's been greatly vexing."

Sorin raised an eyebrow. "You're a two-star physician, Marcus. Are you sure you want to consult with me, a former one-star physician?"

"Your talent as a physician is legendary, regardless of family politics," said Marcus. "Moreover, your expertise on poison might give you another perspective. I'm also worried about potential reoccurrences in the Bloodwood Outpost. As you well know, environmental factors can often complicate simple cases."

Sorin pursed his lips and thought for a few seconds before answering. "The case?"

"A middle-aged female came to the Growing Branches four days ago," Marcus explained. "A one-star physician diagnosed her condition as a minor lung infection. He fed her a standard Sun and Star Purification Potion that should have cleared out her infection within four hours. We kept her for observation, as per protocol. Two hours after the treatment, she began suffering from sudden onset heart arrhythmia."

Sorin's frown deepened as he thought of a possible diagnosis. *If it's not the lungs, then it's something connected to them. Heart? No, the symptoms don't match. Then it can only be...* "It was chronic invasive blood corruption, wasn't it?"

"Indeed, it was," confirmed Marcus. "Of the second type. By the time I discovered the oversight, her condition was critical. As you know, second-type blood corruption varies greatly across cases and has no standard treatment. I, therefore, attempted a blood burn treatment while stimulating her lung, liver, and heart meridians."

"Experimental, but not ungrounded," said Sorin, fondling his chin. "Were there any adverse effects to the blood burn treatment?"

"Indeed, there were," said Marcus. "She went into anaphylactic shock. A standard throat-opening acupuncture failed to liberate her airway, forcing us to perform a physical tracheotomy. Further, her lungs began to fill with fluid. I had to use my two-star life mana to maintain her vitality until her body processed whatever was going on with her."

Sorin visualized the treatment and symptoms and sketched out multiple different explanations. In the end, he settled on the most likely explanation. "It's the Sun and Star Purification Potion that's responsible. It interacted with the blood burn treatment, causing anaphylaxis and pulmonary edema."

Marcus's brows furrowed. "I thought so at first, but the interaction between these two shouldn't result in such symptoms. I checked the history. There are only sparse records of negative interactions between both medications."

"That is indeed the case," said Sorin. "She would have been fine with either the Sun and Star Purification Potion or the Blood Burn Potion. And if not for her original symptoms, taking both would not have any adverse effects."

Marcus's eyes narrowed. "Wait. Are you saying that the invasive blood corruption contributed as well?"

Sorin nodded. "It was a three-way poison interaction. The Sun and Star Purification Potion and Blood Burn Potion are both low-grade poisons. When they mix, they form a third poison, a weak one. This poison is normally not strong enough to affect even a weakened patient, but…"

"But corruption can amplify poisons," muttered Marcus. "Ingenious. No wonder the second treatment failed."

"It's not a common situation," Sorin reassured him. "Usually, invasive blood corruption wouldn't be missed. I imagine that some other symptoms pointed in multiple directions. The physician in question made a judgment call and chose the most likely disease. But in the end, his choice was proven wrong."

"That's indeed the case," said Marcus with a sigh. "I can't blame the man, as I would have probably made the same choices at his level. It was only after the fact that we discovered the underlying cause."

"Such is the case with so many of our diagnoses," said Sorin. "We're always making best guesses, and it isn't until the situation turns for the worse that we realize the mistakes we've committed."

"Very good," said Marcus. "I'm both relieved at the explanation and more confident in applying the blood burn treatment for this condition. I'll also have my staff look out for cases of invasive blood corruption. Environmental factors in the Bloodwood Outpost may produce cases with similar symptoms." He then tapped his fingers on the table and gave Sorin an appraising look. "I'll see if I can get some of your things returned. Glassware. Reference books. The medical mannequin. These objects are not problematic, so I see no reason to keep them from you. But the Divine Medical Codex can't be returned. The elders were strict on this."

Sorin smiled lightly. "What is it that you want in return for this favor?"

"This is simply how things would have developed in a few months," said Marcus. "The idea was to beat you down, then to give you a consolation prize to shut you up. But given your growth, I've chosen to accelerate the process."

"And what exactly would that consolation prize be?" asked Sorin. "My own things don't exactly qualify."

"The family has decided to allow you *one* designation," said Marcus. "Apothecary."

Sorin frowned. "That's a half-baked alchemist at best. They're allowed to concoct poisons only and attract a great deal of prejudice from all levels of society."

"Apothecaries are valuable individuals," corrected Marcus, "regardless of what people think. Moreover, they operate under the jurisdiction of both the Alchemists Guild and the Medical Association to prevent adverse outcomes.

"This is a legitimate career and can be pursued in conjunction with your adventuring. Moreover, it will further alienate you from the physician and alchemist occupations. All the family asks in return is that you agree to consult on difficult cases that are within your capabilities. They will otherwise not interfere with your activities and will even issue you commissions on occasion. For example, I'm in great need of help concocting certain poisons useful in my clinic."

Sorin nodded slowly. This *did* solve a few of his pressing matters, namely access to a lab and certain restricted one-star poisons. "Fine," he said. "I agree."

"Excellent," said Marcus. "Your things are in storage, and I'll have them sent back in no more than three days. As for the paperwork with the Alchemists' Association, there should be no issues. We'll use your prior status as a one-star physician to bypass the need for an extensive examination."

Marcus then made up an excuse about a cauldron of pills needing his attention and left the Kepler Manor. Sorin was still deep in thought an hour later.

"Dinner will be ready soon, Mister Kepler," said Percival. "Perhaps you would like to wash up before then?"

"What's your read on Marcus?" Sorin asked Percival. Given his prior occupation and his extended service to the Kepler Clan, he would have unique insight into the situation.

"He's a snake," said Percival without hesitation. "A manipulator."

"I thought so," said Sorin, looking out the window. "You and Clarice can go ahead and eat, Percival. I'll be in my office for the next few hours, making plans. I don't expect I'll be done until well into the evening."

"I'll bring up a plate once dinner is done," said Percival.

"Make it four," said Sorin. "Otherwise, Lorimer will cause a mess again."

54

APPRAISAL

At noon the next day, Sorin traveled to the Adventurers Guild for a meeting with his team. A guild employee hailed him as he entered and escorted him to a conference room at the back, where a healthy spread of food had just been set out.

Naturally, Stephan and Gareth were already there, and Lawrence followed ten minutes later. An older man in mage's robes and a pointed hat arrived five minutes after that, alongside Daphne. He wore a monocle in one eye, and from it, Sorin could sense intense fluctuations of magic.

Stephan waited for Daphne to grab a sandwich and fried potatoes before kicking things off. "Everyone, this is Marik Wentworth, one of the best appraisers in the Mages Guild. I handed the goods off to him shortly after we arrived, and he has been working diligently on the case ever since."

"Indeed I have," said Marik in an aged but succinct voice. He retrieved a bag from his belt pouch, and from that small bag, he took out a few medium-sized bags, each one labeled and with its own attached piece of paper. "It took me all night to go over these things, as some of them are quite rare, but I was able to accomplish the deed in the allotted time."

The appraiser took out a few sheets of paper and began reading their contents. "Mundane goods are as follows:

"Mixed one-star cores from Manabane Swamp and surrounding area. Estimated Value: 5,325 gold. Corresponding Bounty: 4,686 gold, to be paid out by the Adventurers Guild.

"Mixed one- and two-star cores from Dedalus's Labyrinth. Estimated Value: 9,267 gold. Due to the location of their acquisition, no bounty shall be paid.

"Miscellaneous one-star medicinal ingredients, 4,130 gold according to Adventurers Guild list price.

"Jasmine Bone Fruit, 23 count, 500 gold apiece. As a representative of the Mages Guild, I can offer you—"

"We won't be selling these fruits and will be storing them at the Adventurers Guild," Stephan cut in. "But if we have any extra Bone-Forging Pills after everything is said and done, we will consider the Mages Guild."

The appraiser seemed to have expected this response and nodded. "Then I'll exclude these items from the list.

"Antique coins, valued at approximately 1,500 gold.

"Rubies, Magic-Grade, one-star, 1,400 gold. However, I see here that you've already exchanged 2500 gold worth of rubies from the Adventurers Guild.

"Sapphires, Magic-Grade, one-star, 2,200 gold.

"Topazes, Magic-Grade, one-star, 1,600 gold.

"These mundane items are liquid, and the Adventurers Guild will surely provide you with compensation as per my appraisal. Just include a copy of my report when you submit these items."

"Thank you very much for your hard work," said Stephan.

"It's what you're paying me to do," said the appraiser. "Moreover, I still haven't completed appraisals on the equipment you took with you. If you'd all be so kind as to produce the magical items that you obtained on your journey?"

Stephan took out a small pile of items, including the boots, gauntlets, and helm he'd acquired. The others did the same with the things they'd looted—no, that they'd *recovered.* This included Sorin's dagger, ring, and magical string.

The appraiser spent a few minutes with each pile of items and took notes as he worked. Unlike Daphne, who required vast amounts of mana and time to perform appraisals, the man was systematic and stayed energized. He only consumed one mana potion during the process.

Finally, Marik sat down, took off his monocle, and began reading off the list he'd compiled.

"Boots of Strength, claimed by Stephan—1,500 gold. These boots will increase the physical strength of the wearer by 30 percent, but to a maximum of 200 pounds of total composite strength. Can be bonded with an armor set for improved synchronicity of enchantments.

"Gauntlets of Shearing, claimed by Stephan—1,600 gold. The claws are adamantine-tipped and enchanted with a Lesser Shearing spell. They will cut through one-star bone and metal with no issues. Grip strength will improve up to 50 percent but will only be effective on one-star strength. Can be bonded with an armor set for improved synchronicity of enchantments.

"Helm of Intimidation, claimed by Stephan—1,800 gold. Aside from the obvious benefit of additional protection, the helm will automatically project an aura that will weaken one-star enemies by up to 6 percent in all attributes. This stacks with curses and poisons and other similar effects, but not with mood-altering spells and spell-like abilities. Can be bonded with an armor set for improved synchronicity of enchantments."

He then moved on to Gareth's pile of two items.

"Bracers of Amplification, claimed by Gareth—2,200 gold. These bracers will enhance skills performed with arms and hands by 30 percent, adequate only for one-star skills. They will not amplify regular attacks.

"Endless Quiver, one-star, claimed by Gareth—1,800 gold. The quiver will endlessly produce arrows at the lesser one-star grade with enchantments in random elements. Please note that the term endless is purely theoretical. The quiver holds up to 500 arrows, and once used, these arrows will recharge at a rate of one arrow per minute.

Daphne's loot was relatively easy to appraise, as it only consisted of one item.

"Pyromancer's Staff, claimed by Daphne—3,400 gold. Much more effective than a wand, this ruby-tipped staff will increase the area of effect of fire spells by 50 percent and reduce their cost by 30 percent—an excellent weapon for a talented mage.

Next up were Sorin's items.

"Dagger of Lesser Curse, claimed by Sorin—2,000 gold. The weakening curse will stack up to fifteen times, and each instance will add a 1 percent weakening effect to the opponent's attributes that will wear off after sixty seconds.

"Ring of Poison Manipulation, claimed by Sorin—1,200 gold. I'll note that if the element were fire, frost, or lightning, the price would be closer to 2,500 gold. In addition to increasing the efficiency of poison mana manipulation, the ring can be used as a focus for poison-element spells. But unlike a wand or staff, it will not reduce their costs. The amplification effect is also less than that of a wand or staff. Still, in exchange for these detriments, the hand may be used to form spell seals or carry additional items.

"As for this piece of string... well, it's useless now. Non-magical outside the dungeon you were in. It retains traces of ancient divination magic, however, so I can offer you 500 gold for the object on behalf of the Mages Guild.

"Done," said Stephan. "Unless you want to keep it?" he asked Sorin.

"I have no use for it," replied Sorin. "Sell away."

"Then next, we'll look at Lawrence's items." The way the appraiser said his name was odd. "You never thought we'd meet again, did you, you little runt? Did you enjoy what you saw six and a half weeks ago at 24 Durling Street?"

"This..." said Lawrence with a laugh. "It was just a tiny peek. Nothing was seen! Surely you wouldn't let such things interfere with your work?"

The man snorted. "Fortunately, I am a professional. Very much unlike you and that scoundrel you call father.

"Sword of Keen Edge, claimed by Lawrence—1,900 gold. The keen edge enchantment will cut through mana shields with excellent efficiency. It will function like a standard enchanted weapon against physical items.

"Cloak of Obscurity, claimed by Lawrence—1,800 gold. Projects a small area of shadows around the wearer, increasing the ease of activating shadow techniques.

"Boots of Silent Passage, claimed by Lawrence—1,200 gold. Deafens footsteps. Reduces noise caused by movement in general.

Having finished the personal piles, the mage moved on to the last pile. "That only leaves these items obtained from the boss monster:

"Minotaur Leather, two-star, degraded. Salvageable quantity: unknown. Estimated value—1,500 gold. This is based purely on the results of my divination.

"Minotaur Horns, two-star, intact—1,000 gold each. They can likely be worked into weapons or armor as supplementary material.

"Core of Violence, two-star—2,000 gold. It can be used to make an offering at the Temple of Hope with a specific wish in mind. It is less variable than standard offerings, though it should be noted that the potency of the offering is only equal to 1,500 gold worth of demon cores.

The appraiser then placed the sheet he'd been reading on the table and stamped it with his seal. The seal was a magical green color and gave off a unique mana signature. "If that's everything, I'll be on my way. The total appraisal amount is listed on the top page for your reference, as is the invoice for my services."

"Are you willing to take magic-grade gems as payment?" asked Stephan.

"Of course," said the appraiser. "In fact, that's my preferred payment method. May I choose them myself?"

"You can pick your choice of sapphires and topazes, as Daphne may want rubies for her spells," replied Stephan.

The mage nodded and picked a few dozen gems from two of the

three gem bags and placed these into what Sorin now identified as a bag of holding. "Many thanks for the business. Do keep in touch."

"It was our pleasure," said Stephan. He waited until the mage was out of the room before sitting down and slumping in his seat. "These appraisers are basically robbers. It cost us 2,500 gold coins to identify everything."

"They've got the market cornered, unfortunately," said Daphne. "Pyromancers are great at torching things, but when it comes to appraising items, we can't even determine specific functions."

"It's an unavoidable expense," agreed Gareth. "And speaking of expenses…"

"Right," said Stephan. "The expenses. I've got a list here:

"Boat destruction—2,000 gold.

"Boat rental—500 gold."

"Are you serious?" said Lawrence. "They're dinging us for rental *and* damages?"

"Unfortunately, that's what we agreed to in the contract," said Stephan. "Moving on,

"Ruin map—500 gold.

"We used up all our mana and health potions, and we should really be keeping two of each per team member. I'm allocating 2,000 gold to this expense total.

"There's also what we owe for the Boots of Strength and Dagger of Lesser Curse. Unless you want to return it to the Adventurers Guild instead?"

"I'll keep it," said Sorin. "I like the weight."

"I've also taken a liking to these boots," said Stephan. "Next up are communal expenses, including reparations to families and other miscellaneous items. It all adds up to 2,800 gold apiece. Don't argue; we'll never see that money if we want to retain our memberships. On the bright side, we're receiving 2,100 gold for artifacts sold from the ruin's main floor.

"In all, our group has netted 50,408 gold in items, cores, and gems, excluding the Jasmine Bone Fruit. Unless, of course, any of you want your cut now instead of later when we bargain with the Alchemists Guild to make us Bone-Forging Pills."

None of their group members took up his offer, so Stephan tallied up individual loot counts. Aside from the three items he'd claimed, he expressed his desire for the Minotaur horns, and no one fought him on it.

Gareth was also interested in the Minotaur leather, so Sorin and Lawrence agreed to visit a leatherworker to see if they could each get a suit of enchanted leather armor made. In this case, Sorin and Lawrence would get priority.

"That just leaves cores, gems, gold, and the core of violence," said Stephan. "Lawrence and I are tapped out, so we can't take priority. Daphne, you're least in debt, so you get the first pick."

"I'll take gems or cash; either is fine," said Daphne. "I mostly want to buy spell books. Everything else is irrelevant."

"I'm looking to purchase some skills," said Gareth. "I'll pass on the Temple of Hope, even if it's statistically the better option."

"Hm…" Sorin looked at the crimson core on the table that positively reeked of violence. "The appraiser was saying this could be used to make specific wishes?"

"Making specific wishes might be embellishing the matter," said Stephan. "At most, you can make a request, and Hope will decide how to meet this request. The request also can't be too specific."

"That sounds about right," said Sorin. A part of him was tempted to sell the thing for gold, which he desperately needed. Still, another part of him couldn't help but think about the golden seals blocking off his last extraordinary meridian. "I'll take the Core of Violence, then. Unless someone else wants it?"

"Are you sure?" asked Stephan. "We could always sell it."

"Positive," said Sorin. "There's something I want, and this is likely my best chance."

"Then that makes things simple," said Stephan. "Since no one wants demon cores, we'll just sell them for cash. We'll do the same for the collector's gold, the gems, the medicinal ingredients, etc. After everyone gets what they claimed, Daphne will get 6,150 gold, Gareth will get 5,550 gold, Sorin will get 3,350 gold, Lawrence will get 4,150 gold, and I will get 3,650 gold. We'll make the exchange here at the Adventurers Guild and put the Jasmine Bone Fruits into guild storage."

The gold involved was mind-numbing to Sorin. *I've dealt with such amounts before, but only when dealing with an entire clinic. Is this why people become adventurers?* But as soon as he thought of the rewards, he also thought of the costs. Many adventurers had died in the ruin, and there were also adventurers like Collin and Lise who'd suffered crippling injuries and would not be able to continue as adventurers.

With the appraiser's documentation, it was a simple matter to complete the exchange. Sorin received six cards worth 500 gold and three cards worth 100 gold, as well as two healing potions, two mana potions, and 50 gold in change.

He was about to leave when Lorimer suddenly squirmed in his pocket. He remembered the matter of rations and promptly exchanged for 200 gold in miscellaneous one-star cores.

"It's still pretty early in the afternoon," said Gareth when they walked out of the guild. "Do any of you have plans? If not, why don't we go over to the leatherworker? I hear he's busy these days, but he *might* be able to make time for us, given the materials we're offering."

"I've got nothing planned for today," said Sorin. "How about you, Lawrence? Wait, are you shivering?"

"I think I've been cursed!" Lawrence whispered. "It must be the appraiser! I can't think of anyone else who'd do such a thing!"

Sorin rolled his eyes. "Serves your right, given your hobbies. Seriously, you should consider finding a new one."

Lawrence sighed. "Everyone misunderstands us explorers. If not for people like me, we'd always be stuck in the mundane and the routine, forever adhering to the boundaries set by society."

"Less talking and more walking," said Gareth. "I have an image to maintain."

"Same," said Sorin. He put his hands in his pockets and followed Gareth as he led the way to the east end of town.

55

THE LEATHERWORKER

The leatherworker was located three streets from the outpost wall, in an eight-by-eight-block section of the city reserved for metalwork, leather-work, slaughterhouses, and other similar businesses.

There was a total of twelve leatherworkers in the city. Gareth swore by Sanderson's Leather Outfitting and refused to see any others. "He only does custom work with one-star leathers or greater," explained Gareth as they approached the shop. "Moreover, he's a Bone-Forging cultivator and two-star leatherworker, so every piece he makes can be enchanted."

A small bell rang when they entered the shop. To the right, Sorin spotted racks of sample materials along with images of popular designs. Dozens of sample works were mounted on mannequins on the left side, showcasing leather armor, leather bags, shoes, and gloves, along with long leather coats made from cold-resistant leather and lined with the finest sheep's wool.

They casually looked around for a few minutes before a bald man with huge biceps and a pair of circular glasses walked out. "What can I help you with today, gentlemen?" asked the man. "Ah, it's you, Gareth. You should know that I'm so busy that it's tough to make time even for a strapping young man like yourself."

"We can come back at a more convenient time if that works better for you, Mr. Sanderson," said Gareth.

"I'm not in a hurry with this specific piece, though I do have to finish the cut within the hour," said Mr. Sanderson, cutting him off. "So spare me the pleasantries and get right down to business. "I'll have to warn you if it's not interesting, I have a waiting list six weeks long, and…" His voice trailed off as his eyes caught the rolled-up piece of leather Lawrence was holding.

"My word. What a beautiful specimen. Quick, set it on the work-bench!" Lawrence could only do as he said, and he was quickly pushed aside by the man, who now had a passionate glint in his eyes. "Yes, this is definitely a premium material compared to what I usually see here. The smell of it. The feel of it. I don't suppose you'd be willing to sell it to me? I'll definitely give you a satisfactory price."

He then adjusted his glasses and looked over their group of three in more detail. "You must be Lawrence Holt. Yes, there's no mistaking the beautifully sharp features on your face. You're much more handsome than your father."

"Um, thanks?" said Lawrence uncertainly.

"And you," said Mr. Sanderson, focusing on Sorin. A prickling sensation ran up Sorin's spine as he felt the man's powerful mana and spiritual senses gently probe him. "You have the scent of poison on you, though you look nothing like those despicable fellows I sometimes deal with."

"Sorin was once a one-star physician," said Gareth, introducing Sorin. "But later, he recovered his cultivation and began cultivating poison."

"Sorin… Kepler, is it?" said Mr. Sanderson. "I heard about you. There are conflicting opinions about your choice of occupation. Still, knowing those old fogies from the Medical Association, you likely had no choice in the matter."

"Let's not talk about such things," said Sorin. "We're here to get three suits of leather armor made, one for each of us. Will that be an issue?"

"Hm…" The leatherworker looked from them to the leather, then took out careful measuring tools. He traced out patterns with chalk directly on the hide that avoided the most dreadful burns and cuts on the material. "It'll suffice. Barely."

"I hope they'll be enchantable with custom properties?" asked Gareth.

"Naturally," said Mr. Sanderson. "Anything else would be a waste. These are two-star materials, degraded as they are. They'll be able to accommodate the most powerful enchantments at one-star grade. Now strip. All three of you." The three men exchanged uncomfortable looks and then began unbuttoning their shirts. "Not here, you savages! In the changeroom out back!"

He chased them over to a curtained-off area, where all three took off everything short of underwear. Mr. Sanderson entered just as they were finished and produced a tape that he used to measure their arms, legs, waists, and chests. "Yes, the materials should do quite nicely. However, I might have to substitute certain parts for four-horned demon ox leather. This material is a little *too* flexible and will need a bit of reinforcement. Have you decided on your enchantments? Or a certain design?"

The three of them exchanged looks. "We can pick our enchantments?" asked Lawrence with mild surprise.

"Of course, you can pick your enchantments!" said Mr. Sanderson. "These are premium materials. You won't find better leather at the one-star grade." He walked over to a shelf and slapped three books down in front of them. "There. That should cover enchantments, styles, and customizations. You three should look over these while I finish my cut. With clothes on, of course." He excused himself and retreated to the back of the workshop, where a pristine white hide lay stretched out over a cutting table. Sorin shivered as he saw the man run his hand on the hide's smooth surface as though it were a horse in need of soothing.

Lawrence grabbed the book on customizations, while Gareth grabbed the one dealing with style. Sorin was new to the topic of armor, so he leafed through the book on enchantments. *Interesting,* thought

Sorin as he reviewed what was available. *These aren't piecemeal enchantments but sets that confer compatible properties.*

These properties tended to follow the description of demons—for example, the Three-Ringed Python enchantment, which emphasized strength and flexibility. There was the Night Wraith enchantment that provided passive cover and even temporary phasing abilities—but only for three seconds and only against weapons and arrows, not physical obstructions.

"I'll probably be going for the Wind Blessed enchantment myself," said Gareth as he flipped through the style book. "The basic enchantment improves wind-based movement skills by 30 percent and base movement speed by 15 percent. The only problem is that you gain a weakness to fire-type mana."

"A small price to pay, in my opinion," said Lawrence. "Huh. That's an exciting way to hold throwing knives. And the pockets on this thing!"

"You'd think it's not a problem, but that's because you're not usually a target of enemy fire spells," said Gareth.

"Maybe," said Lawrence. "I'll go with the one-star Night King enchantment." They'd clearly both researched this topic before coming here.

"Doesn't that improve your night vision and attack speed?" asked Gareth. "Why not prioritize evasion and movement speed?"

Lawrence snorted. "Who needs movement speed when it's much more useful to attack and kill something in a single exchange? Besides, it's not *just* night vision. It's *predatory* night vision, with predatory being the main aspect. It'll let me better identify enemy weaknesses and their remaining health and mana stores."

Sorin had never heard of these abilities before, so he flipped through the book with interest. Should he get something that could poison his enemies or retaliate, or something like Gareth's, to increase his mobility?

He took his time reviewing the enchantment book and completely ignored the style and add-ons book. Such things were more important to

Lawrence, who needed to use tools in battle, and Gareth, who often had to track down or repel enemies.

Unfortunately, he couldn't decide before Mr. Sanderson finally returned from the back. He smelled strongly of treating chemicals but seemed to have developed a resistance to such things.

"Have you all decided yet?" asked Mr. Sanderson.

"Night King Armor, Midnight Assassin Style, trapping and poison vial accessories," replied Lawrence. "I'd also like to be able to store a few throwing knives up my sleeves.

"Wind Blessed Armor, Deep Woods Warder Style," said Gareth. "No additional accessories required. Minimalistic."

"Those are both good choices for a rogue and an archer," said Mr. Sanderson. "But are you sure you don't want something more flexible? Maybe something that will accommodate close combat armaments?"

"I'm not very good at swordsmanship, and I'd rather focus on my strong points," said Gareth, shaking his head.

"As long as you're aware," said Mr. Sanderson. "What about you, young man? You look a little lost."

"In truth, I have no idea what I should get," Sorin said, closing the book. "Do you have any suggestions?"

The man shrugged. "That depends on your role in combat."

"I'm usually in close combat, though I might also use the occasional spell," said Sorin. "But my main concern is compatibility with my blood."

"With your blood?" Mr. Sanderson asked, frowning. "Let me draw some and see." He came up to Sorin with a needle and poked him, but the needle instantly dissolved. "I see what's going on. That narrows our options significantly."

He flipped through the book and revealed snake-patterned leather armor. "Stygian Viper enchantment. It adds a poisonous element to attacks and has a retaliation effect. It should be resistant to your poisonous blood." He then flipped forward a few dozen pages to a rock-patterned armor. "Stone Skin Armor. It'll make you heavy, but not so heavy that spells will fail. You'll be slower, but you'll be able to take a lot more hits than someone with standard leather armor."

Finally, he flipped over to the end of the book. "This is my recommendation, though. Blood Drinker Armor."

"Blood Drinker?" asked Sorin. "You mean I'll be able to drink the blood of my enemies?"

"Heavens no!" said Mr. Sanderson. "That's a two-star ability at the very least. This armor only feeds on the blood that spills on it, gaining its properties and repairing itself. So whenever you suffer wounds, the armor will theoretically drink enough blood to regenerate itself, saving a lot on repairs and also preventing enemies from slowly wearing you down.

"There's another advantage: If you feed it poisonous blood, it should theoretically gain contact poison properties. That means that just by touching you, demons will get afflicted. Of course, the premise is that you're basically hugging them, but what can you do? That's the limitation of one-star armor."

"Does it have any other properties?" asked Sorin.

"Of course," said Mr. Sanderson. "Its most significant advantage is its berserker property. You healed fast from that needle puncture wound, and it took me a bit of strength to get past your defenses. This tells me that you're not someone to shy away from taking hits.

"You're saying the berserker property will make me stronger as I take damage?" asked Sorin, intrigued by the possibility.

"Your stats will increase tremendously," said Mr. Sanderson. "Your defenses will increase as well. Your armor won't be as good as theirs in an undamaged state, but once you take enough hits, its enhancement effect could become twice to three times stronger than theirs, in theory. I believe the theoretical limit of the enchantment is a 35 percent increase in defense, strength, and agility, assuming you're on the cusp of death."

"That... doesn't seem very safe," said Sorin.

"Unfortunately, it's the only armor I can guarantee will have full compatibility with your blood," said Mr. Sanderson. "You're currently at the eighth stage of Blood-Thickening. But what about the ninth stage?

The tenth stage? Bone-Forging? Other enchantments *might* be able to tolerate your blood at the ninth stage, but after that, you'd be gambling."

"Shouldn't you mention the cost of the armor," said Gareth. "He's obviously never bought proper leather armor before."

"And you have?" snapped Mr. Sanderson. "And what's the big deal about costs? The average adventurer spends 500 gold fixing their enchanted leather armor after coming back from an expedition. And that's for medium damage. If it's overly damaged, there won't even be a chance to repair it. With Blood Drinker Armor, there'll be no need—even if 10 percent of the armor is left, it will regenerate given enough blood."

"But since you asked, I'll outline the costs. You're supplying the leather, which I'm happy to work with, so we'll cut that part out. Next is the leatherworking, which will cost about 750 gold apiece, with slight fluctuations for customizations. That'll give you a masterwork armor capable of holding an enchantment.

"A Night King enchantment is worth 400 gold. A Wind Blessed enchantment is worth 600 gold. As for the Blood Drinker enchantment, it's worth 700 gold. The functionality is basic, but believe me when I say you'll be saving in the long run on repairs."

Sorin nearly choked when he heard the number. "You're saying this is going to cost me 1,450 gold, even after we supply the materials?"

"It's honestly not bad, given the quality," assured Gareth. "Custom leather armor can't be compared to stock armor that you adjust as well as you can with straps. This will fit you like a glove."

But Sorin was crying inwardly. *I already have so many expenses, and I still need to go to the Mages Guild and the Alchemists Guild,* he thought. But safety was a priority, so he bit back on these words and ultimately accepted the cost. "Fine. 1450 gold it is."

Lawrence and Gareth were also agreeable to the price he quoted. They signed an agreement and then began choosing colors, which could be added free of charge. Sorin was partial to navy blue coloring, so he picked a combination of blue and black.

"That about does it," said Mr. Sanderson. "At least for you two. As for you, Mr. I Have Poison For Blood; I'll be needing a couple of buckets."

"A couple of buckets?" asked Sorin, confused.

"Of your blood, obviously," said Mr. Sanderson. "Otherwise, how am I going to increase its compatibility with the enchantment? How are the mages going to train the enchantment?"

When the leatherworker put it that way, Sorin could only accept the buckets and cut open his arm. He leaked a pint into it but stopped when he realized there was now a gaping hole in the shop's sturdy wooden floor.

Mr. Sanderson seemed to expect this. He escorted Sorin three buildings down, where he borrowed four large specialty bottles and a glass funnel covered in anti-corrosion runes.

Two hours later, Sorin, Gareth, and Lawrence made their way over to a bar for dinner. "You should have seen the look on his face when you melted the funnel," joked Lawrence. "Something tells me it was expensive."

Sorin couldn't help but laugh as well. "Who cheaps out on the funnel when they're using two-star laboratory-grade glass bottles? Actually, I think he was less upset about the funnel and more upset at the person who'd sold it to him in the first place."

"Still, it'll be a while before the armor's ready," said Gareth. "A week at the very least."

"Ten days for mine," said Sorin. "It's a good thing we were planning on taking a couple of weeks off anyway."

"What can you do," said Lawrence. "They've got all the mages in the city running around touching up the wall spells and fixing equipment. Adventurers like us are seen as extras, so we have to make the best of the situation."

"Downtime is a good thing," said Gareth. "We've had a tense couple of weeks, and I have quite a few things I need to work on."

Sorin, as well. He needed to experiment with poisons and spells, as well as figure out how to open his companions' extraordinary meridians.

"As much as I like relaxing, I'm afraid I won't have much time for it," said Gareth. "I almost guarantee that my father will conscript me to fletch arrows till my hands bleed."

"I'm glad I don't have a dad like that," said Lawrence. "He usually lets me do whatever he wants, so I'll take the chance to do a bit of local sightseeing. Ouch! What was that for?" Gareth had elbowed him hard enough to crack a rib.

"Have you learned nothing in the past few weeks?" asked Gareth. "I'm sure I speak for everyone in our party when I say that we're tired of you damaging our reputation."

"Agreed," said Sorin. "Less peeping and a little more growing up would be a nice development."

"You're all a bunch of spoilsports," Lawrence mumbled. "Anyway, it's dinner time. Who's up for noodles?"

"Noodles would be a nice change," said Gareth.

"I'm okay with noodles," said Sorin.

"Then follow me, gentlemen," said Lawrence. "I know the best place in town."

56

COFFEE-ADDICTED MAGES

The following day, Sorin ate a light breakfast before heading off to the Mages Guild, located just south of the outpost's central square. The guild was a different sight during the day than at night, so Sorin was finally able to appreciate the wondrous glass building nestled within a giant hedge maze.

Said building was a multi-story complex whose five stories some-what resembled a mage's hat. Its multiple facets caught and refracted sunlight and also used said light to power the many spells that controlled the building's inner environment.

A pillar of pure mana ran from the bottom to the top of the cylinder, then spread out like veins that lit up the entire structure. This included the public library on the first floor, the most popular building in the guild by far.

It was early morning, so the guild was dead quiet. The staff manning the many desks in the lobby were chatting amiably while drinking extra-large cups of coffee. Their relaxed demeanor made Sorin temporarily forget some of the building's surprising features, like the automatic sliding glass doors, the well-heated air, and the flashy noticeboards that cycled through various announcements without the need for ink or paper.

"Hello?" said Sorin, stepping up to an unmanned desk nearest one such group of coffee-drinking mages. *Did they even hear me? Should I try again?* Fortunately, one of the nearby coffee drinkers sighed and shuffled over to the desk.

"How can I help you, Mr…"

"Kepler," said Sorin. "Sorin Kepler. I'm here to see a friend. Daphne Phillips."

"Mage Phillips?" said the man, blinking slowly. He took a sip from his giant coffee mug before swiping at a glass interface and bringing up a list of names and titles. "According to the registry, Mage Philips is currently in her room. I could send her a message notifying her that a visitor is here for her, but given the time…"

"Please send the message," said Sorin. "I'm sure that in her case, it doesn't matter what time it is. Also, she's somehow developed the ability to sleepwalk and sleepread. Time and location are no longer a factor.

"Fair enough," said the mage, pressing on a rune beside Daphne's name and injecting mana into it. "Take a seat, and feel free to peruse the public library while you wait. As a non-member, you'll need to remain in the public-access areas."

"Speaking of membership, how does one go about becoming a member?" asked Sorin. "How much does a membership cost? What are the benefits?"

At the prospect of registering a new member, the man woke up slightly. "Becoming a member is very easy," the man explained. "The first requirement is that the potential member demonstrate a Tier 0 spell."

Sorin directly summoned a mana needle, then a mana ball. These were, in fact, Tier 0 spells that he'd learned to support his activities as a physician many years ago. He'd since modified the simple spells to accommodate poison mana.

"Are there any other requirements?" asked Sorin.

"No, we're fairly liberal about recruiting members," the man said. "The fact that you've learned a Tier 0 spell is proof that you have sufficient talent in spellcraft to at least learn a Tier 1 spell if you work hard enough.

"The cost of registration is a fifty-gold initial fee. Renewal costs ten gold every year. The main benefit of membership is free coffee and the ability to browse higher levels of the library. It also grants one the ability to rent out practice rooms."

Sorin was surprised by the generous benefits. "I expected membership to be much more expensive. I've been told learning spells is a money sink."

"The expenditure of our members relies solely on their inclinations to study and learn magic," said the man cheerfully. "Would you like to proceed with a membership application?"

Sorin had thought long and hard about how to improve himself for their next adventure, and learning some minor spells was one of these ways. Joining the Mages Guild was unavoidable, so he didn't hesitate to spend the small amount of gold and filled out the surprisingly brief registration form.

Ten minutes later, the clerk handed him a light blue card showing his photograph, name, and member number. The card could be used to gain access to member-only areas and secure free coffee.

"The card is linked to your member account," the clerk explained. "You'll need to top up your account with gold for when you'll inevitably want to make a purchase." Sorin was confused by the certainty of his words. Still, he nodded and made his way to the café to secure a free coffee before heading over to the library.

The Mages Guild is way better than the Adventurers Guild, thought Sorin as he sipped his coffee. The coffee had been given to him in a spell-insulated mug and came complete with a lid. It was possible to drink *through* the lid via a small opening that would only activate when pressing against it with one's upper lip. The cup was of high quality, but it strictly couldn't be taken out of the Mages Guild. Failing to return a cup would result in fines.

This place has free coffee, it's clean, and it has enchantments for everything, thought Sorin as he walked through the lobby. *The food is reasonably cheap, and there's no need to deal with cockroaches and unsanitary adventurers.*

Another perk afforded to members was the freedom to walk their familiars. Familiars of all kinds were allowed to scurry about within a hundred feet of their owners, though their owners would be responsible for any damages they caused.

Lorimer was overjoyed by this development and was, therefore, on his best behavior. Incurring a fine was the best way to upset the miser known as Sorin Kepler. In fact, he proved downright helpful in chasing away more annoying familiars who tried to brush up against Sorin despite the warnings of their owners.

The Mages Guild's library was one of the largest libraries Sorin had ever laid eyes on. It dwarfed Kepler Clan's comprehensive medical library, which he'd only scanned through a part of despite his quick reading speed and near-photographic memory.

The first floor was reserved for public use. Sorin was pleased to discover thousands of Tier 0 spells and tens of thousands of introductory magical theory books, works of fiction, and papers written by beginner academics, free for perusal even by non-members.

Sorin was still determining how long Daphne would be, so he located several Tier 0 spells that he felt he should have learned as a child and tossed the books on one of the many tables. These included the Light spell, the original Poison Needle spell, Poison Spray, Poison Blade, and Poison Orb. Unlike the Mana Blade, Mana Needle, and Mana Orb spells, the poison versions of these spells were optimized for use with poison mana. They would be able to increase the effects of the spells in his possession by over 50 percent.

The Light spell was first on his list. He read the introductory page but stopped to take a quick sip of coffee. Yet no sooner had he opened the first page did a startling but stern voice speak out. "Rule Violation: Drinking non-water beverages next to an open book. Fine: 5 gold coins."

Sorin's eye twitched. He looked around the library and saw a smattering of pitying but unsurprised expressions. *This is ridiculous,* thought Sorin. *No one warned me of such a rule.* He carefully set his coffee down before replying to the voice. "There were no rules posted anywhere. I didn't do anything wrong."

The voice spoke again, but not in the manner he expected. "Rule Violation: Yelling loudly in the public library: 5 gold coins. In reply to your earlier words, ignorance of the rules is no excuse for breaking them. You may pay your fines at the membership desk and familiarize yourself with the complete rules handbook upon leaving the library."

Sorin grumbled inwardly but knew that there was nothing to be done. He didn't wish to be continuously fined, however, so he abandoned the spell books he'd picked out and made his way for the entrance. As he crossed the threshold, however, the stern voice reprimanded him once again. "Abandoning books without returning them to a librarian, custodian, or clerk: 5 gold coins."

"Oh, come on," said Sorin, storming off. His initial positive impression of the Mages Guild was now tarnished. These mages weren't just addicted to coffee—they were addicted to extorting money from people as well!

Several hours later, Sorin was seated in front of a pile of Tier 0 spell books. He read at a slow and steady pace. Occasionally, he stopped his reading, used his finger as a bookmark, and took a sip from his enchanted coffee mug, taking special care not to spill a single drop.

Finger bookmarking was the agreed-upon best way to keep one's spot in a book without breaking the rules. Dog-earing was unacceptable and punishable by mandatory attendance at a 3-day seminar on appropriate book-handling practices.

Reviewing and updating his Mana Blade, Mana Needle, and mana orb spells only required a half-hour for each spell, as their spell frameworks were almost identical to the versions he already knew. As for the poison spray spell, it was only a Tier 0 spell and functioned on similar principles, so it took him a full hour. The light spell, however, took two hours to master.

But two hours is much faster than the first time I tried learning spells, thought Sorin. He remembered learning Mana Needle for the first time; it had been a three-day headache-inducing ordeal that had strengthened his determination never to learn advanced spells. *It seems Assessor Haley's assessment of my mage potential is accurate. Learning simple spells isn't challenging at all, and I might even be able to learn higher-tier spells if I'm willing to spend time on them.*

After learning the light spell, Sorin was at a loss for what to do. Fortunately, this was when a familiar sleep-deprived figure entered the library with a coffee and an open book in hand. Her actions were mechanical and well-practiced.

As she brought the coffee cup to her lips for a drink, she closed her book, leaving a finger in place to mark her spot. By the time her cup was back down again, the book was fully open, and she continued where she left off.

"You came," said Daphne as she arrived at Sorin's study table. "How much did you get fined before you went to read the rule book?"

"Twenty-five gold coins," said Sorin grumpily. "This system is seriously messed up. Why wouldn't they just have you read the book before breaking the rules and getting punished for it?"

"Cash cow," said Daphne, taking another long sip of coffee. "Also, it's easier to make people remember the rules when they'd been stung. I believe they tried mandatory classes and seminars for a while, but people just guessed for the exam and squeaked a pass, then proceeded to break the rules anyway. Also, there were a few unfortunate incidents involving younger mages trying to summon female demonic familiars."

"I noticed you don't have a familiar," said Sorin.

Daphne shrugged. "They're troublesome. Not very useful. Maybe I'll consider it when I can summon a Stygian Firebat or something. By the way, you should pick a better time to visit. Most of us mages go to bed at three or four in the morning." She let out a loud yawn to accentuate her point.

"For some reason, I thought you'd all be enthusiastic early birds," said Sorin. "Also, you're always half asleep. I figured it didn't matter."

"Reasonable," said Daphne as she took a seat. She flipped through the books Sorin had been studying. "Light. Blade. Spray. Orb. Needle. Different shapes for the same mana. All useful in different situations, especially given your lack of ranged options. You're clearly here to learn spells, so I assume you're here for advice from an expert on what to learn. What are your needs? What is your budget?"

"My budget is 1,400 gold," said Sorin. He knew that only the basics were free. Learning anything above the first floor would require additional payment.

"Tight," said Daphne. "But money's always tight for spellcasters. Continue."

"I'm in need of close and mid-range spells," said Sorin. "I usually find myself in close combat, but there's no reason not to support you if the situation arises. I made a small wish list—can you tell me your thoughts?"

"First, I want a medium-ranged spell that can help me supplement your superior bombardment in case we're surrounded. I can use an acid-type poison for this spell.

"Second, I'd like a needle-type spell. My paralytic poison isn't potent, so I need a way to pierce defenses. I'm a decent shot at short range, and my reaction speed is very high. With practice, I'll be able to strike acupoints.

"Finally, I'd like a blade spell and a spray spell. I already have a close-combat technique, but fighting the Minotaur, I found it difficult to penetrate his mana shields and physical defenses. As for the spray spell, I need it because lobbing an orb of acid isn't very practical when you've got six demons in your face."

Daphne took another sip of coffee. "Well analyzed. And you also recognized the superiority of fire magic. Very good. Spell potential? Mana reserves?"

"My spell potential is garbage," said Sorin. "B-grade."

"The cut-off for mage material is B-grade, so I'd hardly call that garbage," said Daphne.

"As for my mana reserves, they're impressive," said Sorin.

"Most men usually think their mana reserves impressive," said Daphne. "Until they compare them to others and find they could always be larger."

Sorin, who'd taken the opportunity to sip on his coffee, choked on the hot liquid. Fortunately, he reacted quickly to shield the books on the table with his sleeves so that not a drop of liquid fell on them.

"S-grade," said Sorin. "Apologies for not being more specific."

"S-grade mana reserves but only B-grade mage potential?" said Daphne. "What a strange combination. With such mana reserves, I'd normally advise a mage to go for bigger, flashier spells. Unfortunately, you wouldn't be able to learn one even if I gave you a full year."

"It took me two hours to learn the light spell," said Sorin. "Please be gentle."

"Don't worry," said Daphne with a wink. "I'll take care of you. This young lady has a lot more experience than you think."

57

THREADING THE SPEAR

Daphne asked Sorin a few more questions before leading him up to the library's second floor. Most of them pertained to his mana control and his ability to separate his mana into different natures.

"Different spell shapes are more suited to different types of mana," Daphne explained. "And variable mana cultivators, though uncommon, are numerous enough that this matter gets special attention in spell theory books."

"Acid-type mana is the most common type of poison mana. It's best applied as an orb or spray. It's almost never applied in the form of a needle or blade. Paralytic-style mana is more multipurpose and can be applied in various shapes. As for anti-mana... you need a solid framework like a blade or an orb. A spray form is too loose and will lead to uncontrollable results. At the same time, a needle or a flower has too many fine details and will likely explode before it reaches its target."

"I'm a little confused about the acid mana restrictions," said Sorin. "Why can't they be used to form blades and needles?"

"I thought you were a physician," said Daphne. "Don't you know how acid functions?"

Sorin thought about this and realized that acid wounds were evenly distributed and indiscriminate. They took time to act. "You're saying they're too slow."

"They're not instantaneous forms of damage," Daphne confirmed. "Blade spells and needle spells usually require a sharp characteristic or an effect of some kind. An acid blade would lack piercing power, while a needle would be lacking in quantity."

"I understand," said Sorin. "Please recommend whatever you think is appropriate."

The second level of the library was much like the first in that it had plenty of study tables and a vast assortment of books. To a tee, all those present had mastered the technique of drinking coffee while reading.

There was also a powerful mage on this floor of the library. Based on the mage's aura, Sorin could tell that he was a Bone-Forging cultivator.

"I take it he's here to protect the books?" said Sorin as they passed the old mage.

"These books are worth hundreds of thousands of gold coins, and that's only for this floor alone," explained Daphne. "I would imagine that the Medical Association would have strict guards as well, or at the very least, a strict vetting process for access to their precious tomes."

Daphne then let Sorin know that due to his lack of magical knowledge, he would only be able to learn relatively low-tier spells. If he wanted to learn anything better, he would need to commit himself to learning magic for a few years.

At first, Sorin thought this was Daphne being snobby. But then she told him she'd been studying magic for ten years despite having S-Class mage potential, so he wisely shut his mouth, as anything else would be insulting.

Daphne was the oldest individual in their group but had a similarly low cultivation stage. This had less to do with her talent and more to do with the way she spent her time and money. Instead of purchasing expensive cultivation-boosting medicine, Daphne had opted to strengthen her fundamentals in spellcraft. It was only recently that she'd started steadily increasing her cultivation.

"Given your budget limitations, I recommend choosing this as your orb spell," Daphne said, picking out a book. "It's only a C-Tier spell, but that's mostly because of its range limitation of 300 feet. Its power is somewhat lacking, but its cast time is low."

"Veridian Smoke Bomb?" muttered Sorin as he opened the cover. He read the description and saw that the veridian in the name referred to the name of the inventor. The smoke bomb portion described the mechanism of poison propagation. "'Compatible with all types of poison mana. An honestly disappointing spell with low commitment. Useful for eliminating trash demons not worthy of attention.' This Albus Veridian was quite the character."

"*Archmage* Veridian was indeed quite the character," said Daphne, placing her hand firmly on the first page before Sorin could turn it. "And remember, if you read it, you rent it."

"Thanks for the save," said Sorin.

"Not a problem," said Daphne. "Archmage Veridian was a controversial figure. He was a fan of efficient and multipurpose spells and had variable poison mana, similar to yours. The orb is, therefore, very compatible with both paralytic mana and acid mana. The afflictions will propagate through skin contact and the victim's airways."

"Do I have any other options?" asked Sorin.

"A variant of the Fireball spell called Poison Explosion," said Daphne. "It basically uses the same spell framework but emphasizes blast radius instead of power. The range is 1500 feet, and it'll drain a quarter of a B-Class's mana stores. There are other spells, of course, but I don't recommend you learn them unless you want to learn magical theories and tailor your spells."

"How much does either option cost?" asked Sorin.

"Veridian Smoke Bomb is worth 300 gold, while Poison Explosion is worth 500 gold, same as Fireball," said Daphne. "I'll have you note that Poison Explosion is nothing like my personally customized Fireballs. Please don't be disappointed if you buy that one."

"Both budget and practicality point to the Veridian Smoke Bomb," said Sorin.

"I thought so," said Daphne. "Now, let's get to the most difficult part —needle spells."

She led Sorin down several shelves, picking up a few books from each shelf in the process. By the end of it, she'd picked out twenty different spells for him to choose from. "Are you sure you don't have any specific recommendations?" asked Sorin, looking at each of their introductory pages. "And why do some of these say 'arrow' instead of 'needle'? And is this a *spear* spell?"

"The 'needle-type' definition is unfortunately broad," said Daphne. "I'm not sure how this came about, but there was a lot of disagreement on what a needle was and quite a few debates on the semantics of it. In the end, there were three main camps: the needle camp, the arrow camp, and the spear camp."

"Why spears?" asked Sorin.

"Well, if you think about it, needles are just very small spears," said Daphne. "And they were dead set on using the verbiage. The many fierce debates led to a Mages Guild Council deliberation, and the mages in charge, very much annoyed by the situation, settled on a solution that no one liked.

"The standard verbiage used would be needle-type spells, but all introductory spell books would contain a note about the ongoing debate and the merit of using arrow and spear to describe these spells. Spells could also retain their original names using arrows and spears, even if, technically, said spears were the size of sewing needles. This gave a way for each camp to liberally plagiarize each other's spells and create different name variants just to stick it to their opponents.

"That sounds very... childish," said Sorin.

"Mages are often eccentric characters," said Daphne. "I'm actually pro-spear camp and was captain of my debate team in arguing the matter. But semantics aside, this is good news for you—needle spells are extremely cheap as a result."

She then went on to introduce the main spell variants—darts, arrows, spears, and, of course, needles. Needles also had a corresponding spray-type variant, while spears had a variant that could be physically carried.

Almost all of them had the option of adding additional needles. Doing so would result in decreased efficiency and accuracy.

"I'll pick this one," Sorin finally said, picking a spell called Threading the Spear. It was not at all like a spear spell, as its base spell involved launching tiny needles at a range of 30 feet. But the spell *did* have detailed instructions on how to produce 'spears' as small as half an inch and as large as ten feet long and two inches thick. Those larger than four feet could effectively be used as spears in battle, and could be thrown at much farther targets.

"A good choice," said Daphne with a smile. "Note the wonderfully infuriating wordplay."

"It's nothing compared to 'Archmage Syracuse's Tiny and Ineffective Spear,'" said Sorin.

"Archmage Syracuse was pro-spear, and an unfortunate incident in the bedroom had the entire anti-spear camp smearing him in publications for five whole years," said Daphne. "*Anyway*, because this is technically a gag spell, it only costs 200 gold."

Sorin was relieved at the price because, on top of the other spells he was looking to acquire, he still needed to purchase and formulate poisons. The ninth and tenth poisons for the Ten Thousand Poison Canon had strict requirements, as they needed to conform with his existing poisons.

Having secured two good spells, Sorin needed a blade-type spell. There weren't many anti-mana spells available, however, so Sorin could only grit his teeth and purchase the one-star, B-Tier spell, Anti-Mage's Blade, for 600 gold, leaving him with 525 gold and change.

They were about to leave the second floor when suddenly, a book caught Sorin's eye. "A vision-type spell?" he said, pulling it out of the bookshelf. "Ophidian Eye?"

"It's one of those niche vision spells," explained Daphne. "Everybody likes to put their own spin on them, like Pyromancer's Eye or Frost Wyvern's Gaze. They help beginners manipulate and sense mana. Judging by the price, this one was a failure."

Indeed, the spell was classified as a D-Tier enchantment. Its only purpose was to highlight a person's meridians. Ideally, the spell would have also lit up the target's acupoints, vitals, and bones.

For someone like Sorin, however, this spell was a godsend. *A hundred gold for something that can allow me to determine a target's anatomy without touching or striking them? I'll take it!* He wished there were more spells like these.

Sorin added the book to his pile and made his way to the checkout counter on the first floor. "Interesting," said an old librarian as he placed the books on a spell circle and extracted an illusory copy from them. "Poison mana spells. You don't see a lot of plague mages these days. Though they used to be a lot more popular a few hundred years back, or so I hear."

"I believe the Medical Association had a lot to do with that," said Sorin, accepting the illusory copies.

"Indeed, they did," said the librarian. "Them and the Olympian Council both. There were also shadows of the Demon Hunters Association in this matter, though books on the subject are hard to find these days."

"Many thanks for helping us out," said Sorin politely. "How long can I keep these?"

"Normally? Four weeks," said the librarian. "But for a student of history like yourself, I'll add another two weeks. Don't be in a hurry to remember them. Learning a spell isn't the same as mastering a spell. It's not unusual for mages to take out a book two or three times before they're satisfied."

Sorin winced at the thought of wasting so much money. "Many thanks for your pointers. And for the extended grace period as well."

"Not a problem," said the man. "The vice guild master told me to look out for a good seedling that cultivates poison. You can thank him instead."

"Why didn't you tell me you knew the vice guild master?" hissed Daphne when they left the counter. "If I'd known, I'd have asked for a discount!"

Sorin shook his head. "I only met him in passing. He helped me get out of a difficult situation. I'd hate to impose on him, given that it's me who owes him a favor. How exactly do mages survive, by the way? These books are all grossly expensive."

"Most have rich families," answered Daphne. "Those that don't have rich relatives normally charge mana crystals in exchange for gold. They can also enchant items, maintain spell circles and formations, etc. Many become adventurers. There's a lot of demand for mages, but not enough mages to go around. Also, theory books are much cheaper than spell books. People would typically study the basics for years before picking out their spells, then spend months playing around with them and making them their own."

She escorted Sorin down to the coffee shop, where they both secured an extra coffee. Lorimer wasn't allowed a coffee, however, as he'd damaged a library book on the first floor, and Sorin had needed to pay five gold as a result.

"I guess that's it," said Sorin when they were both done with their coffee. "Thanks a lot for helping me out. I hope you're still free for dinner tomorrow?"

"Of course," said Daphne. "A mage never says no to free food. I believe it was Archmage Worsted who popularized the saying."

"I'll be sure to let Percival and Clarice know about your food preferences," said Sorin. "But please, do be punctual. Percival gets irritated when people are late, and Lorimer starts chewing the furniture when he doesn't eat on time."

"I'm usually stylishly late, but for you, I'll make an exception," said Daphne. "See you tomorrow evening."

"See you tomorrow evening," echoed Sorin.

Having accomplished his mission, he returned to the manor and locked himself in his study. He then cracked open the illusory copy of Threading the Spear and began committing its runes and spell patterns to memory.

58

SELF-EXPERIMENTATION

Sorin was no stranger to spellcraft, as in his younger years, his mentor had forced him to study spell theory to make up for a physician's deficits. Though he'd only begun cultivating six years ago and had spent three of those years unable to cultivate, the years he *had* practiced had been filled to the brim with mana manipulation drills.

Unlike life mages, physicians didn't study complex healing spells. Instead, they focused on the simple application of life mana using various shapes and techniques. They treated specific injuries and provided vital support for individual systems instead of the whole body, thereby avoiding potential complications.

Though Sorin couldn't use life mana, the mana manipulation techniques he'd learned allowed him to bypass many troublesome steps in learning his new spells. He was able to form a proper one-star poison needle after only ninety-eight attempts, complete with all thirty-six runes and twelve mana lines that joined together at two points.

Sharp, small, and concentrated. This was the essence of needle spells. It was also the essence of spear spells, except in this case, one replaced the word small with the word big.

Size control was specifically what Sorin was after. After successfully summoning his first needle, he began experimenting with shrinking the needle down to as small a size as possible and reducing its thickness. He repeatedly banished and summoned needles in various positions inside flexible tubing that had been left after the Kepler Clan's raid on his manor.

Mana composition is essential, thought Sorin as he executed the spell using combinations of paralytic, acidic, and anti-mana properties. *The needle I need relies on a balance between anti-mana and acidic toxins.* After half a day of trying, he was eventually able to achieve his goal—a needle that roughly replicated the meridian-opening tincture in Sirius's research notes.

After that, it was a simple matter to condense two more needle templates, one with anti-mana and paralytic properties and another with pure acid properties. The first would be used in small numbers to paralyze demons in battle. The second would be used in a spray-style arrangement at point-blank range to eliminate small numbers of lesser demons.

Once the fine-tuning of the spell was complete, he used the Ophidian Eye enchantment to enhance his vision. It was a low-tier spell that had required two hours total to comprehend. His improved vision lit up the meridians running through his body. This included all opened meridians, as well as his unopened Belt Vessel, Conception Vessel, and Governing Vessel.

With Ophidian Eye lighting up the way, Sorin inserted his newly formulated paralytic needle into his thigh. The needle pierced into his flesh, stopping just short of his bone. A numbing sensation spread out, completely disrupting his musculature and nervous system. His mana flow grew somewhat chaotic but was still serviceable.

He then stood up and tried to walk before confirming that only limping was possible. *Twenty seconds of paralysis isn't bad, considering my resistance to poison, but I'll need a better test subject,* thought Sorin. *Lorimer? No, he's highly resistant to poison as well. Lawrence?* Given that the risks were very minimal, using the rogue as an unwilling test subject would serve the dual purpose of further science and punishing him for his ethically dubious behavior.

But I can't experiment with meridian opening in the same way, continued Sorin. *Piercing into an acupoint would have little effect. I can already clear out meridians using my mana and spiritual senses. What I need to do instead is inject mana into a living body and form a poison needle despite their natural resistance and mana flow.*

Sorin's regeneration rate was S-Class, meaning that even his internal organs and nerves would regenerate if damaged. He, therefore, didn't hesitate to inject mana from his finger into his arm. He cast Threading the Spear to summon a single needle. His natural mana immediately tried to absorb the spell, but Sorin suppressed it and forced the spell template into existence.

Crap! A small explosion of poison mana ruptured his meridian as the spell collapsed. The collapse had come quickly and without warning. Having expected such an occurrence, however, he numbed his arm. He ignored the pain as he ruminated over the reason for his failure.

What followed was a series of consecutive attempts using different undamaged meridians. With every failure, Sorin switched to a new and undamaged part of his body and repeated the process, as his natural regeneration would eventually heal the injuries.

Sorin grew increasingly skillful as time went by. The first successful needle took two hours to form, but the second only took fifteen minutes. By midnight, he could already form a needle with 95 percent assurance. It wasn't the same as attempting the matter on a separate living host, but it was progress.

"Good morning, Mr. Kepler," greeted Percival the next day. "Up late working?"

Sorin yawned as he accepted a freshly brewed cup of coffee, along with a plate of buttered toast and a few links of fried sausage. "How are the preparations going for tonight's dinner coming along?"

"Everything is proceeding as planned," said Percival. "There's no need to worry about anything, Mr. Kepler. Simply focus on your work and enjoy."

"How's Lorimer doing?" asked Sorin. "I hear you found something interesting to keep him busy?"

"This..." Percival grimaced. "It's frankly impossible to keep that rat out of trouble. I therefore consulted with the city guard on the issue and obtained some intriguing suggestions."

Sorin jumped. "The city guard? Why are you involving them?"

"Relax," Percival assured. "It's nothing bad. The guard is as concerned about his good behavior as you are, as the last thing they want is a swarm of vengeful rats eating them alive in their sleep."

Sorin relaxed substantially. "Then please continue."

"The city has an expansive sewer system running beneath the outpost," Percival explained. "It's a place of filth and corruption that constantly spawns demons that the guards must clear out. But a good portion of the guards have no desire to deal with such problems. I, therefore, approached their captains and struck a deal with them: On their shifts, Lorimer would go down into the sewers and come back with whatever demon cores he collected. He'll get to keep half the demon cores he finds but must turn the rest in for the guards so they have proof of having performed their duties."

This was too much news for Sorin to take in, given his sleep-deprived state. Still, he steadied himself with a sip of hot coffee and gave Percival an approving nod. "Well done, Percival. You're a credit to the force."

"I'm simply a man who knows how to get by on a tight budget," said Percival.

Given Percival's words, Sorin had an inkling of what the man had been doing to keep the house's finances afloat. "There will be no need to worry about such things in the future, Percival. You can rely on me for the house's finances going forward." He then tactfully switched to another topic. "Is there anything I should take note of in the news?" Newspapers were a luxury because they required ink stones from the Mages Guild for printing. It was only recently that they had no issue affording this nicety.

"There are a few important things for you to take note of," reported Percival. "For example, the upcoming demon tide and preparations for winter. Most of the rest is nonsense, but I do recall seeing a mage image of a certain rogue sneaking about on private property." He flipped to the seventh page and showed the dark, barely recognizable image of a man jumping over a fence.

"That's Lawrence all right, though he'll deny it to the end," said Sorin.

"News aside, you had a delivery this morning," said Percival.

"A delivery?" asked Sorin, intrigued. "I don't remember expecting one."

"You can go downstairs to check things out," said Percival with a smile. "I've already taken the trouble to unpack everything in the lab. Your books have also been moved to the study, and your desk is back in your office."

"Marcus is a conniving snake, but he's being honest this time," muttered Sorin. "What in the Seven Evils is his angle? Why would the family suddenly give me back my things?"

Sorin hastily finished breakfast before going upstairs and looking through the books in his study. Virtually all of his books had been returned, with the exception of the Divine Medical Codex. What's more, they'd been cleaned of all dust and organized alphabetically.

Were they looking for something? thought Sorin as he flipped through the books. Even stiff ones he hadn't read through in years were now soft and pliable. The more he looked through his collection, the more stock he gave to this theory. It was just like that time after he'd recovered from his injuries and was able to walk again after his cultivation was crippled.

Upon going through the things in his bedroom, he'd realized that all his belongings had been searched. There hadn't been any attempt at hiding this fact, so his naïve self had pitched a fit. It was the same for his late father's lab and clinic.

Expecting the worst, Sorin finished up in the library and made his way down to the basement. To his surprise, however, his labware was pristinely clean. The ones that had been broken during the search had been replaced, and two items, a ventilation spell plate and a heating spell plate, had been added.

"This is going a bit far for reparations," said Sorin as Percival came down. "What's going on here, Percival?"

"I was just as surprised as you are," said Percival. "So I went to the telegram office and sent a message to one of the elders in the Punishment Bureau that I am in frequent contact with. He simply stated that the punishment Marcus doled out was overly harsh and that the Council of Elders had ordered Marcus's branch of the family to replace your belongings and refurbish the laboratory." Judging by his expression, however, there was more to the story.

"Just say what's on your mind, Percival," said Sorin.

"To be honest, this matter is extremely suspicious," Percival said bluntly. "Moreover, even your books seem like they received a very heavy dusting, if you catch my drift." His comments confirmed Sorin's suspicions. "What do you intend to do, Mr. Kepler? Can I be of assistance in any way?"

Sorin shrugged. "I'll simply proceed as normal. They're clearly looking for something, but I have nothing to hide." He wasn't going to repeat the mistakes of his younger self. Raising the alarm and complaining would only cause people to look down on him and damage his already tarnished image.

"You've grown up," said Percival. "I'm glad you're not walking down the same path as before. If that's everything, I'll be heading upstairs to help Clarice with the preparations for tonight's dinner."

The butler excused himself, leaving Sorin to look through his upgraded laboratory equipment. He swept through the lab in search of surveillance devices but found none. Nothing had been tampered with, and that included the medical mannequin. This object was easily worth 5,000 gold and could only be obtained in a city using the right connections. Of course, the old mannequin had undergone a complete overhaul. It had been completely dismantled and cleaned, and most of its used parts had been replaced.

Having determined that everything was in order, Sorin activated the mannequin with mana crystals and pressed his finger on one of its acupoints. He poured a small dose of poison mana into the mannequin and tried to form a mana needle in its thigh meridian.

It's much more difficult on a mannequin than inside my own meridians, thought Sorin as the needle exploded, damaging the mannequin. Thankfully, the mannequin had a repair enchantment, and it wasn't long before the damaged meridian completely recovered.

Undeterred by a single failure, Sorin repeated the process several dozen times before eventually succeeding. Then, having established that what he was doing was theoretically possible, Sorin perfected the process and then got to work guiding the needle halfway up a meridian. He got about halfway through the meridian before encountering a difficult-to-navigate section and accidentally rupturing the meridian.

Encouraged by this preliminary success, Sorin continued his experiments and formulated a plan for possible future steps. Once the mannequin outlived its usefulness, he would switch to using live demon specimens or cadavers to practice.

As for experimenting with humans, this was to be done at the very end of the research process. He wasn't like his ancestor, Sirius Abberjay Kepler, who was willing to throw thousands of lives away to obtain an answer. A physician should always have a bottom line, no matter how great the benefit might be. Even if this benefit could uplift humanity as a whole.

It was then that Sorin froze. The needle he was guiding exploded in the mannequin and even ruptured the tip of his finger. He ignored the blood that dribbled down onto the stone floor as he connected certain matters, including the death of his parents, his crippling, the searching of his possessions, and the Kepler Clan's strange treatment.

There were, after all, two things that Sorin intended to hide from his family. The first was the Ten Thousand Poison Canon and its origins. As for the second, it was something he'd discovered only a short time ago: Sirus Abberjay Kepler's research notes, which had been inscribed on his bones without his knowledge.

A DINNER WITH FRIENDS

Formal dinners were a staple of upper-class life in big cities. As a member of the Kepler Clan, Sorin had attended many such events and, therefore, knew most of what was expected of him as the host.

Sorin didn't have the same financial ability he used to have, but that didn't stop him from offering his best. His friends deserved no less than his best. A symphony of smells currently filled the Kepler Manor. Percival and Clarice were taking turns in the kitchens while also making sure that the entire house was clean and essentials like mana lamps, tea, and alcohol were fully stocked.

There wasn't much for Sorin to do as the head of the household. Usually, it would fall to him to study his guests and their habits and create a plan on how to keep everyone entertained. Still, since only four guests would be in attendance, this step could be omitted in favor of cleaning up.

A hot bath was precisely what Sorin needed to unwind. He washed his hair and toweled off before donning a white cotton shirt and navy wool pants. These were freshly pressed, courtesy of Percival.

He finished the outfit off with a pair of snake leather shoes, a navy tie, and silver serpentine cufflinks that matched the silver serpentine buckle on his snake leather belt. Unsurprisingly, his family was big on snakes and snake paraphernalia.

Come on, Sorin, pull yourself together, thought Sorin as he oiled his hair. *It's only been three years since you've done something like this. You're a natural. All the people trying to suck up to you in the past said so multiple times.* Once his hair was tidied, he applied a faint mist of cologne. *Just strong enough to make a statement but not strong enough to offend.*

Since Percival and Clarice were busy, it fell to Sorin to groom Lorimer. The rat had been bathed in the morning and had not gone out to the sewers, so Sorin applied a double dose of cologne to the rat, dressed him in a custom suit shirt combo he'd commissioned with a local tailor, and then finished off the ensemble with a tiny bow tie fastened with a silver serpentine clip that matched Sorin's.

"I hope you can be on your best behavior tonight, Lorimer," said Sorin as he adjusted his tie. "If you cause a scene, I'll never tolerate you at such events again. And you know what that means, don't you? It means you'll miss out on your share of expensive food." Said food was going to cost him thirty-two gold coins for a single meal. That didn't even include the cost of wine, whisky, and other drinks, in addition to all the time that was spent preparing.

It was just past five when the first guest arrived. Sorin personally opened the door to welcome Stephan with a firm handshake and half-hug. "I'm glad you could make it," said Sorin, looking the man up and down. "Nice suit. I didn't realize they made them in your size."

Stephan chuckled as he handed his coat to Percival, who was shadowing Sorin. "They're a hassle because I need to get them tailor-made every time I break through. Still, I find it's well worth the trouble. Your expression alone is justification enough for the expense."

"Pardon Mr. Kepler for his rudeness, but would you like something to drink?" Percival asked Stephan. "And please, let's get you out of the cold and into the sitting room."

Sorin escorted Stephan to the living room and gestured to an entire three-person couch. The large man took up half the couch just by himself. He accepted a drink that Percival stealthily placed on a glass coffee table and downed the entire contents before letting out a satisfied sigh.

"Now that hit the spot," said Stephan. "Is this Dalwig?"

"Aged 30 years," said Sorin. He took a sip from his glass and grimaced. "Unfortunately, I don't believe they make alcohol that can affect me anymore. There are advantages and disadvantages to every cultivation method."

Stephan chuckled. "At least you can drink everyone under the table with no effort. And if you don't know them well, you can pretend to be drunk. It's great for information-gathering. Speaking of which..." His ears twitched, then his nose. "I think I smell Lawrence. Dead gods, I think he dressed up. I think he *shaved.*"

Sorin opened the door to find a charming and youthful man grinning from ear to ear. "Stephan was right," said Sorin, ushering him in. "You're practically unrecognizable."

"It's your fault for holding a formal event," said Lawrence, tossing his coat to the nimble Percival. "Do we do the heavy drinking now or after dinner?"

"I believe I'll be teaching you a lesson after the fine meal Sorin's cooks have prepared," Stephan said as Lawrence took a seat. "But feel free to warm up. I'll match you, drink for drink."

Lawrence sat down with uncharacteristic grace and requested wine when Percival asked him for his drink of choice. "Is this Pinot du Lac? Their 467 vintage? It's definitely one of their better years."

"I didn't realize one of Sorin's companions was a man who knew his wine," said Percival. "Perhaps we can discuss the topic a little later?"

"As long as there's wine to drink, I'm happy to chat on the subject," said Lawrence. "What? I *am* capable of refined behavior."

"I didn't say anything," said Stephan. "But I believe Sorin is completely shocked by this revelation."

"I thought your father was an adventurer," said Sorin. "Sorry, but it doesn't quite match the stereotype."

"Adventurers can do non-adventuring things," said Lawrence defensively. "He was quite the social butterfly, you know. As a result, not many people dared cause trouble for him."

"I heard it was because he had a great deal of blackmail on important figures," said Stephan. "I mean, am I wrong? Should I fire my informants?"

Lawrence cleared his throat uncomfortably. "I'm sure there were many reasons. Ah, our two stragglers are at the door." He pounced on the opportunity to change the topic.

"It's exactly quarter after five," said Sorin, checking the old clock in a corner of the living room. "It seems Miss Daphne took my warning about punctuality to heart." He opened the door to find a man wearing a simple suit, Gareth, and a shivering lady in a flimsy dress, Daphne.

"Have you never heard of dressing for the weather?" asked Sorin, ushering them in and shutting the door. "Or maybe you thought yourself immune to cold given your vast and mighty powers?"

"I offered her my coat, but she refused," said Gareth. "Though by then, we were almost here, so I can't blame her for doubling down on her choice of dress."

"I learned a new spell that was *supposed* to stop all this nonsense," said Daphne through chattering teeth. "It's called Fire Within, a Tier 0 spell. Whoever made it was apparently exaggerating the weather protection properties it provided. If he weren't already dead, I'd burn his house down."

"I've always been a fan of the saying dress for the weather, but prepare for the storms," said Gareth, handing his coat to Percival. "Feel free to borrow my coat on the way back."

"That won't be necessary," said Percival to Gareth. "We have spare coats in case of such mishaps, and Miss Phillips is welcome to one or even two of them to see her home safely."

"I'm sure it's just a problem with the fine-tuning," Daphne grumbled. "But I'll bother you for a large cup of tea. Five spoons of sugar. And yes, I'm sure."

"Tea?" asked Sorin, escorting them into the sitting room. "I thought you and the other mages were committed to coffee."

"It's actually quite a contentious topic, similar to the spear versus needle debate," said Daphne as she accepted a hot drink and held it in her hands to thaw them. "There's free 'coffee' in the café at the Mages Guild, but they'll allow substitution with common brands of tea if you ask for it. Wait, is that *Lorimer?* He's adorable!"

The rat had just skittered down the stairs and joined them, completing their party. He even had a small couch, which Percival made for him one day prior. It was the only piece of furniture he *didn't* gnaw on, much to Percival's and Clarice's chagrin.

Lorimer squeaked loudly at Percival, and the butler immediately brought him a cup of coffee. "You can understand him?" asked Sorin, surprised. "I thought you just asked him yes or no questions to communicate."

"We've built a certain rapport over time, and I, therefore, understand a few polite requests," Percival replied. "But they have to be *polite* requests, understand. Made with good timing and with all the best intentions." Lorimer squeaked an affirmative, and the butler answered his squeaks with a warm smile. "By the way, dinner is almost ready. Shall we move into the dining room at your convenience?"

"We'll stay here for another quarter-hour to give Daphne time to warm up," replied Sorin.

"Very good," said Percival. "I'll coordinate with Clarice to set up the silverware and finish the remaining dishes."

The group made small talk as Daphne sipped on her hot drink. Color soon returned to her face. As a mage, she had much less endurance and vitality than other cultivators and, therefore, took much time to stop shivering.

Sorin took the opportunity to evaluate his companions from a social standpoint. Lawrence was obviously middle-class with a decent education, while Daphne was from a wealthy family, as shown by her knowledge of etiquette, the approximate value of her dress, as well as her attendance at classes at the Mages Guild for ten years.

Gareth, on the other hand, was an unknown to Sorin. He was a silent and taciturn man who didn't like to embellish. It was, therefore, difficult to know whether his conservative suit was well-worn due to frequent attendance at similar social events or if it was something second-hand or a hand-me-down that he wore with a grace that belied his status.

Once Daphne finished warming up, they moved into the dining room, where Clarice was currently cutting into a roast of cured black-flame pork. A three-foot roasted shimmer fish lay at the center of the table, alongside pan-fried squash, a corn and pork paté, and a salad so fresh it defied the cold weather that would soon sweep through the outpost.

Percival served them each a glass of red wine and proceeded to hover around the table. "A slice of shimmer fish, please," Lawrence instructed Clarice when she moved on to cutting up the roasted fish.

"I think it should be ladies first," said Stephan. "What would you like, Daphne? Ignore this rude rogue."

"I'll take some cured pork, thank you very much," said Daphne. "Unless Lawrence insists on gender equality?"

"You guys always team up on me," Lawrence grumbled. "Whatever. I don't care. I'll eat last."

Sorin helped himself to a few side dishes as he waited for the main dishes to be served. He looked to Lorimer as he accepted a thick slice of fish and noted that the rat had been given a table with an assortment of delicacies.

I don't think there's ever been such a pampered rat in the history of Pandora, thought Sorin as he dug into his meal. The fish had a slightly metallic taste thanks to the mineral-rich waters it grew in. It was slightly poisonous for commoners, but cultivators could eat as much as they liked.

"I'm thrilled to finally have you all at my place," said Sorin, raising a glass of wine. "I wish I could host you all in my hometown with all the pomp and splendor I once could muster, but times have changed. This is the best I have to offer, and while it's far from enough, I hope you can accept it.

"As many of you know, it's customary to hold toast at the beginning of the meal. I'll keep this toast simple and offer it to friendship, because we've become more than just teammates now. If you ever need help, I won't hesitate to walk on sharp glass and through searing flames to assist you. You can consider whatever is mine as yours."

They each took a sip of their wine and turned to Stephan, the leader of their party. "I'm not sure I can top a toast like that, but so I'll aim for second best. Here's to the continued success of the team: 'We Don't Need a Life Mage.' May our slogan ring true, from Bloodwood Forest all the way to Mount Olympus."

"To wealth and glory," said Gareth, raising his glass next.

"To wonderful stories," said Daphne, issuing the next toast. "And to the success of the book series I just signed, based on our adventures."

"You signed a book deal?" exclaimed Lawrence. "Without telling us? Where's my cut? Oh, wait, it's my turn. To see all the pretty things, to robbing tombs—I mean, to *archeology*—and all that other fun stuff. Yeah, you know what I'm talking about."

"You're not using our names, are you?" Stephan asked Daphne when everyone set their glasses down.

"Of course not," said Daphne. "Most of our names are fine, but who would use Lawrence in a storybook? Honestly."

"Then there's no problem," said Stephan. "Don't let Lawrence badger you for a cut of the profits. You're a mage, and you need all the gold you can get your grubby little hands on."

"Tell me about it," muttered Daphne. "The Mages Guild is claiming partial ownership of the manuscript."

"On what grounds?" asked Sorin.

"The guild publication rules," said Daphne. "But that rule was clearly made for spells and research papers!"

"I'm honestly not surprised," said Sorin, who'd learned of the Mages Guild's shameless money-earning methods firsthand. "Lorimer, do you have anything else to add?" The rat froze and then issued a series of loud squeaks. "He says he's delighted to have such fine companions and hopes that you'll all spare some demon cores for a pitiful and starved rat. Hey, wait, I don't starve you, Lorimer. I feed you as much as I can and according to merit. The reason you don't eat well is because you keep getting in trouble."

"A rat after my own heart," said Lawrence with a sigh. "Why don't you transfer your contract over to me, Little Lorimer? I'll treat you much better than he does."

Lorimer replied with a few squeaks, and when Lawrence asked for a translation, Sorin did so honestly. "He says you aren't worthy. Sorry, Lawrence, but this rat has standards."

60

HERO MEDAL

Sorin wasn't a fan of wine. It was sweet yet tart and had complex flavors that aficionados were insistent existed but that he'd never been able to personally taste.

As a result, Sorin liked more potent drinks like whisky and all its regional variants. Near Bloodwood Forest, the farmers grew rye, so Sorin had adopted rye whisky as his drink of choice.

Stephan seemed to have similar tastes because he was already on his tenth glass of rye whisky. Thankfully, he knew moderation and didn't even attempt to test his robust constitution. "I hear the Adventurers Guild is finally making preparations for the demon tide," the adventurer casually brought up amidst lighter conversation. "I believe they'll be conscripting us any time now."

"Conscripting?" asked Lawrence. "Wait, my old man said I'd definitely be participating in the outpost's defense, but I never expected conscription was the reason why."

"It's not the same as joining the military," Stephan assured him. "There are enough adventurers that we only have to patrol for three days in any given week and remain on call for the rest of it. And if you see battle, you get a bit of a break before your next shift—assuming it's not all hands on deck for the final push."

Like big cities, outposts had their problems. Summer was the domain of Violence, and according to Violence's nature, it would always send demons with their last burst of energy before they entered a deep slumber for the winter.

As for the winter… well, Sorin didn't dwell on that. His own mana and that of his companions were relatively free of corruption. The Madness that accompanied the chill winter winds would be of little concern to them.

"I think it's best if we all take extra precautions during the demon tide," said Sorin, swirling his glass of whisky and then drinking it down in a single gulp. "I've seen far too many adventurers and soldiers die from corruption and demonic wounds. I don't want to see my friends to suffer a similar fate."

"I think our chances of surviving are pretty good," said Gareth. "According to my father, adventurers are more likely to survive than rank-and-file soldiers. Our team is also pretty high-tier compared to the average adventuring team."

"Your father would know," said Stephan with a sigh. "Nighthawks are privy to a lot of information compared to other people."

"Nighthawks?" asked Sorin.

"It's a small town, so it's not surprising that you don't know," said Gareth. "Nighthawks are sort of like policemen, but for cultivators. They're especially active in the winter. Big cities have them too, but they usually get sent out when the police force can't handle something."

"We're all on the upper end of strength for one-star adventurers," Stephan assured them. "But as everyone is likely aware, increasing our strength in the next two weeks is of paramount importance. There's no need to skimp on money in that aspect. There will be plenty of money to be made during the demon tide."

Gareth sighed. "If only we had one more month. Then I could break through to the tenth stage of Blood-Thickening and obtain a large increase in strength." He, Lawrence, and Daphne all had much thicker auras than when they'd arrived at the outpost. They'd clearly all taken the chance to break through to the ninth stage of Blood-Thickening.

"I'm personally in no hurry to break through," said Daphne.

"And why is that?" asked Gareth.

Daphne shrugged. "If the strongest and best-connected person in our party isn't in a hurry to break through, why should we be? Isn't that right, Mr. Hero?"

Stephan stiffened at her words. "Who told you?"

Daphne shrugged. "I heard the vice guild master of the Mages Guild mention a Hero Medal being awarded. I didn't know if it was you who got it, but your reaction confirms it."

Stephan winced. "I guess there's no hiding it." He took out a silver badge engraved with a mountain. Atop the mountain were twelve circles joined together in a semicircle. It was the symbol of Olympia, where the Pandoran government was based.

"A Hero Medal?" asked Lawrence. "What did you do to deserve something like that? We went to the ruins and explored them just like you did."

Stephan shrugged. "I'm afraid I can't speak of it. Not just because my family would forbid it but because they make you swear not to tell anyone during the conferment ceremony. As for Daphne's suggestion that you all not advance... I'm of the same opinion. Advancing to the tenth stage of Blood-Thickening solidifies your foundation, making further improvements more difficult."

"What other improvements can even be made in the Blood-Thickening Realm?" asked Lawrence, only for Gareth to elbow him. "What?"

"When someone from a major family gives you vague hints, there's often a good reason," said Gareth. "Or so my father always says."

"I think I have some idea of what Stephan is talking about," said Sorin. "But first, I was wondering if I could check each of your conditions." He looked around and casually took note of Percival's position. "I've made progress with the meridian-opening method, but there are some things I'd like to verify."

Lawrence sighed and held out his arm. "Go ahead. I'm used to it." Sorin didn't stand on ceremony and directly grabbed his wrist and inserted his spiritual strength.

He's the same as me, thought Sorin, inspecting the silver-sealed Conception Vessel. *Except he's only unlocked three seals out of twenty-four. Aside from that, his blocked extraordinary meridians are showing signs of loosening up.* He then moved on to Daphne and Gareth and confirmed similar developments. *Daphne has unlocked four seals, while Gareth has only unlocked two. Their blocked extraordinary meridians also show signs of opening.*

"Do you mind if I take a look?" Sorin asked Stephan.

"Not at all," said Stephan with a knowing smile. Sorin injected his spiritual strength into the man's giant body and experienced something rare: repulsion.

Usually, Sorin would stop here, but since he'd obtained his friend's permission, he drilled his spiritual force deeper into the man's body to inspect his meridians. *It's like I thought. The silver seals are entirely gone. What should have required a tincture and medical treatment was accomplished through other means.*

"Your condition is good," said Sorin, pulling his hand back. "In fact, your sixth extraordinary meridian has shown slight signs of loosening."

"Really?" asked Stephan. "Why can't I sense anything?"

"It's normal for a physician to be more aware of a patient's body," said Sorin. "On a completely unrelated note, you suddenly transformed in the battle against the Minotaur. Your beastshift form has evolved somehow."

"That's right," confirmed Stephan. "I can now shift into an Arctic Rune Bear. It's a much larger creature than a brown bear. I'd imagine it wouldn't be impossible for me to tackle a weaker two-star demon one-on-one now."

"Why didn't you use that technique earlier?" asked Lawrence. "That Minotaur nearly cut me in two."

Once again, Gareth elbowed him. "What?"

"Read between the lines, will you?" said Gareth.

"Fine," said Lawrence. "Are you at least going to tell us what perks a Hero Medal has?"

"Sure," said Stephan. "There are plenty. Fr one, the medal itself has a small storage space. Also, I get a 10 percent discount at the Alchemists Guild, Mages Guild, and Adventurers Guild. Most shops will give you a 5 percent discount, directly subsidized by the government.

"I'm not sure about the rest of the Medical Association, but my Kepler Clan pays attention to Heroes," Sorin divulged. "There are certain treatments that are reserved for Heroes and influential figures. For example, my clan's meridian-opening treatment." Of course, only the most distinguished figures would qualify to have their extraordinary meridians opened.

"Similarly, my York Clan will adopt Heroes into the family on a regular basis," said Stephan. "They're sought-after individuals wherever they go. I therefore hope that each of you will fight hard and try to distinguish yourselves during the demon tide."

"I just recalled another matter," said Sorin. "Opening additional meridians gets challenging after one's foundation solidifies. I can't do so right now, but I hope to make progress in the next two weeks and aid everyone in opening at least one or two more extraordinary meridians."

"You have such knowledge?" asked Stephan, reevaluating Sorin. While they'd been playing a game this whole time, informing their team of certain things in a roundabout manner, Sorin had never exposed his status in the Kepler Clan.

"My name *is* Sorin Abberjay Kepler," Sorin said to Stephan.

"Interesting," said Stephan. "I think I finally understand why Marcus is causing so much trouble for you."

"Can anyone please fill me in on what's going on?" asked Lawrence. "For the love of Hope, don't elbow me again; my brittle bones can't take it, Gareth."

"Let's just say that not every member of the Kepler Clan is qualified to learn such techniques," Sorin said to Lawrence. Naturally, he didn't tell Lawrence that he wasn't one of these people. His father had passed away before he'd been taught, and the elders had not seen it fit to instruct him on the matter after his cultivation had been crippled.

At the same time, Sorin carefully evaluated Percival's behavior. *He looks composed, but the shaking in his hands and his hesitant actions show that my words shocked him,* thought Sorin. *Will he report my words back to Marcus as I intend him to?*

"Every major clan has secrets that they only pass along to their core members," Stephan added. "Techniques related to extraordinary meridians are such secrets. Each major clan has their own way of going about it, but the Kepler Clan distinguishes itself in that regard. Their way is the least risky."

Sorin had accomplished his goal for the conversation, so he moved things along. "Apart from the demon tide, what else is new?"

"The lumberjacks are pulling back, and so are the farmers," said Gareth. "I expect there will be an abundance of temporary shelters that need to be built. Also, there's a shortage of arrows and bows. If anyone wants to make a quick buck, it's not a bad time to enter Bloodwood Forest to escort lumberjacks."

"I don't have much news," said Lawrence.

Stephan snorted. "As if anyone would believe that."

"Well, sorry if I haven't been doing as much casual reconnaissance as I usually do," said Lawrence. "I've been looking into some matters for Sorin. It's up to him if he wants me to tell everyone else about it."

"Did you find anything interesting?" asked Sorin.

"Nothing," said Lawrence in disappointment. "The guy's too clean. He's practically a saint."

"Who's a saint?" asked Daphne. "Give me a name, and I'll have someone scry out their dirty secrets."

"If you want to scry a two-star physician, be my guest," said Lawrence. "In case it's not obvious, the person I'm talking about is Marcus Kepler." Percival, who'd been pouring Stephan another drink, nearly fumbled the bottle.

"What do you mean, he's too clean?" asked Sorin.

"Marcus is perfect," said Lawrence. "He never gets into trouble. He doesn't do anything underhanded or give out bribes. He even treats a lot of commoners free of charge. For a two-star physician to do something like that, isn't it unheard of? My old man once went to a big city to get someone to look at his leg, and he said they were crooks, the whole lot of them."

"He treats a lot of commoners?" asked Sorin, slightly interested. "That's common for one-star physicians but rare for two-star physicians. Their time is usually better spent teaching or improving their own skills.

"I thought someone was just embellishing things," Lawrence agreed. "But then I went to check it out and confirmed he does indeed treat a lot of commoners. The farmers are all getting prompt treatment, and even a lot of the hopeless cases near the temple have been seen, too. It makes no sense, given my intuition about his character."

"And what does your intuition say?" asked Sorin.

"He's a snake, obviously," said Lawrence. "No offense."

"None was taken," said Sorin. "I have a similar appraisal of the man. That's why I was surprised when he visited me the other day and gave me back my things. He's even getting me a designation at the Alchemists Guild."

"What designation?" asked Gareth.

"Apothecary," said Sorin. "Feel free to let me know what you need when I'm officially allowed to blend and sell poisons."

"Maybe you misunderstood him," suggested Stephan. "Family politics can be complicated."

Daphne snorted in response. "I guarantee that he's a bad apple."

"On what basis?" asked Stephan.

"On the basis of plot requirements," Daphne explained. "Virtually any development can be explained if you look at it from the angle of a storybook. Lawrence, you say he's clean, but didn't he intentionally hurt Sorin? He's nice, but isn't he being too showy about it? Something's obviously off. Just the fact that we're talking about it now is obviously some sort of foreshadowing."

"He *is* a Bone-Forging cultivator," said Gareth. "According to my father, most Bone-Forging cultivators are competitive since resources are scarce. Not just that, he's a two-star physician. Outposts don't normally get high-level physicians since it's more efficient to have people travel to cities."

"He also doesn't seem upset about it," said Daphne. "That alone is very suspicious."

Sorin agreed with her assessment, as ridiculous as her logic was. There were too many things that seemed too perfect. "Let's not talk about Marcus anymore," he said, changing the topic. "Why don't we talk about that local sports team?"

"We... we don't have a local sports team," said Lawrence.

"Oh," said Sorin. "My bad. I never did like sports, but it always seems to be something people like talking about."

"I'm more interested in that piano over there," said Daphne, pointing out an antique instrument in a corner of the room. "Does Percival know how to play? Or maybe Clarice?"

"I'm afraid Mr. Kepler is the only one capable of playing to adequate standards," said Percival, topping up her wine glass. "Though he loathes to inform people of this competency."

All eyes in the room settled on Sorin, who rolled his eyes. "This is exactly why I don't like telling people. I don't suppose you can all spare me and pretend you didn't hear him?"

"Nonsense," said Stephan. "Talents are meant to be shared."

Sorin let out a deep sigh but rose from his chair and walked over to the piano. It was a seventy-year-old grand piano that Percival tuned on a monthly basis.

He took a seat and began running through the many songs in his head. *A fugue would be appropriate,* he thought as his fingers started moving according to muscle memory. *Nothing too complicated. Just a hint of playfulness and inquiry.*

Sorin's mind wandered as music filled the room. He lost himself in the music he'd abandoned for the better part of three years.

It came surprisingly easily to him. Then again, how could it not? Almost a decade of forced lessons and sufficiently strict parents had worked the music into his bones. Even if his mind didn't remember the music, his fingers did.

He was so engrossed in the tune that he only realized he'd stopped playing a minute later. Tears stained his face, and he thanked hope that he was facing *away* from his friends.

Sorin used mana to wipe the tears away, then turned to his audience and bowed. "My apologies for the poor performance."

"That was... that was beautiful," said Lawrence. "Like one of those sound recordings you get in the shops—*ouch!*"

"Don't worry about Lawrence," said Stephan, who'd elbowed him. "I'll be sure to beat some manners into him."

"That's all right," said Sorin. "In fact, his words are high praise, as my meager talents aren't worthy of attention." He had known good musicians and was very aware of his limitations. At most, his talent could impress those not familiar with music.

"The hour is getting late," said Percival from the back of the room. "Moreover, I heard there might be a thunderstorm tonight."

It was a polite way of saying that the party was over. Percival had obviously noticed Sorin's sour mood and was seeking to extricate him from this embarrassing situation.

"There's no need," said Sorin. "We have rooms aplenty in the house. I'll have a whisky, Percival. A double, if you could."

"Mr. Kepler..."

"There's no need to fuss, Percival," Sorin insisted. "There are no strangers here. I couldn't ask for better company."

61

INVESTIGATION

The week following the banquet was uneventful, and Sorin spent most of it learning from the spell books he'd rented from the Mages Guild. Threading the Spear was easy enough at lower levels but learning the 'spear spray' portion of the spell necessitated a practice room with sufficiently durable walls and mannequins.

In the end, Sorin rented a one-star training room for 50 gold per day. The training room contained a total of five training dummies, which allowed him to train Threading the Spear and Veridian Smoke Bomb while simultaneously maintaining Anti-Mage's Blade and Ophidian Eye. The training dummies lasted until he ran out of mana and regenerated by the time he finished his recovery.

Threading the Spear was a tricky spell due to its flexibility. Once one locked in their required size, however—and the suggested size was six feet long and one inch wide—using it became very easy. Sorin naturally assigned acidic mana to the needle spray portion of the spell, but he also generated templates for paralytic poison attacks using one to three needles.

Veridian Smoke Bomb was best suited to acid attacks and paralytic attacks. The method of delivery was starkly different for each case. When used with acid, Veridian Smoke Bomb aerosolized the mana used.

It enhanced its ability to stick to skin, clothes, and armor. The paralytic version, on the other hand, gasified the poisonous mana to make it easier for living creatures to breathe in.

Sorin burned through 150 gold before he was sufficiently familiar with all four spells, reinforcing his theory that only rich people could become successful mages.

It was late in the evening, nearly morning for some early risers. Sorin's eyes were tired from reading, but the helpful caffeine infusion from a near-limitless supply of tea kept his mind and body in peak condition.

The room was dimly lit by candlelight, as mana lamps were hard on the eyes and just didn't feel *right* to Sorin, who enjoyed reading yellowing pages from dusty old tomes.

Candlelight wasn't an optimal lighting source. Shadows danced in the room as the candles flickered, elongating and shortening unpredictably. They were very unlike the slow-moving shadow that was creeping ever closer to Sorin's desk, a shadow he pointedly ignored until it was almost upon him.

"Lawrence, you really need to work on your dramatic entrances," said Sorin, taking a sip from his teacup. "Also, why would you ever sneak up in front of me instead of behind me? Couldn't you just appear over my shoulder and slam a book down on my desk or something?"

"I was going to do that, but then I remembered that you could melt my face off in three seconds flat," said Lawrence, appearing from the shadows. "Also, are we going to do this or not? We don't have a huge opening if we want to avoid the guards."

"Give me a minute to change," said Sorin. "And Lorimer? Go to the clinic and scout things out for us ahead of time." The bleary-eyed rat had been resting in a small bed just beside the office window. He squeaked an affirmative and lazily launched himself on the windowsill before pushing through a crack of an opening and scrambling down the house's brick siding.

Sorin didn't have a thief's getup like Lawrence. He *did* have dark clothes, however, courtesy of Percival, for potential clandestine outings.

He blended in perfectly with the nigh-total darkness found in the market districts past ten o'clock. Only the occasional lamp post and guard light broke up the monotonous nightscape that clung to the Growing Branches Community Clinic like a wet blanket.

"This is it," said Lawrence to Sorin. "Your last chance to turn around and *not* antagonize a two-star physician."

"He's an arrogant fellow, so he'll at most have some recording treasures set up inside the clinic," said Sorin. "Lorimer? Get in there and do your thing."

Lorimer protested Sorin's tyranny but relented when the former physician tossed out a few demon cores. The rat scurried into the clinic, then opened a window five minutes later to indicate the coast was clear.

Sorin followed Lawrence through the window and looked around. The clinic was unrecognizable compared to when he'd last entered. Several more beds had been set up, and bookshelves had been taken down in favor of office space for Marcus, a two-star physician, and his five one-star residents.

"The place is a lot smaller than I remember," said Lawrence. "The office, I understand, but what's that room over there?"

"A lab, I imagine," said Sorin, leafing through the contents of the sole medical bookshelf in the room. They contained standard medical reference books. Three tomes were missing, and a note had been left behind by Gabriella stating that she was borrowing the books for personal study. This reinforced Marcus's claim that she was not being mistreated.

"That animal," said Lawrence, picking up the note. "How *dare* he be nice? He's supposed to be cold and cruel and have a target painted on his face. Ideally, he should be a lot uglier, too."

"Your sarcasm is noted," said Sorin. "Now help me look for incriminating evidence."

"And what exactly am I looking for?" asked Lawrence.

"I don't know," said Sorin. "Data? Purchasing records? Things with detailed information so I don't need to leaf through individual cases? And *please* remember how things are before you take them."

While Lawrence busied himself in Marcus's office, Sorin headed over to the new laboratory. The small medical mixing room had been torn down to accommodate five complete sets of one-star laboratory equipment, including earth flame spell circles, ventilation runes, and safe storage for medicinal ingredients.

Judging by the residual smells, this lab was used just yester-day, thought Sorin. *These equipment sets all smell slightly of cleaning agents, which means that all five sets were used.*

There were also a large number of half-open boxes containing poisons. Many of their contents were depleted, further evidence of Marcus's claim that they were indeed using the poisons they'd obtained from the Alchemists Guild.

Sorin had a great need for these poisons, but he held back from taking them. Instead, he took note of their contents to confirm some initial guesses. *Steelblood Amaranth, Cold Blood extract, Blood Rush Ginseng... The only commonality between these poisons is that they primarily affect the blood and mana circulation systems.*

Six boxes stood out to Sorin. This was because they were critical ingredients for concocting the meridian-clearing tinctures he'd obtained from Sirius's research notes. *But they're not placed together, and I don't see any Manabane Poisons. This indicates that they're not concocting a finished product but experimenting with different mixtures.*

Was the Sovinger branch attempting to replicate the Abberjay branch's secret medicinal formula? There was evidence to suggest this, but it was far from conclusive. He would need clearer proof in order to confirm Marcus's motives.

"I found some purchasing lists," Lawrence called out. "I also found a case summary list."

Sorin took one last look at the poisons before leaving the alchemy workshop. "Let me take a look," said Sorin, grabbing the purchasing list first. He confirmed that large quantities of one-star poisons were getting shipped in from Dustone to replenish the lab's stores.

He then inspected the case summary list with much greater scrutiny than the purchasing list. Unfortunately, it wasn't easy to make out anything from the scattered data points. Even if Marcus was performing meridian-opening trials, they were mixed in with various other cases.

One thing Sorin noted was that the amount of medicine used was inconsistent with the amount of medicine ordered. *Not* by a large margin, but enough that medical trials weren't off the table. Moreover, there are no records of the poisons in the laboratory ever being used, despite the large quantities ordered and the small quantities remaining.

"Put these back where you found them," said Sorin, handing the papers back to Lawrence. "We're leaving."

"Leaving?" asked Lawrence. "But we just got here."

Sorin shook his head. "We won't find anything, Lawrence. It seems I underestimated Marcus."

Inwardly, Sorin analyzed what he'd discovered. *This is clearly a case of research and development. Human experimentation may or may not be involved, as no data supports either situation. The only way I'll know for sure is by finding a notebook with test data.* Given the importance of these experiments, Marcus would either keep such a notebook in a secure laboratory or directly on his person.

Sorin didn't particularly care about the Sovinger branch trying to deduce the Abberjay branch's secret meridian-opening tinctures. He'd never agreed with keeping the method a tight secret, and neither had his father. Moreover, the secret formula had likely changed hands in the past few years. The Mockingjay branch oversaw the Kepler Clan now, and it was much more populous than Sorin's Abberjay branch, which only had 100 members and very little residual influence.

What *did* bother him, however, was the potential for human experimentation. Such things were ethically dubious even in the most reasonably argued cases. As a result, physicians were required to submit proposals for human experimentation to the Medical Association and obtain approval prior to conducting live trials.

The review process was even more stringent now than it had been twenty or thirty years ago. Recent improvements in animal cruelty laws had rendered most medical testing models obsolete, and the entire research community was scrambling to find a replacement.

Since Sorin had no proof, he decided to silently keep an eye on things. He also had an opening to exploit: Marcus had hinted that he would be willing to issue commissions to Sorin once he obtained his apothecary designation. In fact, Marcus might actively pursue the matter since it was entirely possible for Sorin to be privy to the secret meridian-opening formula—something Percival would confirm for Marcus very shortly.

Lawrence returned after 'tidying up' Marcus's office. "Unless he's super obsessive about cleanliness, he won't know we were ever here."

"Our tracks?" asked Sorin.

"Dusted," said Lawrence. "And Lorimer doesn't leave tracks for some reason. Good job, Lorimer." The rat squeaked as he climbed up Sorin's pant leg and scurried into his shirt pocket.

They left the clinic through the window and successfully evaded detection. The rogue went off to another part of town to continue his nighttime peeping. In contrast, Lorimer went straight towards the sewer entrance, only to be stopped by Sorin.

"Lorimer," Sorin said to the rat. "You're hiding something from me, aren't you?" The rat shook his head aggressively. "Fine. Then how do you explain the lack of footprints?" The rat hesitated before activating an ability. His fur blended in with the shadows, much like Lawrence did. "A stealth ability. That's very useful, but only if I know about it." The rat squeaked to protest his innocence. "You were looking to surprise me? I'm not a three-year-old, Lorimer. Keep this up, and I'll confiscate a part of your sewer earnings."

Dejected, the rat crawled over to the sewer grate and disappeared into the smelly darkness that was the outpost's underground. Sorin felt a *little* guilty about chewing the rat out but was convinced that a firm approach was best with tamed demons.

THE APOTHECARY

The following day, Sorin headed out to Sanderson's Leather Outfitting to retrieve his leather armor. The shop was empty except for the sole employee and proprietor of the shop, Mr. Sanderson. "An early riser, I see," said Mr. Sanderson. "Not like those good-for-nothing rich folk I'm used to dealing with. I take it you're here for your armor?"

"Lawrence said it would be ready by today," said Sorin. "I hope I'm not too early?"

"I have a habit of finishing things up the day before," said Mr. Sanderson. He reached beneath the counter to retrieve a footlong square package. "I'll trouble you to slip this beauty on so I can make the final adjustments."

Sorin went to the back dressing room and donned the armor. He felt an intimate connection to the armor the instant his skin made contact. *Is it because it's been drinking my blood?* thought Sorin as he tightened the belt straps until they were comfortably snug.

"Fits you like a glove, right?" said Mr. Sanderson as Sorin walked out. "But the legs are off. You're best off tightening them a little more." He bent down and yanked at the leather straps until the leggings felt uncomfortably tight.

"This feels… not right," said Sorin, bending down. To his surprise, however, the armor flexed along with him. "This is... this is *nice*. I might as well be wearing long underwear."

"The armor has a lot of flex to it." Mr. Sanderson nodded. "Actually, your arms could use tightening as well." He tightened the six straps in turn, then allowed Sorin to familiarize himself with the armor by swinging around his dagger. "Remember that feeling whenever you put it on. And don't forget to feed the thing a pint of blood every week when you're not out adventuring and getting hurt."

Sorin had no issues with this, as a pint of blood wasn't much for a Blood-Thickening cultivator. "Do you have any other advice for me? Maintenance routines I should perform?"

"There's no maintenance to speak of for Blood Drinker Armor," said Mr. Sanderson. "The blood lubricates the leather and keeps it supple. It's the same for the buckles. One thing to watch out for, though—it's weak to fire. Try not to get hit by a Fireball or something because it'll take twice as long to regenerate. Oh, and take this thing." He pulled out a small bundle from the package.

"A whip?" asked Sorin in surprise. "I don't remember ordering this."

"I had a bunch of scraps lying around and thought I'd throw it into the mix," said Mr. Sanderson. "Those mages are cheap bastards, but they ultimately agreed to link it with the Blood Drinker enchantment. You'll need to feed it, just like the armor. A tablespoon a week should do the trick."

Sorin accepted the whip and directly used Python Coil to test out its abilities. The whip wrapped around one of the wooden pillars supporting the building's roof but pulled it back when the wood started hissing and warping. "Apologies," said Sorin to Mr. Sanderson. "I'm used to using this technique with a mithril string. I didn't realize it would be so potent. Please have someone assess it and send me the bill."

"Don't worry about it," said Mr. Sanderson. "It's a small matter. I'll get Mr. Woodworth to take a look at it, and he'll make it good as new."

Sorin went to the back and peeled off his armor. "Any big plans for the day?" asked Mr. Sanderson as he emerged. "You can settle your bill now or arrange for installments."

"I'll pay right now," said Sorin, handing over 1,450 gold in coins and gold cards. "As for plans, I was going to stop by the Alchemists Guild. I have an appointment with Mr. Primrose."

"The apothecary?" asked Mr. Sanderson. "Makes sense, given your cultivation path."

"You know him?" asked Sorin.

"We've collaborated during a few demon tides when things got tough," said Mr. Sanderson. "Us support cultivators usually don't get involved, but when push comes to shove, we *are* Bone-Forging cultivators."

"So he's a Bone-Forging cultivator as well," said Sorin.

"One of three at the Alchemists Guild," said Mr. Sanderson. "Similarly, the Blacksmiths Guild, the Mages Guild, the Adventurers Guild, and the Governor's Manor also have three apiece."

They seem to maintain a specific number on purpose, thought Sorin. *Is it for balance reasons? Do they ship extras to the big cities?*

"Any tips on interacting with him?" asked Sorin. "What's Mr. Primrose like?"

"Jaded," said Mr. Sanderson. "Pragmatic. Hard-working. Likes raising insects."

"Insects?" asked Sorin.

"It's a poison thing, or so I'm told," said Mr. Sanderson. "He's a handsome man after my own heart, but he makes himself emotionally unavailable. A shame, really.

"The only advice that I can offer is to show interest but to keep your thoughts to yourself. The last thing you want to do is upset a poisoner. In terms of damage potential, he's probably in the top five of the entire city. Now, will you be taking this away yourself, or would you like it delivered?"

"Please send the armor over to the Kepler Manor," said Sorin, not wanting to be burdened with the package all day. "Is there a delivery fee?"

Mr. Sanderson shook his head. "It's included with your purchase. It should get there before dinner time—let me know if it doesn't."

"I'll be sure to come by if I need anything else," said Sorin.

"Don't be a stranger," said Mr. Sanderson. "Especially if you find some more premium materials for me to work with!"

The Alchemists Guild, like the Mages Guild, was located close to the town's central square. It wasn't as grand as the Mages Guild, as it occupied only a single city block. Still, it was no less critical to cultivators and non-cultivators alike.

A steady stream of customers entered the guild every day to purchase purification, healing, and mana potions. The guild also sold a considerable number of Blood-Thickening Potions to the city's cultivators, an essential resource for cultivators looking to increase their cultivation realms.

The guild's storefront was much less busy than usual due to the impending demon tide. News that the guild was no longer producing non-healing and non-mana potions had spread. Most cultivators were forced to put their cultivation on hold and instead prepare for battle.

There were roughly a thousand combat-ready cultivators in the outpost. This figure did not include the city's supporting cultivators, which numbered nearly 1,500. To Sorin's knowledge, there were only twenty official alchemists in the city to support all these cultivators. This included the three Bone-Forging alchemists that Mr. Sanderson had mentioned.

Sorin skipped Henry's storefront and directly proceeded to the guild's reception, where customers could meet with alchemists for custom orders. "Can I help you?" asked the receptionist, barely looking up from an alchemy textbook.

"I have an appointment with Mr. Primrose in five minutes," said Sorin.

The receptionist shook when he mentioned the name. "Apothecary Primrose, you say? He's on the second floor, Workshop 22. You... you don't need someone to lead you there, do you?" She seemed highly reluctant to go anywhere near the apothecary's workshop.

"That won't be necessary," said Sorin. "I know my way around."

The receptionist let out a sigh of relief but leaned over to issue him a friendly warning. "Be sure to keep your questions short and your comments to yourself. And if you smell anything funny or out of the ordinary, don't run. If he wants to kill you, no one in the outpost will be able to save you."

Sorin made his way up the building's familiar stone steps. The workshops were organized in such a manner that each one had a window as an emergency exit. At the center of the building's second floor stood several vats of powder. These powders were mostly non-reactive and could be used to extinguish even magical fires.

Workshop 22 was the furthest workshop from the entrance. It was also separated from the other workshops via thick stone double walls. Warning signs were plastered all over the door, along with a giant list of rules that needed to be followed. This included the golden rule: no eating or drinking in the laboratory.

The door took a great deal of strength to open and automatically slammed shut once Sorin was inside. The workshop was much larger than the ones he was used to but only had one occupant.

Mr. Primrose was a tidy man. He was tall and thin and wore black pants with a white cotton shirt that he rolled up past his elbows. He had long black hair that he kept tied up in a ponytail and a pair of circular spectacles that sat too far up his thin nose. Sorin immediately recognized him as the representative from the Alchemists Guild who had witnessed the matter with Orpheus at the Adventurers Guild.

"Mr. Sorin Kepler, I presume," said the man, not bothering to turn around. The man was standing near a fume hood, where he was busy dripping drops of blue liquid into a beaker of glowing green liquid. "Formerly a one-star physician. Currently a poison cultivator and adventurer. Training includes rudimentary alchemy and laboratory skills. Due to political machinations within the Kepler Clan, he is prohibited from obtaining the 'alchemist' designation without prior approval from the

Kepler Clan. The apothecary designation is acceptable, pending a quali-fied assessment."

"Looks like they've got an extensive dossier on me," said Sorin.

"A necessity when dealing with potential recruits into the ranks of my lowly profession," said Mr. Primrose. "After all, we wouldn't want a person with criminal tendencies learning to make poisons on a large scale, would we?"

"I suppose not," agreed Sorin.

"Then let's not waste time and get on with it," said Mr. Primrose, still not looking up. "Tell me - If an individual were to cook an ash swamp toad and stew it with tomatoes on the vine and caramelized onions before consuming it, what harm might you expect to befall him?" White snowflake-like precipitates appeared in the green beaker under the fume hood. Though they seemed harmless, Sorin could tell that this was the actual poison being concocted by the two-star apothecary.

"Though I can't see why anyone would ever do such a thing, can I ask some questions first?" asked Sorin.

"You may," said the man.

"Was any salt added to the stew?" asked Sorin. "Were any spices, herbs, or fragrant roots added to the mix?"

"Standard table salt, non-iodized," said the man, taking the beaker over to a filter flask. He used his mana to form a vacuum that sucked away the liquid and began drying the white snowflakes. "Also, he added thyme, red ginger, and garlic. Oh, and some beef stock because he heard frog meat wasn't delicious."

Sorin quickly discarded what information wasn't relevant and kept what was. "Then there are several possibilities," said Sorin. "The first possibility is death within 5 seconds, caused by seizing of the heart and immediate loss of blood circulation to the brain.

"The second possibility is that in the preparation process, he wisely removed the internal organs and washed the frog meat, leaving only paralytic poisons to leach into the stew. In this case, he'd fall over, stiff as a board, but awaken the following day. That was all assuming he didn't suffer head trauma or anything similar on the way down.

"The third possibility is that the red ginger you described isn't the common red ginger used in cooking, but the red ginger alchemists use in creating antidotes. In this case, there are two outcomes. First, the heart seizure will be delayed and become a standard heart attack. It's possible to survive with the help of a life mage or a physician's intervention. As for the paralytic effect, it would be completely neutralized by the red ginger. If the frog had its innards removed and the medicinal red ginger was used, the stew would be a marvelous, albeit tasteless, meal made with over 200 gold of medicinal ingredients."

"Anything else?" asked the man.

"There's nothing else unless I've missed other factors related to the water, the person's general health, and contact with other substances," said Sorin. "This is what I would answer if a physician requested a consultation."

THANKLESS BUT LUCRATIVE

Mr. Primrose took his time in evaluating Sorin's answer. The white snowflake-like powder was now fully dehydrated, so the man peeled off a sheet of filter paper from the filter flask's funnel, then carefully knocked the dry contents into a pouch, which he weighed and labeled before placing on a shelf. He then took a seat by the waist-height lab bench and gestured for Sorin to do the same.

"What if you were wrong?" Mr. Primrose quizzed. "What treatment would you recommend to guarantee success in eliminating the poison from the patient's body?"

"There are many treatment options," said Sorin. "And to my knowledge, no treatment would guarantee success. Moreover, you only asked about the poison. I can only recommend something with further knowledge of the patient's situation or other symptoms.

"More to the point, is this a question of treatment methods or the symptoms? Because symptoms were what you inquired about, not treatment options. I could use the symptoms and descriptions to recognize the poisons utilized and even formulate an antidote. Still, I'm afraid this would do little good for the patient by the time a physician realized what was going on."

"Well said," said Mr. Primrose with a tight smile. "By the time the physician came to us for help, it would be too late. Because that's what we do, Mr. Kepler: We study poisons to better understand them and, therefore, better assist professionals in their work. This includes physicians. This includes the Governor's Manor. This includes the Adventurers Guild.

"We are *not* assassins. We do not sell poisons to the unqualified. We do not formulate cure-alls. We do not diagnose patients. Full stop.

"Apothecaries only fill out approved orders to make a living. This includes orders or consultations requested by a physician's official prescription and those vetted by the Alchemists Guild. Private dealings are strictly prohibited. The only exceptions that can be made in your case are poisons for self-defense and to support your profession. You can brew poisons for you and your teammates, but no one else. Understood?"

"Understood," said Sorin, realizing that he'd barely passed the man's test. There was no need to question Sorin's knowledge of poison because, as a physician, half his education revolved around the subject.

"Your relationship with the Medical Association and your relatives doesn't interest me one whit," said the man, walking up to a desk. He opened a small wooden drawer, revealing an emblem that resembled an alchemist's emblem, except that it had a slightly green tinge and had a snake wrapped around the cauldron, baring its fangs. He tossed the emblem to Sorin. "I am merely instructing you on the rules of our profession absent any other factors.

"If you one day regained your status as a physician, unlikely as that is given their views on poison users, you will be able to skip several steps. But the *rules* will not change.

"I understand," Sorin reiterated. "I will hold myself to the highest of standards and adhere to the rules of the apothecary profession."

Mr. Primrose nodded. "That covers most of it. You may use this workshop if you keep it clean. You may *only* use this workshop in the guild, as it is the only one that is properly equipped to deal with poisonous explosions or other incidents, up to and including two-star poisons. Do you have an earth flame?"

"I do," said Sorin. "Though he *is* a living creature. Will that be a problem?"

"A beast flame," said Mr. Primrose. "How interesting. No, it won't be a problem as long as he abides by the rules of the laboratory." He then gestured to a board where several papers were pinned. The board was separated into two sections. The one-star section was the largest of the two. "There is great demand for poisons of late, so feel free to take on any commissions you are capable of concocting. Feel free to read any books you see in the reference library. You may also take on private commissions directly from physicians or consult with physicians on cases. However, these must be reported to the Alchemists Guild for due diligence."

"May I perform experiments?" asked Sorin.

"You may," said Mr. Primrose. "Though I advise you not to bite off more than you can chew. Otherwise, I'll be left with the unfortunate task of picking your bones and melted flesh off the floor and sending your remains to the furnace for cremation."

"You may also come to me for advice, though I must warn you— until the demon tide is over, my time is limited. Speaking of which, I still have 50 kilos' of veridian ash poison to make by day's end. Its concoction is troublesome, so I'll be isolating a portion of the laboratory until I'm finished. You may now do as you please." The man then hopped off his bar stool and walked over to a corner of the laboratory. A mana shield sprang up, separating the room's airspace.

Sorin looked around the laboratory. A large shelf of ingredients was located near the entrance. Sorin had assumed these ingredients belonged to Mr. Primrose, but when he saw an inventory sheet and price list next to the highly poisonous ingredients, he realized that this was simply the toxic ingredient dispensary and storage space. The ones found for sale on the first floor were merely the least lethal of the bunch.

The inventory sheet and sign-out system were self-explanatory. Sorin or any other alchemist or apothecary in the Alchemists Guild could buy ingredients on credit. The cost of ingredients would be directly deducted from the reward when turned in. This was fortunate because Sorin was low on funds and wouldn't be able to invest much upfront.

The mission board was of particular interest to Sorin. The number of one-star commissions wasn't small; roughly half the commissions were helpful in medicine, while another half were poisons that he recognized as being applicable to adventurers.

There was also a brightly labeled request in a prominent position on the board. *An open mission for unlimited amounts of lung rot powder and scorching bramble ash?* thought Sorin. The Governor's Manor had issued the mission, so Sorin could only assume these were in preparation for defending the outpost during the demon tide. A similar mission was issued on the two-star board for Veridian Bone Corroding Ash, the long-form name of the veridian ash poison Mr. Primrose was concocting.

Sorin decided to focus on medical missions to start. He was sensitive to the costs of such ingredients since he was used to purchasing them for his clinic. *How lucrative...* That was his first impression of apothecary missions. *Too lucrative. Don't they know how easy this stuff is to make? The failure rate is basically negligible.*

Sorin wasn't a qualified alchemist by any means. He needed the proper flame control and knowledge of herbology required for the profession. But that didn't mean he was utterly ignorant of poison-crafting methods.

In general, an alchemist's success rate ranged between one success per three potions brewed and one success per two potions brewed. Potions that were made often might have a higher success rate, on the order of two successes per three potions brewed.

The margins generally reflected this. Failing twice but succeeding once would allow a one-star alchemist to roughly break even. If they wanted to make money doing alchemy, they would need to increase their success rate.

But for poisons, it was a different matter. Everything was priced on the same principle, but the difficulty in *brewing* them was much lower. Sorin had a broad knowledge of different poison concoction methods thanks to the Ten Thousand Poison Canon and, therefore, knew that poison concocting was significantly easier than potion making.

Success was almost guaranteed for creating 2-3 poison blends. Even complex poisons requiring ten or more ingredients had failure rates lower than 33 percent.

"Here's your meal ticket, Lorimer," said Sorin, pointing to the board. The small rat poked his head out of Sorin's chest pocket. "I know you hate being a beast flame, but if you can suffer through it, I'll split my earnings with you 9:1." Lorimer squeaked in protest, but Sorin shook his head. "I'll find an earth flame to rent if you don't accept. Choose wisely."

Thankfully, Lorimer was still a rat and, as such, was a terrible negotiator. He didn't know that renting an earth flame was extremely expensive and accounted for roughly 25 percent of an alchemist's expenses. A 10 percent cut was a steal of a deal for Sorin, further increasing his already lucrative margins.

The simplest poisons are small money items, but at my level, they're the most efficient to make, thought Sorin. *They don't require a lot of time, so I can mix them up in an hour with time to spare.*

One-star alchemists and apothecaries were limited to small quantities of reagents. A cauldron was the typical quantity used to measure potions. Up to ten potions could be extracted from a single cauldron, and the success rate was based on the quantity of extractable potions rather than the success of an individual cauldron.

Having made his decision, Sorin picked up the first mission, five cauldrons of crimson juniper extract. This poison was helpful in treating liver corruption. There was a high demand for this poison in the clinics, and the Alchemists Guild was often behind on orders, forcing patients to wait until their conditions worsened and the treatment was no longer as effective.

The main ingredients for the poison were 100 milliliters of liquified mana extract, ten mature Blood Juniper Cones, five grams of Crimson Fire Bark, and three drops of condensed sun extract, which the Mages Guild produced via sun-converging spell formations.

Sorin signed out the ingredients from storage and grabbed a mortar and pestle, a cauldron, and some fire essence crystals. Lorimer adopted his position in the earth's flame formation, keeping a fire essence crystal at the ready in case he ran low on energy.

Preparing the poison was extremely easy. Sorin measured out the liquified mana extract and added it to the cauldron, leaving it to Lorimer to increase its spirituality. Meanwhile, he used the mortar and pestle to grind the juniper cones and crimson fire bark, taking care to wash them carefully between uses.

Once the liquified mana extract began to glow healthily, Sorin directly tossed the two ingredients into the cauldron and used his mana to extract the poisonous ingredients from their powdered forms and into the liquids.

Extraction is the most essential part of the process, thought Sorin as he worked. *Failing to extract enough poisonous ingredients will result in a reduction in the total amount of active poison produced.*

Fortunately, Sorin's cultivation technique was extremely overbearing in this regard. By consuming a small amount of each ingredient, he was able to mimic these poisons in his mana and, therefore, exert additional influence on them.

He also had a second advantage: the Ring of Poison Manipulation. Thanks to the ring he wore on his left hand, Sorin was able to enhance his connection to the poisons and further facilitate the extraction process.

It wasn't long before the potion began glowing with a crimson light, which Sorin carefully nourished with Lorimer's flames. After thirty minutes of nurturing, the potion's glow reached a peak. Sorin stopped heating the solution and brought it over to a separatory funnel.

He then poured three drops of condensed sun extract into the funnel and mixed the solution thoroughly. A small, gritty film formed atop the funnel, which Sorin separated from the final potion by draining out the bottoms. In the end, he was left with 98 milliliters of Crimson Juniper Extract.

"Your control isn't bad," said a voice from behind Sorin. Sorin jumped when he saw that Mr. Primrose was standing behind him.

"Aren't you supposed to be concocting something, Mr. Primrose?" asked Sorin.

"I had a bit of downtime and thought I'd see how you were doing," said Mr. Primrose. "And please, call me Alexis. Mr. Primrose is what strangers call me. We're not strangers anymore—we're coworkers."

"Many thanks for the feedback... Mr. Primrose," Sorin said. He couldn't get around to calling him Alexis. "Do you have any recommendations?"

"At this level? No," said Mr. Primrose. "Your poison control can probably allow you to manipulate up to five poisons at similar success rates. If you want to maximize your profits, I suggest going for slightly more complex poisons. On the other hand, you may want to clear some backlog for the clinics. As a former physician, I'm sure you are more sensitive to their needs than others."

"I'll give it some thought," said Sorin. "At the very least, I know this poison is in high demand. I'll clear out four more cauldrons before the end of the day and make my decision then."

"You're free to do as you wish, of course," said Mr. Primrose. "Clearing out the backlog will only take a few days, anyhow. And I don't have any time to spare to concoct such low quantities of low-grade poisons."

Alexis returned to his side of the workshop, leaving Sorin to tally up his profits and losses. *One cauldron is roughly ninety to a hundred milliliters,* thought Sorin, jotting 88 gold down as the reward for ninety-eight milliliters of extract. *My costs were roughly 23 gold in ingredients, leaving me with 65 gold as my commission.*

Even *after* Lorimer's 10 percent cut, this was a huge profit. It wouldn't be long before he'd saved up enough for his ninth poison.

64

PROBING

Sorin spent the next three days concocting all manner of poisons. He cleared the simpler requests by the outpost's physicians first, then moved on to custom requests from the Adventurers Guild.

It was impossible for an apothecary to sustainably concoct poisons all day. Breaks and rests were needed, and sleep requirements rose with the strain on one's spirit. Sorin, therefore, spent much downtime between batches of poison doing mathematics. His end goal: calculating the ideal ninth poison with which to increase his cultivation.

In the end, Stone-Melt and Bone-Melt poison work best for what I'm going for, thought Sorin, tapping a pen to a piece of paper. He had a headache from manipulating Lorimer's earth flame and wouldn't be able to continue concocting for the remainder of the evening. *Nothing short of a top one-star poison will do, but none of these poisons are available in the outpost. The only option is to 'grow' my own poisons.* This would involve first creating a low-level poison, then feeding it compatible poisons until its potency increased to the desired level.

Three days of continuous concoction proved quite lucrative for Sorin. He managed to make 1,700 gold by fulfilling requests, more than half of the required 3,000 gold he would need to grow a suitable poison.

He shuddered at how much it would cost to concoct a suitable tenth poison.

Sorin was about to finish up for the evening when he suddenly heard a knock on the laboratory door. Thinking a one-star alchemist needed reagents again, he yawned and made his way over to the entrance.

Before he could arrive, however, the door opened on its own, revealing a familiar two-star alchemist, Alchemist Avery. It was the same alchemist who had conspired with the Governor's Manor to have him arrested on false charges following his failed assassination.

Sorin's mind raced to find a solution to his predicament; if a two-star alchemist wanted him dead, there was little he could do to resist. Fortunately, the worst didn't come to pass. Instead, the alchemist snorted and turned around, leaving the door open for another individual.

"The one you are looking for is here, Physician Marcus," said Alchemist Avery. "Try not to touch anything, and do make sure to inspect yourself for potential contamination when leaving the premises."

Having been introduced and let inside, Marcus walked into the restricted laboratory, taking extra care to avoid the vats of chemicals near the entrance. "I paid a visit to your manor, but Percival told me you practically live here now," said Marcus. "But this is convenient, too. The guild is much easier to get to than your residence."

"What do you want?" asked Sorin wearily.

"Not going to say hello or offer me something to drink?" asked Marcus. "Oh. Right. Lab rules. I always hated them. And I see you've taken your new occupation to heart and are making money hand over fist. It's good to look ahead instead of dwelling on the past. I applaud your determination."

"What do you want, Marcus?" Sorin reiterated. "In case you haven't noticed, I'm swamped."

"Yes, I see you're very busy resting your drained spirit," said Marcus. His eyes flickered to the paper on the table. "Brainstorming poison recipes. Admirable. You can't just wait for opportunities to fall on your lap—true cultivators *create* opportunities."

"What do you want?" asked Sorin a third time. "If you don't say it soon, I'll have you evicted."

Marcus shrugged. "I've come to obtain your assistance, of course. A consultation, if you will."

Sorin directly held out his hand. "Consultation fee."

Marcus's mouth twitched, but he reached into his belt pouch and took out a card worth 100 gold. "Will this suffice?"

"It's enough to start the conversation," said Sorin. He gestured for Marcus to take a seat at his desk.

"I have a case," said Marcus, accepting the seat. "A female patient. Bone-Forging Realm. She is fifty-two years old and belongs to the Nighthawks. She has awoken abruptly from her latest round of seclusion and experienced cultivation deviation. Though she survived, her cultivation is currently in a crippled state.

"As you can imagine, the outpost places great importance on her recovery. There are less than thirty Bone-Forging experts in the entire outpost, and each one is a strategic asset. I therefore prioritized this case, inspected her body, and discovered obstructions in her meridians.

"Normally, dislodging obstructions wouldn't be a problem. In this case, however, dislodging the obstructions in her meridians could easily prove fatal. Ultimately, I decided not to proceed and seek assistance. I would be very grateful if you would accompany me in trying to resolve this tricky case."

Sorin frowned when he heard this. *A blocked meridian? Do you think I'm a child that can't see what you're doing?* "I'd need to inspect the patient to make a determination," he replied after a lengthy wait. "I can't think of any tinctures or potions that can aid the situation."

"How unfortunate," said Marcus. "Many lives depend on this. As you well know, a Bone-Forging cultivator is a powerhouse that even ten elite Blood-Thickening cultivators would have trouble fighting."

"I understand the severity of the situation," said Sorin, "and I didn't say I had no solutions. I just need to personally inspect the patient before making any recommendations."

"Thank you for not directly rejecting me," said Marcus. "If you can come up with a solution, I'm sure the Nighthawks will reward you handsomely."

"I definitely won't hold back," said Sorin. "No matter the reward." In other words, some things couldn't be bought with money.

The two checked out of the Alchemists Guild and made their way to the west of the settlement. They arrived at a walled manor guarded by two Blood-Thickening cultivators. "It's me, Physician Marcus," said Marcus when they arrived. "I've secured a helper and would like to give healing the madame's condition another attempt."

The two guards exchanged looks before one of them ran inside the building. "Apologies, but these are sensitive times," said the guard who remained. "We must obtain permission before anyone enters or leaves the premises."

"Very understandable," said Marcus. "We'll wait here until we're cleared to enter."

The guard returned two minutes later and nodded to his companion. "They can both enter but must register first." Both Sorin and Marcus took out their identity plates and professional emblems. They quickly scanned over Marcus's credentials before looking at Sorin's with great scrutiny. "An apothecary? Only one star?"

"Trust me, this is the helper I need," said Marcus. "If he can't help, we'll need to call another high-ranking two-star physician from a nearby city. The cost and time involved will be astronomical, especially given how closely the timetable aligns with the demon tide."

"If you insist, Physician Marcus," said the guard. "Please follow me to Madam's chambers." He led Sorin and Marcus into a luxurious manor. The walls were covered in tasteful and expensive paintings, and gold trim could be seen even in the textured wallpaper. That wasn't even counting the dozens of gold-plated candlesticks Sorin spotted burning expensive scented candles or the gold-painted porcelain that was proudly displayed in the living room cabinet.

The guard had them take off their shoes and led them up thickly carpeted stairs. The house was warm, even in the hallways, thanks to carefully inscribed spell runes that circulated air between the top and bottom floors.

They passed a library, a study, and six guest rooms before arriving at the master bedroom, where two more guards had been posted. The guards scrutinized their identification documents before instructing them to enter.

Sorin found the patient lying in her bed, deathly pale but otherwise brimming with power. There was a disconnect, however; this power was present but couldn't be mobilized.

"I brought a helper along in the hopes that he might have a solution to your condition, Lady Duchene," said Marcus as he made his way over to the bed. He placed his hand on her forehead, then tapped a few locations on her body. Her symptoms were instantly alleviated with the introduction of two-star life mana. "Unfortunately, all I can do with my limited abilities is temporarily ameliorate your vitals. As you know, this isn't a sustainable solution. It's better to resolve the problem quickly rather than waiting two weeks for another physician to arrive."

The lady in the bed sighed softly. She was a beautiful woman with not the slightest wrinkle despite being in her early fifties. The streaks of white hair on her head were a symptom of her current health problems and would quickly vanish, assuming they could treat her condition.

"Let him take a look and see if he can sort me out," said Lady Duchene. "Though I'll be honest, I am not optimistic about this attempt of yours. There's nothing a Blood-Thickening cultivator can do to improve my condition. Of this, I am convinced."

"Sorin Kepler, one-star apothecary, at your service," said Sorin, bowing lightly before approaching the lady. He first placed his hand on several key acupoints to map out her mana circulatory system. He then used Ophidian Eye to confirm the obstructions in her mana flow. Both actions required intense concentration and a large quantity of mana since two-star mana created natural interference that was difficult to overcome even with a patient's consent.

"There are obstructions in her large intestine, heart, and spleen meridians," said Sorin to Marcus. "There is also a minor obstruction in her Belt Vessel, but this problem will resolve itself over time."

"Can you do anything to clear these out?" asked Marcus. "I know of many different treatment methods, but nothing that can help against these specific blockages." Sorin nearly rolled his eyes at Marcus's almost complete lack of subterfuge.

Lady Duchene's condition was intriguing, to say the least. The blockages in her body were akin to 'natural' blockages that would be cleared using meridian-opening tinctures. If not for the near impossibility of replicating this condition, Sorin would have suspected that Marcus had staged the whole affair. According to what Sorin could deduce, these obstructions were caused by debris from within the lady's own body that had been shaken loose via the sudden interruption in her cultivation.

"I have a solution," Sorin directly admitted. "But unfortunately, it's a little experimental. There is a risk of damaging her meridians during the process. Judging by the state of her body, she will be unable to heal from this damage.

"Moreover, the situation is worse than you described. Lady Duchene's cultivation isn't just damaged—her life force is also slowly draining away. If this isn't resolved, she'll die within the next two months. The longer we take to treat her, the more her life span will be affected. Every day that goes by will effectively reduce her lifespan by a single year."

Lady Duchene didn't seem surprised by his comment, which showed that Marcus had already deduced as much. "If you and Physician Marcus believe the risks are justified, I'm prepared to accept an experimental treatment."

"Just about anything would be better than the alternative of waiting for assistance," said Marcus. "We're a long way from Delphi or Olympia. Even if I *can* call in another two-star physician, there's no guarantee he'll be of any help."

"Then I'll be frank," said Sorin. "I can use a certain poison to clear her obstructions, but her meridians can't withstand the treatment. Do you have any way to heal meridians or perhaps shield them?" His message was simple: he had access to the tincture formula, but he'd need something in return.

"Healing meridians is beyond what I'm capable of," said Marcus, frowning. "As you well know, this sort of thing relies mostly on one's natural regeneration capabilities."

Or someone with a python's regeneration prowess, thought Sorin, though he didn't voice any objections to Marcus's statement.

"Likewise, I recommend against meridian strengthening concoctions since they simultaneously strengthen and embrittle meridians," continued Marcus. "The mere shock of dislodging an obstruction might cause them to shatter."

"So you don't have a solution?" asked Sorin. "That's a pity because I'm truly helpless unless you can help me with this small matter."

"There *is* a way to support her meridians," said Marcus hesitantly. "I haven't used the procedure much myself, but I believe I have a 95 percent chance of succeeding. The process is called a mana stent. It's an inner protective layer that a physician coats over a patient's meridians. The coating is intentionally tough and malleable, making it easy to retrieve and unlikely to burst if damaged."

A stent, thought Sorin. He knew of such things but only knew of physical stents. They were largely impractical things used on important arteries susceptible to bursting. Typically, such supports weren't needed since damage to these arteries could quickly be healed with life mana. As a result, their creation wasn't part of the core curriculum for becoming a physician.

"If you can reinforce the section of meridian one foot in either direction of the obstruction, I can attempt to dissolve it," said Sorin. "But you should know that Lady Duchene is a Bone-Forging cultivator and that my solution involves my mana. There's a huge imbalance in strength."

"It's not a concoction?" asked Marcus, confused.

"Not a concoction," confirmed Sorin. "And I'm sure you understand how difficult it is to shape mana inside an active meridian."

"Can't he just peel my mana away?" mumbled Lady Duchene. "I had a physician do that for me once to treat a bad case of corruption."

"This..." Marcus nodded slowly. "Since we're at a similar cultivation stage, I can give it a try. This shouldn't be too difficult since mana flow has already been interrupted. Your thoughts, Sorin?"

"If you can clear her mana, my odds of success shoot up to 80 percent," said Sorin. In truth, it was close to 90 percent, but Sorin didn't want to overplay his hand.

"Then, if Lady Duchene has no objections, prepare for the procedure," instructed Marcus. "I'll begin with peeling back the patient's mana." He then placed a finger on Lady Duchene's abdomen and injected a thick stream of life mana. The color drained from the lady's skin as her flesh lost the blocked meridian's support. Her flesh began to wither as the surgery's countdown began.

65

STENT AND SPEAR

Lady Duchene had a total of three obstructed meridians. For a mortal, that wasn't a big deal, but for a Bone-Forging cultivator, this was not only a massive impediment to their cultivation but a lethal flaw.

In Lady Duchene's case, the obstructions are causing some organs to be exposed to too much mana. Meanwhile, other organs are starved for mana. A Bone-Forging cultivator's body might be powerful, but it similarly required high levels of mana and adequate mana circulation to maintain.

Marcus was a skilled doctor, and fortunately for Sorin, he made no move to hide his techniques as he first applied them to the spleen meridian. "We'll use this meridian as proof of concept," Marcus explained as he worked. "Our success will only slightly improve the lady's condition; conversely, failure will not lead to a significant decline in her condition."

"Agreed," said Sorin. "Is that a general spell structure you're using for your stent? I expected it to be a specialized life mana spell."

Marcus chuckled. "Actually, you could also create a stent if you set your mind to it. The key is mana shaping practice and maintaining a stable structure. The nature of the mana involved is irrelevant.

"Of course, there are benefits to each type of mana. Metal mana will create the strongest stent. Wood mana and water mana will create flexible stents. As for fire mana... well, I wouldn't recommend making a fire mana stent because it would result in an explosion if it failed."

"What about life mana?" asked Sorin.

"Life mana stents can regenerate from damage," explained Marcus. "As for poison stents... I'd say the benefit is that they will be completely sterile. If a life mana stent bursts, the uncontrolled release of life mana can result in pathogen mutation and cancerous growth. As for poison mana, it will simply poison the patient and can be cured with the right antidote."

Marcus then proceeded to carefully peel away Lady Duchene's mana, fully exposing the work site and the stent. It had a hexagonal mana structure, like a beehive filled with tiny amounts of honey. *It's simpler than I imagined,* thought Sorin while Marcus completed the framework.

"Your turn," said Marcus.

"Got it," said Sorin. "Commencing the treatment."

With the stent in place and the patient's mana cleared, the operation was now similar to operating on a mannequin. A poison needle formed from Sorin's meridian clearing cocktail appeared in needle shape, then slowly wandered over to the obstruction.

Once the needle and the obstruction made contact, Sorin activated its acidic and anti-mana properties and had them attack the obstruction. A mixture of flesh, corruption, and mana crystals melted away at a noticeable pace until, finally, the obstruction was cleared.

"Removing the treatment solution," Sorin said, pulling the needle-shaped mass of mana back into his body.

"Removing the stent," said Marcus, dismantling the mana structure plate by plate. He then proceeded to test the integrity of the meridian. "The meridian is clear and undamaged. I'll begin restoring mana flow in increments."

Thanks to his Ophidian Eye enchantment, Sorin was able to see the mana slowly trickle in and fill the previous void. Marcus slowly unraveled his isolation plug until the meridian's mana flow reached 90 percent of its original rate. He then entirely removed the plug, fully restoring function to the corresponding body parts.

"That worked much better than I expected," said Marcus. "I take it your mana has special properties?"

"Indeed," said Sorin. "Acid, paralytic, and other special properties." Anti-mana was the fundamental property, but he did not share this detail.

"Regardless, the treatment seems effective," said Marcus. "Why don't we move on to the large intestine?"

"Sure," said Sorin. "You stent, and I'll spear."

The duo quickly replicated their solution, with Marcus isolating part of the meridian while Sorin dissolved the obstruction. This time, however, it took much longer to wear down the obstruction, as it was more crystalline than fleshy. Sorin didn't want to increase the amount of anti-mana in the needle for fear that it would result in residual damage.

Unfortunately, the third obstruction was even worse than the first. "I can't dissolve the obstruction with my current mana composition," Sorin was forced to admit. "Please allow me some time to recalibrate." Without waiting for an answer, he altered his Mana Needle template until it was 50 percent anti-mana and 50 percent acid. Though he was somewhat worried about clashing with Marcus's mana, he was confident that the man's Bone-Forging mana wouldn't be greatly affected if push came to shove.

"Please reinforce the stent when I pierce the obstruction," said Sorin. "I'm afraid clearing it will exert more pressure on the meridian membrane than previously."

"Reinforcing," said Marcus, who then signaled for Sorin to make a second attempt.

Sweat rolled off Sorin's face as he tore into the crystalline obstruction like a drill, slowly but surely wearing away at what appeared to be a large chunk of rock until it shattered into pieces. He then attacked the pieces that fell to prevent them from causing any further issues.

"That should be it," said Sorin, withdrawing his mana.

"Let's see if all our efforts paid off," said Marcus. "Withdrawing stent. Inspecting the meridian for damage." A minute later, he let out a sigh of relief. "The meridian is clear. I'll begin retrieving the plug at a controlled rate."

Mana slowly poured into Lady Duchene's body, instantly filling the area around her chest with warmth. Her heartbeat strengthened by the second until, finally, the plug collapsed like a dam. The sudden shock to her body was too much for the lady to handle; she coughed out a mouthful of black blood filled with impurities and corruption.

"Congratulations, Lady Duchene," said Marcus. "You're going to make a full recovery. I'll have to trouble you to stop by the clinic every day for the next three days for follow-up treatments, as much of the latent corruption in your body has been released and will require purging."

Lady Duchene cleared her throat. "That's quite possibly the most uncomfortable mouthful of blood I've ever spat up. And believe me when I say that I've coughed up many mouthfuls."

"Lady Duchene is part of the Winter Enforcement Team in the Nighthawk Division," Marcus explained, noticing Sorin's confusion.

"You mean… when people go mad in the winter…" said Sorin.

"That's right," said Marcus. "It's their team who hunts down crazed cultivators and cultists for bounties. Thanks to their efforts, regular citizens can sleep soundly in the winter."

"You grossly exaggerate our efforts," mumbled Lady Duchene. "If anything, our contributions are much higher during the demon tides. Madness is a pervasive problem that requires the occasional nip, but Violence is a powerful and persistent force in this outpost." She bent forward and spat out another mouthful of blood. This time, it was primarily red and devoid of the previous corruption. "I always underestimated corruption in my younger days. It's not until you reach higher realms that you realize how much of an impact it has."

"Corruption is the root of 90 percent of all cultivation problems," agreed Marcus. "I often tell our clan's elders that they should really do more for the outpost cultivators in this regard. Unfortunately, their ideas are old and outdated. All they know is how to fight for power and keep it in their bony hands."

"I'll make a trip to the Alchemists Guild tomorrow to square accounts," said Lady Duchene. "Once again, thank you ever so much for the treatment, Apothecary Sorin, Physician Marcus. I must also apologize—in my current state, I won't be able to see you out."

"No apology required," said Marcus. "I believe the guard outside is more than capable of seeing us off the premises."

"It was nice meeting you, Lady Duchene," said Sorin.

"Likewise, Apothecary Sorin," said Lady Duchene.

Five minutes later, Sorin and Marcus were walking outside on the chilly street. The hour was late, so there was no point in going back to the guild. "That stent procedure was interesting," Sorin said as they walked. "I'm surprised I never learned it."

"It's not something physicians use often," said Marcus. "Even two-star physicians."

"Where do you think I should read up on it if I'd like to learn specifics?" asked Sorin. "I ask purely for academic reasons, of course. To improve my ability to consult on future cases."

"I'm equally curious about the peculiarities of your poison mana," answered Marcus. It was an offer to exchange knowledge.

In Sorin's opinion, Marcus's knowledge was much less valuable than his secrets. He could only let the matter drop for now. *There are better things to exchange the meridian-opening formula for. Information on my parents, for instance. Information about their deaths.* Directly requesting such information could backfire, however, so he opted to wait until it was naturally brought up in conversation.

Judging by the recent batch of poisons his clinic has requested, they're making steady progress in determining the meridian-opening formula. He'll definitely breach the topic when they perfect the primary meridian formulas. After that, it becomes difficult to prevent casualties while fine-tuning the final tinctures.

"Well, I'd best get going," said Marcus when they reached a fork in the road. One led toward the Kepler Manor, and the other led toward the Governor's Manor, where Marcus was currently residing. "I'm glad we could collaborate again to achieve such wonderful results. Don't be a stranger, Sorin. And please prioritize my clinic's concoctions if you're able to."

"I always prioritize medical poisons, so there's no need to worry about that," said Sorin. "Have a good evening, Marcus. Please let me know about any developments with Lady Duchene's treatment."

The lights were still on when Sorin arrived at the manor. A sumptuous dinner had been left in the kitchen, so Sorin and Lorimer helped themselves before retiring to the office.

Several hours later, Sorin put down his pen and looked through several sheets of notes on possible mana structures. *What a pain,* he thought, rubbing his tired eyes. *The only way to know for sure is to test everything.*

66

THIRD ENCOUNTER

Sorin spent the days that followed amassing gold by concocting the more lucrative poisons on the apothecary request board. He managed to earn 3,500 gold before realizing that this was the limit of easy money to be earned.

With all the lucrative missions out of the way, there's only the recurring one-star mission issued by the Governor's Manor. The poison is a simple one that alchemists probably wouldn't mind concocting. But with the low margins, I'll only be able to make 150–200 gold per day.

Compared to his previous situation as a quasi-one-star physician, Sorin was swimming in gold. The problem wasn't that he couldn't earn money, but that he couldn't earn it quickly enough.

Having collected the necessary funds, Sorin purchased some minor poisons and began actively growing what would become his ninth poison. He settled on stone melt instead of bone melt, mainly because damage to one's bones was tricky to deal with and could impact his ability to become a Bone-Forging cultivator.

The initial concoction required fifteen simple poisons worth 500 gold in total. Sorin used these poisons to form a 'seed' that he then proceeded to nourish with increasingly powerful poisons.

Unfortunately, it was when Sorin had just finished the seed that he received a piece of critical news: the demon tide was starting, and the first of many skirmishes had taken place. All registered adventurers were to report for mandatory patrols. Only cultivators serving as critical craftsmen or logistics personnel were exempt.

Those in other critical roles are also exempt, but that's left entirely to the discretion of the Governor's Manor. Fortunately, serving as an apothecary will allow me to avoid the first waves and finish nourishing my ninth poison. He didn't want to abandon his friends, but he similarly couldn't give up on his cultivation. Moreover, his research into the stent procedure was showing promise; only concocting would give him enough time to develop the procedure.

Sorin, therefore, got busy concocting Lung Rot Powder and Scorching Bramble Ash. He requested a large batch of ingredients from the Alchemists Guild and informed them that he would be participating in the war as an apothecary for the time being.

As expected, he soon received a letter from the guild master instructing him that he need not report to the Adventurers Guild for duty. The condition was that he submit a minimum of 750 grams of either of the one-star poisons requested by the Governor's Manor every day.

Sorin quickly did the math and found these conditions acceptable. *Concocting 750 grams will take me about eight hours per day. I'll also be able to earn 150 gold per day, 15 of which will go to Lorimer.* The hard-working rat was getting increasingly demanding about the quality of the demon cores in his diet and was, therefore, quite happy to serve as a beast flame to facilitate this.

Meanwhile, feeding the Stone-Melt Poison will only require two hours per day. That will leave me with two to four hours of research time in the Mages Guild. Ultimately, the stenting procedure was a spell-like application of mana. By spending the income that he earned crafting poisons, he would be able to secure a tutor to help him craft a framework compatible with poison mana.

Having made his decision, Sorin sent a letter to Stephan through the guild courier informing him of his future activities. He received a reply later that day stating that the team had no problems with this as long as he convened with them before the demon tide grew more violent.

Relieved, Sorin began feeding the Stone-Melt Poison in earnest and crafted a bit of extra scorching bramble ash in case he encountered any mishaps in the laboratory that would prevent him from meeting his quota.

Three days later, he squeezed out time to hire a tutor. The man was a retired adventurer who handled pure mana and was, therefore, experienced in a variety of spell forms. They scrapped the initial stenting framework and built a more suitable one from the ground up.

As far as tutors went, he was one of the more expensive ones; fortunately, Lady Duchene's bounty added up to a total of 1,500 gold, an impressive amount for less than two hours of work, especially if it allowed him to open extraordinary meridians in the future.

On the fourth day, Sorin reached initial success in growing his ninth poison. The Stone-Melt Poison reached the middle one-star grade and showed no signs of stalling. On the fifth day, it reached the peak of the middle grade, and it would only be a matter of time until it reached the highest grade.

On the fifth day, Sorin finally managed to extricate himself from other duties and tie up a loose end. He made his way to the temple just outside the Bloodwood Outpost. Despite the corpses that were piling up outside the city as the guards and adventurers repelled wave after wave of demons, the path to the cathedral remained clear and untainted.

There were many beggars, homeless people, and refugees residing in a small tent village near the temple. Small fires burned in each camp as the refugees took turns cooking thin stews that were distributed amongst the poor and the helpless, courtesy of the Temple of Hope, the Governor's Manor, and the guilds and associations.

Out of habit, Sorin cast the Ophidian Eye spell and inspected their conditions. He confirmed Lawrence's report on Marcus's behavior and corroborated the patient data they'd found in the clinic. The vibrant mana signatures he saw on each of them would only be seen in perfectly healthy people, relatively free of corruption.

There was an oddness he couldn't quite place in these people, but time was pressing. He made his way over to the side temple used by adventurers, where he was quickly ushered to a private altar, complete with wish-fire and freshly cut kindling.

Sorin reverently placed his offering, the Core of Violence, on the altar and lit up the kindling. Like the two times before, Sorin found himself in a dark space. Nine black chains with a hint of gold whipped in the night sky, only joining together at their point of origin, the nine-tailed fox that went by the name of Hope.

"We meet again, Sorin Abberjay Kepler," whispered the fox from its elevated position. "And this time, you've brought along a proper offering. How *delightful.* Have you decided on what you wish to pursue? Will it be power? Information? The games you humans play never bore me."

It took some time for Sorin to get used to the stifling sensation of the dark space. The nature of the temple corrupted as surely as entering Bloodwood Forest would. In this case, it kindled the deepest and most desperate desires hidden away in one's heart.

In Sorin's case, it was a bubbling desire for vengeance against those who wronged him, along with an insatiable curiosity for the truth behind the deaths of his parents and the Abberjay branch's fall from grace.

Hope was a strange and counter-intuitive feeling. It filled a person with energy and allowed them to break free from their predicaments. At the same time, it was suffocating, for it could only be felt alongside despair.

Sorin, therefore, reined in his emotions and banished his deeper desires. He hadn't come here for the truth, nor had he come here for power. He'd come here for knowledge that only a deity could grant.

"I am too weak for vengeance and can only accommodate so much power," said Sorin. "But I have faith that you, the Lord of Hope and the Light of the Desperate, can answer a question that's been bothering me for quite some time."

The fox snorted. "Do you really think that flattery will change the way an Evil conducts its business?"

"Not at all," said Sorin. "I wanted to clarify that, unlike before, I don't want straight answers. I don't want a specific boon. What I want... is Hope.

"There are shackles that bind humanity. They are divine chains that prevent us from unlocking our fullest potential. My request is this: I wish for a way to break through these limits. I wish for a hint at how to break these shackles, something the ancient gods of Pandora forbade my ancestor from delving into."

The fox chuckled. "Do you think you're the only one who's ever wished for such a thing, Sorin Abberjay Kepler? Tens of thousands have asked for the same, yet after all these years, no one has ever succeeded.

"I would never dare ask for certainty," said Sorin. "But I have gazed upon these golden shackles and found them most repugnant."

Several tense seconds passed while the fox considered his request. "Very well, Sorin Abberjay Kepler," said the fox. "I will grant you your wish, though I guarantee that you will regret making it." He then sent Sorin flying out of the dark space and back into his body, which was still kneeling and piously praying.

Sorin felt weak, like he hadn't eaten in days. His spirit was drained to the point that he would be unable to wield mana without resting for an hour. The fire on the altar was just going out, with not even ashes remaining of the Core of Violence.

When the last of the wish flames burned out, a small bottle appeared on the altar. It contained a single black pill that filled even Sorin with revulsion. Attached to the pill was a note.

Violent Awakening Pill, Sorin read. *Poison taboo pill. Consumable. The consumer of this pill will experience a significant increase in mana potency and physical strength, equivalent to roughly half of a cultivation realm. Effect duration: 5–10 minutes.*

Sorin frowned as he continued reading the description.

Using this pill will result in the corruption of one's mana attribute with the Violence aspect. Invasive corruption is inevitable. Should the user survive the contamination, their life order will change. They will no longer be considered human but a fully-fledged demon instead.

"This... what is this nonsense?" said Sorin after reading the bottle. "Is this a *joke*? I asked for a way to break humanity's shackles, not for a way to leave one's humanity behind and become a demon."

This wasn't a pill to be casually consumed. The least terrible consequence for doing so was death. Demonification was naturally the most terrifying outcome, as the accompanying madness would lead one to turn on their companions.

Sorin sighed as he picked up the pill bottle. What had he expected—an actual solution? Besides, the pill was still worth something. Selling it would be impossible, but it would serve as a form of insurance or possibly as a deterrent.

Having made his decision, Sorin stored the pill bottle and left the temple of hope. He didn't have much time remaining until the demon tide reached its most deadly stages.

LAB RAT

On the sixth day since the start of the demon tide, Sorin received a letter from Stephan informing him that he should prepare to return to the team. The demons were becoming increasingly aggressive, and there was no telling how long it would be before intense fighting broke out.

The ninth poison had reached a critical point, so Sorin spent the entire night nurturing it. At dawn, the poison finally broke through to become a substance that could melt one-star enchanted stone with little effort.

Sorin placed several drops of the poison on his skin to test it out. He felt his bones soften as the poison attacked the minerals in his body. Still, he recovered when the eight other poisons in his body subdued the intruder.

He then continued dripping the poison until he finished off three ten-milliliter vials of it. His body reached its saturation limit, and the amount he could absorb per day sharply decreased.

Sorin spent the seventh day practicing his stent technique and creating one last batch of poison. He also took the time to concoct a few poisons for Marcus. These requests were lucrative and gave Sorin some insight into Marcus's progress in deciphering the meridian-opening formula.

By the looks of it, he's deduced about 70 percent of the formula for opening extraordinary meridians, thought Sorin as he reviewed the potential poison combinations. *I also haven't heard anything about excess casualties. Is he testing the concoction on demons before moving on to human trials?*

It was eight in the evening when he finally finished the last mandatory batch of poisons. He tidied up his things before heading over to Mr. Primrose's office. The pale man was taking a break between batches of two-star poison. Like Sorin, he was required to concoct a minimum amount of poison every day.

"I see you've finished up with your experiment," said Mr. Primrose. "Judging by the change in your aura, you're using it to change the nature of your mana?"

"Something like that," said Sorin. He'd never heard of people cultivating by ingesting poisons before, so he chose to keep this information under wraps. "Pardon me for saying this, but you look exhausted, Mr. Primrose. "Even if you *can* concoct more poison than required, it doesn't mean you *have* to."

Mr. Primrose shook his head. "The more poison I concoct, the easier repelling the most intense waves of the demon tide will be. You've never experienced a tide firsthand, Sorin, so you naturally can't imagine what it feels like to lose your closest companions."

"It's something I hope never to experience," said Sorin. "Which is why I'll be reporting for adventuring duty first thing in the morning."

Mr. Primrose nodded. "I was wondering when you would. After all, you're not *really* an apothecary. You're an adventurer who happens to concoct poisons on the side."

"Do you need any last-minute help with anything?" asked Sorin.

"No," said Mr. Primrose. "If I need assistance, I'll request the guild leader to assign me a few reluctant alchemists."

"Then I wish you all the best," said Sorin. "Please don't hesitate to see a physician if your health deteriorates. It's dangerous to keep your mana in a constant state of overdraft."

"I didn't become a two-star apothecary through sheer dumb luck," said Mr. Primrose.

"I apologize," said Sorin. "Old habits die hard."

Though it was late in the evening, Sorin didn't immediately return home. He instead traveled to the Holt residence in the north end of town.

A handsome middle-aged man with blond hair opened the door when Sorin knocked. "Hello there. How can I help you?" The years had not been kind to the man, as evidenced by his missing leg. A metallic prosthesis from the Mages Guild had been installed on the limb, restoring part of his mobility.

"Hello, Mr. Holt," said Sorin. "I'm Sorin Kepler, a friend of Lawrence's. I was working late, so I missed his return to the Adventurers Guild. Is he in?"

"Lawrence!" Mr. Holt yelled over his shoulder. "Get your butt down here. Your friend is waiting. And heat some water on your way down, or else he'll think we're uncivilized barbarians!" He then waved Sorin in. "Make yourself at home, dear. He'll be right down."

Indeed, Sorin caught a human-shaped blur whipping about the house, picking things up. A kettle landed on the stove in the kitchen just before a chair was pulled out from beneath the table. A few seconds later, the human-shaped blur transformed into Lawrence, whose hair was still drying after taking a bath.

"Sorin," said Lawrence, a little out of breath. "You should have told me you were coming."

"I wasn't sure when I'd finish work today," said Sorin, handing over his coat. "I hope I'm not causing you too much trouble."

"Not at all," said Lawrence. "I just got back an hour ago. Had dinner and washed up. It's going to be another early start tomorrow, but I imagine it'll be corpse cleanup again. Never gets old."

"Corpse cleanup?" asked Sorin, taking a seat in the living room. Lawrence zipped into the kitchen and poured him a cup of hot water before zipping back. Then, realizing he'd forgotten tea leaves, he zipped back into the kitchen and brought over a tin. "Wait, is this green tea? It's not easy to find leaves out here."

Lawrence shrugged. "It's what my family drinks. It's a bit more expensive than what most people have, but I think it's well worth it. So? What do you think of the place? It's different than you expected, isn't it?"

"It's cleaner than I expected, given your behavior," Sorin admitted. The place had a homely feel to it, as though a housewife had spent the past ten years adding small decorations to the place to liven it up. "Isn't it just you and your father here?"

"My father has some interesting hobbies," said Lawrence. "Painting, for example. He paints all sorts of things he saw back during his adventuring days."

"I bet," said Sorin, peeling his eyes away from a picture of three half-naked women bathing. Their scant clothes tastefully covered critical parts of their bodies, barely dragging the painting's category down from offensive to almost modest. "You said something about corpse duty?" Sorin said, adding a small pinch of tea leaves into his cup and waiting for them to steep.

"Right. Corpse duty," said Lawrence. "Most of the demons get killed by mortal archers on the walls. The rest get killed by mages or by wall enchantments.

"If no one clears them out, the corpses will corrupt the land. Their cores will also disintegrate and transform into demonic energy, which will strengthen their brethren.

"It's up to the adventuring teams to clean up the corpses, pick up cores and arrows, and other useful demon parts. It'll be up to farmers and mages to perform a proper cleanup after the demon tide is over."

"I imagine this is just a warm-up activity before the *real* fighting starts," said Sorin.

"That's right," said Lawrence. "According to my old man, it won't be long before they stop sending out adventuring teams and assign everyone to certain walls in rotation."

"Seems like I chose the best time to join in," said Sorin.

"A good thing, too," said Lawrence. "Gareth and Stephan have been getting on my nerves. Only Daphne will give me the time of day—but only when she's not distracted by her spell book or her stories."

"I'll be joining Gareth and Stephan's faction if you don't mind," said Sorin. "Lorimer is with me on this one." The small rat poked his head out of Sorin's pocket, nodded, and then squeaked. "He's asking if you have coffee, by the way."

"My dad hates the stuff," said Lawrence. "So that's a hard no. Does he… does he like cookies?"

"Is *that* what I've been smelling?" said Sorin. As if to answer his question, the door to the kitchen burst open, revealing Lawrence's father. The man had a heart-pattern apron on and was holding a plate of cookies in each hand.

"Here you go, Sorin," said Mr. Holt. "Eat 'em while they're hot. Your rat can have a few, but if he dares gnaw on my furniture, there'll be rat cakes on the menu this time tomorrow."

To Sorin's surprise, Lorimer nodded politely and hopped onto the table to help himself to a cookie. He nodded to Sorin and gestured to the plate, forcing Sorin to pick out three cookies and place them on the smaller plate.

The rat then nibbled at a cookie and nodded before giving a claw up to Mr. Holt. "Not bad, right?" said Mr. Holt. "Let me know if you need anything else, Sorin. My son doesn't have the best of manners, as much as I've tried to teach him proper etiquette."

Lawrence chuckled awkwardly as his father retreated. "Please pretend you didn't see that. Men baking with such enthusiasm… isn't a common sight."

Sorin shrugged. "Percival bakes all the time. Though not with as much *flare* as your father does, I'll admit. By the way, these cookies are *delicious*."

"He's seduced a fair number of ladies over the years with this recipe," said Lawrence, nodding. "If it weren't for his insistence on not remarrying, there'd be people lining down the street to propose."

Sorin was highly suspicious of this statement because, as far as he'd gathered, Mr. Holt had as bad a reputation as Lawrence. *Then again, these cookies are amazing. I wonder how the rest of his cooking is. Should I find a way to invite myself for dinner?*

Lawrence cleared his throat. "*Anyway*, that's the situation outside the walls. We're going to loot bodies and burn them. You can dissect some as long as it doesn't affect our schedule."

"Very good," said Sorin, grabbing another cookie. "Then that brings me to the reason for my visit. I just finished researching a technique. It's a work of art, if I do say so myself. I came here to show it off—and to test it, of course. For science."

"For science?" said Lawrence. At first, he was confused, but then realization dawned on him. "No, no, no!" he said, standing up. "I am *not* a lab rat. Besides, you have Lorimer. Use him!"

"Come on," said Sorin. "I've already experimented on a medical mannequin and demon corpses. This is a perfectly safe procedure. Mostly."

"Absolutely not," said Lawrence. "This is unethical. A breach of your sacred oath as a physician."

"Don't exaggerate," said Sorin. "This is a perfectly safe test. Worst case, you'll have sore meridians for the next few days."

Lawrence groaned. "I *hate* being a lab rat. And why is it always me? Why not Gareth?"

"My preferred choice is actually Stephan because his physical capabilities are higher," said Sorin. "Unfortunately, I probably can't open his last blocked meridian. That only leaves you, Gareth, and Daphne. Daphne's body is weakest, and Gareth is too much of a coward. Not the kind of person willing to take one for the team."

Lawrence nodded and slowly sat down. "That's right. Gareth would never dare take one for the team. Plus, his pain tolerance is terrible. We can't have him fainting mid-procedure, can we?"

"According to what I can tell, there's just mild discomfort," said Sorin. "But *yes,* it would be far too much for Gareth until I've fine-tuned the procedure."

"Fine," said Lawrence. "You have my permission."

Relieved at not having to detain his friend and forcefully experiment on him, Sorin retrieved his paralysis poison from Lawrence's teacup and activated Ophidian Eye. The mana in Lawrence's body lit up in Sorin's eyes. It superimposed itself on the many anatomical maps he'd memorized over the years.

"First, I'll assess your condition," said Sorin, placing his hand on his chest. "You're a little exhausted and not at your peak, but I believe it's safe to begin the experimental treatment." Inwardly, he noted that Lawrence had unsealed ten out of twenty-four of the silver seals on his Conception Vessel.

"You were born with naturally unlocked Yin Hell Vessel and Yang Heel Vessel," Sorin said as he finished his inspection. "This has given you higher movement speed compared to your peers.

"You, therefore, have four remaining options for your next meridian-opening. There are the Yin Link Vessel and Yang Link Vessel, which will increase your coordination and control. There's the Thrust Vessel, which will increase the rate at which you can expel and circulate mana. Finally, there's the Belt Vessel, which will let you better leverage your mana and strength."

"Thrust, then Belt," replied Lawrence without any hesitation. "I'm lacking in offense. It's hard for me to finish off enemies before I disengage these days."

"I'll do my best," said Sorin. He placed his finger on Lawrence's chest and poured a stream of poison mana into two neighboring meridian pathways. He then shaped that mana and had it form a complex stent. The supporting structure snugged up against the meridians, all save a single bare point where the meridians would eventually connect.

He then formed a mana needle and drilled it into the connecting wall. Lawrence's face contorted in pain, but thanks to a paralytic he'd injected in his body as a precaution, he was unable to utter a sound. A combination of flesh, crystalized mana, and corruption rapidly melted away, establishing a connection between the two meridians.

Lawrence trembled as his mana flow abruptly changed and sped up. Sorin had expected this, however, and pre-emptively stabilized his needle and stent as Lawrence's blood thickened slightly and his mana flow adjusted.

Ten minutes later, Lawrence's condition stabilized, enabling Sorin to continue the meridian-opening procedure. He widened the poison needle and continued drilling until, finally, there were no obstructions to mana flow.

"There," said Sorin, retracting the stent. "That wasn't that bad, was it?"

"That *hurt*," snapped Lawrence. "And how could you paralyze me without my consent?"

"I was afraid I'd alarm your father," said Sorin.

"Darn right you were afraid," said Lawrence. "If he'd heard what I wanted to shout while paralyzed, he would have come here and shoved a rolling pin up your—"

"Language!" hollered Mr. Holt from another room.

"It wasn't *that* bad," said Sorin. "Trust me, I've done this kind of thing before. On myself." Of course, he didn't mention that his meridians naturally opened as he cultivated and that no piercing was required during this process.

"So we're done?" said Lawrence. "You can go ahead and do your thing on the others?"

"Almost," said Sorin. "But first, I think I can unblock your Belt Vessel. Assuming you're brave enough to risk it."

Lawrence hesitated but ultimately nodded. "Fine. If it'll increase my strength before the demon tide intensifies, I'm game."

Sorin nodded. "Prepare yourself, then. "This one will be a lot more painful than the last since opening a blockage stiffens the other meridian-openings."

"You know what, on second thought, I'm good," said Lawrence, standing up. He managed to take two steps before falling to the ground. Lorimer blinked and looked from Lawrence to Sorin uneasily.

"What?" said Sorin. "He chickened out, but he's still willing. On a subconscious level."

"Everything all right in there?" said Mr. Holt, poking his head out of the kitchen.

"Everything's fine," Sorin assured. "He might *look* paralyzed and unable to respond, but that's because he's putting on a strong front. This is good for him. Trust me—I was a doctor once."

"Heh," said Mr. Holt, limping into the room and turning Lawrence over. "That'll teach him to not let his guard down. More cookies?" He didn't wait for Sorin's answer before placing another plate on the table. Lorimer immediately grabbed one and retreated to his spot at the table, taking extra care not to drop any crumbs in the process.

"Sure, why not," said Sorin, grabbing another delicious cookie. "Unblocking meridians is hungry work."

"I'll make sure no one bothers you," said Mr. Holt. "Just make sure you don't injure him too badly, all right?"

CORPSE PATROL

Shortly after seeing Lawrence, Sorin paid Gareth a visit to the east end of town. He arrived late at night, but fortunately, the archer was not yet asleep. Upon hearing of Sorin's success with Lawrence, Gareth had Sorin unlock his Thrust Vessel and Yin Link Vessel, which would greatly improve the power and accuracy of his arrows.

Next, Sorin went to the Mages Guild to find Daphne. He found her half asleep, trying to figure out a spell model. Sorin successfully unlocked her Yin and Yang Link Vessels, greatly increasing her mana manipulation abilities.

Sorin got about two hours of sleep before forcing himself out of bed and donning his blood-drinker armor. He filled a pouch with crystal needles, some medical-grade stitching string, and bandages in acid-proof bottles. He then strapped his whip and dagger of lesser curse to his belt, completing the ensemble.

In an effort to fit in with the team, Lorimer smeared demon blood beneath his eyes like war paint before hopping into the custom pocket built into Sorin's armor. "You ready, partner?" Sorin asked. The rat squeaked an acknowledgment. "You've been very well-behaved lately, Lorimer. Keep up the good work."

Sorin met his companions just outside the north gate. The Temple of

Hope was technically the closest building to Bloodwood Forest, but no demons dared invade it. Instead, they broke up to attack either the north or the south in a seemingly random pattern.

"Glad you could make it," greeted Stephan, pulling Sorin into a tight bear hug. "I heard about your research breakthrough from Lawrence. Good work."

"There's still a long way to go," said Sorin. "I expect I'll be able to unlock five extraordinary meridians after my next breakthrough. As for the sixth, it'll have to wait until I break through to the tenth stage of Blood-Thickening."

"You heard the man," said Stephan to the others. "Try not to break through to the tenth stage before Sorin. The foundations we lay out now will impact the future of our team. Try to distinguish yourselves in battle, and who knows? Maybe another Hero will appear in Team 'We Don't Need a Life Mage.'"

Not long after they arrived, an adventurer approached Stephan and handed him a report.

"Any news?" asked Gareth.

"There was an attack three hours ago," said Stephan, handing him the scroll. "So we can expect some quiet for the first part of our shift."

"Is it corpse duty again?" asked Daphne.

"It's corpse duty again," said Stephan. "So you can take it easy and keep learning your new spell while you torch the odd corpse. We aim to get everything cleaned up in the next two hours."

Ten minutes after they left the north gate, they encountered a pile of 200 or so one-star wolf demon corpses. It was difficult to tell exactly how many there were because the corpses were mutilated and burnt beyond recognition. An exact count would need to wait until after they'd collected the individual cores.

It was Gareth who explained their group's duties to Sorin. "Strictly speaking, we're here to guard the mortal soldiers and their carts as they harvest beast parts. We only participate in the clean-up operations if there are hazards or the soldiers need help removing the demon cores."

As the team's rogue and archer, it fell to Lawrence and Gareth to scout out for danger. With Daphne studying spells, it fell to Sorin and Stephan to walk around, splitting open skulls and extracting their demon crystals.

Corpse duty was ideal for Lorimer, who'd been starved for over a week. He ravenously ate corpses but held off on the cores while Sorin clarified the situation with Stephan.

"Since they're not our kills, we only get 25 percent of the harvest," Stephan explained. "We can't take anything until the governor's men tally everything up, though. They'll pay us out by the end of the day."

"Lorimer won't get in trouble for eating corpses, will he?" asked Sorin.

"As long as he doesn't eat anything valuable, all is well," said Stephan. "The leftovers will get cremated via wish-fire either way."

It didn't take long for Stephan and Sorin to extract the cores, leaving them with nothing to do while the mortal soldiers cleared up the remainder of the corpses and burned the rest. This left Sorin ample time to practice his poison spells on looted corpses.

Sorin was also interested in demon anatomy. He performed the odd autopsy to better understand the demons and their weaknesses. Some had two hearts, and others lacked major organs. Meridian patterns varied greatly between demon types; knowing these details would give Sorin a distinct advantage in future battles.

Two hours passed in this fashion. They moved from battlefield to battlefield like wandering nomads. When their carts were full, what remained of the corpses were burned on pyres as offerings to Hope.

Shortly after returning to the gates, a horn sounded, and their team lined up on the walls to see a veritable sea of demons surging out of the forest. Only then did Sorin truly understand why they called it a demon *tide*. They washed out like waves, collapsing upon themselves as they rushed towards the outpost walls in a thoughtless frenzy.

"Why do demon tides happen?" Sorin found himself asking.

"There is substantial debate on the topic," answered Daphne. "And unfortunately, there are no definitive answers."

"Then what's your best guess?" asked Sorin.

"Domain transition," answered Daphne. "Each of the Seven Evils has its own domain. Of the seven, only three evils can unleash demons upon the mortal world. Death is omnipresent and controls the deceased. Violence dominates the summer months and corrupts wildlife to devour each other and proliferate. As for Madness, it controls darkness, inconsistency, and the unknown. The creatures it spawns are horrifying, random, and often the product of cultivators losing their minds.

"There is much debate on why demon tides only occur when transitioning from summer to winter, but not vice versa. Personally, I think that it's due to the characteristics of Violence. 'He' spurs demons to mate and proliferate. 'He' pushes them past their natural limitations. And when 'He' is about to go dormant, there is a need to release all the built-up potential that would otherwise be wasted.

"But why isn't there a similar event for Madness?" asked Sorin.

"Because Madness is something that lurks deep within our hearts." It was Gareth who answered the question. "Humans aren't cyclical creatures like beasts in the wild or the rising or falling of seasons. Madness is always present, lurking where one least expects it. It acts up in the winter when darkness and uncertainty are at their strongest."

Sorin shivered as he recalled his experiences treating patients during the winter. It's why he fought so hard to purge corruption whenever he could. The more corruption one accumulated, the more likely they were to experience visual and auditory hallucinations that pushed them to commit unspeakable acts. Some would even transform into true demons that infiltrated cities and outposts and plotted the downfall of humanity.

"I believe the demons are retreating into the forest," said Gareth, breaking the uncomfortable silence that had settled on the group. "It won't be long before the guard opens the gates and lets us out again."

They returned outside the walls twenty minutes later, burning corpses with wish-fire and collecting demon cores. This time, it was a large wave. Hence, soldiers were escorted and requested that they help extract arrows and demon parts in addition to the usual demon cores.

They were halfway done when, suddenly, Sorin felt discomfort deep in his gut. He looked towards the wilderness and drew his dagger as Lawrence and Gareth returned from their scouting.

"There are demons nearby," said Gareth. "Somewhere behind the tree line."

"What are your recommendations?" asked Stephan, yielding to their group's archer.

"I recommend we escort our soldiers back to the settlement and report the situation to the higher-ups," said Gareth.

"It's a little late for that, I'm afraid," interrupted Lawrence. "Look over there!" A group of a hundred or so one-star demons had emerged from Bloodwood Forest and were charging at the group nearest to them.

The adventuring team escorting the distant soldiers drew their weapons and initiated a strategic retreat. Meanwhile, the leader of their team's soldiers took out a brass horn and blew out a loud note, which was immediately answered with a call from the wall for all teams to retreat.

"We're dropping the carts and pulling back," said the leader of the fifty guards they were escorting.

"Retreat in an orderly fashion," Stephan instructed. "My companions and I will prepare for battle."

"Another group of demons just emerged," said Gareth, pointing in another direction. "The first group we saw consists of roughly 100 Blood Tusk Boars, while this second group contains about 200 Flame Antler Deer."

"Looks like those deer are also heading towards that other group of adventurers," said Lawrence. "Anyone know who that is?"

"It should be Barbara's team," muttered Stephan. "A hundred might be doable for them, but three hundred? Impossible."

"Our assignment is to escort *this* group of soldiers," Gareth reminded Stephan.

"But won't it become tricky to see them safely back if Barbara's group falls?" asked Sorin. "Those demons could cut us off." He wasn't sure how correct his words were, but it didn't sit well with Sorin to leave Barbara's team to fend for themselves.

"It's not exactly a good idea to waste time," said Lawrence. "Why don't we just flip a coin?"

Daphne snorted. "Coins have terrible variance. I can think of ten different methods that are much better than—"

"We're *not* going to make decisions based on coin flips, dice rolls, or card draws," said Stephan, cutting Lawrence off. "Daphne, pros and cons."

Daphne frowned, then calmly provided her analysis.

"Pros for breaking formation: we're lowering overall group risk," said Daphne. "The cons, however, are that we're throwing ourselves in danger. Ten one-star adventurers against 300 demons at point-blank range? Forgive me for not being optimistic."

"What are the odds that the demons ignore us?" Stephan asked Gareth.

"They definitely won't do that," said Gareth, shaking his head. "These demons are crazed because of Violence's influence. They'll charge for the nearest target, no exceptions."

Stephan sighed as he came to a decision. "We're going in," he said to the leader of the soldiers they were escorting. "Please return to the city and inform the commander of our strategic decision."

"We'll do so at once," said the leader. Like the rest of the soldiers, he wasn't a cultivator. As far as he was concerned, these decisions were beyond his pay grade.

"Let's make haste," said Stephan. "We don't have a minute to waste. Lawrence, Sorin, run ahead. Gareth, Daphne, on my back."

"On your back?" said Daphne, her eyes lighting up. "Yes!!! We're riding into battle on an armored polar bear, Gareth! This is going to be awesome!"

Sorin immediately set off towards Barbara's team, which had already engaged with the first group of a hundred demons. They did their best to prevent the demons from wrapping around them and attacking the mortal soldiers. This bought the soldiers precious seconds to pull back from the front line but ruined their formation, resulting in one of their members getting injured.

"What do you see, Lawrence?" Sorin asked as he grabbed his dagger. An orb of poison appeared in his hand, ready to be thrown.

"They're surrounded and using a three-point formation while their life mage heals their injured member," said Lawrence. "It's not a problem fighting off the Blood Tusk Boars since Barbara is a beast, but it'll be a different story when those Flame Antler Deer get here. Also... I think those deer might have a leader."

Sorin's expression fell. "A two-star demon?"

"Probably," said Lawrence. "Why don't we pull back and abort the mission?"

"Not happening," said Sorin, tightening his grip on his dagger. "As long as we can buy time for Stephan to arrive, we have a chance." As a Hero, Stephan was capable of fighting demons above his rank.

"Pushing past them is going to be difficult," said Lawrence.

"I'll throw in a ball of paralyzing mist and dive in first," said Sorin. "Can you cover me?"

"You only live once, I guess," said Lawrence, blending into Sorin's shadow. Sorin tossed a Veridian Smoke Bomb, stunning a group of ten Blood Tusk Boars before heading into their midst.

RESCUE

Time slowed to a crawl as Sorin weaved through ten stunned boars, cutting three of them in passing to inject a lethal dose of poison while evading their sharp tusks.

Due to the constraints of the Veridian Smoke Bomb spell, the paralytic poison keeping the boars in place was insufficient to support their stunned state; it wasn't long before Sorin ran into a fully functional enemy that lifted its horned snout to gore him.

Sorin moved his dagger to defend but aborted when he saw a blade flick out of his shadow and pierce into the boar's neck. He hopped over the boar's corpse and slammed his dagger into the boar's side, injecting a generous dose of acidic poison into its spleen. Its innards liquified and spilled out onto the ground, creating a hazardous pool of poison and further hindering the horde's movements.

Sorin caught a glimpse of Barbara's group through the crowd of demons. Two of her companions wielded swords to hold back the tide of crazed boars, while Barbara wielded a short spear and shield to significant effect.

As Barbara ran a boar through, Sorin angled his left hand and cast Threading the Spear at three adjacent boars to pierce their bodies with a shower of acid arrows. Their corpses melted as they fell, creating a gap in the encirclement that Sorin used to join the group of beleaguered adventurers.

"Look out!" Barbara shouted as Sorin reached their defensive line. A boar jumped out and tried to cut him off. Fortunately, Sorin didn't just have Lawrence, but Lorimer as well. The rat flung himself into the boar's eye socket and then exited out the other. The boar fell to the ground, dead, and was soon joined by many of its companions.

"You shouldn't have come," said Barbara through labored breaths as Sorin joined her team.

"What are you going to do? Send us back the way we came?" said Lawrence, popping out of Sorin's shadow. He took out a small crossbow and an arrow into a boar's eye from the safe center. "Do you need help, Miss Healer? Team 'We Don't Need a Life Mage' has a unique take on how to treat wounds, but I'm sure we could come to some sort of compromise."

"There's no need to bother yourselves," said the mage as she pulled her bloody hands away from her patient and pulled her clothes and armor back into place. "Do I need to kick you for you to get back to work, Suzanne?"

"I'm getting up," said the groggy tank. "It's just a bit of lost blood. Not a big deal." She picked up her shield and shoved it past Sorin. "This is my position, thank you. A lightly armored fellow like you shouldn't be fighting on the front lines."

Sorin agreed with that assessment. His new Blood Drinker Armor was still leather armor in the end. It would only give him partial protection against tusks and do nothing against hooves and headbutts.

He, therefore, retreated to the center with Lawrence and summoned a ball of acidic poison. The Veridian Smoke Bomb shot past a tiring swordswoman, melting three blood-tusk boars to the ground and creating a threatening area that no boars dared approach for the next five seconds.

The moment of respite was enough for Audrey, Barbara's life mage, to cast a stamina restoration spell and relieve her fatigue.

Sorin and Lawrence's arrival created a chain reaction that significantly reduced the pressure on Barbara's team. They were able to focus on killing boars instead of defending, which, in the long term, increased everyone's odds of survival.

When only twenty boars remained, Sorin jumped out of the encirclement alongside Lawrence and Lorimer. The rat was in his element and had even single-handedly dispatched fifteen Blood Tusk Boars. Sorin turned a blind eye to the cores the rat 'accidentally' devoured, as antagonizing him wouldn't do anyone any good.

"These boars aren't what's worrying me," Barbara said as she pierced the last boar through the neck. "They're cannon fodder. They're not even worth a second look. The real problem is that group of 200 Flame Antler Deer. They're much larger and stronger than the boars, and they seem to be accompanied by a two-star demon. Wait, is that Gareth and Daphne riding on *Stephan*?"

Compared to Lawrence and Sorin, the rest of Team 'We Don't Need a Life Mage' was either extremely slow or fragile. Gareth, for example, was quick enough to outrun Lawrence and Sorin but wouldn't survive charging into the encirclement of boars. The archer had, therefore, settled for shooting arrows from Stephan's back as the twelve-foot bear trudged along. Daphne had similarly cast two well-placed Fireballs from atop Stephan's back to eliminate problematic boars before they could become a problem.

"Sorry we took so long," said Stephan as Gareth and Daphne hopped off. He maintained his Arctic Rune Bear form, complete with the half plate he'd modified using the Minotaur's tusks and other armor pieces obtained from Daedalus's Labyrinth.

"That's a lot of Flame Antler Deer," said the staff-wielding Daphne. "I hate Flame Antler Deer. My fire spells won't even be half as effective against them."

"I'm less worried about that and more worried about their buck," said Gareth. "I spotted it hiding amongst the rest and can confirm it exists."

"They've finished grouping up and are readying for a charge,"

Barbara said to Stephan. "Suzanne and I can hold some of them back, but we'll need help against the buck."

"Don't worry about the buck," said Stephan. "I'll hold him back. Keep a safe distance from me, and everything will be fine."

The demonic deer were much faster than the demonic boars. They crossed half the thousand-foot distance separating them in under ten seconds. There was no time for advanced tactics, so Stephan placed himself just ahead of their group and prepared to receive the charge. Barbara and Suzanne took his flanks, while Sorin and Lawrence remained on standby.

Three. Two. One. Now!

Stephan launched himself forward at the last second, crashing into the front row of deer and knocking them backward. Barbara used her spear to catch a larger deer mid-charge while Suzanne raised her large shield and blocked a set of kicking hooves.

Fire erupted around Sorin and company as the deer, unable to adjust their charge on the fly, resorted to using long-ranged fire attacks against their team. Daphne countered this by summoning a fire shield around their group and holding on until it exploded, knocking back the dozen nearest deer without causing them much harm.

The charging deer were a problem for Sorin, who was used to fighting with a dagger at close range. He cast Threading the Spear to take out three charging deer as they approached. The 'spears' of acid caught them in the torso but failed to kill them. Clawed hooves stamped down on Sorin's arms, chest, and legs, thankfully missing vitals thanks to the help of his blood-drinker armor.

Sorin chugged a healing potion and trusted it to work its magic. *A total of seventeen bruises and accompanying crush injuries. Cracked bones, but none are broken. Setting of bones and removal of splinters are unnecessary.*

Even with the potion, Sorin's vitality was significantly depleted. Fortunately, the initial charge was done, and the deer were no longer fast-moving targets. Instead, the nightmarish demons attacked with reckless abandon, using their hooves, sharp teeth, and burning horns.

In battles like these, it was Lorimer who was most reliable. The rat had keen survival instincts, and thanks to its small size and sharp teeth and claws, he could burrow into his prey and eat it from the inside out. Sorin winced as he witnessed such a scene not more than ten feet away from him. A demonic deer let out an agonizing shriek as Lorimer burst out of its torso before diving back in to nibble at its insides.

Barbara's group had already formed a defensive encirclement around Gareth, Daphne, and Audrey. Arrows and Fireballs blasted apart demonic deer, covering the battlefield in a slick layer of fresh corruption and gore.

Meanwhile, Stephan had already engaged the two-star stag. He matched the creature blow for blow, creating a zone that one-star demons instinctively avoided, stabilizing their group's defensive perimeter.

I need to conserve mana, thought Sorin as the battle wore on. He'd already expended a fifth of his mana in the previous fight. He was constantly expending mana despite taking a sip from his potion. *Ophidian Eye, Viper Strike, and Adder Rush require very little mana, but they prevent my mana stores from regenerating. Still, they're the most efficient use of my mana for now. They will help us solidify our formation and mount a counterattack.*

An added benefit to Ophidian Eye was that it highlighted a target's mana system and lit up when techniques were being utilized. This allowed him to predict when a deer was about to use their movement technique and dispatch them before the activation was finalized.

The technique also allowed Sorin to analyze the condition of his teammates. Suzanne, for example, had sluggish mana and was barely holding on, courtesy of Audrey's restoration spells. Thankfully, Daphne and Gareth had diverted most of their attention to supporting the poor tank.

Stephan's condition is worsening, Sorin thought as he cast Threading the Spear once again to eliminate a small cluster of demons. *His mana fluctuations are about equal to the stag's. Still, the stag has a higher cultivation base and can maintain the expenditure for much longer.*

"Gareth! Daphne! Cover me while I break out to help Stephan!" Sorin shouted. He rushed out of the enclosure like a winding serpent, coiling around the confused demonic deer and trying to break through their defenses.

Sorin's movements naturally attracted the aggression of the demonic deer, and he soon became the target of sharp teeth, sharp hooves, and searing horns that had similar effects to a firebrand enchantment.

Arrows and Fireballs flew in to support Sorin, but avoiding everything was impossible. His body became littered with cuts and puncture wounds; his armor, soaked through with his poisonous blood, did its best to regenerate and cover his vitals.

Not much farther now, thought Sorin. He dodged a pair of sharp hooves and rolled beneath another deer, provoking an instinctual stomp. Left with no other options, he cast Threading the Spear and sprayed twelve acidic needles into the deer, melting the flesh off its bones.

Sorin dragged his body out of a pile of corrupted entrails and smashed a Veridian Smoke Bomb down on his location. A paralytic mist enveloped his surroundings, causing the demonic deer nearest him to stumble and stagger. Sorin was unaffected by the poison; he took advantage of their stunned state to dart between two deer and execute them with consecutive Viper Strikes to the neck.

The two deer were the last opponents he faced before entering a zone of extreme heat and cold. Fire was on the winning side. Ice was almost entirely restricted to a twelve-foot Arctic Rune Bear mauling a two-star demonic stag with surprising agility.

"I'm here to help, Stephan!" Sorin shouted out.

"Take your time," said Stephan, grunting as the stag forced him back. "It's not like I'm losing or anything."

BEAR VS STAG

The two-star stag was extraordinarily nimble and liked to jump in battle and kick out with its clawed hooves. Thanks to its thick demonic energy, its body had further mutated, granting the deer two additional legs and additional joints on each leg that made them resemble scorpion stingers.

Stephan wasn't fighting like he usually did. Instead of his trademark reckless style, he mostly opted for cautious swipes at the demon while maintaining a defensive posture. In many ways, he reminded Sorin of a badger defending his lair.

But Stephan won't be able to hold out much longer, thought Sorin. *His energy stores aren't as deep, even if he* can *match the stag blow for blow, thanks to his abilities as a Hero.* There was also the fact that the deer had mana shields, while Stephan didn't. His armor served to mitigate some of the damage, but it was already half-destroyed from the exchange and continued to deteriorate.

Having determined their respective strengths and weaknesses, Sorin activated Anti-Mage's Blade and covered his dagger with a network of solid but poisonous mana that specialized in tearing through mana shields. He kept his left hand empty in preparation for casting any spells he might require in the future, then began circling the stag in search of an opening.

Sensing the threat Sorin posed, the stag immediately adjusted its wild fighting style. Its horns lit up and blasted Sorin with a wave of heat that licked his flesh and burned his skin.

Sorin dodged the flame wave and dove in to try his luck with his dagger. He then pulled back on instinct, barely avoiding a clawed hoof that came flying from an inconceivable angle.

Sorin responded by throwing out a spray of three paralytic needles with his left hand. These needles contained Manabane Poison and easily pierced through the deer's mana shields and struck its side, disrupting the mana flow in its hip and preventing it from moving properly.

The deer pulled back its limp leg to protect it from future needle sprays; Sorin used the opportunity to close the distance. He avoided another flying hoof with Adder Rush, then stabbed his dagger two consecutive times into the same paralyzed hip. A large dose of Manabane Poison infiltrated the stag's body, temporarily causing its flames to go out.

Stephan took advantage of the stag's dimmed flames to drastically lower the temperature in the region, weakening the many one-star deer still besieging their companions. His two paws then rent through the deer's mana armor and tore into its tough leather, delivering a solid dose of cold energy and slowing its movements.

This gave Sorin the opening he needed to throw another paralytic needle. This time, he targeted the creature's neck, causing it to stagger and opening it up to Stephan's gauntleted claws.

Unfortunately, the difference in strength between this two-star demon and the Minotaur caused him to overestimate the duration of his poisons. Just as his latest batch of poison took effect, the first batch faded away, freeing up its hooves to slice Sorin's chest open and tear away a large chunk of flesh.

Another clawed hoof followed, but this time, Sorin used Cobra's gaze to stun the stag for an instant, giving him more than enough time to avoid it. Thanks to his armor's berserker effect, his speed was now greatly increased; he dodged the deer's follow-up attack and used Viper Strike twice more.

This time, Sorin didn't bother with paralytic poison and directly injected acidic mana into its system. The deer twisted in mid-air to retaliate, but Stephan, anticipating such a reaction, struck down with a Lunisolar Paw, interrupting its movements. The hoof barely grazed Sorin as he made his way to the creature's neck and slammed a poison-filled agger into its spine.

Sorin's deadly attack caused the two-star deer to go berserk. It slammed into Stephan's shoulder as he tried to assist Sorin, then bit into Sorin's left shoulder. Unable to free himself, Sorin grabbed his whip and tangled up the deer with Python Coil to prevent it from thrashing about and crushing him in the process.

Heavy damage to muscle tissues and nerves, Sorin analyzed as the deer thrashed. *Mana flow is disrupted along critical meridians. Recommendation: use Flesh-Melt Poison to close off key arteries, then apply a healing potion to regenerate lost flesh. Remove melted flesh to restore blood flow once a critical amount of flesh is restored.*

Like a puppet, Sorin acted on these instructions. He stabbed three points on his shoulder to stop the bleeding, then splashed a healing potion on his shoulder. He then pressed those same two spots, materializing a simple mana needle to break apart the obstruction he'd created.

All of this was very difficult while riding on a bucking deer, and while his actions weren't enough to restore the use of his arm, he could now rest easy knowing that his arm wouldn't be crippled for the foreseeable future.

Eventually, the deer realized that getting rid of Sorin in this way would be impossible. Flames burst out of the deer's flesh and threatened to roast Sorin alive, forcing him to release python coil and roll away before the deer could trample him.

Fortunately, Stephan was ready for him and attacked the berserk deer with steel-tipped claws. Blood splashed on the ground as both sides abandoned defense in favor of offense. Stephan's wounds were worse, but his critically low health seemed to trigger an ability in his armor that covered him in a light shield, rendering him temporarily impervious to damage.

Taking advantage of this period of invulnerability, the bear launched itself at the deer and tackled it to the ground. Sorin didn't hesitate to dive in and stab at the creature repeatedly, injecting it with heavy doses of paralytic poison.

The creature's thrashing grew increasingly weak as Stephan bit into the creature's neck, and Sorin's previous poisonous attacks erupted uncontrollably. Little by little, the creature lost its life, and finally, after ten seconds of limp thrashing, it collapsed, dead.

"You can relax now," Sorin said, confirming its demise with Ophidian Eye.

"That much is obvious," said Stephan, pulling back from the creature. "The demonic deer are routed. It won't be long before they scatter and return to the wilderness." Gareth and Daphne were picking off what demonic deer they could. Barbara had also taken out a bow, though her skills were lacking compared to Gareth's.

A minute later, the battle was at an end. Half the demonic deer had been slain, while the other half had run back into the wilderness. Having no further prey to hunt down, Stephan unshifted and took out a dagger, which he used to cut open the demonic stag's skull and retrieve a bloody crystal filled with violet energy.

"Its horns should also be excellent two-star materials," Stephan said to Sorin. "Its hooves, on the other hand, are full of corruption and can't be utilized."

The experienced adventurers quickly broke down into two camps: the healing camp and the gathering camp. Lawrence spearheaded the gathering, while Sorin joined Audrey. Sorin cleared corruption using poison, while the latter used her thick life mana to heal critical injuries. She had clearly received some medical education and was, therefore, able to avoid common errors and prevent accidental over-healing.

Five minutes later, horns sounded. A group of soldiers who had left the fort shortly after their battle made their way over. Sorin joined the other adventurers under Barabara and Stephan's lead and met with an old friend of theirs: the leader of this group of soldiers, Orpheus.

"We rushed out as soon as we heard about your predicament but were unable to verify the situation given the density of the demons present," Orpheus said to Stephan and Barbara. "I hope you'll forgive my understandable lateness."

"You could have easily made your way over if you wanted to," snapped Barbara, but she stopped when Stephan placed a burly hand on her shoulder.

"Don't worry, I'll take care of this," said Stephan. "Orpheus, it's nice to see you again. Did you come to assist us in looting the battlefield?"

"Looting the battlefield?" asked Orpheus. "The battlefield belongs to the Governor's Manor. I'll naturally need to trouble you to turn in all those demon cores you've collected."

"I'm afraid things don't work that way, Orpheus," said Stephan. "If you check the agreement between the Adventurers Guild and the Governor's Manor, you'll see that kills belong to those who made them. In cases of ambiguity, there is an equal split. It's too bad you took so long to get here that even a blind soldier standing on the walls would know you weren't here before the fighting ended."

Orpheus's jaw clenched. "Our presence on the battlefield exerted pressure on the deer horde."

"A tenuous argument," said Stephan. "It might even hold weight. But are you sure the governor wants to provoke the Adventurers Guild at such a crucial juncture? I believe the outpost's adventurers would be most upset if their income were suddenly put at risk because of the greed of a few corrupt soldiers."

Orpheus snorted. "Fine. The battlefield is yours. But the responsibility for clearing it also falls on your team."

"You don't need to worry about that," said Stephan. "We'll naturally take the best of it. As for what we can't carry, we'll torch it. Better to offer these things to Lord Hope instead of wasting them on ungrateful individuals."

Having failed to achieve his objective, Orpheus retreated. "That's it?" said Barbara. "That bastard basically tried to kill us just now, and all that happens is that he loses a share of the spoils he never earned?"

"Don't worry, he'll suffer immensely in the future," said Stephan.

"There's no love lost between him and the Adventurers Guild. When word breaks out about what happened—through no direct effort of my own, of course—you can be sure that no adventurer will dare support any troop he's in. Vice Governor Marsh will have no choice but to kick him down a notch and keep him inside the city to prevent further incidents."

"I never realized you were a schemer," said Lawrence, holding his thumb out. "Well done."

"I don't think the matter is so simple," said Sorin, shaking his head. "Don't you think this was too blatant on Orpheus's part?"

"Blatant?" asked Lawrence. "Hasn't he always been blatant?"

"Sorin's right," said Barbara. "He was blatant in the labyrinth, but that's because he could hide things if he succeeded. But this... this was just downright stupid."

"Are you saying he *wants* to get punished?" asked Stephan incredulously.

Sorin sighed. "It just reminds me of an incident in the Kepler Clan. A family member didn't have the contribution points to study in the library. Instead of going out to earn contribution points, he broke several library rules, which resulted in him getting punished with scribe duty. Two years later, he learned enough to pass the physician examination. By then, it was obvious what he did, but his value became too high for the family to punish him."

"I don't think we have enough information to assemble this puzzle," said Daphne. "Unless you all have some dirt on him or awareness of the situation inside the Governor's Manor?"

"We don't," said Barbara. "Though Audrey might. She *is* related to Governor Marsh."

They all looked at the bloody-handed life mage washing her hands. "What?" Audrey said. "It's a distant relation. I haven't visited my uncle, the governor, since Physician Kepler moved in as a guest."

"I agree with Daphne," said Sorin. "We don't know enough. But I'll wager that we'll soon find out what he's after. For him to go through this much risk, whatever he's after must be quite lucrative."

Their two teams retrieved the rest of the demon cores and cut off as many deer horns as they could carry. According to Daphne, mages could use the dust of their ground-up horns. Artificers could also use them as a base for flame brand enchantments or premium fuel for their furnaces. Some of the higher-quality pieces could even be used as core components for wands.

"*Lorimer*," Sorin warned when he noticed the rat trying to embezzle. "You only get to eat the cores of the demons you killed. And those cases are obvious. Don't try to sneak in extra portions for yourself."

Lorimer let out a few aggrieved squeaks, and Sorin shook his head. "No. You *can't* eat the horns. Not until after we're done packing up what we can. You can have the leftovers." As for the corpses, Lorimer could eat as many as he liked.

They returned to the settlement an hour later and split up the loot. After a ten-way split, the horns, cores, and bounties totaled up to 1,760 gold apiece. After replacing his health potions, Sorin had 1,500 gold remaining.

Stephan was the worst off in the exchange. Not only was he stuck spending 500 gold for materials to repair his damaged half-plate armor, but Haley also took the rest of his gold as part of his repayment to the York Clan. Fortunately, this was the last payment, and he would be free to keep all the spoils going forward and begin shoring up his lacking skillset.

CASUALTIES

Sorin and Barbara's teams were taken off rotation one day early due to their unexpected and intense battle. "I just got here, and now we're already getting time off?" asked Sorin, wincing as he rolled his shoulder. Flesh-Melt Poison and healing potions had prevented complications, but his arm would still need surgery to regain full functionality.

"Don't get too comfortable," said Stephan. "The current shifts are three days on and one day off. We won't find out till later if we're stuck on days or nights."

"Nights are the *worst*," added Lawrence. "You can't see anything out there, and sometimes, the dead rise and start attacking us."

"Then I guess I'd better not delay my trip to the clinic," said Sorin. "How about you? How are your wounds?"

"My hide is a lot tougher than it used to be," said Stephan. "I only suffered superficial injuries."

"You realize you volunteered to be the team's tank, don't you?" said Gareth.

"It doesn't make getting hurt less painful," Stephan snapped. "Since you and Lawrence are so idle, how about you go restock our potions and consumables?"

"I'm afraid I can't," said Gareth. "I finally saved up enough for the skill I want, and I need to practice. It looks like Lawrence will have to go on his own."

"Hey, why do I get saddled with mule duty again?" Lawrence complained.

"It's not nice to insult mules," said Daphne, taking a sip from her mana potion. She was pale, and her hands were shaking due to over-drafting her mana to summon fire shields throughout the battle.

The medical clinic was located just north of the southern gate. This was because the gate saw 50 percent more demons on average compared to the northern gate. The Temple of Hope's placement just north of the western entrance was responsible for this anomaly. One-star or even two-star demons didn't dare approach the temple's sacred boundary.

The clinic had a capacity of roughly fifty beds. A total of three physicians and two apprentices were on duty, including Marcus, the city's only two-star physician, and Gabriella, Sorin's former student.

These individuals were all hard at work, with the apprentices mostly performing triage and the physicians doing their best to heal critical injuries before they became irreparable.

There's a lot of critically wounded patients, thought Sorin as he tallied the severity of their injuries. *Eight patients are beyond saving and have been administered anesthetics. Twelve are critically wounded but should pull through given prompt treatment.* As for the others, there would be no long-term issues as long as they were seen in the next twenty-four hours.

"Apothecary Sorin, what brings you here?" Sorin was surprised by Marcus's respectful form of address but refrained from making any snide remarks.

"I was injured in the scuffle outside the northern wall," Sorin replied as Marcus approached him. "Things look quite busy here. Do you require my assistance?"

Marcus shook his head. "All the critical cases are being addressed, so that won't be necessary. We're busy but far from overwhelmed."

"Did the southern wall suffer an attack as well?" asked Sorin.

"Indeed, they did," answered Marcus. "And unlike the northern wall's relatively organized defense, only one team dared to stand up against the demons and buy their comrades time to retreat. As a result, the slower soldiers and adventurers were hunted down. Those you see here are those fortunate enough to survive that disaster.

Sorin's eyes quickly scanned the wounded and spotted a familiar face: the ice mage from Haster's team. His leg had been torn off, and the physicians had been unable to stop him from bleeding out. His corpse was still warm and had yet to be covered.

"How's Haster?" asked Sorin.

"I can't discuss specific patients for confidentiality reasons," said Marcus apologetically. "But patients are allowed friendly visitors. Does your shoulder need to be looked at now, or can it wait an hour?" He was clearly looking to start treating the next patient.

"It can wait," said Sorin. "A half-day, if needed. After that, nerve damage might start setting in."

"It shouldn't be so long," said Marcus. "I'll send someone over once things settle down."

Since Gabriella was busy, Sorin entered the temporary clinic in search of Haster. The building was made of clean canvas. The walls had been scrubbed clean less than four hours prior, and the place smelled of disinfectant and freshly boiled fever medicine.

A helpful nurse brought Sorin to a bed on the far side of the clinic. He breathed out a sigh of relief when he saw that Haster's limbs were intact. The man's beard was starting to fill in, connecting his thick side-burns to what might become a bushy mustache if he let it grow any longer.

The usual redness on the swordsman's face was nowhere to be found, though judging by the flask on his bedside table, Sorin suspected that had more to do with loss of blood than lack of liquor.

"I'm surprised they let you keep your alcohol," said Sorin, pulling up a seat. "It doesn't usually affect the medicine, but it puts an unnecessary strain on your liver and other organs."

Haster groaned as he turned his head toward Sorin. "I told them I'd refuse treatment if they refused me liquor. They were halfway to kicking me out when that uppity physician, Marcus, told them I was obviously chronically dependent on alcohol, and keeping me from drinking would probably kill me."

Sorin frowned and looked over Haster's condition with Ophidian Eye. "There's some truth to that. Less because of your dependency but more because of your mana. I've never seen such violent mana in a cultivator."

"I don't know about *that*, but I do know I've always had terrible headaches," said Haster. "Drinking is the only way to chase them off. Numbing the feeling of losing my companions is just a bonus."

"I'm sorry for your loss," said Sorin, deactivating Ophidian Eye. "They struck us up north, too. We managed to reach Barbara's team just in time. The soldiers on corpse duty were able to get away as a result."

Haster sighed. "They were right to run away. I don't resent them. All they did was follow the plan. Hell, half my team wanted to do the same. But I saw what would happen if we didn't hold those demons back. I should have died out there, but here I am."

The adventurer reached over for his flask but dropped it as pain arced through his arm. Sorin picked up the flask, opened it, and handed it to the man. "Do you need me to get you something stronger?"

"No need," said Haster. "This stuff is actually not bad, strength-wise. It's the taste that makes me flinch." He sighed once again. "I don't think I'm cut out for this adventuring gig, Sorin. A drunken swordsman is good at killing, but it comes at a price. The drink makes us reckless, and that recklessness gets people killed."

"Your recklessness saved a lot of good men and women," said Sorin. "Don't second-guess yourself. You did the right thing."

"I know," whispered Haster. "I just wish doing the right thing didn't hurt so damn much."

Seeing that his presence wasn't too helpful, Sorin tactfully retreated to the curtain. "Do you need me to pass along any messages?"

"Yeah," said Haster. "Tell the guild I'm retiring. Tell them to split my loot up and give it to my team's families. It's not worth as much as their lives, but it should help them get through the worst of it."

"I'll pass on the word, but no guarantees they'll listen to me," said Sorin, closing the curtain behind him.

Many cases were much worse than Haster's. Most of the outpost's soldiers were non-cultivators, and it was these lesser soldiers who went out to collect the loot, arrows, and cores that had gotten caught by the invading demons.

Three painful hours passed before a familiar figure approached Sorin. "Gabriella," he greeted. "I saw you earlier, but you were busy. I didn't want to interrupt your work."

"As if I'd let such a small thing affect my work," said Gabriella. "You should have said hello at the very least."

"Are you here to assist a physician?" asked Sorin.

"Actually, I've been assigned to your case alone," said Gabriella smugly. "Assuming you think my skills are up to the challenge."

"I think you'll do all right," replied Sorin. "The procedure is relatively low risk, though I should warn you to take precautions against poisonous blood."

"Don't worry, I made preparations for that," said Gabriella, rubbing her hands together—a shroud of protective life mana wrapped around them.

"The jade hand technique," said Sorin with approval. "It looks like you took the reading I assigned to heart."

"Most of us in the clinic had to learn the skill," said Gabriella. "Marcus's orders. It's mostly for handling poisonous ingredients in the lab, but it *does* have a few practical applications in the clinic."

Gabriella led Sorin to a curtained-off area. The hospital bed had already been covered in a sheet of protective mana foil. A thick layer of non-reactive absorbent pads would catch any blood that spilled. "We normally just take these out for extreme cases of corruption," Gabriella explained. "They were collecting dust in the back until Marcus told us to pull them out for your treatment."

"Speaking of Marcus, how is he treating you?" asked Sorin.

"Very well, actually," said Gabriella. "The trial period was difficult, but I understood what he was doing. If all goes well, I should be able to take the physician's examination in the new year."

"That's good," said Sorin, wincing as Gabriella pressed his shoulder with her mana-covered hands. Streams of life mana poured into his arm, probing his wounds and outlining the teeth marks that had crushed his flesh and even chipped his bones.

"No infection. Surprising," said Gabriella. "Is your constitution immune to disease?"

"Highly resistant," Sorin admitted. "To corruption as well, assuming it's not too high-grade."

"Your regenerative abilities are very impressive," said Gabriella, pressing into the deepest wound. Sorin couldn't help but gasp in pain. "Though, in this case, that isn't a good thing. Your wounds have healed over foreign objects." She pulled out an enchanted scalpel and cut at the boundaries of the 'room,' isolating it from the outside world. A silver light flashed as the enchantment on the scalpel purified all elements of disease and corruption floating in the air and on Sorin's clothes and skin.

Only then did Gabriella proceed to mark key areas on Sorin's shoulder using a mana pen. There were three places where his bones had chipped, resulting in obstructions to blood flow. The largest mark, however, was reserved for the tooth fragment that had embedded itself in Sorin's bones and tangled with his nerves and meridians.

"I thought Marcus was exaggerating when he said your blood was corrosive," Gabriella muttered as she cut into Sorin's flesh. A small amount of blood seeped out before she managed to block his artery with life mana. Sorin's own mana instinctively fought against it, but he managed to control the interaction enough for her to clamp it off.

Gabriella then proceeded to pull out the obstructing bone chip with tweezers. "I think I'll have to throw away this scalpel and these tweezers when I'm done with you."

"Just send the bill to the Adventurers Guild," said Sorin. "I'm sure they'll handle it."

"I'm sure they will, given the situation outside," said Gabriella. She repeated the procedure for the two other minor injuries before prepping to extract the tooth fragment. "Do you need any anesthetic?" she asked.

"Won't work," said Sorin, shaking his head. "My poison resistance is too high."

"A pity," said Gabriella, making a face. "Hopefully, you're tougher than you used to be."

Sorin gasped lightly as Gabriella cut deep into his flesh and used forceps to pry apart his skin. A small piece of decaying yellow bone was lodged in his shoulder joint, where a mass of nerves, veins, and one of his meridians met.

This confirms that I'm not completely immune to corruption, thought Sorin as he watched her pull out the tooth fragment from a mass of black flesh. Gabriella then quickly blocked off the blood flow and scraped away the corrupt tissue, leaving only raw, regenerating flesh where a putrid infection had once been.

Sorin had to admit that Gabriella had improved since his departure. Marcus had clearly been tutoring her and was not neglecting her as he'd first thought.

Her cultivation has improved substantially as well, thought Sorin, activating Ophidian Eye. Her network of twelve naturally opened primary meridians and four naturally opened extraordinary meridians lit up in his eyes. Her talent was one of the reasons he'd taken her in despite his body's poor condition.

It took her only a few minutes to stitch up his wound. She tried healing him, but due to the violent interactions between life mana and poison mana, she was forced to relent and use a healing potion to promote local regeneration instead.

"Judging from your natural regeneration response, you should be good as new in half a day," said Gabriella, tidying up the blood in the area and throwing the bloodied materials in a mithril bin for later disposal. "You should watch out for yourself, Sorin. You might be an adventurer now, but that doesn't mean your life is disposable."

"But if I don't get hurt, how am I going to get to see you?" asked Sorin with a grin.

Gabriella chuckled. "Silly boy. You're older than I am, but you still can't figure out that you don't *need* a reason to visit someone, assuming you enjoy their company."

"I don't suppose you have time for a coffee or something?" asked Sorin.

"I'm afraid not," said Gabriella, shaking her head. "The clinic is extremely busy, and we've got a strict rotation to ensure that we're prepared for emergencies at all times. Also, there's the drug trials that are still ongoing."

"Drug trials?" asked Sorin. Her words piqued his interest. Was Marcus being so blatant as to perform drug trials out in the open?

"It's an experimental treatment proposed by the Kepler Clan," said Gabriella. "The idea is to use a simplified version of the Kepler Clan's meridian-opening procedure to allow wounded veterans to partially recover their capabilities. They could then return to work or combat, depending on their preferences."

"Any results so far?" asked Sorin.

"There are a few promising subjects," said Gabriella. "Some soldiers in the garrison, for example. They'd retired due to their wounds but can now properly wield mana and weapons."

Sorin was skeptical about the validity of this so-called treatment but gave no indication of this to Gabriella. *According to the potions being brewed, he's clearly trying to zero in on the original formula. This isn't a fine-tuning but an actual drug trial in disguise.* Fortunately, the ingredients were all geared towards the primary meridian-opening tincture. There were few permanent adverse consequences to receiving treatment with a sub-optimal tincture. At worst, the meridians in question wouldn't open.

Even so, Sorin vowed to investigate the matter. If Marcus got too ambitious and attempted dangerous experiments, he would do everything he could to put a stop to it.

Sorin and Gabriella chatted for a few more minutes before she escorted him out of the tent. He passed Marcus on his way out. The man was reviewing reports now that the number of critical patients had been reduced.

"Gabriella, make sure to bring those bandages to the hazardous waste bin," Marcus called out behind them. "We wouldn't want anyone to get poisoned because they're unaware of the risks."

"Right away, sir," said Gabriella. She gave Sorin an apologetic look before rushing back into the clinic.

Having finished recovering, Sorin decided to retire early and get some rest. The half-day he needed to recover would require active effort on his part. Moreover, the demon tide was still ongoing. All adventurers were still on call, and there was no telling when the emergency bell would toll, mustering everyone for one last bloody battle.

———

Shortly after Sorin left the clinic, Marcus personally took it upon himself to dispose of the clinic's hazardous waste. Most of it was just simple contaminated waste that required incineration, but there was one exception: the bandages and absorbent pads that had been used during Sorin's surgery.

Marcus gingerly recovered these materials before making his way back to the Growing Branches Community Clinic. The small laboratory was currently not in use.

A short while later, Marcus walked out of the laboratory and took a seat in his office to review the test results. "Mostly acidic components, with a minor paralytic component," he muttered. "The tests can't determine what the mysterious element in his poisonous blood is, but fortunately, I can."

There was only one poison that was corrosive enough to inhibit his two-star mana: Manabane Poison.

72

TOXICOLOGY ASSESSMENT

The next day was an off-shift day for Team 'We Don't Need a Life Mage.' After verifying that his companions were fine and that they'd all unlocked a few additional silver meridians, Sorin returned to the poison workshop in the Alchemists Association, where Mr. Primrose was hard at work.

The older man greeted Sorin briefly before turning back to a large cauldron of poison he was busy concocting for the defense effort. Sorin recognized the poison as scorching bramble ash, a one-star poison with unlimited demand on the mission board. As a two-star apothecary, Mr. Primrose could concoct ten times as much scorching bramble ash as Sorin could, though his time was normally spent crafting rarer poisons.

"Are you here to fulfill missions or to craft personal poisons?" Mr. Primrose asked after a while.

"I'm here for personal poisons and cultivation," replied Sorin. "Do we have any Dream Butterfly Wings and Asphyxiating Sage Root in stock?"

"We've got a limited quantity of both," answered Mr. Primrose. "I'll pull them aside so that no one nabs them to make sleeping medicine or other similarly useless things. By the way, do you have a few hours to spare?"

"What do you need?" asked Sorin.

"There's a toxicology assessment request that came in from Physician Lim's clinic," said Mr. Primrose. "A patient is experiencing severe diarrhea. No blood in the stool. Dr. Lim and a life mage he sent the sample to have detected no disease, so they wanted to see if poisons were responsible."

"How's the patient?" asked Sorin.

"Recovering," said Mr. Primrose. "It's just a routine procedure. No need to bother yourself if you have something better to do."

"I'm a little busy right now," said Sorin. "And can't any alchemist do this?"

"They always pass these requests on to us for priority since they're higher-risk jobs than alchemical requests," said Mr. Primrose. "Since you're not free, I'll let them know to assign this to a junior alchemist."

Sorin went to the back of the workshop, where a small cultivation chamber lay, and retrieved the seven vials of Stone-Melt Poison that remained. He directly drank one and felt it dissipate throughout his body, weakening his bones temporarily as the other eight poisons in his body confronted and consumed the invading poison.

Thanks to the intense combat the previous day, it took Sorin only a few hours to completely digest four vials of Stone-Melt Poison. He kept the remaining three vials for later, as absorbing them would take too much time.

Sorin now had a considerable amount of wealth to throw around and had seen the shortcomings of his personal poisons. While they grew with his cultivation realm and the potency of his blood, they were somewhat lacking compared to stronger prepared poisons that could be applied mid-battle.

Three poisons stood out to Sorin as particularly useful—Dream Butterfly Powder, Blisterlung Powder, and Dream Blade Ointment. The first of these poisons was ideal for knocking crowds of lesser demons unconscious. The second could kill said demons within ten seconds, while the third could be applied to bladed weapons in order to achieve a more potent sleeping effect.

Sorin spent eight hours preparing multiple batches of said poisons before he was forced to stop by a splitting headache. In total, he'd managed to produce two pouches of Dream Butterfly Powder, four pouches of Blisterlung Powder, and three vials of Dream Blade Ointment.

While Sorin had not chosen any overly complex features for his armor, Mr. Sanderson had worked in several useful pockets where pouches could be stored. Sorin carefully arranged the poison pouches in easy-to-remember locations. As for ointment, he placed the tubes on his belt for quick breaking and application.

Sorin wanted to continue crafting but was ultimately forced to stop. Not because of fatigue but because of funding—whatever gains he'd experienced in battle had been completely used up on raw ingredients.

Since further concocting was impossible, Sorin spent his time letting out blood for use as application poison to be used by his teammates. Since the blood was thin and would pit most steel arrows, he had Lorimer heat the blood until it congealed. The resulting jelly was mixed with compatible oils, which he poured into custom vials for Lawrence and a small cylinder that Gareth could dump a handful of arrows into.

It was late at night when Sorin finished his work, so he decided to sleep in one of the workshop's two cots. The Alchemists Guild was relatively quiet at nighttime, except for the occasional explosion, so he quickly drifted off to sleep.

It felt like only an hour had passed when Sorin was abruptly awakened by fierce knocking on the workshop's door. Tired but functional, Sorin walked over to the door and opened it to see a frantic alchemist.

"Thank goodness you're here!" said the alchemist, who looked to be barely older than seventeen years old. "Quick, take a look at this." He barged past Sorin and laid down a test kit on the table. "It's poison, all right. Some kind of condensed corruption. But it's unlike anything I've ever seen."

Sighing, Sorin made his way over to the test tubes in question. He took the original sample and sniffed it. "This is the patient's blood? The one with the diarrhea?"

"Yes," said the alchemist. "Though I can scarcely believe it after finishing the tests. Did you know it's closer to—"

"Demon blood," said Sorin, cutting him off. "This blood is so corrupted that it's bordering on mutation. Is this a new sample? And how exactly did the doctors not spot this? And what's the patient's status?"

"He's dead," said the alchemist with a gulp. "I received word ten minutes ago. Moreover, there are a hundred additional toxicology report requests, all with the same symptoms."

Sorin massaged his brow and pieced together what little information he had. *This can't be an epidemic since corruption doesn't spread like a disease except in specific cases. To affect so many people, it must be environmental.* He quickly ran through the many options for possible contamination sources. "Are all the cases from the same address?"

"No, they're from all across the city," said the alchemist.

"Then it must come from the water," said Sorin, returning the vial of blood to the panicking alchemist. "Go downstairs and have the receptionist alert the guild master."

"But the receptionist has already gone home," said the alchemist.

"Then activate the fire alarm," Sorin snapped. "Anything to grab his attention. After that, arrange for someone to send this vial of blood to Mr. Primrose. I'll run over to the Mages Guild and let them know about the situation." Then, remembering that they had a very important ally to draw on, he amended his statement. "Once you send word to Mr. Primrose, find a way to deliver a message to Physician Marcus Kepler. This situation is going to spiral out of control quickly."

"Right away!" said the alchemist, breaking into a run. He returned a few seconds later to grab the test results he'd forgotten on the table.

Sorin left the Alchemists Guild and broke into a run. He didn't stop until he arrived at the Mages Guild. "Can I help you?" asked a sleepy receptionist. Fortunately, the Mages Guild never really shut down and had staff available at all hours.

"I need either the guild master or vice guild master here right now," said Sorin. "This is an emergency. Do it, and I'll take responsibility for the fallout."

"What's all this ruckus?" said an elderly voice. A blurry figure walked from the library at an impossible speed and arrived before Sorin. "Well? You said it was an emergency, didn't you? Speak up!"

Sorin immediately explained the issue with the test tube, the hundred toxicology requests, as well as his speculations about aqueduct contamination. "I realize I'm cutting through a lot of red tape, but if it's corruption of the water supply, we don't have much time to waste."

"Indeed," said the elder. "I'll apprise the guild master and vice guild master of the situation and send word to the Adventurers Guild. "You've already sent word to key members of the Alchemists Guild, correct?"

"Yes," said Sorin. "I plan to head to the northwest, where the river enters the outpost next."

"Very well," said the elder. "But if the matter is beyond your ability to handle, be sure to wait until reinforcements arrive."

Sorin ran out the door and rushed over to the northwest guard house. He thanked his lucky stars when he saw a crowd of senior cultivators there, along with Mr. Primrose, who'd evidently gotten his message.

"How bad is it?" asked Sorin.

"I've never seen such heavy contamination in a river," said Mr. Primrose. "I'm also uncertain as to the source of the contamination. I sent a message to the Mages Guild, and they've informed me that they're divining potential solutions."

"Has Marcus been informed?" asked Sorin.

"He's currently being awoken from seclusion, or so I'm told," said Mr. Primrose. "As for the governor, he's at a critical moment in his cultivation. Waking him will be harmful to the defense efforts, so we won't do so unless we have no choice. Ah, there you are, Derrek."

"I came as soon as I heard what was going on, Alexis," said Vice Guild Master Thomas to Mr. Primrose. "The guild master has gone to the eastern wall where the aqueduct leaves the outpost to get a better picture of the problem. Meanwhile, Elder Book will analyze the soil for contamination."

Sorin groaned when he heard this. "You're saying this isn't just limited to the water itself, but the soil as well?"

"That appears to be the case," the vice guild master said. "But we'll confirm the extent soon enough. Ah, here's Elder Book's familiar. Let's see what he has to say."

A small sparrow swooped down from the sky and deposited a small scroll in Thomas's outstretched palm. The man opened the scroll and scanned its contents. "Soil corruption is confirmed. That can only mean that the corruption in the water is extremely high."

"Did either of them pinpoint the source?" asked Mr. Primrose.

"Negative," said Vice Guild Master Thomas. "Also, the number of afflicted villagers has increased to 300. It appears that the corruption snuck into the water supply, and anyone who drank any water in the past twelve hours is slowly succumbing.

"I'll trust you to inform the outpost residents to refrain from drinking any more water unless it's confirmed to be pure," said Mr. Primrose. "As for you, Sorin, I have a very important task for you."

"Anything," said Sorin.

"Think," said Mr. Primrose, his expression turning serious. "Because if we don't discover the nature of this poison very shortly, there will be no saving this entire outpost."

73

BLOOD CORRUPTION POISON

Mr. Primrose was experienced in assessing environmental contamination. In the time that Sorin was able to brainstorm ten ideas as to what might be the cause of the corruption, the man had thought up dozens and taken out an array of test tubes, each with their own corresponding test medium.

"Have that earth flame rat of yours heat ten of these vials, then add three drops of river water into each one," directed Mr. Primrose as he took out two portable heating arrays. "You'll need to use your spiritual strength and mana to merge the drops and the test solution. A color change will indicate a positive or negative response for a specific type of contaminant.

Sorin immediately got to work according to the apothecary's arrangements. As he tested, he also used his mana to probe the water samples and assimilate their poisons.

Unfortunately, the amount of poison present in the vials was too minute, so Sorin couldn't fully identify the contaminant. He *did*, however, discover that it specialized in attacking an individual's bloodstream, not the intestines, as initially diagnosed. Excessive diarrhea was just an extra, meaningless symptom.

As the two apothecaries busied themselves with testing the river water, the Alchemists Guild, in conjunction with the Mages Guild, began brewing possible anti-toxins and drafting river water remediation plans. The sheer volume of water in the aqueduct was difficult to manage for the mages, but if it were just dispersing anti-toxins, that wouldn't be a problem.

"It's not a mineral contaminant or a metal," said Sorin. "I've also confirmed that it's not a disease."

"It's not an acid or an emulsifier," said Mr. Primrose. "It's not pure corruption either, though it contains corruption in large amounts."

"Could it be a different poison, amplified by corruption?" asked Sorin. "Then it would have dual characteristics and would resonate with the strong aura of violence near Bloodwood Forest."

"You're suggesting the virulence of the poison is indirect?" asked Mr. Primrose.

"It's merely speculation," said Sorin.

"It's a workable idea," said Mr. Primrose. "Unfortunately, none of these tests would be able to identify it. We should finish these and see if we're so lucky as to find the answer with standardized testing first."

Twenty minutes later, they were no closer to a solution, as the potential poisons that could be involved were reclusive and unknown. Sorin naturally had access to a full database of potential poisons, but like Mr. Primrose, he was limited in his ability to match highly specific information to the test results and symptoms they'd discovered.

"What if we looked at this from a different angle?" Sorin thought out loud. "For one, the carrying mechanism. We've confirmed that the poison is a colloidal solution."

"Colloidal solutions are rare," Mr. Primrose reluctantly agreed. "It *does* narrow it down somewhat. But most of these would need to be intentionally added to the river. The Season of Madness isn't upon us yet, so I'm skeptical that there's a saboteur among our cultivators causing all of this."

"Since it's happening during the demon tide, it must be the work of demons," agreed Sorin. "Intelligent demons exist, or so I'm told."

"But a demon strong enough to corrupt this water could flatten the outpost," said Mr. Primrose. "Why bother corrupting the river water and the land along with it?"

"That just narrows it down even further," said Sorin. "What could demons access in large quantities that would form a colloidal solution?"

Mr. Primrose's eyes widened. "Blood. Demon blood."

"That's indeed a strong possibility," agreed Sorin. "The blood of certain demons is highly toxic. Moreover, it will naturally carry corruption, which would result in a corrupted poison."

"Contaminating our water supply wouldn't be difficult either," added Mr. Primrose. "All they'd need to do is dump some bloody corpses upstream of the river and have them leak down into the outpost using the water's natural flow."

"Doing so in this fashion would also bypass the temple of hope's measures against corruption," said Sorin. "It's a known fact that temples are situated outside of their outposts in part to purify the water supply coming in. Against normal corruption flowing from the wilderness, it's enough, but against poisonous blood? It wouldn't be very effective."

Having determined the likely source of the contamination, Mr. Primrose shot a wave of poisonous mana into the air. Five figures immediately appeared—Vice Guild Master Victor from the Adventurers Guild, Vice Guild Master Thomas from the Mages Guild, Vice Guild Master Young from the Alchemists Guild, and Vice Governor Marsh from the Governor's Manor.

"We just finished damming off the water supply," said Vice Governor Marsh. "All that's left is purifying the water supply inside the outpost. What progress would you like to appraise us on, Alexis?"

"I'm afraid that given the source of the contamination, simply damming off the water supply won't suffice," said Mr. Primrose. "We've yet to verify this, but our best guess is that poisonous demon blood is responsible for the contamination."

Vice Guild Master Victor frowned. "Are you saying there are poisonous demon carcasses leaking blood into our water supply? That wouldn't have such a disproportionate impact. Unless…"

"Unless the number of corpses numbered in the dozens," finished

Vice Governor Marsh. "Fortunately, something like this is easy to verify. Ashley, can I trouble you to scout out this matter? Once we confirm if there are corpses and how difficult they are to remove, we'll mobilize additional forces."

"I'll take Haley and go immediately," said Vice Guild Master Victor.

"Since the water supply is dammed off, the most pressing issue isn't the source of the corruption, but how to deal with this corrupted water," said Vice Guild Master Thomas.

"Indeed it is," said Vice Guild Master Young in a rare display of intraguild agreement. "Otherwise, the outpost's soil will need to be changed out. Judging by the rate of corruption, over a fifth of the outpost's territory will become unlivable in the next twenty-four hours."

"Unfortunately, there are no aggressive ways to handle this sort of contamination," said Mr. Primrose. "Only basic poison manipulation would be able to dredge out the contaminants. The only other solution I can think of is having the priests from the Church of Hope cast their blessings on the river to weaken its corruption and slow the spread. Boiling the water will also work, but the amount of energy required is astronomical."

"This is our number one priority," said Vice Governor Marsh to those in attendance. "Moreover, it is clear that an intelligent demon is presiding over this year's demon tide and is using underhanded tactics. Derek, how many fire mages can you round up quickly?"

"Probably a hundred," said Vice Guild Master Thomas. "It's the most popular specialization by far."

"I'll trouble you to mobilize them and also to mobilize your guild's geomancers to isolate sections of the river just like you did the water source," said Vice Governor Marsh. "Compartmentalization, then purification. The fire mages will boil the water, as Mr. Primrose suggested. Ellest?"

"Yes?" answered Vice Guild Master Young.

"Has the Alchemists Guild come up with a cure for this poison?" asked Vice Governor Marsh.

"Alexis thought up a solution, and we already have every alchemist in the city making anti-toxins for the afflicted," said Vice Guild Master Young. "With the guild master, Alchemist Avery, and I joining forces, we'll be able to concoct enough to treat the worst of cases."

"Please do so," said Vice Governor Marsh. "Alexis, it seems Ashley's back with our answer already. What's the word, Ashley?"

"I've located 50 corpses, all cut up and piled up ten miles up, just at the edge of the woods," said Vice Guild Master Victor. "Haley went to get Guild Master Roy. We'll send all the adventurers we can spare to assist in the cleanup, though life mages will be assigned to assisting Marcus and the other physicians, who are currently organizing temporary clinics."

"Very good," said Vice Governor Marsh. "Please take Wesley and a contingent of soldiers along in case of trouble."

"Affirmative," said Vice Guild Master Victor before disappearing.

"Alexis, Sorin, we'll have to trouble you to join the mages in purifying as much of the water as you can," said Vice Governor Marsh.

"We'll do as you say," said Mr. Primrose. "Sorin, I take it you know how to separate poisons from water?"

"I've got a ring of poison manipulation to help me along, so I'll be fine," said Sorin. "Where would you like me to start?"

"In the middle, where the poison isn't too weak or too strong," said Mr. Primrose. "The mages and I will start at the river entrance and work their way towards you."

Sorin set out without any hesitation. On his way, he passed adventurers and soldiers evacuating villagers away from the river. Included was his own team, excluding Daphne, who was to assist in boiling river water.

By the time Sorin arrived, the geomancers had already sectioned the river using small dams of stone. The aqueduct was actually a more appropriate term, as its walls were reinforced, though many people still called it 'the river.' It was thirty feet wide and three feet deep. As a result, even a 300 foot section contained a substantial amount of water.

As ordered, Sorin began extracting poison from the river water and dumping it into a barrel. The corrupt blood was a muddy color since not all water could be separated from it.

Unfortunately, there's too much water. I'll die of exhaustion before I finish this small section.

Yet, there was little else Sorin could do. He continued separating poison from water and managed to extract a full three barrels of diluted demon blood before he finally sat down on the ground, exhausted. *I didn't even fully purify a single section yet.* The land nearest the river was already showing signs of blight.

The mages and Mr. Primrose weren't having a much better time of it. In the time that Sorin half-cleaned a single segment, they only managed to clean five despite their superior numbers. Mr. Primrose was responsible for two of these sections. *At this rate, we'll be able to prevent half the potential corruption. Not nearly enough, given the stakes involved.*

Seeing no better solution to their problem, Sorin could only turn to his last resort. *My body has already begun absorbing the Stone-Melt Poison, but it's not an irreversible process. If I absorb this Blood Corruption Poison, I'll then be able to use my own body to extract the poison instead of using my spiritual strength. I'll be able to speed up the process by ten, if not twenty, times!*

There was naturally a drawback to this solution—by taking in so much poison that his body had yet to assimilate, Sorin would inevitably be poisoned. There was also corruption to worry about. But Sorin was beyond caring.

I can worry about corruption later, Sorin thought as he made his way into the river, ignoring the warning calls of the guards beside him. *If the land is contaminated too severely, water distribution will become an issue. Non-cultivators will be the first to perish.*

74

TOXIC METABOLISM

Given Sorin's resistance to poison, the river water flowing through the aqueduct was minimally harmful to him. That all changed when he began circulating the Ten Thousand Poison Canon to absorb poison through his skin, directly drawing it into his blood and mana.

Thirty percent. Forty percent. Fifty percent. Sixty! Sorin rapidly drained one section of poison by replacing his Stone-Melt Poison. He excreted the old poison through a trickle of blood into a flask that he placed on the aqueduct's stone wall.

Having finished the purification, he wasted no time jumping into the next section and repeating the poison absorption process. "You should be careful of how much contamination you take in," warned a priest who witnessed Sorin's antics. "Corruption is a dangerous poison. Even us priests have difficulty neutralizing it in high doses."

"Many thanks for the warning," said Sorin. "I know what I'm doing."

"Hope bless," said the priest of Hope, who continued past him downstream of the river.

Having gotten rid of the meddlesome priest, Sorin began the absorption process once again. Unfortunately, he hit a wall in his efforts seconds after he began. This was because his blood had reached its limits and found it difficult to assimilate additional poison and transform itself.

Left with no better choice, Sorin ignored this limitation and forcibly absorbed the poison into his body. This brought the poison well above his tolerance limit but still succeeded in purifying the section of the aqueduct.

By the time he reached the next section, the poison had begun to affect Sorin. Blood-red veins had appeared all over his body. He ejected what poison he could into one of the many barrels placed on the river's edge, but doing so also removed what was keeping the corruption in his body in check. Fortunately, he still had Lorimer to help him deal with the situation.

While fully ridding himself of corruption was impossible, he was able to concentrate it at certain points in his body, forming small blobs, cists, and blisters that Lorimer devoured to enhance his cultivation. The rat's aura grew increasingly menacing as he broke through to the tenth stage of Blood-Thickening.

Unfortunately, that's only a part of the corruption, thought Sorin. A second part remained inside his flesh and bones, striking a tenuous balance with the existing poisons in his body. Mercifully, the same priest of Hope that had warned him appeared then and placed his hands on Sorin. His body was engulfed in a white fire that burned away the pustules and excess corruptive elements.

"My Lord has instructed me to stay here and purify you periodically," said the priest with a smile. "But there are limits, Sorin Abberjay Kepler. Very few human beings exceed them and live to tell the tale."

"Don't worry," said Sorin. "I value my life very much. But I can risk a bit of long-term contamination and delays to my cultivation to limit the corruption. Otherwise, there's no telling how many people will go mad from exposure in the winter."

He moved on to the next segment, once again absorbing more poison than he could bear. His organs were showing early signs of failure, and puss oozed out from cracks on his skin as he used his body as a conduit to eject the poison from the river.

"Do you not care about your own life?" asked the priest as Sorin concentrated his corruption into pustules once again. "Do you not care about the truth you seek?"

"Bite my shoulder and draw blood," said Sorin to Lorimer, ignoring the priest. "I'm going to force a large amount of corruption back out and into you." He did so, and the priest followed up by purifying him a second time.

With Lorimer's and the priest's help, Sorin completely absorbed the third segment's poison and moved on to the fourth. Unfortunately, it became impossible to eject the poison completely. Moving became difficult, and Sorin danced on the edge of unconsciousness.

This was his limit, Sorin realized. This was where he stopped. *Four segments are already more than enough. The mages and Mr. Primrose will take care of the rest.*

As was his habit, he performed a full inspection of his body. *Organ failure is imminent but is being kept in check by my natural regeneration. Mana and blood contamination are high, but my poisons are currently maintaining a balance. Recommendation: Absorb additional poisons to eject corruption. Nurture the hemotoxin in my body to promote its growth and eventual role as my ninth poison.*

Having confirmed his vitals, he moved onto his meridians. Though they were strained from all the poison coursing through his body, they were still elastic and free from perforation. Corruption had begun settling into them and was forming preliminary blockages, but those were nothing he couldn't handle with the Ten Thousand Poison Canon.

Sorin also performed a cursory inspection on his Conception Vessel. He wasn't expecting any changes since he wasn't in combat, but he was surprised to see that many of the seals had cracked open. *Is it not combat that breaks open seals but exertion instead?* thought Sorin. *Or maybe challenging my limits like I've been doing with this poison?*

The smart thing would be stopping now, but if opening the Conception Vessel was possible, that would change the equation. And not just for opening his own, but also for understanding how the seals were opened in the first place.

Few were like Sorin, who could actively monitor their condition. Physicians rarely opened their Conception Vessel, likely because opening it required pressure that very few encountered while practicing medicine.

Sorin cautiously lowered himself into the fifth segment and once again drank in its poison and corruption. As the strain on his body mounted, so too did the strain on the silver seals until, finally, a seal cracked open, followed by a second and a third, sending streams of silver energy that poured into his blood and mana, alleviating his condition somewhat and allowing him to go just a little further.

Once the fifth segment was done and the priest and Lorimer finished their purification, Sorin proceeded to the sixth segment. There, his hair turned white. And in the seventh segment, his eyes took on a sickly green tinge. By the eighth, his bones had grown brittle, and three of his ribs had fractured. The corruption became unmanageable even with the priest and Lorimer controlling it.

"Sorin Abberjay Kepler, you have done enough," said the priest as Sorin pulled himself out of the water. "If you stop now, it is still possible to use a wish to save yourself. At the very least, you can preserve your life and continue as a mortal physician."

"You're saying that if I stop now, I'll be able to live, but I'll be crippled?" Sorin asked the priest.

"You had hope of coming out unscathed if you'd listened to my advice earlier," said the priest in a stern tone. "But you declined my advice, so here we are. Life is the only thing you can hope for now. For giving Hope to so many lives, I believe there's a good chance that my Lord will grant such a request."

Sorin knew the risk to his life was real, but he'd known it when he'd decided to continue despite reaching his limits. By pushing himself, he'd unlocked all but one last silver seal, and his instincts told him that breaking this seal would be a game-changer and reverse the entire situation.

"There's no difference between living and dying if I go back to the way I was before," said Sorin, shaking his head. "So I'll continue as before."

"A human cannot withstand additional poison," said the priest of Hope. "This is not my opinion as a priest, but a revelation from my lord."

"Then I'll have to become something more than human," said Sorin.

Though he was willing to risk his own life for a breakthrough, others were a different matter. He grabbed the fattened Lorimer, who was now brimming with corruption. "You've eaten enough for now. If you keep on going, you'll lose yourself to Violence." He tossed the rat to the priest, who caught it with a deft hand. "Keep an eye on him, will you? I've got work to do." Then, laboriously, he dragged his body over to the next segment.

The tenth river segment felt like a bucket of ice water, fresh from the Mages Guild, courtesy of the many ice mages practicing their magic in the warm summer weather. As a physician, Sorin could tell that his body was on the verge of shutting down. His mana was showing signs of losing control, and it wouldn't be long before he lost consciousness and never awakened.

Yet he also felt the strain in that silver seal and the resonance with the rest of his body. The Ten Thousand Poison Canon trembled with joy every time a seal broke, and likewise, the corruption in his body quivered in fear.

Sorin, therefore, urged the Ten Thousand Poison Canon to drink in the corrupted poison in the river, knowing full well that should he fail, there would be no saving him. His consciousness began to fade when, suddenly, he felt something inside him shatter. He grinned as he felt his gamble paying off, and the last silver seal broke. Mana flooded his conception vessel, dyeing his blood and mana with a potent silver hue.

The fresh injection of mana filled Sorin's body with warmth and vitality. His blood was reinvigorated. His mana thickened. His body underwent an earth-shaking transformation.

Corresponding to this change, a vast whirlpool spread outward from his body, expanding to the river and adjoining earth and sucking out a familiar substance—the poison corrupting the outpost's water supply!

Poison poured into Sorin's body without reservation, pushing him to the brink of failure a second time. But the sudden influx and his thickened mana broke the balance in his body, forcing his eight fused poisons to suddenly fuse with the ninth.

The moment it fused with his poisonous mana and blood, Sorin instantly became aware of its properties and the way to cure it. *Furious Blood Invasion Poison. One-star poison. Produced with the mixed blood of Blood Invasion Bats, Furious Demonic Badger Mice, and Crimson Blood Rats.*

Sorin wanted nothing more than to inform Mr. Primrose about this critical information, but before he could do so, he felt something else in his body shatter. His mana flow once again changed as his belt meridian was forced open, completing his meridian network. All primary meridians and the seven out of eight meridians permitted by the gods were now fully functional, bringing Sorin to the peak of what a Blood-Thickening cultivator was capable of.

This power... thought Sorin as he reached out to the vortex surging from his body. A stream of information appeared inside his mind.

Heroic Ability: Toxic Metabolism.

Description: All toxins beneath the tolerance limit can be metabolized into mana and life force. Efficiency depends on poison compatibility. Excess energy will be stored as lifeforce that will gradually dissipate unless utilized.

Sorin also vaguely sensed that thanks to Toxic Metabolism, the rate at which he could ingest and absorb poisons through the Ten Thousand Poison Canon had greatly improved. It was still limited to absorption by touch or with liquid as a medium, but now it was so fast that it would only take a second to retrieve all his poisons from a corpse or even a living target.

But that doesn't at all explain why I'm able to absorb so much poison so quickly, thought Sorin. *Does my breakthrough have a grace period?* Whatever it was, he didn't question it. He immediately hopped out of the purified water segment and into the next toxic segment. The river water was detoxified in record time, as was the poison in the drenched soil leaching through the cracks in the stone-covered aqueduct.

The infusion of poison was too much for Sorin to handle. Fortunately, any excess was quickly converted to life force, which he immediately used to heal the damage to his corrupted body and meridians. As for the corruption itself, his nine fused poisons were much more potent than before. By collaborating with the priest who was purifying his body without reservation, Sorin was able to exterminate the bulk of the corruption at the expense of his mana, which was quickly regenerated by converting excess poisons absorbed from the river into mana and life force.

Sorin rapidly cleansed five more segments in quick succession, after which he started feeling bloated. *The corruption in my body is gone now, and so is the excess poison. My life force, on the other hand, is too concentrated. In a sense, I'm 'full' and won't be able to continue until I finish metabolizing the remaining poison in my body. I need... I need to stop.*

It was then that he realized that he'd caught up to Mr. Primrose and the mages. The entire group was looking at him slack-jacked. Brimming full of poison, Sorin collapsed to one knee. "I'm fine," he said, holding up his hands when Mr. Primrose tried approaching him. "My blood is poisonous. Don't... don't let anyone approach me. I'm fine. More than fine."

Mr. Primrose didn't take his word for it and inspected his body using his powerful poison mana and spiritual force. "The river segments on the way?" he asked after confirming his condition.

"All cleaned since my starting location," answered Sorin between breaths. "Only the less-contaminated segments remain."

"Then we'll continue," said Mr. Primrose. "You rest up, and we'll get your companions to come guard you while you recover."

What seemed like seconds but was likely minutes later, Sorin heard Stephan calling out to him. Lawrence tried approaching him, but

Daphne cursed him out and summoned a wall of flame to hold him back.

Sorin's head was swimming. His body was fine, but the spiritual strain was too much. He could barely understand what was going on. But his friends were there, so he knew that he was safe.

Having done everything he could for the outpost and unable to move a single finger, Sorin collapsed on the cobblestone road. He was naked, as his clothes had completely disintegrated, but he wore a contented smile on his face.

In an alley not far from where Sorin had fainted, a priest of Hope was grinning from ear to ear. Reverse psychology worked wonders for certain kinds of people and often led to miraculous outcomes.

"I told him a human couldn't withstand that much poison," said the priest with a chuckle. "But a *Hero* can. They're all about exceeding human limitations." The rat in his hand squeaked and demanded to be released, but the priest kept a firm grip. "Are you indignant, little rat? Are you upset at your current situation?" The rat squeaked an affirmative.

"Well, *forgive* me for not caring one whit about what you want. You're more stubborn than Sorin is, and that's saying something. You say you want freedom, but is that what you really want? Freedom would only bring you years of starvation. Even if you did manage to break through, an Envoy of Violence would surely have come to claim you. The so-called freedom you'd obtained would evaporate like a fine morning mist."

Lorimer squeaked out words of defiance. "You're asking how I know that? I'm sure you've guessed it by now. You might begrudge my little game, Lorimer Prescott Rockeater, but you'll eventually realize the truth: Companionship with Sorin Abberjay Kepler isn't a guaranteed bet, but it's the best hope you'll ever have. Trust me when I say that when it comes to hope and fate, no one knows better than little old me."

The priest then placed the rat on the floor and watched it scramble away. "How terrible it is not to have anyone appreciate your genius. If only the other Seven were a bit more intelligent. It would make this game far more interesting to play." Unsurprisingly, the rat turned around when he heard his words and squeaked out a question. "Who am I? I'm just a normal priest, obviously. No one of consequence." When Lorimer squeaked out that this was clearly nonsense, the priest chuckled. "How could I possibly be anything more than a normal priest, little rat? That would be a clear violation of the Eight Evils Pact."

The rat squeaked uncertainly, then dashed off towards the group of adventurers circling the physician who claimed he wasn't one. "This project is far more entertaining than I expected," muttered the priest. "I wonder how far he'll get before his time runs out?"

The priest had many projects, but they all had one thing in common: their lifespans were dreadfully short.

75

HERO

Sorin woke to find himself inside the Adventurers Guild on a bed reserved for recovering patients. The room was a semi-private one, with only two other occupied beds.

"Urgh…" said Sorin, feeling for his head. He had a pounding headache, though a quick inspection using his spirituality and mana confirmed his condition was perfect.

Organs are fully functional, thought Sorin as he checked items off a list. *Heartbeat is elevated compared to normal, but blood flow remains unchanged. Blood is much thicker than before the unexpected break-through, with mana density as much as 30 percent higher than before.*

He then moved on to the circulation of mana in his body, which was now much faster and smoother than normal. *All twelve primary meridians remain open. All seven extraordinary meridians are still open. Mana flow has increased substantially. Meridian elasticity and width have greatly improved. Speculation: Mana transference and expulsion greatly improved—assumption to be verified.*

The increase in his mana density was partly due to his breakthrough into the ninth stage of Blood-Thickening. Another part was due to the overall enhancement he'd received by unlocking his Conception Vessel. The same change that had widened and enhanced his meridians had also dyed his mana with a silvery sheen, the same sheen that had been present on the seals locking away his Conception Vessel.

Mana fluctuations have returned to normal levels. Spirituality is back to reasonable levels. Conclusion: Mana and spirituality were greatly enhanced during the breakthrough, allowing for the completion of a short-term, urgent task. This outburst is akin to displays of hysterical strength observed in mortal patients. Further verification is required.

"Hey!" Sorin opened his eyes to see a half-blind man with short red hair. "Are you going to sit around all day like a goldfish?" said the man. "Sorry, but we already have one of those."

Sorin's eyes flickered to the third bed in the room, where an acquaintance was lying down. "Don't bother Haster," he said to the half-blind patient. "He's suffering from severe trauma, and harassment could easily trigger him."

"I heard about what happened to him," said the half-blind adventurer. "Actually, I saw it. I was one of the people who ran. Only a handful of us survived out of a group of twenty. My name's Robert, by the way. Robert Aston."

"Sorin. Sorin Kepler. We're not on forced bed rest, are we?"

"No," said the man. "We're free to go whenever we like. But you won't get free food if you leave now. Lunch should be up in about an hour."

"I'll pass," said Sorin, sitting up from his bed. Aside from the headache, he felt fantastic.

Sorin's belongings had been laid out in a neat pile beside his bed. Since these were uncertain times, Sorin opted for the new clothes that Percival had evidently delivered. He finished off his ensemble by donning his leather armor, his dagger, and the waterproof poison pouches that someone had retrieved from the Alchemists Guild.

Speaking of Percival, the man had left a note on the clothes. *I would have stayed, but the guild forbade it. I shall visit around noon every day to check on your welfare.*

"How many days have I been here?" asked Sorin.

"Less than a day," said Robert. "You were a mess, and no one seemed to want to clean you up. I think a man called Mr. Primrose came by to decontaminate your body before they gave the all-clear to transfer you to a bed."

"Many thanks," said Sorin. "I wish you a speedy recovery."

"Enjoy!" said the half-blind man.

On his way out, Sorin placed a hand on Haster's foot, sending a stream of spirituality to double-check that the man's body was fine. "It wasn't your fault, Haster. You did what you could." He wasn't sure if the man heard him, but he walked out the door and headed over to the guild lobby.

"There he is!" shouted Lawrence, holding up a mug of ale as Sorin walked through the door. "Cheers to our newest Hero!" All the adventurers in the room echoed his shout.

"How long have you guys been here?" asked Sorin, walking up to their table.

"Since a few hours ago," said Stephan. "I figured you wouldn't be out for long, given your breakthrough. Heroes heal fast, you know."

"Physician Marcus said that the trauma to your body was extreme," Daphne cut in. "But he also said that the life force inside you was so potent that you would likely regenerate from all the damage in less than an hour."

"That much I remember," said Sorin. "Glad you could all make it. Wait, where's Gareth?"

"He's outside the walls tracking the last of the poisonous creatures in the vicinity with all the best archers and a dozen Bone-Forging cultivators," said Stephan.

"Fair enough," said Sorin. "How... how many people didn't make it?"

Stephan's expression turned dark. "A total of 231 non-cultivators died from invasive corruption. Only seven cultivators died because they're naturally more resilient to such things. The rest were treated quickly enough by the alchemists and physicians that they managed to pull through."

"What about the contamination?" asked Sorin.

It was Daphne who answered. "I've heard some influential mages say that 7 percent of the outpost's land is contaminated and in need of remediation. Residents in these locations have been evacuated to temporary shelters as remediation during the demon tide would be unwise." This was within Sorin's expectations and also made it clear that his gamble had saved the outpost much future trouble.

"Ah, there he is!" said Stephan. He raised his hand to call out his friend but paused mid-motion when he saw the person walking next to Gareth.

"What's eating you?" asked Haley, pulling up a chair. "Gareth isn't so reserved when interacting with me. How could you, my younger brother, be so insensitive?"

"Yeah, Stephan," said Gareth, pulling up his chair. "Don't be mean to your older sister. And I can't believe how *mean* you were to her growing up. The stories she tells—if it were in my family, you would have been beaten black and blue."

Stephan's eye twitched. "I *was* beaten black and blue. By that witch you seem to have a good impression of!"

"Well, you definitely deserved it," said Gareth, calling over a waitress and ordering a mug of ale. "What does our Hero want? It's on me."

"Actually, it's on the house," said the waitress, pulling up. "Heroes drink for free."

"In that case, I'll have whisky," said Sorin. "Make it a triple. Adventurers don't get a bad rep for drinking before noon here, do they?"

"Only if they get drunk, dear," said the waitress. "I'll bring that drink right up. And what about you? The usual?"

"I'll take a midnight flower this time, thank you very much," said Haley. She waited until the waitress was back with their drinks before raising her hand. A curtain of light sprang up around their table, isolating them from the rest of the pub.

"To what do we owe the pleasure, dear sister?" asked Stephan once everyone had taken a sip.

"I thought that was obvious," said Haley, tossing a silver medallion over to Sorin. "Here you go. Your very own Hero Medal."

"Shouldn't this be done in a confidential setting?" asked Stephan, eyeing his strictly non-Hero companions.

Haley shook her head. "There's two of you on the team now. That changes things. As for everyone else in the pub, they won't be able to hear crap unless they're a Bone-Forging Hero or stronger."

"What exactly *is* a Hero?" asked Sorin. "Does it have to do with the Conception Vessel we've slowly been unlocking?"

"Sharp," said Haley. "Only physicians notice the specifics. But yes, it's the Conception Vessel."

Daphne raised her hand. "Conception Vessel?"

"You explain it," said Haley to Sorin.

"Everyone has twelve primary meridians and eight extraordinary meridians," Sorin explained. "The twelve primary meridians are common knowledge. The eight extraordinary meridians are hidden knowledge. In essence, they're the reason for various disparities in talent.

"Two of these extraordinary meridians are even more special—the Conception Vessel and the Governing Vessel. They aren't like the other extraordinary meridians, which only link together other meridians and change their circulation patterns—they actually have their own acupoints. Also, they aren't just blocked by crystalized mana and debris. They're physically blocked by seals. In the Conception Vessel's case, those seals are silver. According to my observations, these seals can wear away as cultivators challenge their limits."

"What about the Governing Vessel?" asked Daphne, showing her usual thirst for knowledge.

"There's no point in talking about it because it's completely sealed off," said Sorin. To my knowledge, it's forbidden by the ancient gods and locked up by divine energy. Unless the York Clan knows something that I don't?"

"We don't," said Haley. "To my knowledge, humans can only unlock the Hero Meridian. Oh. Since it's normally done by exceeding one's limits, and it's easiest to do that in the heat of battle against extremely powerful enemies or by risking one's life, they named it so. Someone who unlocks this meridian will transform and gain something called a Heroic Ability."

"Mine is called Toxic Metabolism," Sorin muttered. "It's honestly the only reason I'm still here."

"One second," cut in Lawrence. "Why exactly is this knowledge secret?"

"Isn't that obvious?" said Gareth. "Stephan got his Hero Medal after the Minotaur almost ripped him in half. Sorin got his by nearly poisoning himself to death. I'm pretty sure the only reason we're learning about all this is because it won't take us long to put two and two together since there are two Heroes on our team."

"That... makes a lot of sense," said Lawrence. "Please continue, Assessor York."

"I mean, that's all there is to it, really," said Haley. "The other extraordinary meridian knowledge Sorin spoke of is forbidden knowledge for power reasons. As for the Hero Medal, I trust Stephan will go over its alert functions and the perks. It has a small storage space. In bigger cities, you can find Hero Halls that offer things you can't find anywhere else."

"Are you a Hero?" asked Lawrence.

"How else would I have the clearance to talk about this?" Haley chuckled. "By the way, you're all officially sworn to secrecy. Sign this contract or die." She said these words with a complete lack of humor as she handed out four silver scrolls to each member of their team.

After viewing the associated rules, Sorin signed the contract and instantly felt a silver shackle settle around his soul. *It's not that Stephan didn't want to talk about it, but that he* couldn't *talk about it,* Sorin realized. He'd only used the most indirect ways to make his point.

"I get telling us and all, but aren't you worried about us getting ourselves killed?" asked Lawrence.

"Idiot," said Gareth. "She's obviously telling us so that we know exactly what's at stake."

"That's right," said Haley. "Heroes tend to take on tougher missions. Their cultivation tends to rise a lot faster than that of others. If you don't all take risks and become Heroes, Sorin and Stephan are going to leave you behind."

"That makes sense," said Lawrence. "Given that I was destined to be awesome, it'd be silly if my companions weren't as well."

"If by awesome, you mean an awesome peep, then maybe?" said Daphne. "By the way, the vice guild master came to see me yesterday. He did *not* enjoy your voyeurism during an emergency."

"I was *scouting*," said Lawrence. "Why doesn't anyone ever believe me?"

"I'm more interested in what it means to *be* a Hero," said Sorin. "I find I'm much stronger than before."

"Three things," said Haley, holding up her fingers. "The first is an enhancement. Heroes are superior compared to other cultivators depending on the enhancement. For example, Stephan here. He got a strength enhancement. He's easily three times stronger than another non-Hero cultivator at the same level. The ones specializing in strength."

"In my case, it was my mana circulation and output that were enhanced," said Sorin.

"Really?" asked Daphne. "How was it enhanced?"

"I don't know for sure," said Sorin. "But three times seems about right."

Palpable jealousy could be seen on Daphne's face. "Looks like we're going to have to modify those spells you learned," she said. "Otherwise, you'll blow your spell matrices."

Sorin frowned. "I never thought of it that way. I guess there's no way around it. What about the other two advantages?"

"The second thing about Heroes is that they get to ignore realm suppression partially," said Haley. "Of course, it's limited to a single realm."

"Realm suppression?" asked Gareth, intrigued. "You mean the gap between stars?"

"There's an overall tenfold difference between Blood-Thickening and Bone-Forging cultivators," answered Haley. "But that's only in terms of absolute strength. Any abilities or strength or weapons of a lower tier used against superior creatures will see a great reduction in effectiveness. The Hero enhancement allows one to close the absolute gap in strength. More importantly, it reduces the realm suppression effect by two-thirds."

"No wonder my poisons are so ineffective against two-star demons," said Sorin.

"It's the same for my spells," muttered Daphne. "They should really tell us about these things up front."

"They don't tell you because the gap is large enough to make people despair," said Haley with mixed emotions. "At least with Hope, anything is possible."

"What about the third factor?" said Sorin. "You said something about Heroic Abilities."

Haley nodded. "Most Heroes get Heroic Abilities. Mine is called Blink."

76

OVERHAUL

"Blink?" said Daphne when Haley confessed her Heroic Ability. "You mean, like the spell?"

"Like the spell, but without magic," said Haley, looking quite pleased with herself.

"But that's... that's at least a Flesh-Sanctification–level spell," said Daphne, flabbergasted.

"Which is why I can only use the ability once every minute and only within thirty feet," said Haley. "Oh, and it has no cast time and reduced mana cost."

"But that's..." said Daphne.

"*Broken*," said Stephan. "Which is why Blood-Thickening Heroes are theoretically able to come out on top against weaker two-star demons in a one-on-one battle. Though I remember the cooldown time being closer to three minutes."

"Breaking through to Bone-Forging fixed that," said Haley. "In any case, broken is exactly what you should call a Heroic Ability. Heroes are rule-breakers. Convention-breakers."

"Doesn't Lawrence already do that?" asked Sorin, confused. "He teleports behind enemies all the time."

"I specifically *don't* teleport behind my enemies, thank you very much," said Lawrence. "It's actually an optical illusion. I just move extremely quickly under stealth, making it *look* like teleportation. But in the end, just moving really fast."

"What about your ability, Stephan?" asked Sorin. "It's that Arctic Rune Bear form you acquired recently, isn't it?"

"Actually, my Heroic Ability is a bit more flexible than that," said Stephan. "Normally, I can only beastshift into creatures that I've seen before and only of the weaker variety. My ability has evolved to allow me to shift into superior creatures with magical abilities."

"Wait," said Lawrence. "Are you saying you could shift into a dragon?"

"A dragon?" mused Stephan. "Maybe I could if I cultivated for a hundred years. But wouldn't it just be better to shift into a dragon bear?"

"Sheesh," said Lawrence. "What's with you and bears?"

"It's got nothing to do with personal opinion," said Stephan. "Bears are objectively the best beast shape. In all aspects."

"What about speed?" pressed Lawrence. "Wouldn't a hawk be more efficient? Or a rabbit?"

"That's why I'll eventually obtain the pigmy bear transformation and the hawk bear transformation," said Stephan. Sorin had no idea if he was actually serious about these transformations.

"There are obviously limitations to which forms he can take," said Haley. "Nevertheless, Stephan can exceed the normal limitations of his level, bringing his core ability up to par with a two-star cultivator's core ability. The ability will also continue to be useful even after he advances to the Bone-Forging Realm."

Sorin felt that, compared to these two abilities, his own ability was somewhat lackluster. Then again, maybe he needed to think on it? The ability to metabolize poisons had a lot of potential applications. "The name of the ability is Toxic Metabolism. I can already metabolize poisons to an extent, but this increases my ability to do so substantially. Though, I have a feeling that the strength I displayed out on the river isn't my actual strength."

"What you experienced is called a Heroic Outburst," Haley

explained. "You only get one of those, and you'll never be able to match up to what you did with your current cultivation realm."

"Like Stephan holding down the Minotaur?" asked Sorin.

"That's right," said Haley. "Are there any particulars about your ability? You should have an instinctual grasp of the ability and be able to explain it."

"This…" Sorin thought back to his ability description and laid it out for everyone else to analyze. "First, I can digest poisons much more quickly. At least… one hundred times more quickly."

"Doesn't that make you basically immune to poisons?" asked Gareth.

"I suppose it does," said Sorin. "One-star poisons, at least. And wait, I have partial immunity to two-star poisons. Also, this used to tire me out, but now it replenishes me. It converts the excess poisons into mana and life force."

"Lifeforce means you can regenerate at an accelerated rate," said Haley. "It's a tier higher than life mana and will allow you to regenerate from deeper wounds; much more efficiently than a healing potion too."

"So, wait, you're saying Sorin should go around carrying vials of poison instead of healing potions?" said Lawrence jokingly.

"So it seems," said Sorin thoughtfully. "The ability has some other benefits. For one, it's improved my ability to retrieve my poisons. Whether it's my poisonous blood or the mana I've injected into a target, I can retrieve it with high efficiency. And if I use external poisons to damage or incapacitate my enemies, I could then absorb the poison and digest it for a healing effect."

Most of his teammates seemed to like his ability, but Daphne stood out as the lone voice of dissent. "If it isn't an offensive ability, isn't it terrible? Don't get me wrong, I'm sure it'll work wonders with your staying power, given how much your mana circulation speed has increased, but it's not exactly going to make the difference when fighting a two-star demon."

"Maybe it's because you're a mage, Daphne, but regeneration is much more powerful than you're giving it credit for," said Stephan.

"Especially for someone like Sorin, who needs time to wear down an enemy. He also needs to take risks to land those first strikes."

"I suppose," Grumbled Daphne.

When Stephan put it that way, Sorin couldn't help but agree. His fighting style was currently too cautious, and he often didn't dare approach two-star demons for short burst attacks. If he had access to life force in battle, he wouldn't need to worry about silly things like organ trauma and cracked bones and torn ligaments.

"Anyway, that about covers it," said Haley. "Only one question remains: Are you going to continue as a team, or will you split up?"

"Question!" said Daphne, immediately raising her hand.

"Shoot," said Haley.

"Must we fight stronger enemies, or can one become a Hero by laying waste to an army of demons?" asked Daphne.

"This... honestly, I have no idea," said Haley. "But I like your pitch. Let's see if you can pull it off."

"That didn't sound like a no," said Daphne. "In that case, I'll give it a go."

"I'm obviously in," said Lawrence. "I mean, I've finally found team-mates that are as good-looking and brilliant as *ah!*" He yelped as Stephan tapped his other shoulder with a giant bear claw. "Hey! That's not fair. You didn't give me time to prepare."

"Hm..." Gareth was the only one who seemed undecided. "I'll stay. For now. If I start holding you all back, I'll leave the team."

"I'm sure you won't hold us back," Stephan started, but Gareth cut him off.

"I'll be the one to decide if I'm holding you all back or not," said Gareth. "You heard what she said. Becoming a Hero involves risking your life. I'm a very risk-averse individual. Are you fine with my answer, Miss York?"

"I'm not pushing anyone to make any specific decisions," said Haley. "As long as you realize that since you're part of a Hero's team you'll be called out to the same missions, I'm fine."

"Got it," said Gareth. Out of all their team members, he was the most pragmatic.

Once Haley departed, Sorin led his teammates back to a private room to investigate the situation with their meridians. Daphne and Gareth were well on their way to opening their Hero Meridian and had already unlocked 14 out of 24 seals. Lawrence, on the other hand, had stalled out at ten seals. Given Haley's explanation, Sorin theorized it had to do with his cowardly fighting style.

"I'm not a coward," said Lawrence. "I'm just very careful about when I attack."

"You're going to have to take risks if you want to keep up with Papa Bear here," said Stephan. "Stick your neck out a little, Lawrence, and I'm sure you'll figure it out. Actually, it's nice to have someone who can tell us exactly how much progress we're making. No one in the York clan can visualize extraordinary meridians so clearly."

"I also wouldn't let Haley discourage everyone," said Sorin. "In case you didn't notice, my cultivation stage just increased."

"Which means…" said Lawrence. His eyes widened when a whip coiled around his body like a snake and injected him with paralytic poison. "No! Sorin! Spare me!"

Sorin ignored Lawrence's pleas and injected a stream of mana into his meridians. With the changes to his meridian network and the overall transformation in his body, it was a simple matter to materialize a poison needle and scaffolding. Lawrence's Yin Link Vessel was pierced through without any problems; unfortunately, he failed in opening Lawrence's sixth extraordinary meridian and would need to wait for his next breakthrough to make an attempt.

Following his success with Lawrence, Sorin successfully unlocked a portion of Gareth and Daphne's potential until they each had a total of five unlocked extraordinary meridians.

"I bet the Kepler Clan would spit blood if they found out what Sorin was doing," said Stephan heartily. "I mean, I've *heard* of the Kepler Clan's meridian-opening method, but it's obviously not this potent. My clan's elders said there's at least a 50 percent chance of failure during the process, but you didn't even fail once."

"It has to do with my cultivation method," Sorin admitted. "Thus my confidence in unlocking an additional meridian once I break through."

"Don't worry, we'll keep your secret," said Gareth. "Stephan, what's next on our agenda?"

"Rest and stand by," said Stephan. "Apparently, our team is too important to send out on corpse duty now."

"Then how are we supposed to become Heroes?" whined Lawrence.

"There'll be plenty of time for that," said Stephan. "Judging by the situation with the poison, this demon tide is going to be much more dangerous than usual. So, if anyone has been hoarding money, spend it. Don't save up in situations like this, or it won't just be you that ends up dead, but your friends as well."

Sorin nodded solemnly and vowed to mix up additional poisons during his downtime.

The next thing Sorin did was follow Daphne back to the Mages Guild. They rented a training room and began the painful process of modifying spell forms. "No! I said faster and more perfectly, not slower and clumsier!"

"Faster and more perfectly isn't exactly the best pointer," said Sorin. "Any specific things I should look out for?"

Daphne massaged her brow. "I hate non-fire spells. They're so complicated and unrefined. Um… how about you tighten your weave around the mana injection point?"

"Like this?" said Sorin, summoning a much larger Veridian Smoke Bomb than he was used to.

"Exactly!" said Daphne. "That should about double how much poison you can deliver. The efficiency on this spell is bad, so that's all we can accomplish."

"What about Anti-Mage's Blade?" asked Sorin.

"Can't alter it," said Daphne. "Same with Ophidian Eye. It's just not responsive to an increase in mana output."

Threading the Spear was, fortunately, much easier to modify than the

Veridian Smoke Bomb. Sorin's output was less restricted by his spiritual sense and more by his mana throughput. Since it wasn't practical to charge a spell for more than three seconds, he'd only been able to blast out around twenty mana needles at a time in a random spray. Now, he was able to increase the count to forty. The distance he could send them flying also increased by 50 percent. The potency of the individual needles, however, remained unchanged.

Once the spell forms were finalized, Sorin bid Daphne farewell and returned to the poison workshop, where Mr. Primrose was hard at work creating large batches of poison for the defense effort.

Sorin's immediate goal was to make money, so he quickly cleared the one-star medical missions. He paid special attention to Marcus's mission and noticed that anti-mana poisons had been added to the request.

How did he figure it out? thought Sorin as he looked through the list of poisons. *It isn't obvious from the earlier formulas to use some anti-mana poison. Wait a minute—my blood!* He cursed inwardly as he realized he'd slipped up. Of course, Marcus was able to figure it out—he had an entire absorptive pad full of poisonous blood to analyze in the laboratory!

Refusing to craft the poison would only arouse suspicion, given the high price. Moreover, testing such a concoction would be difficult, as a high fatality rate accompanied it. Sorin could only accept the mission.

At least a two-star physician presiding over the process will increase the odds of survival. Permanent injuries can't be prevented, so he'll need to be discrete in how he carries out his experiments.

There were quite a few possibilities. First, Marcus could experiment on captured demons. Alternatively, he could experiment on cadavers. While it was theoretically possible to experiment on death row prisoners with approval, the Bloodwood Outpost did not have many such individuals, and the data would not be statistically significant.

Wait a minute. Sorin froze halfway through concocting Vermillion Heart Poison. The slight pause was enough to burn the mixture irredeemably, leading to the loss of seventy-five gold in medicinal ingredients. But Sorin didn't care—he quickly picked up the cauldron and upended it into a waste bucket before continuing his train of thought. *The veterans! The veterans are signing up for an experimental treatment! I overlooked it before because I was assuming he was performing primary meridian-openings, but extraordinary meridian-openings are extremely risky!*

Realizing his abnormal state, Sorin forced himself to calm down. At this point, it was all conjecture and speculation on his part. Just because Marcus was zeroing in on the formula, it didn't mean he would immediately start carrying out live human trials.

Still, it was best to be prudent with this sort of thing. This was especially the case since Sorin was aware of the tincture formulas and knew firsthand from Sirius Kepler's research notes how deadly the experiments would be. Sighing, Sorin cleaned up the workshop and left the Alchemists Guild. There was only one person he could rely on in a situation like this: his trusty lab assistant, Lawrence Holt.

77

ESPIONAGE

"Absolutely not," said Lawrence, throwing himself down on a comfy chair and picking up a cup of hot chocolate. "You listen to me, Sorin Kepler. Drink some hot cocoa and have a few cookies to calm down. You'll soon realize that life is worth living and that sneaking into the Governor's Manor is basically suicide. Seriously—ask my dad. Dad, it's suicide, isn't it?"

"It's only suicide if you get caught!" said Mr. Holt from the kitchen. "How long are you staying, Sorin? Lawrence, should I make pie? You know what, I'll just start making pie."

"I think we're good on the pie front, Dad!" yelled Lawrence. "See? Straight out of the old man's mouth—it's suicide. We'll get caught."

"I'm not deaf, Lawrence," said Sorin. "Besides, weren't you looking for a way to become a Hero? I think sneaking into a Flesh-Sanctification cultivator's manor to look for traces of human experimentation conducted by a Bone-Forging physician when you're only a Blood-Thickening cultivator is pretty damn heroic."

"But it's not *me*," said Lawrence. "I peep on casual things. *Meaningless* things. Peeping is sightseeing, not military espionage."

"Fine. Don't come," said Sorin, taking a big gulp of hot cocoa. "Wow. That's *good*."

"The secret ingredient is freshly shaved chocolate imported from Dumas," said Lawrence, raising his mug. "You won't find anything like it even in the nearest city."

"Is *that* what your dad spends his adventuring savings on?" asked Sorin.

"What else is he going to spend them on?" asked Lawrence. "It's baking and hot chocolate or hard drugs. Take your pick."

"Fair enough," said Sorin. "Well, if you're not game, I guess I can only talk to Haley. She *is* the better rogue, after all."

"Pft," said Lawrence. "She's not a rogue. She's an assassin."

"Is there a difference?" asked Sorin.

"A big one," said Lawrence. "She's a stickler for the rules, for one. She definitely won't volunteer to break into the Governor's Manor."

"But you already said no, and I don't know anyone else who could succeed," said Sorin.

Lawrence sighed. "It's a sin to be so talented, Sorin. And so good-looking. I can see why you came knocking on my door, begging for a favor."

"Who said anything about begging?" asked Sorin. "Actually, you know what? There's no need to bother. I'll get Lorimer to sneak in." Lorimer, who'd been nibbling on a cookie, froze mid-nibble and shook his head. "Come on, don't be a coward, Lorimer. I'll buy you... a thousand gold in demon cores. You can even pick them." Once again, Lorimer shook his head. "Fine, Haley it is. Enjoy your cookies and hot cocoa, Lawrence."

"Wait, wait, wait," said Lawrence, intercepting Sorin before he could leave the residence. "It's not out of the question. But I'll need support. You'll need to come with me. And Lorimer will need to as well."

"Won't that make us more likely to be discovered?" asked Sorin.

"Only if we're stupid about it," said Lawrence. "In truth, it's not as risky as you're making it out to be. It takes energy to monitor a whole castle—and the Governor's Manor is basically a castle. You think a Flesh-Sanctification cultivator can just casually monitor two square miles, three stories, and a super-basement through solid stone?"

"You make a good point," Sorin admitted. "Though the level of detail you're giving me is telling me you've done this before."

"Indeed, I have," said Lawrence. "And *without* getting caught. So there are good reasons why I need you to come along. Firstly, Lorimer makes a good distraction. No one expects rats to collude with people. They won't even think about it even if they know you have a rat familiar. Rats are disgusting creatures that no one would ever cooperate with.

"Second, your poisons might come in handy. Not to melt off faces, but from a utility point of view."

"My spells aren't exactly stealthy," said Sorin.

"But you don't *have* to use spells," said Lawrence. "And you can do cool things like melt locks and paralyze people with your whip. You might not be good at sneaking around and stabbing things, but knocking them out? You're a pro!"

"Fine," said Sorin. "Lorimer and I will accompany you. But we need to do this tonight. I just processed a few batches of Manabane Poison, and I imagine Marcus will want to begin experimenting right away, assuming he's using the demon tide as cover for his experiments."

"Are you sure you're not overreacting?" asked Lawrence. "Just because he's zeroing in on your clan's secret formula doesn't mean he's going to start experimenting on people. Besides, isn't he a nice guy?"

"Both you and my butler said he was obviously a snake," said Sorin. "I happen to feel the same way."

"Fine," said Lawrence. "We'll go tonight. But not till two in the morning."

"What happens at two?" asked Sorin.

"Shift change, obviously," said Lawrence. "What? Why are you looking at me like that?"

"Have you seriously gone peeping inside the Governor's Manor before?" asked Sorin. "Then why were you fighting me so hard on this?"

"Woah, slow down," said Lawrence. "I've only snuck around the first floor. Possibly the second, and perhaps only near a young lady's bedroom. But sneaking into an evil basement laboratory is a whole other story. I didn't get very far before they chased me out."

"You got caught?" groaned Sorin. "And how are you so sure it's in the basement?"

"You said this procedure is painful and possibly lethal, right?" said Lawrence. "It's pretty hard to hide that kind of stuff when a gardener could just look through the window and casually witness evil as it happens, don't you think? Pretty much all dangerous things happen in basements. It's a rule. And I'd bet my dad's hot cocoa recipe that the governor's cultivation chamber is in a secondary basement, somewhere not easily accessed by even his most trusted people."

"But probably not on the same floor as the experiments," said Sorin.

"Probably not," said Lawrence. "High-level cultivators hate getting distracted the most."

"Then what are we waiting for?" asked Sorin. "There's a lot to prepare."

"Pie," said Lawrence. "Because no one sneaks into an evil basement on an empty stomach."

Several hours and two pies later, two men and one pet rat launched themselves above a ten-foot wall just as one guard's mana lamp faded and another took its place. The three interlopers squeezed through the narrow opening in the manor's defenses and rolled underneath an irregular opening beneath a narrow hedge.

They waited for the patrolling guard's heavy footsteps to pass, then cut across the yard just beside a lamp-lit entrance. Their target: a small window covered in steel bars. The bars were loose, and with a bit of work on Lawrence's part, they managed to sneak through them and into a dark room on the first floor of the Governor's Manor.

"This is the first banquet room," Lawrence explained as they edged over to the closed door and cracked it open. "As far as I know, there are two entrances to the basement, each of them under guard. There are stairs near the front entrance, the most obvious route, and there's also the entrance the servants use. It's tiny and single-file, but it's much more discreet. Follow me!"

The two men and their trusty rat scurried across the floor. Lawrence blended with the shadows while Sorin kept inhumanly low using Adder Rush. "Do we just run across—"

"Freeze!" hissed Lawrence. Sorin didn't move an inch as a small curtain of shadows spread out from Lawrence's cloak, completely obscuring him as a pair of maids walked by with a basket of laundry. "We're fine now," said Lawrence, dispelling the cloak and breaking into a casual walk. "At least, until the kitchen we are. Getting past them is going to be tricky. But that's all right—I have a plan."

As with most large residences, the Governor's Manor never truly slept. There were servants awake at all times of day and night to keep the place perpetually spotless, as well as two chefs and support staff constantly preparing delicacies for the governor, his family, and his guests to enjoy.

Wondrous smells wafted out of the kitchen when they arrived. Lawrence pulled Sorin to the wall just as a pot-bellied man with stained white clothes stormed out the door and shouted to a nearby attendant. "Bring zis one up to the second floor for Mizz Penelope and her friends to enjoy."

"I'm afraid they might be sleeping," said the attendant nervously.

"Tiz no concern of mine," said the cook. "If zey don't answer ze door, simply place it ouzzide so zey will know zey were served ze best."

Sorin relaxed as the man re-entered the kitchen without seeing them. "How exactly are we supposed to get past him?" he whispered to Lawrence.

"Obviously, with the help of our fine companion," said Lawrence. "Well? Do the thing, Lorimer. Go in there and bait them off." Lorimer sniffed and rolled his eyes before letting out a few moderately loud squeaks. "Come on now. The night isn't getting any younger."

"You should probably do what he says," urged Sorin. "He *is* the expert. Wait, is that scurrying I hear?" He turned around and nearly jumped when he saw two dozen rats line up like soldiers.

Lorimer stood up on his two hind paws and began squeaking out what appeared to be a prepared speech. The awestruck rats stood by for the entire thing, then stood up on their hind paws and saluted before scurrying into the kitchen.

"He can do that?" said Lawrence. "How come we didn't know he could do that?"

"Thinking about it, he *did* command a bunch of rats when we brought him into town," said Sorin, glaring at the rat. "He really does like keeping secrets."

It only took thirty seconds for a commotion to erupt inside the kitchen. Screams cut through the slightly chilly air, immediately followed by footsteps and five furious cooks and one very disgruntled chef chasing after two dozen rats with various cooking implements.

"Let's go!" shouted Lawrence, leading the way into the kitchen. Aside from a few messes worth of dropped food, the kitchen was surprisingly clean. An entire pig was roasting on a spit at the back, along with three chickens, two ducks, and one quail.

At the back of the kitchen lay a larder, which happened to lead into a wine cellar inside the basement's first level. "Help me move these wine barrels," said Lawrence.

"What wine barrels?" muttered Sorin. "Oh, bother. Light!" A small pale-green sphere of illumination appeared in his left hand and floated into the air. Without his intervention, it would shine for five minutes before dissipating.

The wine barrels in question were mercifully of the normal variety. Thanks to his above-average strength for a cultivator, Sorin was able to move aside the rack in question in a matter of minutes.

"This doesn't exactly look like a servant entrance," said Sorin.

"About that…" said Lawrence. "I *may* have used this entrance once, so they sealed it off. But look: the door remains!"

Said door was made of pure metal and painted dark green. A large glob of melted metal lay where a handle had once been. "What now?"

"This is only a minor problem," said Lawrence. "After all, we have *you,* don't we?"

"Hm…" Sorin eyed the sealed door and agreed that unsealing it was feasible. "No problem. But I'm still nervous about this. What's our exit strategy? How will we get past the cooks on our way out?"

"That…" Lawrence winced. "My plan only took us this far. I figured we could just run once we confirmed our guesses."

"From a Bone-Forging cultivator?" said Sorin. "Don't be an idiot, Lawrence. You're naughty, but you're not stupid."

"Fine, I *do* have a plan," said Lawrence. "And it involves Lorimer. Doesn't he have sharp teeth that can bite through rocks? We'll tunnel our way out!"

Sorin gave Lawrence a flat look. "Only if we *want* them to know we were here." Then he sighed and took out a pouch. "Looks like we can only rely on money to solve the problem."

"Poison?" exclaimed a horrified Lawrence. "You want to silence them?"

Sorin rolled his eyes. "Just get ready to scout the hallway behind this door. Leave the escaping part to me."

78

A DIFFERENT KIND OF HERO

Having a workable escape plan, Sorin focused on the steel door connecting the cellar to the rest of the basement. The door was conspicuous now that they'd rolled the barrels away, so they kept the barrels ready to move back in case they had more time on their hands for their getaway.

Sorin used mostly acidic mana in the shape of a blade to melt away the mass of metal that was locking the door in place. Its composition was mostly Iron-Melt Poison, which was extremely effective in melting down the blob but had the unfortunate side effect of releasing corrosive substances in the form of smelly gases.

"That should about do it," said Sorin. He dug his hands into a handle he'd melted into the door but was stopped by Lawrence before he could pull it.

"One second here," said Lawrence, pulling out a small vial from his jacket. He dripped a few drops onto the door's hinges, then gave Sorin a thumbs-up. "Try not to make it squeak. The oil will take care of the hinges, but if the door rubs—"

Lawrence's voice cut off as Sorin pulled the door open with barely a sound. Only a slight rubbing could be heard from where a little rust remained between the door and the frame. "I melted away the rust at the edges while I was at it. In case it caused us problems."

"It's good to work with sensible people," said Lawrence, putting away his vial and dropper.

A dimly lit hallway appeared behind their door, which was nestled in an alcove away from prying eyes. Shadows extended from the darkness, and Sorin, Lawrence, and Lorimer used said shadow to rush over to a small, dark patch where the mana lamp lighting failed to overlap.

"From what I remember, this is where the armory and the manor's guardhouse are located," whispered Lawrence. "They patrol the halls in ten-minute intervals, so we'll need to wait for the next set of guards to walk past."

Five minutes later, a pair of guards came by, as predicted. Once again, Lawrence used his cloak of shadows to hide them. When the guards finished their rounds and returned to the guard house through the doorway, Lawrence nodded to Lorimer, who scampered over as planned and slowly shut the door as though a draft of wind had blown it shut. Sorin and Lawrence used the blind spot this created to cross the guard house and make their way toward a small stairwell.

"And how exactly are we supposed to get past those two?" asked Sorin, pointing to two sleepy guards. "It's one thing if the cooks fall asleep because they ate too much, but guards passing out at the same time? Obviously fishy."

"I didn't know there'd be guards here," argued Lawrence. "It's my first time trying to go down to the second level."

Sorin sighed as he handed a pouch of poison to Lawrence. "Use about half of that. I'll recover it on our way back. Make sure you make it look like they naturally fell asleep."

"No problem," said Lawrence. "But wait a second. I think they're talking about something."

Indeed, the two guards were having a friendly conversation about events in the manor. "Looks like the experiments are starting up again," said the short, stocky guard. "Something about a new formula. Except only those who got through the first treatment successfully can take part."

"It's a hell of a gamble they're taking," said the skinny guard. "I hear a bunch of people died trying it out earlier today."

"That was because they were wounded veterans," said the stocky guard. "There are fewer complications when you have a whole body. Plus, I heard Orpheus is going to be part of this batch. Not a fan of the way he does things, but he sure knows how to ingratiate himself to the right people."

"Let's do this," said Sorin.

Lawrence stuck out a thumb, then blended with the shadows and crept over to the two guards. Ten seconds later, the guards collapsed into silent heaps. Lawrence dragged the tall one into the alcove and leaned him against the wall, then placed his stocky companion in his arms. "That's how people usually sleep together, right?"

"Are you thinking they won't say anything in case people think they're having an illicit relationship?" asked Sorin. Typically, military institutions were very strict about such things and would go to great lengths to separate couples.

"That's actually a good reason, in hindsight," said Lawrence. "I just thought it'd be funny." He then looked down at the pair. "How long does that give us?"

"Ten minutes," said Sorin. "Possibly longer if the guards don't make a big deal of this." He turned to Lorimer and signaled for him to go down the stairs first. "Don't look at me that way. You're as sneaky as Lawrence is, and you're also a smaller target."

Lorimer squeaked a complaint but did as he was told. He returned thirty seconds later and signaled for them to follow.

The second basement's lighting was much worse than the first. It evidently didn't receive as much foot traffic. There were no guards at the few doors that could be seen, though Lorimer said that another stairwell existed around the corner. He felt a terrifying presence from that stairwell and refused to investigate further.

"Lorimer says there's a half-open door halfway through the main hallway," said Sorin. "He said he smelled poisons in there—the kind I work with. But he didn't want to go in because there's a scary cultivator in there."

"That's probably Marcus," said Lawrence. He was about to step into the shadows when his foot suddenly paused. "Lorimer. Why didn't you tell me this place was trapped?" Lorimer squeaked and confessed that he didn't know what Lawrence was talking about. "Oh, I see. It's a trip-wire alarm, and you're too short to trip it. That's easy enough to get past."

"I think the tricky part is going to be sneaking up on Marcus," said Sorin. "He's not just a Bone-Forging cultivator—he's a physician. Physicians have strong souls."

"That's why I'll need to completely retract my aura," said Lawrence solemnly. "While simultaneously trying to sense these stupid alarm threads. They're not just on the floor, you know."

Taking a deep breath, Lawrence took his first step into the dimly lit stone hallway. He took a second step, then leaped forward to land on his hands, only to contort sideways to avoid an invisible obstruction.

Sorin had always seen Lawrence as a bit of a clown, but it was when things got tricky like this that his talents really shone through. *His composure is admirable, given the risks he's taking. Wait—not good!*

A pulse of spiritual force swept through the corridor. Whether Lawrence sensed it or not, he instinctively froze and withdrew his mana and spirituality.

The spiritual force lingered for a moment before returning to the room. Lawrence breathed out a sigh of relief and continued on his way.

The alarm web seems to be getting tighter the closer he gets. More-over, he needs to time things perfectly so that he doesn't trigger Marcus's senses.

The pulses of spirituality came in periodic waves, making it obvious that this was just something Marcus was doing out of habit. Most of his attention would naturally be reserved for monitoring his experiments.

Soon enough, Lawrence was just outside the door. He signaled to

Sorin that he could see what was going on but couldn't progress any further.

Sorin shook his head and waved for Lawrence to come back. *It's not worth getting caught. No one knows we're here, so it won't be difficult for Marcus to silence us and dump our corpses.*

Unfortunately, non-verbal communication was impossible, and neither of them dared whisper for fear of catching Marcus's attention. Lawrence ultimately decided *not* to pull back. He edged closer and closer to the door, desperate to get a better look but running the constant risk of catching Marcus's attention.

Eight minutes were up when Sorin suddenly caught a flicker of something in his mind. It was an image, a three-dimensional one, centered around Lawrence of all people. *Wait, how did he do that?* thought Sorin. *He would have told us if he had this kind of ability.* Lawrence was many things, but humble was not one of them.

The image projected was impressive, Sorin had to admit. It didn't just include what was in Lawrence's line of sight but pierced through walls as well. Through this strange, shared vision, Sorin could see the entire laboratory. There were ten patients strapped to beds, partially sedated but awake. Orpheus and his teammates were among them, their bodies covered in needles and black from the meridian-opening tincture's invasion.

Marcus was also there, though only as a faint outline. It seemed Lawrence didn't dare spy on him directly with his ability. Moreover, a certain halo of danger could be seen surrounding Marcus and even leaking out of the room, slightly overlapping with Lawrence's figure. This indicated that Lawrence was directly at the edge of Marcus's perception and could get caught at any moment.

The poisons required for the tincture are confirmed, thought Sorin, scanning the surprisingly detailed image. *Marcus is doing his best to stabilize the patients, but given that the composition of the tincture is only 90 percent replicated, the risk of death is increased.*

Sorin spotted a notebook and tried to sneak a peek, but it was then that Lawrence's projected image faded. The rogue quickly retreated from the trapped hallway like a practiced acrobat and landed beside Sorin.

"There," said Lawrence, out of breath. "I saw everything."

"I'm aware," said Sorin.

"Wait, you are?" said Lawrence, frowning.

Sorin tapped his friend's body and confirmed that he had indeed unlocked his Hero Meridian. "You awakened as a Hero and transmitted what you saw. You likely just experienced an enhanced version of your Heroic Ability."

Lawrence was ecstatic at the development but clearly knew what to prioritize. He led the way back up alongside Lorimer, and Sorin, not wanting to stack coincidences, withdrew the sleeping poison from the two sleeping guards via touch transmission and used Toxic Metabolism to break down the foreign poisons. They ducked past the armory and guard house just in time to avoid the incoming patrol.

The patrol found the two sleeping guards, but fortunately, they seemed to find the sleeping duo an extremely funny occurrence and even took out picture crystals to capture the image. By the time they were done, Sorin and Lawrence were back in the wine cellar. Sorin used Iron-Melt Poison to seal the door shut once again, then teamed up with Lawrence to roll the barrels back into place.

"You know what to do," said Sorin, handing Lawrence another pouch of poison. A minute later, Sorin re-entered the poisoned kitchen and absorbed the poison lingering in the air. Lawrence arranged the small group of cooks into a circle and placed a half-eaten roast beside one of them. A few grease stains on their hands and mouths, along with some spilled wine, courtesy of Lorimer, was all the incriminating evidence they needed to plant before withdrawing the poison and ducking through the window.

"A Hero!" said Lawrence, raising his hands as they left the premises. "I'm a Hero, baby! Wait till Gareth and Stephan hear about this."

"You're definitely not the standard sort of Hero," said Sorin, massaging his brow. "We'll need to sort out the details of your ability, but it clearly has to do with perception."

"It's called Near-Sighted," said Lawrence. "It lets me narrow my vision to a 50-foot radius and lets me see *everything*. That includes traps, magic, and all sorts of things. But I can't transmit continuous images to my friends like I just did. Just still-shots here and there to alert them about stuff."

"It sounds like an extremely useful ability," said Sorin. He was still deeply regretful about the limits of his own ability.

"Cheer up, mate," said Lawrence. "You're basically unkillable. I wonder if you could regenerate an arm."

"I can't," said Sorin with certainty. "If I lose more than a certain amount of flesh, I can't get it back. But I *might* be able to reattach an arm. I'm not completely certain."

"See, *that's* an awesome ability," said Lawrence. "An unkillable Hero. As for me, I can just see things really well. In the end, that's just a support ability."

Having achieved their goals for the evening, Sorin returned to the workshop. He used the remaining dream butterfly powder on the receptionist to mask his return and signed the guest book with an incorrect time before returning to their shared laboratory.

"Up late doing interesting things, I imagine?" asked Mr. Primrose.

"No," said Sorin, shaking his head. "Nothing interesting." He needed a sufficiently good reason and damning evidence if he was to expose Marcus. Otherwise, the governor would simply buy him time to clean up the laboratory and cover up any wrongdoing.

"That's good," said Mr. Primrose. "Boring is always good in times like these. You look exhausted. Don't you have a shift tomorrow morning?"

"I completely forgot," said Sorin. "What time is it anyway? Four o'clock? That means I've still got a couple of hours to sleep."

Mr. Primrose let out a soft chuckle. "To be young again. I have extra potent coffee for Bone-Forging cultivators if you're willing to give it a try. Worst case, you'll be poisoned. Nothing you can't handle, am I right?"

79

CLAN POLITICS

Mr. Primrose's coffee awoke Sorin to a whole new world of possibilities. "I just—I just can't stop thinking about it," Sorin confessed in an all-too-quick voice. "Poisons. Lots of poison! And no side effects!"

His four companions blinked, sipped coffee from their mugs, then turned their attention back to the city wall just outside the coffee shop. They were officially on standby but were free to do whatever they liked as long as they wore their armor and carried their weapons and were physically within a half mile of their assigned position.

"I know I've said this before, but you really need to calm down," said Gareth. "Yes, we understand that you're poisoned. And yes, we understand that you can take care of it. But some of us aren't awake yet —Daphne, for example." He flicked his fingers in front of the mage's glazed eyes and elicited no response.

Sorin, frustrated by his inability to gesticulate what he'd figured out, took in a deep breath and processed an additional portion of Bone-Forging strength caffeine. This pushed him back from the brink of losing his mind and allowed him to slow down his thought process just enough for everyone to understand him.

"Sorry about that," said Sorin. "It's tough to digest two-star poisons.

Mr. Primrose makes really strong coffee—much stronger than I expected, at least."

"Isn't he an apothecary?" said Stephan. "Don't they *only* make poisons?"

Sorin shrugged. "Coffee can technically be considered a poisonous stimulant. Also, it's for personal use, not for sale."

"So what *did* you figure out during your caffein-induced fever dream?" asked Gareth. "We picked up bits and pieces here and there but weren't able to figure it out."

Sorin took a moment to organize his thoughts before continuing. "Mr. Primrose's coffee enlightened me on a few things. Namely, poisonous potions and poisonous pills. They aren't usually made since their downsides are often extreme, and most cultivators won't dare use them. My thoughts are as follows: Since I can absorb and digest poisons, shouldn't we be carrying such potions with us?"

"That's... not a bad idea, actually," said Gareth. "Though I can't think of where we'd purchase such medicines off the top of my head."

"That's because they're not standardized," said Stephan. "At least most of them aren't, anyway. The most common types on the market are potential-burning pills. They fill you with strength for a short moment, but they exhaust your talent and make it difficult to break through in the future."

"Those wouldn't work," said Sorin, shaking his head. "They damage your system to get you that extra energy. But something like a mana potion that instantly replenishes a lot of mana but results in an exhausted state one minute later due to poison accumulation? Or maybe a potent healing potion that leaves you weakened? A potion that increases your power for a short amount of time but leaves your muscles full of toxins that take a while to clean?"

"It's definitely worth investigating," said Stephan. "But like I said, such things aren't standardized. Apothecaries sometimes produce them, but they're only used as a last resort. Now, since you're back to normal, let's get this meeting started. Daphne? Your book is on fire!"

"What? Fire!?" said Daphne, rousing from her half-asleep state.

"Hey, there's no fire. In fact, my books are all fireproof." She glared at Stephan. "How dare you trick me?"

"I just wanted you to wake up so we could ask young Mr. *Hero* here about how he managed to defy the odds," said Stephan. "Also, it looks like I owe Gareth some money."

"Same," grumbled Daphne. She and Stephan handed over a small pouch of gold to the smug-looking archer. "Now spill it, or should we get Sorin to tell us the *real* story."

Lawrence set down his breakfast and let out a satisfied sigh. "It's a wonderful day, isn't it, fellow Heroes? And fellow *non*-Heroes."

"It seems I have no choice but to risk my life and break through," said Gareth with a sigh. "Otherwise, there'll be no stopping him."

Daphne shrugged. "He can keep acting smug. If he takes it too far, I'll set him on fire until he begs for mercy."

Lawrence shuddered slightly but continued grinning. "I suppose that, as the newly inducted Hero, it falls to me to tell the story.

"It was late last night when Sorin and I infiltrated a villain's den. It was a risky thing we did, and there were dozens of Bone-Forging cultivators with specialized senses keeping watch. Sorin wanted to retreat, but I knew that for the good of the outpost, we had no choice but to put our lives on the line. We used everything we had at our disposal—poison, steel, and my wondrous good looks. Many female villains were seduced over the evening until, finally, we arrived at a grim dungeon."

Sorin, unable to take it anymore, cut him off. "We snuck into the Governor's Manor."

"You *what?*" Stephan hissed. "You're... you're serious, aren't you?"

Lawrence shrugged. "It wasn't a big deal. I've done it before when I was much weaker."

"Just because you survived once doesn't make it not risky," said Stephan. "Gareth, tell him!"

Gareth sighed. "According to the outpost's laws, the governor has the right to put anyone but a Bone-Forging cultivator or a Hero to death. It's a right that can only be vetoed by a vice guild master or someone of higher rank."

"*Seriously?*" said Lawrence. "That's… *ridiculous*. I've never heard of this ever happening to anyone. Ever."

"It's a little obscure because, generally, the outpost governor doesn't use this power except in extreme circumstances," said Gareth. "It's bad for morale. But he could probably say you were a spy for the demons or something if he found you sneaking around his manor in the middle of a demon tide."

"Wow," said Lawrence. "Am I ever glad we didn't get caught? Wait, did you know this, Sorin?"

"Obviously," said Sorin. "The first thing I did when I moved to the outpost was look up the rules and regulations."

"And you didn't *tell* me?" said Lawrence.

"I thought you knew," said Sorin with a shrug. "Apologies. I thought you were just brave. Turns out the ignorant know no fear."

"*Anyway*," said Lawrence, glaring at Sorin. "We snuck into the first basement through the kitchen, then made our way to the second basement, where Marcus's secret laboratory is hidden."

"Wait, you were doing all this to spy on *Marcus?*" said Stephan, raising his hands. "This just keeps getting better!"

"We had no choice," said Sorin. "Based on the poisons he's having me concoct, I had strong suspicions that he might be carrying out live human experiments."

"If that's indeed the case, you should inform the guild master about it," Stephan scolded. "It's like no one cares about the rules one whit!"

"And why would I do that?" Sorin challenged. "If there was an official investigation, that would leave Marcus more than enough time to clean up after himself. Moreover, I wasn't sure about it. Until last night, at least."

Stephan frowned. "Are you saying you caught him in the act of performing human experiments?"

"I was just as surprised as you were," said Lawrence. "I thought Sorin was just being paranoid. But there I was, looking in on a group of volunteers strapped to beds. Orpheus was one of them. I think they called them meridian-opening trials?"

"Meridian-opening..." muttered Stephan. "So, it's not just Marcus, but the Kepler Clan that's involved. *Wait a minute.* Sorin. You're part of the Abberjay branch of the family, aren't you? Your parents... *ah.* This all makes sense now."

"What makes sense?" asked Sorin. "What do you *know*?"

"Not much," said Stephan. "But based on what I overheard from my father speaking to the clan's elders, the Kepler Clan's meridian-opening formula and method are a carefully guarded secret. According to my lessons, the Abberjay branch controls the formula. But only the formula for the first eight primary meridians is widely circulated within the Abberjay branch. The higher-level formulas are passed on from clan leader to clan leader."

"My father was the former clan leader," Sorin directly admitted. "But my parents passed away three years ago. I'm not sure about the specifics."

"I'm not too sure either," said Stephan. "But what I *do* know is that three years ago, just after the Kepler Clan experienced an internal upheaval, they started limiting advanced meridian-opening procedures. My father inquired about obtaining one for me but was outright refused. He was so angry he broke a family heirloom."

Sorin frowned. "So you're saying my parent's death is related to this sudden change in attitude?"

"Undoubtedly," said Stephan. "The consensus is that the late clan leader concocted the advanced tinctures and also kept the advanced formula on his person. With his death, the formula was lost."

Sorin suddenly thought of his ransacked residence and Marcus's confiscation of his assets. The experimentation, combined with the carrot and stick approach the Kepler Clan's Council of Elders was taking with him... All of it made sense now.

"I would appreciate it if no one spoke of the treatments I've been providing you all," Sorin said with a sigh. "Otherwise, things will get troublesome. Hm, I'll probably need to see if Percival already spilled the beans or if he kept that to himself."

"Why would you hide it?" asked Daphne.

"Um… because I'm a weak Blood-Thickening cultivator that they could capture with little effort?" said Sorin. "Do you have a different take on it?"

"To be honest, this situation has a lot of story potential," said Daphne. "And if *I* was writing the story, I'd get you—obviously the main character—to blatantly use said formula and make it known to your elders."

Sorin massaged his brow. "Can you explain the logic to me, please? I'm still dealing with the after-effects of Mr. Primrose's coffee."

"I think I see what she's saying," said Gareth. "It's like in warfare. Sometimes, famous generals expose a secret weapon since its greatest value is not to be used but to serve as a deterrent."

"That's right," said Daphne. "If everyone knows that I can cast a Meteor spell to destroy the entire outpost, will they dare stop me from stealing cake from a child in broad daylight? You hold a lot of power if you possess the formula and they don't, Sorin. In fact, even if they do possess the formula, having it provides you with certain advantages. Assuming they don't just assassinate you, you'll possess the ability to retaliate if they upset you too badly."

"Um, can we get back to the *real* important stuff?" said Lawrence. "Like me being a Hero?"

"One second, Lawrence," said Sorin. "So, you're saying I should find a way to expose what I know, but in a subtle way?"

"That's right," said Daphne. "That will give you a level of what I like to call 'plot armor.'"

Sorin nodded. "Fine. I'll give it some thought. But I'd appreciate it if everyone kept quiet about this for the time being. I'm not sure about the exact situation, and I don't want to take any unnecessary risks until I confirm a few things."

"Our lips are sealed," said Stephan. "Now cough it up, Lawrence. You obviously did some life-risking peeping, which is why your Hero Meridian was unlocked. What enhancement did you receive? What Heroic Ability did you get?"

Lawrence, excited about all the attention he was getting, insisted on having Stephan buy everyone a round of drinks before continuing. "That hit the spot," said Lawrence, sipping on hot chocolate. "It's not as good as my dad's, but it'll do. Now, where was I? Ah yes. My wonderful ability." He proceeded to explain the details and limitations.

"Three-dimensional vision within 50 feet that detects traps, magical or otherwise?" said Gareth. "Useful. Especially if you can share the vision periodically."

"Only for a bit," said Lawrence. "It's very tiring. But activating the ability itself doesn't take a lot of energy. It's just mentally taxing."

"A peeping ability for a peeper," said Stephan. "How fitting. What about your enhancement? What kind of ability increase did you get?" Sorin's ears perked up because Lawrence hadn't yet told him about this part.

"It's *lame*," said Lawrence with a sigh.

"It can't be that bad," said Gareth. "There are no useless abilities."

Lawrence shrugged. "My reflexes just got better. That's all. And they were already pretty good."

Gareth frowned. "So you're saying you didn't see a big improvement in your overall abilities?"

"It's not a *bad* improvement," said Lawrence. "Just... underwhelming."

Sorin was also confused. His own increase in mana throughput was extremely powerful. He refused to believe Lawrence's enhancement wasn't equally impressive.

Maybe it's not just his reflexes that improved. Maybe... Sorin had a bold hypothesis he decided to test out. He covertly took his whip out of his belt pouch and controlled it to loop under the table. Then, after winding up slowly to avoid alerting Lawrence, he directed the whip to crack towards Lawrence's head.

"Hey! What was that for?" said Lawrence, jumping suddenly. "Sorin, what the hell? I thought we were friends!"

"We are," said Sorin with a grin. "I was just testing you."

"I think I see what's going on here," said Gareth. "Your reflexes didn't improve. It's your senses."

"And why don't I feel that way at all?" asked Lawrence. "My eyesight didn't change. Neither did my hearing."

"I think Gareth's right," said Stephan. "Except it's not your basic senses that got enhanced. Instead, it's your sixth sense."

"That…" said Lawrence, raising his finger. "Huh. That's pretty cool. And it explains why I was able to avoid a skillet to the face when I walked into the kitchen this morning. Don't ask."

"A sixth sense ability," muttered Daphne. "Aren't those rare? Sorry, I spent some gold to read up on Heroic Abilities and stuff. Found some statistics."

"Very rare," agreed Stephan. "And only useful for certain types of cultivators. For rogues, it's an especially valuable skill."

"There you go!" said Lawrence, once again very smug about his newly acquired title. "Hero Lawrence is at your service. Please try to keep up."

"Does shooting a Hero in the unmentionables make you a Hero?" asked Gareth.

"Unfortunately not," said Stephan. Then he turned towards the wall and frowned. Lawrence did the exact same thing.

"Trouble?" asked Sorin.

"Most definitely," said Stephan.

"Wait, you have a sixth sense, too?" asked Lawrence. "Didn't you get a huge strength boost?"

"That's just a part of being a beastshift warrior," said Stephan with a wink. "Try to keep up, Lawrence."

"The soldiers on the walls are scrambling," said Gareth. "There's no bell, but—" His words were cut off by a loud toll.

"Looks like things are heating up," said Stephan. "No time to finish. Drinks are on me." He tossed a gold coin on the table and picked up his gauntlets and helmet. Sorin followed, looking worriedly towards the dark clouds rolling in from the forest.

THE TIDE COMES IN

The bell tolled a total of six times before letting out, sending a loud and clear message that this was *not* a drill. Soldiers and cultivators scrambled to their stations, some of them carrying large bundles of arrows and alchemical supplies, as well as entire crates full of mana, health, and stamina potions.

"This is our assigned section," said Stephan as he led them up a set of wooden stairs. "Remember: we're here to assist. We'll be conserving our energy for hotspots if possible. Most one-star demons won't be a threat to us or the defenders, but given the numbers involved, there may be complications.

"Stay sharp. If you spot opportunities, let me, or preferably Gareth, know."

The walls were thirty feet high and built using entire tree trunks harvested from the Bloodwood Forest. After being processed, refined, and enchanted by the many mages in the city, their surfaces had then been etched with spells used to destroy and repel lower-level demons.

Despite their relatively low numbers, mortal soldiers were the bread and butter of the outpost's defenses. It was they who activated the wall spells using mana crystals and shot arrows by the hundreds using mechanical contraptions.

The mortal-guided spells were powerful and cleared one-star demons by the thousands. But they were not omnipotent and required charging up using bucketloads of mana crystals.

While the spells recharged, mortal soldiers killed demons attempting to crawl up the walls with arrows or knocked them down using long spears. And when the demons managed to close the gap, it was then that the cultivating soldiers came in to support them.

Corpses piled up by the thousands. Compared to the earlier waves, there were a hundred times more demons. Accompanying them were dozens of two-star demons, all of them wary and calculating as they coldly watched their brethren perish.

"It seems we were assigned a particularly difficult stretch of wall," said Gareth, peering into the distance.

"Especially if you consider who's guarding the wall with us," chimed in Lawrence.

Sorin let out a groan as he noticed a team of five adventurers climb onto the same section of the wall. Their leader was none other than Orpheus, who'd clearly survived the meridian-opening treatment. "Didn't they recently pull him off duty because he tried to sabotage us?"

"Alas, no punishment is forever, and the severity of a punishment often depends on the value of the individual," said Stephan. "According to what you described, there's a high chance that Marcus succeeded and that his value went through the roof."

Sorin cast Ophidian Eye and inspected Orpheus and his companions to be sure. "Eighteen unlocked meridians," he confirmed. "As for his companions, they've unlocked sixteen, fourteen, thirteen, and thirteen respectively. Twelve of those are primary meridians, obviously. The rest are extraordinary meridians."

Stephan's eyes narrowed. "Are you saying he's unlocked everything but the Hero Meridian?"

"Even that one's halfway unsealed," said Sorin. "Further proving that character does not a Hero make. How about I sick Lorimer on him mid-battle? A mercy, compared to what I'd do to him?"

Stephan shook his head. "As much as I want to deal with him, we can't do anything directly." He shot Gareth a meaningful look, and the archer, fully focused on the ongoing battle, only spared him a glance to confirm he was listening.

The weakest of the demons were the first to attack, both to waste the wall's energy and to consume ammunition. Their corpses eventually piled up high enough to serve as a corpse ladder that subsequent demons used to climb the deadly palisade.

Mid-tier demons arrived once most of the lower-tier demons were expended. There were wolves, deer, badgers, and boars. Birds dive-bombed the defenders overhead with the help of three two-star demons that required Vice Guild Master Victor to keep in check.

With the mid-tier demons joining in, the defense revealed the alchemical cannons they'd hidden and used them to blast larger clusters of stronger demons. They utilized explosive alchemical reagents and spell runes to propel large balls of iron. These balls, in turn, were enchanted with one-time glyphs that either detonated on impact or flooded the surrounding area in a sea of fire.

"Why don't I see any Bone-Forging cultivators?" asked Sorin as the battle grew increasingly fierce.

"You don't see them because they're not here," said Gareth. "I over-heard a few soldiers talking. Apparently, the southern wall is getting hit far worse. We've only got Vice Guild Master Victor, Haley, and one of the city's Nighthawks to help us out."

"Wait, are you saying it's up to *us* to take care of those huge demons?" Lawrence pointed with a gulp.

"That's proper Hero duty, isn't it?" teased Stephan. "Don't tell me you're *scared*."

"Could I trouble the two of you to protect me from those annoying birds instead of bantering with one another?" asked Daphne. The mage had been silently chanting and tracing sigils all this time. In her hands were two dozen glowing sigils that were showing signs of instability.

"Are those traps?" asked Gareth. Daphne nodded. "Remotely deto-nated or proximity traps?"

"Remotely detonated," said Daphne. "Though I have to be within range. Do you have any thoughts as to where to best place them?"

"I've got a few ideas," said Gareth. "Does our dear leader have any preferences?"

"You're the tactician," said Stephan. "I'm just a front-line general. Hardly important. Say what you need, and I'll make it happen."

"Then, for starters, let's place a healthy barrier between us and Orpheus," said Gareth. Their team jogged halfway between their two groups and screened Daphne as she placed a small cluster of sigils onto the stones lining the wooden wall.

"Out of curiosity, is the wall fireproof?" asked Sorin. "It *is* made of wood."

"Relax, an expert enchanted the wall," said Daphne as she poured her mana into the glyph to complete a spell circle. "Now stop distracting me. One mistake, and they go boom."

Surprisingly, Orpheus did not come over to engage them and instead placed all his focus on the battle outside. The two-star demons were creeping in, and judging by his expression, he was clearly planning on fighting said demons.

Just because Heroes are contractually prevented from sharing their experiences doesn't mean political families won't have access to this information, thought Sorin.

According to Percival, Orpheus's Valmer family was formerly an influential one. They would have no shortage of restricted information and above-average cultivation techniques and would, therefore, know a thing or two about how Heroes were made.

"That's enough for up here," said Gareth once Daphne finished placing the fifth trap glyph. "How are your mana stores?"

"More than good enough to activate all the traps I prepared," said Daphne. "As for detonating them, it doesn't require much. Just a thought on my part."

"Then how do you feel about going on patrol?" asked Gareth. "Out there, obviously. We can't wait for the two-star demons to come to us."

"Is this about your cousin again?" asked Lawrence. "Because I swear, it was completely consensual."

"Are you sure about this?" Stephan asked Gareth.

"Positive," said Gareth. "Otherwise, who's to say those two-star demons will really attack? The way I see it, they're just analyzing. Unless they have good reasons to do otherwise, they'll only push forward during the final wave. Besides—how else will we get to see brave Orpheus in action?"

"You're the commander," said Stephan with a shrug. White hair burst out of his skin as he transformed into an Arctic Rune Bear. "Everyone, hop on!"

Gareth and Lawrence activated their movement techniques and landed on the Arctic Rune Bear's back. As for Sorin, he used Adder Rush to pick up Daphne before joining them atop Stephan's shoulder blades.

Stephan launched himself down the thirty-foot wall, releasing a shockwave of frosty and violent energy in all directions. One-star demons that had survived their encounter with the wall were pulverized, giving Sorin and Lawrence sufficient time to hop off Stephan and protect his flanks.

Ever since receiving his Heroic Empowerment, Stephan had been a monster on the battlefield. Every swipe of his claws slew several lesser one-star demons. Only the strongest of one-star demons could survive a blow, and even then, they were either too damaged to fight properly or bled out a few seconds later.

Sorin and Lawrence were also monsters in their own right. Sorin was far faster and stronger than he'd ever been. Dispatching one-star demons consisted of thrusting out with Viper Strike, injecting maximal poison into his prey, and withdrawing said poison back into his body with the aid of Toxic Metabolism. The entire process took less than half a second and could be repeated in near perpetuity.

Lawrence, on the other hand, was a different type of nightmare. He didn't have Sorin's strength or his ability to take blows, but he had speed, awareness, and reflexes in spades. His signature movement technique could now be utilized to its fullest. It was to the point that Triple Stab Execution, a single-target skill, could be used on three separate targets. His ability to take advantage of critical weaknesses was even greater than Sorin's, which made it so that he was able to take out all enemies he attacked in one hit despite his lacking offense.

With Stephan taking point and Lawrence and Sorin guarding his flanks, Gareth was free to spam his latest skill, Power Shot, on key targets. Their group had no issue pushing a hundred feet away from the wall. Once they crossed that invisible boundary, Daphne twisted a ring on her finger and turned invisible. The only indication of her presence was the faint glow of fire affinity mana that appeared whenever she set a trap rune.

"Put the next one down ten feet to the south," said Gareth once she'd installed the first.

"Is that much planning really necessary?" asked Daphne.

"I thought we had an understanding," said Gareth. "I tell you who to burn and where, and you cast spells to your heart's content."

"I like this understanding," said Daphne. "Please instruct me, exalted commander."

"Everyone, pull back slightly," shouted Gareth. "Daphne, use that opening to lay down your next trap." He used his archery and footwork to cover their retreat and proceeded to trace a squiggly pattern with seemingly no rhyme or reason, all the while drawing closer to the two-star demons.

A few of the two-star demons in the distance edged closer upon detecting their presence. Unfortunately, they didn't seem to have any intentions of participating in this battle.

"We need someone to volunteer to piss them off," said Gareth when Daphne finished installing the last of her traps.

"I won't do it," said Lawrence immediately. "I refuse. I might be a Hero, but I'm not going to randomly stab a two-star demon in the back and hope to get away with it."

"No need to worry, everyone," said Sorin with a light chuckle. "I already enlisted a volunteer. All he asks is for a full share of the demon cores."

"What could a rat possibly do to—" Gareth's voice cut off as an unearthly shriek filled the air. The Curly-Horned Demonic Bull nearest to them suddenly fell to the ground, writhing. Shortly after, a Tiger-Pawed Musk Deer joined him, as did a Shadow-Pawed Demonic Badger.

Gareth hopped onto Stephan, who was still mid-combat, and peered in the distance. "I'd ask what you instructed your rat to do, but given that they're all male and bleeding between the legs…"

Sorin grinned as he stabbed one of the few demons brave enough to approach their group in the neck. "Lorimer is an expert at provoking such creatures. Have faith in Lord Lorimer and gain eternal life."

"Aren't three two-star demons a few too much?" muttered Daphne.

"I'm sure Gareth has a plan," said Stephan. "What's the plan, Gareth?"

"What plan?" asked Gareth. "The traps are all random."

"You son of a—" Lawrence shouted suddenly. He raised his dagger as a small blur broke past him, avoiding his attack. Demons parted to reveal three ferocious creatures. Their eyes were red, and they were focused on a single individual: Lawrence, whose body was now spattered with blood and whose belt pouch now contained three bloody… *appendages,* courtesy of Lord Lorimer.

"They don't look so happy to see you, Lawrence," said Stephan.

"I've been framed!" said Lawrence. "Your bloody rat framed me! By the way, I think I see Orpheus heading our way."

"Nice," said Gareth, a rarely seen wild gleam appearing in his eyes. "Now let's see how badly he overextends."

SKIRMISH OUTSIDE THE WALL

The Curly-Horned Demonic Bull was the fastest of the three demons, with the Tiger-Pawed Musk Deer, in all its vampiric glory, being only slightly slower. As for the Shadow-Pawed Demonic Badger, Sorin had lost track of it. Only a parting wave of demons confirmed that it was circling around their group and cut off the perpetrator—obviously Lawrence—from retreating.

"This is ridiculous!" said Lawrence, splitting off from their group and attracting the demonic bull's attention. "It was the rat! The rat!" Yet he did not throw away the looted reproductive organs, as the demons had already chosen their target. More to the point, no other team member would be able to survive the wrath of all three demons simultaneously.

Sorin had yet to find time to craft more poisons for himself, but there were a few existing one-star poisons that could be found on the black market. Most were alchemical stimulants with adverse effects so severe they were outlawed—something he personally didn't need to worry about.

He drained a vial of one of these illegal stimulants and braced himself as colors grew more intense, and the sound of pounding hooves and ripping claws rattled his eardrums. It took only a few seconds for

Sorin to adapt to his improved senses and increased strength and dexterity. He could feel the strain on his body as it overcame its natural limitations but felt comfortable in being able to recover from this damage thanks to his S-Class regeneration.

The poisonous effects of the stimulant were threefold. Firstly, the stimulant would exhaust Sorin's body due to overexertion. Secondly, it would leave dangerous toxins in his nervous system, which would accumulate with each use. Thirdly, the perception-enhancing stimulant would degrade upon expending itself and transform into a toxin that would cause irreparable brain damage. This was why even military application of these stimulants was restricted to one use per person per year and three-lifetime doses maximum. These last two properties were naturally no problem for Sorin. Thanks to Toxic Metabolism, he could both avoid these negative effects and even convert them to vitality stores, thereby making up for the drawback of overexertion.

By now, the Curly-Horned Demonic Bull had already charged at Lawrence and missed. But the Shadow-Pawed Demonic Badger was cunning and appeared behind Lawrence while he was still recovering, swiping at him with its two-foot-long claws.

Sorin used his enhanced reflexes and speed to close the gap and pull Lawrence back before the claws hit him. Simultaneously, Stephan appeared to intercept the badger with a Lunisolar Paw and prevent it from retreating.

The impact of the clashing Shadow-Pawed Demonic Badger and the Arctic Rune Bear sent Sorin and Lawrence tumbling backward. Sorin, being much more difficult to put down than Lawrence, used his body as a shield and suffered lacerations on his back from the collision that ripped away armor and skin and exposed his bare bones.

Lawrence moved to help Sorin apply a healing potion but was forced to retreat when the Tiger-Pawed Musk Deer pounced over Stephan and dove straight for Lawrence. The rogue dodged its first attack but was forced to the ground. An arrow pierced down from above and chained the musk deer to another point in the earth, thereby diverting it before it could trample the rogue to death.

That must be Gareth's newest skill—Shackle Shot, thought Sorin. The skill was an expensive one for archers that could chain down and stun either a single enemy or entire groups for up to three seconds. It joined Power Shot, Triple Shot, Quick Shot, and Eagle Eye, as well as Gareth's wind-based movement technique, to make the archer the most prolific member of their party when it came to skills.

Shackle Shot normally boasted a one-to-three-second stun length, but its effect was short-lived due to rank suppression. However, the half-second stun bought Lawrence more than enough time to pick himself off the ground before using the creature's shadow to maneuver around it and performing Triple Stab Execution.

Having gained the upper hand, Lawrence was able to control the momentum of their battle, freeing up the rest of their team to take care of the other two demons. "Sorin, disable the badger's mana if you can!" shouted Gareth. He led off their counter-offensive by blasting the badger with a power shot to the side of the head, enabling Stephan to push it back onto its uncertain hind legs.

Sorin didn't think twice before using Adder Rush to close the gap. The badger saw him coming and tried to intercept him, but Sorin leaned in, taking a few more deep gashes to his back to strike at the creature's left leg and inject a heavy dose of Manabane Poison, disabling its mana flow and disrupting its mana shielding.

The demon in question was 25 feet tall when standing on its hind legs. Sorin's attack naturally provoked a counterattack from the giant badger in the form of a sweeping kick, but Sorin used his trusty whip and Python Coil to yank himself forward toward the wounded leg. He then jumped off said leg to attack another acupoint, injecting a second dose of Manabane Poison. It joined with the first in disabling any movement techniques the Shadow-Pawed Demonic Badger might use for the foreseeable future.

There was a second benefit to the exchange—destabilizing the badger's footing enough for Stephan to push it backward. "Explode!" shouted Daphne from their safe center when the badger reached a cluster of fire sigils.

What amounted to three fully charged Fireballs detonated just behind the badger, scorching its lower limbs beyond recognition and infuriating the creature.

Losing the remainder of its reason, the demon activated a berserk ability and began mindlessly mauling Stephan, but the bear-man fought back with one charged Lunisolar Paw after another, enforcing a stalemate that was rapidly transforming into an advantaged position for the beastshift warrior.

The Tiger-Pawed Musk Deer is still chasing down Lawrence, and having a damn hard time of it too, thought Sorin. *As for the Curly-Horned Demonic Bull, Orpheus and his team are taking care of it.* For once, Sorin was glad they were on the same battlefield; the demonic bull was a powerful opponent and was difficult to stop with a single adventurer.

Meanwhile, Lawrence was doing a great job stalling the musk deer using his quick reflexes and enhanced sixth sense. Unfortunately, the musk deer soon grew tired of his antics and activated a vampiric ability. Vitality began to steadily drain from Lawrence to empower the musk deer. Daphne and Gareth were similarly affected.

Sensing the threat the creature posed, Gareth changed his target to the musk deer. His charged Power Shots didn't pack much of a punch unless they hit vitals, but they still forced the musk deer to react and gave Lawrence the openings he needed.

Unfortunately, Lawrence couldn't deal a lot of damage to the creature, and Daphne, under the direction of Gareth, had snuck out to lay down additional runes nearby. It, therefore, fell to Sorin to expedite its demise.

"Lorimer, help me out," Sorin called out. The rat, who'd been hiding amongst the lesser demons not far away, charged at the musk deer and instantly provoked an extreme response. The Tiger-Pawed Musk Deer abandoned all defenses as it began recklessly attacking the rat, giving Lawrence an opening to attack its neck vertebrae.

Sorin simultaneously closed in on its flank; the deer responded to his charge by swiping at him with its left tiger paw but wasn't able to catch

Sorin, who was now enhanced by both the stimulant poison and his Blood Drinker Armor's enchantment.

Sorin's body was covered in his own blood, giving him access to a convenient source of external poison. He swiped his cursed dagger on his bloody chest while avoiding the tiger paw, then proceeded to use Viper Strike to inject a combination of mana and blood into the musk deer's hindquarters.

The Tiger-Pawed Musk Deer shrieked as its internal mana circulation was disrupted. It flailed and managed to catch Sorin and throw him to the ground, where it proceeded to trample him. Sorin felt his bones crack and his organs shift.

As durable as he was, Sorin was unable to withstand a sustained attack by a two-star demon. Fortunately, he wasn't alone. One final Shackle Shot, courtesy of Gareth, and a vicious counterattack, courtesy of Sorin's Lord and Savior, Lorimer Rockeater. The well-timed Shackleshot pierced through the creature's mana-disrupted body and pinned it to the ground. Lorimer took advantage of its stunned condition to crawl through Sorin's dagger wound and ravage the demon's innards.

The demon contorted in pain, giving Sorin the time he needed to use Python Coil and pull two of the creature's legs out from under it. It fell to the ground, prone, and both Sorin and Lawrence launched themselves onto the creature's exposed underbelly and stabbed at its vitals.

Combined with Lorimer's intense offensive, the creature was eventually unable to hold out. It shivered as it reached its limits, and what remained of its poor life left it.

Sorin first confirmed the creature's death with Ophidian Eye, then placed his hand on the creature's underbelly to retrieve his poisons. Retrieving his poison back from the creature's body restored only half of his initial mana reserves. This was because a two-star demon like the musk deer was resistant to his poisons and able to destroy them before they could invade its body.

"Incoming shenanigans," warned Gareth as Sorin took a much-needed breather and drank back a health option. "Orpheus and the bunch."

"Aren't they taking this a bit too far?" said Sorin, noticing that they were maneuvering closer to Stephan to use him and the demon he was fighting as a distraction.

"What are you talking about?" said Gareth with a grin. "They're helping us. Daphne?"

"On it," said Daphne, focusing on a cluster of five sparks she'd laid. "Activating the rune cluster in five, four, three, two, one… *Now!*" An explosion blasted the Curly-Horned Demonic Bull Orpheus was baiting towards them into the air. It landed near Sorin and Lawrence, who exchanged a look before repeating the previous process and easily dispatching another two-star demon.

"Hey, that was our kill!" yelled Orpheus.

"Tell someone who cares," said Sorin. Lorimer emerged from the musk deer carcass just as Sorin finished retrieving his poisons. The rat tossed a demon core to Sorin's outstretched hand, then dug into the bull's eye socket to excavate another demon core.

"That's *our* core," said Orpheus.

"Then come take it, coward," said Sorin. Unfortunately, Orpheus's self-control was high, and he didn't pursue the matter.

As they continued exchanging hostile banter, Gareth leaped into the air and launched another Power Shot. *It's coated with my blood poison,* thought Sorin as the arrow built up power and pierced into another two-star demon—an Earth-Shaping Termite. It and two other two-star companions were drawn towards their battlefield, as was a Wind-Shaping Hawk up above them.

"Finish off the badger," said Gareth. "Orpheus, you look like you could use a good fight; take care of these termites, will you?"

"I'm *not* yours to command," said Orpheus, only to realize that he had no choice in the matter. Gareth used arrows to lure the termites toward his group, and Orpheus, unable to avoid them on time, chose to face them in battle.

"Let's go kill ourselves a badger," Sorin said to Lawrence.

"How about we go for a good ole-fashioned pincer attack?" suggested Lawrence. "Simple, but effective."

HIT AND RUN

Stephan and the shadow-pawed demon badger were both in rough shape. A mixture of red blood and black gore covered their bodies, and Stephan's armor, newly repaired and upgraded since their last round of corpse collection, was in tatters.

Despite the heavy damage he'd suffered, Stephan didn't hesitate to taunt the badger as Sorin and Lawrence closed in. Sorin took advantage of the badger's distracted state to inject two doses of Flesh-Melt Poison straight into its heart while Lawrence stabbed it in the back of the neck.

"It's on its last legs!" roared Stephan, wrestling the creature to the ground. Lorimer, ever the opportunist, crawled into its eye and ate through its heavily corrupted brain.

"Gareth is getting pretty ambitious, isn't he?" said Sorin, once again retrieving his poisons from the demon's corpse. He felt the stimulants in his body wearing off, forcing him to drink another toxic vial to stave off exhaustion.

"Most of the enemy demons are focused on the south side," said Stephan, breaking a healing potion onto his bloodied chest. "Now's naturally the best time for us to lay on some preemptive damage."

"I don't know if provoking that hawk was the best idea, though," said Sorin, noting the powerful bird diving down at them with malicious intent.

"I wouldn't worry about that hawk too much," said Stephan.

The demonic hawk in question had its claws stretched out and was halfway to the ground when an arrow shot all the way from the outpost wall, struck the creature, and knocked it to the ground. It landed conveniently near a cluster of three fire trap glyphs, which Daphne promptly detonated to finish off the creature.

This left only the termites and a group of three two-star demonic wolves nearby. Gareth tried to bait the wolves but failed to catch their attention. Lorimer squeaked to Sorin, but the man shook his head. "Those wolves look smart. I doubt they'd fall for it."

"The demons are gone, and the army's going to close in soon," said Gareth. "Let's retreat."

"What about Orpheus and the rest?" asked Lawrence.

"I don't see how that's our problem," said Gareth.

"Let's kill the termites before we leave," Stephan interrupted. "Wouldn't want them to become Heroes, would we?"

"That *does* make sense," said Gareth, stroking his chin. "Sorin? Lawrence?"

"On it," said Sorin, taking note of Gareth's strange body language. The duo split, with Lawrence taking on the termite engaged with four of Orpheus's men, while Orpheus tried his best to single-handedly take down the remaining termite.

A risky move with a high payoff, thought Sorin, further convinced that Orpheus was armed with the knowledge on how to become a Hero. *Too bad you chose to try breaking through near me.*

Sorin launched himself at the termite, ignoring one of its many clawed appendages tearing into his right arm and nicking his bone in favor of piercing through its exoskeleton and injecting a dose of poison. Insects were more difficult to poison properly due to their organ structures and, therefore, didn't react as violently as Sorin expected. *Is it because it has its own acids?* he wondered.

Regardless, Sorin's attack ignored realm suppression and was disproportionately painful as a result. The termite immediately turned its attention to Sorin, knocking him past Orpheus, who took advantage of the opening to stab the creature in the abdomen.

"Don't... meddle... in other people's battles," said Orpheus with gritted teeth.

"Rich words coming from you," said Sorin, picking himself up on the ground. He stepped forward, only to suddenly realize that the termite's two-star poison was invading his system. He fell to one knee as his body struggled to metabolize the toxins. "By the way, nice job 'getting yourself in trouble' to land on Marcus's list."

"So, you're not completely brainless," said Orpheus, parrying a spur and rolling out of the way of the second. "It's too bad my mana type wasn't fully compatible with the treatment method. Otherwise, I wouldn't need to go through all this just to unlock a stupid Hero Meridian."

Orpheus was a gifted fighter and had clearly received premium lessons on swordsmanship. His techniques were also aligned with death mana, a rare affinity for a cultivator. Sorin could only imagine what kind of money his family had spent to obtain them.

Incompatible body type? Sorin wondered as he continued to metabolize the two-star poison. As far as he knew, death mana was quite compatible with the meridian-opening treatment. It was life mana that was difficult to reconcile with the Kepler Clan's meridian-opening procedure.

He swiftly set aside the passing thought to focus on the termite poison. It was a weak toxin that was quickly converted to nourishment and life force via Toxic Metabolism.

Orpheus continued to land one strike after another, whittling down the creature's defenses until an opening presented itself. Orpheus dodged to land the finishing blow. "Look out!" Sorin shouted, finally purging the last of the poison and leaping over to 'help' him. This placed him in Orpheus's way, foiling his attempt and placing him in an unfavorable position.

It was, of course, entirely possible for Orpheus to dodge the termite's counterattack. But Orpheus had gotten his fair share of termite poison, slowing his reflexes. Dodging became all but impossible once Sorin discretely used Cobra's Glare to temporarily paralyze the man and force him to block.

A deadly spur smashed down onto Orpheus's sword at just the right angle, shoving it deep into his shoulder and through his collarbone. *Drat,* thought Sorin. *Not through the vitals.* He blocked the termite's follow-up attack so as to avoid suspicion. Sabotaging Orpheus had surprisingly little effect on Sorin's mental state.

Seeing their captain fall to the termite's attack, his remaining team members split apart to defend him. Lawrence finished off the remaining termite, and Gareth joined in, along with Daphne. With Fireballs and arrows striking it from behind, the termite quickly fell.

Heavy meridian damage and light nervous system damage, thought Sorin as he evaluated Orpheus's injuries. His teammates were doing their best to bandage him up and apply strong healing potions, but the blood wouldn't stop. They could only watch on helplessly as his blood continued to pool beneath his cooling body.

"We need to leave," said Gareth, running up to them. "Cut out the cores and prepare to retreat."

"Can't you see our captain is dying?" snapped one of Orpheus's teammates.

Gareth chuckled. "Given our relationship and the shit he's tried to pull on us, why should we care? Also, good job, Sorin. Who knows what kind of state he'd be in if you hadn't stepped in to defend him."

"Guys," said Daphne, huffing as she made her way over to them. "We have a problem."

Sorin's eyes narrowed as he suddenly sensed a threat to his life. It was the sort of sixth sense every cultivator had, but that rarely triggered. This time, everyone sensed a powerful presence stemming from Blood-wood Forest, whipping up the nearby demons into a frenzy. This included the remaining two-star demons.

"We have to run. *Now!*" snapped Gareth.

"But he's going to bleed out," urged one of Orpheus's teammates. "Aren't you a physician?"

"Former physician," said Sorin. Hesitating, he placed a hand on Orpheus's unconscious body and spotted the key arteries spurting blood, then used Flesh-Melt Poison to block them off. "This is all I can do for now. Please note that his injuries are severe and that my treatment will lead to necrosis, nerve damage, and meridian damage that will only increase as treatment is delayed. At best, I've preserved his life, assuming we can get him to a competent surgeon quickly enough."

The four clearly had no idea what had transpired in battle and could only thank Sorin and pick up their leader. A bloody-furred Stephan trotted over to Daphne and picked her up. Gareth hopped onto Stephan's back and pulled out three arrows.

Sorin and Lawrence fell into position beside Stephan. All four of Orpheus's teammates, hardy warriors by the looks of them, fell in line behind them. Gareth and Daphne did their best to rain fire and arrows down on any demons that drew too close, but their enemies were far too numerous.

It didn't take long for Lawrence and Sorin to suffer multiple wounds. Stephan's sides became bloody and raw from repeated attacks, and corruption was beginning to set in. Even Sorin, gifted as he was at purging corruption, predicted that treating him would be far from easy.

"Incoming!" shouted Gareth as a massive eagle dove towards them. His arrows did nothing to stop it, but thankfully, an arrow shot from the outpost walls forced it to veer off course and miss them by a few feet. "We're too slow. We need to push in faster."

"I'm trying," said Stephan, making his way towards a large basket being lowered from the wall to retrieve them.

"We've got three minutes, tops," said Gareth, eyeing the demons closing in on them. He scanned their surroundings, then pointed. "Go that way."

"That's hardly the best direction," argued Stephan.

"It's the path of least resistance," said Gareth. "*Move!*"

Upon hearing the man's voice, Sorin felt power surge through his limbs and a want—no, a *need*—to follow his orders. It was the same for their entire team.

Sorin suddenly gained a high-level awareness of their surroundings. It wasn't a precise view like the occasional pulse Lawrence sent their way to make them aware of nearby threats, but more a bird's eye view of their surroundings.

It showed Sorin that they were indeed cutting across a map filled with thousands of different creatures in a pattern that pushed through their respective groupings and through weaker enemies. Moreover, those enemies seemed to instinctively avoid them, as though something— *someone*—repelled them.

Gareth wasn't the only one to experience a stark change in demeanor. Something seemed to shatter around Daphne as she drank down a mana potion. She didn't throw out a Fireball as she usually would but instead summoned one from the center of a group of demons. The Fireball exploded like a fire trap, clearing a swath of demons out of their way just before they reached it.

Gareth shot down a strong demon trying to fill in the gap, while Sorin lobbed a Veridian Smoke Bomb to disable lesser enemies trying to fill it using paralytic poison. "Here, use this," said Sorin, tossing two vials of Dream Blade Ointment to Gareth. The ointment wouldn't be as potent on arrows, but it was better than nothing. The archer promptly used the ointment to empower several arrows, enabling him to disable five high-threat one-star demons before they became a problem.

"Prepare to board the rescue platform!" shouted Gareth just as they reached the wall.

"We won't make it," said one of Orpheus's companions. "They won't be able to pull us up before the two-star demons get to us." Sorin frowned as he pondered their options. He could *maybe* buy time against the five two-star demons heading straight for them but wouldn't be able to intercept their momentum.

"Leave them to me," said Daphne, over-drafting her mana to summon several orbs of fire in the middle of enemy ranks. They didn't immediately detonate but accumulated much like her original fire traps.

By virtue of her breakthrough as a Hero, she was able to quickly summon a full twenty trap orbs, once again depleting her mana. "There. That'll keep them busy."

"Your meridians are under heavy strain," noted Sorin as he observed Daphne's condition.

"I'm *fine*," said Daphne.

"What are you all waiting for?" yelled Gareth, nocking an arrow. "Pull us up!" He unleashed a Shackle Shot that entangled a demonic stag reminiscent of the stag and chained it to a large demonic hedgehog.

An additional barrage of arrows further impeded the demons. These were shot out by none other than Vice Guild Master Victor, who could literally shoot out a rain of arrows with a single shot. But he could only spare one shot every few seconds, as the three two-star demons flying overheard would tear him apart once he showed any signs of weakness.

They'd reached two thirds of the way up when suddenly, one of the two-star demons broke through, forcing Daphne to prematurely detonate the group Fireballs she'd planted. She coughed up blood and collapsed as the explosion rocked the platform and threatened to shove everyone off.

"The rope's frayed!" shouted Lawrence, transmitting an image to their team. One of the two ropes pulling up their basket was singed, likely from the shrapnel the explosion had thrown up, and was mere seconds from letting go.

Sorin, thinking quickly, used Python Coil in conjunction with his whip and grabbed the end of the rope, preventing them from falling just as the rope snapped. The strain was enormous, especially given Stephan's weight. He felt his ligaments tearing as the basket was slowly hauled upwards.

They were barely five feet away from the top of the wall when one of the avian demons decided enough was enough. A Steelfeather Eagle —a stronger cousin of the Steelfeather Sparrow—dove down at them despite Victor and Gareth's heavy barrage.

It was about to make contact when suddenly, a blade swept upward and caught the creature in the neck, decapitating it. Two powerful sets of hands then caught the ropes attached to the basket and yanked it up the rest of the way.

"Some would call what you all did the epitome of foolishness," said a stern voice. It was none other than Vice Governor Marsh, who'd caused Sorin much trouble in the past. "Fortunately, I'm a man who appreciates ten two-star demons getting taken out of the equation before the final push."

"I'm sure my urging had nothing to do with you coming here," said Haley, appearing beside him.

"Politics have no place on this battlefield," said Vice Governor Marsh. "Heroes that can take down so many two-star demons before Bone-Forging are an asset that must be protected."

For a moment, Sorin felt shame wash over him. Shame over how he'd sabotaged Orpheus. But then he remembered everything Orpheus had done and reaffirmed that he'd made the right decision. *Who knows how many people died because of his sabotage over the years? Who knows how many more would die in the future if he was left unchecked?* As a physician, it was his duty to excise malignant tumors before they became a problem.

The battle that followed didn't take long to wrap up. The remaining demons threw themselves against the wall to expend ammunition, poisons, and alchemical explosives.

While the soldiers wrapped things up, Sorin and his team were quickly ushered off to the medical tent. Stephan's wounds were the worst of the bunch, but they paled in comparison to Orpheus's. Sorin marked him as a lost cause, but it seemed his family had a lot of influence; he was ushered off to a surgical room where doctors tried their best to restore his vital functions.

Sorin was sure that Orpheus would pull through with this much attention. His only consolation was that while his life was not in danger, Sorin's subtle tampering would make it impossible for him to continue to cultivate.

A SOMBER INTERLUDE

No one mentioned Orpheus's condition upon returning to the guild. To any outside observer, it was clear that the greedy cultivator's plan to take advantage of the questionable presence of Team 'We Don't Need a Life Mage's on the battlefield had backfired. He only had himself to blame for his injuries.

Sorin only felt the vaguest twinge of guilt. Not for the man himself or for what he'd done, but for the valuable physician time wasted on restoring the functionality of his right arm. Could he have applied a stronger dose of poison? Naturally. But doing so would have been potentially traceable by an experienced physician, so he had refrained from doing so.

Guild members slowly trickled in as the battle in the south tapered off. Fighters were given a cursory inspection by the physicians in the clinic and cleared for duty almost immediately. Adventurers returned to the guild with snippets of information, and it was quickly confirmed that two Bone-Forging cultivators had perished in battle, including the nighthawk leader, Lady Duchene, and Commander Zenol of the Governor's Manor.

"I can't believe this isn't even the final push," said Stephan as he felt his bloody bandages. "Bone-Forging cultivators don't typically fall until then."

"There's something unusual about this demon tide," agreed Gareth. "But that's only to be expected after what happened to our water system."

"I guess corpse patrol will be working overtime?" said Sorin.

"Naw," said Lawrence. "I heard from Dad that the temple has a way of clearing a lot of corpses and cores all at once. It's just a waste to do it until there are a lot of them. Takes energy or something. What's eating you, Daphne?"

The mage was currently frowning, which was uncharacteristic given her recent Heroic Empowerment. *She's not even muttering something about new spells and adjusting her spell matrices. Wait, is she channeling a spell right now?*

"I just overheard a conversation in conference room about casualties," said Daphne a couple minutes later. "See Barbara over there, all on her lonesome?"

"Yeah?" asked Lawrence. "What about her?"

"Her entire team just died," said Daphne. "She only survived by the skin of her teeth and became a Hero as a result."

"Should we go say hello or something?" asked Lawrence, attracting a stern glare from Gareth.

"If she wants to be alone, then let her be alone," said Gareth. "Besides, can't you feel the bloodlust she's giving off? She's primed to kill demons and is in no state to interact with other people."

"There was one other Heroic Breakthrough," said Daphne. "A surprising one, though. It seems Nale is now a Hero as well. He cut his way through the battlefield to save Barbara and her team and is arguably the only reason Barbara managed to make it out alive."

"He might be scum, but at least he's *redeemable* scum," muttered Stephan. "Unlike *someone* we know." Once again, no names were said, but everyone knew whom he was speaking of.

The rest of their discussion revolved around the team's two newest

Heroes: Gareth and Daphne. Gareth had unlocked a similar ability to Lawrence, which allowed him a bird's-eye view of the battlefield and allowed him to share it like Lawrence could. As for his Heroic Empowerment, it came in a unique form: presence. Stephan now radiated an aura of command and was able to make his full intentions known to the team, with or without words. He would also unconsciously repel weaker demons and slightly influence their decision-making.

Daphne's ability was, unsurprisingly, the most useful on offense. "Instead of casting Fireballs from a distance, I can now cast them anywhere within fifty feet and detonate them at point-blank range. I can only do it every sixty seconds, but that's more than often enough."

"Isn't that just like Haley's ability?" said Lawrence. "Why does everyone else get an overpowered ability and not me?"

"And why just Fireballs?" asked Stephan. "It's unusual for abilities to be so specific."

"It's not specific to any single spell, but it only really works if an explosion is involved," said Daphne. "So, Fireball and Flame Rune Trap, in my case. The casting delay is also unaffected by my Quick Cast Skill, so it takes a good second to pull off. I need to account for any delays on my own. Also, physical overlap with the spell matrices will cancel the casting."

"It still sounds like a powerful ability," said Sorin bitterly. Once again, he was reminded of the relative uselessness of his ability.

"Your ability's not bad, Sorin," reassured Stephan. "Didn't you just basically pump yourself full of life-threatening stimulants and increase your combat potential by 20 percent with zero consequences? And can't you drink potions twice as frequently as we can by sheer virtue of metabolizing toxins better?"

"I suppose," said Sorin. These abilities were indeed useful. It was too bad he couldn't retrieve said toxins from his companions and expedite their own healing. "Any idea when the final push is coming?"

"It should be soon, or so Haley says," said Stephan. "It could be hours. It could be minutes." The adventurers gathered were all on standby and would be reassigned once the last phase of the demon tide started.

Waiting around was a waste of time, in Sorin's opinion. "I'm going to go see Haster," he finally decided. "See if I can talk some sense into him."

"You sure?" asked Stephan. "His mental state is fragile."

"It can't get any worse than it already is," said Sorin. "Besides, isn't this demon tide much worse than usual? We need all the help we can get."

The cots in the Adventurers Guild were not for critical patients. They were there to accommodate those that were ready to be discharged but had trouble returning to their duties. In addition to Haster and the half-blind man from before, there was one more patient. He had suffered a traumatic head injury and was still recovering from the shock.

"Hello, Haster," said Sorin, walking up to the man's cot. As usual, the bearded man was staring at the ceiling. A flask of wine could be seen on his bedside, an allowance given only due to the recommendation of his attending physician.

"What do you want?" grumbled Haster.

"I'm just checking up on a friend," said Sorin, placing his hand on the man's legs. His mana and spiritual force quickly scanned his body and mapped out his meridians. *Eleven naturally unlocked primary meridians, and three naturally unlocked extraordinary meridians. Genius grade.*

"Didn't anyone tell you it's rude to inspect people without their consent?" Haster said, glaring at Sorin. "I'm fine. I don't need a physician. Get out."

"No can do," said Sorin. "The situation outside is getting pretty bad. Barbara lost her team. We're also down two Bone-Forging cultivators."

"And how exactly is that my problem?" asked Haster.

"I'm pretty sure it's everyone's problem," said Sorin. "Now, hold still; this might hurt."

"What are you—" Haster gritted his teeth as Sorin shot a stream of poison into an acupoint using his finger. He repeated the process twenty more times over the span of a minute, completely unlocking Haster's final primary meridian.

This was followed by a burst of sword energy that lacerated Sorin's still-repairing armor. "How dare you inject me with poison without my consent. Get *out!*" barked Haster.

"Make me," said Sorin. He used Python Coil to restrain the man, provoking an uproar from the half-blind man.

"Relax. I'm just helping out a friend," Sorin assured him.

"I'm... going to see myself out," said the half-blind man, running out the door.

"I don't *need* your help, Sorin," said Haster through gritted teeth. He mobilized his mana and blasted Sorin using his body as a medium. Sorin's leather armor was severely damaged, and blood oozed out of his wounds, forcing Sorin to pull the toxins back into his body lest they harm Haster.

"You forced me," said Sorin. He grabbed his remaining vial of dream blade ointment and shoved a handful of mana needles into it before sticking said needles into the thrashing man's left leg, heavily sedating him.

"This is... *unethical*..." slurred Haster as he tried to free himself from Python Coil and failed.

"I won't argue with that," said Sorin. "Feel free to report me to the Medical Association. I'm sure they'd jump at the opportunity to put me in my place."

He then put his palm on the man's chest and quickly identified his blocked Yin Link Vessel. He formed a stent and spear and pierced through the obstruction, unlocking the meridian and restoring a semblance of balance to the man's violent sword-aligned mana.

Next came the Yin Heel Vessel. "Your mana is a mess because your meridians are severely lacking in the yin element," said Sorin as he unblocked the meridian. "As a result, exerting your full power has been self-destructive. Of course, that might have more to do with your mutated mana. Sword-aligned mana is rare and often causes problems."

Once again, a poisonous needle pierced through a blockage and opened an extraordinary meridian. Only two openable meridians remained sealed: his Belt Vessel and the Conception Vessel. Ironically enough, only a single cracked silver seal still blocked off the Conception Vessel, likely because he'd risked everything to hold back demons from hunting down the outpost's soldiers.

"Stay here and mope if you want," said Sorin, retracting his poison and releasing Haster just as guild support staff came pouring into the room.

"We're going to have to ask you to leave, Hero Kepler," said a stern administrator flanked by two wary adventurers wielding swords.

"I was just on my way out," said Sorin, shooting her a smile. "Think about it, Haster. How many lives are you willing to sacrifice for the privilege of inaction?" He knew these words were a bit hypocritical coming from him, but *someone* had to try jolting him out of his stupor.

Sorin rejoined his companions at their table. When they inquired as to Haster's health, he simply shook his head. "I did what I could for him. Unlocked his latent potential and fixed some of his issues. Physically, he's perfectly fine. But mentally... he has a block he needs to overcome."

"People who've experienced traumatic situations need space, Sorin," said Gareth. "You can't force them out of their little world. When my mother passed, it took my father years to pull himself back together. Until then, it was me taking care of him instead of the other way around."

Sorin nodded. It was the first time Gareth had ever volunteered information about his family. "All I did was give him a nudge. As for what he does with it? That's up to him. But I do hope to see him once again on the battlefield. He seemed so alive down in the ruins."

Haster's situation also reminded Sorin of his own state three years ago. It had taken him half a year to gain any semblance of motivation after his cultivation was crippled. He moved to the Bloodwood Outpost to run a clinic at the Grand Elder's suggestion. It was only thanks to the flood of patients that he was able to force himself out of his state.

In the end, it was Gabriella who really woke Sorin up. Her eyes were much brighter than everyone else's, and she was passionate about becoming a physician despite coming from a poor family and having received very little education.

Without her, he would never have found the courage to face the fox and change his destiny.

BREACH

Sorin and his team soon discovered that it wasn't just two but *four* Bone-Forging cultivators who died in battle that day. The heavy casualties provoked a shuffling in the assigned adventurers, as well as the conscription of Bone-Forging cultivators who normally avoided battle.

Team 'We Don't Need a Life Mage' was one of many teams sent to the southern wall. They were joined by Mr. Primrose, who was arguably one of the more deadly cultivators in battle thanks to his powerful poison mana, and Haley, as a representative of the Adventurers Guild. Barbara and Nale also came with them, along with three other Heroes who had broken through mid-battle.

An endless tide of demons could be seen from their vantage point atop the bloodwood walls. A small portion fell to arrows and spell bombardments, and the rest fell to devastating spell waves powered by their freshly topped-up supply of demon cores.

Poison had also been brought to the forefront. Wind mages used gentle drafts to drizzle lung rot powder and scorching bramble ash on the demonic invaders. Packs of hundreds of wolves erupted in flames before they could even reach the wall, and demonic herds numbering in the thousands simply collapsed as lung rot powder corroded their internal organs, leaving them to suffocate out on the open plain as the endless tide of demons trampled them into mush.

It wasn't just poisons that were deployed. Barrels of alchemical reagents were launched into the enemy horde, detonating on impact. An alchemist's fire filled large swaths of land, scorching everything in its wake. The copious amounts of blood did nothing to put out the fires but instead served as fuel for the alchemical concoctions, spreading them farther and wider than their initial payload warranted.

Like the other adventurers, Sorin and his team were on standby, ready to respond to any eventualities. Many of these eventualities took the form of two-star demons that lumbered toward the wall with no regard for their safety. They fell under arrow and spell, including a few poisonous spears, courtesy of Sorin. But for the most part, Sorin conserved his mana, as it would be needed when the fighting reached its climax.

Mana potions were consumed by the thousands. Demon cores and mana crystals saved up over the course of an entire year were burned up at an alarming rate. Before long, demon corpses were piled up high enough even for one-star demons to launch themselves onto the parapets, where cultivators of the Governor's Manor and the Adventurers Guild cut them down before they could cause too much damage.

"I see termites up ahead," said Gareth, his gaze penetrating deep into the wilderness. "Tens of thousands of them." The swarm skittered over to the wall as soon as it emerged, unleashing acid upon the battlements that ate away at the enchanted wood, destabilizing its enchantments.

"Unleash the insecticide!" called out Commander Zenol's replacement, Command Ven. A hundred mortal soldiers each hauled up a 25-kilogram bag of powder onto the wall and fed them into a wind funnel powered by dozens of mages. The potent poison had little to no effect on the mammalian one-star demons but struck the swarm of demonic termites with such a blow that only a few two-star guardians and the two-star queen lurking just behind the tree line remained.

"It's going back for reinforcements," said Commander Ven. "Commander Resh?"

"On it," said the Bone-Forging archer supporting the southern wall. He pulled a black arrow out of his quiver and shot it at the retreating queen in one fluid motion. Its guardians, sensing the threat to their hive, attempted to block the shot with their bodies—only to discover that the shot was not something an ordinary two-star demon could block. The two guardian termites collapsed and were quickly followed by their queen.

"Is there no end to them?" muttered Sorin. He didn't remember the demon tides being so bad. That said, he'd always experienced them from the safety of the medic tent.

"This is as bad as it gets," said Stephan. "A push like this only comes once every century."

Sorin nodded and continued observing the battle that took place. The demons employed swarm tactics that differed depending on the species, and the defending humans countered with what appeared to be well-practiced responses. Poison for termites. Fire for wolves. Normal arrows in most cases, but enchanted arrows against trickier targets.

Two-star demons were difficult for Blood-Thickening cultivators to take down, but that didn't mean it was impossible. Through sheer numbers, the defenders of the outpost took down monstrous creatures well before they could reach the bloodwood walls.

It's a good thing the outpost didn't skimp on wall enchantments, thought Sorin, his eyes wandering to the palisade holding back a moat of contaminated blood. The moat had been accumulating all battle, and if not for the wood's blood-absorbing and recycling properties, the level of liquid would have been much higher.

Wait a minute. Sorin's eyes narrowed when he saw that the wall was glowing a blood red color. That in itself wasn't worrying—what *was* worrying was that the single stretch of wall they were on was glowing a different color than the rest. *It's filled with green sparks. They're spreading out throughout the wood.* What was worse, they contained something Sorin would recognize anywhere he found it—life energy.

"I'm not feeling so well," mumbled Lawrence as he clutched his chest. "I feel sick. How about we get off this wall?"

"Something's happening," said Stephan, sniffing. "Something strange."

"We need to get off the wall. Now!" shouted Sorin. He quickly used Python Coil to grab Daphne and any surrounding soldiers, interrupting them mid-fire in some cases. His companions did the same, as did Commander Ven.

Haley also appeared on the wall with a blink and threw off mortal soldiers before launching herself off the wall with a kick. Moments later, the wall *exploded* in a mess of wooden stakes that impaled the remaining defenders and ripped into the city.

Seconds later, a dozen spires of wood shot out from the ground via well-hidden roots, destroying fortifications and piercing into bunkers filled with civilians. The attack slew hundreds of non-combatants before the defenders could react.

Further complicating matters, the corrupted soil near the aqueduct suddenly sprouted a small forest of vines that immediately gobbled up all available water and used the incoming water flow to fuel its expansion.

Sorin mourned the loss of so many and cursed the enemy for its trickery. The poisoning of the water supply hadn't been done with the intention to kill them, but to plant the seeds for an attack within.

Even so, his eyes were glued to a small figure that walked through the breach, birthing flowers with every step she took. She looked mostly human, but the natural energies that she gave off and the corruption infesting every fiber of her being marked her as being something more.

She was a demon, and a powerful one at that. A three-star demon that inspired fear and reverence in even Bone-Forging cultivators.

The demon looked around at the surrounding adventurers with disdain and only stopped when another powerful entity interposed himself between her and the rest of the outpost.

"I expected a powerful opponent," said the new arrival. "But never in my wildest dreams did I think a corrupted dryad would be behind this attack. Has your kind not seen enough bloodshed? Has it not learned its lesson over the centuries?"

The man had short black hair with graying sides and wore silver armor inlaid with powerful black runes. Every inch of his body pulsed with power far stronger than that of Bone-Forging cultivators, confirming that he was indeed Governor Marsh, father of Vice Governor Marsh, the strongest cultivator in the outpost.

"My kind will never forget the injustice done to us, Governor Marsh," said the demon in a soul-soothing voice. "Not in a hundred years, and not in a thousand years either."

"You know me?" asked the governor in an even tone. "It seems we underestimated your patron's intelligence network. And his intelligence, for that matter."

"It was only a matter of time before we made our appearance," said the dryad. "Your kind shamelessly stole this land that rightfully belongs to us. The Herald of Violence has returned and has instructed us to reclaim it."

At the mention of this so-called Herald of Violence, the governor's expression turned grave. "So, the herald has awakened at last. But judging by your weak energies, he is still recuperating from his injuries."

"Injured or not, his very presence has revitalized our kind," said the dryad. "Even if you survive this demon tide, will you survive a second? Or a third? Things will only get worse from here on out."

Governor Marsh snorted at these words. "So what if your kind has recovered slightly? We humans pushed you back after the Twilight of the Gods, and we will do so again. The Seven Evils might back your resurgence, but we have the Almighty Hope as our ally. With Hope on our side, we will never falter."

Upon hearing his words, the dryad chuckled. "Hope is the patron of the desperate, Governor Marsh. He would never support humanity unless it were facing an uphill battle. The era of humanity is over. It is us, the rightful inheritors of Pandora, the children of the now-dead gods, who will reign supreme."

"You are but a pale imitation of what you once were," said Governor

Marsh, drawing his sword. "And you might be powerful, but my cultivation counters yours. Do your worst, spirit of the forest."

Parley finished, Governor Marsh and the dryad shot into the air, where they engaged in a battle far beyond what mere mortals could comprehend. Out of consideration for the demons and humans below, the shockwaves were contained.

"Soldiers, assemble!" yelled Commander Ven as demons began pouring forth through the gap. "Adventurers, support!"

Gareth ushered them toward the formation of soldiers, but they were stopped by Stephan's sister, Haley. "A team of five Heroes has no business in an army formation," said Haley. "Each of you is theoretically capable of taking down a two-star demon, so we'll have you focus on those instead."

"Do you mean to have us go outside the walls like the other Bone-Forging experts?" asked Gareth. Over a dozen powerful auras had already hopped off the walls to engage in battle with the enemy's elites. The Vice Guild Master and the Librarian of the Mages Guild also stood atop the breached wall, unleashing deadly magics upon the enemy horde.

Haley snorted. "You are Heroes, not Bone-Forging cultivators. You wouldn't last two minutes out there. No, I have a much more important job for you all. It'll become apparent soon enough."

A dreadful silence spread out across the southern outpost. Powerful mana signatures erupted where stakes had shot out of the ground, destroying fortifications. The masses of broken wood twisted as life energy animated them to create lumbering tree constructs that began attacking their surroundings indiscriminately.

Five more Heroes ran up to where Sorin's team was gathered and joined them. Among them were Barbara and Nale, as well as three other Heroes Sorin had yet to meet. But they glowed with silver light and an energy signature that exceeded their realms, making it clear that none of them were to be underestimated.

"Stephan, your team will head east," said Haley. "Barbara, you'll lead these other four west. Your mission is to take out as many treants as pop up."

Commands issued, she disappeared into the shadows.

DEFORESTATION

Sorin and his companions raced across what used to be the well-maintained cobblestone roads of the Bloodwood Outpost. Vines and tangled roots were spreading rampantly across entire city blocks, barring roads and tearing down buildings.

What's worse, an entire square mile of civilization had been transformed by the dryad near the aqueduct, with more land falling under her control with each passing moment. It sent a statement to the defenders: time was not on their side, and soon, not even ruins would remain where the outpost once stood.

The governor was doing his best to tie up the dryad, but he was unable to completely lock away her influence. Thick vital energy rained down on the outpost, further fueling the rampant growth of the vine forest and the treants as they lumbered about and doled out destruction.

"First contact will be with a single treant," said Gareth, directing them to an isolated treant. "Be aware that we're fighting an elemental; conventional tactics may not prove effective. I have only one request for this round: Daphne, you're sitting this one out."

The fire mage looked downright miffed at being left out but didn't overly complain. After all, there were plenty of trees to burn, and there was only so much mana she could draw on.

Sorin was personally very grateful for Gareth's consideration. Both he and Lawrence had attacks that were highly dependent on his opponent's physiology. Sorin had no idea how a treant would react to his poisons.

The target in question was a 'short' treant, barely twenty feet tall. It towered over the row housing it was halfway through demolishing with exaggerated oaken fists the size of a small horse.

"On my mark," said Gareth, nocking an arrow. "Get set. Go!" He struck the treant with Shackle Shot, tethering it to a half-broken house. Thanks to his Heroic attribute, the stun effect lasted a little longer than it had with prior two-star enemies, exerting its influence for a full second before wearing out.

In that time, Lawrence worked his way to the creature's leg and sliced it up and down, leaving shallow gashes that quickly healed over.

"My attacks aren't doing much," said Lawrence. "I'll try to hit its eyes? Maybe its joints?"

"The key is trying as many things as possible," called out Gareth. "Maybe Sorin can help us out with some poison once he figures out what works and what doesn't."

The treant freed itself from Shackle Shot's influence just before Sorin arrived and greeted him with a large fist to the face. Sorin used Adder Rush to dodge the lumbering attack and struck what appeared to be an ankle with his dagger. He infused it with a combined poison and cast Ophidian Eye to analyze how it traveled.

Paralytic has little to no effect, thought Sorin as he dodged a follow-up attack. Vines shot out from the earth—he barely avoided them but ended up in an awkward position. The treant tried to kick him, but he used Cobra's Glare to lock it down. To his surprise, this was very effective. *Soul resistance is minimal, with all resources spent on physical strengthening, life magic, and recovery. Python Coil will likely have little to no effect.*

Sorin sent out a Python Coil for good measure to confirm his hypothesis. As expected, it barely affected the treant's movements. After avoiding a stray vine sent his way, Sorin stabbed at a tangle of vines that appeared to be the creature's calf. *Manabane Poison is extremely effective and causes disintegration and seeming necrosis of the creature's wooden 'flesh,' which is curious because the invasive blood poison component has little to no effect. Acidic poisons are also minimally effective.*

Having completed his initial analysis, Sorin attuned his blood to deliver an optimized poison consisting of primarily Manabane Poison. He then used Viper's Strike to deliver quick payloads to the creature's legs, disabling movement in its lower limbs.

In tandem, Lorimer shot out of Sorin's chest pocket and adopted his flame form. He scurried up the treant amid Lawrence's probing blows and located what Sorin figured was its 'heart.'

Three seconds later, there was a loud *crunch*. The treant froze mid-motion, then fell to the ground as a pile of sawdust. Lorimer hopped out of the pile holding a half-eaten demon core, which he gobbled up greedily.

"Looks like their cores are their critical weakness," said Sorin, retrieving his poisons from the pile of sawdust. "By the way, where's Stephan?"

Stephan, it turns out, had willfully ignored Stephan's orders and had decided to take on a treant by himself. In terms of offense, he was the most frightening on their team but was, unfortunately, a bit slow. The lumbering treant proved an excellent matchup.

Compared to the treant's powerful body, the vines it summoned were weak and couldn't hold back the Arctic Rune Bear. The aura of frost Stephan gave off further embrittled the wooden enemy and hampered its strange bodily functions.

What followed next was a brutal and one-sided mangling, with the nimble armored bear slashing at openings like a boxer, breaking away pieces of frozen wood until the treant could no longer keep up. He finished it off by biting into its chest and retrieving its core, which he directly tossed into the small storage space attached to his Hero Medal.

"Can I start burning things now?" Daphne asked Gareth once Stephan returned.

"Sure," said Gareth. "Knock yourself out." Daphne sent three Fireballs she'd pre-cast streaking towards a treant, setting it on fire. This didn't seem to be enough, so she sent a fourth Fireball, finishing it off. "Feeling better now?"

"Much better," replied Daphne. "What are we waiting for guys? Let's go burn ourselves some trees."

Seeing that five-on-one tactics weren't efficient, Gareth split them up into three groups. Sorin and Lorimer consisted of one group, and Lawrence and Daphne a second. Stephan was a one-man team, but in all fairness, Lawrence mostly served to distract Daphne's targets as she torched them to oblivion.

Gareth was a floater, as his normal arrows had little to no effect. He mostly used Shackle Shot to support their team and used his commanding presence to optimize their movements as they worked further into the city.

It wasn't long before they finished off ten treants—a full third of the number spawned in their area. "How's everyone holding up?" asked Gareth. "Mana-wise, I mean." No one had suffered any serious injuries thus far.

Sorin had Toxic Metabolism to rely on to reabsorb his poisons and was, therefore, good to go after consuming half a mana potion. Daphne, on the other hand, was greatly fatigued. After unleashing hell on a few elementals, she discovered that *maybe* spamming Fireballs was not the answer to everything. She, therefore, shifted her strategy and focused on providing pointed assistance to Sorin and Stephan in the form of Fireballs cast directly into their blind spots.

They continued killing treants as before, but it soon became clear that they could not continue in this fashion. "I don't like where those treants are heading," said Gareth. "We need to increase our pace and ignore some of the nearer treants."

"What's got you worried?" asked Stephan.

"They're just getting awfully close to a cluster of shelters," said Gareth. "A good half of the remaining ones are at least. Is everyone ready to move fast?"

Gareth once again sent a map to everyone and used his command ability to guide them down the least cluttered pathway. The dryad's ability to provoke growth was difficult to deal with, and many of the streets were blocked off by tangled vines.

They avoided one such blockade and were about to enter what used to be a small business hub when Lawrence suddenly bolted to the side. An image flashed in Sorin's mind, alerting him to a pit trap full of wooden stakes, which he managed to jump away from before the 'ground' beneath them collapsed.

"Why didn't you see that coming?" asked Gareth. "As far as I know, your vision at close range is near perfect. Daphne, would you mind?"

"Sure thing, boss," said Daphne, torching the pit trap and killing the elemental creature governing it.

"My ability works fine," said Lawrence. "It just gets a little blurry when dealing with entities summoned by three-star demons."

"Fair point," said Gareth. "There's a shelter with three treants getting a little too close just up ahead." He nocked an arrow and fired a Power Shot at an elemental's head but failed to provoke a response. "Shackle shot it is, then," he muttered, rushing up ahead and firing a shot that tangled two treants together. "Watch your fire, Daphne. Make sure it doesn't spread."

"No problem," said Daphne, summoning a Fireball opposite the bunker and detonating it straight into the elementals' unprotected backs.

Meanwhile, Lawrence and Sorin closed the gap. As the creatures broke free from the Shackle Shot, Sorin ran onto a vined leg, executed Cobra's Glare, and stabbed a dagger filled with Manabane Poison where Ophidian Eye detected the creature's core.

As for Lawrence, he was carrying their most potent weapon of all—Lorimer. Lawrence carried the rat up to the scorched treant's back and tossed the rat onto the core's approximate location. The rat proceeded to burrow into the creature's wooden flesh to seek out the delicious treasure within.

Stephan arrived shortly after and began mauling the treant Sorin had disrupted with his Manabane Poison. Having taken Manabane Poison to the core, the creature was easy prey for the Arctic Rune Bear. This freed Sorin to launch an attack on the third two-star treant attacking the shelter. This one was a willow and proved to be nimbler than its companions. It evaded his initial attack with a poison spear and whipped its willowy branches at him, slapping him down onto the broken stone streets.

Three fractures, thought Sorin, picking himself up. *Minor muscle trauma. Two partially torn ligaments.* He shot back a cocktail of stimulant poison and rolled his shoulder as his regenerative powers kicked in. He then shot out towards the willow, ducking beneath its branches to reach its main body, only to find himself facing another row of thin branches arranged as a prison. Yet Sorin wasn't troubled by this development because his contract with Lorimer made him fully aware of the small creature flying the willow's way on a collision course for its thin, willowy arm.

The treant shrieked in what seemed to be rage or annoyance as the rat gnawed off the arm. It brought up its branches to sweep away the rat, but in doing so, it freed Sorin. He stabbed its thin legs with Viper Strike, filling them with Manabane Poison until their wood failed. It wasn't long before it fell to the ground in a pile of wood chips, revealing a grinning rat with a large demon core tucked in its cheek.

"It looks like the second team has everything under control," said Gareth, peering off in the distance. Barbara and her group of five were tackling a second group of three treants.

It was Sorin's first time seeing Barbara fight since her awakening as a Hero; what he saw left a great impression on him. The armored fighter started off with a fiery spear to initiate, only to rapidly switch to a sword mid-combat. A shield appeared as the treant she was engaged with slapped at her with a vine-covered arm, only to disappear as she summoned the spear once again and pierced it straight into the creature's heart.

"Speed enhancement, I think?" commented Sorin.

"And a weapon ability," said Stephan. "By the looks of it, she can switch between different weapons at will. It's a happy coincidence that they all have fire-related enchantments."

"Not to spoil the mood, but I think we have more important things than watching an Amazon goddess kill treants," said Lawrence.

"What's the problem?" asked Stephan but cut off when Gareth launched himself into the air to get a better look at his surroundings.

"He's right," said Gareth upon returning. He sent a quick image to the group to apprise them of the situation. "Those treants tricked us. While we were fighting this group, another small group made a quick break toward the next shelter."

HIDDEN CARDS

By the time Gareth noticed the elementals, it was too late. Their team could only try to make ground as the shelter collapsed under the weight of the many fists smashing down on it.

The intentions of the elementals were clear: by threatening a large enough population, they would force the governor to divert his attention away from fighting the creator of the treants, the dryad.

This tactic proved effective; seeing that Sorin's group wouldn't make it on time, the governor struck out with mana blades to try taking out the treants from a distance. The dryad would have none of this, however. She intercepted the governor's attacks, cutting off any hope left for the humans in the shelter.

Sorin cringed as he watched the treants wind back for one final attack. Yet before they could unleash it, a brilliant silver flash streaked past several city blocks. A sword left its sheath and released a blade of silver mana, slicing off a treant's arm before it could land the finishing blow.

"Who in Hope's name is *that*?" asked Stephan.

"I think it's—" said Gareth.

"Haster," said Sorin with a grin.

The silver flash slowed down to reveal a drunken man in green robes who appeared beside the treant and cut through its chest, where its core typically lay. The creature was instantly reduced to a pile of wood chips. Before it hit the ground, the Haster staggered like a drunk and seemingly tripped—just in time to avoid a carriage-sized fist as it came crashing down on his initial position.

The fist kicked up large amounts of dust that obscured the shelter's surroundings. Just as the dust started clearing, a silver flash cut down a second elemental, and it was followed by a third and a fourth. A single step and a single slash were all it took for Haster to cut down a two-star demon.

And he didn't stop. He couldn't stop. Momentum carried Haster into a drunken spin, throwing him towards the fifth treant. It tried to kick him, only to miss as he once again staggered in an unpredictable manner, sweeping his sword in a wide arc that cut through its core and lopped off another treant's arm.

The deadly drunken swordsman's assault forced the remaining three treants to reconsider their assault and focus on the lone cultivator. Willowy branches whipped down with rapid frequency, barely missing the staggering swordsman every time, until finally, he rolled beneath the creature's feet and once again sliced it in two.

Only two treants remained. They tried to flee, but their large sizes worked against them. Haster poured his remaining energy into a final attack that cut through the two demons in quick succession, averting the crisis. One Blood-Thickening cultivator had single-handedly slain eight treants, saving 300 civilians from an untimely death.

"I think he got a speed enhancement," said Stephan.

"Definitely," agreed Gareth. "And I think his ability is speed-related as well."

"It's not an offensive upgrade?" asked Daphne, confused.

"Speed equals power for some cultivators," answered Stephan. "And look—using that ability wasn't easy on him. It looks like he just collapsed."

"Should I go help him?" asked Sorin.

"No can do," said Gareth. "Since that shelter's taken care of, let's clean these few treants out. The sooner we take care of them, the sooner we can help out the soldiers on the wall."

They set off once again and systematically cleaned up the remaining treants. Daphne was already exhausted and focused on recovering her energy, so it took them twice as long for each kill. Even so, her kill count was the highest in the entire group, with Lorimer coming in close second.

"Will the governor be all right?" Sorin wondered aloud as he looked up above the city. The dryad and the governor were still fighting, though the governor seemed to be exhausted, while the dryad was still brimming with energy.

"It's hard to tell with fighters at their level," answered Stephan. "Besides, it's not just the governor that the dryad needs to worry about."

"You mean…" Sorin had barely finished speaking when a spell circle lit up above the Mages Guild. It was an elaborate circle and so complex that looking at it gave Sorin a headache. It also happened to be located just beneath the dryad.

The dryad attempted to retreat but was cut off by the cunning governor. Multiple streaks of lightning shot up from the Mages Guild and blasted the dryad from below.

"You think pitiful tricks from a Bone-Forging mage can wound me?" said the dryad as the spell circle finally let out. Her bark-like skin was charred, and her hair had burned away. Only a stump remained of one of her legs, but it was quickly regenerating.

"You think I'll let you stall?" said Governor Marsh. He struck out with his silver sword, summoning forth a storm of blades that attacked her from eight directions at once. Her charred flesh began whittling away faster than it could regenerate. "Not going to defend? Then die!"

One of the eight blades solidified as Governor Marsh appeared behind it and stabbed forth with all his strength. Yet just as his blade pierced her wooden flesh, she exploded into a cloud of sawdust that reformed behind the governor and stabbed toward his back with an oakwood spear.

Despite his awkward position, Governor Marsh managed to pivot midair and parry with his silver sword. Yet the spear was unusually flexible and managed to sneak past his guard. It struck him in the breastplate and flung him toward the ground.

The dryad flew downward to finish the governor off but was forced to retreat as an assassin appeared beside her and struck out with a poisoned blade. The assassin was none other than Haley, who'd been hiding for the entire battle.

"So you finally reveal yourself," said the dryad, abandoning her pursuit of the governor. Another oakwood spear shot out of her outstretched arm and stabbed towards the assassin. By now, Haley was fully committed to her strike and could only redirect the fatal blow to a less critical location, her shoulder.

The force of the blow sent her flying—fortunately, towards Sorin and his team. Stephan shifted out of bear form, caught her as she fell, and immediately brought her to Sorin, who used Flesh-Melt Poison to seal off her arteries and then splashed a healing potion on the wounds as a stopgap.

Yet before Sorin could do any more than that, his body broke into a cold sweat. The three-star dryad suddenly appeared in the airspace above their small group, oakwood spear at the ready and grinning from ear to ear.

"What have we here?" said the dryad. "No less than five Blood-Thickening Heroes and a Bone-Forging Hero as well? What a joyous occasion it is to find such promising human saplings to prune."

The dryad tossed the oakwood spear in their general direction with so much energy that the air rippled. Due to the three-star pressure she exerted, none of them could move, let alone avoid the dangerous and seemingly all-encompassing attack.

The spear was about to hit them when suddenly, a sigh cut through the outpost. A flash of red metal cut through the oakwood spear as a *second* Flesh-Sanctification cultivator appeared. It was none other than Guild Master Roy, the supposed Bone-Forging cultivator overseeing the Adventurers Guild.

"Isn't it below you to attack a group of Blood-Thickening pups?"

said Guild Master Roy, hefting his own spear over his shoulder. "Why don't you pick on someone your own size?"

"It's as we suspected," said the dryad with a smile. "The conflict between the Governor's Manor and the Adventurers Guild—the meaningless spats and the absurd amount of bad blood between the two factions. It was a ploy all along, wasn't it?"

"I was hoping to surprise your helper in a pinch moment, but certain factors forced my hand," said Guild Master Roy. "Well? Are you going to reveal yourself, or will you stand by as we slaughter this corrupted dryad and destroy your pitiful army?"

Clap. Clap. Clap.

A second three-star demon walked out from behind a collapsed building and ascended to the skies. This creature was short compared to the dryad and had the legs and horns of a goat. It bore no weapon but carried instead an instrument: a pan flute, the likes of which one might find in a museum.

"I didn't think anyone here was capable of sensing me," said the creature. "What gave me off?"

"You did," said Guild Master Roy. "Just now. So thank you kindly for saving me the trouble. A corrupted satyr on land is just as hard to find as a dryad in her forest."

"If not harder," agreed the satyr. "Oh well. Since you know what I am, there's no point dragging this out. I just wonder what gives you the confidence to step out and fight me when you know you're so clearly outmatched."

"I do," said a fifth voice. It was a priest—or at least someone Sorin had assumed was a priest. The old preacher, who'd been presiding over offerings since before Sorin's arrival, now surprised everyone with an aura that hovered between that of a Bone-Forging cultivator and a Flesh-Sanctification cultivator.

The satyr's expression fell. "So what if you're halfway into the Flesh-Sanctification realm? Such power is lacking compared to the likes of us."

"But it's more than enough to wield this wish-fire lantern," said the preacher with a smile. He pulled out a pole supporting a glass-covered case. Inside it floated an orb of fire with a presence that didn't lose out to the governor's.

"I'll shoot your words right back at you," said Governor Marsh, who'd splashed a high-quality healing potion over his shattered breast-plate. "What gives you the confidence to fight the three of us at once?"

The satyr's eye twitched. "It's an even battle, at best. If you want to fight, let's fight!"

The satyr put his pan flute to his lips and began playing. A fierce melody ripped through the entire outpost, disrupting mana and invigo-rating those who relied on corruption to cultivate.

The demons at the walls grew violent and began fighting the defenders with no regard for their lives. It took them less than thirty seconds to create several openings on the front lines and force the human soldiers to abandon sections of the wall.

Initially, Sorin thought this was the pan flute's main effect. However, upon seeing the disproportionate reaction from the governor and Guild Master Roy, he realized this was not the case. The flute was a targeted attack intended to weaken Flesh-Sanctification cultivators enough that the dryad was able to split into two identical bodies and still put up a good fight.

Fortunately, the preacher was there to help them and used his wish-fire to counteract the satyr's spell. As a result, the two warriors were able to take the upper hand and slowly force the dryad back.

"Sorin, she's not looking too good," Stephan urged as the Flesh-Sanctification powerhouses rose from the ground. "You can help her, can't you?"

"I'm not sure I can," said Sorin, inspecting her wounds. "She's a Bone-Forging cultivator, and I was only a one-star physician at my best; forget me as I am now. Stephan, can you carry her while I stabilize her? We need to find a place that's relatively safe to perform an emergency surgery."

"No problem," said Stephan. He gently picked his sister up while

Sorin applied pressure to key acupoints to prevent blood from pouring out and mana from dispersing.

"Lawrence, I'll need you to go to the emergency clinic and fetch physician Marcus to perform an emergency corruption extraction, bone repair, and a major flesh restoration," continued Sorin. "We'll need a bone mend tincture, a nerve regeneration tincture, and a two-star healing potion."

"Are you sure you can trust the guy after what you've seen him do?" asked Lawrence.

"We don't exactly have a choice," snapped Sorin. "Go!"

"I scouted out a location not far away," said Gareth, jumping off a piece of rubble. "The building is mostly intact, as are a few of the surrounding buildings."

"Then let's get her to a better place," said Sorin. "Daphne, can you run along with Gareth and set up a bed? Preferably with clean sheets and some hot water?"

"No problem," said Daphne. She ran off after Gareth while Stephan and Sorin slowly transported Haley, taking great care not to disturb her limp body as they travelled.

THE ROLE OF A PHYSICIAN

Sorin had always been a composed person, especially around critical patients, so he found it odd to suddenly reminisce about his childhood as Haley's situation worsened and Stephan grew increasingly frantic.

As his hands pierced needles into her skin to guide the mana in her body around obstructions, he thought of the practical structure of Pandora's educational curriculum.

First came primary education, which lasted six years and covered general topics. Next came secondary education in the form of internships, where children learned their parent's trade or that of a relative.

It wasn't a perfect system. Many people were left behind and trained in dead-end jobs. But it was an *efficient* system, one that allowed humanity to survive as they reclaimed land from the Seven Evils under the banner of their savior, Hope.

Sorin's father was a physician, and his mother was an alchemist. As an only child, he'd been required to study medicine. That included after-school lessons he'd attended concurrently with primary school.

When younger children were out playing in the streets, Sorin had been studying medical theory and practicing with his hands to develop the required dexterity for his profession. Thus, the piano. He performed his first surgical procedure at the ripe old age of twelve years old. It was during this procedure that he'd lost his first patient.

"Physician Gregory and Physician Lim are inbound, along with a small group of soldiers," said Gareth, popping into the broken building they'd repurposed as an operating room.

"How's the hot water coming along?" asked Sorin.

"I just fixed the water runes destroyed by the impact, so I've got as much as you need," said Daphne.

As Daphne heated water and Stephan peeled away clothing and washed Haley's bloodied flesh, Sorin's mind returned to a critical moment in his development.

"What is the role of a physician, in your opinion, Sorin?" his father had asked him.

Sorin had answered that it was saving lives and preserving the vitality in their bodies and their bodily functions.

His father had disagreed. "A physician is primarily a decider and a killer. A decider in that he chooses who lives and chooses what part of the patient to save. He's also a killer. A killer of flesh. A killer of disease. A killer of poison and corruption."

Physician Gregory and Physician Lim cleansed themselves upon arriving and ushered Stephan and Daphne to the outskirts of the room as they sealed the room against corruption and disease. Sorin refused to budge, so they could only hand him a clearmist vial. He used it to clean himself out of habit, then used his own personal poisons to further disinfect his body and key pieces of equipment.

Physician Gregory and Physician Lim then began arguing about how to proceed. Physician Lim wanted to restore blood flow, while Physician Gregory was concerned about Haley's bones. Which begged the question: why were they even having this conversation?

"Where's Physician Marcus?" Sorin asked, finally returning to the present moment.

"We don't know," said Gregory snapped. "And that's not relevant. The patient needs care, and we're all she has."

"How is that not relevant?" Sorin pressed. "She needs a two-star physician, and there's only one two-star physician in the entire outpost. Why didn't anyone go find him?"

"This…" said Gregory.

"None of us can go find him because he told us he had something else to attend to, on order of the governor," said Physician Lim. "Now how would you approach this problem, Sorin? I'm afraid to say that this is beyond either of us."

"What are you asking him for?" asked Gregory. "He's no physician."

His words jabbed painfully at one of Sorin's regrets. *He's right,* thought Sorin. *I abandoned this path. I should just let them go about their work.*

Yet as the two continued to talk, Sorin quickly saw problems with their logic and reasoning. Their approaches would work for a one-star cultivator, but they didn't quite apply to a two-star cultivator. What might kill a one-star cultivator wouldn't necessarily kill a two-star cultivator, and vice versa. What was even worse, these two physicians were being indecisive, a cardinal sin for any doctor to make.

"Haley doesn't have the time for you both to bicker," Sorin reminded them.

"She also doesn't have time for your unqualified input," snapped Gregory.

The words bothered Sorin. "Unqualified?" muttered Sorin. "Is my input really unqualified, Physician Gregory?"

"Naturally, Apothecary Sorin," the man replied. "The Medical Association withdrew its support for your licensure for reasons we are both aware of."

"You mean politics?" said Sorin, his temper flaring. "I was a qualified one-star physician at twelve years of age. I ran my own practice for three years not because the Medical Association pitied my loss of cultivation, but because my performance in their eyes warranted that I continue practicing."

"Now isn't the time for—" started Gregory.

"This is exactly the time for me to clarify this issue," said Sorin. "If I was qualified without a cultivation base, why should I be disqualified now? Physicians use poison all the time, and I would go so far as to say that in this entire outpost, there is no more qualified person to judge my competency in using them and any potential dangers I might pose to my patients."

"Sorin, what Gregory means is that—" said Physician Lim.

"Haley is officially my patient," said Sorin, cutting him off. "And no matter what the Medical Association says, I *am* the most qualified person in this room. I *am* a physician. If Marcus can't deign to come treat Haley, then it is my *duty* as a physician to attend to her."

A physician was a decider, first and foremost. He decided who lived and who died. And most importantly, he decided when and where he practiced and where his skills were most needed.

"You and Physician Lim will assist me," said Sorin. "Physician Lim, please prepare the surgical equipment. Physician Gregory, prepare the two-star bone-mend tincture and the nerve regeneration tincture you brought, as well as the two-star health potion for layered application." He then glared at the two of them, as if daring them to disobey.

Gregory was ultimately the first to cave. "We'll follow your lead, Physician Sorin, for the good of the patient. But you should be aware that we'll need to report everything to the association."

"I care not one whit about getting reported," said Sorin. "What's important now is Haley York's critical condition and my ability to save her.

He then fully embraced his old profession and his father's teachings as he prepared Haley for her operation by using poison mana to purge all influence of Disease and any remnant corruption on her body.

"The patient's shoulder is a terrible mess," said Sorin to the two attending physicians. "Most of her flesh is so mangled that corruption has worked its way into every inch of it. Her arteries are blocked off, and her flesh is necrotizing. What's worse, her mana flow is impeded. Her bones, where the bulk of a Bone-Forging cultivator's energy is stored, have splintered, sending fragments deep into her flesh, further disrupting the flow of blood and mana.

"Our course of action will be as follows: First, retrieve the bone fragments; Second, destroy and purify the contaminated tissue; Third, repair damage to the bone. Fourth, regrow and reconnect tissues as best as possible. Once we're finished, the patient's recovery will depend upon her own capabilities."

"Scalpel," said Sorin, holding out his hand. Physician Lim handed him the sterilized surgical instrument, and Sorin used it to cut open her flesh. Haley had passed out, but this was fortunate because they didn't have any two-star anesthetics on hand. "Physician Gregory, please tie off the main arteries while I retrieve the bone fragments."

Sorin used forceps to pull apart the flesh and cut deeper into the mana-powered tissue in Haley's pectoral. He reached in and pulled out a small shard the size of his pinky nail. It was covered by ruby-red runes that simultaneously sealed the bones and served as a conduit for their power.

There were a total of seventeen such shards in her shoulder. Sorin retrieved them one by one and placed them in a disinfectant solution before turning his attention to the greatest problem: corruption. "I'll be removing the worst of the corrupted flesh before we re-introduce blood flow."

"Wouldn't it be wiser to ensure proper blood flow first?" asked Gregory. "I mean no disrespect, sir. I just have the patient's best interest at hand. Regardless of the decision made, I will follow your lead."

"Negative," said Sorin, shaking his head. "I never properly studied two-star anatomy, but I do know that their flesh is more resilient to loss of blood and associated necrosis. Meanwhile, their tissues are highly infused with mana, making them more susceptible to high-level corruption. We're lucky the spear that stabbed her didn't splinter like her bones. Otherwise, there would be no saving her."

The dryad was a three-star entity, and her summoned weapon, that oakwood spear, was therefore a three-star weapon. The weapon clearly placed an emphasis on stability, which was why the contamination Sorin found was two-star at best.

Yet even two-star corruption was a huge problem for a one-star physician. Sorin's poisons simply couldn't fight it off and could, at best, suppress it. Concocting and activating a decontamination solution was something only a two-star physician or apothecary could do, so Sorin could only do the next best thing: amputation. Amputating her entire shoulder was out of the question, but removing corrupted flesh was not. He cut out large chunks of tissue until barely more than bones remained of her shoulder.

Fortunately, Haley was a two-star cultivator and could handle such trauma. She could even hold out while Sorin mobilized his personal poisons to seek and destroy the remaining one-star corruption and the tiny pockets of two-star corruption infecting her body. It took a half-hour to fully eliminate all the corruption, at which point Sorin was thoroughly exhausted.

"We've eliminated all pathogens and corruption and can now move on to rebuilding her shoulder," said Sorin. "We'll start with the bones. Please stand by to assist with life mana as directed. Bone-mend tincture." Physician Gregory handed him a light blue vial.

The potion in question was a two-star potion that could fill in gaps in a patient's bone structure. The regenerated bone wouldn't be as effective as the original bone, however, so it was best to fuse pieces of the original bone together.

This was where the bone fragments came in. Sorin slowly assembled them like a jigsaw puzzle until only a few missing pieces were left. "The few missing pieces won't overly affect her recovery," said Sorin to the two physicians. "That being said, I doubt a Bone Mend Potion will do her much good. Better to leave the bones incomplete and let them recover on their own."

"Assessor Haley *is* a Hero," said Physician Gregory. "She should have access to advanced bone regeneration potions through the Hero Association."

"That is my hope as well," said Sorin. "From now on, I'll be relying on the two of you. Please make use of the healing potion and nerve regeneration tincture as I direct. You'll find it difficult to mobilize your life mana due to her own two-star mana, but it's essential to use it to catalyze growth. A potion has limitations and must be guided. Otherwise, the patient will suffer serious residual trauma."

Neither physician argued with Sorin, and they even seemed relieved he'd pointed this out. Sorin was a poison user, after all, and his strengths lay in killing. Killing flesh. Killing corruption. Killing disease.

Modern physicians focused on healing, as potions and poisons could be applied to make up for a life cultivator's shortcomings. But according to Sorin's late father, it had once been the opposite. Poison users were the original physicians, and they had made extensive use of healing potions, wands, and other implements to facilitate their practice.

The three built up Haley's flesh in layers, carefully regenerating small pieces of nerves as they worked. Fortunately, Bone-Forging cultivators could recover from most fleshly wounds using their bones as an energy source and template.

The one thing that couldn't be saved were her meridians. These were tricky to heal, and Sorin didn't have the ability to do so. Even Marcus had been helpless in healing Lady Duchene's meridians; Sorin suspected that only three-star physicians could properly mend such injuries.

"She'll have a difficult time using her skills and cultivating going forward," Gregory commented. "Let's hope we made the right decision. Assassins are especially prone to losing their tempers once they gain consciousness."

"Haley would never do such a thing," said Stephan, who'd been watching all this time. "You have my word on it."

"I would never impact a patient's well-being on mere speculation," said Gregory as he poured the last of the healing potion onto her shoulder.

"Two-star corruption is not something any of us could underestimate," said Sorin, shaking his head. "We amputated that tissue because it was the best decision to make with the knowledge we had." A doctor was a decider, but in the end, it was the patient who would need to live with the consequences of their actions. "Will the two of you return to the clinic now?"

"We'll have the soldiers we brought along transport Miss York on a stretcher and rush back to the clinic as soon as possible," said Physician Gregory.

"She's in good hands," said Physician Lim to Stephan. "But you're more than welcome to come along with us if you wish."

"No," said Stephan. "We're still needed on the battlefield. Rest up, Sorin. We'll head out once you're finished recovering."

Sorin took out a mana potion and took a sip. "If you find yourself overworked, push more onto Gabriella," Sorin said to Physician Gregory. "She's a bright girl and can stand the pressure."

"I will if I get a chance," said Physician Greogry. "Unfortunately, she's currently off shift, as she exhausted herself to treat a large influx of patients."

Sorin no longer paid them any mind as they left the broken building. He focused instead on replenishing his mana stores and returning to a battle-ready state. Half an hour later, he rose from his cross-legged posture and sought out his teammates, who'd moved up to the roof of the building to watch the fight as it unfolded.

"Did I miss anything important?" asked Sorin.

"Oh, just a few humble exchanges by cultivators that exceed our imagination," said Gareth. "That satyr pulled out an artifact, forcing the bishop to draw on the temple's wish-fire stores. The temple was then overrun by two-star demons.

"This proved to be a trap, however; the temple had already been evacuated, and the bishop detonated something inside it, filling the battlefield with wish-fire and eliminating over thirty two-star demons in the span of a few seconds."

"That's... intense," said Sorin. "And way above our pay grade."

"Definitely," agreed Gareth. "But as a result of all these things, the battlefield has stabilized. Things aren't looking good for the demons. It's going to be a bloody battle, though. I'm not sure where we can best contribute."

"We should go to the most violent battlefield, obviously," said Stephan.

"You know, I was thinking the exact opposite," said Lawrence. "You know—pick the low-hanging fruit? Support me on this one, Daphne."

The mage snorted. "Coward."

"I prefer the non-discriminatory term—cautious Hero," said Lawrence. "It rolls off the tongue, don't you think?"

"How about you, Sorin?" asked Stephan. "You've been oddly quiet."

"I was thinking that before hopping onto a battlefield, we could make a quick stop by the Governor's Manor," said Sorin. "I can't shake the feeling that something is going on in there."

"Whatever Marcus is doing is hardly more important than repelling the demons," countered Stephan. "Besides, what will you do once you catch him in the act? Kill him in the name of justice? Kill the only two-star physician in the outpost?"

Sorin shook his head. "No. Too many lives are at stake. It makes more sense to pressure him into returning to the battlefield earlier and stop whatever he's doing. There's no way he can kill and silence five Heroes, right? This way, we'll have our physician back earlier *and* join the battle. Win-win."

"Honestly, it's not a bad idea," said Gareth. "Besides, he's a physician. A Bone-Forging physician, but still a physician. Our chances of intimidating him are rather high."

"Maybe," said Stephan, unconvinced. "Daphne? Lawrence?"

"Why am I last?" asked Lawrence.

"Because your opinion counts the least, obviously," said Daphne. "I also support this plan. As a bonus, we'll get to figure out exactly what Marcus is doing. Whatever it is, it seems to require a pitched battle taking place to cover up its existence."

It was now four in favor, meaning that Stephan was outnumbered either way. "Fine," said Stephan. "Let's make a quick stop at the Governor's Manor. We'll *peacefully* make our demands to Marcus and escort him onto the battlefield. But mark my words—physicians aren't to be underestimated. Moreover, there's a big difference between each stage of the Bone-Forging Realm."

FURY

The Governor's Manor was not too far from the building they'd been hiding in. The only signs of life they saw was the occasional soldier on patrol, who scanned them with a demonic detection device before continuing with their missions.

Likewise, the Governor's Manor was completely empty. Sturdy as it was, it wasn't a bunker; all its inhabitants had been evacuated to the nearest shelter prior to the final wave of the demon tide. Its unattended garden was overrun under the influence of the dryad, substantially slowing their entry into the premises.

"You'd think they'd leave a skeleton crew or something," said Stephan, kicking down the front door. "If just to guard the governor's valuables."

"Honestly, I didn't see that many valuables kicking around last time we were here," said Lawrence. "That must be why. No need to keep pretty things lying around when your house could suddenly become overrun by demonic rats." Lorimer squeaked indignantly when he heard this. "No, I'm not discriminating against rats," said Lawrence. Lorimer squeaked again. "Sorin, I can't understand what he's saying."

"He's asking if you like rats," said Sorin, petting Lorimer's little head. "Because there's about a thousand of them lurking around the manor. He could arrange for an extended petting session."

As if to accentuate Sorin's words, rats scurried out of their hiding places as they walked past them. Some were hiding in cracks between stones, while others had tunneled into the manor's stone walls to create an impressive network. The rats came in various sizes, but without exception, they came out to pay homage to their king, who seemed content with telling them to keep up the good work and return to their stations.

The first basement was as empty as the main floor. All armor and weaponry had been taken by the guards, both on and off shift. All the troops had been mobilized to cope with the last wave of the demon tide.

The second basement was just as they'd found it the last time they visited. The same alarm trap had been set up and was easily dismantled by Lawrence. After much ducking and weaving, he made his way to a device on the wall that deactivated the alarm and allowed their group to proceed without alerting Marcus.

Sorin pushed open the door to the laboratory. There were two individuals present: Marcus Kepler and his patient, a naked woman with needles inserted all over her body. At first, Sorin didn't recognize her. But realization struck him like a bolt of lightning, and rage bubbled up from the pit of his stomach.

"Marcus! Sovinger! Kepler! What the hell is going on?!" Sorin could barely contain himself, for in front of Marcus lay Gabriella Michka, Sorin's former student.

Sorin's first instinct was to rush forward as Gabriella's body twitched from the insertion of another poisoned needle. But then he stopped himself as the rational part of his brain kicked in.

"So what was the experiment this time?" asked Lawrence as they walked in. "Because you look mad as hell, Sorin. You—*oh*."

Stephan, Gareth, and Daphne stepped into the room after Lawrence, but sensing the mood in the room, they remained silent. As for Sorin, he did his best to control his temper as needle after needle was inserted into Gabriella's naked body.

"I predicted people might come forcibly fetch me, but I'm glad it's a more reasonable group that came," said Marcus, looking up from his 'project.' "The slightest mistake could break the tenuous balance in Miss Michka's body, after all. Not even *I*, the creator of this tincture, can predict what would happen if the process were to be interrupted midway."

Sorin had many things to say, many emotions he wanted to let out, but everything boiled down to a single word. "Why?" Sorin asked. "Why go to such lengths? Why take all these risks? And why her, of all people?"

"Why her?" asked Marcus as though it were the most nonsensical question out of the three. "Because she happened to be a prime specimen for experimentation, of course. One with an amazing life-oriented constitution. And one all too willing to undergo the experimental procedure, dangerous as it is."

"You're trying to tell me she knew what she was getting into and risked her life regardless?" asked Sorin, a hint of scorn in his voice.

"I don't expect you to believe me, but... *yes*," said Marcus, inserting another needle. "Sorin, you can't even begin to imagine the sort of red tape one must go through for these sorts of experiments. It's not even about people dying so much as how much suspicion it would arouse and how badly it would damage the reputation of all physicians. I'm sure you can see why I would choose an outpost during the demon tide, of all locations, to conduct my experiments in secret.

"And don't think I'm the only one who does it, Sorin. The Governor's Manor and the Adventurers Guild use the demon tides to uncover potential heroes and prodigies. The Alchemists Guild and the Mages Guild use the demon tides to try out new spells and weapons.

"All these things have a single goal in mind: to increase the power of humanity. And I am no exception. In fact, I aim to do mankind a great service."

"Your logic is twisted and ignores the most basic pillars of justice," Stephan cut in. "Perhaps many dark deeds are done behind the scenes, but at least on the surface, what you do is condemned by every institution on Pandora."

Meanwhile, Sorin was doing his best to identify both the components of the tincture being used and the pattern it was applied in. There were a total of forty needles currently inserted into Gabriella's body, and quite a few of them were inserted in the Conception Vessel's meridians.

"You're trying to unlock a life mana cultivator's Hero Meridian with a tincture, aren't you? said Sorin. "That's insane, Marcus, and you know it."

"It has been quite the conundrum, yes," said Marcus, not slowing his placement of the needles. Like Sorin, he too wished to see Gabriella pull through this alive and leave nothing to chance. "The Kepler Clan is known for its meridian-opening tinctures and application techniques. It's the only clan that can open high-level extraordinary meridians, and it's not unheard of for the clan head to directly unlock a cultivator's Conception Vessel.

"Yet despite possessing such means, our clan suffers from a major weakness: the difficulty in opening a life cultivator's meridians. The methods developed by other great families are not transferable to our clan. Opening the Conception Vessel is monstrously difficult for life mana cultivators; forget physicians who never see the front lines."

"That's because poison and life mana conflict," said Sorin. "Life mana supports existing bodily functions, while poisons forcefully manipulate the human body, often to damage it and disable its key functions. As a result, the two types of mana react violently when brought into contact. The backlash can easily kill a life mana cultivator." It was also the reason why life mana cultivators had difficulties treating poison mana cultivators and why these cultivators had trouble using wands and rings of the opposite element.

"That is the common thought process, yes," said Marcus. "I thought so as well, until I realized that one poison in particular does *not* react violently. It directly snuffs out life mana before it can react."

"Necrotic poisons," muttered Sorin. "You're madder than I thought, Marcus. You're not just trying to reclaim the family's lost tinctures;

you're trying to improve upon them to create a tincture for life mages. Does the family even know what you're doing?"

"So you know about the incident with the meridian-opening tinctures," said Marcus with a smile that was not a smile. "Unsurprising, given your companions. Unsurprising, given that you've fully opened your own meridians. This lends credence to the theory that your parents not only passed on the tincture formulas to you but also the family's lost poison cultivation technique. As for the treasure they lost, it's unlikely that you obtained it. A pity, because the reward for retrieving it is astronomical."

This was a lot of information to process, but Sorin didn't allow himself to be distracted. The needle placement was almost complete. Thanks to the poisons on the counter, Sorin had a good idea of what sort of tincture Marcus was using. The poisons were reminiscent of those used in Trials 307-332, Potential Unlocking of the Conception Vessel Using a Mixture of Manabane Poison and Necrotic Erosion Toxins. It was the experiment with the lowest fatality rate amongst those attempted, but the odds of death were still upward of 30 percent.

"There," said Marcus, placing the last needle and completing the network. "The necrotic poison is slow acting to avoid tissue death. It does, however, lack a certain amount of... force. Which is why there's one last step to this experiment."

He raised his hand, summoning a life shield that suddenly forced their entire group backwards and out of the door, slamming them into the wall. Marcus Kepler walked out after them, and moments later, a spell circle lit up inside the room, provoking ghostly howls as death mana was rapidly drawn into the circle and into Gabriella's body.

"It's a forbidden ritual!" said Daphne, picking herself up off the ground. "A two-star version of the death convergence ritual. This kind of ritual uses sites of mass death to gather the death mana that accumulates. It was outlawed because of the intentional disasters caused by those who used it."

"You don't really believe that we'll just watch and wait while you use a forbidden ritual to perform an experiment on an innocent lady, do you, Marcus?" asked Stephan, shifting into his bear form. "You've crossed a line, and we can only consider you a demonic infiltrator in human skin."

"Then I'm looking forward to seeing what a group of five Heroes plans on doing against a physician who's experienced his third forging," said Marcus. "Because the only way to deactivate the life shield blocking off the laboratory is to kill me."

SECRETS OF LIFE MANA

"Are you sure you want to do this?" Stephan asked Sorin as Marcus's body lit up with light green runes. The runes were complex and originated from his bones—a trait shared by all Bone-Forging cultivators. It was from these empowered bones that mana shields were generated, and mana circulation outside the body was facilitated. "I'm not going to lie, Sorin. The odds of us being able to beat him aren't great."

"Still better than Gabriella's," said Sorin. "If it were just the meridian-opening tinctures, I'd put her odds of survival at 30 percent. The influx of death mana will greatly increase the potency of those poisons and weaken her life mana affinity. I can't be sure how everything will interact, but I'd bet my life on her odds of survival being less than 50 percent. Conversely, I'm 90 percent confident in being able to save her if I can get in that room and draw the poison out of her."

"Then let's hope he's just book smart," said Stephan. "Cover me." He launched himself at Marcus, who'd pulled back into the long and wide corridor, seemingly uncaring about the life mana shield blocking the operating room. Metal-coated claws smashed through a hastily assembled life shield, but not quick enough to catch Marcus as he expertly dodged and kicked away the armored bear.

Stephan smashed into the wall. Hard. Marcus was about to take advantage of his dazed state to stab him with a knife when he suddenly stopped; Lawrence's short sword pierced through where Marcus would have been, forcing the rogue to pull back before the physician could counter-attack.

Marcus turned his attention back to Stephan, but three arrows shot down the hallway, distracting him. He responded to Gareth's barrage by summoning a tall wooden staff and spinning it, deflecting two arrows and taking a third to the chest. He then rushed forward, barely avoiding a Fireball as it detonated near his prior position and colliding into Sorin.

Sorin's bones cracked from the impact, though he managed to twist his arm to strike Marcus in the side using Viper Strike, injecting a large dose of acidic poison and melting away a mass of flesh.

Stephan had now fully recovered from his dazed state; he jumped in to engage Marcus, but the physician, having had enough of the bear, slammed his staff into the ground. "Serpentine Guardian!" he shouted, injecting a large dose of life mana into the staff. "Tie that bear down!" The staff knocked down Stephan and wrestled him to the floor before he could so much as touch Marcus's robes.

Dealing with Stephan took a lot of time and energy. In exchange for tying down Stephan, he took three Fire Bolts and two arrows to chest. The Fire Bolts were deflected by his robes, as was one of the arrows, but the second arrow drew blood.

Encouraged by the wounds they managed to inflict, Sorin tossed a poison spear at Marcus and attacked him along a curved path according to Gareth's instructions. This allowed Gareth to fire off a Power Shot and for Daphne to launch a powered Fire Bolt while Marcus received Sorin's charge.

Yet before their attacks could land, Marcus's body suddenly sped up and dodged. His dagger pierced into Sorin's shoulder, cutting through bone and ligaments but missing his organs. "I would have thought that you of all people would know that physicians should never be underestimated."

He then pulled back just as Lawrence appeared and parried his short sword using his dagger. *He's using his superior spiritual senses to predict our attack patterns,* thought Sorin. *His speed and strength are also very exaggerated. Is he surpassing his limitations by manipulating his body using life mana?* Such a thing was impossible for a one-star physician to do, but that was not necessarily the case for Marcus, a two-star physician.

Moreover, Marcus seemed to be able to shrug off all their attacks. Whatever poison Sorin launched at him was immediately purified, while any wounds caused by arrows or Fire Bolts that managed to bypass his robes were immediately healed over with life mana. Sorin's own acid-laced attack had already been neutralized.

Fortunately, Sorin had a secret ally and just needed to buy him a few seconds. This time, he approached Marcus cautiously and coordinated with Lawrence for a simultaneous attack. A split second before they struck, Sorin activated Cobra's Gaze and engaged in a spiritual collision with Marcus. Both sides suffered damage in the process, but Sorin had Lawrence to back him up, and as a result, Marcus was unable to avoid either of their attacks.

It was during this exchange that Lorimer finally managed to gnaw through the snake staff entangling Stephan and set him free. The bear, having experienced nothing but failure at the hands of Marcus, attacked him with a fully empowered Lunisolar Paw. Cornered and wounded by Lawrence and Sorin, Marcus was unable to avoid Stephan's taunt skill and was therefore forced to meet the attack head on.

Despite Stephan's great strength, he and the physician were evenly matched. But during the exchange, Sorin was able to stab Marcus thrice in the back, injecting a heavy dose of Manabane Poison into his bloodstream.

Lorimer took advantage of this disruption to crawl through Marcus's shielding and gnaw at the man's flesh. "That's enough playing around," said Marcus. "Life Drain!" Sorin suddenly felt a large chunk of his vitality leave him and every one of his companions and pour into Marcus. The wounds they'd inflicted instantly healed over.

"Vampiric spells? Really?" said Sorin. "You realize the Medical Association really frowns upon those sinister spells, don't you?"

"You speak as though you actually respect that politically charged regulatory body," said Marcus, summoning his damaged staff back into his hand. "You of all people should understand that they're a bunch of short-sighted fools."

Sorin agreed with that assessment. Truth be told, vampiric spells weren't particularly nefarious—they just came off that way to a significant portion of the population. The ban was imposed to preserve the image of physicians, who preferred to avoid combat in the first place.

"It looks like all the old tricks are on the table then," said Stephan, smacking a healing potion on his chest. "Life syphoning. Body amplification. Also, it looks like he actually knows how to fight. I hope you have something up your sleeve, Sorin, or we're cooked."

Sorin glanced over to Gabriella, whose body was now covered in small black veins. "You go. I'll stay."

"That isn't how this sort of thing works," said Stephan.

"And I still don't think you realize how outmatched you are," said Marcus. "I would prefer to avoid the death of a member of the York Clan, if possible, and would like to avoid killing you as per the wishes of the Grand Elder, Sorin, but I'm not against killing your other three party members before disabling the both of you. Snake Staff—Coil!"

He threw the staff over to Gareth and Daphne like a spear. The archer tried to deflect it with an arrow but was unable to stop it. Daphne, on the other hand, gave up on intercepting the staff and opted to launch a Fireball she'd been charging at Marcus, damaging both Sorin and Stephan in the process.

"Naïve," said Marcus, appearing from the smoke. His body was burnt but his flesh was rapidly regenerating. "Let's first deal with the member of the York Clan. Concussive Strike!" He flitted over to the bear with a speed that defied the limitations of Bone-Forging cultivator and slapped his hand on the side of Stephan's head. The bear crumpled to the ground, unconscious.

"You're very difficult to lock onto for a rogue, but don't think that you're impossible to detect," continued Marcus. "Spiritual Paralysis!" The attack knocked Lawrence out of Marcus's shadow and opened him up to a lethal dagger strike—one that Sorin predicted and intercepted by stabbing his dagger towards Marcus's unprotected heart.

"Lorimer! Now!" shouted Sorin as Marcus turned around and grabbed Sorin's neck.

"Reee!" The rat, who'd been lurking in the shadows, erupted into flames and jumped onto Marcus's back.

"Get off me, you filthy vermin!" snarled Marcus. He tossed Sorin at a nearby stone wall and grabbed Lorimer before he could dig too deep, then proceeded to drain what little vitality the rat possessed before throwing him down the hall, half-dead.

"Lorimer..." said Sorin, picking himself up. The rat wasn't dead, and Sorin could still feel his life flame. But his companions were falling one after another. Lawrence was now unconscious, and Gareth and Daphne were following in his footsteps. Thankfully, none of them had received fatal wounds.

"As you can see, this was all quite pointless, Sorin," said Marcus. "If it were anyone else, I would teach a harsher lesson, but it's like I said: the Grand Elder is quite interested in your situation, quite possibly because of your cultivation technique and the knowledge you've acquired. You also possess the purest blood of the Abberjay branch."

Realizing he was sorely outclassed and that Gabriella's life hung in the balance, Sorin could only go all out. He took out a flask of stimulant poison and chugged down its entire contents, ingesting a quadruple dose in a single instant. He shuddered as his metabolism sped up and his body's natural limiters were released, enabling him to unleash 40 percent more strength and speed than normal at great cost to his endurance.

What followed was a fast-paced exchange of blows. Marcus naturally came out on top. He was stronger and faster than Sorin, and he also could purify and heal any poisons or injuries he suffered. "Well?" said Marcus after they'd exchanged fifty odd blows. "Are you ready to give up and accept your situation?"

"Not quite yet," said Sorin. If it were anyone else, he'd take the pragmatic approach. Unfortunately, this involved Gabriella. He took out a pill bottle and popped out a pitch-black pill. It was none other than the Violent Awakening Pill, the poison pill he'd obtained from Hope when he'd requested a way to exceed his human limitations.

Marcus's eyes narrowed when he saw the pill. "That's a taboo poison pill, Sorin. Are you sure you want to eat that? I sense thick demonic energies inside it—there may be no recovering from consuming it."

"You're not leaving me much of a choice, are you?" asked Sorin. "Or will you move aside and let me detoxify her?"

Marcus's eyes narrowed. "You can't begin to comprehend how valuable this experiment is. How valuable *she* might potentially be. If my predictions are accurate, this won't just open her Conception Vessel, but also activate her dormant constitution. There's no telling how powerful she'll become as a result of this."

"And you're willing to risk her death to accomplish this?" asked Sorin.

"I am, and she is too," said Marcus. "This is beyond you and me, Sorin. If the Kepler Clan gains such a powerful life cultivator, our enemies will not be able to keep knocking us down. We will awaken the potential of the entire continent and reclaim the land that humanity has lost."

"You're insane," said Sorin flatly. "Even Sirius, the butcher that he was, realized his limits in the end."

"*You're* the insane one," said Marcus. "What is a single life, one *willing* to sacrifice herself, compared to the good of the entire continent? A great battle is coming, Sorin. The Evils are stirring. We must be prepared to face them in battle."

Unfortunately for Marcus, Sorin didn't care much about his reasons. Not because a life was at stake, but because it was Gabriella's.

She had done far too much for Sorin. She was the light that had lit up his grim world when everything seemed hopeless. She had given him the courage he needed to move on and to approach Hope like many desperate people had before him.

Without her, he would be nothing. Without her, he would be on his last legs and might have already succumbed to his internal injuries.

He, therefore, didn't hesitate to toss the Violent Awakening Pill into his mouth and absorb its potent corruption. His aura soared, and strength that far exceeded the Blood-Thickening Realm filled his body.

"You said it was impossible for a Blood-Thickening cultivators at my level to defeat you," said Sorin. "Let's put that theory to the test, shall we?"

EMBRACING VIOLENCE

The stones lining the basement floor cracked as Sorin pushed himself forward with no technique, no deception, only raw and unadulterated violence. Marcus summoned his snake staff to intercept him, but Sorin used his own arm to catch its bite, taking a small injury to land a Viper Strike into Marcus's side and unleash three times as much poison as was normally possible.

Sorin's swift hands followed up to land another hit, forcing Marcus to use a spiritual attack to try and paralyze him. But in Sorin's crazed state, the attack had no effect. Marcus suffered a second poison-filled wound and was unable to evade the follow-up Python Coil that violently gripped him.

"Arrogant!" said Marcus, activating his life mana full force. A life shield appeared and forced Sorin back. But Sorin caught himself with what appeared to be claws coming out of his hands and feet and crazily launched himself forward once again.

The aggressive offense was taxing on Sorin, but every time he reached his limit, something seemed to break inside him, filling him with an additional burst of energy. It caused his mana and blood to boil and seek out any outlet possible.

When Marcus finally had enough and used his two-star dagger to intercept Sorin's own dagger, cutting it in half, Sorin abandoned his weapon and launched himself at the Bone-Forging physician with his bare hands.

"This isn't me," said a small voice inside of Sorin.

But Sorin didn't listen. He continued his assault even when Marcus used his dagger to stab him in the chest, puncturing his lung.

The wound *hurt*, but it didn't overly slow Sorin down; his regeneration was operating at several times the usual speed. The small wound closed seconds after Marcus caused it.

"You've lost all sense of reason," muttered Marcus, once again pushing Sorin back with a life shield. "You're hardly better than animal now, Sorin. Was it worth it? In the end, you saved no one and have simply handed yourselves to the demons on silver platter."

Sorin ignored the question and once again launched himself at Marcus like a wild animal. He knew he was becoming predictable, but he didn't care.

Marcus, finally having enough of the ordeal, stabbed Sorin in the leg. Sorin managed to tear a gash into Marcus's chest with his claws, in exchange, but the two-star physician quickly purged his poisons and corruption, then used his life drain ability on Sorin's leg before tossing him back onto the ground.

Leg hobbled, Sorin was no longer able to ignore Marcus's dagger, and neither was he able to avoid the serpent staff's biting attacks. His leather armor had been reduced to rags, and bloody holes appeared on his bedeviled body, challenging its ability to regenerate.

I can't...

He couldn't think. He couldn't react properly. And now he'd lost the initiative, and Marcus had him on the ropes.

If only I had an opening. If only I hadn't lost myself.

He braced himself as the snake pulled its head back and went for his throat.

"Reeeee!" A blazing rat shot past Sorin and collided with the snake staff, then wrestled it to the ground. Sorin wondered how Lorimer could have possibly recovered but noticed an open belt pouch near Stephan's unconscious body, with demon cores and coins spilling out of it.

On paper, the staff was vastly more powerful than the rat, but against the mutated Rockgnaw Rat's teeth, it soon suffered a crack. "Lorimer," muttered Sorin, regaining a bit of his lucidity. Violence's effect was indeed very potent and had completely overpowered Sorin's conscious mind.

Now able to think a little clearer, Sorin drew on his poisonous mana but discovered it to be unstable. Complex spells were no longer an option.

Simple, then, thought Sorin, summoning a mass of violent poison mana into his hand and forming it into a six-foot-long spear. It was stable and tangible, and most importantly, he could use it to leverage his now-immense strength.

Sorin once again launched himself at Marcus despite his hobbled leg.

Having lost the protection of his staff, the physician summoned a life shield to repel Sorin. But he underestimated Sorin's new spear, which was filled with Sorin's poisons, including his pernicious Manabane Poison.

Sorin's first attack failed to penetrate the shield, but it managed to weaken it enough so that with the second strike, the shield shattered, hitting Marcus with a heavy backlash. Sorin was also affected by the breaking shield, but once again, something broke inside Sorin, filling him with strength. Enough to push past the secondary shield Marcus summoned and force the battle into a melee brawl.

Reacting quickly, Marcus stepped in to prevent Sorin from using the spear effectively. Sorin drew the weapon back into his body and caught Marcus's dagger with his bare hands. He then used the only weapon he had remaining—his teeth—to attack him.

"Argh!" Marcus yelled as Sorin's unnaturally sharp teeth bit into his shoulder. "You *monster!*"

"Interesting words coming from a total psychopath," said Sorin, spitting out blood. "A person like you who has no regard for boundaries or basic principles is effectively a monster in human skin."

Marcus cackled madly. "Do you even know how you look, Sorin? If there's a monster here, it's you!" He then pulled back his dagger, severely lacerating Sorin's fingers. Fortunately, Sorin's hands were now covered in scales, negating over half of the damage, including that caused by the fire-based enchantment on the dagger.

This time, Marcus didn't let up. Sorin was forced to pull back and summon another spear. He threw the spear at Marcus, piercing yet another hole through his defenses. "You'll run out of energy if you keep going like this," said Marcus. "I, on the other hand, have energy for days." Sorin knew it was true, but he also knew he had no choice but to fight on. If he didn't, Violence would consume him.

Crack.

Yet another sensation of breaking finally alerted Sorin that something was amiss. It wasn't his bones breaking, and neither was it his meridians. He quickly inspected his body but discovered nothing wrong. In fact, everything was better than it should be. His natural abilities and strength had improved, and his mana was thicker than ever.

"Enough of this," said Marcus. "You know the kinds of preparations our family makes when sending out members for important missions. Given that I was sent to this outpost in the middle of nowhere, these trinkets happen to counter you perfectly."

Sorin's eyes narrowed as Marcus summoned a medallion in his hands. "An anti-demon talisman?" said Sorin.

"Precisely," said Marcus. "Since you've embraced the darkness, then this medallion will consume it and you with it." The medallion shattered in Marcus's hands, filling the room with white flames. They weakened both Sorin and Lorimer, who'd gotten the upper hand with the staff, instantly turning the tides against them.

The staff, under the direction of Marcus, coiled around Lorimer and attempted to gobble down the rat. Fortunately, Sorin was ready—he used his powerful claws to grasp the snake staff just beneath the head and pulled it back, giving Lorimer just enough time to free himself.

"Go!" said Sorin, punting the rat away. "I probably won't survive this, so get the hell out of here!"

"I don't think I'll be letting any demons wander about this manor, thank you very much," said Marcus, summoning a bubble of life mana around Lorimer. The rat attempted to gnaw at the bubble, only to find that it was extremely flexible and not susceptible to sharp teeth.

Simultaneously, the staff attacked Sorin and attempted to coil around him. Being experienced with such attacks, Sorin was able to avoid the worst of it but found himself under constant pressure that once again caused something inside him to break.

A seal? thought Sorin, inspecting his body. That wasn't theoretically possible since he'd already fully unlocked his Conception Vessel.

Unless...

He turned his inner spiritual senses towards his last remaining blocked meridian: the Governing Vessel.

But it's impossible to unlock these seals. Even Sirius was forced to give up.

Unless... unless he was trying something Sirius hadn't tried? Something that had been impossible before now? Was corruption the hidden key?

Sorin's body was now rife with corruption thanks to the poison pill, to the point that his bones were unstable and on the verge of permanently mutating. This corruption had also wandered over to his meridians and was corrupting his blood and mana. Then, upon encountering his unopened meridian, it found its nemesis in the form of divine seals blocking off the meridian's twenty-eight acupoints and instinctively attacked them.

Six out of twenty-eight seals are broken, resulting in a significant increase in strength. But passively waiting for them to open won't work. Like the Conception Vessel, breaking them open requires a concerted effort in conjunction with high-level impacts.

Another thing Sorin realized was that with every seal that broke, a portion of the corruption in the Violent Awakening Pill was eliminated. While it might not save his cultivation, eliminating corruption might allow him to regain his faculties after defeating Marcus, at least enough to save Gabriella.

He, therefore, threw himself at Marcus and continued his assault. Each exchange broke a seal, flooding him with another sudden surge of strength.

But Marcus clearly didn't see this. "You're losing this battle of attrition, Sorin," said Marcus. "But I can also see that you've not completely lost control. Give up, Sorin, and I'll pull some strings to preserve your life and have the Temple of Hope purify you. The Grand Elder holds you in high esteem, after all."

Mentioning the Grand Elder, the one person who *should* have supported him when his parents died, only fueled Sorin's rage. He redoubled his attacks, shattering five more golden seals before once again pulling back. Such a speed was too slow, however, and breaking seals was becoming more difficult. He would need to commit if he was going to break through in this battle.

Sorin analyzed the corruption in his body and immediately discovered how to speed up the breaking of the golden seals. Currently, the corruption was a foreign entity and was only passively attacking the seals. The quickest way to obtain its help would be to assimilate the corruption into his mana and blood and directly impact the seals.

There was no time to hesitate. Indecision was a cardinal sin for a physician. He directly activated Toxic Metabolism. The Heroic Ability wasn't made to handle corruption and, therefore, showed signs of sluggishness. But corruption, by nature, wished to contaminate. It therefore willingly fused Sorin's nine poisons and initiated a breakthrough.

"And here I thought that you could still be saved," said Marcus, shaking his head. He sighed as he pulled out another talisman—one made to trap demons instead of purifying them. "I will not kill you, as the Grand Elder has specifically requested it, but even so, I doubt he will be able to save one who has so thoroughly embraced corruption."

White fire appeared as Marcus broke the talisman and formed a wish-fire prison around Sorin. The prison suppressed him, and the suppression only grew stronger as Violence fused with his nine other poisons and propelled him to the tenth stage of Blood-Thickening.

Sorin grinned wickedly as his power rose. "If you hadn't messed with Gabriella, I wouldn't have committed to this path, Marcus. I would have never discovered the key. You can only blame yourself for what's about to happen."

"What are you talking about?" asked Marcus. "Is babbling nonsense all you corrupt cultivators do? I've heard of your deceptive ways and how you can influence the minds and hearts of others with only a few words. I refuse to listen."

Crack. Crack. Crack.

Marcus's eyes widened as he took a step back. "What's going on?"

Crack. Crack. Crack. CRACK!

"You can't possibly undergo another breakthrough so shortly after reaching the tenth stage of Blood-Thickening," continued Marcus.

Crack. Crack. Crack. CRACK. **CRACK!**

Sorin smiled toothily as one seal after another broke under the force of his corrupt mana until, finally, the last seal broke, and a tarnished golden light flooded every cell in his body. Strength filled Sorin as holy energy coursed through his meridians and invigorated his blood.

But along with these positive changes came some extreme side effects. Violence, for one, had become an inseparable part of Sorin. It rampaged inside him, wanting to be let out. And rather than fight against it, Sorin pursued the most sensible option.

He embraced it.

91

HAND OF THE MEDICINE GOD

Outside the Governor's Manor and high above the Bloodwood Outpost, Guild Master Roy and Governor Marsh collaborated to severely punish the mythical invaders for underestimating their defenses. The seeds of deception sown over decades finally paid off as the guild master pierced the dryad through her wooden heart with a burning spear, and Governor Marsh lopped off her head with his silver blade.

Just like many times before, the dryad reformed from her own sawdust, greatly weakened by the effort. She was joined by the satyr, who could no longer support the spiritual expenditure needed to play his instrument.

"It seems we underestimated you humans once again," said the satyr. "But no matter. We will return, and when we do, this outpost and any adjoining cities will fall."

"You think we'll let you out of the net we wove with such great difficulty?" said Governor Marsh. "Naïve."

"It is you who is naïve," said the satyr. "Did you think we didn't come prepared? Let's see who you value more—the residents of this outpost or the lives of us three-star demons." He summoned a sphere of corrupt energy in his hand and dropped it.

"It's not even a question," answered Governor Marsh. "We'll do both!" He gripped his sword and made to execute his Heroic Ability.

Yet just as he was about to activate it, a flash of gold emanated from his manor, accompanied by an intense aura of corruption. It was only a single instant, but that instant made all the difference. The satyr took advantage of it to push the sphere of corrupt energy downward, forcing Guild Master Roy and the mysterious preacher to catch it and suppress it.

As for Governor Marsh, he belatedly activated his Heroic Ability, Infinite Blade Storm. His blade bit into the satyr and the dryad multiple times, but in the end, he missed a strike due to their head start, bringing an untimely end to his chaining ability. "Till we meet again!" yelled the satyr, dragging the half-dead dryad alongside him.

"It'll be impossible to catch up once they reach the forest," said Guild Master Roy, working with the bishop to seal the corrupt sphere. Governor Marsh immediately identified it as an unstable three-star core of Violence.

"Someone has invaded my manor," said the governor, frowning. "I sense corruption... and something else."

"We'll be right there," said Guild Master Roy. "You go on ahead. Don't worry about us." Sighing, Governor Marsh took one last look at the walls and the retreating demons before flying over to his manor, wondering what the hell Marcus was doing inside it instead of the clinic and what in the Seven Evils was going on with that strange energy signature.

Having incorporated corruption into his cultivation, Sorin found himself at a disadvantage against the prison of wish-fire Marcus had summoned. Yet thanks to the golden light that was now part of his mana, he was able to place both hands on the intangible prison and inject Manabane Poison into the framework.

Sorin circulated his mana in a familiar pattern: Viper Strike. As he did so, a stream of information entered his mind and informed him that his ability was no longer so limited. He would now be as gifted at injecting, withdrawing, and manipulating poisons in anything he touched. The ability's name had changed to reflect this and now went by the much more impressive title: Hand of the Medicine God.

Using his powerful spiritual perception, Sorin quickly identified nodes in the wish-fire prison. The prison was powerful against demons and corruption, but weak against humans. The enhanced Manabane Poison rapidly eroded the wish-fire prison, rendering it susceptible to physical breakage.

As a Blood-Thickening cultivator, Sorin would normally be unable to exert this much strength, but thanks to Violence's empowerment, he was able to repurpose his mana and strengthen his physique. The prison shattered, revealing a shocked Marcus with blood dribbling from the corner of his mouth.

"Impossible," said Marcus. "How can this be? Escaping that prison should be impossible."

"I took a risk, and it paid off," said Sorin, looking at his clawed and scaled hand.

Sorin's body was littered with wounds. His vitality stores and mana stores were still quite low despite having unlocked what he decided to dub the Divine Meridian. Fortunately, it wasn't just Viper Strike that received an upgrade, but his Toxic Metabolism as well. It was now a divine ability that was extremely effective regarding corruption, something he immediately put to good use.

The claws on his hands pulled back inside his body, where he subsequently metabolized it. The core aspect of Violence remained and could not be separated from him, but he could still purge the excess corruption in his flesh.

Just like any other poison, Toxic Metabolism converted the corruption into mana and life force, something Sorin was in dire need of.

Despite his wounded state, Sorin didn't give Marcus time to react. He launched himself at the physician without a weapon and took a dagger to the chest in the process.

In exchange, he laid both hands on Marcus and used Hand of the Medicine God to inject a heavy dose of mixed manabane and acidic poison—straight into the man's weakest point, his internal organs.

Marcus forced Sorin back with a life shield, but Sorin, having yet to land, summoned a dark spear filled with mixed poison and corruption. The spear shattered the life shield and pierced through Marcus's mana shields like they didn't exist, burning a hole in his protective robes and melting away a significant amount of flesh.

Marcus reacted quickly. He swiftly chopped off the corrupted flesh and mobilized his life-affinity mana to heal the injury. He then drank a healing potion and an all-purpose antidote to fight off the poisons burning his innards.

He'd just finished drinking the antidote when Sorin used Adder Rush to attack him from the side. Marcus went for the kill. A dagger shot out, this time aiming for Sorin's head.

Yet he underestimated Sorin once again. A half second before the dagger made contact, Sorin activated Cobra's Gaze, paralyzing Marcus. The ability broke through what remained of the realm suppression between them, dragging out its duration significantly. This bought Sorin the time he needed to use Python Coil around Marcus's arm and then Hand of the Medicine God to quickly inject Manabane Poison into the arm's acupoints.

Sorin's mana was weak against two-star mana, but realm suppression no longer seemed to apply to him. The Divine Empowerment he'd received was responsible, and eliminated the concept of realm suppression entirely, at least between their two cultivation stages.

As a result, Marcus was a step too slow in purging the Manabane Poison, giving Sorin the last opening he needed to press his hands on Marcus's poison-filled torso. "**Violence,**" Sorin whispered, injecting corruption into his body and causing the initial poison and acid he'd injected to flare. The poison expanded violently, melting away half of Marcus's organs before he could even react and eating away at the forged bones forming his rib cage.

It was impossible for Marcus to speak in his condition. It was equally impossible for him to recover, even with his life mana. He simply stared ahead blankly as he collapsed to his knees, waiting for his brain to get the message that the fight was over, that he would soon be dead.

Finally, Marcus collapsed. With defeat, the orb around Lorimer vanished. The rat looked up at Sorin fearfully, and Sorin, for once, smiled. "You did good, Lorimer," said Sorin. "Enough to deserve a good reward." He then summoned Lorimer's contract rune and tossed it over to the rat. "Sorry for being anything less than a friend. In my defense, you *did* try to kill me."

Lorimer stared at him for a moment. Then, to Sorin's surprise, he tossed the rune back at him. "You want to come with me?" said Sorin, surprised.

"Reee!" squeaked Lorimer.

"But you want to actually get paid instead of getting ripped off," said Sorin with a chuckle. "You're smarter than I realized."

Sorin then turned his eyes over to his unconscious companions. "Help me take care of them for now, will you? I have something important to do. Something that just might kill me."

He walked over to the laboratory, which was no longer protected by a life shield. Gabriella's body was completely covered in black veins, and a silver glow was beginning to appear on her skin.

Despite the glow, she was not in good condition. Yet, thanks her inherently high vitality and the subdued nature of the poison, she was still holding strong despite the ample death mana flooding into the ritual circle and empowering the poison.

Sorin was not in a hurry to remove the poison—the slightest loss of balance could easily result in her death. But he *did* take the flask of poison Marcus had injected into her and drink it, then used Toxic Metabolism to sort out the poisons and identify them.

The formula was 70 percent identical to the original tincture from similar experiments. As for the missing ingredients, they'd been made up for using various necrotoxins. He identified Life Bane Lily, Nightshade Vine, Demonic Wolf Spider Venom, and Death Touch Toad

Poison—all high-level one-star poisons that interacted in wondrous ways to delay sudden necrotic damage.

Gabriella's meridians were a mess, as was her mana. Life mana and death mana were opposites and therefore eliminated each other in a surprisingly peaceful fashion. There were occasional holes in her meridians, as well as dead flesh, but for the most part, her body was undamaged.

A surprising development, considering the death-aligned ritual circle, thought Sorin. The ritual was still steadily gathering death-aligned mana, thereby enhancing the poisons in her body at a steady rate. He confirmed from Marcus's notes that this was all according to calculation. Marcus had apparently mapped out Gabriella's abilities long before formulating his hypothesis. Originally, Marcus had been sent to the outpost to try and improve the Kepler Clan's primary meridian-opening tinctures.

It didn't take long for Sorin to finish extracting everything valuable from the notebook. He first used Hand of the Medicine God to gradually control the poisons and draw them towards the half-opened Hero Meridian in Gabriella's body. He then extracted the necrotic poison through subsequent acupoints, breaking open the cracked silver seals on her Conception Vessel one at a time. A silver light flashed when the final acupoint opened, and Gabriella's body began to recover at a visible rate.

Sorin then moved to withdraw the necrotoxins and death mana coursing through her veins. Yet before he could do so, Gabriella's body began to glow with a silver light. Her body began to actively devour the toxins and the death mana contaminating her body.

Is this her Heroic Ability? Purification? thought Sorin, relieved at the direction of her recovery. With her intense life force and purification abilities, her life was no longer in danger.

All that was left was disabling the death-aligned ritual drawing death mana from outside the manor. He was no expert in rituals but knew that destabilizing them would likely interrupt their core functions. Removing the gems in the circle would likely be enough, something Sorin attempted to do, but failed.

No worries, thought Sorin. *I'll just wait until Daphne is awake. She should be able to disable this thing, right?*

But once again, Sorin's hopes were dashed. The force in Gabriella's body erupted following the initial round of purification and reached out to the ritual circle, which began operating at several times its original frequency. The initial trickle of death mana became a stream that poured into Gabriella's body, causing it to glow like a torch in the darkness.

If I can't stop the ritual, I'll take her out, Sorin decided. He moved to pick her up, but a powerful energy forced him back. What's more, it was a familiar energy to Sorin. A *golden* energy not dissimilar to the one present in his own body.

Before he could even process what was happening, the stream of death mana turned into a river of anguished souls that filled the room. Sorin could only escape and drag his friends out of range before their life flames were snuffed out.

Crisp, shattering sounds filled the air much like they had during Sorin's breakthrough. Then, after an extended pause, the final seal broke open. A golden light filled the room, causing plant life to erupt from the stone walls and the stone floor.

Similarly, Sorin's companions received a large dose of life energy.

"Urgh." Stephan was the first to regain consciousness in their group. "What happened?"

"My head... hurts," moaned Daphne, picking herself up.

"Um, why are there plants randomly growing in this dark base-ment?" asked Lawrence.

"I'm so confused," said Gareth.

"Ree!" agreed Lorimer.

Sorin was confused as well, but he had his suspicions about what happened to Gabriella. "Let's get her out of here," he said as the pres-ence of death in the room faded, leaving only the purest life energy that continued to heal their wounds, including Sorin's.

They found Gabriella still unconscious on the operating table, with a remnant golden glow leaking out from her bare skin. A strange symbol could be seen on her forehead—one of a torch glowing in the darkness, bringing forth new life after a cold winter.

Sorin quickly picked a blanket off a chair and tossed it onto her naked body.

"What happened to her?" asked Lawrence. "And why is she glowing?"

"I think you're better off not asking that question," said Stephan. "Assuming what I'm thinking just happened actually happened."

Sorin had many questions for Stephan, but before he could elaborate, a powerful presence bore down on their group. It entered the manor and swiftly crossed two floors before entering the laboratory.

"What have we here?" said the man Sorin immediately recognized as Governor Marsh. The man's silver eyes zeroed in on Sorin. "High-level demonic corruption? No, based on the energy signature, that's impossible. If you don't peel off your disguise, demon, I'll do it for you!"

The pressure Governor Marsh gave off intensified and immediately scattered Sorin's energy. Regardless of the benefits the divinity in his blood and mana granted him, he couldn't deal with the sheer raw power of a Flesh-Sanctification cultivator.

"Governor, you're killing him!" shouted Stephan. "And what's this about corruption?"

"Know your place, boy, and let me deal with this scum," said Governor Marsh. "Kneel, boy. I said **kneel!**"

The man's imposing nature skyrocketed, and Sorin immediately felt an urge to prostrate himself. His knees buckled, but he caught himself just before they touched the ground.

"**Piss off**," said Sorin, channeling every ounce of divinity in his body to fight off the governor's influence.

"Interesting," said Governor Marsh. "You give off a surprisingly holy presence for a demon. Are you a hybrid or some sort of experiment? No matter. We'll get to the bottom of it and obtain justice for Physician Marcus."

"Justice?" said Sorin, infuriated by the man's words. "The man conducted human experiments in your basement, and you're calling for justice? And here I was hoping you were just complacent. Instead, it appears that you're complicit."

Governor Marsh frowned at these words. "Human experimentation? What nonsense is this? Marcus was just borrowing the laboratory space to treat sensitive patients and conduct the veteran rehabilitation trials. Something that proved quite effective, according to what I've been told."

Sorin had already reviewed Marcus's notes, so he wasn't surprised by the man's words. Yet he still had his suspicions—what kind of man wouldn't know what was happening inside his own basement?

Fortunately, it seemed the matter wasn't solely up to him because seconds later, two other powerful cultivators descended into the basement and joined the governor.

"Kepler?" said Guild Master Roy upon seeing Sorin.

"You know this man?" asked Governor Marsh.

"He's the young member of the Kepler Clan Marcus Kepler kept causing problems for," said Guild Master Roy.

"Right, you told me about that," said Governor Marsh. "Is he the one my idiot son decided to corrupt justice over?"

"The very same," said Guild Master Roy.

Sorin was surprised by the exchange; by all rights, these two should be at each other's throats. Instead, it seemed that they were actually on friendly terms and even shared a long history together.

"Then that explains his reason for coming down here and killing Marcus," said Governor Marsh. "What a diplomatic bomb."

"Not as much as letting those two demons slip away," said Guild Master Roy. "Don't worry, though—I'll help you clean it up, but only if you let me figure out what's going on here. Also, could you explain why there's a naked female Hero strapped to hospital bed in your basement, along with what appears to be an apothecary's worth of poison concoctions and laboratory notes? Wait, is that golden light trickling off her body?"

The two Flesh-Sanctification cultivators and the bishop instantly rushed past Sorin and his companions and ignored them. "Hope be praised," said Governor Marsh.

"Is she..."

"Yes, I can confirm it," said Bishop Harold. "She's a God Seed. Whatever experiments Marcus performed on her awakened her inner divinity."

Having confirmed his suspicions, Governor Marsh's vision trained on Sorin and his team. Sorin felt killing intent from the man and highly suspected that silencing them was suddenly on the table, damn the political ramifications.

Fortunately, Bishop Harold cleared his throat. "I believe the death of five promising Heroes would not go unnoticed. Moreover, the one that appears to be affected by demonic corruption is someone Lord Hope has taken interest in."

Governor Marsh grunted. "Fine. But I expect a full investigation of these individuals, as well as the imposition of an Order of Silence. Regardless of our disastrous ambush, the God Seed's safety is paramount.

"Meanwhile, we'll conduct an investigation into Marcus's activities. We'll involve the Medical Association, the Alchemists Guild, and the Kepler Clan. None of us are to reveal the appearance of a God Seed. Is that understood?"

"Understood," said Guild Master Roy.

"Everything will be as you say," said Bishop Harold. "Now come along, you five. And you too, little rat. I'm afraid your stay won't be comfortable, especially Sorin's, but I believe everything will be fine as long as everyone cooperates.

92

REDACTED

Sorin was kept in a separate cell from his companions. A separate prison, actually, which made time flow by at an agonizing pace. Fortunately, Sorin wasn't overly restricted. He was allowed to perform mana manipulation exercises and familiarize himself with the hybrid energy inside his body.

During his stay, he felt only the occasional probe from the kindly Bishop Harold, but it was an inquisitive probe that bore no ill-will. The man seemed equally interested in the golden light in his mana and the tarnished coloring that accompanied it.

Contrary to his expectations, Lord Hope was not summoned, and neither was Sorin taken in for questioning or inquisition. His stay therefore became a weeklong session that Sorin used to prepare for his breaking through to the Bone-Forging Realm.

Sorin was far from the only corrupted prisoner beneath the temple. The other prisoners showed no overt signs of corruption, but occasionally, he heard mad ravings in the night. These only grew worse as the nights grew colder, and Violence's influence was steadily replaced by the Madness of Winter.

On the eighth day, light trickled into Sorin's cell for the first time.

The clouds above the outpost dispersed as a final dose of warmth descended before the dreaded winter snows.

The door to the prison opened, revealing Bishop Harold. He came accompanied by the jailor, who walked over to Sorin's cell and unlocked the demonbane door with a rune-covered key.

"You're free to go," said the jailor, nodding to Bishop Harold.

"I'll take him from here," said the bishop. "Do you need any time to prepare yourself? To clean up?"

"I'm fine," said Sorin, who'd gotten ample water and hadn't been mistreated. "Lead the way."

The bishop accompanied Sorin up to a side entrance to the temple, which was still recovering from the damage it had suffered from the demon tide.

"My investigation reveals that while you have been corrupted, this corruption has found a balance with your mana," explained Bishop Harold. "It is a complex case that required that I directly consult with Lord Hope. Lord Hope assures me that this development is intentional and has authorized me to release you. I could have done so four days ago, but I kept you in custody for your own protection."

"I'm sure you have a lot of questions, but first, accept this gift." He held out a black and gold fox-head pendant, which Sorin accepted but didn't immediately wear. "It was issued by Lord Hope to hide your... condition. It might cost you an equipment slot, but I suggest you prioritize the protection it offers."

Sorin ultimately chose to put on the pendant. "Where's Lorimer?" he asked. His voice was hoarse, as he hadn't spoken in a full week.

"Ah, the rat," said the bishop. He pulled out a small cage and opened its door. Lorimer scurried out and jumped onto Sorin's shoulder. "He was not mistreated in any way, and I assure you that he was fed well during his stay."

"Reee!" said Lorimer in an aggrieved voice. It was obvious that he didn't agree with that statement.

"The investigation?" asked Sorin.

"This..." said the bishop with a complicated expression. "The

Medical Association and the Alchemists Association always take great interest in these sorts of cases. As you well know, the matters you accused Marcus of are highly regulated, and permission for such experiments was clearly not given."

"And?" pressed Sorin. "The result?"

"I'm afraid there was no result to the investigation," said the bishop. "A government agent arrived five days after you were taken to the temple, and shortly after, the investigation team dispersed. No orders were issued. No statement was given. I can only advise you to keep this matter to yourself and not pry into it."

"What about Gabriella?" asked Sorin, dreading the answer. Whatever had happened to her down in the basement wasn't normal. Was she recovering well? Had she truly unlocked her Governing Vessel like he suspected? "The words God Seed were used, and I believe that regardless of the contract I signed, someone in my situation should know certain things."

Bishop Harold nodded slowly. "Be sure not to share this information with your companions unless you absolutely have to, Sorin. This regards not only your safety but meticulous plans crafted by Lord Hope himself."

"Naturally," said Sorin. None of his companions, save Lorimer, had witnessed his Divine Awakening. In fact, he believed the only reason the governor had not discovered Sorin's anomaly was because of Gabriella's transformation.

"As you can imagine, a God Seed is someone who's embarked on the path of the divine," continued Harold. "Each God Seed is a candidate to accept the mantle of a god, should they pass the trials assigned to them. Your own path is a unique one, but Gabriella has embarked on the path of Persephone. It is a path that seeks life in death and renews what is aged and corrupted.

"God Seeds are the hope of humanity and will be nurtured at all costs. In fact, the loss of this entire outpost would be considered a small price to pay for Gabriella's awakening. So, while you might loathe Marcus's actions, many would consider him a hero. Alas, he will never be known as such; to protect the God Seed, the experiments that led to her awakening have been classified, and all those involved have been sworn to secrecy."

"What about the Kepler Clan?" asked Sorin.

"They sent a representative, who seemed genuinely horrified by what was reported," said Bishop Harold. "But unlike the others, he was made privy to Gabriella Michka's situation. Perhaps this is a compensation of sorts to the Kepler Clan and their hard work? The man naturally agreed to take on Gabriella as his final apprentice."

"What was his name?" asked Sorin.

"I believe he went by the name of Elder Ignis Mockingjay Kepler," said Bishop Harold.

Elder Ignis was the strictest elder of the Kepler Clan. He had a reputation for impartiality and was a peak Flesh-Sanctification cultivator. In terms of power, he was ranked third in the family, right after his uncle, the Clan Leader. And unlike the Grand Elder, who *should* have supported him, Elder Ignis had protected Sorin's life after the Mockingjay branch's rebellion had succeeded. Sorin was relieved, in a sense, since Gabriella would be much safer with him than his uncle or the Grand Elder.

Sorin let out a deep sigh. His emotions towards Gabriella were complicated. Now, even more so, as she'd just inadvertently joined his uncle's faction. "Is she still here, or did she leave with the elder?" asked Sorin.

"I'm afraid she left just yesterday," said Bishop Harold. "She wanted to see you, but the elder assured her that she would get to see you soon as long as your growth remained unimpeded." Sensing his disappointment, the bishop placed his hand on Sorin's shoulder. "I'm sorry, Sorin. Sometimes, things don't develop the way we plan. The truth is often more complicated than anyone ever gives it credit for. Even I, a bishop of the Temple of Hope, only know a fraction of it. And even that would break most men and women on Pandora."

"Then I'll thank you for your hospitality and be on my way," said Sorin.

"That would be for the best," said Bishop Harold. "Stay safe and be sure to keep that pendant on. It's not something just anyone is allowed to have."

With that, the bishop left Sorin to rejoin the stoic Gareth, who'd been waiting silently by the Temple Gate. "I hope you didn't wait too long?" said Sorin upon reaching him.

"We waited in shifts," said Gareth, stepping off his stone perch. "You know, it's·a good thing it hasn't snowed yet. Otherwise, we'd all be at Lawrence's place enjoying a delicious cup of hot cocoa instead of waiting for you at this uncomfortable temple."

The archer's cultivation remained unchanged at the ninth stage of Blood-Thickening. Yet his presence was sharper than before they'd parted. It was clear that he could break through to the tenth stage at any time and had chosen to wait for Sorin's release.

The streets of the Bloodwood Outpost were a flurry of activity. The governor had released building materials stockpiled for the past decade in warehouses, and everyone, including the soldiers and adventurers, was hard at work rebuilding the city's basic infrastructure.

"There's a lot more people here than there used to be," Sorin noted as they walked.

"Indeed, there are," said Gareth. "Apparently, the provincial government has decided to double the outpost's population over the next three years. And now that Guild Master Roy has come out as a Flesh-Sanctification cultivator, the Mages Guild, the Alchemists Guild, and the Nighthawks will all be getting reinforcements in the form of their own Flesh-Sanctification cultivators.

"That seems pretty biased against the Governor's Manor," said Sorin.

"It does indeed," said Gareth. "Word is that the provincial government is shaking things up. They're not too happy that the dryad and the satyr managed to escape, so they're sending a bunch of Bone-Forging cultivators to 'assist' the governor. They're also transferring Vice Governor Marsh to a bigger city. A punishment, some say, though

Stephan insists it's a promotion in disguise. A... compensation, of sorts. For services rendered."

The team had been informed about Sorin's impending release. He found them in the Adventurers Guild. Sorin ordered a drink, adopted his usual spot at the table, and even ordered a drink in a bowl for Lorimer, much to the displeasure of the waitress.

"We had an intense debate about what to do about you when you got back," said Stephan when they finally settled down. "I suggested one punch each for getting us into this mess, though Daphne suggested that was unfair to her since her physical strength is much lower than ours. I was willing to compromise with a straight shot to the family jewels, but Lawrence and Gareth convinced us that since Gabriella was involved, corporal punishment was going a bit overboard."

"Sorry," said Sorin with a guilty smile. "When I saw her on that table... When I saw Marcus with those needles... Even if you'd all stood by and watched, I wouldn't have been able to."

Stephan grimaced when he heard this. "Let's... not talk about that event in detail ever again. In fact, let's pretend we never went to the manor. I heard there's a *lot* of scrutiny over what happened there, and a huge amount of political power went into suppressing it."

"Got it," said Sorin. Little did Stephan know that it wasn't just Gabriella's secrets that were suppressed, but his own.

"Lawrence, any word on when the final rewards will be calculated?" asked Stephan.

"It's apparently going to take a couple more weeks," grumbled Lawrence. "That being said, the Alchemists Guild was willing to take an order for a cut of the pills produced."

"Are those..." said Daphne as Lawrence took out a few pill bottles.

"Bone-Forging Pills," said Lawrence with a grin. "Our cut, at least. We had to give up 20 percent to the Alchemists Guild to cut to the front of the line, but it was that or wait two months till they filled our order."

"Twenty percent isn't bad," said Stephan. "Hero discount?"

"Hero discount," said Lawrence with a nod. "There's a lot of perks I've been made aware of, perks that I fully intend to take advantage of.

I'm not sure how many of these we'll need, but five each should be enough, shouldn't it?"

"I don't need mine," said Sorin, pushing his vial forward, only for Lorimer to squeak loudly. "Wait, you can actually eat those?" Lorimer confirmed this, and Sorin took them back. "Sorry guys. It seems my gluttonous little friend has reserved them."

"Speaking of Lorimer, you two seem to be quite a bit closer," said Daphne. "A logical plot development, I suppose. Relationships were made, mended, and severed. Secrets were discovered, and more secrets were introduced."

"Speaking of stories, how are your royalties coming along?" asked Gareth.

"Very well, actually," said Daphne, perking up. "In fact, I've already earned out my advance. Apparently, hope sells quite well in dark times like these. Also, the tense three-way relationship between Stephan, Gareth, and Lawrence—not at all related to you three, of course—was received well.

Gareth's smile faded, and Lawrence and Stephan both glared murderously at Daphne. "You wrote *what* now?" said Stephan. "You know what? I take it back. We're going to need some royalties if you're going to be taking advantage of us like this."

"Damn straight," said Gareth.

"Not to derail the discussion, but there's something I'd like to get out of the way," said Sorin. They all looked at him expectantly, then at Lawrence. "As is tradition, it only makes sense for you to go first, my precious laboratory assistant."

"Hey! Not this again!" protested Lawrence. The rogue froze as a current of poisonous energy traveled into his body and gently pierced open his remaining extraordinary meridian. "Wait, just like that?"

"Just like that," said Sorin. He repeated the process for each of his companions and finally, for good measure, unsealed several blocked meridians in Lorimer's strange body. In the rat's case, corruption was key to unlocking the demon constitution. He had no silver or golden seals like humans had.

By the end of the treatment, each of them glowed with a silver light as their meridian networks were finally completed. In turn, each of them broke through their current limits, entering the tenth stage of Blood-Thickening, the final stage before becoming a Bone-Forging cultivator. The process completely exhausted Sorin, but compared to prior openings, it was quite relaxing.

"I'm sorry, Sorin, but that ability is completely overpowered," said Stephan. "And don't think I'm exaggerating. With a talent like this, I wouldn't be surprised if every faction on Pandora wanted to either recruit you or kill you."

"Which is why I'm not going to do this often," said Sorin. "It's greatly draining, you know. In fact, there seems to be a hard limit on how many meridians I can unlock per week."

Stephan flashed him a grin. "Got it. Imposing scarcity to not tilt the political landscape too much. I take it you're going to reveal your ability to the Kepler Clan to obtain their protection?"

"According to Marcus, they really did run into issues," said Sorin with a frown. "I'm hoping that by revealing a bit of what I can do, I'll be able to discover more. Unfortunately, I'll have to relocate soon. Likely to Delphi, the provincial capital."

Though most of the political power in the Kepler Clan was based in Olympia, its origins were still tied to Asclepius and Apollo, the patrons of Delphi. It was where the family library was located, as well as its famed medical academy. The Medical Association was also based there.

"Delphi, huh?" said Stephan. "It might be tricky to arrange, but I think we can probably take on a few missions on our way there after we break through to Bone-Forging."

"Wait, you're bringing the team to Delphi?" asked Sorin, confused. It was with great reluctance that he'd announced his intentions to return to his family's city of origin. He was, after all, an adventurer and would need to find a new team once he relocated.

"It got brought up a few times while you were locked under the temple," said Stephan. "We discussed several options since none of us want to stay here once we break through to the Bone-Forging Realm.

Don't get me wrong, this is a fine place to get military contributions. But for adventurers, there are much better places to grow and develop."

"Don't you want to return to Ephesus?" asked Sorin. The York Clan was from a neighboring province and shared a city of origin with the Atlan Clan. Both clans were rivals in the adventuring scene.

"Maybe one day," said Stephan. "But would you go there if we did?"

Sorin thought about it, then shook his head. "I have things to do in Delphi. Messy family things. Honestly, you even bothering to—"

"Then it's settled," said Stephan. "We're all agreed?"

"I'm game," said Lawrence. "I hear Delphi has a nice temple with cute fortune tellers."

"They're called oracles," Gareth said scathingly. "And you'd better control yourself because I hear there's a legitimate demigod holding fort in the city. One that is very protective of said oracles. He's a mean archer, or so I'm told."

"I guess I pretty much *have* to follow you guys?" said Daphne. "How else am I going to keep writing these books?"

"Speaking of books, we really should get back to this issue of royalties," said Stephan.

The rest of the conversation passed like a dream. Though the losses to the outpost were disastrous, they avoided speaking about casualties. They laughed, they drank, and Sorin once again felt that warmth that he'd been missing in his own clan.

These people were his family. Much more so than the Kepler Clan that had raised him. And if he was being completely honest with himself, he was glad they were coming to Delphi with him despite the dangers it would bring them.

Later that night, Sorin dragged his weary bones over to the Kepler Manor. Their team meeting had only lasted two hours before Haley had walked in and commandeered them for wood-carrying duty. Sorin was exhausted, both physically and spiritually. It was reassuring, in a sense, knowing that despite the changes his body was undergoing, he was still human in the end.

"Mr. Kepler!" greeted Percival when he entered the house.

"Mr. Kepler!" said Clarcie as she rushed out of the kitchen. "Let me fix you a plate. We weren't sure if you'd be coming back today."

"The food can wait," said Sorin. "Come over here, Percival."

"What—" Percival started, but he froze when Sorin pressed a finger on his chest and injected a stream of mana into his body.

Sorin first got a general idea of Percival's wounds, then struck him over a hundred times on the limbs and chest using his finger. Like with his friends, he channeled poison into the butler's body to break open his sealed meridians, break up the corruption and mana clogging up his body, and absorb them into his own.

His two staff members had once been decently strong cultivators, but having been wounded and having stagnated for over a decade, their mana and their spirits were weak. Combined with the shock at having their injuries disappear little by little, it was no wonder they remained silent during the entire procedure, which finished up with Sorin taking out a healing potion and guiding the fluid to fix the worst of their meridian damage.

Sorin performed a full unsealing for their twelve primary meridians but stopped after that. Their injuries were simply too severe. But that didn't mean there wasn't hope—if they broke through to the Bone-Forging Realm, most of their injuries would heal, and their opened meridians would be forged anew.

It took an hour to perform both treatments, at which point he and his two patients were fully exhausted. But tired as he was, Sorin showed no outward signs of fatigue.

"This is all I can do for you," Sorin said to his two employees. "I know you'll need to report this to the family head. Just know that I support you doing this. In fact, it would be doing me a favor. But please relay this information to your *secondary* contact, the Grand Elder, as well."

He knew full well that two different factions were interested in his circumstances. They each had their goals, he was sure, but he was banking that his knowledge and abilities would provide him some sort of protection.

Percival and Clarice looked exceedingly guilty about the whole thing but confirmed the contents of the message. "Is there anything else you would like me to tell them, Mr. Kepler?" asked Percival.

"Yes," said Sorin. "Tell them they can expect me in Delphi in the near future. There's no need for them to fetch me—I'll find them myself."

Having said this, Sorin retreated from the living room and went up the stairs. He was in no mood to eat, and Percival and Clarice were likely in no mood to cook.

Exhausted but unable to sleep, Sorin sat in his office, thinking and planning. He wasn't a great political mind by any means, but he would need to have his wits about him in the coming days.

He took solace in the fact that he would not be alone on his journey.

He now had friends to rely on. Friends he could trust.

Pandora Unchained will continue in Book Two!

THANK YOU FOR READING RETURN OF THE PANDORA UNCHAINED

We hope you enjoyed it as much as we enjoyed bringing it to you. We just wanted to take a moment to encourage you to review the book. Follow this link: Pandora Unchained to be directed to the book's Amazon product page to leave your review.

Every review helps further the author's reach and, ultimately, helps them continue writing fantastic books for us all to enjoy.

Also in series:

Pandora Unchained
Pandora Unchained 2

Check out the entire series here! (Tap or scan)

Want to discuss our books with other readers and even the authors? Join our Discord server today and be a part of the Aethon community.

Facebook | Instagram | Twitter | Website

You can also join our non-spam mailing list by visiting www. subscribepage.com/AethonReadersGroup and never miss out on future releases. You'll also receive three full books completely Free as our thanks to you.

Looking for more great LitRPG?

Check out our new releases!

Betrayed by his guild... Left for dead... He must become stronger than they ever imagined. *Ever since Arwin was summoned as a child, all he has known is war. And now, to claim the demon queen's life and end the war, he has to sacrifice himself. But, as he deals the final blow, the Hero of Mankind is betrayed. Caught in a magical explosion thought to end him, Arwin awakens a month later to find that everyone has already moved on. His* [Hero] *class has changed to a unique blacksmith Class called* [The Living Forge] *that is empowered by consuming magical items, but some of his old passive* [Titles] *remain, giving him the power to forge his new future exactly the way he wants to. Arwin isn't going to settle for anything less than completely surpassing the powers he wielded as the Hero. After all, you are what you eat – and Arwin's diet just became legendary.* **Don't miss the next epic LitRPG Saga from Actus, bestselling author of** Return of the Runebound Professor. **With nearly 7-million views on Royal Road, this definitive edition is perfect for fans of Seth Ring, Jonathan Brooks, Michael Chatfield and lovers of all things Progression Fantasy and Crafting. About the Series:** *Features a healthy mix of crafting and combat, a strong-to-stronger MC, power progression, a detailed magic system, item enchantment, smithing, unforgettable characters, and much more!*

Get Rise of the Living Forge Now!

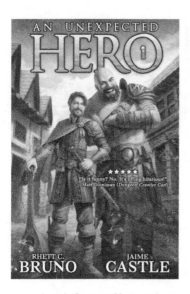

Order Now!

(Tap or Scan)

A magical new world. An ancient power. A chance to be a Hero. Danny Kendrick was a down-on-his luck performer who always struggled to find his place. He certainly never wanted to be a hero. He just hoped to earn a living doing what he loved. That all changes when he pisses off the wrong guy and gets transported to another world. Stuck in a fantasy realm straight out of a Renaissance Fair, Danny quickly discovers that there's more to life. Like magic, axe-wielding brutes, super hot elf assassins, and a talking screen that won't leave him alone. He'll need to adapt fast, turn on the charm, and get stronger if he hopes to survive this dangerous new world. But he has a knack for trouble. Gifted what seems like an innocent ancient lute after making a questionable deal with a Hag, Danny becomes the target of mysterious factions who seek to claim its power. It's up to him, Screenie, and his new barbaric friend, Curr, to uncover the truth and become the heroes nobody knew they needed. And maybe, just maybe, Danny will finally find a place where he belongs. Don't miss the start of this isekai LitRPG Adventure filled with epic fantasy action, unforgettable characters, loveable companions, unlikely heroes, a detailed System, power progression, and plenty of laughs. From the minds of USA Today bestselling and Award-winning duo Rhett C Bruno & Jaime Castle, An Expected Hero *is perfect for fans of* Dungeon Crawler Carl, Kings of the Wyld, *and* This Trilogy is Broken!

Get An Unexpected Hero now!

He has a year left to live... unless he gains the power to kill the Gods first. Each year, the Nightlords choose a new Emperor to rule Yohuachanca. Delicious food graces his palate. The realm's most beautiful women fill his vast palace. Four priestesses counsel him in all matters. The life of an emperor is good, luxurious, and short... For at the year's end, he is sacrificed to the Nightlords under the light of the Scarlet Moon. Iztac is the piss-poor orphan chosen to be this year's emperor. A sacrifice bound for the altar. But the Nightlords have made a mistake this time. For Iztac is a sorcerer, whose soul journeys into the secret underworld to plunder the secret spells of the dead. There, in the darkness, hides the power to drag the Nightlords off their throne. He has a year to find it, or perish for good. Iztac may not be the first emperor, but he will be the last. ***Don't miss this action-packed Progression Fantasy saga with a unique spin from Maxime J. Durand, bestselling author of* Vainqueur the Dragon, The Perfect Run, *and* Apocalypse Tamer.**

Get The Last Emperor Now!

For all our LitRPG books, visit our website.

ABOUT THE AUTHOR

I'm Patrick Laplante, and I write cultivation fantasy. In cultivation stories, the main character powers up and trains all the time to fight even stronger villains. Think Dragon Ball Z. Or Naruto. Or any RPG game.

I wasn't always a writer. I started off my adult life as a humble engineer. It took me seven years of working for a soul-sucking corporation to realize that my true love was writing all along (please don't tell my wife and child).

I like games. Board games. Role-playing games. Computer games. You name it. I like strategy games like Chess and Go as well. I used to do martial arts, but then I got injured too often, so I don't do too much of that anymore.

There is nothing on this earth more satisfying than reading a good book. You know the kind I'm talking about – it takes your heart and smashes it to pieces, then builds you a new heart. A better heart.

That's the kind of book I look for as a reader. It's also the kind of book I try to deliver as a writer.

Website: www.paintingthemists.com

ALSO BY PATRICK LAPLANTE

Made in the USA
Las Vegas, NV
15 November 2024

11883992R00395